THE ENEMY

Back in Reacher's army days, a general is
found dead on his watch.

ONE SHOT

A lone sniper shoots five people dead in a heartland city.
But the accused guy says, 'Get Reacher'.

THE HARD WAY

A coffee on a busy New York street leads to a shoot-out
three thousand miles away in the Norfolk countryside.

BAD LUCK AND TROUBLE

One of Reacher's buddies has shown up dead in the California
desert, and Reacher must put his old army unit back together.

NOTHING TO LOSE

Reacher crosses the line between a town called
Hope and one named despair.

GONE TOMORROW

On the New York subway, Reacher counts
down the twelve tell-tale signs of a suicide bomber.

61 HOURS

In freezing South Dakota, Reacher hitches
a lift on a bus heading for trouble.

WORTH DYING FOR

Reacher runs into a clan that's terrifying the Nebraska locals,
but it's the unsolved case of a missing child that he can't let go.

THE AFFAIR

Six months before the events in *Killing Floor*,
Major Jack Reacher of the US Military Police goes
undercover in Mississippi, to

Jack Reacher: CV

Name: Jack Reacher (no middle name)

Born: 29 October

Height:
6 foot 5 inches/
1.95 metres

Weight:
220-250 lbs/
100-113 kg

Size:
50-inch/127cm chest,
3XLT coat, 37-inch/
95cm inside leg

Eyes: Blue

Distinguishing marks:
scar on corner of left
eye, scar on upper lip

Education:
US Army base schools in
Europe and the Far East;
West Point Military Academy

Service:
US Military Police,
thirteen years; first CO
of the 110th Division;
demoted from Major to
Captain after six years,
mustered out with rank
of Major after seven

Service awards:
Top row: Silver Star, Defense
Superior Service Medal,
Legion of Merit
Middle row: Soldier's Medal,
Bronze Star, Purple Heart
Bottom row: 'Junk awards'

Last known address:
Unknown

Family:
Mother, Josephine Moutier
Reacher, French national;
Father, Career US
Marine, served in
Korea and Vietnam;
Brother, Joe, five years in
US Military Intelligence,
Treasury Dept.

Special skills:
Small arms expert, outstanding
on all man-portable
weaponry and
hand-to-hand combat

Languages:
Fluent English and French,
passable Spanish

What he doesn't have:
Driver's licence; credit cards;
Federal benefits; tax returns;
dependents

Jack Reacher – a hero for our time

'**Clint Eastwood**, **Mel Gibson** and **Bruce Willis** all rolled into one, a **superman** for our time' *Irish Times*

'Thinking girl's beefcake'
The Times

'TOUGH-BUT-FAIR'
Mirror

'ONE OF THE GREAT
ANTIHEROES'
Independent

'**Admired** by his male readers and **lusted** after by his female ones'
Daily Express

'Arms the size of **Popeye's**'
Independent

'The lonest of **lone wolves**... **too cool** for school'
San Francisco Chronicle

'Part-**Robin Hood**, part-**gorilla**'
Sunday Times

'One of the truly memorable **tough-guy heroes**' Jeffery Deaver

'This is Jack **Reacher** for pity's sake, he'll **eat you** for breakfast!' *Los Angeles Times*

Have you read them all?

The Jack Reacher thrillers by Lee Child – in the order
in which they first appeared.

KILLING FLOOR

Jack Reacher gets off a bus in a small town in Georgia.
And is thrown into the county jail, for a murder he didn't commit.

DIE TRYING

Reacher is locked in a van with a woman claiming to be FBI.
And ferried right across America into a brand new country.

TRIPWIRE

Reacher is digging swimming pools in Key West when a detective
comes round asking questions. Then the detective turns up dead.

THE VISITOR

Two naked women found dead in a bath filled with paint. Both
victims of a man just like Reacher.

ECHO BURNING

In the heat of Texas, Reacher meets a young woman whose
husband is in jail. When he is released, he will kill her.

WITHOUT FAIL

A Washington woman asks Reacher for help. Her job?
Protecting the Vice-President.

PERSUADER

A kidnapping in Boston. A cop dies.
Has Reacher lost his sense of right and wrong?

NOTHING TO LOSE

Lee Child

BANTAM BOOKS

LONDON · TORONTO · SYDNEY · AUCKLAND · JOHANNESBURG

TRANSWORLD PUBLISHERS
61–63 Uxbridge Road, London W5 5SA
A Random House Group Company
www.transworldbooks.co.uk

NOTHING TO LOSE
A BANTAM BOOK: 9780553824414

First published in Great Britain
in 2008 by Bantam Press
a division of Transworld Publishers
Bantam edition published 2009

Addresses for Random House Group Ltd companies outside
the UK can be found at: www.randomhouse.co.uk
The Random House Group Ltd Reg. No. 954009

The Random House Group Limited supports The Forest Stewardship
Council (FSC®), the leading international forest certification organisation.
Our books carrying the FSC label are printed on FSC® certified paper. FSC is
the only forest certification scheme endorsed by the leading environmental
organisations, including Greenpeace. Our paper procurement policy can be
found at www.randomhouse.co.uk/environment

Typeset in Times by
Kestrel Data, Exeter, Devon.

Printed and bound by
CPI Group (UK) Ltd, Croydon, CR0 4YY

6 8 10 9 7

If I listed all the ways she helps me, this dedication would be longer than the book itself. So I'll just say: to my wife Jane, with a lot of thanks.

ONE

The sun was only half as hot as he had known sun to be, but it was hot enough to keep him confused and dizzy. He was very weak. He had not eaten for seventy-two hours, or taken water for forty-eight.

Not weak. He was dying, and he knew it.

The images in his mind showed things drifting away. A rowboat caught in a river current, straining against a rotted rope, pulling, tugging, breaking free. His viewpoint was that of a small boy in the boat, sitting low, staring back helplessly at the bank as the dock grew smaller.

Or an airship swinging gently on a breeze, somehow breaking free of its mast, floating up and away, slowly, the boy inside seeing tiny urgent figures on the ground, waving, staring, their faces tilted upward in concern.

Then the images faded, because now words seemed more important than pictures, which was absurd, because he had never been interested in words before. But before he died he wanted to know which words were his. Which applied to him? Was he a man or a boy? He had been described both ways. *Be a man*, some had said.

Others had been insistent: *The boy's not to blame*. He was old enough to vote and kill and die, which made him a man. He was too young to drink, even beer, which made him a boy. Was he brave, or a coward? He had been called both things. He had been called unhinged, disturbed, deranged, unbalanced, delusional, traumatized, all of which he understood and accepted, except unhinged. Was he supposed to be *hinged*? Like a door? Maybe people were doors. Maybe things passed through them. Maybe they banged in the wind. He considered the question for a long moment and then he batted the air in frustration. He was babbling like a teenager in love with weed.

Which is exactly all he had been, a year and a half before.

He fell to his knees. The sand was only half as hot as he had known sand to be, but it was hot enough to ease his chill. He fell face down, exhausted, finally spent. He knew as certainly as he had ever known anything that if he closed his eyes he would never open them again.

But he was very tired.

So very, very tired.

More tired than a man or a boy had ever been.

He closed his eyes.

TWO

The line between Hope and Despair was exactly that: a line, in the road, formed where one town's blacktop finished and the other's started. Hope's highway department had used thick dark asphalt rolled smooth. Despair had a smaller municipal budget. That was clear. They had top-dressed a lumpy roadbed with hot tar and dumped grey gravel on it. Where the two surfaces met there was an inch-wide trench of no-man's-land filled with a black rubbery compound. An expansion joint. A boundary. A line. Jack Reacher stepped over it mid-stride and kept on walking. He paid it no attention at all.

But he remembered it later. Later, he was able to recall it in great detail.

Hope and Despair were both in Colorado. Reacher was in Colorado because two days previously he had been in Kansas, and Colorado was next to Kansas. He was making his way west and south. He had been in Calais, Maine, and had taken it into his head to cross the continent diagonally, all the way to San Diego in California. Calais was the last major place in the northeast,

15

San Diego was the last major place in the southwest. One extreme to the other. The Atlantic to the Pacific, cool and damp to hot and dry. He took buses where there were any and hitched rides where there weren't. Where he couldn't find rides, he walked. He had arrived in Hope in the front passenger seat of a bottle green Mercury Grand Marquis driven by a retired button salesman. He was on his way out of Hope on foot because that morning there had been no traffic heading west towards Despair.

He remembered that fact later, too. And wondered why he hadn't wondered why.

In terms of his grand diagonal design, he was slightly off course. Ideally he should have been angling directly southwest into New Mexico. But he wasn't a stickler for plans, and the Grand Marquis had been a comfortable car, and the old guy had been fixed on Hope because he had three grandchildren to see there, before heading onward to Denver to see four more. Reacher had listened patiently to the old guy's family tales and had figured that a saw-tooth itinerary first west and then south was entirely acceptable. Maybe two sides of a triangle would be more entertaining than one. And then in Hope he had looked at a map and seen Despair seventeen miles further west and had been unable to resist the detour. Once or twice in his life he had made the same trip metaphorically. Now he figured he should make it for real, since the opportunity was right there in front of him.

He remembered that whim later, too.

The road between the two towns was a straight

two-lane. It rose very gently as it headed west. Nothing dramatic. The part of eastern Colorado that Reacher was in was pretty flat. Like Kansas. But the Rockies were visible up ahead, blue and massive and hazy. They looked very close. Then suddenly they didn't. Reacher breasted a slight rise and stopped dead and understood why one town was called Hope and the other Despair. Settlers and homesteaders struggling west a hundred and fifty years before him would have stopped over in what came to be called Hope and would have seen their last great obstacle seemingly within touching distance. Then after a day's or a week's or a month's repose they would have moved on again and breasted the same slight rise and seen that the Rockies' apparent proximity had been nothing more than a cruel twist of topography. An optical illusion. A trick of the light. From the top of the rise the great barrier seemed once again remote, even unreachably distant, across hundreds more miles of endless plains. Maybe thousands more miles, although that too was an illusion. Reacher figured that in truth the first significant peaks were about two hundred miles away. A long month's hard trekking on foot and in mule-drawn carts, across featureless wilderness and along occasional decades-old wheel ruts. Maybe six weeks' hard trekking, in the wrong season. In context, not a disaster, but certainly a bitter disappointment, a blow hard enough to drive the anxious and the impatient from hope to despair in the time between one glance at the horizon and the next.

Reacher stepped off Despair's gritty road

and walked through crusted sandy earth to a table rock the size of a car. He levered himself up and lay down with his hands behind his head and stared up at the sky. It was pale blue and laced with long high feathery clouds that might once have been vapour trails from coast-to-coast redeye planes. Back when he smoked he might have lit a cigarette to pass the time. But he didn't smoke any more. Smoking implied carrying at least a pack and a book of matches, and Reacher had long ago quit carrying things he didn't need. There was nothing in his pockets except paper money and an expired passport and an ATM card and a clip-together toothbrush. There was nothing waiting for him anywhere else, either. No storage unit in a distant city, nothing stashed with friends. He owned the things in his pockets and the clothes on his back and the shoes on his feet. That was all, and that was enough. Everything he needed, and nothing he didn't.

He got to his feet and stood on tiptoe, high on the rock. Behind him to the east was a shallow bowl maybe ten miles in diameter with the town of Hope roughly in its centre, eight or nine miles back, maybe ten blocks by six of brick-built buildings and an outlying clutter of houses and farms and barns and other structures made of wood and corrugated metal. Together they made a warm low smudge in the haze. Ahead of him to the west were tens of thousands of flat square miles, completely empty except for ribbons of distant roads and the town of Despair about eight or nine miles ahead. Despair was harder to see than Hope. The haze was thicker in the west. Details were not decipherable, but the place looked larger than Hope had been, and teardrop-shaped, with a conventional Plains downtown mostly south of the main drag and then a wider zone of activity beyond it, maybe industrial in nature, hence the smog. Despair looked less pleasant than Hope. Cold, where Hope had looked warm; grey, where Hope had been mellow. It looked unwelcoming. For a brief moment Reacher considered backtracking and striking out south from Hope itself, getting back on course, but he dismissed the thought even before it had fully formed. Reacher hated turning back. He liked to press on, dead ahead, whatever. Everyone's life needed an organizing principle, and relentless forward motion was Reacher's.

He was angry at himself later, for being so inflexible.

He climbed off the rock and followed a long diagonal in the sand and rejoined the road twenty yards west of where he had left it. He stepped up on to the left-hand edge and continued walking, long strides, an easy pace, a little faster than three miles an hour, facing oncoming traffic, the safest way. But there was no oncoming traffic. No traffic in either direction. The road was deserted. No vehicles were using it. No cars, no trucks. Nothing. No chance of a ride. Reacher was a little puzzled, but mostly unconcerned. Many times in his life he had walked a lot more than seventeen miles at a stretch. He raked the hair off his forehead and pulled his shirt loose on his shoulders and kept on going, towards whatever lay ahead.

THREE

The edge of town was marked by a vacant lot where something had been planned maybe twenty years before but never built. Then came an old motor court, closed, shuttered, maybe permanently abandoned. Across the street and fifty yards west was a gas station. Two pumps, both of them old. Not the kind of upright rural antiques Reacher had seen in Edward Hopper's paintings, but still a couple of generations off the pace. There was a small hut in back with a grimy window full of quarts of oil arrayed in a pyramid. Reacher crossed the apron and stuck his head in the door. It was dark inside the hut and the air smelled of creosote and hot raw wood. There was a guy behind a counter, in worn blue overalls stained black with dirt. He was about thirty, and lean.

'Got coffee?' Reacher asked him.

'This is a gas station,' the guy said.

'Gas stations sell coffee,' Reacher said. 'And water, and soda.'

'Not this one,' the guy said. 'We sell gas.'

'And oil.'

'If you want it.'

'Is there a coffee shop in town?'

'There's a restaurant.'

'Just one?'

'One is all we need.'

Reacher ducked back out to the daylight and kept on walking. A hundred yards further west the road grew sidewalks and according to a sign on a pole changed its name to Main Street. Thirty feet later came the first developed block. It was occupied by a dour brick cube, three storeys high, on the left side of the street, to the south. It might once have been a dry goods emporium. It was still some kind of a retail enterprise. Reacher could see three customers and bolts of cloth and plastic household items through its dusty ground floor windows. Next to it was an identical three-storey brick cube, and then another, and another. The downtown area seemed to be about twelve blocks square, bulked mostly to the south of Main Street. Reacher was no kind of an architectural expert, and he knew he was way west of the Mississippi, but the whole place gave him the feel of an old Connecticut factory town, or the Cincinnati riverfront. It was plain, and severe, and unadorned, and out of date. He had seen movies about small-town America in which the sets had been artfully dressed to look a little more perfect and vibrant than reality. This place was the exact opposite. It looked like a designer and a whole team of grips had worked hard to make it dowdier and gloomier than it needed to be. Traffic on the streets was light. Sedans and pick-up trucks were moving slow and lazy. None of them was newer than three years old. There were few pedestrians on the sidewalks.

Reacher made a random left turn and set about finding the promised restaurant. He quartered a dozen blocks and passed a grocery store and a barber shop and a bar and a rooming house and a faded old hotel before he found the eatery. It took up the whole ground floor of another dull brick cube. The ceiling was high and the windows were floor-to-ceiling plate glass items filling most of the walls. The place might have been an automobile showroom in the past. The floor was tiled and the tables and chairs were plain brown wood and the air smelled of boiled vegetables. There was a register station inside the door with a *Please Wait to be Seated* sign on a short brassed pole with a heavy base. Same sign he had seen everywhere, coast to coast. Same script, same colours, same shape. He figured there was a catering supply company somewhere turning them out by the millions. He had seen identical signs in Calais, Maine, and expected to see more in San Diego, California. He stood next to the register and waited.

And waited.

There were eleven customers eating. Three couples, a threesome, and two singletons. One waitress. No front of house staff. Nobody at the register. Not an unusual ratio. Reacher had eaten in a thousand similar places and he knew the rhythm, subliminally. The lone waitress would soon glance over at him and nod, as if to say *I'll be right with you*. Then she would take an order, deliver a plate, and scoot over, maybe blowing an errant strand of hair off her cheek in a gesture designed to be both an apology and an appeal for sympathy. She would collect a menu from a stack and lead him to a table and bustle away and then revisit him in strict sequence.

But she didn't do any of that.

She glanced over. Didn't nod. Just looked at him for a long second and then looked away. Carried on with what she was doing. Which by that point wasn't much. She had all her eleven customers pacified. She was just making work. She was stopping by tables and asking if everything was all right and refilling coffee cups that were less than an inch down from the rim. Reacher turned and checked the door glass to see if he had missed an opening-hours sign. To see if the place was about to close up. It wasn't. He checked his reflection, to see if he was committing a social outrage with the way he was dressed. He wasn't. He was wearing dark grey pants and a matching dark grey shirt, both bought two days before in a janitorial surplus store in Kansas. Janitorial supply stores were his latest discovery. Plain, strong, well-made clothing at reasonable prices. Perfect. His hair was short and tidy. He had shaved the previous morning. His fly was zipped.

He turned back to wait.

Customers turned to look at him, one after the other. They appraised him quite openly and then looked away. The waitress made another slow circuit of the room, looking everywhere except at him. He stood still, running the situation through a mental database and trying to understand it. Then he lost patience with it and stepped past the sign and moved into the room and sat down alone at a table for four. He scraped his chair in and made himself comfortable. The waitress watched him do it, and then she headed for the kitchen.

She didn't come out again.

Reacher sat and waited. The room was silent. No talking. No sounds at all, except for the quiet metallic clash of silverware on plates and the smack of people chewing and the ceramic click of cups being lowered carefully into saucers and the wooden creak of chair legs under shifting bodies. Those tiny noises rose up and echoed around the vast tiled space until they seemed overwhelmingly loud.

Nothing happened for close to ten minutes.

Then an old crew-cab pick-up truck slid to a stop on the kerb outside the door. There was a second's pause and four guys climbed out and stood together on the sidewalk. They grouped themselves into a tight little formation and paused another beat and came inside. They paused again and scanned the room and found their target. They headed straight for Reacher's table. Three of them sat down in the empty chairs and the fourth stood at the head of the table, blocking Reacher's exit.

FOUR

The four guys were each a useful size. The shortest was probably an inch under six feet and the lightest was maybe an ounce over two hundred pounds. They all had walnut knuckles and thick wrists and knotted forearms. Two of them had broken noses and none of them had all his teeth. They all looked pale and vaguely unhealthy. They were all grimy, with ingrained grey dirt in the folds of their skin that glittered and shone like metal. They were all dressed in canvas work shirts with their sleeves rolled to their elbows. They were all somewhere between thirty and forty. And they all looked like trouble.

'I don't want company,' Reacher said. 'I prefer to eat alone.'

The guy standing at the head of the table was the biggest of the four, by maybe an inch and ten pounds. He said, 'You're not going to eat at all.'

Reacher said, 'I'm not?'

'Not here, anyway.'

'I heard this was the only show in town.'

'It is.'

'Well, then.'

'You need to get going.'

'Going?'

'Out of here.'

'Out of where?'

'Out of this restaurant.'

'You want to tell me why?'

'We don't like strangers.'

'Me either,' Reacher said. 'But I need to eat somewhere. Otherwise I'll get all wasted and skinny like you four.'

'Funny man.'

'Just calling it like it is,' Reacher said. He put his forearms on the table. He had thirty pounds and three inches on the big guy, and more than that on the other three. And he was willing to bet he had a little more experience and a little less inhibition than any one of them. Or than all of them put together. But ultimately, if it came to it, it was going to be his two hundred and fifty pounds against their cumulative nine hundred. Not great odds. But Reacher hated turning back.

The guy that was standing said, 'We don't want you here.'

Reacher said, 'You're confusing me with someone who gives a shit what you want.'

'You won't get served in here.'

'Won't I?'

'Not a hope.'

'You could order for me.'

'And then what?'

'Then I could eat your lunch.'

'Funny man,' the guy said again. 'You need to leave now.'

'Why?'

26

'Just leave now.'

Reacher asked, 'You guys got names?'

'Not for you to know. And you need to leave.'

'You want me to leave, I'll need to hear it from the owner. Not from you.'

'We can arrange that.'

The guy who was standing nodded to one of the guys in the seats, who scraped his chair back on the tile and got up and headed for the kitchen. A long minute later he came back out with a man in a stained apron. The man in the apron was wiping his hands on a dish towel and didn't look particularly worried or perturbed. He walked up to Reacher's table and said, 'I want you to leave my restaurant.'

'Why?' Reacher asked.

'I don't need to explain myself.'

'You the owner?'

'Yes, I am.'

Reacher said, 'I'll leave when I've had a cup of coffee.'

'You'll leave now.'

'Black, no sugar.'

'I don't want trouble.'

'You already got trouble. If I get a cup of coffee, I'll walk out of here. If I don't get a cup of coffee, these guys can try to throw me out, and you'll spend the rest of the day cleaning blood off the floor and all day tomorrow shopping for new chairs and tables.'

The guy in the apron said nothing.

Reacher said, 'Black, no sugar.'

The guy in the apron stood still for a long moment and then headed back to the kitchen. A minute later the waitress came out with a single cup balanced on a saucer. She carried it across the room and set it down in front of Reacher, hard enough to slop some of the contents out of the cup and into the saucer.

'Enjoy,' she said.

Reacher lifted the cup and wiped the base on his sleeve. Set the cup down on the table and emptied the saucer into it. Set the cup back on the saucer and squared it in front of him. Then he raised it again and took a sip.

Not bad, he thought. A little weak, a little stewed, but at heart it was a decent commercial product. Better than most diners, worse than most franchise places. Right in the middle of the curve. The cup was a porcelain monstrosity with a lip about three-eighths of an inch thick. It was cooling the drink too fast. Too wide, too shallow, too much mass. Reacher was no big fan of fine china, but he believed a receptacle ought to serve its contents.

The four guys were still clustered all around. Two sitting, two standing now. Reacher ignored them and drank, slowly at first, and then faster as the coffee grew cold. He drained the cup and set it back on the saucer. Pushed it away, slowly and carefully, until it was exactly centred on the table. Then he moved his left arm fast and went for his pocket. The four guys jumped. Reacher came out with a dollar bill and flattened it and trapped it under the saucer.

'So let's go,' he said.

The guy standing at the head of the table moved out of the way. Reacher scraped his chair

28

back and stood up. Eleven customers watched him do it. He pushed his chair in neatly and stepped around the head of the table and headed for the door. He sensed the four guys behind him. Heard their boots on the tile. They were forming up in single file, threading between tables, stepping past the sign and the register. The room was silent.

Reacher pushed the door and stepped outside to the street. The air was cool, but the sun was out. The sidewalk was concrete, cast in five-by-five squares. The squares were separated by inch-wide expansion joints. The joints were filled with black compound.

Reacher turned left and took four steps until he was clear of the parked pick-up and then he stopped and turned back, with the afternoon sun behind him. The four guys formed up in front of him, with the sun in their eyes. The guy that had stood at the head of the table said, 'Now you need to get out.'

Reacher said, 'I am out.'

'Out of town.'

Reacher said nothing.

The guy said, 'Make a left, and then Main Street is four blocks up. When you get there, turn either left or right, west or east. We don't care which. Just keep on walking.'

Reacher asked, 'You still do that here?'

'Do what?'

'Run people out of town.'

'You bet we do.'

'You want to tell me why you do?'

'We don't have to tell you why we do.'

29

Reacher said, 'I just got here.'

'So?'

'So I'm staying.'

The guy on the end of the line pushed his rolled cuffs above his elbows and took a step forward. Broken nose, missing teeth. Reacher glanced at the guy's wrists. The width of a person's wrists was the only failsafe indicator of a person's raw strength. This guy's were wider than a long-stemmed rose, narrower than a two-by-four. Closer to the two-by-four than the rose.

Reacher said, 'You're picking on the wrong man.'

The guy that had been doing all the talking said, 'You think?'

Reacher nodded. 'I have to warn you. I promised my mother, a long time ago. She said I had to give folks a chance to walk away.'

'You a momma's boy?'

'She liked to see fair play.'

'There are four of us. One of you.'

Reacher's hands were down by his sides, relaxed, gently curled. His feet were apart, securely planted. He could feel the hard concrete through the soles of his shoes. It was textured. It had been brushed with a yard broom just before it dried, ten years earlier. He folded the fingers of his left hand flat against his palm. Raised the hand, very slowly. Brought it level with his shoulder, palm out. The four guys stared at it. The way his fingers were folded made them think he was hiding something. *But what?* He snapped his fingers open. *Nothing there.* In the same split second he moved sideways and heaved his right fist up like a convulsion and caught the guy that had stepped forward with a colossal uppercut to the jaw. The guy had been breathing through his mouth because of his broken nose and the massive impact snapped his jaw shut and lifted him up off the ground and dumped him back down in a vertical heap on the sidewalk. Like a puppet with the strings cut. Unconscious before he got halfway there.

'Now there are only three of you,' Reacher said. 'Still one of me.'

They weren't total amateurs. They reacted pretty well and pretty fast. They sprang back and apart into a wide defensive semicircle and crouched, fists ready.

Reacher said, 'You can still walk away.'

The guy that had been doing the talking said, 'I don't think so.'

'You're not good enough.'

'You got lucky.'

'Only suckers get sucker-punched.'

'Won't happen twice.'

Reacher said nothing.

The guy said, 'Get out of town. You can't take us three on one.'

'Try me.'

'Can't be done. Not now.'

Reacher nodded. 'Maybe you're right. Maybe one of you will stay on your feet long enough to get to me.'

'You can count on it.'

'But the question you need to ask is, which one of you will it be? Right now you've got no way of knowing. One of you will be driving the other three to the hospital for a six-month stay. You want me out of town bad enough to take those odds?'

Nobody spoke. Stalemate. Reacher rehearsed his next moves. A right-footed kick to the groin of the guy on his left, spin back with an elbow to the head for the guy in the middle, duck under the inevitable roundhouse swing incoming from the guy on the right, let him follow through, put an elbow in his kidney. One, two, three, no fundamental problem. Maybe a little clean-up afterwards, more feet and elbows. Main difficulty would be limiting the damage. Careful restraint would be required. It was always wiser to stay on the right side of the line, closer to brawling than homicide.

The tableau stayed frozen. Reacher upright and relaxed, three guys in a crouch, one sprawled face down on the floor, breathing but bleeding and not moving. In the distance beyond the three guys Reacher could see people going about their lawful business on the sidewalks. He could see cars and trucks driving slow on the streets, pausing at four-way stops, moving on.

Then he saw one particular car blow straight through a four-way and head in his direction. A Crown Victoria, white and gold, black push bars on the front, a light bar on the roof, antennas on the trunk lid. A shield on the door, with *DPD* scrolled across it. *Despair Police Department*. A heavyset cop in a tan jacket visible behind the glass.

'Behind you,' Reacher said. 'The cavalry is here.' But he didn't move. And he kept his eyes on the three guys. The cop's arrival didn't necessarily guarantee anything. Not yet. The three guys looked mad enough to move straight from a verbal warning to an actual assault charge. Maybe they already had so many they figured one more wouldn't make any difference. *Small towns.* In Reacher's experience they all had a lunatic fringe.

The Crown Vic braked hard in the gutter. The door swung open. The driver took a riot gun from a holster between the seats. Climbed out. Pumped the gun and held it diagonally across his chest. He was a big guy. White, maybe forty. Black hair. Wide neck. Tan jacket, brown pants, black shoes, a groove in his forehead from a Smokey the Bear hat that was presumably now resting on his passenger seat. He stood behind the three guys and looked around. Surveyed the scene. *Not exactly rocket science*, Reacher thought. *Three guys surrounding a fourth? We're not discussing the weather here.*

The cop said, 'Back off now.' Deep voice. Authoritative. The three guys stepped backward. The cop stepped forward. They swapped their relative positions. Now the three guys were behind the cop. The cop moved his gun. Pointed it straight at Reacher's chest.

'You're under arrest,' he said.

FIVE

Reacher stood still and asked, 'On what charge?'

The cop said, 'I'm sure I'll think of something.' He swapped the gun into one hand and used the other to take the handcuffs out of the holder on his belt. He held them on the flat of his palm and one of the guys behind him stepped forward and took them from him and looped around behind Reacher's back.

'Put your arms behind you,' the cop said.

'Are these guys deputized?' Reacher asked.

'Why would you care?'

'I don't. But they should. They put their hands on me without a good reason, they get their arms broken.'

'They're all deputized,' the cop said. 'Especially including the one you just laid out.'

He put both hands back on his gun.

'Self-defence,' Reacher said.

'Save it for the judge,' the cop said.

The guy behind him pulled Reacher's arms back and cuffed his wrists. The guy that had done all the talking opened the cruiser's rear door and stood there holding it like a hotel doorman with a taxicab.

'Get in the car,' the cop said.

Reacher stood still and considered his options. Didn't take him long. He didn't have any options. He was handcuffed. He had a guy about three feet behind him. He had a cop about eight feet in front of him. Two more guys three feet behind the cop. The riot gun was some kind of a Mossberg. He didn't recognize the model, but he respected the brand.

'In the car,' the cop said.

Reacher moved forward and looped around the open door and jacked himself inside butt-first. The seat was covered in heavy vinyl and he slid across it easily. The floor was covered in pimpled rubber. The security screen was clear bullet-proof plastic. The seat cushion was short, front to back. Uncomfortable, with his hands cuffed behind him. He braced his feet, one in the left foot well and one in the right. He figured he was going to get bounced around.

The cop got back in the front. The suspension yielded to his weight. He reholstered the Mossberg. Slammed his door and put the transmission in drive and stamped on the gas. Reacher was thrown back against the cushion. Then the guy braked hard for a stop sign and Reacher was tossed forward. He twisted as he went and took the blow against the plastic screen with his shoulder. The cop repeated the procedure at the next four-way. And the next. But Reacher was OK with it. It was to be expected. He had driven the same way in the past, in the days when he was the guy in the front and someone else was the guy in the back. And it was a small town. Wherever the police station was, it couldn't be far.

The police station was four blocks west and two blocks south of the restaurant. It was housed in another undistinguished brick building on a street wide enough to let the cop park nose-in to the kerb on a diagonal. There was one other car there. That was all. Small town, small police department. The building had two storeys. The cops had the ground floor. The town court was upstairs. Reacher guessed there were cells in the basement. His trip to the booking desk was uneventful. He didn't make trouble. No point. No percentage in being a fugitive on foot in a town where the line was twelve miles away in one direction and maybe more in the other. The desk was manned by a patrolman who could have been the arresting officer's kid brother. Same size and shape, same face, same hair, a little younger. Reacher was uncuffed and gave up the stuff from his pockets and his shoelaces. He had no belt. He was escorted down a winding stair and put in a six-by-eight cell fronted by ancient ironwork that had been painted maybe fifty times.

'Lawyer?' he asked.

'You know any?' the desk guy asked back.

'The public defender will do.'

The desk guy nodded and locked the gate and walked away. Reacher was left on his own. The cell block was otherwise empty. Three cells in a line, a narrow corridor, no windows. Each cell had a wall-mounted iron tray for a bed and a steel toilet with a sink built in to the top of the tank. Bulkhead lights burned behind wire grilles on the ceilings. Reacher ran his right hand under cold water at the sink and massaged his knuckles. They were sore, but not damaged. He lay down on the cot and closed his eyes.

Welcome to Despair, he thought.

SIX

The public defender never showed. Reacher dozed for two hours and then the cop that had arrested him clattered down the stairs and unlocked the cell and gestured for him to get up.

'The judge is ready for you,' he said.

Reacher yawned. 'I haven't been charged with anything yet. I haven't seen my lawyer.'

'Take it up with the court,' the cop said. 'Not with me.'

'What kind of a half-assed system have you got here?'

'The same kind we've always had.'

'I think I'll stay down here.'

'I could send your three remaining buddies in for a visit.'

'Save gas and send them straight to the hospital.'

'I could put you in handcuffs first. Strap you to the bed.'

'All by yourself?'

'I could bring a stun gun.'

'You live here in town?'

'Why?'

'Maybe I'll come visit you one day.'

'I don't think you will.'

The cop stood there waiting. Reacher shrugged to himself and swung his feet to the floor. Pushed himself upright and stepped out of the cell. Walking was awkward without his shoelaces. On the stairs he had to hook his toes to stop his shoes falling off altogether. He shuffled past the booking desk and followed the cop up another flight. A grander staircase. At the top was a wooden double door, closed. Alongside it was a sign on a short post with a heavy base. Same kind of thing as the restaurant sign, except this one said: *Town Court*. The cop opened the left-hand panel and stood aside. Reacher stepped into a courtroom. There was a centre aisle and four rows of spectator seating. Then a bullpen rail and a prosecution table and a defence table, each with three wheelback chairs. There was a witness stand and a jury box and a judge's dais. All the furniture and all the structures were made out of pine, lacquered dark and then darkened more by age and polish. The walls were panelled with the same stuff, up to three-quarters height. The ceiling and the top of the walls were painted cream. There were flags behind the dais, Old Glory and something Reacher guessed was the state flag of Colorado.

The room was empty. It echoed and smelled of dust. The cop walked ahead and opened the bullpen gate. Pointed Reacher towards the defence table. The cop sat down at the prosecution table. They waited. Then an inconspicuous door in the back wall opened and a man in a suit walked in. The cop jumped up and said, 'All rise.' Reacher stayed in his seat.

The man in the suit clumped up three steps and slid in behind the dais. He was bulky and somewhere over sixty and had a full head of white hair. His suit was cheap and badly cut. He picked up a pen and straightened a legal pad in front of him. He looked at Reacher and said, 'Name?'

'I haven't been Mirandized,' Reacher said.

'You haven't been charged with a crime,' the old guy said. 'This isn't a trial.'

'So what is it?'

'A hearing.'

'About what?'

'It's an administrative matter, that's all. Possibly just a technicality. But I do need to ask you some questions.'

Reacher said nothing.

The guy asked, 'Name?'

'I'm sure the police department copied my passport and showed it to you.'

'For the record, please.'

The guy's tone was neutral and his manner was reasonably courteous. So Reacher shrugged and said, 'Jack Reacher. No middle initial.'

The guy wrote it down. Followed up with his date of birth, and his Social Security number, and his nationality. Then he asked, 'Address?'

Reacher said, 'No fixed address.'

The guy wrote it down. Asked, 'Occupation?'

'None.'

'Purpose of your visit to Despair?'

'Tourism.'

40

'How do you propose to support yourself during your visit?'

'I hadn't really thought about it. I didn't anticipate a major problem. This isn't exactly London or Paris or New York City.'

'Please answer the question.'

'I have a bank balance,' Reacher said.

The guy wrote it all down. Then he sniffed and skipped his pen back over the lines he had already completed and paused. Asked, 'What was your last address?'

'An APO box.'

'APO?'

'Army Post Office.'

'You're a veteran?'

'Yes, I am.'

'How long did you serve?'

'Thirteen years.'

'Until?'

'I mustered out ten years ago.'

'Unit?'

'Military Police.'

'Final rank?'

'Major.'

'And you haven't had a permanent address since you left the army?'

'No, I haven't.'

The guy made a pronounced check mark against one of his lines. Reacher saw his pen move four times, twice in one direction and twice in the other. Then the guy asked, 'How long have you been out of work?'

'Ten years,' Reacher said.

'You haven't worked since you left the army?'

'Not really.'

'A retired major couldn't find a job?'

'This retired major didn't want to find a job.'

'Yet you have a bank balance?'

'Savings,' Reacher said. 'Plus occasional casual labour.'

The guy made another big check mark. Two vertical scratches, two horizontal. Then he asked, 'Where did you stay last night?'

'In Hope,' Reacher said. 'In a motel.'

'And your bags are still there?'

'I don't have any bags.'

The guy wrote it down and made another check mark.

'You walked here?' he asked.

'Yes,' Reacher said.

'Why?'

'No buses, and I didn't find a ride.'

'No, why here?'

'Tourism,' Reacher said again.

'What had you heard about our little town?'

'Nothing at all.'

'Yet you decided to visit?'

'Evidently.'

'Why?'

'I found the name intriguing.'

'That's not a very compelling reason.'

'I have to be somewhere. And thanks for the big welcome.'

The guy made a fourth check mark. Two vertical lines, two horizontal. Then he skipped his pen down his list, slowly and methodically, fourteen answers, plus four diversions to the margin for the check marks. He said, 'I'm sorry, but I find you to be in contravention of one of Despair's town ordinances. I'm afraid you'll have to leave.'

'Leave?'

'Leave town.'

'What ordinance?'

'Vagrancy,' the guy said.

SEVEN

Reacher said, 'There's a vagrancy ordinance here?'

The judge nodded and said, 'As there is in most Western towns.'

'I never came across one before.'

'Then you've been very fortunate.'

'I'm not a vagrant.'

'Homeless for ten years, jobless for ten years, you ride buses or beg rides or walk from place to place performing occasional casual labour, what else would you call yourself?'

'Free,' Reacher said. 'And lucky.'

The judge nodded again, and said, 'I'm glad you see a silver lining.'

'What about my First Amendment right of free assembly?'

'The Supreme Court ruled long ago. Municipalities have the right to exclude undesirables.'

'Tourists are undesirable? What does the Chamber of Commerce think about that?'

'This is a quiet, old-fashioned town. People don't lock their doors. We don't feel the need. Most of the keys were lost years ago, in our grandparents' time.'

'I'm not a thief.'

'But we err on the side of caution. Experience elsewhere shows that the itinerant jobless have always been a problem.'

'Suppose I don't go? What's the penalty?'

'Thirty days' imprisonment.'

Reacher said nothing. The judge said, 'The officer will drive you to the town line. Get a job and a home, and we'll welcome you back with open arms. But don't come back until you do.'

The cop took him downstairs again and gave him back his cash and his passport and his ATM card and his toothbrush. Nothing was missing. Everything was there. Then the cop handed over his shoelaces and waited at the booking desk while he threaded them through the eyelets in his shoes and pulled them tight and tied them off. Then the cop put his hand on the butt of his gun and said, 'Car.' Reacher walked ahead of him through the lobby and stepped out the street door. The sun had gone. It was late in the day, late in the year, and it was getting dark. The cop had moved his cruiser. Now it was parked nose-out.

'In the back,' the cop said.

Reacher heard a plane in the sky, far to the west. A single engine, climbing hard. A Cessna or a Beech or a Piper, small and lonely in the vastness. He pulled the car door and slid inside. Without handcuffs he was a lot more comfortable. He sprawled sideways, like he would in a taxi or a town car. The cop leaned in after him, one hand on the roof and one on the door, and said, 'We're serious. You come back, we'll arrest you, and you'll spend thirty days in that same cell. Always assuming you don't look at us cross-eyed and we shoot you for resisting.'

'You married?' Reacher asked.

'Why?'

'I thought not. You seem to prefer jerking off.'

The cop stood still for a long moment and then slammed the door and got in the front. He took off down the street and made a right and headed north. *Six blocks to Main Street*, Reacher figured. *If he turns left, takes me onward, to the west, maybe I'll let it go. But if he turns right, takes me back east to Hope, maybe I won't.*

Reacher hated turning back.

Forward motion was his organizing principle.

Six blocks, six stop signs. At each one the cop braked gently and slowed and looked left and looked right and then rolled forward. At Main Street he came to a complete halt. He paused. Then he hit the gas and nosed forward and swung the wheel.

And turned right.

East.

Back towards Hope.

EIGHT

Reacher saw the dry goods emporium and the gas station and the abandoned motor court and the vacant unbuilt lot slide by and then the cop accelerated to a steady sixty miles an hour. The tyres rumbled over the rough road and stray pebbles spattered the underside and bounced and skittered away to the shoulders. Twelve minutes later the car slowed and coasted and braked and came to a stop. The cop opened his door and climbed out and put his hand on the butt of his gun and opened Reacher's door.

'Out,' he said.

Reacher slid out and felt Despair's grit under his shoes.

The cop jerked his thumb, to the east, where it was darker.

'That way,' he said.

Reacher stood still.

The cop took the gun off his belt. It was a Glock nine-millimetre, boxy and dull in the gloom. No safety catch. Just a latch on the trigger, already compressed by the cop's meaty forefinger.

'Please,' the cop said. 'Just give me a reason.'

Reacher stepped forward, three paces. Saw the moon rising on the far horizon. Saw the end of Despair's rough gravel and the start of Hope's smooth blacktop. Saw the inch-wide trench between, filled with black compound. The car was stopped with its push bars directly above it. The expansion joint. The boundary. The line. Reacher shrugged and stepped over it. One long pace, back to Hope.

The cop called, 'Don't bother us again.'

Reacher didn't reply. Didn't turn around. Just stood and faced east and listened as the car backed up and turned and crunched away across the stones. When the sound was all gone in the distance he shrugged again and started walking.

He walked less than twenty yards and saw headlights a mile away, coming straight at him out of Hope. The beams were widely spaced, bouncing high, dipping low. A big car, moving fast. It came at him out of the gathering darkness and when it was a hundred yards away he saw it was another cop car. Another Crown Vic, painted black and white, police spec, with push bars, lights, and antennas. It stopped short of him and a spotlight mounted on the windshield pillar lit up and swivelled jerkily and played its beam all the way up and down him twice, coming to rest on his face, blinding him. Then it clicked off again and the car crept forward, tyres hissing on the smooth asphalt surface, and stopped again with the driver's door exactly alongside him. The door had a gold shield painted on it, with *HPD* scrolled across the middle. *Hope Police Department*. The window buzzed down and a hand went up and a dome light came on inside. Reacher saw a woman cop at the wheel, short blond hair backlit by the weak yellow bulb above and behind her.

'Want a ride?' she asked.

'I'll walk,' Reacher said.

'It's five miles to town.'

'I walked out here, I can walk back.'

'Riding is easier.'

'I'm OK.'

The woman was quiet for a moment. Reacher listened to the Crown Vic's engine. It was idling patiently. Belts were turning, a muffler was ticking as it cooled. Then Reacher moved on. He took three steps and heard the car's transmission go into reverse and then the car came alongside him again, driving backward, keeping pace as he walked. The window was still down. The woman said, 'Give yourself a break, Zeno.'

Reacher stopped. Said, 'You know who Zeno was?'

The car stopped.

'Zeno of Cittium,' the woman said. 'The founder of Stoicism. I'm telling you to stop being so long-suffering.'

'Stoics have to be long-suffering. Stoicism is about the unquestioning acceptance of destinies. Zeno said so.'

'Your destiny is to return to Hope. Doesn't matter to Zeno whether you walk or ride.'

'What are you anyway, a philosopher or a cop or a cab driver?'

'The Despair PD calls us when they're dumping someone at the line. As a courtesy.'

'This happens a lot?'

'More than you'd think.'

'And you come on out and pick us up?'

'We're here to serve. Says so on the badge.'

Reacher looked down at the shield on her door. *HPD* was written across the scroll in the centre, but *To Protect* was written at the top of the escutcheon, with *And Serve* added at the bottom.

'I see,' he said.

'So get in.'

'Why do they do it?'

'Get in and I'll tell you.'

'You going to refuse to let me walk?'

'It's five miles. You're grumpy now, you'll be real cranky when you arrive in town. Believe me. We've seen it before. Better for all of us if you ride.'

'I'm different. Walking calms me down.'

The woman said, 'I'm not going to beg, Reacher.'

'You know my name?'

'Despair PD passed it on. As a courtesy.'

'And a warning?'

'Maybe. Right now I'm trying to decide whether to take them seriously.'

Reacher shrugged again and put his hand on the rear door handle.

'Up front, you idiot,' the woman said. 'I'm helping you, not arresting you.'

So Reacher looped around the trunk and opened the front passenger door. The seat was all hemmed in with radio consoles and a laptop terminal on a bracket, but the space was clear. No

50

hat. He crammed himself in. Not much leg room, because of the security screen behind him. Up front the car smelled of oil and coffee and perfume and warm electronics. The laptop screen showed a GPS map. A small arrow was pointing west and blinking away at the far edge of a pink shape labelled *Hope Township*. The shape was precisely rectangular, almost square. A fast and arbitrary land allocation, like the state of Colorado itself. Next to it Despair township was represented by a light purple shape. Despair was not rectangular. It was shaped like a blunt wedge. Its eastern border matched Hope's western limit exactly, then it spread wider, like a triangle with the point cut off. Its western line was twice as long as its eastern and bordered grey emptiness. Unincorporated land, Reacher figured. Spurs came off I-70 and I-25 and ran through the unincorporated land and clipped Despair's northwestern corner.

The woman cop buzzed her window back up and craned her neck and glanced behind her and K-turned across the road. She was slightly built under a crisp tan shirt. Probably less than five feet six, probably less than a hundred and twenty pounds, probably less than thirty-five years old. No jewellery, no wedding band. She had a Motorola radio on her collar and a tall gold badge bar pinned over her left breast. According to the badge her name was Vaughan. And according to the badge she was a pretty good cop. She seemed to have won a bunch of awards and commendations. She was good-looking, but different from regular women. She had seen stuff they hadn't. That was clear. Reacher was familiar with the concept. He had served with plenty of women, back in the MPs.

He asked, 'Why did Despair run me out?'

The woman called Vaughan turned out the dome light. Now she was front-lit by red instrument displays from the dash and the pink and purple glow from the GPS screen and white scatter from the headlight beams on the road.

'Look at yourself,' she said.

'What about me?'

'What do you see?'

'Just a guy.'

'A blue collar guy in work clothes, fit, strong, healthy and hungry.'

'So?'

'How far did you get?'

'I saw the gas station and the restaurant. And the town court.'

'Then you didn't see the full picture,' Vaughan said. She drove slow, about thirty miles an hour, as if she had plenty more to say. She had one hand on the wheel, with her elbow propped on the door. Her other hand lay easy in her lap. Five miles at thirty miles an hour was going to take ten minutes. Reacher wondered what she had to tell him, that less than ten minutes wouldn't cover.

He said, 'I'm more green collar than blue.'

'Green?'

'I was in the army. Military cop.'

'When?'

'Ten years ago.'

'You working now?'

'No.'

'Well, then.'

52

'Well what?'

'You were a threat.'

'How?'

'West of downtown Despair is the biggest metal recycling plant in Colorado.'

'I saw the smog.'

'There's nothing else in Despair's economy. The metal plant is the whole ballgame.'

'A company town,' Reacher said.

Vaughan nodded at the wheel. 'The guy that owns the plant owns every brick of every building. Half the population works for him full time. The other half works for him part time, when and if he needs them. The full-time people are happy enough. The part-time people are insecure. They don't like competition from outsiders. They don't like people showing up, looking for casual labour, willing to work for less.'

'I wasn't willing to work at all.'

'You tell them that?'

'They didn't ask.'

'They wouldn't have believed you anyway. Company towns are weird places. Standing around every morning waiting for a nod from the foreman does things to people. It's kind of feudal. The whole place is feudal. The money the owner pays out in wages comes right back at him, in rents. Mortgages, too. He owns the bank. No relief on Sundays, either. There's one church and he's the lay preacher. You want to work, you have to show up in a pew from time to time.'

'Is that fair?'

'He likes to dominate. He'll use anything.'

'So why don't people move on?'

'Some have. Those that haven't never will.'

'Doesn't this guy want people coming in to work for less?'

'He prefers stability. He likes the people he owns, not strangers. And it doesn't really matter what he pays, anyway. He gets it right back in rents and profits from his stores.'

'So why were those guys worried?'

'People always worry. Company towns are weird.'

'And the town judge toes their line?'

'He has to. It's an elected position. And the vagrancy ordinance is for real. Most towns have one. We do, for sure, in Hope. No way around it, if someone complains.'

'But nobody complained in Hope. I stayed there last night.'

'We're not a company town.'

Vaughan slowed. Hope's first built-up block was ahead in the distance. Reacher recognized it. A mom-and-pop hardware store. That morning an old guy had been putting stepladders and wheelbarrows out on the sidewalk, building a display. Now the store was all closed up and dark.

He asked, 'How big is the Hope PD?'

Vaughan said, 'Me and two others and a watch commander.'

'You got sworn deputies?'

'Four of them. We don't use them often. Traffic control, maybe, if we've got construction going on. Why?'

'Are they armed?'

'No. In Colorado deputies are civilian peace officers. Why?'

'How many deputies does the Despair PD have?'

'Four, I think.'

'I met them.'

'And?'

'Theoretically, what would the Hope PD do if someone showed up and got in a dispute with one of your deputies and bust his jaw?'

'We'd throw that someone's sorry ass in jail, real quick.'

'Why?'

'You know why. Zero tolerance for assaults on peace officers, plus an obligation to look after our own, plus pride and self-respect.'

'Suppose there was a self-defence issue?'

'Civilian versus a peace officer, we'd need some kind of amazing reasonable doubt.'

'OK.'

'You'd have felt the same in the MPs.'

'That's for damn sure.'

'So why did you ask?'

Reacher didn't answer directly. Instead he said, 'I'm not a Stoic, really. Zeno preached the passive acceptance of fate. I'm not like that. I'm not very passive. I take challenges personally.'

'So?'

'I don't like to be told where I can go and where I can't.'

'Stubborn?'

'It annoys me.'

Vaughan slowed some more and pulled in at the kerb. Put the transmission in Park and turned in her seat.

'My advice?' she said. 'Get over it and move on. Despair isn't worth it.'

Reacher said nothing.

'Go get a meal and a room for the night,' Vaughan said. 'I'm sure you're hungry.'

Reacher nodded.

'Thanks for the ride,' he said. 'And it was a pleasure to meet you.'

He opened the door and slid out to the sidewalk. Hope's version of Main Street was called First Street. He knew there was a diner a block away on Second Street. He had eaten breakfast there. He set out walking towards it and heard Vaughan's Crown Vic move away behind him. He heard the civilized purr of its motor and the soft hiss of its tyres on the asphalt. Then he turned a corner and didn't hear it any more.

An hour later he was still in the diner. He had eaten soup, steak, fries, beans, apple pie, and ice cream. Now he was drinking coffee. It was a better brew than at the restaurant in Despair. And it had been served in a mug that was cylindrical in shape. Still too thick at the rim, but much closer to the ideal.

He was thinking about Despair, and he was wondering why getting him out of town had been more important than keeping him there and busting him for the assault on the deputy.

NINE

The diner in Hope had a bottomless cup policy for its coffee and Reacher abused it mercilessly. He drank most of a Bunn flask all on his own. His waitress became fascinated by the spectacle. She didn't need to be asked for refills. She came back every time he was ready, sometimes before he was ready, as if she was willing him to break some kind of a world record for consumption. He left her a double tip, just in case the owner fined her for her generosity.

It was full dark when he left the diner. Nine o'clock in the evening. He figured it would stay dark for another ten hours. Sunrise was probably around seven, in that latitude at that time of year. He walked three blocks to where he had seen a small grocery. In a city it would have been called a bodega and in the suburbs it would have been franchised, but in Hope it was still what it had probably always been, a cramped and dusty family-run enterprise selling the things people needed when they needed them.

Reacher needed water and protein and energy. He bought three one-litre bottles of Poland

Spring and six chocolate chip Powerbars and a roll of black thirteen-gallon garbage bags. The clerk at the register packed them all carefully into a paper sack and Reacher took his change and carried the sack four blocks to the same motel he had used the night before. He got the same room, at the end of the row. He went inside and put the sack on the night stand and lay down on the bed. He planned on a short rest. Until midnight. He didn't want to walk seventeen miles twice on the same day.

Reacher got off the bed at midnight and checked the window. No more moon. There was thick cloud and patches of distant starlight. He packed his purchases into one of the black garbage bags and slung it over his shoulder. Then he left the motel and headed up to First Street in the darkness and turned west. There was no traffic. No pedestrians. Few lit windows. It was the middle of the night in the middle of nowhere. The sidewalk ended twenty feet west of the hardware store. He stepped off the kerb on to the asphalt and kept on going. Route-march speed, four miles an hour. Not difficult on the smooth flat surface. He built up a rhythm to the point where he felt he could keep on walking for ever and never stop.

But he did stop. He stopped five miles later, a hundred yards short of the line between Hope and Despair, because he sensed a shape ahead of him in the blackness. A hole in the darkness. A car, parked on the shoulder. Mostly black, some hints of white.

A police cruiser.

Vaughan.

The name settled in his mind and at the exact same time the car's lights flicked on. High beams. Very bright. He was pinned. His shadow shot out behind him, infinitely long. He shielded his eyes, left-handed, because his bag was in his right. He stood still. The lights stayed on. He stepped off the road and looped out over the crusted sand to the north. The lights died back and the spot on the windshield pillar tracked him. It wouldn't leave him. So he changed direction and headed straight for it.

Vaughan turned the light off and buzzed her window down as he approached. She was parked facing east, with two wheels on the sand and the rear bumper of the car exactly level with the expansion joint in the road. Inside her own jurisdiction, but only just. She said, 'I thought I might see you here.'

Reacher looked at her and said nothing.

She asked, 'What are you doing?'

'Taking a stroll.'

'That all?'

'No law against it.'

'Not here,' Vaughan said. 'But there is if you take three more steps.'

'Not your law.'

'You're a stubborn man.'

Reacher nodded. 'I wanted to see Despair and I'm going to.'

'It isn't that great of a place.'

'I'm sure it isn't. But I like to make my own mind up about things like that.'

'They're serious, you know. Either you'll spend thirty days in jail or they'll shoot you.'

'If they find me.'

'They'll find you. I found you.'

'I wasn't hiding from you.'

'Did you hurt a deputy over there?'

'Why do you ask?'

'I was thinking about the question you asked me.'

'I don't know for sure what he was.'

'I don't like the idea of deputies getting hurt.'

'You wouldn't have liked the deputy. If that's what he was.'

'They'll be looking for you.'

'How big is their department?'

'Smaller than ours. Two cars, two guys, I think.'

'They won't find me.'

'Why are you going back?'

'Because they told me not to.'

'Is it worth it?'

'What would you do?'

Vaughan said, 'I'm an oestrogen-based life form, not testosterone. And I'm all grown up now. I'd suck it up and move on. Or stay in Hope. It's a nice place.'

'I'll see you tomorrow,' Reacher said.

'You won't. Either I'll be picking you up right here a month from now or I'll be reading about you in the newspaper. Beaten and shot while resisting arrest.'

'Tomorrow,' Reacher said. 'I'll buy you a late dinner.'

He moved on, one pace, two, three, and then he stepped over the line.

TEN

He got off the road immediately. The Hope PD had predicted that he would rise to the challenge. It was an easy guess that the Despair PD would make the same assessment. And he didn't want to blunder into a parked Despair cruiser. That event would have an altogether different conclusion from a pleasant chat with the pretty Officer Vaughan.

He looped fifty yards into the scrub north of the road. Near enough to retain a sense of direction, far enough to stay out of a driver's peripheral vision. The night was cold. The ground was uneven. The going was slow. No chance of getting close to four miles an hour. No chance at all. He stumbled on. He had no flashlight. A conscious decision. A light would hurt him more than help him. It would be visible for a mile. It would be worse than climbing up on a rock and yelling *Here I am*.

A slow mile later the clock in his head told him it was quarter to two in the morning. He heard an aero engine again, far away to the west, blipping and feathering. A single-engine plane, coming in to land. A Cessna, or a Beech, or a Piper. Maybe the same one he had heard take off, hours before. He listened to it until he imagined it had touched down and taxied. Then he started walking again.

Four hours later dawn was about seventy-five minutes away and he was about level with the centre of downtown, three hundred yards out in the scrub. He knew he must have left a healthy trail of footprints, but he didn't particularly care. He doubted that the Despair PD maintained a kennel full of bloodhounds or ran aerial surveillance from a helicopter. As long as he stayed off the roads and the sidewalks he was as good as invisible.

He moved another fifty yards north and sensed the bulk of another boat-sized table rock and hunkered down behind it. The night was still cold. He unwrapped his stuff and drank water and ate a Powerbar. Then he repacked his bag and stood up behind the rock and turned to study the town. The rock was chest high to him and he leaned against it with his elbows out and his forearms flat on its top surface and his chin resting on his stacked fists. At first he saw nothing. Just darkness and stillness and the hidden glow from occasional lit windows. Further in the distance he saw more lights and sensed more activity. The residential areas, he guessed, south of downtown. Houses and apartment buildings, perhaps. Maybe trailer parks. He figured people were getting up for work.

Ten minutes later he saw headlight beams coming north. Two, three sets. Their light funnelled through the cross streets and bounced and dipped and threw long shadows straight towards him. He stayed where he was, just watching. The beams paused at Main Street and then swept west through huge right-angle swings. More came after them. Soon every cross street was lit up bright by long processions of vehicles. It was like the day was dawning in the south. There were sedans and pick-up trucks and old-model SUVs. They all drove north to Main Street and paused and jostled and swung west, towards where Vaughan had said the recycling plant was.

A company town.

Six o'clock in the morning.

The people of Despair, going to work.

Reacher followed them on foot, four hundred yards to the north. He stumbled on through the crusted scrub, tracking the road. He was doing about three miles an hour. They were doing more than thirty. But still it took ten minutes for them all to pass him. They made a long convoy. Then the last truck got ahead of him and he followed the red chain of tail lights with his eyes. A mile or more ahead the horizon was lit up with an immense glow. Not dawn. That was going to happen behind him, to the east. The glow to the west was from arc lighting. There seemed to be a huge rectangle of lights on poles surrounding some kind of a massive arena. It looked to be about a mile long. Maybe a half-mile wide. *The biggest metal recycling plant in Colorado*, Vaughan had said.

No kidding, Reacher thought. *Looks like the biggest in the world*.

White steam and dirty black smoke drifted here and there in the glow. In front of it the long convoy of vehicles peeled off left and right and parked in neat rows on acres of beaten scrub. Their headlights swung and bounced and then shut down, one by one. Reacher holed up again, a quarter-mile short and a quarter-mile north of the gate. Watched men file inside, shuffling forward in a long line, lunch pails in their hands. The gate was narrow. A personnel entrance, not a vehicle entrance. Reacher guessed the vehicle entrance was on the other side of the complex, convenient for the highway spurs.

The sky was lightening behind him. Landscape features were becoming visible. In an overall sense the terrain was basically flat, but up close it was pitted with enough humps and dips and rocks to provide decent concealment. The earth was sandy and tan. There were occasional scrubby bushes. There was nothing interesting anywhere. Nothing to attract hikers. Not attractive picnic territory. Reacher expected to spend the day alone.

The last worker filed inside and the personnel gate closed. Reacher moved on, wheeling north and west in a wide circle, staying hidden, but looking for elevation where he could find it. The recycling plant was truly enormous. It was ringed by an endless solid wall welded out of metal plates painted white. The wall was topped with a continuous horizontal cylinder six feet in diameter. Impossible to climb. Like a supermax prison. His initial estimate of the size of the place had been conservative. It looked bigger than the town itself. Like a tail that wags a dog. Despair was not a town with a plant attached. It was a factory with a dormitory outside its gates.

Work was starting inside. Reacher heard the

groan of heavy machinery and the ringing sound of metal on metal and saw the flare and spark of cutting torches. He moved all the way around to the northwest corner, fifteen minutes' fast walk, still a quarter-mile out in the scrub. The vehicle gate was visible now. A section of the west wall was standing open. A wide road ran from the horizon straight to it. The road looked to be smooth and solid. Built for heavy trucks.

The road was a problem. If Reacher wanted to continue his counterclockwise progress, he would have to cross it somewhere. He would be exposed. His dark clothes would stand out in the coming daylight. But to who, exactly? He guessed the Despair cops would stay in town east of the plant. And he didn't expect any roving surveillance teams out of the plant itself.

But that was exactly what he got.

He watched from four hundred yards away and two white Chevy Tahoes came out of the vehicle gate. They drove fifty yards down the road and then plunged off it, one to the left and one to the right, on to beaten tracks of packed scrub created by endless previous excursions. The Tahoes had raised off-road suspensions and big white-lettered tyres and the word *Security* stencilled in black across their doors. They drove slowly, maybe twenty miles an hour, one clockwise, one counter-clockwise, as if they intended to lap the plant all day long.

Reacher crouched low and backed off another hundred yards. Found a suitable rock and got down behind it. The Tahoes were on perimeter tracks maybe fifty yards from the walls. If the plant was a mile or more long and a half mile or more wide, then each circuit was about three and a half miles long. At twenty miles an hour, each circuit would take each truck a little more than ten minutes to complete. Therefore with two trucks moving in opposite directions any one point would be free of surveillance for slightly more than five minutes. That was all. And that was if the two trucks kept pace with one another.

Reacher hated turning back.

He struck out due west, staying in the dips and washes as far as possible and keeping boulders between himself and the plant. Ten minutes later the natural terrain gave way to where the land had been cleared and graded for the road. The near shoulder was maybe ten yards wide, made of packed sand dotted with stunted second-growth weeds. The roadbed was fifteen or sixteen yards wide. Two lanes, with a bright yellow line between. Smooth blacktop. The far shoulder was another ten yards wide.

Total distance, thirty-five yards, minimum.

Reacher was no kind of a sprinter. As any kind of a runner, he was pretty slow. His best attempt at speed was barely faster than a quick walk. He crouched just east of the last available table rock and watched for the Tahoes.

They came around much less often than he had predicted. The intervals were closer to ten minutes than five. Which was inexplicable, but good. What wasn't good was that the road itself was starting to get busy. Reacher knew he should have seen that coming. The largest recycling plant in Colorado clearly needed input, and it clearly

66

produced output. They didn't dig stuff out of the scrub and then bury it again. They trucked scrap in and then trucked ingots out. A lot of scrap, and a lot of ingots. Shortly after seven o'clock in the morning a flat-bed semi roared out of the gate and lumbered on to the road. It had Indiana plates and was laden with bright steel bars. It drove a hundred yards and was passed by another flat-bed heading inward. This one had Oregon plates and was loaded with crushed cars, dozens of them, their chipped and battered paint layered like thin stripes. A container truck with Canadian plates left the plant and passed the Oregon semi. Then the counterclockwise Tahoe showed up and bounced across the roadbed and kept on going. Three minutes later its clockwise partner rotated in the opposite direction. Another semi left the plant and another headed in. A mile west Reacher saw a third approaching, wobbling and shimmering in the morning haze. Way behind it, a fourth.

It was like Times Square.

Inside the plant giant gantry cranes were moving and cascades of welding sparks were showering everywhere. Smoke was rising and fierce blasts of heat from furnaces were distorting the air. There were muted noises, the chatter of air hammers, clangs of sheet metal, metallic tearing sounds, deep sonorous rings like massive impacts on a blacksmith's anvil.

Reacher drank more water and ate another Powerbar. Then he repacked his plastic sack and waited for the Tahoes to pass one more time and just got up and walked across the road. He passed within forty yards of two speeding trucks, one inbound, one outbound. He accepted the risk of being seen. For one thing, he had no real choice. For another, he figured it was a question of degrees of separation. Would a truck driver tell a plant foreman he had seen a pedestrian? Would the plant foreman call the security office? Would the security office call the town cops?

Unlikely. And even if it happened, response time would be slow. Reacher would be back in the weeds well before the Crown Vics showed up. And the Crown Vics would be no good off-road. The Tahoes would stick to their own private itineraries.

Safe enough.

He made it onward to where the rocks and the humps and the dips resumed and headed south, tracking the long side of the plant. The wall continued. It was maybe fourteen feet high, welded out of what looked like the roofs of old cars. Each panel had a slight convex curve. They made the whole thing look quilted. The six-foot cylinder along the top looked to be assembled from the same material, moulded in giant presses to the correct contour, and welded together in a seamless run. Then the whole assembly had been sprayed glossy white.

It took Reacher twenty-six minutes to walk the length of the plant, which made it more than a mile long. At its far southwest corner he saw why the Tahoes were so slow. There was a second walled compound. Another huge rectangle. Similar size. It was laid out along an axis running from the northeast to the southwest, not quite in line with the plant. Its northeastern corner was maybe fifty yards from the plant's southwestern corner. Tyre tracks showed that the Tahoes were lapping it too, passing and repassing through the fifty-yard bottleneck in a giant distorted figure-eight. Reacher was suddenly exposed. His position was good, relative to the first compound. Not so good, relative to the second. The clockwise Tahoe would sweep through the gap and make a wide turn and come pretty close. He backed off west, aiming for a low boulder. He got halfway across a shallow pan of scrub.

Then he heard tyres on dirt.

He dropped flat to the floor, face down, watching.

69

ELEVEN

The white Tahoe came through the bottleneck at twenty miles an hour. Reacher heard its tyres on the scrub. They were wide and soft, squirming on the loose surface, squelching small stones, shooting them left and right. He heard the hiss of a power steering pump and the wet throb of a big V-8 as the vehicle turned. It came through a shallow curve, close enough for Reacher to smell its exhaust.

He lay still.

The truck drove on. Didn't stop. Didn't even slow. The driver was high up in the left-hand seat. Reacher guessed like most drivers his eyes were following the turn he intended to make. He was anticipating the curve. Looking ahead and to his left, not sideways to his right.

Bad technique, for a security guard.

Reacher lay still until the Tahoe was long gone. Then he stood up and dusted himself off and headed west and sat down again behind the low boulder he had been heading for.

*　　*　　*

The second compound was walled with field-stone, not metal. It was residential. There was ornamental planting, including screens of trees placed to block any view of industrial activity. There was a huge house visible in the distance, built out of wood in a chalet style more suitable to Vail than Despair. There were outbuildings, including an oversize barn that was probably an aircraft hangar, because inside the whole length of the far wall was a wide graded strip of dirt that could only be a runway. It had three wind-socks on poles, one at each end and one in the middle.

Reacher moved on. He stayed well away from the fifty-yard bottleneck. Too easy to be spotted. Too easy to be run over. Instead, he looped west again and aimed to circle the residential compound too, as if both enclosures were one giant obstacle.

By noon he was holed up way to the south, looking back at the recycling plant from the rear. The residential compound was closer, and to his left. Far beyond it to the northwest was a small grey smudge in the distance. A low building, or a group of buildings, maybe five or six miles away. Indistinct. Maybe close to the road. Maybe a gas station or a truck stop or a motel. Probably outside Despair's town limit. Reacher narrowed his eyes and squinted, but he couldn't make out any detail. He turned back to the nearer sights. Work continued inside the plant. Nothing much was happening at the house. He saw the Tahoes circling and watched the trucks on the distant road.

There was a continuous stream of them. Mostly flat-beds, but there were some container trucks and some box trucks. They came and went and the sky stained dark with diesel in a long ribbon all the way to the horizon. The plant belched smoke and flame and sparks. Its noise was softened by distance, but up close it must have been fearsome. The sun was high and the day had gotten warm.

He hunkered down and watched and listened until he got bored and then he headed east, for a look at the far side of town.

It was bright daylight, so he stayed cautious and moved slow. There was a long empty gap between the plant and the town itself. Maybe three miles. He covered them in a straight line, well out in the scrub. By the middle of the afternoon he was level with where he had been at six o'clock in the morning, but due south of the settlement, not due north, looking at the backs of houses, not the fronts of commercial buildings.

The houses were neat and uniform, cheaply but adequately built. They were all one-storey ranches with shingle siding and asphalt roofs. Some were painted, some were stained wood. Some had garages, some didn't. Some had picket fences around their yards, some yards were open. Most had satellite dishes, tilted up and facing southwest like a regiment of expectant faces. People were visible, here and there. Mostly women, some children. Some men. They were getting in and out of cars, doing yard projects, moving slow. The part-time workers, Reacher guessed, unlucky today. He moved along a hundred-yard arc, left and right, east and west, changing his point of view. But what he saw didn't change much. Houses, in a strange little suburb, tight in to the town, but miles from anywhere else, with empty vastness all around. The skies were high and huge. Away to the west the Rockies looked a million miles away. Reacher suddenly understood that Despair had been built by people who had given up. They had come over the rise and seen the far horizon and had quit there and then. Just pitched camp and stayed where they were. And their descendants were still in town, working or not working according to the plant owner's whim.

Reacher ate his last Powerbar and drained the last of his water. He hacked a hole in the scrub with his heel and buried the wrappers and the empty bottles and his garbage bag. Then he dodged from rock to rock and got a little closer to the houses. The low noise coming from the distant plant was getting quieter. He guessed it was close to quitting time. The sun was low to his left. Its last rays were kissing the tops of the distant mountains. The temperature was falling.

The first cars and pick-up trucks straggled back close to twelve hours after they had left. A long day. They were heading east, towards darkness, so they had their headlights on. Their beams swung south down the cross streets, bouncing and dipping, coming Reacher's way. Then they turned again, variously left and right, and scattered towards driveways and garages and car ports and random patches of oil-stained earth. They stopped moving, one after another, and the beams died. Engines stopped. Doors creaked open and slammed shut. Lights were on inside houses. The blue glow of televisions was visible behind windows. The sky was darkening.

Reacher moved closer. Saw men carrying empty lunch pails into kitchens, or standing next to their cars, stretching, rubbing their eyes with the backs of their hands. He saw hopeful boys with balls and mitts looking for a last game of catch. He saw some fathers agree and some refuse. He saw small girls run out with treasures that required urgent inspection.

He saw the big guy who had blocked the end of the restaurant table. The guy who had held the police car's door like a concierge with a taxicab. The senior deputy. He got out of the old listing crew-cab pick-up truck that Reacher had seen outside the restaurant. He clutched his stomach with both hands. He passed by his kitchen door and stumbled on into his yard. There was no picket fence. The guy kept on going, past a cultivated area, out into the scrub beyond.

Reacher moved closer.

The guy stopped walking and stood still on planted feet and then bent from the waist and threw up in the dirt. He stayed doubled up for maybe twenty seconds and then straightened, shaking his head and spitting.

Reacher moved closer. He got within twenty yards and then the guy bent again and threw up for a second time. Reacher heard him gasp. Not in pain, not in surprise, but in annoyance and resignation.

'You OK?' Reacher called, out of the gloom.

The guy straightened up.

'Who's there?' he called.

Reacher said, 'Me.'

'Who?'

Reacher moved closer. Stepped into a bar of light coming from a neighbour's kitchen window.

The guy said, 'You.'

Reacher nodded. 'Me.'

'We threw you out.'

'Didn't take.'

'You shouldn't be here.'

'We could discuss that further, if you like. Right now. Right here.'

The guy shook his head. 'I'm sick. Not fair.'

Reacher said, 'It wouldn't be fair if you weren't sick.'

The guy shrugged.

'Whatever,' he said. 'I'm going inside now.'

'How's your buddy? With the jaw?'

'You bust him up good.'

'Teeth OK?'

'What do you care?'

'Calibration,' Reacher said. 'It's an art. Doing what you need to, no more, no less.'

'He had lousy teeth to start with. We all do.'

'Too bad,' Reacher said.

'I'm sick,' the guy said again. 'I'm going inside. I didn't see you, OK?'

'Bad food?'

The guy paused. Then he nodded.

'Must have been,' he said. 'Bad food.'

He turned his back and headed for his house, slow and stumbling, holding his belt one-handed, like his pants were too big for him. Reacher watched him go, and then he turned and walked back to the distant shadows.

He moved fifty yards south and fifty yards east of where he had been before, in case the sick guy changed his mind and decided he had seen something after all. He wanted some latitude, if the cops started a search in the guy's back yard. He wanted to begin the chase outside a flashlight beam's maximum range.

But no cops showed up. Clearly the guy never called. Reacher waited the best part of thirty minutes. Way to the west he heard the aero engine again, straining hard, climbing. The small plane, taking off once more. Seven o'clock in the evening. Then the noise died away and the sky went full dark and the houses closed up tight. Clouds drifted in and covered the moon and the stars. Apart from the glow from draped windows the world went pitch black. The temperature dropped like a stone. Night-time, in open country.

A long day.

Reacher stood up and loosened the neck of his shirt and set off east, back towards Hope. He kept the lit houses behind his left shoulder and when they fell away he looped left into the dark and skirted where he knew the dry goods emporium and the gas station and the abandoned motor court and the vacant lot must be. Then he moved left again and strained to make out the line of the road. He knew it must be there. But he couldn't see it. He moved towards where he figured it must be, as close as he dared. Eventually he saw a black stripe in the darkness. Indistinct, but different from the black plain that was the scrubland. He lined himself up with it and fixed its direction in his mind and retreated sideways a safe ten yards and then moved on forward. Walking was difficult in the dark. He stumbled into bushes. He held his hands out in front of him to ward off table rocks. Twice he tripped on low football-sized boulders, and fell. Twice he got up and brushed himself off and staggered onward.

Stubborn, Vaughan had said.

Stupid, Reacher thought.

The third time he tripped was not on a rock. It was on something altogether softer and more yielding.

TWELVE

Reacher sprawled forward and some kind of a primitive instinct made him avoid landing right on top of the thing he had tripped on. He kicked his legs up and tucked his head in and rolled, like judo. He ended up on his back, winded, and hurting from having landed on sharp stones, one under his shoulder and one under his hip. He lay still for a moment and then rolled on his front and pushed himself to his knees and shuffled around until he was facing the way he had come. Then he opened his eyes wide and stared back into the blackness.

Too dark to see.

No flashlight.

He shuffled forward on both knees and one hand, with the other held low in front of him and curled into a fist. A slow yard later it touched something.

Soft.

Not fur.

Cloth.

He spread his fingers. Clamped them loosely. Rubbed his fingertips and the ball of his thumb left and right. Squeezed.

A leg. He had his hand on a human leg. The size and heft of a thigh was unmistakable. He could feel a hamstring under his fingers and a long quadriceps muscle under his thumb. The cloth was thin and soft. Probably cotton twill, worn and washed many times. Old chinos, maybe.

He moved his hand to the left and found the back of a knee. The leg was face down. He pushed his thumb around and underneath and found the kneecap. It was jammed down in the sand. He skipped his hand three feet to the right and slid it up a back to a shoulder blade. Walked his fingers to a neck, and a nape, and an ear.

No pulse.

Cold flesh. No warmer than the night-time air.

Below the ear was a collar. Knit, rolled, faintly abrasive. A polo shirt, maybe. He shuffled closer on his knees and opened his eyes so wide the muscles in his face hurt.

Too dark to see.

Five senses. Too dark to see, nothing to hear. He wasn't about to try tasting anything. That left smell, and touch. The smell was fairly neutral. Reacher had smelled more than his fair share of deceased organisms. This one wasn't particularly offensive. Unwashed clothes, stale sweat, ripe hair, dry sunbaked skin, the faintest trace of methane from early decomposition. No voided bowel or bladder.

No blood.

No perfume, no cologne.

No real information.

So, touch. He used both hands and started with the hair. It was not long, not short, and tousled.

Maybe an inch and a half or two inches. Wiry, with a tendency to wave. Caucasian. Impossible to say what colour. Under it was a small, neat skull.

Man or woman?

He ran his thumbnail the length of the spine. No bra strap under the shirt, but that didn't necessarily mean anything. He poked and probed the back of the ribcage like a blind man reading Braille. Light skeleton, pronounced backbone, light and stringy musculature. Narrow shoulders. Either a thin boy, slightly wasted, or a fit woman. The kind that runs marathons or rides her bike for a hundred miles at a time.

So, which?

Only one way to find out.

He found folds of cloth at the hip and the shoulder and rolled the body on its side. It was reasonably heavy. The way his hands were spaced told him it was maybe five-eight in height, and the weight was probably close to one-forty, which made it probable it was male. A woman marathon runner would have been much lighter, maybe a hundred and five. He kept hold of the bunches of cloth and eased the body past the vertical and let it flop on its back. Then he spread his fingers and started again at the head.

A man, for sure.

The forehead was ridged and bony and the chin and the upper lip were rough with maybe four days of stubble. The cheeks and the throat were smoother.

A young man, not much more than a boy.

The cheekbones were pronounced. The eyes were hard and dry, like marbles. The facial skin was firm and shrunken. It was slightly gritty with grains of sand, but not much had stuck. The skin was too dry. The mouth was dry, inside and out. The tendons in the neck were obvious. They stood out like cords. No fat anywhere. Barely any flesh at all.

Starved and dehydrated, Reacher thought.

The polo shirt had two buttons, both of them undone. No pocket, but it had a small embroidered design on the left chest. Under it there was a thin pectoral muscle and hard ribs. The pants were loose at the waist. No belt. The shoes were some kind of athletic sneakers, hook-and-loop closures, thick waffle soles.

Reacher wiped his hands on his own pants and then started again from the feet upward, looking for a wound. He went at it like a conscientious airport screener starting a patient full-body search. He did the front and rolled the body again and did the back.

He found nothing.

No gashes, no gunshot wounds, no dried blood, no swellings, no contusions, no broken bones.

The hands were small and fairly delicate, but a little calloused. The nails were ragged. No rings on the fingers. No pinkie ring, no class ring, no wedding band.

He checked the pants pockets, two front, two rear.

He found nothing.

No wallet, no coins, no keys, no phone. Nothing at all.

He sat back on his heels and stared up at the sky, willing a cloud to move and let some moonlight through. But nothing happened. The night stayed dark. He had been walking east, had fallen, had turned around. Therefore he was now facing west. He pushed back off his knees and stood up. Made a quarter-turn to his right. Now he was facing north. He started walking, slowly, with small steps, concentrating hard on staying straight. He bent and swept his hands flat on the scrub and found four stones the size of baseballs. Straightened again and walked on, five yards, ten, fifteen, twenty.

He found the road. The packed scrub gave way to the tarred pebbles. He used his toe to locate the edge. He bent and butted three of his stones together and stacked the fourth on top, like a miniature mountain cairn. Then he turned a careful one-eighty and walked back, counting his paces. Five yards, ten, fifteen, twenty. He stopped and squatted and felt ahead of him.

Nothing.

He shuffled forward with his arms out straight, patting downward, searching, until his right palm came down on the corpse's shoulder. He glanced up at the sky. Still solid.

Nothing more to be done.

He stood up again and turned left and blundered on through the dark, east towards Hope.

THIRTEEN

The closer he got to the Hope town line, the more he let himself drift left towards the road. Hope wasn't a big place, and he didn't want to miss it in the dark. Didn't want to walk on for ever, all the way back to Kansas. But he drifted slow enough that when he hit the shoulder and felt the first tarred pebbles under his feet he figured he had less than a mile to go. The clock in his head said that it was midnight. He had made good progress, close to three miles an hour, despite falling four more times and detouring every thirty minutes to confirm he wasn't drastically off course.

Despair's cheap road crunched loudly under his feet but the hard level surface allowed him to speed up. He hit a good rhythm and covered what was left of the last mile in less than fifteen minutes. It was still very cold. Still pitch dark. But he sensed the new blacktop ahead. He felt it coming. Then he felt the surface change under his feet. His left foot pushed off rough stones and his right foot landed on velvet-smooth asphalt.

He was back over the line.

He stood still for a second. Held his arms wide

and looked up at the black sky. Then bright head-lights hit him head on and he was trapped in their beams. A spotlight clicked on and played over him, head to foot and back again.

A cop car.

Then the beams died as suddenly as they had appeared and a dome light came on inside the car and showed a small figure at the wheel. Tan shirt, fair hair. Half a smile.

Vaughan.

She was parked head-on, with her push bars twenty yards inside her own jurisdiction, just waiting in the dark. Reacher walked towards her, moving left, skirting her hood and her fender. He stepped to the passenger door and put his hand on the handle. Opened it up and crammed himself into the space inside. The interior was full of soft radio chatter and the smell of perfume.

He asked, 'So are you free for a late dinner?'

She said, 'I don't eat with jerks.'

'I'm back, like I said I would be.'

'Did you have fun?'

'Not really.'

'I'm working the graveyard shift. I don't get off until seven.'

'Breakfast, then. Drinking coffee with jerks is not the same as eating with them.'

'I don't drink coffee for breakfast. I need to sleep in the daytime.'

'Tea, then.'

'Tea has caffeine too.'

'Milk shake?'

'Maybe.' She was resting easy in the seat, one elbow on the door and the other hand in her lap.

'How did you see me coming?' Reacher asked. 'I didn't see you.'

'I eat a lot of carrots,' Vaughan said. 'And our video has night vision enhancement.' She leaned forward and tapped a black box mounted high on the dash. 'Traffic camera and a hard disc recorder.' She moved her hand again and hit a key on the computer. The screen changed to a ghostly green wide-angle image of the scene ahead. The road was lighter than the scrub. It had retained more of the daytime heat than its surroundings. Or less. Reacher wasn't sure.

'I saw you half a mile away,' Vaughan said. 'A little green speck.' She tapped another key and spooled back through the time code and Reacher saw himself, a luminous sliver in the dark, getting bigger, coming closer.

'Very fancy,' he said.

'Homeland Security money. We all got zillions. Got to spend it on something.'

'How long have you been out here?'

'An hour.'

'Thanks for waiting.'

Vaughan started the motor and backed up a little and then turned across the width of the road, in a wide arc that took the front wheels off the blacktop and through the sand on the shoulder. She got straightened up and accelerated.

'Hungry?' she asked.

'Not really,' Reacher said.

'You should eat anyway.'

'Where?'

'The diner will still be open. It stays open all night.'

'In Hope? Why?'

'This is America. It's a service economy.'

'Whatever, I might go take a nap instead. I walked a long way.'

'Go eat in the diner first.'

'Why?'

'Because I think you should. Nutrition is important.'

'What are you, my mother?'

'I think you should eat, that's all.'

'Are you on commission? Is the chef your brother?'

'Someone was asking about you.'

'Who?'

'Some girl.'

'I don't know any girls.'

'She wasn't asking about you personally,' Vaughan said. 'She was asking if anyone had been thrown out of Despair more recently than her.'

'She was thrown out?'

'Four days ago.'

'They throw women out too?'

'Vagrancy isn't a gender-specific offence.'

'Who is she?'

'Just some kid. I told her about you. No names, but I said you might be eating in the diner tonight. I was assuming you would get out OK. I try to live on the sunny side of the street. So I think she might come looking for you.'

'What docs shc want?'

'She wouldn't tell me,' Vaughan said. 'But my impression was her boyfriend is missing.'

FOURTEEN

Reacher got out of Vaughan's cruiser on First Street and walked straight down to Second. The diner was all lit up inside and it was doing some business. Three booths were occupied. A guy on his own, a young woman on her own, two guys together. Maybe some Hope residents commuted for work. Not to Despair, obviously, but maybe to other towns. Maybe to other states, like Kansas or Nebraska. And those were big distances. Maybe they all got back too late to face cooking at home. Or maybe they were shift workers, just starting out, with long trips ahead of them.

The sidewalks close to the diner were deserted. No girls hanging around. No girls watching who was going in and coming out. No girls leaning on walls. No girls hiding in the shadows. Reacher pulled the door and went in and headed for a booth in the far corner where he could sit with his back protected and see the whole room at once. Pure habit. He never sat any other way. A waitress came over and gave him a napkin and silverware and a glass of ice water. Not the same waitress he had met before, during his caffeine marathon.

This one was young, and not particularly tired, even though it was very late. She could have been a college student. Maybe the diner stayed open all night to give people jobs, as well as meals. Maybe the owner felt some kind of a civic responsibility. Hope seemed to be that kind of a town.

The menu was in a chromium clip at the end of the table. It was a laminated card with pictures of the food on it. The waitress came back and Reacher pointed to a grilled cheese sandwich and said, 'And coffee.' The waitress wrote it down and walked away and Reacher settled back and watched the street through the windows. He figured that the girl who was looking for him might pass by once every fifteen or twenty minutes. It was what he would have done. Longer intervals might make her miss his visit. Most diner customers were in and out pretty fast. He was sure there was a trade association somewhere with the exact data. His personal average was certainly less than half an hour. Shorter if he was in a hurry, longer if it was raining. The longest stay he could recall might be upward of two hours. The shortest in recent memory was the day before, in Despair. One fast cup of coffee, supervised by hostile glares.

But nobody passed by on the sidewalk. Nobody glanced in through the windows. The waitress came over with his sandwich and a mug of coffee. The coffee was fresh and the sandwich was OK. The cheese was sticky in his mouth and less flavourful than a Wisconsin product would have been, but it was palatable. And Reacher was no kind of a gourmet. He rated food quality as either adequate or not adequate, and the adequate category was always by far the larger of the two. So he ate and drank and enjoyed it all well enough.

After fifteen minutes he gave up on the girl. He figured she wasn't coming. Then he changed his mind. He quit staring out at the sidewalk and started looking at the other customers inside the diner and realized she was already in there, waiting for him.

The young woman, sitting three booths away.

Stupid, Reacher, he thought.

He had figured that if their relative positions had been reversed he would have walked by every fifteen or twenty minutes and checked through the windows. But in reality, he wouldn't have done that. Instead, he would have come in out of the cold and sat down and waited for his mark to come to him.

Like she had.

Pure common sense.

She was maybe nineteen or twenty years old, dirty blond hair with streaks, wearing a short denim skirt and a white sweatshirt with a word on it that might have been the name of a college football team. Her features didn't add up all the way to beauty, but she had the kind of irresistible glowing good health that he had seen before in American girls of her station and generation. Her skin was perfect. It was honey-coloured with the remnant of a great summer tan. Her teeth were white and regular. Her eyes were vivid blue. Her legs were long, and neither lean nor heavy. *Shapely*, Reacher thought. An old-fashioned word, but the right one. She was wearing sneakers with tiny white socks that ended below her ankles. She had a bag. It was beside her on the bench. Not a purse, not a suitcase. A messenger bag, grey nylon, with a broad flap.

She was the one he was waiting for. He knew that because as he watched her in his peripheral vision he could see her watching him in hers. She was sizing him up and deciding whether to approach.

Deciding against, apparently.

She had had a full fifteen minutes to make her decision. But she hadn't gotten up and walked over. Not because of good manners. Not because she hadn't wanted to disturb him while he was eating. He suspected her concept of etiquette didn't quite stretch that far, and even if it did, then a missing boyfriend would have overwhelmed it. She just didn't want to get involved with him. That was all. Reacher didn't blame her. *Look at yourself*, Vaughan had said. *What do you see?* He had no illusions about what the girl three booths away was seeing. No illusions about his appearance or his appeal, in the eyes of someone like her. It was late at night, she was looking at an old guy twice her age, huge, untidy, dishevelled, somewhat dirty, and surrounded by an electric stay-away aura he had spent years cultivating, like a sign on the rear end of a fire truck: *Stay Back 200 Feet*.

So she was going to sit tight and wait him out. That was clear. He was disappointed. Primarily because of the questions surrounding the dead boy in the dark, but also because in a small corner of his mind he would have liked to be the kind of guy that pretty girls could walk up to. Not that he would have taken it anywhere. She was wholesome and he was twice her age. And her boyfriend was dead, which made her some kind of a widow.

She was still watching him. He had moved his gaze so that he could see her reflection in the window next to her. She was looking up, looking down, kneading her fingers, glancing suddenly in his direction as new thoughts came to her, and then glancing away again as she resolved them. As she found reasons to stay well away from him. He gave it five more minutes and then fished in his pocket for cash. He didn't need a check. He knew what the sandwich and the coffee cost, because the prices had been printed on the menu. He knew what the local sales tax percentage was, and he was capable of calculating it for himself in his head. He knew how to work out a fifteen per cent tip, for the college-age waitress who had also stayed well away from him.

He folded small bills lengthwise and left them on the table. Got up and headed for the door. At the last minute he changed direction and stepped over to the young woman's booth and slid in opposite her.

'My name is Reacher,' he said. 'I think you wanted to talk to me.'

The girl looked at him and blinked and opened her mouth and closed it again and spoke at the second attempt.

She said, 'Why would you think that?'

'I met a cop called Vaughan. She told me.'

'Told you what?'

'That you were looking for someone who had been to Despair.'

'You're mistaken,' the girl said. 'It wasn't me.'

She wasn't a great liar. Not great at all. Reacher had come up against some real experts, in his previous life. This one had all the tells on display. The gulps, the false starts, the stammers, the fidgets, the glances to her right. Psychologists figured that the memory centre was located in the left brain, and the imagination engine in the right brain. Therefore people unconsciously glanced to the left when they were remembering things, and to the right when they were making stuff up. When they were lying. This girl was glancing right so much she was in danger of getting whiplash.

'OK,' Reacher said. 'I apologize for disturbing you.'

But he didn't move. He stayed where he was, sitting easy, filling most of a vinyl bench made for two. Up close the girl was prettier than she had looked from a distance. She had a dusting of freckles and a mobile, expressive mouth.

'Who are you?' she asked.

'Just a guy,' Reacher said.

'What kind of a guy?'

'The judge in Despair called me a vagrant. So I'm that kind of a guy, I guess.'

'No job?'

'Not for a long time.'

She said, 'They called me a vagrant too.'

Her accent was unspecific. She wasn't from Boston or New York or Chicago or Minnesota or the deep south. Maybe somewhere in the southwest. Arizona, perhaps.

He said, 'In your case I imagine they were inaccurate.'

'I'm not sure of the definition, exactly.'

'It comes from the old French word *waucrant*,' Reacher said. 'Meaning one who wanders idly from place to place without lawful or visible means of support.'

'I'm in college,' she said.

'So you were unfairly accused.'

'They just wanted me out of there.'

'Where do you go to school?'

She paused. Glanced to her right.

'Miami,' she said.

Reacher nodded. Wherever she went to school, it wasn't Miami. Probably wasn't anywhere in the east. Was probably somewhere on the west coast. Southern California, possibly. Unskilled liars like her often picked a mirror image, when lying about geography.

'What's your major?' he asked.

She looked straight at him and said, 'The history of the twentieth century.' Which was probably true. Young people usually told the truth about their areas of expertise, because they were proud of them, and they were worried about getting caught out on alternatives. Often they didn't have alternatives. Being young, it came with the territory.

'Feels like yesterday to me,' he said. 'Not history.'

'What does?'

'The twentieth century.'

She didn't reply. Didn't understand what he meant. She remembered maybe eight or nine

93

years of the old century, maximum, and from a kid's perspective. He remembered slightly more of it.

'What's your name?' he asked.

She glanced to her right again. 'Anne.'

Reacher nodded again. Whatever her name was, it wasn't Anne. Anne was probably a sister's name. Or a best friend's. Or a cousin's. Generally people liked to stay close to home, with phoney names.

The girl who wasn't called Anne asked, 'Were *you* unfairly accused?'

Reacher shook his head. 'A vagrant is exactly what I am.'

'Why did you go there?'

'I liked the name. Why did you go there?'

She didn't answer.

He said, 'Anyway, it wasn't much of a place.'

'How much of it did you see?'

'Most of it, the second time.'

'You went back?'

He nodded. 'I took a good look around, from a distance.'

'And?'

'It still wasn't much of a place.'

The girl went quiet. Reacher saw her weighing her next question. How to ask it. Whether to ask it. She put her head on one side and looked beyond him.

'Did you see any people?' she asked.

'Lots of people,' Reacher said.

'Did you see the airplane?'

'I heard one.'

'It belongs to the guy with the big house. Every

night he takes off at seven and comes back at two o'clock in the morning.'

Reacher asked, 'How long were you there?'

'One day.'

'So how do you know the plane flies every night?'

She didn't answer.

'Maybe someone told you,' Reacher said.

No reply.

Reacher said, 'No law against joyriding.'

'People don't joyride at night. There's nothing to see.'

'Good point.'

The girl was quiet for another minute, and then she asked, 'Were you in a cell?'

'Couple of hours.'

'Anyone else in there?'

'No.'

'When you went back, what people did you see?'

Reacher said, 'Why don't you just show me his picture?'

'Whose picture?'

'Your boyfriend's.'

'Why would I do that?'

'Your boyfriend is missing. As in, you can't find him. That was Officer Vaughan's impression, anyway.'

'You trust cops?'

'Some of them.'

'I don't have a picture.'

'You've got a big bag. Probably all kinds of things in there. Maybe a few pictures.'

She said, 'Show me your wallet.'

'I don't have a wallet.'

'Everyone has a wallet.'

'Not me.'

'Prove it.'

'I can't prove a negative.'

'Empty your pockets.'

Reacher nodded. He understood. *The boyfriend is some kind of a fugitive. She asked about my job. She needs to know I'm not an investigator. An investigator would have compromising ID in his wallet.* He lifted his butt off the bench and dug out his cash, his old passport, his ATM card, his motel key. His toothbrush was in his room, assembled, standing upright in a plastic glass next to the sink. The girl looked at his stuff and said, 'Thanks.'

He said, 'Now show me his picture.'

'He's not my boyfriend.'

'Isn't he?'

'He's my husband.'

'You're young, to be married.'

'We're in love.'

'You're not wearing a ring.'

Her left hand was on the table. She withdrew it quickly, into her lap. But there had been no ring on her finger, and no tan line.

'It was kind of sudden,' she said. 'Kind of hurried. We figured we'd get rings later.'

'Isn't it a part of the ceremony?'

'No,' she said. 'That's a myth.' Then she paused a moment and said, 'I'm not pregnant, either, just in case that's what you're thinking.'

'Not for a minute.'

'Good.'

'Show me the picture.'

She hauled the grey messenger bag into her lap and raised the flap. Rooted around for a moment and came out with a fat leather wallet. There was a billfold part straining against a little strap, and a change purse part. There was a plastic window on the outside with a California driver's licence behind it, with her picture on it. She unpopped the little strap and opened the billfold and riffed through a concertina of plastic photograph windows. Slid a slim fingertip into one of them and eased a snapshot out. She passed it across the table. It had been cut down out of a standard six-by-four one-hour print. The edges were not entirely straight. It showed the girl standing on a street with golden light and palm trees and a row of neat boutiques behind her. She was smiling widely, vibrant with love and joy and happiness, leaning forward a little as if her whole body was clenching with the onset of uncontrollable giggles. She was in the arms of a guy about her age. He was very tall and blond and heavy. An athlete. He had blue eyes and a buzz cut and a dark tan and a wide smile.

'This is your husband?' Reacher asked.

The girl said, 'Yes.'

The guy was way more than a head taller than she was. He was huge. He towered right over her. His arms were as thick as the palm trunks behind him.

Not the guy Reacher had tripped over in the dark.

Not even close.

Way too big.

FIFTEEN

Reacher squared the snapshot on the tabletop in front of him. Looked at the girl across from him and asked, 'How old is this photo?'

'Recent.'

May I see your driver's licence?'

'Why?'

'Something I need to check.'

'I don't know.'

'I already know your name isn't Anne. I know you don't go to school in Miami. My guess would be UCLA. This photograph looks like it was taken somewhere around there. It has that LA kind of feel.'

The girl said nothing.

Reacher said, 'I'm not here to hurt you.'

She paused and then slid her wallet across the table. He glanced at her licence. Most of it was visible behind the milky plastic window. Her name was Lucy Anderson. No middle name. Anderson, hence Anne, perhaps.

'Lucy,' he said. 'I'm pleased to meet you.'

'I'm sorry about not telling you the truth.'

'Don't worry about it. Why should you?'

'My friends call me Lucky. Like a mispronunciation. Like a nickname.'

'I hope you always are.'

'Me too. I have been so far.'

Her licence said she was coming up to twenty years old. It said her address was an apartment on a street he knew to be close to the main UCLA campus. He had been in LA not long before. Its geography was still familiar to him. Her sex was specified as female, which was clearly accurate, and her eyes were listed as blue, which was an understatement.

She was five feet eight inches tall.

Which made her husband at least six feet four. Maybe six feet five. In the picture he looked to be well over two hundred pounds. Maybe Reacher's own size. Maybe even bigger.

Not the guy in the dark. The guy in the dark had been Lucy Anderson's size.

He slid the wallet back across the table. Followed it with the photograph.

Lucy Anderson asked, 'Did you see him?'

Reacher shook his head.

'No,' he said. 'I didn't. I'm sorry.'

'He has to be there somewhere.'

'What's he running from?'

She looked to the right. 'Why would he be running from something?'

'Just a wild guess,' Reacher said.

'Who are you?'

'Just a guy.'

'How did you know my name wasn't Anne? How did you know I'm not in school in Miami?'

'A long time ago I was a cop. In the military. I still know things.'

She went quiet and a little pale. Her skin whitened behind her freckles. She fumbled the photograph back into its slot and fastened the wallet and thrust it deep into her bag.

'You don't like cops, do you?' Reacher asked.

'Not always,' she said.

'That's unusual, for a person like you.'

'Like me?'

'Safe, secure, middle class, well brought up.'

'Things change.'

'What did your husband do?'

She didn't answer.

'And who did he do it to?'

No answer.

'Why did he go to Despair?'

No response.

'Were you supposed to meet him there?'

Nothing.

'Doesn't matter, anyway,' Reacher said. 'I didn't see him. And I'm not a cop any more. Haven't been for a long time.'

'What would you do now? If you were me?'

'I'd wait right here in town. Your husband looks like a capable guy. He'll probably show up, sooner or later. Or get word to you.'

'I hope so.'

'Is he in school too?'

Lucy Anderson didn't answer that. Just secured the flap of her bag and slid off the bench sideways and stood up and tugged the hem of her skirt down. Five-eight, maybe one-thirty, blond and blue, straight, strong, and healthy.

100

'Thank you,' she said. 'Good night.'

'Good luck,' he said. 'Lucky.'

She hoisted her bag on her shoulder and walked to the door and pushed out to the street. He watched her huddle into her sweatshirt and step away through the cold.

He was in bed before two o'clock in the morning. The motel room was warm. There was a heater under the window and it was blasting away to good effect. He set the alarm in his head for six thirty. He was tired, but he figured four and a half hours would be enough. In fact they would have to be enough, because he wanted time to shower before heading out for breakfast.

SIXTEEN

It was a cliché that cops stop in at diners for doughnuts before, during, and after every shift, but clichés were clichés only because they were so often true. Therefore Reacher slipped into the same back booth at five to seven in the morning and fully expected to see Officer Vaughan walk in inside the following ten minutes.

Which she did.

He saw her cruiser pull up and park outside. Saw her climb out on to the sidewalk and press both hands into the small of her back and stretch. Saw her lock up and pirouette and head for the door. She came in and saw him and paused for a long moment and then changed direction and slid in opposite him.

He asked, 'Strawberry, vanilla, or chocolate? It's all they've got.'

'Of what?'

'Milk shakes.'

'I don't drink breakfast with jerks.'

'I'm not a jerk. I'm a citizen with a problem. You're here to help. Says so on the badge.'

'What kind of problem?'

'The girl found me.'

'And had you seen her boyfriend?'

'Her husband, actually.'

'Really?' Vaughan said. 'She's young to be married.'

'I thought so too. She said they're in love.'

'Cue the violins. So had you seen him?'

'No.'

'So where's your problem?'

'I saw someone else.'

'Who?'

'Not saw, actually. It was in the pitch dark. I fell over him.'

'Who?'

'A dead guy.'

'Where?'

'On the way out of Despair.'

'Are you sure?'

'Completely,' Reacher said. 'A young adult male corpse.'

'Are you serious?'

'As a heart attack.'

'Why didn't you tell me last night?'

'I wanted time to think about it.'

'You're yanking my chain. There's what out there, a thousand square miles? And you just happen to trip over a dead guy in the dark? That's a coincidence as big as a barn.'

'Not really,' Reacher said. 'I figure he was doing the same thing I was doing. Walking east from Despair to Hope, staying close enough to the road to be sure of his direction, far enough away to be safe. That put him in a pretty specific channel. I might have missed him by a yard, but I was never going to miss him by a mile.'

Vaughan said nothing.

'But he didn't make it all the way,' Reacher said. 'I think he was exhausted. His knees were driven pretty deep in the sand. I think he fell on his knees and pitched forward on his front and died. He was emaciated and dehydrated. No wounds, no trauma.'

'What, you autopsied this guy? In the dark?'

'I felt around.'

'Felt?'

'Touch,' Reacher said. 'It's one of the five senses we rely on.'

'So who was this guy?'

'Caucasian, by the feel of his hair. Maybe five-eight, one-forty. Young. No ID. I don't know if he was dark or fair.'

'This is unbelievable.'

'It happened.'

'Where exactly?'

'Maybe four miles out of town, eight miles short of the line.'

'Definitely in Despair, then.'

'No question.'

'You should call the Despair PD.'

'I wouldn't piss on the Despair PD if it was on fire.'

'Well, I can't help you. It's not my jurisdiction.'

The waitress came over. The day shift woman, the witness to the coffee marathon. She was busy and harassed. The diner was filling up fast. Small-town America, at breakfast time. Reacher ordered coffee and eggs. Vaughan ordered coffee, too. Reacher took that as a good sign. He waited until the waitress had bustled away and said, 'You *can* help me.'

Vaughan said, 'How?'

'I want to go back and take a look, right now, in the daylight. You can drive me. We could be in and out, real fast.'

'It's not my town.'

'Unofficial. Off duty. Like a tourist. You're a citizen. You're entitled to drive on their road.'

'Would you be able to find the place again?'

'I left a pile of stones on the side of the road.'

'I can't do it,' Vaughan said. 'I can't poke around over there. And I sure as hell can't take *you* there. You've been excluded. It would be unbelievably provocative.'

'Nobody would know.'

'You think? They've got one road in and one road out and two cars.'

'Right now they're eating doughnuts in their restaurant.'

'You sure you didn't dream this?'

'No dreaming involved,' Reacher said. 'The kid had eyeballs like marbles and the inside of his mouth was parched like shoe leather. He'd been wandering for days.'

The waitress came back with the coffee and the eggs. The eggs had a sprig of fresh parsley arrayed across them. Reacher picked it off and laid it on the side of the plate.

Vaughan said, 'I can't drive a Hope police cruiser in Despair.'

'So what else have you got?'

She was quiet for a long moment. She

105

sipped her coffee. Then she said, 'I have an old truck.'

She made him wait on the First Street sidewalk near the hardware store. Clearly she wasn't about to take him home while she changed her clothes and her vehicle. A wise precaution, he thought. *Look at yourself*, she had said. *What do you see?* He was getting accustomed to negative answers to that question. The hardware store was still closed. The window was full of tools and small consumer items. The aisle behind the door was piled high with the stuff that would be put out on the sidewalk later. For many years Reacher had wondered why hardware stores favoured sidewalk displays. There was a lot of work involved. Repetitive physical labour, twice a day. But maybe consumer psychology dictated that large utilitarian items sold better when associated with the rugged outdoors. Or maybe it was just a question of space. He thought for a moment and came to no firm conclusion and moved away and leaned on a pole that supported a crosswalk sign. The morning had come in cold and grey. Thin cloud started at ground level. The Rockies weren't visible at all, neither near nor far.

Close to twenty minutes later an old Chevrolet pick-up truck pulled up on the opposite kerb. Not a bulbous old classic from the Forties or a swooping space-age design from the Fifties or a muscly El Camino from the Sixties. Just a plain second-hand American vehicle about fifteen years old, worn navy blue paint, steel rims, small tyres. Vaughan was at the wheel. She was wearing a red

106

windbreaker zipped to the chin and a khaki ball cap pulled low. A good disguise. Reacher wouldn't have recognized her if he hadn't been expecting her. He used the crosswalk and climbed in next to her, on to a small vinyl seat with an upright back. The cab smelled of leaked gasoline and cold exhaust. There were rubber floor mats under his feet, covered with desert dust, worn and papery with age. He slammed the door and Vaughan took off again. The truck had a wheezy four-cylinder motor. *In and out real fast*, he had said. But clearly *fast* was going to be a relative concept.

They covered Hope's five miles of road in seven minutes. A hundred yards short of the line Vaughan said, 'We see anybody at all, you duck down.' Then she pressed harder on the gas and the expansion joint thumped under the wheels and the tyres set up a harsh roar over Despair's sharp stones.

'You come here much?' Reacher asked.

'Why would I?' Vaughan said.

There was no traffic ahead. Nothing either coming or going. The road speared straight into the hazy distance, rising and falling. Vaughan was holding the truck at a steady sixty. A mile a minute, probably close to its comfortable maximum.

Seven minutes inside enemy territory, she started to slow.

'Watch the left shoulder,' Reacher said. 'Four stones, piled up.'

The weather had settled to a luminous grey light. Not bright, not sunny, but everything was illuminated perfectly. No glare, no shadows. There was some trash on the shoulder. Not much, but enough to ensure that Reacher's small cairn was not going to stand out in glorious isolation like a beacon. There were plastic water bottles, glass beer bottles, soda cans, paper, small unimportant parts of vehicles, all caught on a long ridge of pebbles that had been washed to the side of the road by the passage of tyres. Reacher twisted around in his seat. Nobody behind. Nobody ahead. Vaughan slowed some more. Reacher scanned the shoulder. The stones had felt big and obvious in his hands, in the dark. But now in the impersonal daylight they were going to look puny in the vastness.

Vaughan drifted to the crown of the road and slowed again.

'There,' Reacher said.

He saw his little cairn thirty yards ahead on the left. Three stones butted together, the fourth balanced on top. A speck in the distance, in the middle of nowhere. To the south the land ran all the way to the horizon, flat and essentially featureless, dotted with pale bushes and dark rocks and pitted with wash holes and low ridges.

'This is the place?' Vaughan asked.

'Twenty-some yards due south,' Reacher said.

He checked the road again. Nothing ahead, nothing behind.

'We're OK,' he said.

Vaughan passed the cairn and pulled to the right shoulder and turned a wide circle across both lanes. Came back east and stopped exactly level with the stones. She put the transmission in park and left the engine running.

'Stay here,' she said.

'Bullshit,' Reacher said. He got out and stepped

108

over the stones and waited on the shoulder. He felt tiny in the lit-up vastness. In the dark the world had shrunk to an arm's length around him. Now it felt huge again. Vaughan stepped alongside him and he walked south with her through the scrub, at a right angle to the road, five paces, ten, fifteen. He stopped after twenty paces and confirmed his direction by glancing behind him. Then he stood still and checked all around, first on a close radius, and then wider.

He saw nothing.

He stood on tiptoe and craned his neck and searched.

There was nothing there.

SEVENTEEN

Reacher turned a careful one-eighty and stared back at the road to make sure he hadn't drifted too far either west or east. He hadn't. He was right on target. He walked five paces south, turned east, walked five more paces, turned around, walked ten steps west.

Saw nothing.

'Well?' Vaughan called.

'It's gone,' he said.

'You were just yanking my chain.'

'I wasn't. Why would I?'

'How accurate could you have been, with the stones? In the dark?'

'That's what I'm wondering.'

Vaughan walked a small quiet circle, all around. Shook her head.

'It isn't here,' she said. 'If it ever was.'

Reacher stood still in the emptiness. Nothing to see. Nothing to hear, except Vaughan's truck idling patiently twenty yards away. He walked ten more yards east and started to trace a wide circle. A quarter of the way through it, he stopped.

'Look here,' he said.

He pointed at the ground. At a long line of shallow crumbled oval pits in the sand, each one a yard apart.

Vaughan said, 'Footprints.'

'My footprints,' Reacher said. 'From last night. Heading home.'

They turned west and backtracked. Followed the trail of his old footprints back towards Despair. Ten yards later they came to the head of a small diamond-shaped clearing. The clearing was empty.

'Wait,' Reacher said.

'It's not here,' Vaughan said.

'But it was here. This is the spot.'

The crusted sand was all churned up by multiple disturbances. There were dozens of footprints, facing in all directions. There were scrapes and slides and drag marks. There were small depressions in the scrub, some fairly precise, but most not, because of the way the dry sand had crumbled and trickled down into the holes.

Reacher said, 'Tell me what you see.'

'Activity,' Vaughan said. 'A mess.'

'A story,' Reacher said. 'It's telling us what happened.'

'Whatever happened, we can't stay here. This was supposed to be in and out, real fast.'

Reacher stood up straight and scanned the road, west and east.

Nothing there.

'Nobody coming,' he said.

'I should have brought a picnic,' Vaughan said.

Reacher stepped into the clearing. Crouched down and pointed two-fingered at a pair of neat parallel depressions in the centre of the space. Like two coconut shells had been pressed down into the sand, hard, on a north–south axis.

'The boy's knees,' he said. 'This is where he gave it up. He staggered to a stop and half turned and fell over.' Then he pointed to a broad messed-up stony area four feet to the east. 'This is where I landed after I tripped over him. On these stones. I could show you the bruises, if you like.'

'Maybe later,' Vaughan said. 'We need to get going.'

Reacher pointed to four sharp impressions in the sand. Each one was a rectangle about two inches by three, at the corners of a larger rectangle about two feet by five.

'Gurney feet,' he said. 'Folks came by and collected him. Maybe four or five of them, judging by all the footprints. Official folks, because who else carries gurneys?' He stood up and checked and pointed north and west, along a broad ragged line of footprints and crushed vegetation. 'They came in that way, and carried him back out in the same direction, back to the road. Maybe to a coroner's wagon, parked a little ways west of my cairn.'

'So we're OK,' Vaughan said. 'The proper authorities have got him. Problem solved. We should get going.'

Reacher nodded vaguely and gazed due west. 'What should we see over there?'

'Two sets of incoming footprints,' Vaughan said. 'The boy's and yours, both heading east out of town. Separated by time, but not much separated by direction.'

'But it looks like there's more than that.'

They skirted the clearing and formed up again west of it. They saw four separate lines of footprints, fairly close together. The aggregate disturbance was less than seven feet wide.

'Two incoming, two outgoing,' Reacher said.

'How do you know?' Vaughan asked.

'The angles. Most people walk with their toes out.'

'Maybe there's an inbred family of pigeon-toed people.'

'That's possible, in Despair. But unlikely.'

The newer of the incoming tracks showed big dents in the sand a yard or more apart, and deep. The older showed smaller dents, closer together, less regular, and shallower.

'The kid and me,' Reacher said. 'Heading east. Separated in time. I was walking, he was stumbling and staggering.'

The two outgoing tracks were both brand new. The sand was less crumbled and therefore the indentations were more distinct, and fairly deep, fairly well spaced, and similar.

'Reasonably big guys,' Reacher said. 'Heading back west. Recently. Not separated in time.'

'What does it mean?'

'It means they're tracking the kid. Or me. Or both of us. Finding out where we'd been, where we'd come from.'

'Why?'

'They found the body, they were curious.'

'How did they find the body in the first place?'

'Buzzards,' Reacher said. 'It's the obvious way, on open ground.'

Vaughan stood still for a moment. Then she said, 'Back to the truck, right now.'

Reacher didn't argue. She had beaten him to the obvious conclusion, but only by a heartbeat.

EIGHTEEN

The old chevy was still idling patiently. The road was still empty. But they ran. They ran and they flung the truck's doors open and dumped themselves inside. Vaughan slammed the transmission into gear and hit the gas. They didn't say a word until they thumped back over the Hope town line, eight long minutes later.

'Now you're really a citizen with a problem,' Vaughan said. 'Aren't you? The Despair cops might be dumb, but they're still cops. Buzzards show them a dead guy, they find the dead guy's tracks, they find a second set of tracks that show some other guy caught up with the dead guy along the way, they find signs of a whole lot of falling down and rolling around, they're going to want a serious talk with the other guy. You can bet on that.'

Reacher said, 'So why didn't they follow my tracks forward?'

'Because they know where you were going. There's only Hope, or Kansas. They want to know where you started. And what are they going to find?'

'A massive loop. Buried Powerbar wrappers and empty water bottles, if they look hard enough.'

Vaughan nodded at the wheel. 'Clear physical evidence of a big guy with big feet and long legs who paid a planned clandestine visit the night after they threw a big guy with big feet and long legs out of town.'

'Plus one of the deputies saw me.'

'You sure?'

'We talked.'

'Terrific.'

'The dead guy died of natural causes.'

'You sure? You felt around in the dark. They're going to put that boy on a slab.'

'I'm not in Despair any more. You can't go there, they can't come here.'

'Small departments don't work homicides, you idiot. We call in the State Police. And the State Police can go anywhere in Colorado. And the State Police gets cooperation anywhere in Colorado. And you're in my logbook from yesterday. I couldn't deny it even if I wanted to.'

'You wouldn't want to?'

'I don't know anything about you. Except that I'm pretty sure you beat on a deputy over there. You practically admitted that to me. Who knows what else you did?'

'I didn't do anything else.'

Vaughan said nothing.

Reacher asked, 'What happens next?'

'Always better to get out in front of a thing like this. You should call in and volunteer information.'

'No.'

'Why not?'

'I was a soldier. I never volunteer for anything.'

'Well, I can't help you. It's out of my hands. It was never *in* my hands.'

'You could call,' Reacher said. 'You could call the State Police and find out what their thinking is.'

'They'll be calling us soon enough.'

'So let's get out in front, like you said. Early information is always good.'

Vaughan didn't reply to that. Just lifted off the gas and slowed as they hit the edge of town. The hardware guy had his door open and was piling his stuff on the sidewalk. He had some kind of a trick stepladder that could be put in about eight different positions. He had set it up like a painter's platform good for reaching second-storey walls. Vaughan made a right on the next block and then a left, past the back of the diner. The streets were broad and pleasant and the sidewalks had trees. She pulled into a marked-off parking space outside a low brick building. The building could have been a suburban post office. But it wasn't. It was the Hope Police Department. It said so, in aluminum letters neatly fixed to the brick. Vaughan shut off the engine and Reacher followed her down a neat brick path to the police station's door. The door was locked. The station was closed. Vaughan used a key from her bunch and said, 'The desk guy gets in at nine.'

Inside, the place still looked like a post office. Dull, worn, institutional, bureaucratic, but somewhat friendly. Accessible. Oriented

117

towards service. There was a public enquiry counter and a space behind it with two desks. A watch commander's office behind a solid door, in the same corner a postmaster's would be. Vaughan stepped past the counter and headed for a desk that was clearly hers. Efficient and organized, but not intimidating. There was an old-model computer front and centre, and a console telephone next to it. She opened a drawer and found a number in a book. Clearly contact between the Hope PD and the State Police was rare. She didn't know the number by heart. She dialled the phone and asked for the duty desk and identified herself and said, 'We have a missing persons inquiry. Male, Caucasian, approximately twenty years of age, five-eight, one-forty. Can you help us with that?' Then she listened briefly and her eyes flicked left and then right and she said, 'We don't have a name.' She was asked another question and she glanced right and said, 'Can't tell if he's dark or fair. We're working from a black and white photograph. It's all we have.'

Then there was a pause. Reacher saw her yawn. She was tired. She had been working all night. She moved the phone a little ways from her ear and Reacher heard the faint tap of a keyboard in the distant state office. Denver, maybe, or Colorado Springs. Then a voice came back on and she clamped the phone tight and Reacher didn't hear what it had to say.

Vaughan listened and said, 'Thank you.'

Then she hung up.

'Nothing to report,' she said. 'Apparently Despair didn't call it in.'

'Natural causes,' Reacher said. 'They agreed with me.'

Vaughan shook her head. 'They should have called it in anyway. An unexplained death out in open country, that's at least a county matter. Which means it would show up on the State Police system about a minute later.'

'So why didn't they call it in?'

'I don't know. But that's not our problem.'

Reacher sat down at the other desk. It was a plain government-issue piece of furniture, with steel legs and a thin six-by-three fibreboard top laminated with a printed plastic approximation of rosewood or koa. There was a modesty panel and a three-drawer pedestal bolted to the right-hand legs. The chair had wheels and was covered with grey tweed fabric. Military Police furniture had been different. The chairs had been covered with vinyl. The desks had been steel. Reacher had sat behind dozens of them, all over the world. The views from his windows had been dramatically different, but the desks had been all the same. Their contents, too. Files full of dead people and missing people. Some mourned, some not.

He thought of Lucy Anderson, called Lucky by her friends. The night before, in the diner. He recalled the way she had wrung her hands. He looked across at Vaughan and said, 'It is our problem, kind of. The kid might have people worried about him.'

Vaughan nodded. Went back to her book. Reacher saw her flip forward from *C* for *Colorado State Police* to *D* for *Despair Police Department*. She dialled and he heard a loud reply in her ear, as if physical proximity made for more powerful electrical current in the wires. She ran through the same faked inquiry, missing person, Caucasian male, about twenty, five-eight, one-forty, no name, colouring unclear because of a monochrome photograph. There was a short pause and then a short reply.

Vaughan hung up.

'Nothing to report,' she said. 'They never saw such a guy.'

NINETEEN

Reacher sat quiet and Vaughan moved stuff around on her desk. She put her keyboard in line with her monitor and put her mouse in line with her keyboard and squared her phone behind it and then adjusted everything until all the edges were either parallel or at perfect right angles to each other. Then she put pencils away in drawers and flicked at dust and crumbs with the edge of her palm.

'The gurney marks,' she said.

'I know,' Reacher said. 'Apart from them, I could have invented this whole thing.'

'If they were gurney marks.'

'What else could they have been?'

'Nothing, I guess. They were from one of those old-fashioned stretchers, with the little skids, not the wheels.'

'Why would I invent anything anyway?'

'For attention.'

'I don't like attention.'

'Everyone likes attention. Especially retired cops. It's a recognized pathology. You try to insinuate yourselves back into the action.'

'Are you going to do that when you retire?'

'I hope not.'

'I don't, either.'

'So what's going on over there?'

'Maybe the kid was local,' Reacher said. 'They knew who he was, so he wasn't a candidate for your missing persons inquiry.'

Vaughan shook her head. 'Still makes no sense. Any unexplained death out of doors has got to be reported to the county coroner. In which case it would have showed up on the state system. Purely as a statistic. The State Police would have said well, hey, we heard there was a dead guy in Despair this morning, maybe you should check it out.'

'But they didn't.'

'Because nothing has been called in from Despair. Which just doesn't add up. What the hell are they doing with the guy? There's no morgue over there. Not even any cold storage, as far as I know. Not even a meat locker.'

'So they're doing something else with him,' Reacher said.

'Like what?'

'Burying him, probably.'

'He wasn't road kill.'

'Maybe they're covering something up.'

'You claim he died of natural causes.'

'He did,' Reacher said. 'From wandering through the scrub for days. Maybe because they ran him out of town. Which might embarrass them. Always assuming they're capable of embarrassment.'

Vaughan shook her head again. 'They didn't run him out of town. We didn't get a call. And they always call us. Always. Then they drive them to the line and dump them. This week there's been you and the girl. That's all.'

'They never dump them to the west?'

'There's nothing there. It's unincorporated land.'

'Maybe they're just slow. Maybe they'll call it in later.'

'Doesn't compute,' Vaughan said. 'You find a dead one, you put one hand on your gun and the other on your radio. You call for backup, you call for the ambulance, you call the coroner. One, two, three. It's completely automatic. There and then.'

'Maybe they aren't as professional as you.'

'It's not about being unprofessional. It's about making a spur-of-the-moment decision to break procedure and not to call the coroner. Which would require some kind of real reason.'

Reacher said nothing.

Vaughan said, 'Maybe there were no cops involved. Maybe someone else found him.'

'Civilians don't carry stretchers in their cars,' Reacher said.

Vaughan nodded vaguely and got up out of her chair. Said, 'We should get out of here before the day guy gets in. And the watch commander.'

'Embarrassed to be seen with me?'

'A little. And I'm a little embarrassed that I don't know what to do.'

They got back in Vaughan's old truck and headed for the diner again. The breakfast rush was over. A degree of calm had been restored. Reacher ordered coffee. Vaughan said she was happy with tap water. She sipped her way through half a glass and drummed her fingers on the table.

'Start over,' she said. 'Who was this guy?'

'Caucasian male,' Reacher said.

'Not Hispanic? Not foreign?'

'I think Hispanics are Caucasians, technically. Plus Arabs and some Asians. All I'm going on is his hair. He wasn't black. That's all I know for sure. He could have been from anywhere in the world.'

'Dark-skinned or pale?'

'I couldn't see anything.'

'You should have taken a flashlight.'

'On balance I'm still glad I didn't.'

'How did his skin feel?'

'Feel? It felt like skin.'

'You should have been able to tell something. Olive skin feels different from pale skin. A little smoother and thicker.'

'Really?'

'I think so. Don't you?'

Reacher touched the inside of his left wrist with his right forefinger. Then he tried his cheek, under his eye.

'Hard to tell,' he said.

Vaughan stretched her arm across the table. 'Now compare.'

He touched the inside of her wrist, gently.

She said, 'Now try my face.'

'Really?'

'Purely for research purposes.'

He paused a beat and touched her cheek, with the ball of his thumb. He took his hand away and said, 'Texture was thicker than either one of us.

Smoothness was somewhere between the two of us.'

'OK,' she said. She touched her own wrist where he had touched it, and then her face. Then she said, 'Give me your wrist.'

He slid his hand across the table. She touched his wrist, with two fingers, like she was taking his pulse. She rubbed an inch north and an inch south and then leaned over and touched his cheek with her other hand. Her fingertips were cold from her water glass and the touch startled him. He felt a tiny jolt of voltage in it.

She said, 'So he wasn't necessarily white, but he was younger than you. Less lined and wrinkled and weather-beaten. Less of a mess.'

'Thank you.'

'You should use a good moisturizer.'

'I'll bear that advice in mind.'

'And sunscreen.'

'Likewise.'

'Do you smoke?'

'I used to.'

'That's not good for your skin either.'

Reacher said, 'He might have been Asian, with the skimpy beard.'

'Cheekbones?'

'Pronounced, but he was thin anyway.'

'Wasted, in fact.'

'Noticeably. But he was probably wiry to start with.'

'How long does it take for a wiry person to get wasted?'

'I don't know for sure. Maybe five or six days in a hospital bed or a cell, if you're sick or on hunger

125

strike. Less if you're moving about out of doors, keeping warm, burning energy. Maybe only two or three days.'

Vaughan was quiet for a moment.

'That's a lot of wandering,' she said. 'We need to know why the good folks of Despair put in two or three days' sustained effort to keep him out of there.'

Reacher shook his head. 'Might be more useful to know why he was trying so hard to stay. He must have had a damn good reason.'

TWENTY

Vaughan finished her water and Reacher finished his coffee and asked, 'Can I borrow your truck?'

'When?'

'Now. While you sleep.'

Vaughan said, 'No.'

'Why not?'

'You'll use it to go back to Despair, you'll get arrested, and I'll be implicated.'

'Suppose I don't go back to Despair?'

'Where else would you want to go?'

'I want to see what lies to the west. The dead guy must have come in that way. I'm guessing he didn't come through Hope. You would have seen him and remembered him. Likewise with the girl's missing husband.'

'Good point. But there's not much west of Despair. A lot of not much, in fact.'

'Got to be something.'

Vaughan was quiet for a moment. Then she said, 'It's a long loop around. You have to go back practically all the way to Kansas.'

Reacher said, 'I'll pay for the gas.'

'Promise me you'll stay out of Despair.'

'Where's the line?'

'Five miles west of the metal plant.'

'Deal.'

Vaughan sighed and slid her keys across the table.

'Go,' she said. 'I'll walk home. I don't want you to see where I live.'

The old Chevy's seat didn't go very far back. The runners were short. Reacher ended up driving with his back straight and his knees splayed, like he was at the wheel of a farm tractor. The steering was vague and the brakes were soft. But it was better than walking. Much better, in fact. Reacher was done with walking, for a day or two at least.

His first stop was his motel in Hope. His room was at the end of the row, which put Lucy Anderson in a room closer to the office. She couldn't be anywhere else. He hadn't seen any other overnight accommodation in town. And she wasn't staying with friends, because they would have been with her in the diner the night before, in her hour of need.

The motel had its main windows all in back. The front of the row had a repeating sequence of doors and lawn chairs and head-high pebbled glass slits that put daylight into the bathrooms. Reacher started with the room next to his own and walked down the row, looking for the white blur of underwear drying over a tub. In his experience women of Lucy Anderson's station and generation were very particular about personal hygiene.

The twelve rooms yielded two possibilities. One had a larger blur than the other. Not necessarily more underwear. Just bigger underwear. An older or a larger woman. Reacher knocked at the other door and stepped back and waited. A long moment later Lucy Anderson opened up and stood in the inside shadows, warily, with one hand on the handle.

Reacher said, 'Hello, Lucky.'

'What do you want?'

'I want to know why your husband went to Despair, and how he got there.'

She was wearing the same sneakers, and the same kind of abbreviated socks. Above them was a long expanse of leg, smooth and toned and tanned to perfection. Maybe she played soccer for UCLA. Maybe she was a varsity star. Above the expanse of leg was a pair of cut-off denims, frayed higher on the outside of her thighs than the inside, which was to say frayed very high indeed, because the effective remaining inseam had to have been less than three-quarters of an inch.

Above the shorts was another sweatshirt, mid-blue, with nothing written on it.

She said, 'I don't want you looking for my husband.'

'Why not?'

'Because I don't want you to find him.'

'Why not?'

'It's obvious.'

'Not to me,' Reacher said.

She said, 'I'd like you to leave me alone now.'

'You were worried about him yesterday. Today you're not?'

She stepped forward into the light, just a pace, and glanced left and right beyond Reacher's shoulders. The motel's lot was empty. Nothing there, except Vaughan's old truck parked at Reacher's door. Lucy Anderson's sweatshirt was the same colour as her eyes, and her eyes were full of panic.

'Just leave us alone,' she said, and stepped back into her room and closed the door.

Reacher sat a spell in Vaughan's truck, with a map from her door pocket. The sun was out again and the cab was warm. In Reacher's experience cars were always either warm or cold. Like a primitive calendar. Either it was summer or winter. Either the sun came through the glass and the metal, or it didn't.

The map confirmed what Vaughan had told him. He was going to have to drive a huge three-and-a-half-sided rectangle, first east almost all the way back to the Kansas line, then north to I-70, then west again, then south on the same highway spur the metal trucks used. Total distance, close to two hundred miles. Total time, close to four hours. Plus four hours and two hundred miles back, if he obeyed Vaughan's injunction to keep her truck off Despair's roads.

Which he planned to.

Probably.

He pulled out of the lot and headed east, retracing the route he had come in on with the old guy in the Grand Marquis. The mid-morning sun was low on his right. The old truck's battered exhaust was leaking fumes, so he kept the windows cracked. No electric winders. Just old-fashioned handles, which he preferred for the precision they

130

permitted. He had the left window down less than an inch, and the right window half as much. At a steady sixty the wind whistled in and sounded a mellifluous high-pitched chord, underpinned by the bass growl of a bad bearing and the tenor burble of the tired old motor. The truck was a pleasant travelling companion on the state roads. On I-70 it was less pleasant. Passing semis blew it all over the place. The geometry was out and it had no stability. Reacher's wrists ached after the first ten highway miles, from holding it steady. He stopped once for gas and once for coffee and both times he was happy to get a break.

The spur came off I-70 west of Despair and ran back south and east and petered out into a heavy-duty county two-lane within thirty miles. Reacher recognized it. It was the same piece of road he had observed leaving the plant at the other end. Same sturdy construction, same width, same coarse blacktop, same sand shoulders. Exactly four hours after leaving the motel he slowed and coasted and crossed the rumble strip and came to a stop with two wheels in the sand. Traffic was light, limited to trucks of all types heading in and out of the recycling plant twenty miles ahead. They were mostly flat-bed semis, but with some container trucks and box vans mixed in. Plates were mostly from Colorado and its adjacent states, but there were some from California and Washington and New Jersey and some from Canada. They barrelled past and their bow waves rocked the old truck on its suspension.

Despair itself was invisible in the far distance,

except for the hint of a smudge on the horizon and a thin pall of smog hanging motionless in the air. Five miles closer but still fifteen miles away was the group of low grey buildings Reacher had seen before, now on his right, a tiny indistinct blur. A gas station, maybe. Or a motel. Or both. Maybe a full-blown truck stop, with a restaurant. Maybe it was the kind of place he could get a high-calorie meal.

Maybe it was the kind of place Lucy Anderson's husband and the unidentified dead guy might have gotten a high-calorie meal, on their way into Despair. In the case of the unidentified dead guy at least, maybe his last meal ever.

Maybe someone would remember them.

Maybe the place was outside Despair's city limit.

Maybe it wasn't.

Reacher checked his mirror and put the truck in gear and bumped his right-hand wheels back on to the road and headed for the horizon. Twelve minutes later he stopped again, just short of a pole that held a small green sign that said: *Entering Despair, Pop. 2691*. A hundred yards the wrong side of the line was the group of low buildings.

They weren't grey. That had been a trick of light and haze and distance.

They were olive green.

Not a gas station.

Not a motel.

No kind of a truck stop.

132

TWENTY-ONE

There were six low green buildings. They were identical metal prefabrications clustered together according to exact specifications and precise regulations. They were separated by roadways of uniform width graded from raw dirt and edged with white-painted boulders of small and consistent size. They were ringed by a razor wire fence, tall, straight, and true. The fence continued west to enclose a parking lot. The lot was filled with six up-armoured Humvees. Each one had a quick-release machine gun mount on top. Next to the parking lot there was a slender radio mast protected by a fence all its own.

Not a motel.

Not a truck stop.

A military facility.

Specifically, an army facility. More specifically, a military police facility. More specifically still, a temporary advanced encampment for a combat MP unit. An FOB, a forward operating base. Reacher recognized the format and the equipment mix. Confirmation was right there on a board at the gate. The gate was a white counterbalanced pole with a guard shack next to it. The board was on stilts next to the shack and was painted glossy army green and had a formal unit ID stencilled on it in white.

Not a National Guard unit.

Not reservists.

A regular army unit, and a pretty good one too. At least it always had been, back in Reacher's day, and there was no reason to believe it had gotten sloppy in the intervening years. No reason at all.

How sloppy it hadn't gotten was proved almost immediately.

The guard shack was a metal affair with tall wide windows on all four sides. Four guys in it. Two stayed where they were, and would for ever, no matter what. The other two came out. They were dressed in desert BDUs and boots and armoured vests and helmets and they were carrying M-16 rifles. They ducked under the boom and formed up side by side and sloped arms and stepped out to the roadway. They executed a perfect left turn and jogged towards Reacher's truck, exactly in step, at exactly seven miles an hour, like they had been trained to. When they were thirty yards away they separated to split the target they were presenting. One guy headed for the sand and came up on Reacher's right and stood off ten yards distant and swapped his rifle into the ready position. The other guy stayed on the blacktop and looped around and checked the truck's load bed and then came back and stood off six feet from Reacher's door and called out in a loud clear voice.

He said, 'Sir, please lower your window.'

And keep your hands where I can see them,

Reacher thought. *For your own safety.* He wound the window all the way down and glanced left.

'Sir, please keep your hands where I can see them,' the guy said. 'For your own safety.'

Reacher put his hands high on the wheel and kept on staring left. The guy he was looking at was a specialist, young but with some years in, with pronounced squint lines either side of his eyes. He was wearing glasses with thin black frames. The name tape on the right side of his vest said *Morgan*. In the distance a truck's air horn sounded and the soldier stepped closer to the kerb and a semi blasted past from behind in a howl of sound and wind and grit. There was a long whine of stressed tyres and Reacher's truck rocked on its springs and then silence came down again. The soldier stepped back to where he had been before and took up the same stance, wary but challenging, in control but cautious, his M-16 held barrel-down but ready.

'At ease, corporal,' Reacher said. 'Nothing to see here.'

The guy called Morgan said, 'Sir, that's a determination I'll need to make for myself.'

Reacher glanced ahead. Morgan's partner was still as a statue, the stock of his M-16 tucked tight into his shoulder. He was a private first class. He was sighting with his right eye, aiming low at Reacher's front right-hand tyre.

Morgan asked, 'Sir, why are you stopped here?'

Reacher said, 'Do I need to have a reason?'

'Sir, you appear to me to be surveilling a restricted military installation.'

'Well, you're wrong. I'm not.'

'Sir, why are you stopped?'

'Stop calling me sir, will you?'

'Sir?'

Reacher smiled to himself. An MP with Morgan's years in had probably read a whole foot-thick stack of orders titled *Members of the Public, Domestic, Required Forms of Address*, endlessly revised, revisited, and updated.

'Maybe I'm lost,' Reacher said.

'You're not local?'

'No.'

'Your vehicle has Colorado plates.'

'Colorado is a big state,' Reacher said. 'More than a hundred thousand square miles, soldier, the eighth largest in the Union. By land area, that is. Only the twenty-second largest by population. Maybe I come from a remote and distant corner.'

Morgan went blank for a second. Then he asked, 'Sir, where are you headed?'

Which question gave Reacher a problem. The spur off I-70 had been small and hard to find. No way could a driver headed for Colorado Springs or Denver or Boulder have taken it by mistake. To claim a navigation error would raise suspicion. To raise suspicion would lead to a radio check against Vaughan's plates, which would drag her into something she was better left out of.

So Reacher said, 'I'm headed for Hope.'

Morgan took his left hand off his rifle and pointed straight ahead.

'That way, sir,' he said. 'You're on track. Twenty-two miles to downtown Hope.'

Reacher nodded. Morgan was pointing

southeast but hadn't taken his eyes off Reacher's hands. He was a good soldier. Experienced. Well turned out. His BDUs were old but in good order. His boots were worn and scratched but well cared for and immaculately brushed. The top of his eyeglasses frame ran exactly parallel with the lip of his helmet. Reacher liked soldiers in eyeglasses. Eyeglasses added a vulnerable human detail that balanced the alien appearance of the weapons and the armour.

The face of the modern army.

Morgan stepped in close to Reacher's fender again and another truck blew by. This one was a New Jersey semi loaded with a closed forty-foot shipping container. Like a giant brick, doing sixty miles an hour. Noise, wind, a long tail of swirling dust. Morgan's BDU pants flattened against his legs and skittering miniature tornadoes of dust danced all around his feet. But he didn't blink behind his glasses.

He asked, 'Sir, does this vehicle belong to you?'

Reacher said, 'I'm not sure you're entitled to information like that.'

'In the vicinity of a restricted military installation I would say I'm entitled to pretty much any information I want.'

Reacher didn't answer that.

Morgan said, 'Do you have registration and insurance?'

'Glove box,' Reacher said, which was a pretty safe guess. Vaughan was a cop. Most cops kept their paperwork straight. Too embarrassing, if they didn't.

Morgan asked, 'Sir, may I see those documents?'

Reacher said, 'No.'

'Sir, now it seems to me that you're approaching a restricted military installation in a stolen load-bearing vehicle.'

'You already checked the back. It's empty.'

Morgan said nothing.

'Relax, corporal,' Reacher said. 'This is Colorado, not Iraq. I'm not looking to blow anything up.'

'Sir, I wish you hadn't used those words.'

'At ease, Morgan. I was speaking negatively. I was telling you what I wasn't going to do.'

'No laughing matter.'

'I'm not laughing.'

'I need to see those vehicle documents, sir.'

'You're overstepping your authority.'

'Sir, I need to see them real quick.'

'You got a JAG lawyer on post?'

'Negative, sir.'

'You happy to make this decision on your own?'

Morgan didn't answer. He stepped close to the fender again and a tanker truck blasted by. It had an orange hazardous chemicals diamond on the back and a stainless steel body polished so bright that Reacher saw himself reflected in it like a funhouse mirror. Then its slipstream died away and Morgan stepped back into position and said, 'Sir, I need you to show me those documents. Just wave them at me, if you like. To prove to me you can put your hands on them.'

Reacher shrugged and leaned over and opened

the glove box lid. Dug through ballpoint pens and envelopes of facial tissues and other miscellaneous junk and found a small plastic wallet. The wallet was black and was printed with a silver shape resembling a steering wheel. It was the kind of cheap thing found for sale at gas stations and car washes, alongside air fresheners shaped like conifer trees and ball compasses that attached to windshields with suction cups. The plastic was stiff and brittle with age and the black colour had leached out to a dusty grey.

Reacher opened the wallet, out of Morgan's sight. On the left behind a plastic window was a current insurance certificate. On the right, a current registration.

Both were made out to David Robert Vaughan, of Hope, Colorado.

Reacher kept the wallet open with his thumb and waved it in Morgan's direction, long enough for the documents to register, short enough for neither of them to be read.

Morgan said, 'Sir, thank you.'

Reacher put the wallet back in the glove box and slammed the lid.

Morgan said, 'Sir, now it's time to be moving along.'

Which gave Reacher another problem. If he moved forward, he would be in Despair township. If he U-turned, Morgan would wonder why he had suddenly gotten cold feet and abandoned Hope as a destination, and would be tempted to call in the plate.

Which was the greater danger?

Morgan, easily. A contest between the Despair

PD and a combat MP unit was no kind of a contest at all. So Reacher put the truck in gear and turned the wheel.

'Have a great day, corporal,' he said, and moved off the shoulder. He hit the gas and a yard later he passed the little green sign and temporarily increased Despair's population by one, all the way up to 2692.

TWENTY-TWO

The sturdy two-lane continued basically straight for five miles to the recycling plant's vehicle gate. A hundred yards before it got there an unsignposted left fork speared off into the brush and formed the western end of Despair's only through road. Reacher recognized it easily. The lumpy camber, the cheap top dressing, the grit and the pebbles. He paused for an approaching semi loaded with bright steel bars and then waited again for a container truck heading for Canada. Then he made the left and bounced up on to the uneven surface and drove on and saw all the same stuff he had seen the day before, but in reverse order. The plant's long end wall, welded metal, bright white paint, the sparks and the smoke coming from the activity inside, the moving cranes. He stretched a long arm across the cab and dropped the passenger window and heard the noise of clanging hammers and smelled the acrid odours of chemical compounds.

He got to the acres of parking near the personnel gate and saw the clockwise security Tahoe bouncing across the scrub in the distance

141

far to his right. Its counterclockwise partner was much closer. It was right there in the lot, doing twenty miles an hour, blank tinted windows, coming on slow, looking to cross the road at a right angle. Reacher speeded up and the Tahoe slowed down and crossed right behind him. Reacher saw it slide past, huge in his mirror. He drove on and then the plant was behind him and downtown Despair was looming up three miles ahead on the right. The low brick cubes, sullen in the afternoon light. The road was clear. It rose and fell and meandered gently left and right, avoiding any geological formation larger than a refrigerator. Cheap engineering, never graded or straightened since its origin as a cart track.

A mile ahead, a cop car pulled out of a side street.

It was unmistakable. A Crown Vic, white and gold, black push bars on the front, a light bar on the roof, antennas on the trunk lid. It nosed out and paused a beat and turned left.

West.

Straight towards Reacher.

Reacher checked his speed. He was doing fifty, which was all that was comfortable. He had no idea of the local limit. He dropped to forty-five, and cruised on. The cop was less than a mile away, coming on fast. Closing speed, more than a hundred miles an hour. Time to contact, approximately thirty-five seconds.

Reacher cruised on.

The sun was behind him, and therefore in the cop's eyes, which was a good thing. The old Chevy truck had a plain untinted windshield, which was a bad thing. Ten seconds before contact Reacher took his left hand off the wheel and put it against his forehead, like he was massaging his temple against a headache. He kept his speed steady and stared straight ahead.

The cop car shot past.

Reacher put his hand back on the wheel and checked his mirror.

The cop was braking hard.

Reacher kept one eye on the mirror and ran a fast calculation. He had maybe fifteen miles to go before the Hope town line and the arthritic old Chevy would top out at about seventy, max, which gave him a thirteen-minute trip. The Crown Vic was not a fantastically powerful car but the Police Interceptor option pack gave it a low axle ratio for fast acceleration and twin exhausts for better breathing. It would do ninety, comfortably. Therefore it would overhaul him within three minutes, just about level with the abandoned motor court, at the start of twelve whole miles of empty road.

Not good.

Behind him the Crown Vic was pulling through a fast U-turn.

Why?

Despair was a company town but its road had to be a public thoroughfare. Any Hope resident would use it to head home off the Interstate. Some Kansas residents would do the same. Unfamiliar vehicles in Despair could not possibly be rarities.

Reacher checked the mirror again. The Crown Vic was accelerating after him. Nose high, tail squatting low.

Maybe the security guy in the counterclockwise

Tahoe had called it in. Maybe he had seen Reacher's face and recognized it. Maybe the deputies from the family restaurant took turns as the security drivers.

Reacher drove on. He hit the first downtown block.

Ten blocks ahead, a second Crown Vic pulled out.

And stopped, dead across the road.

Reacher braked hard and hauled on the wheel and pulled a fast right into the chequerboard of downtown streets. A desperation move. He was the worst guy in the world to win a car chase. He wasn't a great driver. He had taken the evasive driving course at Fort Rucker during the MP Officers' Basic School and had impressed nobody. He had scraped a passing grade, mostly out of charity. A year later the School had moved to Fort Leonard Wood and the obstacle course had gotten harder and he knew he would have failed it. Time and chance. Sometimes it helps a person.

Sometimes it leaves a person unprepared.

He hit three four-way stops in succession and turned left, right, left without pausing or thinking. The streets were plain and narrow and boxed in tight by dour brick buildings but his sense of direction was better than his driving and he knew he was heading east again, parallel to and two blocks south of Main Street. Downtown traffic was light. He got held up by a woman driving slow in an old Pontiac but the blocks were short and he solved his problem by turning right and left again and bypassing her one block over.

The chase car didn't show behind him. Statistics

144

were on his side. He figured the downtown area was about twelve blocks square, which meant there were about 288 distinct lengths of road between opportunities to turn off, which meant that if he kept moving the chances of direct confrontation were pretty low.

But the chances of ever getting out of the maze were pretty low, too. As long as the second cop was blocking Main Street at its eastern end, then Hope was unavailable as a destination. And presumably the metal plant Tahoes were on duty to the west. And presumably Despair was full of helpful citizens with four-wheel-drive SUVs that would be a lot quicker over open ground than Vaughan's ancient Chevy. They could get up a regular posse.

Reacher turned a random left, just to keep moving. The chase car flashed through the intersection, dead ahead. It moved left to right and disappeared. Reacher turned left on the same street and saw it in his mirror, moving away from him. Now he was heading west. His gas tank was more than a quarter full. He turned right at the next four-way and headed north two blocks to Main Street. He turned east there and took a look ahead.

The second Crown Vic was still parked across the road, blocking both lanes, ten yards east of the last developed block, just beyond the dry goods store. Its light bar was flashing red, as a warning to oncoming traffic. It was nearly eighteen feet long. One of the last of America's full size sedans. A big car, but at one end it was leaving a gap of about four feet between the front of its hood and the kerb, and about three feet between its trunk and the kerb at the other.

No good. Vaughan's Chevy was close to six feet wide.

Back at Fort Rucker the evasive driving aces had a mantra: *Keep death off the road: drive on the sidewalk.* Which Reacher could do. He could get past the cop with two wheels up on the kerb. But then what? He would be faced with a twelve-mile high-speed chase, in a low-speed vehicle.

No good.

He turned right again and headed back to the downtown maze. Saw the first Crown Vic flash past again, this time hunting east to west, three blocks away. He turned left and headed away from it. He slowed and started looking for used car lots. In the movies, you parked at the end of a line of similar vehicles and the cops blew past without noticing.

He found no used car lots.

In fact he found nothing much at all. Certainly nothing useful. He saw the police station twice, and the grocery store and the barber shop and the bar and the rooming house and the faded old hotel that he had seen before, on his walk down to the restaurant he had been thrown out of. He saw a storefront church. Some kind of a strange fringe denomination, something about the end times. The only church in town, Vaughan had said, where the town's feudal boss was the lay preacher. It was an ugly one-storey building, built from brick, with a squat steeple piled on top to make it taller than the neighbouring buildings. The steeple had a copper lightning rod on it and the grounding strap

146

that ran down to the street had weathered to a bright verdigris green. It was the most colourful thing on display in Despair, a vivid vertical slash among the dullness.

He drove on. He looked, but he saw nothing else of significance. He would have liked a tyre bay, maybe, where he could get the old Chevy up on a hoist and out of sight. He could have hidden out and gotten Vaughan's bad geometry fixed, all at the same time.

He found no tyre bays.

He drove on, making random turns left and right. He saw the first Crown Vic three more times in the next three minutes, twice ahead of him and once behind him in his mirrors. The fourth time he saw it was a minute later. He paused at a four-way and it came up at the exact same moment and paused in the mouth of the road directly to his right. Reacher and the cop were at right angles to each other, nose to nose, ten feet apart, immobile. The cop was the same guy that had arrested him. Big, dark, wide. Tan jacket. He looked over and smiled. Gestured *Go ahead* like he was yielding, as if he had been second to the line.

Reacher was a lousy driver, but he wasn't stupid. No way was he going to let the cop get behind him, heading in the same direction. He jammed the old Chevy into reverse and backed away. The cop darted forward, turning, aiming to follow. Reacher waited until the guy was halfway through the manoeuvre and jammed the stick back into Drive and snaked past him, close, flank to flank. Then he hung a left and a right and a left again until he was sure he was clear.

147

Then he drove on, endlessly. He concluded that his random turns weren't helping him. He was as likely to turn into trouble as away from it. So mostly he stayed straight, until he ran out of street. Then he would turn. He ended up driving in wide concentric circles, slow enough to be safe, fast enough that he could kick the speed up if necessary without the weak old motor bogging down.

He passed the church and the bar and the grocery and the faded old hotel for the third time each. Then the rooming house. Its door slid behind his shoulder and opened. In the corner of his eye he saw a guy step out.

A young guy.

A big guy.

Tall, and blond, and heavy. An athlete. Blue eyes and a buzz cut and a dark tan. Jeans and a white T-shirt under a grey V-neck sweater.

Reacher stamped on the brake and turned his head. But the guy was gone, moving fast, around the corner. Reacher shoved the stick into reverse and backed up. A horn blared and an old SUV swerved. Reacher didn't stop. He entered the four-way going backward and stared down the side street.

No guy. Just empty sidewalk. In his mirror Reacher saw the chase car three blocks west. He shoved the stick back into Drive and took off forward. Turned left, turned right, drove more wide aimless circles.

He didn't see the young man again.

But he saw the cop twice more. The guy was nosing around through distant intersections like he had all the time in the world. Which he did. Two thirty in the afternoon, half the population hard at work at the plant, the other half cleaning house or baking pies or slumped in armchairs watching daytime TV, the lone road bottlenecked at both ends of town. The cop was just amusing himself. He had Reacher trapped, and he knew it.

And Reacher knew it, too.

No way out.

Time to stand and fight.

TWENTY-THREE

Some jerk instructor at the Fort Rucker MP school had once trotted out the tired old cliché that *to assume makes an ass out of you and me*. He had demonstrated at the classroom chalkboard, dividing the word into *ass*, *u*, and *me*. On the whole Reacher had agreed with him, even if the guy was a jerk. But sometimes assumptions just had to be made, and right then Reacher chose to assume that however half-baked the Despair cops might be, they wouldn't risk shooting with bystanders in the line of fire. So he pulled to the kerb outside the family restaurant and got out of Vaughan's truck and crossed the sidewalk and took up a position leaning on one of the restaurant's floor-to-ceiling plate glass windows.

Behind him the place was doing reasonable business. The same waitress was on duty. She had nine customers eating late lunches. A trio, a couple, four singletons, equally distributed around the room.

Collateral damage, just waiting to happen.

The window glass was cold on Reacher's shoulders. He could feel it through his shirt. The sun was still out but it was low in the sky and the streets were in shadow. There was a breeze. Small eddies of grit blew here and there on the sidewalk. Reacher unbuttoned his cuffs and folded them up on his forearms. He arched his back against the cramp he had gotten from sitting in the Chevy's undersized cab for so long. He flexed his hands and rolled his head in small circles to loosen his neck.

Then he waited.

The cop showed up two minutes and forty seconds later. The Crown Vic came in from the west and stopped two intersections away and paused, like the guy was having trouble processing the information visible right in front of him. *The truck, parked. The suspect, just standing there.* Then the pause was over and the car leaped forward and came through the four-ways and pulled in tight behind the Chevy, on the right-hand sidewalk, facing east, its front fender eight feet from where Reacher was waiting. The cop left the engine running and opened his door and slid out into the roadway. Déjà vu all over again. Big guy, white, maybe forty, black hair, wide neck. Tan jacket, brown pants, the groove in his forehead from his hat. He took his Glock off his belt and held it straight out two-handed and put his spread thighs against the opposite fender and stared at Reacher across the width of the hood.

Sound tactics, except for the innocents behind the glass.

The cop called out, 'Freeze.'

'I'm not going anywhere,' Reacher said. 'Yet.'

'Get in the car.'

'Make me.'

'I'll shoot.'

'You won't.'

The guy went blank for a beat and then shifted his focus beyond Reacher's face to the scene inside the restaurant. Reacher was absolutely certain that the Despair PD had no Officer Involved Shooting investigative team, or even any kind of Officer Involved Shooting protocol, so the guy's hesitation was down to pure common sense. Or maybe the guy had relatives who liked to lunch late.

'Get in the car,' the guy said again.

Reacher said, 'I'll take a pass on that.' He felt the chill against his shoulder blades but stayed relaxed, leaning back, unthreatening.

'I'll shoot,' the cop said again.

'You can't. You're going to need backup.'

The cop paused again. Then he shuffled to the left, back towards the driver's door. He kept his eyes and the gun tight on Reacher and fumbled one-handed through the car window and grabbed up his Motorola microphone and pulled it all the way out until its cord went tight. He brought it to his mouth and clicked the button. Said, 'Bro, the restaurant, right now.' He clicked off again and tossed the microphone back on the seat and put both hands back on the gun and shuffled back to the fender.

And the clock started ticking.

One guy would be easy.

Two might be harder.

The second guy had to move, but Reacher couldn't afford for him to arrive.

No sound, except the idling cruiser and the distant clash of plates inside the restaurant kitchen.

'Pussy,' Reacher called. 'A thing like this, you should have been able to handle it on your own.'

The cop's lips went tight and he shuffled towards the front of the car, tracking with his gun, adjusting his aim. He reached the front bumper and felt for the push bars with his knees. Came on around, getting nearer.

He stepped up out of the gutter on to the sidewalk.

Reacher waited. The cop was now on his right, so Reacher shuffled one step left, to keep the line of fire straight and dangerous and inhibiting. The Glock tracked his move, locked in a steady two-handed grip.

The cop said, 'Get in the car.'

The cop took one step forward.

Now he was five feet away, one cast square of concrete sidewalk.

Reacher kept his back against the glass and moved his right heel against the base of the wall.

The cop stepped closer.

Now the Glock's muzzle was within a foot of Reacher's throat. The cop was a big guy, with long arms fully extended, and both feet planted apart in a useful combat stance.

Useful if he was prepared to fire.

Which he wasn't.

Taking a gun from a man ready to use it was not always difficult. Taking one from a man who had already decided not to use it verged on the easy. The cop took his left hand off the gun and made ready to grab Reacher by the collar. Reacher slid right, his back hard on the window, washed canvas on clean glass, no friction at all, and moved inside the cop's aim. He brought his left forearm up and over, fast, *one two*, and clamped his hand right over the Glock and the cop's hand together. The cop was a big guy with big hands, but Reacher's were bigger. He clamped down and squeezed hard and forced the gun down and away in one easy movement. He got it pointing at the floor and increased the squeeze to paralyse the cop's trigger finger and then he looked him in the eye and smiled briefly and jerked forward off his planted heel and delivered a colossal head butt direct to the bridge of the cop's nose.

The cop sagged back on rubber legs.

Reacher kept tight hold of the guy's gun hand and kneed him in the groin. The cop went down more or less vertically but Reacher kept his hand twisted up and back so that the cop's own weight dislocated his elbow as he fell. The guy screamed and the Glock came free pretty easily after that.

Then it was all about getting ready in a hurry.

Reacher scrambled around the Crown Vic's hood and hauled the door open. He tossed the Glock inside and slid in the seat and buckled the seat belt and pulled it snug and tight. The seat was still warm from the cop's body and the car smelled of sweat. Reacher put the transmission in reverse and backed away from the Chevy and spun the wheel and came back level with it, in the wrong lane, facing east, just waiting.

TWENTY-FOUR

The second cop showed up within thirty seconds, right on cue. Reacher saw the flare of flashing red lights a second before the Crown Vic burst around a distant corner. It fishtailed a little and got straightened up and accelerated down the narrow street towards the restaurant, hard and fast and smooth.

Reacher let it get through one four-way, and another, and when it was thirty yards away he stamped on the gas and took off straight at it and smashed into it head-on. The two Crown Vics met nose to nose and their rear ends lifted off the ground and sheet metal crumpled and hoods flew open and glass burst and airbags exploded and steam jetted everywhere. Reacher was smashed forward against his seat belt. He had his hands off the wheel and his elbows up to fend off the punch of his airbag. Then the airbag collapsed again and Reacher was tossed back against the head rest. The rear of his car thumped back to earth and bounced once and came to rest at an angle. He pulled the Mossberg pump out of its between-the-seats holster and forced the door

155

open against the crumpled fender and climbed out of the car.

The other guy hadn't been wearing his seat belt.

He had taken the impact of his airbag full in the face and was lying sideways across the front seat with blood coming out of his nose and his ears. Both cars were pretty much wrecked as far back as the windshield pillars. The passenger compartments were basically OK. Full size sedans, five star crash ratings. Reacher was pretty sure both cars were undriveable but he was no kind of an automotive expert and so he made sure by racking the Mossberg twice and firing two booming shots into the rear wheel wells, shredding the tyres and ripping up all kinds of other small essential components. Then he tossed the pump back through the first Crown Vic's window and walked over and climbed into Vaughan's Chevy and backed away from all the wreckage. The waitress and the nine customers inside the restaurant were all staring out through the windows, mouths wide open in shock. Two of the customers were fumbling for their cell phones.

Reacher smiled. *Who are you going to call?*

He K-turned the Chevy and made a right and headed north for Main Street and made another right and cruised east at a steady fifty. When he hit the lonely road after the gas station he kicked it up to sixty and kept one eye on the mirror. Nobody came after him. He felt the roughness under his tyres but the roar was quieter than before. He was a little deaf from the airbags and the twin Mossberg blasts.

Twelve minutes later he bumped over the expansion joint and cruised into Hope, at exactly three o'clock in the afternoon.

He didn't know how long Vaughan would sleep. He guessed she had gotten her head on the pillow a little after nine that morning, which was six hours ago. Eight hours' rest would take her to five o'clock, which was reasonable for an on-deck time of seven in the evening. Or maybe she was already up and about. Some people slept worse in the daytime than the night. Habit, degree of acclimatization, circadian rhythms. He decided to head for the diner. Either she would be there already or he could leave her keys with the cashier.

She was there already.

He pulled to the kerb and saw her alone in the booth they had used before. She was dressed in her cop uniform, four hours before her watch. She had an empty plate and a full coffee cup in front of her.

He locked the truck and went in and sat down opposite her. Up close, she looked tired.

'Didn't sleep?' he asked.

'Is it that obvious?'

'I have a confession to make.'

'You went to Despair. In my truck. I knew you would.'

'I had to.'

'Sure.'

'When was the last time you drove out to the west?'

'Years ago. Maybe never. I try to stay out of Despair.'

157

'There's a military base just inside the line. Fairly new. Why would that be?'

Vaughan said, 'There are military bases all over.'

'This was a combat MP unit.'

'They have to put them somewhere.'

'Overseas is where they need to put them. The army is hurting for numbers right now. They can't afford to waste good units in the back of beyond.'

'Maybe it wasn't a good unit.'

'It was.'

'So maybe it's about to ship out.'

'It just shipped back in. It just spent a year under the sun. The guy I spoke to had squint lines like you wouldn't believe. His gear was worn from the sand.'

'We have sand here.'

'Not like that.'

'So what are you saying?'

The waitress came by and Reacher ordered coffee. Vaughan's cup was still full. Reacher said, 'I'm asking why they pulled a good unit out of the Middle East and sent it here.'

Vaughan said, 'I don't know why. The Pentagon doesn't explain itself to neighbouring police departments.'

The waitress brought a cup for Reacher and filled it from a Bunn flask. Vaughan asked, 'What does a combat MP unit do exactly?'

Reacher took a sip of coffee and said, 'It guards things. Convoys or installations. It maintains security and repels attacks.'

'Actual fighting?'

'When necessary.'

'Did you do that?'

'Some of the time.'

Vaughan opened her mouth and then closed it again as her mind supplied the answer to the question she was about to ask.

'Exactly,' Reacher said. 'What's to defend in Despair?'

'And you're saying these MPs made you drive on through?'

'It was safer. They would have checked your plate if I hadn't.'

'Did you get through OK?'

'Your truck is fine. Although it's not exactly yours, is it?'

'What do you mean?'

'Who is David Robert Vaughan?'

She looked blank for a second. Then she said, 'You looked in the glove box. The registration.'

'A man with a gun wanted to see it.'

'Good reason.'

'So who is David Robert?'

Vaughan said, 'My husband.'

TWENTY-FIVE

Reacher said, 'I didn't know you were married.' Vaughan turned her attention to her lukewarm coffee and took a long time to answer.

'That's because I didn't tell you,' she said. 'Would you expect me to?'

'Not really, I suppose.'

'Don't I look married?'

'Not one little bit.'

'You can tell just by looking?'

'Usually.'

'How?'

'Fourth finger, left hand, for a start.'

'Lucy Anderson doesn't wear a ring either.'

Reacher nodded. 'I think I saw her husband today.'

'In Despair?'

'Coming out of the rooming house.'

'That's way off Main Street.'

'I was dodging roadblocks.'

'Terrific.'

'Not one of my main talents.'

'So how did they not catch you? They've got one road in and one road out.'

'Long story,' Reacher said.

'But?'

'The Despair PD is temporarily understaffed.'

'You took one of them out?'

'Both of them. And their cars.'

'You're completely unbelievable.'

'No, I'm a man with a rule. People leave me alone, I leave them alone. If they don't, I don't.'

'They'll come looking for you here.'

'No question. But not soon.'

'How long?'

'They'll be hurting for a couple of days. Then they'll saddle up.'

Reacher left her alone with her truck keys on the table in front of her and walked down to Third Street and bought socks and underwear and a dollar T-shirt in an old-fashioned outfitters next to a supermarket. He stopped in at a pharmacy and bought shaving gear and then headed up to the hardware store at the western end of First Street. He picked his way past ladders and barrows and wound through aisles filled with racks of tools and found a rail of canvas work pants and flannel shirts. Traditional American garments, made in China and Cambodia, respectively. He chose dark olive pants and a mud-coloured check shirt. Not as cheap as he would have liked, but not outrageous. The clerk made them up into a brown paper parcel and he carried it back to the motel and shaved and took a long shower and dried off and dressed in the new stuff. He crammed his old grey janitor uniform in the trash receptacle.

Better than doing laundry.

The new clothes were as stiff as boards, to the point where walking around was difficult. Clearly the Far Eastern garment industry took durability very seriously. He did squats and bicep curls until the starch cracked and then he stepped out and walked down the row to Lucy Anderson's door. He knocked and waited. A minute later she opened up. She looked just the same. Long legs, short shorts, plain blue sweatshirt. Young, and vulnerable. And wary, and hostile. She said, 'I asked you to leave me alone.'

He said, 'I'm pretty sure I saw your husband today.'

Her face softened, just for a second.

'Where?' she asked.

'In Despair. Looks like he's got a room there.'

'Was he OK?'

'He looked fine to me.'

'What are you going to do about him?'

'What would you like me to do about him?'

Her face closed up again. 'You should leave him alone.'

Reacher said, 'I am leaving him alone. I told you, I'm not a cop any more. I'm a vagrant, just like you.'

'So why would you go back to Despair?'

'Long story. I had to.'

'I don't believe you. You're a cop.'

'You saw what was in my pockets.'

'You left your badge in your room.'

'I didn't. You want to check? My room is right here.'

She stared at him in panic and put both hands on the door jambs like he was about to seize her around her waist and drag her away to his quarters. The motel clerk stepped out of the office, forty feet to Reacher's left. She was a stout woman of about fifty. She saw Reacher and saw the girl and stopped walking and watched. Then she moved again but changed direction and started heading towards them. In Reacher's experience motel clerks were either nosy about or else completely uninterested in their guests. He figured this one was the nosy kind. He stepped back a pace and gave Lucy Anderson some air and held up his hands, palms out, friendly and reassuring.

'Relax,' he said. 'If I was here to hurt you, you'd already be hurt by now, don't you think? You and your husband.'

She didn't answer. Just turned her head and saw the clerk's approach and then ducked back to the inside shadows and slammed her door, all in one neat move. Reacher turned away but knew he wasn't going to make it in time. The clerk was already within calling distance.

'Excuse me,' she said.

Reacher stopped. Turned back. Said nothing.

The woman said, 'You should leave that girl alone.'

'Should I?'

'If you want to stay here.'

'Is that a threat?'

'I try to maintain standards.'

'I'm trying to help her.'

'She thinks the exact opposite.'

'You've talked?'

'I hear things.'

'I'm not a cop.'

163

'You look like a cop.'

'I can't help that.'

'You should investigate some real crimes.'

Reacher said, 'I'm not investigating any kind of crimes. I told you, I'm not a cop.'

The woman didn't answer.

Reacher asked, 'What real crimes?'

'Violations.'

'Where?'

'At the metal plant in Despair.'

'What kind of violations?'

'All kinds.'

'I don't care about violations. I'm not an EPA inspector. I'm not any kind of an inspector.'

The woman said, 'Then you should ask yourself why that plane flies every night.'

TWENTY-SIX

Reacher got halfway back to his room and saw Vaughan's old pick-up turn in off the street. It was moving fast. It bounced up over the kerb and headed through the lot straight at him. Vaughan was at the wheel in her cop uniform. Incongruous. And urgent. She hadn't taken time to go fetch her official cruiser. She braked hard and stopped with her radiator grille an inch away from him. She leaned out the window and said, 'Get in, now.'

Reacher asked, 'Why?'

'Just do it.'

'Do I have a choice?'

'None at all.'

'Really?'

'I'm not kidding.'

'Are you arresting me?'

'I'm prepared to. I'll use my gun and my cuffs if that's what it takes. Just get in the car.'

Reacher watched her face through the windshield glass for a long moment. She was serious about something. And determined. That was for sure. The evidence was right there in the set of her jaw. So he tracked around the hood to the passenger side and climbed in. Vaughan waited until he closed his door behind him and asked, 'You ever done a ride-along with a cop before? All night? A whole watch?'

'Why would I? I *was* a cop.'

'Well, whatever, you're doing one tonight.'

'Why?'

'We got a courtesy call. From Despair. You're a wanted man. They're coming for you. So tonight you stay where I can see you.'

'They can't be coming for me. They can't even have woken up yet.'

'Their deputies are coming. All four of them.'

'Really?'

'That's what deputies are for. They deputize.'

'So I hide in your car? All night?'

'Damn straight.'

'You think I need protection?'

'My town needs protection. I don't want trouble here.'

'Those four won't be any trouble. One of them is already busted up and one was sick the last time I saw him.'

'So you could take them?'

'With one hand behind my back and my head in a bag.'

'Exactly. I'm a cop. I have a responsibility. No fighting in my streets. It's unseemly.'

She hit the gas and pulled a tight U-turn in the motel lot and headed back the way she had come. Reacher asked, 'When will they get here?'

'The plant shuts down at six. I imagine they'll head right over.'

'How long will they stay?'

'The plant opens up again at six tomorrow morning.'

Reacher said, 'You don't want me in your car all night.'

'I'll do what it takes. Like I said. This is a decent place. I'm not going to let it get trashed, either literally or metaphorically.'

Reacher paused and said, 'I could leave town.'

'Permanently?' Vaughan asked.

'Temporarily.'

'And go where?'

'Despair, obviously. I can't get in trouble there, can I? Their cops are still in the hospital and their deputies will be here all night.'

Vaughan said nothing.

'Your choice,' Reacher said. 'But your Crown Vic is a comfortable car. I might fall asleep with my mouth open and snore.'

Vaughan made a right and a left and headed down Second Street towards the diner. She stayed quiet for a moment and then she said, 'There's another one in town today.'

'Another what?'

'Another girl. Just like Lucy Anderson. But dark, not blonde. She came in this afternoon and now she's sitting around and staring west like she's waiting for word from Despair.'

'From a boyfriend or a husband?'

'Possibly.'

'Possibly a dead boyfriend or husband, Caucasian, about twenty years old, five-eight and one-forty.'

'Possibly.'

'I should go there.'

Vaughan drove past the diner and kept on driving. She made a left near the end of town and drove two blocks south and came back east on Fourth Street. No real reason. Just motion, for the sake of it. Fourth Street had trees and retail establishments behind the north sidewalk and trees and a long line of neat homes behind the south. Small yards, picket fences, foundation plantings, mailboxes on poles that had settled to every angle except the truly vertical.

'I should go there,' Reacher said again.

Vaughan nodded.

'Wait until the deputies get here. You don't want to pass them on the road.'

'OK.'

'And don't let them see you leave.'

'OK.'

'And don't make trouble over there.'

'I'm not sure there's anybody left to make trouble with. Unless I meet the judge.'

TWENTY-SEVEN

For the second time that day Vaughan gave up her pick-up truck and walked home to get her cruiser. Reacher drove the truck to a quiet side street near the western edge of town and parked facing north in the shadow of a tree and watched the traffic on First Street directly ahead of him. He had a limited field of view. Maybe thirty yards left to right, west to east. Not a great angle. But there wasn't much to see, anyway. Whole ten-minute periods passed without visible activity. Not surprising. Residents returning from the Kansas direction would have peeled off into town down earlier streets. And no one in their right mind was returning from Despair, or heading there. The daylight was fading fast. The world was going grey and still. The clock in Reacher's head was ticking around, relentlessly.

When it hit six thirty-two he saw an old crew-cab pick-up truck flash through his field of vision. From the left, heading east. Moving smartly, from the Despair direction. A driver, and three passengers inside. Big men, close together. They filled the cramped quarters, shoulder to shoulder.

Reacher recognized the truck.

He recognized the driver.

He recognized the passengers.

The Despair deputies, right on time.

He waited a beat and started the old Chevy's engine and moved off the kerb. He eased north to First Street and turned left. Checked his mirror. The old crew-cab was already a hundred yards behind him, moving away in the opposite direction, slowing down and making ready to turn. The road ahead was empty. He passed the hardware store and hit the gas and forced the old truck up to sixty miles an hour. Five minutes later he thumped over the expansion joint and settled in to a noisy cruise west.

Twelve miles later he slowed and coasted past the vacant lot and the shuttered motor court and the gas station and the household goods store and then he turned left into Despair's downtown maze. First port of call was the police station. He wanted to be sure that no miraculous recoveries had been made, and that no replacement personnel had been provided.

They hadn't, and they hadn't.

The place was dark inside and quiet outside. No lights, no activity. There were no cars on the kerb. No stand-in State Police cruisers, no newly deputized pick-up trucks, no plain sedans with temporary *Police* signs stickered on their doors.

Nothing.

Just silence.

Reacher smiled. Open season and lawless, he thought, like a bleak view of the future in a movie.

The way he liked it. He U-turned through the empty diagonal parking slots and headed back towards the rooming house. He parked on the kerb out front and killed the motor and wound the window down. Heard a single aero engine in the far distance, climbing hard. Seven o'clock in the evening. The Cessna or the Beech or the Piper, taking off again. *You should ask yourself why that plane flies every night*, the motel clerk had said.

Maybe I will, Reacher thought. *One day*.

He climbed out of the truck and stood on the sidewalk. The rooming house was built of dull brick on a corner lot. Three storeys high, narrow windows, flat roof, four stone steps up to a doorway set off-centre in the façade. There was a wooden board on the wall next to the door, under a swan-neck lamp with a dim bulb. The board had been painted maroon way back in its history, and the words *Rooms to Rent* had been lettered in white over the maroon by a careful amateur. A plain and to-the-point announcement. Not the kind of place Reacher favoured. Such establishments implied residency for longer periods than he was interested in. Generally they rented by the week, and had electric cooking rings in the rooms. Practically the same thing as setting up housekeeping.

He went up the stone steps and pushed the front door. It was open. Behind it was a plain square hallway with a brown linoleum floor and a steep staircase on the right. The walls were painted brown with some kind of a trick effect that matched the swirls in the linoleum. A bare bulb was burning dimly a foot below the ceiling.

The air smelled of dust and cabbage. There were four interior doors, all dull green, all closed. Two were in back and two were in front, one at the foot of the staircase and the other directly opposite it across the hallway. Two front rooms, one of which would house the owner or the super. In Reacher's experience the owner or the super always chose a ground-floor room at the front, to monitor entrances and exits. Entrances and exits were very important to owners and supers. Unauthorized guests and multiple occupancies were to be discouraged, and tenants had been known to try to sneak out quietly just before final payment of long-overdue rent had been promised.

He opted to start with the door at the foot of the staircase. Better surveillance potential. He knocked and waited. A long moment later the door opened and revealed a thin man in a white shirt and a black tie. The guy was close to seventy years old, and his hair was the same colour as his shirt. The shirt wasn't clean. Neither was the tie, but it had been carefully knotted.

'Help you?' the old guy said.

'Is this your place?' Reacher asked.

The old guy nodded. 'And my mother's before me. In the family for close to fifty years.'

'I'm looking for a friend of mine,' Reacher said. 'From California. I heard he was staying here.'

No reply from the old man.

'Young guy,' Reacher said. 'Maybe twenty. Very big. Tan, with short hair.'

'Nobody like that here.'

'You sure?'

'Nobody here at all.'

'He was seen stepping out your door this afternoon.'

'Maybe he was visiting.'

'Visiting who, if there's nobody here at all?'

'Visiting me,' the old man said.

'Did he visit you?'

'I don't know. I was out. Maybe he called on me and got no reply and left again.'

'Why would he have been calling on you?'

The old guy thought for a moment and said, 'Maybe he was at the hotel and wanted to economize. Maybe he had heard the rates were cheaper here.'

'What about another guy, shorter, wiry, about the same age?'

'No guys here at all, big or small.'

'You sure?'

'It's my house. I know who's in it.'

'How long has it been empty?'

'It's not empty. I live here.'

'How long since you had tenants?'

The old guy thought for another moment and said, 'A long time.'

'How long?'

'Years.'

'So how do you make a living?'

'I don't.'

'You own this place?'

'I rent it. Like my mother did. Close to fifty years.'

Reacher said, 'Can I see the rooms?'

'Which rooms?'

'All of them.'

'Why?'

'Because I don't believe you. I think there are people here.'

'You think I'm lying?'

'I'm a suspicious person.'

'I should call the police.'

'Go right ahead.'

The old guy stepped away into the gloom and picked up a phone. Reacher crossed the hallway and tried the opposite door. It was locked. He walked back and the old guy said, 'There was no answer at the police station.'

'So it's just you and me,' Reacher said. 'Better that you lend me your pass key. Save yourself some repair work later, with the door locks.'

The old guy bowed to the inevitable. He took a key from his pocket and handed it over. It was a worn brass item with a length of furred string tied through the hole. The string had an old metal eyelet on it, as if the eyelet was all that was left of a paper label.

There were three guest rooms on the ground floor, four on the second, and four on the third. Eleven in total. All eleven were identical. All eleven were empty. Each room had a narrow iron cot against one wall. The cots were like something from an old-fashioned fever hospital or an army barracks. They were made up with thin sheets and blankets. The sheets had been washed so many times they were almost transparent. The blankets had started out thick and rough and had worn thin and smooth. Opposite the beds were chests of drawers and free-standing towel racks. The towels were as thin as the sheets. Near the ends of the beds were pine kitchen tables with two-ring electric burners plugged into outlets with frayed old cords. At the ends of the hallways on each of the floors were shared bathrooms, tiled black and white, with large iron claw-foot tubs and lavatories with cisterns mounted high on the walls.

Basic accommodations, for sure, but they were in good order and beautifully kept. The bathroom fitments were stained with age, but not with dirt. The floors were swept shiny. The beds were made tight. A dropped quarter would have bounced two feet off the blankets. The towels on the racks were folded precisely and perfectly aligned. The electric burners were immaculately clean. No crumbs, no spills, no dried splashes of bottled sauce.

Reacher checked everywhere and then stood in the doorway of each room before leaving it, smelling the air and listening for echoes of recent hasty departures. He found nothing and sensed nothing, eleven times over. So he headed back downstairs and returned the key and apologized to the old guy. Then he asked, 'Is there an ambulance service in town?'

The old guy asked, 'Are you injured?'

'Suppose I was. Who would come for me?'

'How bad?'

'Suppose I couldn't walk. Suppose I needed a stretcher.'

The old man said, 'There's a first-aid post up at the plant. And an infirmary. In case a guy gets hurt on the job. They have a vehicle. They have a stretcher.'

'Thanks,' Reacher said.

*   *   *

He drove Vaughan's old Chevy on down the street. Paused for a moment in front of the storefront church. It had a painted sign running the whole width of the building: *Congregation of the End Times*. In one window it had a poster written in the same way that a supermarket would advertise brisket for three bucks a pound: *The Time is at Hand*. A quotation from the Book of Revelation. Chapter one, verse three. Reacher recognized it. The other window had a similar poster: *The End is Near*. Inside, the place was as dark and gloomy as its exterior messages. Rows of metal chairs, a wood floor, a low stage, a podium. More posters, each one predicting with confident aplomb that time was short. Reacher read them all and then drove on, to the hotel. It was full dark when he got there. He remembered the place from earlier daytime sightings as looking dowdy and faded, and by night it looked worse. It was a forbidding brick cube. It could have been an old city prison, in Prague, maybe, or Warsaw, or Leningrad. The walls were dull and featureless and the windows were blank and unlit. Inside it had an empty and unappealing dining room on the left and a deserted bar on the right. Dead ahead in the lobby was a deserted reception desk. Behind the reception desk was a small swaybacked version of a grand staircase. It was covered with matted carpet. There was no elevator.

Hotels were required by state and federal laws and private insurance requirements to maintain accurate guest records. In case of a fire or an earthquake or a tornado, it was in everyone's interest to know who was resident in the building

176

at the time, and who wasn't. Therefore Reacher had learned a long time ago that when searching a hotel the place to start was with the register. Which over the years had become increasingly difficult, with computers. There were all kinds of function keys to hit and passwords to discover. But Despair as a whole was behind the times, and its hotel was no exception. The register was a large square book bound in old red leather. Easy to grab, easy to swivel around, easy to open, easy to read.

The hotel had no guests.

According to the lines of handwritten records the last room had been rented seven months previously, to a couple from California, who had arrived in a private car and stayed two nights. Since then, no trade. Nothing. No names that might have corresponded to single twenty-year-old men, either large or small. No names at all.

Reacher left the hotel without a single soul having seen him and got back in the Chevy. Next stop was two blocks over, in the town bar, which meant mixing with the locals.

TWENTY-EIGHT

The bar was a half-wide slice of the ground floor of yet another dull brick cube. One long narrow room. It ran the full depth of the building and had a short corridor with restrooms and a fire door way in back. The bar itself was on the left and there were tables and chairs on the right. Low light. No music. No television. No pool table, no video games. Maybe a third of the bar stools and a quarter of the chairs were occupied. The after-work crowd. But not exactly happy hour. All the customers were men. They were all tired, all grimy, all dressed in work shirts, all sipping beer from tall glasses or long-neck bottles. Reacher had seen none of them before.

He stepped into the gloom, quietly. Every head turned and every pair of eyes came to rest on him. Some kind of universal bar-room radar. *Stranger in the house*. Reacher stood still and let them take a good look. *A stranger for sure, but not the kind you want to mess with*. Then he moved on and sat down on a stool and put his elbows on the bar. He was two gaps away from the nearest guy on his left and one away from the nearest guy on his right. The stools had iron bases and iron pillars and shaped mahogany seats that turned on rough bearings. The bar itself was made from scarred mahogany that didn't match the walls, which were panelled with pine. There were mirrors all over the walls, made of plain reflective glass screen-printed with beer company advertisements. They were framed with rustic wood and were fogged with years of alcohol fumes and cigarette smoke.

The bartender was a heavy pale man of about forty. He didn't look smart and he didn't look pleasant. He was ten feet away, leaning back with his fat ass against his cash register drawer. Not moving. Not about to move, either. That was clear. Reacher raised his eyebrows and put a beckoning expression on his face and got no response at all.

A company town.

He swivelled his stool and faced the room.

'Listen up, guys,' he called. 'I'm not a metal-worker and I'm not looking for a job.'

No response.

'You couldn't pay me enough to work here. I'm not interested. I'm just a guy passing through, looking for a beer.'

No response. Just sullen and hostile stares, with bottles and glasses frozen halfway between tables and mouths.

Reacher said, 'First guy to talk to me, I'll pay his tab.'

No response.

'For a week.'

No response.

Reacher turned back and faced the bar again. The bartender hadn't moved. Reacher looked him in the eye and said, 'Sell me a beer or I'll start busting this place up.'

The bartender moved. But not towards his refrigerator cabinets or his draught pumps. Towards his telephone instead. It was an old-fashioned instrument next to the register. The guy picked it up and dialled a long number. Reacher waited. The guy listened to a lot of ring tone and then started to say something but then stopped and put the phone down again.

'Voice mail,' he said.

'Nobody home,' Reacher said. 'So it's just you and me. I'll take a Budweiser, no glass.'

The guy glanced beyond Reacher's shoulder, out into the room, to see if any ad-hoc coalitions were forming to help him out. They weren't. Reacher was already monitoring the situation in a dull mirror directly in front of him. The bartender decided not to be a hero. He shrugged and his attitude changed and his face softened a little and he bent down and pulled a cold bottle out from under the bar. Opened it up and set it down on a napkin. Foam swelled out of the neck and ran down the side of the bottle and soaked into the paper. Reacher took a ten from his pocket and folded it lengthways so it wouldn't curl and squared it in front of him.

'I'm looking for a guy,' he said.

The bartender said, 'What guy?'

'A young guy. Maybe twenty. Suntan, short hair, as big as me.'

'Nobody like that here.'

'I saw him this afternoon. In town. Coming out of the rooming house.'

180

'So ask there.'

'I did.'

'I can't help you.'

'You probably can. This guy looked like a college athlete. College athletes drink beer from time to time. He was probably in here once or twice.'

'He wasn't.'

'What about another guy? Same age, much smaller. Wiry, maybe five-eight, one-forty.'

'Didn't see him.'

'You sure?'

'I'm sure.'

'You ever work up at the plant?'

'Couple of years, way back.'

'And then?'

'He moved me here.'

'Who did?'

'Mr Thurman. He owns the plant.'

'And this bar too?'

'He owns everything.'

'And he moved you? He sounds like a hands-on manager.'

'He figured I'd be better working here than there.'

'And are you?'

'Not for me to say.'

Reacher took a long pull on his bottle. Asked, 'Does Mr Thurman pay you well?'

'I don't complain.'

'Is that Mr Thurman's plane that flies every night?'

'Nobody else here owns a plane.'

'Where does he go?'

'I don't ask.'

'Any rumours?'

'No.'

'You sure you never saw any young guys around here?'

'I'm sure.'

'Suppose I gave you a hundred bucks?'

The guy hesitated a beat and looked a little wistful, as if a hundred bucks would make a welcome change in his life. But in the end he just shrugged again and said, 'I'd still be sure.'

Reacher drank a little more of his beer. It was warming up a little and tasted metallic and soapy. The bartender stayed close. Reacher glanced at the mirrors. Checked reflections of reflections. Nobody in the room was moving. He asked, 'What happens to dead people here?'

'What do you mean?'

'You got undertakers in town?'

The bartender shook his head. 'Forty miles west. There's a morgue and a funeral home and a burial ground. No consecrated land in Despair.'

'The smaller guy died,' Reacher said.

'What smaller guy?'

'The one I was asking you about.'

'I didn't see any small guys, alive or dead.'

Reacher went quiet again and the bartender said, 'So, you're just passing through?' A meaningless, for-the-sake-of-it conversational gambit, which confirmed what Reacher already knew. *Bring it on*, he thought. He glanced at the fire exit in back and checked the front door in the mirrors. He said, 'Yes, I'm just passing through.'

'Not much to see here.'

'Actually I think this is a pretty interesting place.'

'You do?'

'Who hires the cops here?'

'The mayor.'

'Who's the mayor?'

'Mr Thurman.'

'There's a big surprise.'

'It's his town.'

Reacher said, 'I'd like to meet him.'

The bartender said, 'He's a very private man.'

'I'm just saying. I'm not asking for an appointment.'

Six minutes, Reacher thought. *I've been working on this beer for six minutes. Maybe ten more to go*. He asked, 'Do you know the judge?'

'He doesn't come in here.'

'I didn't ask where he goes.'

'He's Mr Thurman's lawyer, up at the plant.'

'I thought it was an elected position.'

'It is. We all voted for him.'

'How many candidates were on the ballot?'

'He was unopposed.'

Reacher said, 'Does this judge have a name?'

The bartender said, 'His name is Judge Gardner.'

'Does Judge Gardner live here in town?'

'Sure. You work for Mr Thurman, you have to live in town.'

'You know Judge Gardner's address?'

'The big house on Nickel.'

'Nickel?'

'All the residential streets here are named for metals.'

Reacher nodded. Not so very different from the way streets on army bases were named for generals or Medal of Honor winners. He went quiet again and waited for the bartender to fill the silence, like he had to. Like he had been told to. The guy said, 'A hundred and some years ago there were only five miles of paved road in the United States.'

Reacher said nothing.

The guy said, 'Apart from city centres, of course, which were cobbled anyway, not really paved. Not with blacktop, like now. Then county roads got built, then state, then the Interstates. Towns got passed by. We were on the main road to Denver, once. Not so much any more. People use I-70 now.'

Reacher said, 'Hence the closed-down motel.'

'Exactly.'

'And the general feeling of isolation.'

'I guess.'

Reacher said, 'I know those two young guys were here. It's only a matter of time before I find out who they were and why they came.'

'I can't help you with that.'

'One of them died.'

'You told me that already. And I still don't know anything about it.'

Eleven minutes, Reacher thought. *Five to go*. He asked, 'Is this the only bar in town?'

The guy said, 'One is all we need.'

'Movies?'

'No.'

'So what do people do for entertainment?'

'They watch satellite television.'

'I heard there's a first-aid post at the plant.'

'That's right.'

'With a vehicle.'

'An old ambulance. It's a big plant. It covers a big area.'

'Are there a lot of accidents?'

'It's an industrial operation. Shit happens.'

'Does the plant pay disability?'

'Mr Thurman looks after people if they get hurt on the job.'

Reacher nodded and went quiet again. Sipped his beer. Watched the other customers sipping theirs, directly and in the mirrors. *Three minutes*, he thought.

Unless they're early.

Which they were.

Reacher looked to his right and saw two deputies step in through the fire door. He glanced in a mirror and saw the other two walk in the front.

185

TWENTY-NINE

The telephone. A useful invention, and instructive in the way it was used. Or not used. Four deputies heading east to make a surprise arrest would not indicate their prior intention with a courtesy telephone call. Not in the real world. They would swoop down unannounced. They would aim to grab up their prey unawares. Therefore their courtesy call was a decoy. It was a move in a game. A move designed to flush Reacher westward into safer territory. It was an invitation.

Which Reacher had interpreted correctly.

And accepted.

And the bartender had not called the station house. Had not gotten voice mail. Had not made a local call at all. He had dialled too many digits. He had called a deputy's cell, and spoken just long enough to let the deputy know who he was, and therefore where Reacher was. Whereupon he had changed his attitude and turned talkative and friendly, to keep Reacher sitting tight. Like he had been told to, beforehand, should the opportunity arise.

Which is why Reacher had not left the bar. If

the guy wanted to participate, he was welcome to. He could participate by cleaning up the mess.

And there was going to be a mess.

That was for damn sure.

The deputies who had come in the back walked through the short corridor past the restrooms and stopped where the main room widened out. Reacher kept his eyes on them. Didn't turn his head. A two-front attack was fairly pointless in a room full of mirrors. He could see the other guys quite clearly, smaller than life and reversed. They had stopped a yard inside the front door and were standing shoulder to shoulder, waiting.

The big guy who had gotten sick the night before was one of the pair that had come in the front. With him was the guy Reacher had smacked outside the family restaurant. Neither one of them looked in great shape. The two who had come in the back looked large and healthy enough, but manageable. Four against one, but no real cause for concern. Reacher had first fought four-on-one when he was five years old, against seven-year-olds, on his father's base in the Philippines. He had won then, easily, and he expected to win now.

But then the situation changed.

Two guys stood up from the body of the room. They put their glasses down and dabbed their lips with napkins and scraped their chairs back and stepped forward and separated. One went left, and one went right. One lined up with the guys in back, and one lined up with the guys in front. The newcomers were not the biggest people Reacher had ever seen, but they weren't the smallest, either. They could have been the deputies' brothers or cousins. They probably were. They were dressed the same and looked the same and were built the same.

So, thirteen minutes previously the bartender had not been glancing into the room in hopes of immediate short-term assistance. He had been catching the ringers' eyes and tipping them off: *Stand by, the others are on their way.* Reacher clamped his jaw and the beer in his stomach went sour. *Mistake.* A bad one. He had been smart, but not smart enough.

And now he was going to pay, big time.

Six against one.

Twelve hundred pounds against two-fifty.

No kind of excellent odds.

He realized he was holding his breath. He exhaled, long and slow. Because: *Dum spiro spero.* Where there's breath, there's hope. Not an aphorism Zeno of Cittium would have understood or approved of. He spoke Greek, not Latin, and preferred passive resignation to reckless optimism. But the saying worked well enough for Reacher, when all else failed. He took a last sip of Bud and set the bottle back on his napkin. Swivelled his stool and faced the room. Behind him he sensed the bartender moving away to a safe place by the register. In front of him he saw the other customers in the body of the room pressing backward towards the far wall, cradling their glasses and bottles, huddling together, hunkering down. Alongside him guys slipped off their stools and melted across the room into the safety of the crowd.

There was movement at both ends of the bar.

Both sets of three men took long paces forward.

Now they defined the ends of an empty rectangle of space. Nothing in it, except Reacher alone on his stool, and the bare wooden floor.

The six guys weren't armed. Reacher was pretty sure about that. The deputies had no official weapons. Vaughan had said that in Colorado police deputies were limited to civilian status. And the other two guys were just members of the public. Plenty of members of the public in Colorado had private weapons, of course, but generally people pulled weapons at the start of a fight, not later on. They wanted to display them. Show them off. Intimidate, from the get-go. Nobody in Reacher's experience had ever waited to pull a gun.

So, unarmed combat, six-on-one.

The big guy spoke, from six feet inside the front door. He said, 'You're in so much trouble you couldn't dig your way out with a steam shovel.'

Reacher said, 'You talking to me?'

'Damn straight I am.'

'Well, don't.'

'You showed up one too many times, pal.'

'Save your breath. Go outside and throw up. That's what you're good at.'

'We're not leaving. And neither are you.'

'Free country.'

'Not for you. Not any more.'

Reacher stayed on his stool, tensed up and ready, but not visibly. Outwardly he was still calm and relaxed. His brother Joe had been two years older, physically very similar, but temperamentally very different. Joe had eased into fights. He had met escalation with escalation, reluctantly, slowly, rationally, patiently, a little sadly. Therefore he had been a frustrating opponent. Therefore according to the peculiar little-boy dynamics of the time his enemies had turned on Reacher himself, the younger brother. The first time, confronted with four baiting seven-year-olds, the five-year-old Reacher had felt a jolt of real fear. The jolt of fear had sparked wildly and jumped tracks in his brain and emerged as intense aggression. He had exploded into action and the fight was over before his four assailants had really intended it to begin. When they got out of the pediatric ward they had stayed well away from him, and his brother, for ever. And in his earnest childhood manner Reacher had pondered the experience and felt he had learned a valuable lesson. Years later during advanced army training that lesson had been reinforced. At the grand strategic level it even had a title: *Overwhelming Force*. At the individual level in sweaty gyms the thugs doing the training had pointed out that gentlemen who behaved decently weren't around to train anyone. They were already dead. Therefore: *Hit early, hit hard*.

Overwhelming Force.

Hit early, hit hard.

Reacher called it: *Get your retaliation in first*.

He slipped forward off his stool, turned, bent, grasped the iron pillar, spun, and hurled the stool head-high as hard as he could at the three men at the back of the room. Before it hit he launched the other way and charged the new guy next to the guy with the damaged jaw. He led with his elbow and smashed it flat against the bridge of the guy's nose. The guy went down like a tree and before he hit the boards Reacher jerked sideways from the waist and put the same elbow into the big guy's ear. Then he bounced away from the impact and backed into the guy with the bad jaw and buried the elbow deep in his gut. The guy folded forward and Reacher put his hand flat on the back of the guy's head and powered it downward into his raised knee and then shoved the guy away and turned around fast.

The stool had hit one of the deputies and the other new guy neck-high. Wood and iron, thrown hard, spinning horizontally. Maybe they had raised their hands instinctively and broken their wrists, or maybe they hadn't been fast enough and the stool had connected. Reacher wasn't sure. But either way the two guys were sidelined for the moment. They were turned away, bent over, crouched, with the stool still rolling noisily at their feet.

The other deputy was untouched. He was launching forward with a wild grimace on his face. Reacher danced two steps and took a left hook on the shoulder and put a straight right into the centre of the grimace. The guy stumbled back and shook his head and Reacher's arms were clamped from behind in a bear hug. The big guy, presumably. Reacher forced him backward and dropped his chin to his chest and snapped a reverse head butt that made solid contact. Not as good as a forward-going blow, but useful. Then Reacher accelerated all the way backward and crushed the breath out of the guy against the wall. A mirror smashed and the arms loosened and Reacher pulled away and met the other deputy in the centre of the room and dodged an incoming right and snapped a right of his own to the guy's jaw. Not a powerful blow, but it rocked the guy enough to open him up for a colossal left to the throat that put him down in a heap.

Eight blows delivered, one taken, one guy down for maybe a seven count, four down for maybe an eight count, the big guy still basically functional.

Not efficient.

Time to get serious.

The bartender had said: *Mr Thurman looks after people if they get hurt on the job*. Reacher thought: *So let him. Because these guys are doing Thurman's bidding. Clearly nothing happens here except what Thurman wants*.

The deputy in the back of the room was rolling around and clutching his throat. Reacher stepped up and kicked him in the ribs hard enough to break a couple and then forced the guy's forearm to the floor with one foot and stamped on it with the other. Then he moved on to the two guys he had hit with the stool. The second deputy, and the new guy. One was crouched down, clutching his forearm, turned away. Reacher put the flat of his foot on the guy's backside and drove him head-first into the wall. The other guy had maybe taken the edge of the seat in the chest, like a dull blade. He was having trouble breathing. Reacher kicked his feet out from under him and then kicked him in the head. Then he turned in time to dodge a right hook from the big guy. He took it in the shoulder. Looked for a response. But his balance wasn't good. Floor space was limited by inert assailants. The big guy threw a straight left and Reacher swatted it away and bulldozed a path back to the centre of the room.

The big guy followed, fast. Threw a straight right. Reacher jerked his head to the side and took the blow on the collarbone. It was a weak punch. The guy was pale in the face. He threw a wild breathless haymaker and Reacher stepped back out of range and glanced around.

One stool damaged, one mirror broken, five guys down, twenty spectators still passive. *So far so good*. The big guy stepped back and straightened like they were in a timeout and called, 'Like you said, one of us would stay on his feet long enough to get to you.'

Reacher said, 'You're not getting to me. Not even a little bit.' Which puzzled him, deep down. He was close to winning a six-on-one bar brawl and he had nothing to show for it except two bruised shoulders and an ache in his knuckles. It had gone way better than he could have hoped.

Then it started to go way worse.

The big guy said, 'Think again.' He put his hands in his pants pockets and came out with two switchblades. Neat wooden handles, plated bindings, plated buttons. He stood in the dusty panting silence and popped the first blade with a precision click and then paused and popped the second.

THIRTY

The two small clicks the blades made were not attractive sounds. Reacher's stomach clenched. He hated knives. He would have preferred it if the guy had pulled a pair of six-shooters. Guns can miss. In fact they usually did, given stress and pressure and trembling and confusion. After-action reports proved it. The papers were always full of DOAs gunned down with seven bullets to the body, which sounded lethal until you read down into the third paragraph and learned that a hundred and fifty shots had been fired in the first place.

Knives didn't miss. If they touched you, they cut you. The only opponents Reacher truly feared were small whippy guys with fast hands and sharp blades. The big deputy was not fast or nimble, but with knives in his hands dodged blows would not mean dull impacts to the shoulders. They would mean open wounds, pouring blood, severed ligaments and arteries.

Not good.

Reacher clubbed a spectator out of his seat and grabbed the empty chair and held it out in front of him like a lion tamer. The best defence against knives was distance. The best countermove was entanglement. A swung net or coat or blanket was often effective. The blade would hang up in the fabric. But Reacher didn't have a net or a coat or a blanket. A horizontal forest of four chair legs was all he had. He jabbed forward like a fencer and then fell back and shoved another guy out of his seat. Picked up the second empty chair and threw it overhand at the big guy's head. The big guy turned away reflexively and brought his right hand up to shield his face and took the chair on the forearm. Reacher stepped back in and jabbed hard. Got one chair leg in the guy's solar plexus and another in his gut. The guy fell back and took a breath and then came on hard, arms swinging, the blades hissing through the air and winking in the lights.

Reacher danced backward and jabbed with his chair. Made solid contact with the guy's upper arm. The guy spun one way and then the other. Reacher moved left and jabbed again. Got a chair leg into the back of the guy's head. The guy staggered one short step and then came back hard, hands low and apart, the blades moving through tiny dangerous arcs.

Reacher backed off. Shoved a third spectator out of his seat and threw the empty chair high and hard. The big guy flinched away and jerked his arms up and the chair bounced off his elbows. Reacher was ready. He stepped in and jabbed hard and caught the guy low down in the side, below the ribs, above the waist, two hundred and fifty pounds of weight punched through the blunt end of a chair leg into nothing but soft tissue.

The big guy stopped fighting.

His body froze and went rigid and his face crumpled. He dropped the knives and clamped both hands low down on his stomach. For a long moment he stood like a statue and then he jerked forward from the waist and bent down and puked a long stream of blood and mucus on the floor. He staggered away in a crouch and fell to his knees. His shoulders sagged and his face went waxy and bloodless. His stomach heaved and he puked again. More blood, more mucus. He braced his spread fingertips either side of the spreading pool and tried to push himself upward. But he didn't make it. He got halfway there and collapsed sideways in a heap. His eyes rolled up in his head and he rolled on his back and he started breathing fast and shallow. One hand moved back to his stomach and the other beat on the floor. He threw up again, projectile, a fountain of blood vertically into the air. Then he rolled away and curled into a foetal ball.

Game over.

The bar went silent. No sound, except ragged breathing. The air was full of dust and the stink of blood and vomit. Reacher was shaky with excess adrenalin. He forced himself back under control and put his chair down quietly and bent and picked up the fallen knives. Pressed the blades back into the handles against the wood of the bar and slipped both knives into one pocket. Then he stepped around in the silence and checked his results. The first guy he had hit was unconscious on his back. The elbow to the bridge of the nose was always an effective blow. Too hard, and it can slide shards of bone into the frontal lobes. Badly aimed, it can put splinters of cheekbone into the eye sockets. But this one had been perfectly judged. The guy would be sick and groggy for a week, but he would recover.

The guy who had started the evening with a busted jaw had added a re-broken nose and a bad headache. The new guy at the back of the room had a broken arm from the stool and maybe a concussion from being driven head-first into the wall. The guy next to him was unconscious from the kick in the head. The deputy that the stool had missed had busted ribs and a broken wrist and a cracked larynx.

Major damage all around, but the whole enterprise had been voluntary from the start.

So, five for five, plus some kind of a medical explanation for the sixth. The big guy had stayed in the foetal position and looked very weak and pale. Like he was hollowed out with sickness. Reacher bent down and checked the pulse in his neck and found it weak and thready. He went through the guy's pockets and found a five-pointed star in the front of the shirt. It was an official badge. It was made of pewter and two lines were engraved in its centre: *Township of Despair, Police Deputy*. Reacher put it in his own shirt pocket. He found a bunch of keys and a meagre wad of paper money in a brass clip. He kept the keys and left the cash. Then he stood up again and looked around until he found the bartender. The guy was where he had started, leaning back with his fat ass against his register drawer.

'Call the plant,' Reacher said. 'Get the ambulance down here. Take care with the big guy. He doesn't look good.'

Then he stepped up to the bar and found his bottle. It was where he had left it, still upright on its napkin. He drained the last of his beer and set the bottle back down again and walked out the front door into the night.

THIRTY-ONE

It took ten minutes of aimless driving south of the main drag before he found Nickel Street. The road signs were small and faded and the headlights on Vaughan's old truck were weak and set low. He deciphered Iron and Chromium and Vanadium and Molybdenum and then lost metals altogether and ran through a sequence of numbered avenues before he hit Steel and Platinum and then Gold. Nickel was a dead end off Gold. It had sixteen houses, eight facing eight, fifteen of them small and one of them bigger.

Thurman's pet judge Gardner lived in the big house on Nickel, the bartender had said. Reacher paused at the kerb and checked the name on the big house's mailbox and then pulled the truck into the driveway and shut it down. Climbed out and walked to the porch. The place was a medium-sized farmhouse-style structure and looked pretty good relative to its neighbours, but there was no doubt that Gardner would have done better for himself if he had gotten out of town and made it to the Supreme Court in D.C. Or to whatever circuit included Colorado, or even to night traffic court in Denver. The porch sagged against rotted under-pinnings and the paint on the clapboards had aged to dust. Millwork had dried and split. There were twin newel posts at the top of the porch steps. Both had decorative ball shapes carved into their tops and both balls had split along the grain, like they had been attacked with cleavers.

Reacher found a bell push and tapped it twice with his knuckle. An old habit, about not leaving fingerprints if not strictly necessary. Then he waited. In Reacher's experience the average delay when knocking at a suburban door in the middle of the evening was about twenty seconds. Couples looked up from the television and looked at each other and asked *Who could that be? At this time of night?* Then they mimed their way through offer and counter-offer and finally decided which one of them should make the trip down the hall. Before nine o'clock it was usually the wife. After nine, it was usually the husband.

It was Mrs Gardner who opened up. The wife, after a twenty-three second delay. She looked similar to her husband, bulky and somewhere over sixty, with a full head of white hair. Only the amount of the hair and the style of her clothing distinguished her gender. She had the kind of large firm curls that women get from big heated rollers and she was wearing a shapeless grey shift that reached to her ankles. She stood there, patterned and indistinct behind an insect screen. She said, 'May I help you?'

Reacher said, 'I need to see the judge.'

'It's awful late,' Mrs Gardner said, which it wasn't. According to an old long-case clock in the

200

hallway behind her it was eight twenty-nine, and according to the clock in Reacher's head it was eight thirty-one, but what the woman meant was: *You're a big ugly customer.* Reacher smiled. *Look at yourself*, Vaughan had said. *What do you see?* Reacher knew he was no kind of an ideal night-time visitor. Nine times out of ten only Mormon missionaries were less welcome than him.

'It's urgent,' he said.

The woman stood still and said nothing. In Reacher's experience the husband would show up if the doorstep interview lasted any longer than thirty seconds. He would crane his neck out of the living room and call, *Who is it, dear?* And Reacher wanted the screen door open long before that happened. He wanted to be able to stop the front door from closing, if necessary.

'It's urgent,' he said again, and pulled the screen door. It screeched on worn hinges. The woman stepped back, but didn't try to slam the front door. Reacher stepped inside and let the screen slap shut behind him. The hallway smelled of still air and cooking. Reacher turned and closed the front door gently and clicked it against the latch. At that point the thirty seconds he had been count-ing in his head elapsed and the judge stepped out to the hallway.

The old guy was dressed in the same grey suit pants Reacher had seen before, but his suit coat was off and his tie was loose. He stood still for a moment, evidently searching his memory, be-cause after ten long seconds puzzlement left his face and was replaced by an altogether different emotion, and he said, 'You?'

Reacher nodded.

'Yes, me,' he said.

'What do you want? What do you mean by coming here?'

'I came here to talk to you.'

'I meant, what are you doing in Despair at all? You were excluded.'

'Didn't take,' Reacher said. 'So sue me.'

'I'm going to call the police.'

'Please do. But they won't answer, as I'm sure you know. Neither will the deputies.'

'Where are the deputies?'

'On their way up to the first-aid post.'

'What happened to them?'

'I did.'

The judge said nothing.

Reacher said, 'And Mr Thurman is up in his little airplane right now. Out of touch for another five and a half hours. So you're on your own. It's initiative time for Judge Gardner.'

'What do you want?'

'I want you to invite me into your living room. I want you to ask me to sit down and whether I take cream and sugar in my coffee, which I don't, by the way. Because so far I'm here with your implied permission, and therefore I'm not trespassing. I'd like to keep it that way.'

'You're not only trespassing, you're in violation of a town ordinance.'

'That's what I'd like to talk about. I'd like you to reconsider. Like an appeals process.'

'Are you nuts?'

'A little unconventional, maybe. But I'm not

armed and I'm not making threats. I just want to talk.'

'Get lost.'

'On the other hand I am a large stranger with nothing to lose. In a town where there is no functioning law enforcement at the moment.'

'I have a gun.'

'I'm sure you do. In fact I'm sure you have several. But you won't use any of them.'

'You think not?'

'You're a man of the law. You know what kind of hassle comes afterwards. I don't think you want to face that kind of thing.'

'You're taking a risk.'

'Getting out of bed in the morning is a risk.'

The judge said nothing to that. Didn't yield, didn't accede. Impasse. Reacher turned to the wife and took all the amiability out of his face and replaced it with the kind of thousand-yard stare he had used years ago on recalcitrant witnesses.

He asked, 'What do you think, Mrs Gardner?'

She started to speak a couple of times but couldn't get any words past a dry throat. Finally she said, 'I think we should all sit down and talk.' But the speculative way she said it showed she wasn't all the way scared. She was a tough old bird. Probably had to be, to have survived sixty-some years in Despair, and marriage to the boss man's flunky.

Her husband huffed once and turned around and led the way into the living room. It was a decent square space, conventionally furnished. A sofa, an armchair, another armchair with a lever on the side that meant it was a recliner. There was a coffee table and a large television set wired to a satellite box. The furniture was covered in a floral pattern that was duplicated in the drapes. The drapes were closed and had a ruffled pelmet made from the same fabric. Reacher suspected that Mrs Gardner had done the needlework herself.

The judge said, 'Take a seat, I guess.'

Mrs Gardner said, 'I'm not going to make coffee. I think under the circumstances that would be a step too far.'

'Your choice,' Reacher said. 'But I have to tell you I'd truly appreciate some.' He paused a moment and then sat down in the fixed armchair. Gardner sat in the recliner. His wife stood for a moment longer and then sighed once and headed out of the room. A minute later Reacher heard water running and the quiet metallic sound of an aluminum percolator basket being rinsed.

Gardner said, 'There is no appeals process.'

'There has to be,' Reacher said. 'It's a constitutional issue. The Fifth and the Fourteenth Amendments guarantee due process. At the very least there must be the possibility of judicial review.'

'Are you serious?'

'Completely.'

'You want to go to federal court over a local vagrancy ordinance?'

'I'd prefer you to concede that a mistake has been made, and then go ahead and tear up whatever paperwork was generated.'

'There was no mistake. You are a vagrant, as defined.'

'I'd like you to reconsider that.'

'Why?'

'Why not?'

'I'd like to understand why it's so important to you to have free rein in our town.'

'And I'd like to understand why it's so important to you to keep me out.'

'Where's your loss? It's not much of a place.'

'It's a matter of principle.'

Gardner said nothing. A moment later his wife came in, with a single mug of coffee in her hand. She placed it carefully on the table in front of Reacher's chair and then backed away and sat down on the sofa. Reacher picked up the mug and took a sip. The coffee was hot, strong, and smooth. The mug was cylindrical, narrow in relation to its height, made of delicate bone china, and it had a thin lip.

'Excellent,' Reacher said. 'Thank you very much. I'm really very grateful.'

Mrs Gardner paused a beat and said, 'You're really very welcome.'

Reacher said, 'You did a great job with the drapes, too.'

Mrs Gardner didn't reply to that. The judge said, 'There's nothing I can do. There's no provision for an appeal. Sue the town, if you must.'

Reacher said, 'You told me you'd welcome me with open arms if I got a job.'

The judge nodded. 'Because that would remove the presumption of vagrancy.'

'There you go.'

'Have you gotten a job?'

'I have prospects. That's the other thing we need to talk about. It's not healthy that this town has no functioning law enforcement. So I want you to swear me in as a deputy.'

There was silence for a moment. Reacher took the pewter star from his shirt pocket. He said, 'I already have the badge. And I have a lot of relevant experience.'

'You're crazy.'

'Just trying to fill a hole.'

'You're completely insane.'

'I'm offering my services.'

'Finish your coffee and get out of my home.'

'The coffee is hot and it's good. I can't just gulp it down.'

'Then leave it. Get the hell out, now.'

'So you won't swear me in?'

The judge stood up and planted his feet wide and made himself as tall as he could get, which was about five feet and nine inches. His eyes narrowed as his brain ran calculations about present dangers versus future contingencies. He was silent with preoccupation for a long moment and then he said, 'I'd rather deputize the entire damn population. Every last man, woman, and child in Despair. In fact, I think I will. Twenty-six hundred people. You think you can get past them all? Because I don't. We aim to keep you out, mister, and we're going to. You better believe it. You can take that to the bank.'

THIRTY-TWO

Reacher thumped back over the expansion joint at nine thirty in the evening and was outside the diner before nine thirty-five. He figured Vaughan might swing by there a couple of times during the night. He figured that if he left her truck on the kerb she would see it and be reassured that he was OK. Or at least that her truck was OK.

He went inside to leave her keys at the register and saw Lucy Anderson sitting alone in a booth. Short shorts, blue sweatshirt, tiny socks, big sneakers. A lot of bare leg. She was gazing into space and smiling. The first time he had seen her he had characterized her as not quite a hundred per cent pretty. Now she looked pretty damn good. She looked radiant, and taller, and straighter. She looked like a completely different person.

She had changed.

Before, she had been hobbled by worry.

Now she was happy.

He paused at the register and she noticed him and looked over and smiled. It was a curious smile. There was a lot of straightforward contentment in it, but a little triumph, too. A little superiority.

Like she had won a significant victory, at his expense.

He lodged Vaughan's keys with the cashier and the woman asked, 'Are you eating with us tonight?' He thought about it. His stomach had settled. The adrenalin had drained away. He realized he was hungry. No sustenance since breakfast, except for coffee and some empty calories from the bottle of Bud in the bar. And he had burned plenty of calories in the bar. That was for sure. He was facing an energy deficit. So he said, 'Yes, I guess I'm ready for dinner.'

He walked over and slid into Lucy Anderson's booth. She looked across the table at him and smiled the same smile all over again. Contentment, triumph, superiority, victory. Up close the smile looked a lot bigger and it had a bigger effect. It was a real megawatt grin. She had great teeth. Her eyes were bright and clear and blue. He said, 'This afternoon you looked like Lucy. Now you look like Lucky.'

She said, 'Now I feel like Lucky.'

'What changed?'

'What do you think?'

'You heard from your husband.'

She smiled again, a hundred per cent happiness.

'I sure did,' she said.

'He left Despair.'

'He sure did. Now you'll never get him.'

'I never wanted him. I never heard of him before I met you.'

'Really,' she said, in the exaggerated and sarcastic way he had heard young people use the

208

word before. As far as he understood it, the effect was intended to convey: *How big of an idiot do you think I am?*

He said, 'You're confusing me with someone else.'

'Really.'

Look at yourself. What do you see?

'I'm not a cop,' Reacher said. 'I was one once, and maybe I still look like one to you, but I'm not one any more.'

She didn't answer. But he knew she wasn't convinced. He said, 'Your husband must have left late this afternoon. He was there at three and gone before seven.'

'You went back?'

'I've been there twice today.'

'Which proves you were looking for him.'

'I guess I was. But only on your behalf.'

'Really.'

'What did he do?'

'You already know.'

'If I already know, it can't hurt to tell me again, can it?'

'I'm not stupid. My position is I don't know about anything he's done. Otherwise you'll call me an accessory. We have lawyers, you know.'

'We?'

'People in our position. Which you know all about.'

'I'm not a cop, Lucky. I'm just a passing stranger. I don't know all about anything.'

She smiled again. Happiness, triumph, victory.

Reacher asked, 'Where has he gone?'

'Like I'd tell you *that*.'

'When are you joining him, wherever he is?'

'In a couple of days.'

'I could follow you.'

She smiled again, impregnable. 'Wouldn't do you any good.'

The waitress came by and Reacher asked her for coffee and steak. When she had gone away again he looked across at Lucy Anderson and said, 'There are others in the position you were in yesterday. There's a girl in town right now, just waiting.'

'I hope there are plenty of us.'

'I think maybe she's waiting in vain. I know that a boy died out there a day or two ago.'

Lucy Anderson shook her head.

'Not possible,' she said. 'I know that none of us died. I would have heard.'

'Us?'

'People in our position.'

'Somebody died.'

'People die all the time.'

'Young people? For no apparent reason?'

She didn't answer that, and he knew she never would. The waitress brought his coffee. He took a sip. It was OK, but not as good as Mrs Gardner's, in terms of either brew or receptacle. He put the mug down and looked at the girl again and said, 'Whatever, Lucy. I wish you nothing but good luck, whatever the hell you're doing and wherever the hell you're going.'

'That's it? No more questions?'

'I'm just here to eat.'

*   *   *

He ate alone, because Lucy Anderson left before his steak arrived. She sat quiet for a spell and then smiled again and slid out of the booth and walked away. More accurately, she skipped away. Light on her feet, happy, full of energy. She pushed out through the door and instead of huddling into her shirt against the chill she squared her shoulders and turned her face upward and breathed the night air like she was in an enchanted forest. Reacher watched her until she was lost to sight and then gazed into space until his food arrived.

He was through eating by ten thirty and headed back to the motel. He dropped by the office, to pay for another night's stay. He always rented rooms one night at a time, even when he knew he was going to hang out in a place longer. It was a reassuring habit. A comforting ritual, intended to confirm his absolute freedom to move on. The day clerk was still on duty. The stout woman. The nosy woman. He assembled a collection of small bills and waited for his change and said, 'Go over what you were telling me about the metal plant.'

'What was I telling you?'

'Violations. Real crimes. You were interested in why the plane flies every night.'

The woman said, 'So you *are* a cop.'

'I used to be. Maybe I still have the old habits.'

The woman shrugged and looked a little sheepish. Maybe even blushed a little.

'It's just silly amateur stuff,' she said. 'That's what you'll think.'

'Amateur?'

'I'm a day trader. I do research on my computer. I was thinking about that operation.'

'What about it?'

'It seems to make way too much money. But what do I know? I'm not an expert. I'm not a broker or a forensic accountant or anything.'

'Talk me through it.'

'Business sectors go up and down. There are cycles, to do with commodity prices and supply and demand and market conditions. Right now metal recycling as a whole is in a down cycle. But that place is raking it in.'

'How do you know?'

'Employment seems to be way up.'

'That's pretty vague.'

'It's a private corporation, but it still has to file, federal and state. I looked at the figures, to pass the time.'

And because you're a nosy neighbour, Reacher thought.

'And?' he asked.

'It's reporting great profits. If it was a public company, I'd be buying stock, big time. If I had any money, that is. If I wasn't a motel clerk.'

'OK.'

'And it's not a public company. It's private. So it's probably making more than it's reporting.'

'So you think they're cutting corners out there? With environmental violations?'

'I wouldn't be surprised.'

'Would that make much difference? I thought rules were pretty slack now anyway.'

'Maybe.'

'What about the plane?'

212

The woman glanced away. 'Just silly thoughts.'

'Try me.'

'Well, I was just thinking, if the fundamentals don't support the profits, and it's not about violations, then maybe there's something else going on.'

'Like what?'

'Maybe that plane is bringing stuff in every night. To sell. Like smuggling.'

'What kind of stuff?'

'Stuff that isn't metal.'

'From where?'

'I'm not sure.'

Reacher said nothing.

The woman said, 'See? What do I know? I have too much time on my hands, that's all. Way too much. And broadband. That can really do a person's head in.'

She turned away and busied herself with an entry in a book and Reacher put his change in his pocket. Before he left he glanced at the row of hooks behind the clerk's shoulder and saw that four keys were missing. Therefore four rooms were occupied. His own, Lucy Anderson's, one for the woman with the large underwear, and one for the new girl in town, he guessed. The dark girl, who he hadn't met yet, but who he might meet soon. He suspected that she was going to be in town longer than Lucy Anderson, and he suspected that at the end of her stay she wasn't going to be skipping away with a smile on her face.

He went back to his room and showered, but he was too restless to sleep. So as soon as the stink of the bar fight was off him he dressed again and went out and walked. On a whim he stopped at a phone booth under a street light and pulled the directory and looked up David Robert Vaughan. He was right there in the book. Vaughan, D. R., with an address on Fifth Street, Hope, Colorado.

Two blocks south.

He had seen Fourth Street. Perhaps he should take a look at Fifth Street, too. Just for the sake of idle curiosity.

THIRTY-THREE

Fifth Street ran east to west the whole length of town. It was more or less a replica of Fourth Street, except that it was residential on both sides. Trees, yards, picket fences, mailboxes, small neat houses resting quietly in the moonlight. A nice place to live, probably. Vaughan's house was close to the eastern limit. Nearer Kansas than Despair. It had a large-size plain aluminum mailbox out front, mounted on a store-bought wooden post. The post had been treated against decay. The box had *Vaughan* written on both sides with stick-on italic letters. They had been carefully applied and were perfectly aligned. Rare, in Reacher's experience. Most people seemed to have trouble with stick-on letters. He imagined that the glue was too aggressive to allow the correction of mistakes. To get seven letters each side level and true spoke of meticulous planning. Maybe a straight edge had been taped in position first, and then removed.

The house and the yard had been maintained to a high standard, too. Reacher was no expert, but he could tell the difference between care and neglect. The yard had no lawn. It was covered with golden gravel, with shrubs and bushes pushing up through the stones. The driveway was paved with small riven slabs that seemed to be the same colour as the gravel. The same slabs made a narrower winding walkway to the door. More slabs were set here and there in the gravel, like stepping stones. The bushes and the shrubs were neatly pruned. Some of them had small flowers on their branches, all closed up for the night against the chill.

The house itself was a low one-storey ranch maybe fifty years old. At the right-hand end was a single attached garage and at the left was a T-shaped bump-out that maybe housed the bedrooms, one front, one back. Reacher guessed the kitchen would be next to the garage and the living room would be between the kitchen and the bedrooms. There was a chimney. The siding and the roof tiles were not new, but they had been replaced within living memory and had settled and weathered into pleasant maturity.

A nice house.

An empty house.

It was dark and silent. Some drapes were halfway open, and some were all the way open. No light inside, except a tiny green glow in one window. Probably the kitchen, probably a microwave clock. Apart from that, no sign of life. Nothing. No sound, no subliminal hum, no vibe. Once upon a time Reacher had made his living storming darkened buildings, and more than once it had been a matter of life and death to decide whether they were occupied or not. He had developed a sense, and his sense right then was that Vaughan's house was empty.

216

So where was David Robert?

At work, possibly. Maybe they both worked nights. Some couples chose to coordinate their schedules that way. Maybe David Robert was a nurse or a doctor or worked night construction on the Interstates. Maybe he was a journalist or a print worker, involved with newspapers. Maybe he was in the food trade, getting stuff ready for morning markets. Maybe he was a radio DJ, broadcasting through the night on a powerful AM station. Or maybe he was a long-haul trucker or an actor or a musician and was on the road for lengthy spells. Maybe for months at a time. Maybe he was a sailor or an airline pilot.

Maybe he was a state policeman.

Vaughan had asked: *Don't I look married?*

No, Reacher thought. *You really don't. Not like some people do.*

He found a leafy cross street and walked back north to Second Street. He glanced west and saw Vaughan's truck still parked where he had left it. The diner's lights were spilling out all over it. He walked another block and came out on First Street. There was no cloud in the sky. Plenty of moon. To his right there was silvery flatness all the way to Kansas. To his left the Rockies were faintly visible, dim and blue and bulky, with their north-facing snow channels lit up like ghostly blades, impossibly high. The town was still and silent and lonely. Not quite eleven thirty in the evening, and no one was out and about. No traffic. No activity at all.

Reacher was no kind of an insomniac, but he

didn't feel like sleep. Too early. Too many questions. He walked a block on First Street and then headed south again, towards the diner. He was no kind of a social animal either, but right then he wanted to see people, and he figured the diner was the only place he was going to find any.

He found four. The college girl waitress, an old guy in a seed cap eating alone at the counter, a middle-aged guy alone in a booth with a spread of tractor catalogues in front of him, and a frightened Hispanic girl alone in a booth with nothing.

Dark, not blonde, Vaughan had said. *Sitting around and staring west like she's waiting for word from Despair.*

She was tiny. She was about eighteen or nineteen years old. She had long centre-parted jet black hair that framed a face that had a high forehead and enormous eyes. The eyes were brown and looked like twin pools of terror and tragedy. Under them were a small nose and a small mouth. Reacher guessed she had a pretty smile but didn't use it often and certainly hadn't used it for weeks. Her skin was mid-brown and her pose was absolutely still. Her hands were out of sight under the table but Reacher was sure they were clasped together in her lap. She was wearing a blue San Diego Padres warm-up jacket with a blue scoopneck T-shirt under it. There was nothing on the table in front of her. No plate, no cup. But she hadn't just arrived. The way she was settled meant she must have been sitting there for ten or fifteen minutes at least. Nobody could have gotten so still any faster.

Reacher stepped to the far side of the register and the college girl waitress joined him there. Reacher bent his head, at an angle, universal body language for: *I want to talk to you quietly*. The waitress moved a little closer and bent her own head at a parallel angle, like a co-conspirator.

'That girl,' Reacher said. 'Didn't she order?'

The waitress whispered, 'She has no money.'

'Ask her what she wants. I'll pay for it.'

He moved away to a different booth, where he could watch the girl without being obvious about it. He saw the waitress approach her, saw incomprehension in her face, then doubt, then refusal. The waitress stepped over to Reacher's booth and whispered, 'She says she can't possibly accept.'

Reacher said, 'Go back and tell her there are no strings attached. Tell her I'm not hitting on her. Tell her I don't even want to talk to her. Tell her I've been broke and hungry too.'

The waitress went back. This time the girl relented. She pointed to a couple of items on the menu. Reacher was sure they were the cheapest choices. The waitress went away to place the order and the girl turned a little in her seat and inclined her head in a courteous little nod, full of dignity, and the corners of her mouth softened like the beginnings of a smile. Then she turned back and went still again.

The waitress came straight back to Reacher and he asked for coffee. The waitress whispered, 'Her check is going to be nine-fifty. Yours will be a dollar and a half.' Reacher peeled a ten and three ones off the roll in his pocket and slid them

219

across the table. The waitress picked them up and thanked him for the tip and asked, 'So when were you broke and hungry?'

'Never,' Reacher said. 'My whole life I got three squares a day from the army and since then I've always had money in my pocket.'

'So you made that up just to make her feel better?'

'Sometimes people need convincing.'

'You're a nice guy,' the waitress said.

'Not everyone agrees with that.'

'But some do.'

'Do they?'

'I hear things.'

'What things?'

But the girl just smiled at him and walked away.

From a safe distance Reacher watched the Hispanic girl eat a tuna melt sandwich and drink a chocolate milk shake. Good choices, nutritionally. Excellent value for his money. Protein, fats, carbs, some sugar. If she ate like that every day she would weigh two hundred pounds before she was thirty, but in dire need on the road it was wise to load up. After she was finished she dabbed her lips with her napkin and pushed her plate and her glass away and then sat there, just as quiet and still as before. The clock in Reacher's head hit midnight and the clock on the diner's wall followed it a minute later. The old guy in the seed cap crept out with a creaking arthritic gait and the tractor salesman gathered his paperwork together and called for another cup of coffee.

The Hispanic girl stayed put. Reacher had seen plenty of people doing what she was doing, in cafés and diners near bus depots and railroad stations. She was staying warm, saving energy, passing time. She was enduring. He watched her profile and figured she was a lot closer to Zeno's ideal than he was. *The unquestioning acceptance of destinies*. She looked infinitely composed and patient.

The tractor salesman drained his final cup and gathered his stuff and left. The waitress backed away to a corner and picked up a paperback book. Reacher curled his fist around his mug to keep it warm.

The Hispanic girl stayed put.

Then she moved. She shifted sideways on her vinyl bench and stood up all in one smooth, delicate motion. She was extremely petite. Not more than five-nothing, not more than ninety-some pounds. Below the T-shirt she was wearing jeans and cheap shoes. She stood still and faced the door and then she turned towards Reacher's booth. There was nothing in her face except fear and shyness and loneliness. She came to some kind of a decision and stepped forward and stood off about a yard and said, 'You can talk to me if you really want to.'

Reacher shook his head. 'I meant what I said.'

'Thank you for my dinner.' Her voice matched her physique. It was small and delicate. It was lightly accented, but English was probably her primary language. She was from Southern California for sure. The Padres were probably her home team.

Reacher asked, 'You OK for breakfast tomorrow?'

She was still for a moment while she fought her pride and then she shook her head.

Reacher asked, 'Lunch? Dinner tomorrow?'

She shook her head.

'You OK at the motel?'

'That's why. I paid for three nights. It took all my money.'

'You have to eat.'

The girl said nothing. Reacher thought, *Ten bucks a meal is thirty bucks a day, three days makes ninety, plus ten for contingencies or phone calls makes a hundred*. He peeled five ATM-fresh twenties off his roll and fanned them on the table. The girl said, 'I can't take your money. I couldn't pay it back.'

'Pay it forward instead.'

The girl said nothing.

'You know what pay it forward means?'

'I'm not sure.'

'It means years from now you'll be in a diner somewhere and you'll see someone who needs a break. So you'll help them out.'

The girl nodded.

'I could do that,' she said.

'So take the money.'

She stepped closer and picked up the bills.

'Thank you,' she said.

'Don't thank me. Thank whoever helped me way back. And whoever helped him before that. And so on.'

'Have you ever been to Despair?'

'Four times in the last two days.'

'Did you see anyone there?'

'I saw lots of people. It's a decent-sized town.'

She moved closer still and put her slim hips against the end of his table. She hoisted a cheap vinyl purse and propped it on the laminate against her belly and unsnapped the clasp. She dipped her head and her hair fell forward. Her hands were small and brown and had no rings on the fingers or polish on the nails. She rooted around in her bag for a moment and came out with an envelope. It was stiff and nearly square. From a greetings card, probably. She opened the flap and pulled out a photograph. She held it neatly between her thumb and her forefinger and put her little fist on the table and adjusted its position until Reacher could see the picture at a comfortable angle.

'Did you see this man?' she asked.

It was another standard one-hour six-by-four colour print. Glossy paper, no border. Shot on Fuji film, Reacher guessed. Back when it had mattered for forensic purposes he had gotten pretty good at recognizing film stock by its colour biases. This print had strong greens, which was a Fuji characteristic. Kodak products favoured the reds and the warmer tones. The camera had been a decent unit with a proper glass lens. There was plenty of detail. Focus was not quite perfect. The choice of aperture was not inspired. The depth of field was neither shallow nor deep. An old SLR, Reacher thought, therefore bought secondhand or borrowed from an older person. There was no retail market for decent film cameras any more. Everyone had moved into digital technology. The print in the girl's hand was clearly recent, but it looked like a much older product. It was a pleasant but unexceptional picture from an old SLR loaded with Fujicolor and wielded by an amateur.

He took the print from the girl and held it between his own thumb and forefinger. The bright greens in the photograph were in a background expanse of grass and a foreground expanse of T-shirt. The grass looked watered and forced and manicured and was probably in a city park somewhere. The T-shirt was a cheap cotton product being worn by a thin guy of about nineteen or twenty. The camera was looking up at him, as if the photograph was being taken by a much shorter person. The guy was posing quite formally and awkwardly. There was no spontaneity in his stance. Maybe repeated fumbles with the camera's controls had required him to hold his position a little too long. His smile was genuine but a little frozen. He had white teeth in a brown face. He looked young, and friendly, and amiable, and fun to be around, and completely harmless.

Not thin, exactly.

He looked lean and wiry.

Not short, not tall. About average, in terms of height.

He looked to be about five feet eight.

He looked to weigh about a hundred and forty pounds.

He was Hispanic, but as much Mayan or Aztec as Spanish. There was plenty of pure Indian blood in him. That was for sure. He had shiny black hair, not brushed, a little tousled, neither long nor short. Maybe an inch and a half or two inches, with a clear tendency to wave.

He had prominent cheekbones.

He was casually dressed, and casually turned out.

He hadn't shaved.

His chin and his upper lip were rough with black stubble.

His cheeks and his throat, not so much.

Young.

Not much more than a boy.

The girl asked, 'Did you see him?'

Reacher asked, 'What's your name?'

'*My* name?'

'Yes.'

'Maria.'

'What's his name?'

'Raphael Ramirez.'

'Is he your boyfriend?'

'Yes.'

'How old is he?'

'Twenty.'

'Did you take this picture?'

'Yes.'

'In a park in San Diego?'

'Yes.'

'With your dad's camera?'

'My uncle's,' the girl said. 'How did you know?'

Reacher didn't answer. He looked again at Raphael Ramirez in the photograph. Maria's boyfriend. Twenty years old. Five-eight, one-forty. The build. The hair, the cheekbones, the stubble.

The girl asked, 'Did you see him?'

Reacher shook his head.

'No,' he said. 'I didn't see him.'

225

THIRTY-FOUR

The girl left the diner. Reacher watched her go. He thought that an offer to walk her back to the motel might be misinterpreted, as if he was after something more concrete for his hundred bucks than a feel-good glow. And she was in no kind of danger, anyway. Hope seemed to be a safe enough place. Unlikely to be packs of malefactors roaming the streets, mainly because nobody was roaming the streets. It was the middle of the night in a quiet, decent place in the middle of nowhere. So Reacher let her walk away and sat alone in his booth and roused the college girl from her book and had her bring him more coffee.

'You'll never sleep,' she said.

'How often does Officer Vaughan swing by during the night?' he asked.

The girl smiled the same smile she had used before, right after she said *I hear things*.

'At least once,' she said, and smiled again.

He said, 'She's married.'

She said, 'I know.' She took the flask away and headed back to her book and left him with a steaming mug. He dipped his head and inhaled the smell. When he looked up again he saw Vaughan's cruiser glide by outside. She slowed, as if she was noting that her truck was back. But she didn't stop. She kept on going. She slid right by the diner's window and drove on down Second Street.

Reacher left the diner at one o'clock in the morning and walked back to the motel. The moon was still out. The town was still quiet. The motel office had a low light burning. The rooms were all dark. He sat down in the plastic lawn chair outside his door and stretched his legs straight out and put his hands behind his head and listened to the silence, eyes wide open, staring into the moonlight.

It didn't work. He didn't relax.

You'll never sleep, the waitress had said.

But not because of the coffee, he thought.

He got up again and walked away. Straight back to the diner. There were no customers in there. The waitress was reading her book. Reacher pulled the door and stepped straight to the register and took Vaughan's truck keys off the counter. The waitress looked up but didn't speak. Reacher stepped back to the door and caught it before it closed. Headed out across the sidewalk to the truck. Unlocked it, got in, started it up. Eased off the kerb, turned left, turned left again, and he was on First Street, heading west. Five minutes later he thumped over the line and was back in Despair.

*   *   *

The first twelve miles of empty road were pre-
dictably quiet. The town was quiet, too. Reacher
slowed at the gas station and coasted down
to twenty miles an hour and took a good look
around. Every building he saw was closed up tight
and completely dark. Main Street was deserted
and silent. He turned left and headed for the
downtown maze. He made random turns and
quartered a dozen blocks and saw not a single
lit window or open door. No cars on the streets,
nobody on the sidewalks. The police station was
dark. The rooming house was dark. The bar was
closed up and shuttered. The hotel was just a blank
façade, with a closed street door and a dozen dark
windows. The church was empty and silent. The
green grounding strap from the lightning rod was
turned grey by the moonlight.

He found a cross street and headed south to
the residential area. It was dark and silent from
end to end. No lights at Judge Gardner's house.
No lights anywhere. No sign of life. Cars were
parked, low and inert and dewed by night-time
cold. He drove on until his street petered out
into half-colonized scrubland. He pulled a wide
circle on the packed sand and stopped and idled
with the whole town laid out north of him. It was
lit up silver by the moon. It was just crouching
there, silent and deserted and insignificant in the
vastness.

He threaded his way back to Main Street.
Turned left and headed onward, west, towards the
metal plant.

*   *   *

The plant was shut down and dark. Still, and silent. The wall around it glowed ghostly white in the moonlight. The personnel gate was closed. The acres of parking were deserted. Reacher followed the wall and steered the truck left and right until its weak low beams picked up the Tahoes' tracks. He followed their giant figure-eight, all the way around the plant and the residential compound. Both were dark and silent. No lights in the house. Nothing in the grounds. The plantings were black and massive. The windsocks hung limp in the air. The plant's vehicle gate was shut. Reacher drove slowly past it and then bumped up across the truck road and drove another quarter-turn through the dirt and stopped where the figure-eight's two loops met, in the throat between the plant's metal wall and the residential compound's fieldstone wall. He shut off his lights and shut down the engine and rolled down the windows and waited.

He heard the plane at five past two in the morning. A single engine, far in the distance, feathering and blipping. He craned his neck and saw a light in the sky, way to the south. A landing light. It looked motionless, like it would be suspended up there for ever. Then it grew imperceptibly bigger and started hopping slightly, side to side, up and down, but mostly down. A small plane, on approach, buffeted by night-time thermals and rocked by a firm hand on nervous controls. Its sound grew closer, but quieter, as the pilot shed power and looked for a glide path.

Lights came on beyond the fieldstone wall. A

229

dull reflected glow. Runway markers, Reacher guessed, one at each end of the strip. He saw the plane move in the air, jumping left, correcting right, lining up with the lights. It was coming in from Reacher's left. When it was three hundred yards out he saw that it was a smallish low-wing monoplane. It was white. When it was two hundred yards out he saw that it had a fixed undercarriage, with fairings over all three wheels, called *pants* by aircraft people. When it was a hundred yards out he identified it as a Piper, probably some kind of a Cherokee variant, a four-seater, durable, reliable, common, and popular. Beyond that, he had no information. He knew a little about small planes, but not a lot.

It came in low left-to-right across his windshield in a high-speed rush of light and air and sound. It cleared the fieldstone wall by six feet and dropped out of sight. The engine blipped and feathered and then a minute later changed its note to a loud angry buzzing. Reacher imagined the plane taxiing like a fat self-important insect, white in the moonlight, bumping sharply over rough ground, turning abruptly on its short wheelbase, heading for its barn. Then he heard it shut down and stunned silence flooded in his windows, even more intense than before.

The runway lights went off.

He saw and heard nothing more.

He waited ten minutes for safety's sake and then started the truck and backed up and turned and drove away on the blind side, with the bulk of the plant between him and the house. He bumped through the acres of empty parking and found the road. He turned left and skirted the short end of the plant and joined the truck route. He put his headlights on and got comfortable in his seat and settled to a fast cruise on the firm wide surface, heading out of town westward, towards the MPs and whatever lay forty miles beyond them.

THIRTY-FIVE

The MPs were all asleep, except for two on sentry duty inside the guard shack. Reacher saw them as he drove past, bulky figures in the gloom, dressed in desert camos and vests, MP brassards, no helmets. They had an orange night light burning near the floor, to preserve their night vision. They were standing back to back, one watching the eastern approach, one the western. Reacher slowed and waved, and then hit the gas again and kept on going.

Thirty miles later the solid truck road swung sharply to the right and speared north through the darkness towards the distant Interstate. But the old route it must have been built over meandered on straight ahead, unsignposted and apparently aimless. Reacher followed it. He bumped down off the flat coarse blacktop on to a surface as bad as Despair's own road. Lumpy, uneven, cheaply top-dressed with gravel on tar. He followed it between two ruined farms and entered an empty spectral world with nothing on his left and nothing on his right and nothing ahead of him except the wandering grey ribbon of road and the silver moonlit mountains remote in the distance. Nothing happened for four more miles. He seemed to make no progress at all through the landscape. Then he passed a lone roadside sign that said: *Halfway County Route 37.* A mile later he saw a glow in the air. He came up a long rise and the road peaked and fell away into the middle distance and suddenly laid out right in front of him was a neat chequerboard of lit streets and pale buildings. Another mile later he passed a sign that said: *Halfway Township.* He slowed and checked his mirrors and pulled to the shoulder and stopped.

The town in front of him was aptly named. Another trick of topography put the moonlit Rockies closer again. Not very close, but definitely much closer than before. The hardy souls who had struggled onward from Despair had been rewarded for forty miles of actual travel with an apparent hundred miles of linear progress. But by then they would have been wise enough and bitter enough not to get carried away with enthusiasm, so they had given their next resting place the suitably cautious name of *Halfway*, perhaps secretly hoping that their unassuming modesty would be further rewarded by finding out that they were in fact more than halfway there. *Which they weren't*, Reacher thought. Forty miles was forty miles, optical illusions notwithstanding. They were only a fifth of the way there. But the wagons had rolled out of Despair with only the optimists aboard, and the town of Halfway reflected their founding spirit. The place looked crisp and bright and livelier in the dead of night than Despair had in the middle of the day. It had been rebuilt, perhaps several times. There was nothing ancient visible. The structures Reacher could make out seemed to be seventies stucco and eighties glass, not nineteenth-century brick. In the age of fast transportation there was no real reason why one nearby town rather than another should be chosen for investment and development, except for inherited traits of vibrancy and vigour. Despair had suffered and Halfway had prospered, and the optimists had won, like they sometimes deserved to.

Reacher pulled back on to the road and coasted down the rise into town. It was a quarter past three in the morning. Plenty of places were lit up but not many were actually open. A gas station and a coffee shop was about all, at first sight. But the town and the county shared the same name, which in Reacher's experience implied that certain services would be available around the clock. County police, for instance. They would have a station somewhere, manned all night. There would be a hospital, too, with a 24-7 emergency room. And to serve the grey area in between, where perhaps the county police were interested and the emergency room had failed, there would be a morgue. And it would be open for business night and day. A county town with a cluster of dependent municipalities all around it had to provide essential services. There was no morgue in Hope or Despair, for instance. *Not even a meat locker*, Vaughan had said, and presumably other local towns were in the same situation. And shit happened, and ambulances had to go somewhere. Dead folks couldn't be left out in the street until the next business day. Usually.

Reacher avoided the centre of town. Morgues were normally close to hospitals, and a re-developed county seat would normally have a new hospital, and new hospitals were normally built on the outskirts of towns, where land was empty and available and cheap. Halfway had one road in from the east, and a spider web of four roads out north and west, and Reacher found the hospital a half-mile out on the second exit road he tried. It was a place the size of a university campus, long, low, and deep, with buildings like elongated ski chalets. It looked calm and friendly, like sickness and death was really no big deal. It had a vast parking lot, empty except for a cluster of battered cars near a staff entrance and a lone shiny sedan in a section marked off with ferocious warning signs: *MD Parking Only*. Steam drifted from vents from a building in back. The laundry, Reacher guessed, where sheets and towels were being washed overnight by the drivers of the battered cars, while the guy from the shiny sedan tried to keep people alive long enough to use them in the morning.

He avoided the front entrances. He wanted dead people, not sick people, and he knew how to find them. He had visited more morgues than wards in his life, by an order of magnitude. Morgues were usually well hidden from the public. A sensitivity issue. They were often not signposted at all, or else labelled something anodyne like *Special Services*. But they were always accessible. Meat wagons had to be able to roll in and out unobstructed.

He found Halfway's county morgue in back, next to the hospital laundry, which he thought was smart design. The laundry's drifting steam would camouflage the output of the morgue's crematorium chimney. The place was another low, wide, chalet-style building. It had a high steel fence, and a sliding gate, and a guard shack.

The fence was solid, and the gate was closed, and there was a guard in the shack.

Reacher parked off to one side and climbed out of the truck and stretched. The guard watched him do it. Reacher finished stretching and glanced around like he was getting his bearings and then headed straight for the shack. The guard slid back the bottom part of his window and ducked his head down, like he needed to line up his ears with the empty space to hear properly. He was a middle-aged guy, lean, probably competent but not ambitious. He was a rent-a-cop. He was wearing a dark generic uniform with a moulded plastic shield like something from a toy store. It said *Security* on it. Nothing more. It could have done double duty at an outlet mall. Maybe it did. Maybe the guy worked two jobs, to make ends meet.

Reacher ducked his own head towards the open section of window and said, 'I need to check some details on the guy Despair brought in yesterday morning.'

The guard said, 'The attendants are inside.'

Reacher nodded as if he had received new and valuable information and waited for the guy to hit the button that would slide the gate.

The guy didn't move.

Reacher asked, 'Were you here yesterday morning?'

The guard said, 'Everything after midnight is morning.'

'This would have been daylight hours.'

The guard said, 'Not me, then. I get off at six.'

Reacher said, 'So can you let me through? To ask the attendants?'

'They change at six, too.'

'They'll have paperwork in there.'

The guard said, 'I can't.'

'Can't what?'

The guard said, 'Can't let you through. Law enforcement personnel only. Or paramedics with a fresh one.'

Reacher said, 'I am law enforcement. I'm with the Despair PD. We need to check something.'

'I'd need to see some credentials.'

'They don't give us much in the way of credentials. I'm only a deputy.'

'I'd have to see something.'

Reacher nodded and took the big guy's pewter star out of his shirt pocket. Held it face out, with the pin between his thumb and forefinger. The guard looked at it carefully. *Township of Despair, Police Deputy.*

'All they give us,' Reacher said.

'Good enough for me,' the guy said, and hit the button. A motor spun up and a gear engaged and drove the gate along a greased track. As soon as it was three feet open Reacher stepped through and headed across a yard through a pool of yellow sulphur light to a personnel door labelled *Receiving*. He went straight in and found a standby room like a million others he had seen. Desk, computer, clipboards, drifts of paper, bulletin boards, low wood-and-tweed armchairs. Everything was reasonably new but already battered. There were heaters going but the air was cold. There was an internal door, closed, but Reacher could smell sharp cold chemicals through it. Two of the low armchairs were occupied by two guys. They were white, young, and lean. They looked equally equipped for either manual or clerical labour. They looked bored and a little irreverent, which is exactly what Reacher expected from people working night shifts around a cold store full of stiffs. They glanced up at him, a little put out by the intrusion into their sealed world, a little happy about the break in their routine.

'Help you?' one of them said.

Reacher held up his pewter star again and said, 'I need to check something about the guy we brought in yesterday.'

The attendant who had spoken squinted at the star and said, 'Despair?'

Reacher nodded and said, 'Male DOA, young, not huge.'

One guy heaved himself out of his chair and dumped himself down in front of the desk and tapped the keyboard to wake the computer screen. The other guy swivelled in his seat and grabbed a clipboard and licked his thumb and leafed through sheets of paper. They both reached the same conclusion at the same time. They glanced at each other and the one who had spoken before said, 'We didn't get anything from Despair yesterday.'

'You sure about that?'

'Did you bring him in yourself?'

'No.'

'You sure he was DOA? Maybe he went to the ICU.'

'He was DOA. No doubt about it.'

'Well, we don't have him.'

'No possibility of a mistake?'

'Couldn't happen.'

'Your paperwork is always a hundred per cent?'

'Has to be. Start of the shift, we eyeball the toe tags and match them against the list. Procedure. Because people get sensitive about shit like dead relatives going missing.'

'Understandable, I guess.'

'So tonight we've got five on the list and five in the freezer. Two female, three male. Not a one of them young. And not a one of them from Despair.'

'Anywhere else they could have taken him?'

'Not in this county. And no other county would have accepted him.' The guy tapped some more keys and his screen redrew. 'As of this exact minute the last Despair stiff we had was over a year ago. Accident at their metal plant. Some guy all chewed up, as I recall, by a machine. Not pretty. He was so spread out we had to put him in two drawers.'

Reacher nodded and the guy spun his chair and put himself back-to against the desk with his feet straight out and his elbows propped behind him.

'Sorry,' he said.

Reacher nodded again and stepped back outside to the pool of sulphur light. The door sucked shut behind him, on a spring closer. *To assume makes an ass out of you and me. Ass, u, me.* The classroom jerks at Rucker had added: *You absolutely have to verify.* Reacher walked back across the concrete and waited for the gate to grind open a yard and stepped through and climbed into Vaughan's truck.

He had verified.

Absolutely.

THIRTY-SIX

Reacher drove a mile and stopped at Halfway's all-night coffee shop and ate a cheeseburger and drank three mugs of coffee. The burger was rare and damp and the coffee was about as good as the Hope diner's. The mug was a little worse, but acceptable. He read a ragged copy of the previous morning's newspaper all the way through and then jammed himself into the corner of his booth and dozed upright for an hour. He left the place at five in the morning, when the first of the breakfast customers came in and disturbed him with bright chatter and the smell of recent showers. He filled Vaughan's truck at the all-night gas station and then drove back out of town, heading east on the same rough road he had come in on, the mountains far behind him and the dawn waiting to happen up ahead.

He kept the speedometer needle fixed on forty and passed the MP post again fifty-two minutes later. The place was still quiet. Two guys were in the guard shack, one facing east and one facing west. Their night light was still burning. He figured reveille would be at six thirty and chow at seven. The night watch would eat dinner and the day watch would eat breakfast all in the same hour. Same food, probably. Combat FOBs were light on amenities. He waved and kept on going at a steady forty miles an hour, which put him next to the metal plant at exactly six o'clock in the morning.

The start of the work day.

The arena lights were already on and the place was lit up bright and blue, like day. The parking lot was filling up fast. Headlights were streaming west out of town, dipping, turning, raking the rough ground, stopping, clicking off. Reacher slowed and turned the wheel and bumped down off the road at an angle and drove across the beaten scrub and parked neatly between a sagging Chrysler sedan and a battered Ford pick-up. He slid out and locked up and put the keys in his pocket and joined a converging crowd of men shuffling their way towards the personnel gate. An uneasy feeling. Same sensation as entering a baseball stadium wearing the colours of the visiting team. *Stranger in the house.* All around him guys glanced at him curiously and gave him a little more space than they were giving each other. But nothing was said. There was no overt hostility. Just wariness and covert inspection, as the crowd shuffled along through the pre-dawn twilight, a yard at a time.

The personnel gate was a double section of the metal wall, folded back on hinges complex enough to accommodate the quilted curves of the wall's construction. The dirt path through it narrowed and was beaten dusty by a million foot-steps. Close to the gate there was no jostling. No impatience. Men sidestepped from the left and the right and lined up neatly like automatons, not fast, not slow, but resigned. They all needed to clock on, but clearly none of them wanted to.

The line shuffled slowly forward, a yard, two, three.

The guy in front of Reacher stepped through the gate.

Reacher stepped through the gate.

Immediately inside there were more metal walls, head high, like cattle chutes, dividing the crowd left and right. The right-hand chute led to a holding pen where Reacher guessed the part-time workers would wait for the call. It was already a quarter full with men standing quiet and patient. The guys going left didn't look at them.

Reacher went left.

The left-hand chute doglegged immediately and narrowed down to four feet in width. It carried the line of shuffling men past an old-fashioned punch-clock centred in a giant slotted array of time cards. Each man pulled his card and offered it up to the machine and waited for the dull thump of the stamp and then put the card back again. The rhythm was slow and relentless. The whisk of stiff paper against metal, the thump of the stamp, the click as the card was bottomed back in its slot. The clock was showing six fourteen, which was exactly right according to the time in Reacher's head.

Reacher walked straight past the machine. The chute turned again and he followed the guy in front for thirty feet and then stepped out into the northeast corner of the arena. The arena was vast. Just staggeringly huge. The line of lights on

the far wall ran close to a mile into the distance
and dimmed and shrank and blended into a tiny
vanishing point in the southwest corner. The far
wall itself was at least a half-mile away. The total
enclosed area must have been three hundred
acres. Three *hundred* football fields.

Unbelievable.

Reacher stepped aside to let the line of men
get past him. Here and there in the vastness small
swarms of guys were already busy. Trucks and
cranes were moving. They threw harsh shadows in
the stadium lights. Some of the cranes were bigger
than anything Reacher had seen in a dockyard.
Some of the trucks were as big as earth moving
machines. There were gigantic crushers set on
enormous concrete plinths. The crushers had
bright oily hydraulic rams thicker than redwood
trunks. There were crucibles as big as sailboats
and retorts as big as houses. There were piles of
wrecked cars ten storeys high. The ground was
soaked with oil and rainbow puddles of diesel
and littered with curled metal swarf and where
it was dry it glittered with shiny dust. Steam and
smoke and fumes and sharp chemical smells
were drifting everywhere. There was roaring and
hammering rolling outward in waves and beating
against the metal perimeter and bouncing straight
back in again. Bright flames danced behind open
furnace doors.

Like a vision of hell.

Some guys seemed to be heading for pre-
assigned jobs and others were milling in groups
as if waiting for direction. Reacher skirted around
behind them and followed the north wall, tiny and

insignificant in the chaos. Way ahead of him in the northwest corner the vehicle gate was opening. Five semi trailers were parked in a line, waiting to move out. On the road they would look huge and lumbering. Inside the plant they looked like toys. The two security Tahoes were parked side by side, tiny white dots in the vastness. Next to them was a stack of forty-foot shipping containers. They were piled five high. Each one looked tiny.

South of the vehicle gate was a long line of pre-fabricated metal offices. They were jacked up on short legs to make them level. They had lights on inside. At the left-hand end of the line two offices were painted white and had red crosses on their doors. The first-aid post. It was big enough to be a residential infirmary. Next to it a white vehicle was parked. The ambulance. Next to the ambulance was a long line of fuel and chemical tanks. Beyond them a sinister platoon of men in thick aprons and black welding masks used cutting torches on a pile of twisted scrap. Blue flames threw hideous shadows. Reacher hugged the north wall and kept on moving. Men looked at him and looked away, unsure. A quarter of the way along the wall his path was blocked by a giant pyramid of old oil drums. They were painted faded red and stacked ten high, stepped like a staircase. Reacher paused and glanced around and levered himself up to the base of the tier. Glanced around again and climbed halfway up the stack and then turned and stood precariously and held on tight and used the elevation to get an overview of the whole place.

He hadn't seen the whole place.

Not yet.

There was more.

Much more.

What had looked like the south boundary was in fact an interior partition. Same height as the perimeter walls, same material, same colour, same construction, with the sheer face and the horizontal cylinder. Same purpose, as an impregnable barrier. But it was only an internal division, with a closed gate. Beyond it the outer perimeter enclosed at least another hundred acres. Another hundred football fields. The gate was wide enough for large trucks. There were deep ruts in the ground leading to it. Beyond it there were heavy cranes and high stacks of shipping containers piled in chevron shapes. The containers looked dumped, as if casually, but they were placed and combined carefully enough to block a direct view of ground-level activity from any particular direction.

The internal gate had some kind of a control point in front of it. Reacher could make out two tiny figures stumping around in small circles, bored, their hands in their pockets. He watched them for a minute and then lifted his gaze again beyond the partition. Cranes, and screens. Some smoke, some distant sparks. Some kind of activity. Other than that, nothing to see. Plenty to hear, but none of it was useful. It was impossible to determine which noises were coming from where. He waited another minute and watched the plant's internal traffic. Plenty of things were moving, but nothing was heading for the internal gate. It was going to stay closed. He turned east and looked at the sky. Dawn was coming.

He turned back and got his balance and climbed down the oil drum staircase. Stepped off to the rough ground and a voice behind him said, 'Who the hell are you?'

THIRTY-SEVEN

Reacher turned slowly and saw two men. One was big and the other was a giant. The big guy was carrying a two-way radio and the giant was carrying a two-headed wrench as long as a baseball bat and probably heavier than ten of them. The guy was easily six-six and three hundred and fifty pounds. He looked like he wouldn't need a wrench to take a wrecked car apart.

The guy with the radio asked again, 'Who the hell are you?'

'EPA inspector,' Reacher said.

No reply.

'Just kidding,' Reacher said.

'You better be.'

'I am.'

'So who are you?'

Reacher said, 'You first. Who are you?'

'I'm the plant foreman. Now who are you?'

Reacher pulled the pewter star from his pocket and said, 'I'm with the PD. The new deputy. I'm familiarizing myself with the community.'

'We didn't hear about any new deputies.'

'It was sudden.'

The guy raised his radio to his face and clicked a button and spoke low and fast. Names, codes, commands. Reacher didn't understand them, and didn't expect to. Every organization had its own jargon. But he recognized the tone and he guessed the general drift. He turned and glanced west and saw the Tahoes backing up and turning and getting set to head over. He glanced south and saw groups of men stopping work, standing straight, preparing to move.

The foreman said, 'Let's go visit the security office.'

Reacher stood still.

The foreman said, 'A new deputy should want to visit the security office. Meet useful folks. Establish liaison. If that's what you really are.'

Reacher didn't move. He glanced west again and saw the Tahoes halfway through their half mile of approach. He glanced south again and saw knots of men walking his way. The crew in the aprons and the welders' masks was among them. Ten guys, clumping along awkwardly in heavy spark-proof boots. Plenty of others were coming in from other directions. Altogether maybe two hundred men were converging. Five minutes into the future there was going to be a big crowd by the oil drums. The giant with the wrench took a step forward. Reacher stood his ground and looked straight at him, and then checked west again, and south. The Tahoes were already close and slowing. The workers were still converging. They were forming up shoulder to shoulder in groups. They were close enough for Reacher to see tools in their hands. Hammers, pry bars, cutting torches, foot-long cold chisels.

The foreman said, 'You can't fight them all.'

Reacher nodded. The giant on his own would be hard, but maybe feasible, if he missed with the first swing of the wrench. Then four-on-one or even six-on-one might be survivable. But not two hundred-on-one. No way. Not two hundred and fifty pounds against twenty tons of muscle. He had two captured switchblades in his pocket, but they would be of limited use against maybe a couple of tons of improvised weaponry.

Not good.

Reacher said, 'So let's go. I can give you five minutes.'

The foreman said, 'You'll give us whatever we want.' He waved to the nearer Tahoe and it turned in close. Reacher heard oily stones and curly fragments of metal crunching under its tyres. The giant opened its rear door and used his wrench to make a sweeping *Get in* gesture. Reacher climbed up into the back seat. The vehicle had a plain utilitarian interior. Plastic and cloth. No wood or leather, no bells or whistles. The giant climbed in after him and crowded him against the far door panel. The foreman climbed in the front next to the driver and slammed his door and the vehicle took off again and turned and headed for the line of office buildings south of the vehicle gate. It drove through the middle of the approaching crowd, slowly, and Reacher saw faces staring in at him through the windows, grey skin smeared with grease, bad teeth, white eyes wide with fascination.

*　　*　　*

The security office was at the north end of the array, closest to the vehicle gate. The Tahoe stopped directly outside of it next to a tangled pile of webbing straps, presumably once used to tie down junk on flat-bed trailers. Reacher spilled out of the car ahead of the giant and found himself at the bottom of a short set of wooden steps that led up to the office door. He went up them and pushed through the door and found himself inside a plain metal prefabricated box that had probably been designed for use on construction sites. It was twenty-some feet long and maybe twelve wide and eight high. There were five small windows fitted with thick plastic glass and covered from the outside with heavy steel mesh. Other than that it looked a lot like the ready room he had seen at the Halfway county morgue. Desk, paper, bulletin boards, armchairs, all of it showing the signs of casual abuse a place gets when its users are not its owners.

The foreman pointed Reacher towards a chair and then left again. The giant dragged a chair of his own out of position and turned it around and dumped himself down in it so that he was blocking the door. He laid the wrench down on the floor. The floor was warped ply board and the wrench made an iron clatter as it dropped. Reacher sat in a chair in a corner. Wooden arms, tweed seat and back. It was reasonably comfortable.

'Got coffee?' he asked.

The giant paused a second and said, 'No.' A short word and a negative answer, but at least it was a response. In Reacher's experience the hardest part of any adversarial conversation was the beginning. An early answer was a good sign. Answering became a habit.

He asked, 'What's your job?'

The giant said, 'I help out where I'm needed.' His voice was like a normal guy's, but muffled by having to come out of such a huge chest cavity.

'What happens here?' Reacher asked.

'Metal gets recycled.'

'What happens in the secret section?'

'What secret section?'

'To the south. Behind the partition.'

'That's just a junkyard. For stuff that's too far gone to use. Nothing secret about it.'

'So why is it locked and guarded?'

'To stop people getting lazy. Someone gets tired of working, dumps good stuff in there, we lose money.'

'You part of management?'

'I'm a supervisor.'

'You want to supervise my way out of here?'

'You can't leave.'

Reacher glanced out the window. The sun was over the horizon. In five minutes it would be over the east wall. *I could leave*, he thought. The vehicle gate was open and trucks were moving out. Time it right, get past the big guy, run for the gate, hop aboard a flat-bed, game over. With the wrench on the floor the big guy was less of a problem than he had been before. He was unarmed, and down in a low chair. He was heavy, and gravity was gravity. And big guys were slow. And Reacher had knives.

'I played pro football,' the big guy said.

'But not very well,' Reacher said.

252

The big guy said nothing.

'Or you'd be doing colour commentary on Fox, or living in a mansion in Miami, not slaving away here.'

The big guy said nothing.

'I bet you're just as bad at this job.'

The big guy said nothing.

I could leave, Reacher thought again.

But I won't.

I'll wait and see what happens.

He waited twenty more minutes before anything happened. The giant sat still and quiet by the door and Reacher whiled the time away in the corner. He wasn't unhappy. He could kill time better than anyone. The morning sun rose higher and came streaming in through the plastic window. The rays cast a clouded beam over the desk. All the colours of the rainbow were in it.

Then the door opened and the giant sat up straight and scooted his chair out of the way and the foreman walked in again. He still had his two-way radio in his hand. Behind him in the bright rectangle of daylight Reacher could see the plant working. Trucks were moving, cranes were moving, swarms of men were beavering away, sparks were showering, loud noises were being made. The foreman stopped halfway between the door and Reacher's chair and said, 'Mr Thurman wants to see you.'

Seven o'clock, Reacher thought. Vaughan was ending her watch. She was heading to the diner in Hope, looking for breakfast, looking for her truck, maybe looking for him. Or maybe not.

He said, 'I can give Mr Thurman five minutes.'
'You'll give him however long he wants.'
'He might own you, but he doesn't own me.'
'Get up,' the foreman said. 'Follow me.'

THIRTY-EIGHT

Reacher followed the foreman out of the trailer and into the one next door. It was an identical metal box, but better appointed inside. There was carpet, the armchairs were leather, and the desk was mahogany. There were pictures on the walls, all of them dime-store prints of Jesus. In all of them Jesus had blue eyes and wore pale blue robes and had long blond hair and a neat blond beard. He looked more like a Malibu surfer than a Jew from two thousand years ago.

On the corner of the desk was a bible.

Behind the desk was a man Reacher assumed was Mr Thurman. He was wearing a three piece suit made of wool. He looked to be close to seventy years old. He looked pink and plump and prosperous. He had white hair, worn moderately long and combed and teased into waves. He had a big patient smile on his face. He looked like he had just stepped out of a television studio. He could have been a game show host, or a televangelist. Reacher could picture him, clutching his chest and promising God would fell him with a heart attack unless the audience sent him money.

And the audience would, Reacher thought. With a face like that, he would be buried under fives and tens.

The foreman waited for a nod and left again. Reacher sat down in a leather armchair and said, 'I'm Jack Reacher. You've got five minutes.'

The guy behind the desk said, 'I'm Jerry Thurman. I'm very pleased to meet you.'

Reacher said, 'Now you've got four minutes and fifty-six seconds.'

Thurman said, 'Actually, sir, I've got as long as it takes.' His voice was soft and mellifluous. His cheeks quivered as he spoke. Too much fat, not enough muscle tone. Not an attractive sight. 'You've been making trouble in my town and now you're trespassing on my business premises.'

'Your fault,' Reacher said. 'If you hadn't sent those goons to the restaurant I would have eaten a quick lunch and moved on days ago. No reason to stay. You're not exactly running the Magic Kingdom here.'

'I don't aim to. This is an industrial enterprise.'

'So I noticed.'

'But you knew that days ago. I'm sure the people in Hope were quick to tell you all about us. Why poke around?'

'I'm an inquisitive person.'

'Evidently,' Thurman said. 'Which raised our suspicions a little. We have proprietary processes here, and methodologies of our own invention, which might all be called industrial secrets, if you like. Espionage could hurt our bottom line.'

'I'm not interested in metal recycling.'

'We know that now.'

256

'You checked me out?'

Thurman nodded.

'We made inquiries,' he said. 'Last night, and this morning. You are exactly what you claimed to be, in Judge Gardner's vagrancy hearing. A passerby. A nobody who used to be in the army ten years ago.'

'That's me.'

'But you're a very persistent nobody. You made a ludicrous request to be sworn in as a deputy. After taking a badge from a man in a fight.'

'Which he started. On your orders.'

'So we ask ourselves, why are you so keen to know what happens here?'

'And I ask myself, why are you so keen to hide it?'

Thurman shook his great white head.

'We're not hiding anything,' he said. 'And you're no danger to me commercially, so I'll prove it to you. You've seen the town, you've met some of the folks who live here, and now I'm going to give you a tour of the plant. I'll be your personal guide and escort. You can see everything and ask me anything.'

They went in Thurman's personal vehicle, which was a Chevy Tahoe the same style and vintage as the security vehicles, but painted black, not white. Same modest interior. A working truck. The keys were already in the ignition. Habit, probably. And safe enough. Nobody would use the boss's car without permission. Thurman drove himself and Reacher sat next to him in the front. Nobody was in back. They were alone in the vehicle. They headed south, close to the west wall, away from the vehicle gate, moving slow. Thurman started talking immediately. He described the various office functions, which in order of appearance were operations management, and purchasing, and invoicing, and he pointed out the first-aid post, and described its facilities and capabilities, and made a mildly pointed comment about the people Reacher had put in there. Then they moved on to the line of storage tanks, and he described their capacities, which were five thousand gallons each, and their contents, which were gasoline for the Tahoes and some of the other trucks, and diesel for the cranes and the crushers and the heavier equipment, and a liquid chemical called trichloroethylene, which was an essential metal de-greaser, and oxygen and acetylene for the cutting torches, and kerosene, which fuelled the furnaces.

Reacher was bored rigid after sixty seconds.

He tuned Thurman out and looked at things for himself. Didn't see much. Just metal, and people working with it. He got the general idea. Old stuff was broken up and melted down, and ingots were sold to factories, where new stuff was made, and eventually the new stuff became old stuff and showed up again to get broken up and melted down once more.

Not rocket science.

Close to a mile later they arrived at the internal partition and Reacher saw that a truck had been parked across the gate, as if to hide it. Beyond the wall no more sparks were flying and no more smoke was rising. Activity seemed to have been abandoned for the day. He asked, 'What happens back there?'

Thurman said, 'That's our junkyard. Stuff that's too far gone to work with goes in there.'

'How do you get it in, with that truck in the way?'

'We can move the truck if we need to. But we don't need to often. Our processes have gotten very developed. Not much defeats us any more.'

'Are you a chemist or a metallurgist or what?'

Thurman said, 'I'm a born-again Christian American and a businessman. That's how I would describe myself, in that order of importance. But I hire the best talent I can find, at the executive level. Our research and development is excellent.'

Reacher nodded and said nothing. Thurman turned the wheel and steered a slow curve and headed back north, close to the east wall. The sun was up and the lights were off. Ahead and to the left the jaws of a giant crusher were closing on about ten wrecked cars at once. Beyond it a furnace door swung open and men ducked away from the blast of heat. A crucible moved slowly on an overhead track, full of liquid metal, all bubbling and crusting.

Thurman asked, 'Are you born again?'

Reacher said, 'Once was enough for me.'

'I'm serious.'

'So am I.'

'You should think about it.'

'My father used to say, why be born again, when you can just grow up?'

'Is he no longer with us?'

'He died a long time ago.'

'He's in the other place, then, with an attitude like that.'

'He's in a hole in the ground in Arlington Cemetery.'

'Another veteran?'

'A Marine.'

'Thank you for his service.'

'Don't thank me. I had nothing to do with it.'

Thurman said, 'You should think about getting your life in order, you know, before it's too late. Something might happen. The Book of Revelation says, the time is at hand.'

'As it has every day since it was written, nearly two thousand years ago. Why would it be true now, when it wasn't before?'

'There are signs,' Thurman said. 'And the possibility of precipitating events.' He said it primly, and smugly, and with a degree of certainty, as if he had regular access to privileged insider information.

Reacher said nothing in reply.

They drove on, past a small group of tired men wrestling with a mountain of tangled steel. Their backs were bent and their shoulders were slumped. *Not yet eight o'clock in the morning*, Reacher thought. More than ten hours still to go.

'God watches over them,' Thurman said.

'You sure?'

'He tells me so.'

'Does he watch over you too?'

'He knows what I do.'

'Does he approve?'

'He tells me so.'

'Then why is there a lightning rod on your church?'

Thurman didn't answer that. He just clamped his mouth shut and his cheeks drooped lower than his jawbone. He drove on slowly, in silence, until they arrived at the mouth of the cattle chute leading to the personnel gate. He stopped the truck and jiggled the stick into Park and sat back in his seat.

'Seen enough?' he asked.

'More than enough,' Reacher said.

'Then I'll bid you goodbye,' Thurman said. 'I imagine our paths won't cross again.' He tucked his elbow in and offered his hand, sideways and awkwardly. Reacher shook it. It felt soft and warm and boneless, like a child's balloon filled with water. Then Reacher opened his door and slid out and walked through the doglegged chute and back to the acres of parking.

Every window in Vaughan's truck was smashed.

THIRTY-NINE

Reacher stood for a long moment and ran through his options and then unlocked the truck and swept pebbles of broken glass off the seats and the dash. He raked them out of the driver's footwell. He didn't want the brake pedal to jam halfway through its travel. Or the gas pedal. The truck was slow enough already.

Three miles back to town, twelve to the line, and then five to the centre of Hope. A twenty-mile drive, cold and slow and very windy. Like riding a motorcycle without eye protection. Reacher's face was numb and his eyes were watering by the end of the trip. He parked outside the diner a little before nine o'clock in the morning. Vaughan's cruiser wasn't there. She wasn't inside. The place was three-quarters empty. The breakfast rush was over.

Reacher went in and took the back booth and ordered coffee and breakfast from the day shift waitress. The college girl was gone. The woman brought him a mug and filled it from a flask and he asked her, 'Did Officer Vaughan stop by this morning?'

The woman said, 'She left about a half hour ago.'

'Was she OK?'

'She seemed quiet.'

'What about Maria? The girl from San Diego?'

'She was in before seven.'

'Did she eat?'

'Plenty.'

'What about Lucy? The blonde from LA?'

'Didn't see her. I think she left town.'

'What does Officer Vaughan's husband do?'

The waitress said, 'Well, not much any more,' as if it was a dumb question to ask. As if that particular situation should have been plain to everybody.

That particular situation wasn't plain to Reacher.

He said, 'What, he's unemployed?'

The woman started to answer him, and then she stopped, as if she suddenly remembered that the situation wasn't necessarily plain to everybody, and it wasn't her place to make it plain. As if she was on the point of revealing something that shouldn't be revealed, like private neighbourhood business. She just shook her head with embarrassment and bustled away with her flask. She didn't speak at all when she came back five minutes later with his food.

Twenty minutes later Reacher got back in the damaged truck and drove south and crossed Third Street, and Fourth, and turned left on Fifth. Way ahead of him he could make out Vaughan's cruiser parked at the kerb. He drove on and pulled up behind it, level with the mailbox with the perfectly aligned letters. He idled in the middle of the traffic lane for a moment. Then he got out and walked ahead and put a palm on the Crown Vic's hood. It was still very warm. She had left the diner nearly an hour ago, but clearly she had driven around a little afterwards. Maybe looking for her Chevy, or looking for him. Or neither, or both. He got back in the truck and backed up and swung the wheel and bumped up on to her driveway. He parked with the grille an inch from her garage door and slid out. Didn't lock up. There didn't seem to be much point.

He found the winding path and followed it through the bushes to her door. He hooked her key ring on his finger and tapped the bell, briefly, just once. If she was awake, she would hear it. If she was asleep, it wouldn't disturb her.

She was awake.

The door opened and she looked out of the gloom straight at him. Her hair was wet from the shower and combed back. She was wearing an oversized white T-shirt. Possibly nothing else. Her legs were bare. Her feet were bare. She looked younger and smaller than before.

She said, 'How did you find me?'

He said, 'Phone book.'

'You were here last night. Looking. A neighbour told me.'

'It's a nice house.'

She said, 'I like it.'

She saw the truck keys on his finger. He said, 'I have a confession to make.'

'What now?'

'Someone broke all the windows.'

She pushed past him and stepped out to the path. Turned to face the driveway and studied the damage and said, 'Shit.' Then it seemed to dawn on her that she was out in the yard barefoot in her nightwear and she pushed back inside.

'Who?' she asked.

'One of a thousand suspects.'

'When?'

'This morning.'

'Where?'

'I stopped by the metal plant.'

'You're an idiot.'

'I know. I'm sorry. I'll pay for the glass.' He slipped the keys off his finger and held them out. She didn't take them. Instead she said, 'You better come in.'

The house was laid out the way he had guessed. Right to left it went garage, mud room, kitchen, living room, bedrooms. The kitchen seemed to be the heart of the home. It was a pretty space with painted cabinets and a wallpaper border at the top of the walls. The dishwasher was running and the sink was empty and the counters were tidy but there was enough disarray to make the room feel lived in. There was a four-place table with only three chairs. There were what Reacher's mother had called *touches*. Dried flowers, bottles of virgin olive oil that would never be used, antique spoons. Reacher's mother had said such things gave a room personality. Reacher himself had been unsure how anything except a person could have personality. He had been a painfully literal child.

But over the years he had come to see what his mother had meant. And Vaughan's kitchen had personality.

Her personality, he guessed.

It seemed to him that one mind had chosen everything and one pair of hands had done everything. There was no evidence of compromise or duelling tastes. He knew that way back a kitchen was considered a woman's domain. Certainly it had been that way in his mother's day, but she had been French, which had made a difference. And since then he had been led to believe that things had changed. Guys cooked now, or at least left six-packs lying around, or put oil stains on the linoleum from fixing motorcycle engines.

There was no evidence of a second person in the house. None at all. Not a trace. From his position by the sink Reacher could see into the living room through an arch that was really just a doorway with the door taken out. There was a single armchair in there, and a TV set, and a bunch of moving boxes still taped shut.

Vaughan said, 'Want coffee?'

'Always.'

'Did you sleep last night?'

'No.'

'Don't have coffee, then.'

'It keeps me awake until bedtime.'

'What's the longest you ever stayed awake?'

'Seventy-two hours, maybe.'

'Working?'

He nodded. 'Some big deal, twenty years ago.'

'A big MP deal?'

He nodded again. 'Somebody was doing

266

something to somebody. I don't recall the details.'

Vaughan rinsed her coffee pot and filled her machine with water. The machine was a big steel thing with *Cuisinart* embossed on it in large letters. It looked reliable. She spooned coffee into a gold basket and hit a switch. She said, 'Last night the deputies from Despair headed home after an hour.'

'They found me in the bar,' Reacher said. 'They flushed me west with the phone call and then came after me. It was a trap.'

'And you fell for it.'

'They fell for it. I knew what they were doing.'

'How?'

'Because twenty years ago I used to stay up for seventy-two hours at a time dealing with worse folks than you'll ever find in Despair.'

'What happened to the deputies?'

'They joined their full-time buddies in the infirmary.'

'All four of them?'

'All six of them. They added some on-site moral support.'

'You're a one-man crime wave.'

'No, I'm Alice in Wonderland.'

Now Vaughan nodded.

'I know,' she said. 'Why aren't they doing anything about it? You've committed assault and battery on eight individuals, six of them peace officers, and you've wrecked two police cars, and you're still walking around.'

'That's the point,' Reacher said. 'I'm still walking around, but in Hope, not in Despair. That's weirdness number one. All they ever want to do is keep people out of there. They're not interested in the law or justice or punishment.'

'What's weirdness number two?'

'They came at me six against one and I walked away with two bruises and sore knuckles from pounding on them. They're all weak and sick. One of them even had to call it quits so he could find time to throw up.'

'So what's that about?'

'The clerk at my motel figures they're breaking environmental laws. Maybe there's all kinds of poisons and pollution out there.'

'Is that what they're hiding?'

'Possibly,' Reacher said. 'But it's kind of odd that the victims would help to hide the problem.'

'People worry about their jobs,' Vaughan said. 'Especially in a company town, because they don't have any alternatives.' She opened a cabinet and took out a mug. It was white, perfectly cylindrical, four inches high, and two and a half inches wide. It was made of fine bone china as thin as paper. She filled it from the pot and immediately from the aroma Reacher knew it was going to be a great one. She glanced at the living room but carried the mug to the kitchen table instead, and placed it down in front of one of the three chairs. Reacher glanced at the boxes and the lone armchair in the living room and said, 'Just moved in?'

'A year and a half ago,' Vaughan said. 'I guess I'm a little slow unpacking.'

'From where?'

'Third Street. We had a little cottage with an upstairs, but we decided we wanted a ranch.'

'We?'

'David and I.'

Reacher asked, 'So where is he?'

'He's not here right now.'

'Should I be sorry about that?'

'A little.'

'What does he do?'

'Not so much any more.' She sat in one of the chairs without the mug in front of it and tugged the hem of her T-shirt down. Her hair was drying and going wavy again. She was naked under the shirt, and confident about it. Reacher was sure of that. She was looking straight at him, like she knew he knew.

He sat down opposite her.

She asked, 'What else?'

'My motel clerk figures the plant makes way too much money.'

'That's common knowledge. Thurman owns the bank, and bank auditors gossip. He's a very rich man.'

'My motel clerk figures he's smuggling dope or something with his little airplane.'

'Do you think he is?'

'I don't know.'

'That's your conclusion?'

'Not entirely.'

'So what else?'

'A quarter of the plant is screened off. There's a secret area. I think he's got a contract to recycle military scrap. Hence the wealth. A Pentagon contract is the fastest way on earth to get rich these days. And hence the MP unit down the road. Thurman is breaking up classified stuff back there, and people would be interested in it. Armour

269

thickness, materials, construction techniques, circuit boards, all that kind of stuff.'

'So that's all? Legitimate government business?'

'No,' Reacher said. 'That's not all.'

FORTY

Reacher took the first sip of his coffee. It was perfect. Hot, strong, smooth, and a great mug. He looked across the table at Vaughan and said, 'Thank you very much.'

She said, 'What else is going on there?'

'I don't know. But there's a hell of a vigilante effort going on about something. After the PD ended up depopulated I went to see the local judge about getting sworn in as a deputy.'

'You weren't serious.'

'Of course not. But I pretended I was. I wanted to see the reaction. The guy panicked. He went crazy. He said he'd deputize the whole population first. They're totally serious about keeping strangers out.'

'Because of the military stuff.'

'No,' Reacher said. 'That's the MPs' job. Any hint of espionage, Thurman's people would get on the radio and the MPs would lock and load and about a minute later the whole town would be swarming with Humvees. The townspeople wouldn't be involved.'

'So what's going on?'

271

'At least two other things.'

'Why two?'

'Because their responses are completely incoherent. Which means there are at least two other factions in play, separate and probably unaware of each other. Like this morning, Thurman had me checked out. Easy enough to do, assuming the computers in the police station are still turned on. He saw that my paper trail went cold ten years ago, and therefore I was no obvious danger to him, and then he ran your plate and saw that I was in some way associated with a cop from the next town, and therefore in some way untouchable, so he played nice and gave me a guided tour. But meanwhile without all that information someone else was busy busting your windows. And nobody busts a cop's windows for the fun of it. Therefore the left hand doesn't know what the right hand is doing.'

'Thurman gave you a tour?'

'He said he'd show me everything.'

'And did he?'

'No. He stayed away from the secret area. He said it was just a junkyard.'

'Are you sure it isn't?'

'I saw activity in there earlier. Smoke and sparks. Plus it's carefully screened off. Who does that, for a junkyard?'

'What are the two other factions?'

'I have no idea. But these young guys are involved somehow. Lucy Anderson's husband and the dead guy. And Lucy Anderson's husband is another example of the left hand not knowing what the right hand is doing. They sheltered him and moved him on but threw his wife out of town like a pariah. How much sense does that make?'

'He moved on?'

'I saw him at the rooming house at three o'clock and he was gone by seven. No trace of him, and nobody would admit he had ever been there.'

'The plane flies at seven,' Vaughan said. 'Is that connected?'

'I don't know.'

'No trace at all?'

'No physical sign, and a lot of zipped lips.'

'So what's going on?'

'When was the last time any normal person entered Despair and stayed as long as he wanted and left of his own accord? To your certain knowledge?'

'I don't know,' Vaughan said. 'Months, certainly.'

'There was an entry in the hotel register from seven months ago.'

'That sounds about right.'

'I met the new girl last night,' Reacher said. 'Sweet kid. Her name is Maria. I'm pretty sure the dead guy was her boyfriend. She showed me his picture. His name was Raphael Ramirez.'

'Did you tell her?'

Reacher shook his head. 'No.'

'Why not?'

'She asked me if I'd seen him. Truth is, I didn't actually see him. It was dark. And I can't give her news like that without being completely sure.'

'So she's still swinging in the wind.'

'I think she knows, deep down.'

'What happened to the body?'

273

'It didn't go to the county morgue. I checked on that.'

'We knew that already.'

'No, we knew it didn't go straight to the morgue. That was all. So I wondered if it had been dumped somewhere out of town and found later by someone else. But it wasn't. Therefore it never left Despair. And the only meat wagon and the only stretcher in Despair belong to the metal plant. And the metal plant has a dozen different disposal methods. It has furnaces that could vaporize a corpse in five minutes flat.'

Vaughan went quiet for a spell and then got up and poured herself a glass of water, from a bottle in the refrigerator. She stood with her hips against the counter and stared out the window. Her heels were on the floor but most of her weight was on her toes. Her T-shirt had one lateral wrinkle where the base of her spine met her butt. The cotton material was very slightly translucent. The light was all behind her. Her hair was dry and there was fine golden down on her neck.

She looked spectacular.

She asked, 'What else did Maria say?'

Reacher said, 'Nothing. I didn't ask her anything else.'

'Why ever not?'

'No point. The wives and the girlfriends aren't going to tell us anything. And what they do say will be misleading.'

'Why?'

'Because they've got a vested interest. Their husbands and their boyfriends aren't just hiding out in Despair on their own account. They're

274

aiming to get help there. They're aiming to ride some kind of an underground railroad for fugitives. Despair is a way station, in and out. The women want to keep it all secret. Lucy Anderson was OK with me until I mentioned I used to be a cop. Then she started hating me. She thought I still was a cop. She thought I was here to bust her husband.'

'What kind of fugitives?'

'I don't know what kind. But obviously the Anderson guy was the right kind and Raphael Ramirez was the wrong kind.'

Vaughan stepped back to the table and took Reacher's mug from him and refilled it from the machine. Then she refilled her glass from the refrigerator and came back and sat down and said, 'May I ask you a personal question?'

Reacher said, 'Feel free.'

'Why are you doing this?'

'Doing what?'

'Caring, I suppose. Caring about what's happening in Despair. Bad stuff happens everywhere, all the time. Why does this matter to you so much?'

'I'm curious, that's all.'

'That's no answer.'

'I have to be somewhere, doing something.'

'That's still no answer.'

'Maria,' Reacher said. 'She's the answer. She's a sweet kid, and she's hurting.'

'Her boyfriend is a fugitive from the law. You said so yourself. Maybe she deserves to be hurting. Maybe Ramirez is a dope dealer or something. Or a gang member or a murderer.'

'And pictures,' Reacher said. 'Photographs. Those can be reasons. Ramirez looked like a harmless guy to me.'

'You can tell by looking?'

'Sometimes. Would Maria hang out with a bad guy?'

'I haven't met her.'

'Would Lucy Anderson?'

Vaughan said nothing.

'And I don't like company towns,' Reacher said. 'I don't like feudal systems. I don't like smug fat bosses lording it over people. And I don't like people so broken down that they put up with it.'

'You see something you don't like, you feel you have to tear it down?'

'Damn right I do. You got a problem with that?'

'No.'

They sat in the kitchen and drank coffee and water in silence. Vaughan took her free hand out of her lap and laid it on the table, her fingers spread and extended. They were the closest part of her to Reacher. He wondered whether it was a gesture, either conscious or subconscious. An approach, or an appeal for a connection.

No wedding band.

He's not here right now.

He put his own free hand on the table.

She asked, 'How do we know they were fugitives at all? Maybe they were undercover environmental activists, checking on the pollution. Like volunteers. Maybe the Anderson guy fooled them and Ramirez didn't.'

'Fooled them how?'

'I don't know. But it worries me, if they're using poisons over there. We share the same water table.'

'Thurman mentioned something called trichloroethylene. It's a metal de-greaser. I don't know whether it's dangerous or not.'

'I'm going to check it out.'

'Why would the wife of an environmental activist be scared of cops?'

'I don't know.'

'The Anderson guy wasn't fooling anyone. He was a guest there. He was sheltered and embraced and protected. He was *helped*.'

'But Lucy Anderson wasn't. She was thrown out.'

'Like I said, the left hand doesn't know what the right is doing.'

'And Ramirez was killed.'

'Not killed. Left to die.'

'So why help one and shun the other?'

'Why shun him at all? Why not just round him up and dump him at the line, like they did with me and Lucy?'

Vaughan sipped her water.

'Because he was different in some way,' she said. 'In a different category. More specifically dangerous to them.'

'Then why not just take him out straight away? Disappear him? The end result would have been the same.'

'I don't understand it.'

'Maybe I'm wrong,' Reacher said. 'Maybe they didn't shun him or keep him out. Maybe they never even knew he was there. Maybe he was sniffing around on the periphery, staying out of sight, trying to find a way in. Desperate enough to keep trying, not good enough to succeed.'

'Or both things,' Vaughan said. 'Maybe they picked him up but he got away.'

'Possible. The cops were clowns, basically.'

'So he hung around, because he needed to be there for some reason, but he had to stay out of sight. Then he timed it wrong. He knew he was failing, he tried to get back here, but he ran out of energy on the way.'

'Possible,' Reacher said again.

Vaughan took her hand off the table.

'We need to know exactly who he was,' she said. 'We need to talk to Maria.'

'She won't tell us anything.'

'We can try. We'll find her in the diner. Meet me there, later.'

'Later than what?'

'We both need to sleep.'

Reacher said, 'May I ask you a personal question?'

'Go ahead.'

'Is your husband in prison?'

Vaughan paused a beat, and then smiled, a little surprised, a little sad.

'No,' she said. 'He isn't.'

FORTY-ONE

Reacher walked back to the motel, alone. Two blocks up, three blocks over. The sun was high. The morning was halfway done. Lucy Anderson's door was open. A maid's cart was parked outside. The bed was stripped and all the towels were on the floor. The closet was empty. *I think she left town*, the waitress had said, in the diner. Reacher watched for a moment and then he moved on. *Good luck, Lucky*, he thought, *whatever the hell you're doing and wherever the hell you're going*. He unlocked his own door and took a long hot shower and climbed into bed. He was asleep within a minute. The coffee didn't fight him at all.

He woke up in the middle of the afternoon with the MPs on his mind. The forward operating base. Its location. Its equipment mix. The place came at him like an analysis problem from the classrooms at Fort Rucker.

What was it for?

Why was it there?

The old county route 37 wandered east to

west through Hope, through Despair, through Halfway, and presumably onward. First he saw it laid out like a ribbon, like a line on a map, and then he pictured it in his head like a rotating three-dimensional diagram, like something on a computer screen, all green webs of origins and layers. Way back in its history it had been a wagon trail. Beaten earth, crushed rock, ruts and weeds. Then it had been minimally upgraded, when Model Ts had rolled out of Dearborn and flooded the country. Then Hope Township had upgraded ten miles of it again, for the sake of civic pride. They had done a conscientious job. Maybe foundation reinforcement had been involved. Certainly there had been grading and levelling. Maybe a little straightening. Possibly a little widening. Thick blacktop had been poured and rolled.

Despair Township had done none of that. Thurman and his father and his grandfather or whoever had owned the town before had ignored the road. Maybe they had grudgingly dumped tar and pebbles on it every decade or so, but fundamentally it was still the same road it had been back when Henry Ford ruled the world. It was narrow, weak, lumpy, and meandering.

Unfit for heavy traffic.

Except west of the metal plant. There, a thirty-five mile stretch had been co-opted and rebuilt. Probably from the ground up. Reacher pictured a yard-deep excavation, drainage, a rock foundation, a thick concrete roadbed, rebar, a four-inch asphalt layer rolled smooth and true by heavy equipment. The shoulders were straight and the camber was good. Then after thirty-five miles the new road had been driven through virgin territory to meet the Interstate and the old Route 37 had wound onward as before, once again in its native state, narrow, weak, and lumpy.

Weak, strong, weak.

There was no military presence east of Despair or west of the fork, across the weak parts of the road.

The MP base straddled the strong part.

The truck route.

Close to Despair, but not too close.

Not sealing the town like a trap, but guarding one direction only and leaving the other wide open.

The base was equipped with six up-armoured Humvees, each one an eight-ton rhinoceros, each one reasonably fast and reasonably manoeuvrable, each one topped with a belt-fed 7.62-calibre M60 machine gun on a free-swinging mount.

Why all that?

Reacher lay in bed and closed his eyes and heard barking voices from the Rucker classrooms: *This is what you know. What's your conclusion?*

His conclusion was that nobody was worried about espionage.

He got out of bed at four o'clock and took another long hot shower. He knew he was out of step with the western world in terms of how often he changed his clothes, but he tried to compensate by keeping his body scrupulously clean. The motel soap was white and came in a small thin paper-wrapped morsel, and he used the whole bar. The shampoo was a thick green liquid in a small plastic bottle. He used half of it. It smelled faintly of apples. He rinsed and stood under the water for a moment more and then shut it off and heard someone knocking at his door. He wrapped a towel around his waist and padded across the room and opened up.

Vaughan.

She was in uniform. Her HPD cruiser was parked neatly behind her. She was staring in at him, openly curious. Not an unusual reaction. *Look at yourself. What do you see?* He was a spectacular mesomorph, built of nothing except large quantities of bone and sinew and muscle. But with his shirt off most people saw only his scars. He had a dozen minor nicks and cuts, plus a dimpled .38 bullet hole in the left centre of his chest, and a wicked spider web of white lacerations low down on the right side of his abdomen, all criss-crossed and puckered by seventy clumsy stitches done quick and dirty in a mobile army surgical hospital. Souvenirs, in the first instance of childhood mayhem, in the second of a psychopath with a small revolver, and in the third, shrapnel from a bomb blast. Survivable, because childhood mayhem was always survivable, and because the .38 that hit him had been packed with a weak load, and because the shrapnel had been someone else's bone, not white-hot metal. He had been a lucky man, and his luck was written all over his body.

Ugly, but fascinating.

Vaughan's gaze travelled upward to his face.

'Bad news,' she said. 'I went to the library.'

'You get bad news at libraries?'

'I looked at some books and used their computer.'

'And?'

'Trichloroethylene is called TCE for short. It's a metal de-greaser.'

'I know that.'

'It's very dangerous. It causes cancer. Breast cancer, prostate cancer, all kinds of cancers. Plus heart disease, problems with the nervous system, strokes, liver disease, kidney disease, even diabetes. The EPA says a concentration of five parts per billion is acceptable. Some places have been measured twenty or thirty times worse than that.'

'Like where?'

'There was a case in Tennessee.'

'That's a long way from here.'

'This is serious, Reacher.'

'People worry too much.'

'This isn't a joke.'

He nodded.

'I know,' he said. 'And Thurman uses five thousand gallons at a time.'

'And we drink the groundwater.'

'You drink bottled water.'

'Lots of people use tap.'

'The plant is twenty miles away. There's a lot of sand. A lot of natural filtration.'

'It's still a concern.'

Reacher nodded. 'Tell me about it. I had two cups of coffee right there. One in the restaurant and one at the judge's house.'

'You feel OK?'

'Fine. And people seem OK here.'

'So far.'

She went quiet.

He said, 'What else?'

'Maria is missing. I can't find her anywhere. The new girl.'

FORTY-TWO

Vaughan hung around in the open doorway and Reacher grabbed his clothes and dressed in the bathroom. He called out, 'Where did you look?'

'All over,' Vaughan called back. 'She's not here in the motel, she's not in the diner, she's not in the library, she's not out shopping, and there isn't anywhere else to go.'

'Did you speak to the motel clerk?'

'Not yet.'

'Then that's where we'll go first. She knows everything.' He came out of the bathroom, buttoning his shirt. The shirt was almost due for the trash, and the buttonholes were still difficult. He ran his fingers through his hair and checked his pockets.

'Let's go,' he said.

The clerk was in the motel office, sitting on a high stool behind the counter, doing something with a ledger and a calculator. But she had no useful information. Maria had left her room before seven o'clock that morning, dressed as before, on foot, carrying only her purse.

'She ate breakfast before seven,' Reacher said. 'The waitress in the diner told me.'

The clerk said she hadn't come back. That was all she knew. Vaughan asked her to open Maria's room. The clerk handed over her pass key immediately. No hesitation, no fuss about warrants or legalities or due process. *Small towns*, Reacher thought. Police work was easy. About as easy as it had been in the army.

Maria's room was identical to Reacher's, with only very slightly more stuff in it. A spare pair of jeans hung in the closet. They were neatly folded over the bar of a hanger. Above them on the shelf were one spare pair of cotton underpants, one bra, and one clean cotton T-shirt, all neatly folded together in a low pile. On the floor of the closet was an empty suitcase. It was a small, sad, battered item. Blue in colour, made from fibreboard, with a crushed lid, as if it had been stored for years with something heavy on top of it.

On the shelf next to the bathroom sink was a vinyl wash bag, white, with improbable pink daisies on it. It was empty, but it had clearly been overstuffed during transit. Its contents were laid out next to it, in a long line. Soaps, shampoos, lotions and ointments and unguents of every possible kind.

No personal items. They would have been in her purse.

'Day trip,' Vaughan said. 'She's expecting to return.'

'Obviously,' Reacher said. 'She paid for three nights.'

'She went to Despair. To look for Ramirez.'

'That would be my guess.'

'But how? Did she walk?'

Reacher shook his head. 'I would have seen her. It's seventeen miles. Six hours, for her. If she left at seven she wouldn't have arrived before one in the afternoon. I was on the road between eight-thirty and nine. I didn't pass her along the way.'

'There's no bus or anything. There's never any traffic.'

'Maybe there was,' Reacher said. 'I came in with an old guy in a car. He was visiting family, and then he was moving on to Denver. He'd head straight west. No reason to loop around. And if he was dumb enough to give me a ride, he'd have given Maria a ride for sure.'

'If he happened to leave this morning.'

'Let's find out.'

They returned the pass key and got into Vaughan's cruiser. She fired it up and they headed north to First Street and then west to the hardware store. The last developed block. Beyond it, nothing but open road. The sidewalk was piled high with an elaborate display. Ladders, buckets, barrows, gasoline-driven machines of various types. The owner was inside, wearing a brown coat. He confirmed that he had been building the display early that morning. He thought hard and memory dawned in his eyes and he confirmed that he had seen a small dark girl in a blue warm-up jacket. She had been standing on the far sidewalk, right at the edge of town, half turned, looking east but clearly aiming to head west, gazing at the empty traffic lane with a mixture of optimism and hopelessness. A classic hitchhiker's pose. Then later the store owner had seen a large bottle green car heading west, a little before eight o'clock. He described the car as looking basically similar to Vaughan's cruiser, but without all the police equipment.

'A Grand Marquis,' Reacher said. 'Same platform. Same car. Same guy.'

The store owner had not seen the car stop or the girl get in. But the inference was clear. Vaughan and Reacher drove the five miles to the town line. No real reason. They saw nothing. Just the smooth blacktop behind and the ragged gritty ribbon ahead.

'Is she in danger?' Vaughan asked.

'I don't know,' Reacher said. 'But she's probably not having the best day of her life.'

'How will she get back?'

'I suspect she decided to worry about that later.'

'We can't go there in this car.'

'So what else have you got?'

'Just the truck.'

'Got sunglasses? It's breezy, without the windshield.'

'Too late. I already had it towed. It's being fixed.'

'And then you went to the library? Don't you ever sleep?'

'Not so much any more.'

'Since when? Since what?'

'I don't want to talk about it.'

'Your husband?'

'I said I don't want to talk about it.'

Reacher said, 'We need to find Maria.'

'I know.'

'We could walk.'

'It's twelve miles.'

'And twelve miles back.'

'Can't do it. I'm on duty in two hours.'

Reacher said, 'She's domiciled in Hope. At least temporarily. Now she's missing. The HPD should be entitled to head over there in a car and make inquiries.'

'She's from San Diego.'

'Only technically.'

'Technicalities matter.'

'She took up residency.'

'With one change of underwear?'

'What's the worst thing that can happen?'

'Despair could ask us for reciprocity.'

'They already grabbed it. Their deputies came by last night.'

'Two wrongs don't make a right.'

'Says who?'

'Are you bullying me?'

'You're the one with the gun.'

Vaughan paused and shook her head and sighed and said, 'Shit.' Then she jammed her foot on the gas and the Crown Vic shot forward. The tyres had traction on Hope's blacktop but lost it on Despair's loose gravel. The rear wheels spun and howled and the car stumbled for a second and then accelerated west in a cloud of blue smoke.

They drove eleven miles into the setting sun with nothing to show for it except eyestrain. The twelfth mile was different. Way ahead in the glare Reacher saw the familiar distant sights, all in sharp silhouette and shortened perspective. Vague smudges, on the horizon. The vacant lot, on the left. The abandoned motor court, low and forlorn. The gas station on the right. Further on, the dry goods store in the first brick building.

Plus something else.

From a mile away it looked like a shadow. Like a lone cloud was blocking the sun and casting a random shape on the ground. He craned his neck and looked up at the sky. Nothing there. The sky was clear. Just the grey-blue of approaching evening.

Vaughan drove on.

Three-quarters of a mile out the shape added dimensions. It grew width, and depth, and height. The sun blazed behind it and winked around its edges. It looked like a low wide pile of something dark. Like a gigantic truck had strewn earth or asphalt right across the road, shoulder to shoulder, and beyond.

The pile looked to be fifty feet wide, maybe twenty deep, maybe six high.

From a half-mile out, it looked to be moving.

From a quarter-mile out, it was identifiable.

It was a crowd of people.

Vaughan slowed, instinctively. The crowd was two or three hundred strong. Men, women, and children. They were formed up in a rough triangle, facing east. Maybe six people at the front. Behind the six, twenty more. Behind the twenty, sixty more. Behind the sixty, a vast milling pool of people. The whole width of the road was blocked. The shoulders were blocked. The rearguard spilled thirty feet out into the scrub on both sides.

Vaughan stopped, fifty yards out.

The crowd compressed. People pushed inward from the sides. The vanguard held steady and people closed up from behind. They made a human wedge. A solid mass. Two or three hundred people. They held together, but they didn't link arms.

They didn't link arms because they had weapons in their hands.

Baseball bats, pool cues, axe handles, broom handles, split firewood, carpenters' hammers. Two or three hundred people, pressed tight together, and moving. Moving as one. They were rocking in place from foot to foot and jabbing their weapons up and down in the air. Nothing wild. Their movements were small and rhythmic and controlled.

They were chanting.

At first Reacher heard only a primitive guttural shout, repeated over and over. Then he dropped his window an inch and heard the words *Out! Out! Out!* He hit the switch again and the glass thumped back up.

Vaughan was pale.

'Unbelievable,' she said.

'Is this some weird Colorado tradition?' Reacher asked.

'I never saw it before.'

'So Judge Gardner went and did it. He deputized the whole population.'

'They don't look drafted. They look like true believers.'

'That's for sure.'

'What are we going to do?'

Out! Out! Out!

Reacher watched for a moment and said, 'Drive on and see what happens.'

'Are you serious?'

'Try it.'

Vaughan took her foot off the brake and the car crept forward.

The crowd crept forward to meet it, short steps, crouched, weapons moving.

Vaughan stopped again, forty yards out.

Out! Out! Out!

Reacher said, 'Use your siren. Scare them.'

'Scare *them*? They're doing a pretty good job in reverse.'

The crowd had quit rocking from side to side. Now people were rocking back and forth instead, one foot to the other, jabbing their clubs and sticks forward, whipping them back, jabbing them forward again. They were dressed in work shirts and faded sundresses and jeans jackets, but collectively in terms of their actions they looked entirely primitive. Like a weird Stone Age tribe, threatened and defensive.

'Siren,' Reacher said.

Vaughan lit it up. It was a modern synthesized unit, shatteringly loud in the emptiness, sequencing randomly from a basic *whoop-whoop-whoop* to a manic *pock-pock-pock* to a hysterical digital cackling.

It had no effect.

No effect at all.

The crowd didn't flinch, didn't move, didn't miss a beat.

Reacher said, 'Can you get around them?'

Vaughan shook her head. 'This car is no good

on the scrub. We'd bog down and they'd be all over us. We'd need a four wheel drive.'

'So fake them out. Drift left, then sneak past on the right real fast.'

'You think?'

'Try it.'

She took her foot off the brake again and crept forward, slowly. She turned the wheel and headed for the wrong side of the road on a slight diagonal. The crowd in front of her tracked the move, slow and infinitely fluid. Two or three hundred people, moving as one, like a pool of grey mercury, changing shape like an amoeba. Like a disciplined herd. Vaughan reached the left shoulder. The crowd had set itself to head her off, but it was still very solid all the way out into the scrub on the right.

'Can't do it,' she said. 'There's too many of them.'

She stopped again, ten feet from the front rank.

She killed the siren.

The chanting grew louder.

Out! Out! Out!

Then the note dropped lower and the rhythm changed down. As one the people started banging their clubs and sticks on the ground and shouting only every other beat.

Out!

Crash!

Out!

Crash!

They were close enough to see clearly. Their faces jerked forward with every shouted word, grey and pink and contorted with hate and rage and fear and anger. Reacher didn't like crowds. He enjoyed solitude and was a mild agoraphobic, which didn't mean he was afraid of wide open spaces. That was a common misconception. He liked wide open spaces. Instead he was mildly un-settled by the *agora*, which was an ancient Greek word for a crowded public marketplace. Random crowds were bad enough. He had seen footage of stampedes and stadium disasters. Organized crowds were worse. He had seen footage of riots and revolutions. A crowd two hundred strong was the largest animal on the face of the earth. The heaviest, the hardest to control, the hardest to stop. The hardest to kill. Big targets, but after-action reports always showed that crowds took much less than one casualty per round fired.

Crowds had nine lives.

'What now?' Vaughan asked.

'I don't know,' he said. He especially didn't care for angry organized crowds. He had been in Somalia and Bosnia and the Middle East, and he had seen what angry crowds could do. He had seen the herd instinct at work, the anonymity, the removal of inhibition, the implied permissions of collective action. He had seen that an angry crowd was the most dangerous animal on the face of the earth.

Out!

Crash!

Out!

Crash!

He said, quietly, 'Put the shifter in Reverse.'

Vaughan moved the lever. The car settled back on its haunches, like prey ready to flee.

He said, 'Back up a little.'

Vaughan backed up and steered and got straight on the centre line and stopped again, thirty yards out. Ninety feet. The distance from home plate to first base.

'What now?' she asked.

The crowd had tracked the move. It had changed shape again, back to what it had been at the beginning. A dense triangle, with a blunt vanguard of six men, and a wide base that petered out thirty feet into the scrub on both sides of the thoroughfare.

Out!

Crash!

Out!

Crash!

Reacher stared ahead through the windshield. He dropped his window again. He felt a change coming. He sensed it. He wanted to be a split second ahead of it.

Vaughan asked, 'What do we do?'

Reacher said, 'I'd feel better in a Humvee.'

'We're not in a Humvee.'

'I'm just saying.'

'What do we do in a Crown Vic?'

Reacher didn't have time to answer. The change came. The chanting stopped. There was silence for a second. Then the six men at the front of the crowd raised their weapons high, with clamped fists and straight arms.

They screamed a command.

And charged.

They bolted forward, weapons high, screaming. The crowd streamed after them. Two or three hundred people, full speed, yelling, falling, stumbling, stampeding, eyes wide, mouths open, faces contorted, weapons up, free arms pumping. They filled the windshield, a writhing mob, a frantic screaming mass of humanity coming straight at them.

They got within five feet. Then Vaughan stamped on the gas. The car shot backward, the engine screaming, the low gear whining loud, the rear tyres howling and making smoke. She got up to thirty miles an hour going backward and then she flung the car into an emergency 180 and smashed the shifter into Drive. Then she stamped on the gas harder. She accelerated east and didn't stop for miles, top speed, engine roaring, her foot jammed down. Reacher had been wrong in his earlier assessment. Way too cautious. A Crown Vic with the Police Interceptor pack was a very fast car. Good for a hundred and twenty, easily.

FORTY-THREE

They got airborne over the peak of the rise that put
the distant Rockies close again and then Vaughan
lifted off the gas and took most of the next mile
to coast to a stop. She craned her neck and spent
a long minute staring out the back window. They
were still deep in Despair's territory. But all was
quiet behind them. She parked on the shoulder
with two wheels in the sand and let the engine die
back to idle. She slumped in her seat and dropped
both hands to her lap.

'We need the State Police,' she said. 'We've
got mob rule back there and a missing woman.
And whatever exactly Ramirez was to them, we
can't assume they're going to treat his girlfriend
kindly.'

'We can't assume anything,' Reacher said. 'We
don't know for sure she's there. We don't even
know for sure that the dead guy was Ramirez.'

'You got serious doubts?'

'The state cops will. It's a fairy story, so far.'

'So what do we do?'

'We verify.'

'How?'

'We call Denver.'

'What's in Denver?'

'The green car,' Reacher said. 'And the guy who was driving it. Three hundred miles, six hours' drive time, call it seven with a stop for lunch. If he left around eight this morning, he'll be there by now. We should call him up, ask him if he gave Maria a ride, and if so, where exactly he let her out.'

'You know his name?'

'No.'

'Number?'

'No.'

'Great plan.'

'He was visiting three grandchildren in Hope. You need to get back to town and check with families that have three kids. Ask them if Grandpa just came by in his green Mercury. One of them will say yes. Then you'll get a number for his next stop. It'll be a brother or a sister in Denver, with four more kids for the old guy to visit.'

'What are you going to do?'

'I'm going back to Despair.'

He got out of the car at five thirty-five, a little more than eight miles west of Hope, a little more than eight miles east of Despair. Right in the heart of no-man's-land. He watched Vaughan drive away and then he turned and started walking. He stayed on the road itself, for speed. He ran calculations in his head. *This is what you know.* Twenty-six hundred inhabitants, possibly a quarter of them too old or too young to be useful. Which left more than eighteen hundred people, with maximum availability after six o'clock in the evening, when the plant closed for the day. Newly deputized, newly marshalled, unsure of themselves, inexperienced. Daytime visibility had enabled deployment in large masses. In the dark, they would have to spread out, like a human perimeter. But they would want to stick fairly close together, for morale and effectiveness and mutual support. Therefore no outliers, and no sentinels. Children would be held close in family groups. Each element of the perimeter would want visual contact with the next. Which meant that groups or individuals wouldn't want to be more than maybe ten feet apart. Some people would have flashlights. Some would have dogs. All in all, worst case, they could assemble a human chain eighteen thousand feet long, which was six thousand yards, which was the circumference of a circle a fraction more than a mile in diameter.

A circle a mile in diameter would barely enclose the town. It couldn't enclose the town and the plant together. And it would bunch up on the road in and the road out, especially the road in, from Hope. Cover would be thin elsewhere. Probably very thin. Possibly guys with trucks would be out in the scrub. Possibly the security Tahoes from the plant would be on the prowl. Teenage boys would be unpredictable. Excited by the adventure, and hungry for glory. But easily bored. In fact all of them would get bored. And tired, and low. Efficiency would peak during the first hour, would wane over the next two or three, would be poor before midnight, and would be non-existent in the small hours of the night.

What's your conclusion?

Not a huge problem, Reacher thought. The sun was down behind the distant mountains. There was a soft orange glow on the horizon. He walked on towards it.

At seven o'clock he pictured Vaughan starting her night watch, in Hope. At seven fifteen he was a mile from where the crowd had gathered before, in Despair. It was going dark. He couldn't see anybody in the distance, and therefore nobody could see him in the distance. He struck off the road into the scrub, south and west, at an angle, hustling, unwilling to slow down. The town ahead was dark and quiet. Very quiet. By seven thirty he was six hundred yards out in the sand and he realized he hadn't heard the plane take off. No aero engine, no light in the sky.

Why not?

He paused in the stillness and put together a couple of possible scenarios. Then he moved on, holding a wide radius, quiet and stealthy and invisible in the darkness.

By eight o'clock he was making his first approach. He was expected out of the east, therefore he was coming in from the southwest. Not a guarantee of safety, but better than a poke in the eye. Competent individuals would be distributed all around, but not equally. He had already outflanked most of the people he needed to worry about. He had seen one truck, a battered pick-up with four lights on a bar on its roof. It had been bouncing slowly along, over rough ground, heading away from him.

He moved up through the scrub and paused behind a rock. He was fifty yards from the back of a long line of workers' housing. Low one-storey dwellings, well separated laterally, because desert land was cheap and septic systems didn't work with too much density. The gaps between the houses were three times as wide as the houses themselves. The sky had a minimal grey glow, moon behind cloud. There were guards in the spaces between the houses. Left to right he could make out an individual, a small group, another individual, and another. They all had sticks or clubs or bats. Together they made a chain that went, armed guard, house, armed guards, house, armed guard, house, armed guard.

They thought the houses themselves were defensive elements.

They were wrong.

He could hear dogs barking randomly here and there in the distance, excited and unsettled by the unfamiliar evening activity. Not a problem. Dogs that barked too much were no more use than dogs that didn't bark at all. The guy second from the right between the houses had a flashlight. He was clicking it on at predictable intervals, sweeping an arc of ground in front of him, and then clicking it off again to save the battery.

Reacher moved left.

He lined himself up behind a house that was entirely dark. He dropped to the ground and low-crawled straight for it. The army record for a fifty-yard low crawl was about twenty seconds. At the other extreme, snipers could spend all day crawling fifty yards into position. On this occasion

301

Reacher budgeted five minutes. Fast enough to get the job done, slow enough to get it done safely. Generally the human brain noticed speed and discontinuity. A tortoise heading inward worried nobody. A cheetah bounding in got everyone's attention. He kept at it, slow and steady, knees and elbows, head down. No pauses. No stop-start. He made it through ten yards. Then twenty. And thirty. And forty.

After forty-five yards he knew he was no longer visible from the spaces between the houses. The angle was wrong. But he stayed low all the way, until he crawled right into the back stoop. He stood up and listened for reaction, either outside the house or inside.

Nothing.

He was outside the kitchen door. The stoop was a simple wooden assembly three steps high. He went up, slowly, feet apart, shuffling, putting his weight where the treads were bolted to the side rails. If a stair squeaked, ninety-nine times in a hundred it squeaked in the centre, where it was weakest. He put his hand on the door handle and lifted. If a door squeaked, ninety-nine times in a hundred it was because it had dropped on its hinges. Upward pressure helped.

He eased the door up and in and stepped through the opening and turned and closed it again. He was in a dark and silent kitchen. A worn linoleum floor, the smell of fried food. Counters and cabinets, ghostly in the gloom. A sink, and a tap with a bad washer. It released a fat drip every twenty-three seconds. The drip spattered against a ceramic surface. He pictured the perfect teardrop exploding into a coronet shape, flinging tinier droplets outward in a perfect circle.

He moved through the kitchen to the hallway door. Smelled dirty carpet and worn furniture from a living room on his right. He moved through the hallway to the front of the house. The front door was a plain hollow slab, with a rectangle of painted beading on it. He turned the handle and lifted. Eased it open, silently.

There was a screen door beyond it.

He stood still. There was no way to open a screen door quietly. No way at all. Lightweight construction, tight plastic hinges, a crude spring mechanism. Guaranteed to raise a whole symphony of screeching and slapping sounds. The door had a horizontal bar in the centre, designed to add strength and resist warping. The upper void was less than three feet square. The lower void, the same. Both were meshed with nylon screen. The screen had been doing its job for many years. That was clear. It was filthy with dust and insect corpses.

Reacher pulled out one of his captured switchblades. Turned back to the hallway to muffle the sound and popped the blade. He slit a large X in the lower screen, corner to corner. Pressed the blade back in the handle and put the knife back in his pocket and sat down on the floor. Leaned back and jacked himself off the ground, like a crab. Shuffled forward and went out through the X feet first. Head first would have been more intuitive. The desire to see what was out there was overwhelming. But if what was out there was an axe handle or a bullet, better that it hit him in the legs than in the head. Much better.

There was nothing out there. No bullet, no axe handle. He ducked and squirmed and got his shoulders through the gap and stood up straight and alert, one swift movement. He was standing on a front stoop made of concrete. A plain slab, four by four, cracked, canted down in one corner on an inadequate foundation. Ahead of him was a short path and a dark street. More houses on the other side. No guards between them. The guards were all behind him now, by a distance equal to half a house's depth. And they were all facing the wrong way.

FORTY-FOUR

Reacher headed due north, straight for the centre of town. He threaded between houses and stayed off the roads where possible. He saw nobody on foot. Once he saw a moving vehicle two streets away. An old sedan, lights on bright. A designated supervisor, possibly, on an inspection tour. He ducked low behind a wooden fence and waited until the car was well away from him. Then he moved on across some open scrub and pressed up behind the first of the brick-built downtown blocks. He stood with his back against a wall and planned his moves. He was reasonably familiar with Despair's geography. He decided to stay away from the street with the restaurant on it. The restaurant was almost certainly still open for business. Close to nine in the evening, maybe late for normal supper hours, but with mass community action going on all night it was probably committed to staying open and supplying refreshments for the troops. Maybe the moving car had been a volunteer ferrying coffee.

He stayed in the shadows and used a narrow cross street and turned and walked past the storefront church. It was empty. Maybe Thurman had been inside earlier, praying for success. In which case he was going to be sadly disappointed. Reacher moved on without a sound and turned again and headed for the police station. The streets were all dark and deserted. The whole active population was on the perimeter, staring out into the gloom, unaware of what was happening behind its back.

The street with the police station on it had one street lamp burning. It cast a weak pool of yellow light. The police station itself was dark and still. The outer door was locked. Old wood, a new five-lever deadbolt inexpertly fitted. Reacher took out the keys he had taken from the deputy in the bar. He looked at the lock and looked at the keys and selected a long brass item and tried it. It worked. The lock turned, with plenty of effort. Either the key was badly cut, or the lock's tongue was binding against the striker plate, or both. But the door opened. It swung back and a smell of institutional floor polish wafted out. Reacher stepped inside and closed the door behind him and walked through the gloom the same way he had walked before, to the booking desk. Like the town's hotel, the Despair PD was still in the pen-and-paper age. Arrest records were kept in a large black ledger with gold-painted edges. Reacher carried it to a window and tilted it so that it caught what little light was coming through. Then he opened it up and flipped forward through the pages until he found his own entry, dated three days previously and timed in the middle of the afternoon: *Reacher, J., male vagrant*. The entry had been made well in advance of the town court hearing. Reacher smiled. *So much for the presumption of innocence*, he thought.

The entry immediately before his own was three days older and said: *Anderson, L., female vagrant.*

He flipped backward, looking for Lucy Anderson's husband. He didn't expect to find him, and he didn't find him. Lucy Anderson's husband had been helped, not hindered. Then he went looking for Ramirez. No trace. Nowhere in the book. Never arrested. Therefore the guy hadn't escaped from custody. He had never been picked up at all. If he had ever been there at all. If the dead guy in the dark wasn't someone else.

He leafed backward, patiently, a random three-month sample. Saw six names, Bridge, Churchill, White, King, Whitehouse, Andrews, five male, one female, all vagrants, roughly one every two weeks.

He flipped ahead again, past his own entry, looking for Maria herself. She wasn't there. There was only one entry after his own. It was in new handwriting, because the desk cop had been driving Despair's second Crown Vic and was therefore currently out sick with whiplash. The new entry had been made just seven hours previously and said: *Rogers, G., male vagrant.*

Reacher closed the book and stacked it back on the desk and walked to the head of the basement stair. He felt his way down and opened the cell block door. It was very bright inside. All the bulkhead lights were burning. But all the cells were empty.

*   *   *

A circle a mile in diameter would barely enclose the town. Reacher's next stop was out of town, which meant passing through the perimeter again, this time heading in the other direction. Easy at first, hard later. Easy to sneak up to the line, relatively easy to penetrate it, hard to walk away with a thousand eyes on his back. He didn't want to be the only thing moving, in front of a static audience. Better that the line moved, and broke over him like a wave over a rock.

He sorted through the bunch of keys.

Found the one he wanted.

Then he put the keys back in his pocket and moved back to the booking desk and started opening drawers. He found what he wanted in the third drawer he tried. It was full of miscellaneous junk. Rubber bands, paper clips, dry ballpoint pens, slips of paper with scratched out notes, a plastic ruler.

And a tin ashtray, and a quarter-full pack of Camel cigarettes, and three books of matches.

He cleared a space on the floor under the booking desk and put the arrest ledger in its centre, standing on its edge, open to ninety degrees, with the pages fanned out. He piled every scrap of paper he could find on it and around it. He balled up memos and posters and old newspapers and built a pyramid. He hid two match books in it, with the covers bent back and the matches bent forward at varying angles.

Then he lit a cigarette, with a match from the third book. He inhaled, gratefully. Camels had been his brand, way back in history. He liked Turkish tobacco. He smoked a half-inch and folded the cigarette into the match book in a *T* shape and used a paper clip to keep it secure. Then he nestled the assembly into the base of his paper pyramid and walked away.

He left the street door open two inches, to set up a breeze.

He headed south, to the big deputy's house. He knew where it was. He had seen it from the back, the first night, when the guy got home from work and threw up in the yard. It was a five-minute walk that took him ten, due to stealth and caution. The house was another swaybacked old ranch. Scoured siding, curled roof tiles, dried-out plantings. No landscaping, no real yard. Just beaten earth, including a foot-wide path to the door and twin ruts leading to a parking place close to the kitchen.

The old crew-cab pick-up was right there on it.

The driver's door was unlocked. Reacher slid in behind the wheel. The seat was worn and sagging. The windows were dirty and the upholstery smelled of sweat and grease and oil. Reacher pulled the bunch of keys and found the car key. Plastic head, distinctive shape. He tried it, just to be sure. He put it in the ignition and turned two clicks. The wheel unlocked and the dials lit up. He turned it back again and climbed over the seats and lay down in the rear of the cab.

It took more than thirty minutes for the townspeople to realize their police station was on fire. By that time it was well ablaze. From his low position in the truck Reacher saw smoke and sparks and an orange glow and the tentative start of leaping flames well before anyone reacted. But eventually someone on the perimeter must have smelled something or gotten bored and shuffled a full circle in the dirt and paused long enough to study the horizon behind.

There was uncertainty and confused shouting for about a minute.

Then there was pandemonium.

Discipline broke down immediately. The perimeter collapsed inward like a leaking balloon. Reacher lay still and people streamed past him, few and hesitant at first, then many and fast. They were running, singly and in groups, yelling, shouting, fascinated, uncertain, looking at nothing except the bright glow ahead of them. Reacher craned his head and saw them coming from all directions. The cross streets were suddenly crowded with dozens of people, then hundreds. The flow was all one way. The downtown maze swallowed them all. Reacher sat up and turned and watched the last of the backs disappear around corners and between buildings.

Newly deputized, newly marshalled, unsure of themselves, inexperienced.

He smiled.

Like moths to a flame, he thought. *Literally*.

Then he scrambled over the seat backs and turned the key all the way. The engine turned over once and fired. He drove away slowly, with the lights off, heading a little south of west, through the deserted scrubland. He saw headlights on the road way to his right. Four moving vehicles. Almost certainly the security Tahoes were coming in from the plant, plus probably the ambulance, plus maybe some firefighting equipment he hadn't seen. He kept on going, looping west through the empty land, slowly, bouncing over washboard undulations and jarring over rocks. The wheel squirmed in his hands. He peered ahead through the dirty windshield and steered left and right around large obstacles. He averaged less than twenty miles an hour. Faster than running, but even so it took more than seven minutes before he saw the white gleam of the plant's wall in the darkness.

FORTY-FIVE

Reacher skirted around south of the plant's southern perimeter and kept on going until the residential compound's fieldstone wall loomed up at him. It was hard to see in the darkness. But it would be easy to climb. Plenty of toeholds, in the unmortared joints. He drove halfway around its circumference and parked the truck opposite where he guessed the oversize barn would be. He killed the engine and got out quietly and was over the wall less than ten seconds later. The runway was right in front of him. Maybe sixty feet wide, maybe nine hundred yards long, beaten flat, carefully graded, well maintained. At each end was a low hump, a concrete emplacement for a floodlight set to wash horizontally along the runway's length. Across it and directly ahead was a wide expanse of scrub, dotted here and there with landscaped areas. The plants were all sharp-leaved things that looked silver under the night sky. Native, adapted to the desert. Xeric plants, or xerophilous, drought tolerant, from the Greek prefix *xero-*, meaning dry. Hence *Xerox*, for copying without wet chemicals. Zeno of Cittium would have been puzzled by Xeroxing, but he would have approved of xeroscaping. He believed in going with the flow. The unquestioning acceptance of destiny. He believed in basking in the sun and eating green figs, instead of spending time and effort trying to change nature with irrigation.

Reacher crossed the runway. Ahead of him and behind the last planted area was the big barn. He headed straight for it. It was a three-sided building, open at the front. Maybe fifty feet wide, maybe twenty high, maybe thirty deep. It was entirely filled with a white airplane. A Piper Cherokee, parked nose-out, settled dead level on its tricycle undercarriage, dormant and still and dewed over with cold. Close to ten o'clock in the evening. Close to the halfway point of its normal nightly flight plan. But that night, it was still on the ground. It hadn't flown at all.

Why not?

Reacher walked right into the barn and skirted the right-hand wing tip. Came back to the fuselage and found the step and climbed on the wing and peered in through the window. He had spent time in small planes, when the army had wanted him to get somewhere faster than a jeep or a train could have gotten him. He hadn't liked them much. He had found them small and trivial and somehow unserious. They were like flying cars. He had told himself they were better built than cars, but he hadn't found much concrete evidence to convince himself with. Thin metal, bent and folded and riveted, flimsy clips and wires, coughing engines. Thurman's Cherokee looked no better than most. It was a plain four-seat workhorse, a little worn,

313

a little stained. It had tinny doors and a divided windshield and a dash less complicated than most new sedans. One window had a small crack. The seats looked caved in and the harnesses looked tangled and frayed.

There was no paperwork in the cabin. No charts, no maps, no scribbled latitudes and longitudes. There was no real freight capacity. Just a couple of small holds in various nacelles and voids, and the three spare seats. *People don't joyride at night*, Lucy Anderson had said. *There's nothing to see*. Therefore Thurman was carrying something, somewhere, in or out. Or visiting a friend. Or a mistress. Maybe that was what *lay preacher* meant. You preached, and you got laid.

Reacher climbed down off the wing and walked out of the barn. He strolled through the gloom and took a look at the other outbuildings. There was a three-car garage, at the end of a straight quarter-mile driveway that led to an ornamental iron gate in the wall. There was another, smaller, barn that might have held garden tools. The house itself was magnificent. It was built of oiled boards that shone halfway between blond and dark. It had numerous peaked gables, like a mountain chalet. Some windows were two storeys high. Panelling glowed dark inside. There were cathedral ceilings. There were fieldstone accents and rich rugs and clubby leather sofas and armchairs. It was the kind of gentleman's retreat that should always smell of cigar smoke. Reacher could still taste the part-smoked cigarette in his mouth. He walked all the way around the house, thinking about Camels, and camels, and the eyes of needles. He arrived back at the big barn, and took a last look at the airplane. Then he retraced his steps through the landscaping, across the runway, to the wall. Ten seconds later he was back in the stolen truck.

He U-turned through the sand and crossed towards the plant's metal wall and followed it counterclockwise. The fieldstone wall had been easy to climb, but the metal wall was going to be impossible. It was a sheer fourteen-foot-high vertical plane, topped with a continuous horizontal cylinder six feet in diameter. Like a toilet roll balanced on a thick hardcover book. It was a design derived from prison research. Reacher knew the theory. He had been professionally interested in prisons, back in the day. Stone walls or brick walls or wire fences could be climbed, however high they were. Broken glass set in the tops could be padded or cushioned. Rolls of barbed wire could be crushed or cut. But six-foot cylinders were unbeatable. Compared to the length of an arm or the span of a hand, their surfaces were slick and flat and offered no grip at all. Getting over one was like trying to crawl across a ceiling.

So he drove on, through the empty acres of parking, hoping against hope that the personnel gate would be open, and if it wasn't, that one of the deputy's keys would unlock it. But it wasn't open, and none of the keys fit. Because it didn't have a keyhole. It had a grey metal box instead, set into the wall well to the right, where the gate's arc of travel wouldn't obscure it. The box was the kind of thing that normally held an outdoor electrical outlet. It opened against a spring closure. Inside was a ten-digit keypad. A combination lock. One through nine, plus zero, laid out like a telephone. A possible 3,628,800 variants. It would take seven months to try them all. A fast typist might do it in six.

Reacher drove on, and turned left, and tracked the north wall in the Tahoes' established ruts, hoping against hope that the vehicle gate would be open. He was slightly optimistic. The Tahoes had left in a hurry, and the ambulance, and maybe a fire truck. And people in a hurry didn't always clean up after themselves.

He slowed to a crawl and turned left again.

The vehicle gate was open.

It was built like a double door. Each half cantilevered outward and then swung through a hundred degrees on a wheeled track. And both halves were standing wide open. Together they made a mouth, a chute, a funnel, a V-shaped invitation leading directly to an empty forty-foot gap in the wall, and to the darkness beyond.

Reacher parked the deputy's truck nose-out, right across the wheeled track, blocking the gates' travel, and he took the keys with him. He figured maybe the gate was motorized, or on a time switch. And come what may, he wanted to keep it open. He didn't want it to close with him on the wrong side. Climbing out would be as impossible as climbing in.

He walked a hundred feet into the plant. Felt the familiar terrain underfoot, heavy and sticky with grease and oil, crunchy with shards of metal. He stood still, and sensed giant shapes ahead. The crushers, and the furnaces, and the cranes. He glanced right, and half saw the line of offices and storage tanks. Beyond them, nearly a mile away and invisible in the night, the secret compound. He turned and took half a step in its direction.

Then the lights came on.

There was an audible *whoomp* as electricity surged through cables thicker than wrists and in a split second the whole place lit up blue and brighter than day. A shattering sensation. Physical in its intensity. Reacher screwed his eyes shut and clamped his arms over his head and tried hard not to fall to his knees.

FORTY-SIX

Reacher opened his eyes in a desperate hooded squint and saw Thurman walking towards him. He turned and saw the plant foreman heading in from a different direction. He turned again and saw the giant with the three-foot wrench blocking his path to the gate.

He stood still and waited, blinking, squinting, the muscles around his eyes hurting from clamping so hard. Thurman stopped ten feet away from him and then walked on and came close and looped around behind him and took up a position alongside him, nearly shoulder to shoulder, as if they were two old buddies standing together, surveying a happy scene.

Thurman said, 'I thought our paths were not going to cross again.'

Reacher said, 'I can't be responsible for what you think.'

'Did you sct our police station on fire?'

'You've got a human wall all around the town. How could I have gotten through?'

'Why are you here again?'

Reacher paused a beat. Said, 'I'm thinking

about leaving the state.' Which was permanently true. Then he said, 'Before I go, I thought I'd drop by the infirmary and pay my respects to my former opponents. To tell them no hard feelings.'

Thurman said, 'I think the hard feelings are all on the other side.'

'Then they can tell me no hard feelings. Clearing the air is always good for a person's mental wellbeing.'

'I can't permit a visit to the infirmary. Not at this hour.'

'You can't prevent one.'

'I'm asking you to leave the premises.'

'And I'm denying your request.'

'There's only one patient here at the moment. The others are all home now, on bed rest.'

'Which one is here?'

'Underwood.'

'Which one is Underwood?'

'The senior deputy. You left him in a sorry state.'

'He was sick already.'

'You need to leave now.'

Reacher smiled. 'That should be your town motto. It's all I ever hear. Like New Hampshire, live free or die. It should be Despair, you need to leave now.'

Thurman said, 'I'm not joking.'

'You are,' Reacher said. 'You're a fat old man, telling me to leave. That's pretty funny.'

'I'm not alone here.'

Reacher turned and checked the foreman. He was standing ten feet away, empty hands by his sides, tension in his shoulders. Reacher turned again and glanced at the giant. He was twenty feet away, holding the wrench in his right fist, resting its weight in his left palm.

Reacher said, 'You've got an office boy and a broken-down old jock with a big spanner. I'm not impressed.'

'Maybe they have guns.'

'They don't. They'd have them out already. No one waits to pull a gun.'

'They could still do you considerable harm.'

'I doubt it. The first eight you sent didn't do much.'

'Are you really willing to try?'

'Are you? If it goes the wrong way, then you're definitely alone with me. And with your conscience. I'm here to visit the sick, and you want to have me beaten up? What kind of a Christian are you?'

'God guides my hand.'

'In the direction you want to go anyway. That's very convenient, isn't it? I'd be more impressed if you picked up a message telling you to sell up and give all your money to the poor and go to Denver to care for the homeless.'

'But that's not the message I'm getting.'

'Well, there's a huge surprise.'

Thurman said nothing.

Reacher said, 'I'm going to the infirmary now. You are, too. Your choice whether you walk there or I carry you there in a bucket.'

Thurman's shoulders slumped in an all-purpose sigh and shrug and he raised a palm to his two guys, one after the other, like he was telling a couple of dogs to stay. Then he set off walking, towards the line of cabins. Reacher walked at his side. They passed the security office, and Thurman's own office, and the three other offices Reacher had seen before on his tour, the one marked *Operations*, the one marked *Purchasing*, the last marked *Invoicing*. They passed the first white-painted unit and stopped outside the second. Thurman heaved himself up the short flight of steps and opened the door. He went inside and Reacher followed.

It was a real sick bay. White walls, white linoleum floor, the smell of antiseptic, soft night lights burning. There were sinks with lever taps, and medicine cabinets, and blood pressure cuffs, and sharps disposal cans on the walls. There was a rolling cart with a kidney-shaped steel dish on it. A stethoscope was curled in the dish.

There were four hospital cots. Three were empty, one was occupied, by the big deputy. He was well tucked in. Only his head was visible. He looked pretty bad. Pale, inert, listless. He looked smaller than before. His hair looked thinner. His eyes were open, dull and unfocused. His breathing was shallow and irregular. There was a medical chart clipped to the rail at the foot of his bed. Reacher used his thumb and tilted it horizontal and scanned it. Neat handwriting. Professional notations. The guy had a whole lot of things wrong with him. He had fever, fatigue, weakness, breathlessness, headaches, rashes, blisters, sores, chronic nausea and vomiting, diarrhoea, dehydration, and signs of complex internal problems. Reacher dropped the chart back into position and asked, 'You have a doctor working here?'

Thurman said, 'A trained paramedic.'

'Is that enough?'

'Usually.'

'For this guy?'

'We're doing the best we can.'

Reacher stepped alongside the bed and looked down. The guy's skin was yellow. Jaundice, or the night light reflected off the walls. Reacher asked him, 'Can you talk?'

Thurman said, 'He's not very coherent. But we're hoping he'll get better.'

The big deputy rolled his head from one side to the other. Tried to speak, but got hung up with a dry tongue in a dry mouth. He smacked his lips and breathed hard and started again. He looked straight up at Reacher and his eyes focused and glittered and he said, 'The . . .' and then he paused for breath and blinked and started over, apparently with a new thought. A new subject. He said, haltingly, 'You did this to me.'

'Not entirely,' Reacher said.

The guy rolled his head again, away and back, and gasped once, and said, 'No, the . . .' and then he stopped again, fighting for breath, his voice reduced to a meaningless rasp. Thurman grabbed Reacher's elbow and pulled him back and said, 'We should leave now. We're tiring him.'

Reacher said, 'He should be in a proper hospital.'

'That's the paramedic's decision. I trust my people. I hire the best talent I can find.'

'Did this guy work with TCE?'

Thurman paused a beat. 'What do you know about TCE?'

'A little. It's a poison.'

322

'No, it's a de-greaser. It's a standard industrial product.'

'Whatever. Did this guy work with it?'

'No. And those that do are well protected.'

'So what's wrong with him?'

'You should know. Like he said, you did this to him.'

'You don't get symptoms like these from a fist-fight.'

'Are you sure? I heard it was more than a fist-fight. Do you ever stop to reflect on the damage you cause? Maybe you ruptured something inside of him. His spleen, perhaps.'

Reacher closed his eyes. Saw the barroom again, the dim light, the tense silent people, the air thick with raised dust and the smell of fear and conflict. *He stepped in and jabbed hard and caught the guy low down in the side, below the ribs, above the waist, two hundred and fifty pounds of weight punched through the blunt end of a chair leg into nothing but soft tissue.* He opened his eyes again and said, 'All the more reason to get him checked out properly.'

Thurman nodded. 'I'll have him taken to the hospital in Halfway tomorrow. If that's what it takes, so that you can move on with a clear conscience.'

'My conscience is already clear,' Reacher said. 'If people leave me alone, I leave them alone. If they don't, what comes at them is their problem.'

'Even if you overreact?'

'Compared to what? There were six of them. What were they going to do to me? Pat me on the cheek and send me on my way?'

'I don't know what their intentions were.'

'You do,' Reacher said. 'Their intentions were your intentions. They were acting on your instructions.'

'And I was acting on the instructions of a higher authority.'

'I guess I'll have to take your word for that.'

'You should join us. Come the Rapture, you don't want to be left behind.'

'The Rapture?'

'People like me ascend to heaven. People like you stay here without us.'

'Works for me,' Reacher said. 'Bring it on.'

Thurman didn't answer that. Reacher took a last look at the guy in the bed and then stepped away and turned and walked out the door, down the steps, back to the blazing arena. The foreman and the guy with the wrench were where they had been before. They hadn't moved at all. Reacher heard Thurman close the infirmary door and clatter down the steps behind him. He moved on and felt Thurman follow him towards the gate. The guy with the wrench was looking beyond Reacher's shoulder, at Thurman, waiting for a sign, maybe hoping for a sign, slapping the free end of the wrench against his palm.

Reacher changed direction.

Headed straight for the guy.

He stopped a yard away and stood directly face to face and looked him in the eye and said, 'You're in my way.'

The guy said nothing back. Just glanced in Thurman's direction and waited. Reacher said, 'Have a little self-respect. You don't owe that old fool anything.'

The guy said, 'I don't?'

'Not a thing,' Reacher said. 'None of you does. He owes you. You should all wise up and take over. Organize. Have a revolution. You could lead it.'

The guy said, 'I don't think so.'

Thurman called out, 'Are you leaving now, Mr Reacher?'

'Yes,' Reacher said.

'Are you ever coming back?'

'No,' Reacher lied. 'I'm all done here.'

'Do I have your word?'

'You heard me.'

The giant glanced beyond Reacher's shoulder again, hope in his eyes. But Thurman must have shaken his head or given some other kind of a negative instruction, because the guy just paused a beat and then stepped aside, one long sideways pace. Reacher walked on, back to the sick deputy's truck. It was where he had left it, with all its windows intact.

FORTY-SEVEN

From the plant to the Hope Town line was fifteen miles by road, but Reacher made it into a twenty-mile excursion by looping around to the north, through the scrub. He figured that the townsfolk would have reorganized fairly fast, and there was no obvious way of winning the consequent twin confrontations at both ends of Main Street. So he avoided them altogether. He hammered the deputy's old truck across the rough ground and navigated by the glow of the fire to his right. It looked to be going strong. In his experience brick buildings always burned well. The contents went first, and then the floors and the ceilings, and then the roof, with the outer walls holding up and forming a tall chimney to enhance the air flow. And when the walls finally went, the collapse blasted sparks and embers all over the place, to start new fires. Sometimes a whole city block could be taken out by one cigarette and one book of matches.

He skirted the town on a radius he judged to be about four miles and then he shadowed the road back east a hundred yards out in the dirt. When the clock in his head hit midnight he figured he was less than a mile short of the line. He veered right and bounced up on to the tarred pebbles and finished the trip like a normal driver. He thumped over the line and Hope's thick blacktop made the ride go suddenly quiet.

Vaughan was waiting a hundred yards ahead.

She was parked on the left shoulder with her lights off. He slowed and held his arm out his window in a reassuring wave. She put her arm out her own window, hand extended, fingers spread, an answering gesture. Or a traffic signal. He coasted and feathered the brakes and the steering and came to a stop with his fingertips touching hers. To him the contact felt one-third like a mission-accomplished high-five, one-third like an expression of relief to be out of the lions' den again, and one-third just plain good. He didn't know what it felt like to her. She gave no indication. But she left her hand there a second longer than she needed to.

'Whose truck?' she asked.

'The senior deputy's,' Reacher said. 'His name is Underwood. He's very sick.'

'With what?'

'He said I did it to him.'

'Did you?'

'I gave a sick man a couple of contusions, which I don't feel great about. But I didn't give him diarrhoea or blisters or sores and I didn't make his hair fall out.'

'So is it TCE?'

'Thurman said not.'

'You believe him?'

'Not necessarily.'

Vaughan held up a plastic bottle of water.

Reacher said, 'I'm not thirsty.'

'Good,' Vaughan said. 'This is a sample. Tap water, from my kitchen. I called a friend of a friend of David's. He knows a guy who works at the state lab in Colorado Springs. He told me to take this in for testing. And to find out how much TCE Thurman actually uses.'

'The tank holds five thousand gallons.'

'But how often does it get used up and re-filled?'

'I don't know.'

'How can we find out?'

'There's a purchasing office, probably full of paperwork.'

'Can we get in there?'

'Maybe.'

Vaughan said, 'Go dump that truck back over the line. I'll drive you to town. We'll take a dough-nut break.'

So Reacher checked the mirror and backed up uncertainly until he felt the change of surface. He steered the truck backward into the sand and left it there, keys in. Way behind him he could see a faint red glow on the horizon. Despair was still on fire. He didn't say anything about it. He just walked forward and crossed the line again and climbed in next to Vaughan.

'You smell of cigarettes,' she said.

'I found one,' he said. 'I smoked a half inch, for old times' sake.'

'They give you cancer, too.'

'I heard that. You believe it?'

'Yes,' she said. 'I do, absolutely.'

328

She took off east, at a moderate speed, one hand on the wheel and the other in her lap. He asked her, 'How's your day going?'

'A gum wrapper blew across the street in front of me. Right there in my headlights. Violation of the anti-littering ordinance. That's about as exciting as it gets in Hope.'

'Did you call Denver? About Maria?'

She nodded.

'The old man picked her up,' she said. 'By the hardware store. He confirmed her name. He knew a lot about her. They talked for half an hour.'

'Half an hour? How? It's less than a twenty-minute drive.'

'He didn't let her out in Despair. She wanted to go to the MP base.'

They got to the diner at twenty minutes past midnight. The college-girl waitress was on duty. She smiled when she saw them walk in together, as if some kind of a long-delayed but pleasant inevitability had finally taken place. She looked to be about twenty years old, but she was grinning away like a smug old matchmaker from an ancient village. Reacher felt like there was a secret he wasn't privy to. He wasn't sure that Vaughan understood it either.

They sat opposite each other in the back booth. They didn't order doughnuts. Reacher ordered coffee and Vaughan ordered juice, a blend of three exotic fruits, none of which Reacher had ever encountered before.

'You're very healthy,' he said.

'I try.'

'Is your husband in the hospital? With cancer, from smoking?'

She shook her head.

'No,' she said. 'He isn't.'

Their drinks arrived and they sipped them in silence for a moment and then Reacher asked, 'Did the old guy know why Maria wanted to go to the MPs?'

'She didn't tell him. But it's a weird destination, isn't it?'

'Very,' Reacher said. 'It's an active-service forward operating base. Visitors wouldn't be permitted. Not even if she knew one of the grunts. Not even if one of the grunts was her brother or her sister.'

'Combat MPs use women grunts?'

'Plenty.'

'So maybe she's one of them. Maybe she was reporting back on duty, after furlough.'

'Then why would she have booked two more nights in the motel and left all her stuff there?'

'I don't know. Maybe she was just checking something.'

'She's too small for a combat MP.'

'They have a minimum size?'

'The army always has had, overall. These days, I'm not sure what it is. But even if she squeezed in, they'd put her somewhere else, covertly.'

'You sure?'

'No question. Plus she was too quiet and timid. She wasn't military.'

'So what did she want from the MPs? And why isn't she back yet?'

'Did the old guy actually see her get in?'

'Sure,' Vaughan said. 'He waited, like an old-fashioned gentleman.'

'Therefore a better question would be, if they let her in, what did they want from her?'

Vaughan said, 'Something to do with espionage.'

Reacher shook his head. 'I was wrong about that. They're not worried about espionage. They'd have the plant buttoned up, east and west, probably with a presence inside, or at least on the gates.'

'So why are they there?'

'They're guarding the truck route. Which means they're worried about theft, of something that would need a truck to haul away. Something heavy, too heavy for a regular car.'

'Something too heavy for a small plane, then.'

Reacher nodded. 'But that plane is involved somehow. This morning I was barging around and therefore they had to shut down the secret operation for a spell, and tonight the plane didn't fly. I didn't hear it, and I found it later, right there in its hangar.'

'You think it only flies when they've been working on the military stuff?'

'I know for sure it didn't when they hadn't been, so maybe the obverse is true too.'

'Carrying something?'

'I assume.'

'In or out?'

'Maybe both. Like trading.'

'Secrets?'

'Maybe.'

'People? Like Lucy Anderson's husband?'

Reacher drained his mug. Shook his head. 'I can't make that work. There's a logic problem with it. Almost mathematical.'

'Try me,' Vaughan said. 'I did four years of college.'

'How long have you got?'

'I'd love to catch whoever dropped the gum wrapper. But I could put that on the back burner, if you like.'

Reacher smiled. 'There are three things going on over there. The military contract, plus something else, plus something else again.'

'OK,' Vaughan said. She moved the salt shaker, the pepper shaker, and the sugar shaker to the centre of the table. 'Three things.'

Reacher moved the salt shaker to one side, immediately. 'The military contract is what it is. Nothing controversial. Nothing to worry about, except the possibility that someone might steal something heavy. And that's the MPs' problem. They're straddling the road, they've got six Humvees, they've got thirty miles of empty space for a running battle, they can stop any truck they need to. No special vigilance required from the townspeople. No reason for the townspeople to get excited at all.'

'But?'

Reacher cupped his hands and put his left around the pepper shaker and his right around the sugar shaker. 'But the townspeople *are* excited about something. *All* of them. They *are* vigilant. Today they all turned out in defence of something.'

332

'What something?'

'I have no clue.' He held up the sugar shaker, in his right hand. 'But it's the bigger of the two unknowns. Because everyone is involved in it. Let's call it the right hand, as in the right hand doesn't know what the left is doing.'

'What's the left hand?'

Reacher held up the pepper shaker, in his left hand. 'It's smaller. It involves a subset of the population. A small, special sub-group. Everyone knows about the sugar, most *don't* know about the pepper, a few know about both the sugar *and* the pepper.'

'And we don't know about either.'

'But we will.'

'How does this relate to Lucy Anderson's husband not being taken out by plane?'

Reacher held up the sugar shaker. A large glass item, in his right hand. 'Thurman flies the plane. Thurman is the town boss. Thurman directs the larger unknown. It couldn't happen any other way. And if the Anderson guy had been a part of it, everyone would have been aware. Including the town cops and Judge Gardner. Thurman would have made sure of that. Therefore Lucy Anderson would not have been arrested, and she would not have been thrown out as a vagrant.'

'So Thurman's doing something, and everyone is helping, but a few are also working on something else behind his back?'

Reacher nodded. 'And that something the few are working on behind his back involves these young guys.'

'And the young guys either get through or they

don't, depending on who they bump into first, the many right-hand people or the few left-hand people.'

'Exactly. And there's a new one now. Name of Rogers, just arrested, but I didn't see him.'

'Rogers? I've heard that name before.'

'Where?'

'I don't know.'

'Wherever, he was one of the unlucky ones.'

'The odds will always be against them.'

'Exactly.'

'Which was Ramirez's problem.'

'No, Ramirez didn't bump into anyone,' Reacher said. 'I checked the records. He was neither arrested nor helped.'

'Why? What made him different?'

'Great question,' Reacher said.

'What's the answer?'

'I don't know.'

FORTY-EIGHT

Reacher got more coffee and Vaughan got more juice. The clock in Reacher's head hit one in the morning and the clock on the diner's wall followed it a minute later. Vaughan looked at her watch and said, 'I better get back in the saddle.'

Reacher said, 'OK.'

'Go get some sleep.'

'OK.'

'Will you come with me to Colorado Springs? To the lab, with the water sample?'

'When?'

'Tomorrow, today, whatever it is now.'

'I don't know anything about water.'

'That's why we're going to the lab.'

'What time?'

'Leave at ten?'

'That's early for you.'

'I don't sleep anyway. And this is the end of my pattern. I'm off duty for four nights now. Ten on, four off. And we should leave early because it's a long ride, there and back.'

'Still trying to keep me out of trouble? Even on your downtime?'

'I've given up on keeping you out of trouble.'

'Then why?'

Vaughan said, 'Because I'd like your company. That's all.'

She put four bucks on the table for her juice. She put the salt and the pepper and the sugar back where they belonged. Then she slid out of the booth and walked away and pushed through the door and headed for her car.

Reacher showered and was in bed by two o'clock in the morning. He slept dreamlessly and woke up at eight. He showered again and walked the length of the town to the hardware store. He spent five minutes looking at ladders on the sidewalk, and then he went inside and found the rails of pants and shirts and chose a new one of each. This time he went for darker colours and a different brand. Pre-washed, and therefore softer. Less durable in the long term, but he wasn't interested in the long term.

He changed in his motel room and left his old stuff folded on the floor next to the trash can. Maybe the maid had a needy male relative his size. Maybe she would know how to launder things so they came out at least marginally flexible. He stepped out of his room and saw that Maria's bathroom light was on. He walked to the office. The clerk was on her stool. Behind her shoulder, the hook for Maria's room had no key on it. The clerk saw him looking and said, 'She came back this morning.'

He asked, 'What time?'

'Very early. About six.'

'Did you see how she got here?'

The woman looked both ways and lowered her voice and said, 'In an armoured car. With a soldier.'

'An armoured car?'

'Like you see on the news.'

Reacher said, 'A Humvee.'

The woman nodded. 'Like a jeep. But with a roof. The soldier didn't stay. Which I'm glad about. I'm no prude, but I couldn't permit a thing like that. Not here.'

'Don't worry,' Reacher said. 'She already has a boyfriend.'

Or had, he thought.

The woman said, 'She's too young to be fooling around with soldiers.'

'Is there an age limit?'

'There ought to be.'

Reacher paid his bill and walked back down the row, doing the math. According to the old man's telephone testimony, he had let Maria out at the MP base around eight thirty the previous morning. She had arrived back in a Humvee at six. The Humvee wouldn't have detoured around the Interstates. It would have come straight through Despair, which was a thirty-minute drive, max. Therefore she had been held for twenty-one hours. Therefore her problem was outside of the FOB's local jurisdiction. She had been locked in a room and her story had been passed up the chain of command. Phone tag, voice mails, secure telexes. Maybe a conference call. Eventually, a decision taken elsewhere, release, the offer of a ride home.

Sympathy, but no help.

No help about what?

He stopped outside her door and listened. The shower wasn't running. He waited one minute in case she was towelling off and a second minute in case she was dressing. Then he knocked. A third minute later she opened the door. Her hair was slick with water. The weight gave it an extra inch of length. She was dressed in jeans and a blue T-shirt. No shoes. Her feet were tiny, like a child's. Her toes were straight. She had been raised by conscientious parents, who had cared about appropriate footwear.

'You OK?' he asked her, which was a dumb question. She didn't look OK. She looked small and tired and lost and bewildered.

She didn't answer.

He said, 'You went to the MP base, asking about Raphael.'

She nodded.

He said, 'You felt they could help you, but they didn't.'

She nodded.

He said, 'They told you it was Despair PD business.'

She didn't answer.

He said, 'Maybe I could help you. Or maybe the Hope PD could. You want to tell me what it's all about?'

She said nothing.

He said, 'I can't help you unless I understand the problem.'

She shook her head.

'I can't tell you,' she said. 'I can't tell anyone.'

338

The way she said the word *can't* was definitive. Not surly or angry or moody or plaintive, but calm, considered, mature, and ultimately just plain informative. As if she had looked at a whole bunch of options, and boiled them down to the only one that was viable. As if a world of trouble was surely inevitable, if she opened her mouth.

She couldn't tell anyone.

Simple as that.

'OK,' Reacher said. 'Hang in there.'

He walked away, to the diner, and had breakfast.

He guessed Vaughan planned to pick him up at the motel, so at five to ten he was sitting in the plastic lawn chair outside his door. She showed up three minutes past the hour, in a plain black Crown Vic. Dull paint, worn by time and trouble. An unmarked squad car, like a detective would drive. She stopped close to him and buzzed the window down. He said, 'Did you get promoted?'

'It's my watch commander's ride. He took pity on me and loaned it out. Since you got my truck smashed up.'

'Did you find the litterbug?'

'No. And it's a serial crime now. I saw the silver foil later. Technically that's two separate offences.'

'Maria is back. The MPs brought her home early this morning.'

'Is she saying anything?'

'Not a word.' He got out of the chair and walked around the hood and slid in beside her. The car was very plain. Lots of black plastic, lots of mouse-fur upholstery of an indeterminate colour. It felt like a beat-up rental. The front was full of police gear. Radios, a laptop on a bracket, a video camera on the dash, a hard disc recorder, a red bubble light on a curly cord. But there was no security screen between the front and the rear, and therefore the seat was going to rack all the way back. It was going to be comfortable. Plenty of leg room. The water sample was on the rear seat. Vaughan was looking good. She was in old blue jeans and a white Oxford shirt, the neck open two buttons and the sleeves rolled to her elbows.

She said, 'You've changed.'

'In what way?'

'Your clothes, you idiot.'

'New this morning,' he said. 'From the hardware store.'

'Nicer than the last lot.'

'Don't get attached to them. They'll be gone soon.'

'What's the longest you ever wore a set of clothes?'

'Eight months,' Reacher said. 'Desert BDUs, during Gulf War One. Never took them off. We had all kinds of supply snafus. No spares, no pyjamas.'

'You were in the Gulf, the first time?'

'Beginning to end.'

'How was it?'

'Hot.'

Vaughan pulled out of the motel lot and headed north to First Street. Turned left, east, towards Kansas. Reacher said, 'We're taking the long way around?'

'I think it would be better.'

Reacher said, 'Me too.'

It was an obvious cop car and the roads were empty and Vaughan averaged ninety most of the way, charging head-on towards the mountains. Reacher knew Colorado Springs a little. Fort Carson was there, which was a major army presence, but it was really more of an air force town. Aside from that, it was a pleasant place. Scenery was pretty, the air was clean, it was often sunny, the view of Pikes Peak was usually spectacular. The downtown area was neat and compact. The state lab was in a stone government building. It was a satellite operation, an offshoot of the main facility in Denver, the capital. Water was a big deal all over Colorado. There wasn't much of it. Vaughan handed over her bottle and filled out a form and a guy wrapped the form around the bottle and secured it with a rubber band. Then he carried it away, ceremoniously, like that particular quart had the power to save the world, or destroy it. He came back and told Vaughan that she would be notified of the results by phone, and to please let the lab know some figures for Despair's total TCE consumption. He explained that the state used a rough rule-of-thumb formula, whereby a certain percentage of evaporation could be assumed, and a further percentage of absorption by the ground could be relied upon, so that what really mattered was how much was running off and how deep an aquifer was. The state knew the depth of Halfway County's aquifer to the inch, so the only variable would be the exact amount of TCE heading down towards it.

'What are the symptoms?' Vaughan asked. 'If it's there already?'

The lab guy glanced at Reacher.

'Prostate cancer,' he said. 'That's the early warning. Men go first.'

They got back in the car. Vaughan was distracted. A little vague. Reacher didn't know what was on her mind. She was a cop and a conscientious member of her community, but clearly she was worrying about more than a distant chemical threat to her water table. He wasn't sure why she had asked him to travel with her. They hadn't spoken much. He wasn't sure that his company was doing her any good at all.

She pulled out off the kerb and drove a hundred yards on a tree-lined street and stopped at a light at a T-junction. Left was west and right was east. The light turned green and she didn't move. She just sat there, gripping the wheel, looking left, looking right, as if she couldn't choose. A guy honked behind her. She glanced in the mirror and then she glanced at Reacher.

She said, 'Will you come with me to visit my husband?'

FORTY-NINE

Vaughan turned left into the hills and then left again and headed south, following a sign for Pueblo. Years before, Reacher had travelled the same road. Fort Carson lay between Colorado Springs and Pueblo, south of one and north of the other, bulked a little ways west of the main drag.

'You OK with this?' Vaughan asked him.

'I'm fine with it.'

'But?'

'It's an odd request,' he said.

She didn't answer.

'And it's an odd word,' he said. 'You could have said, come and meet my husband. Or see him. But you said visit. And who gets visitors? You already told me he isn't in jail. Or in the hospital. So where is he? In a rooming house, working away from home? Permanently on duty somewhere? Locked in his sister's attic?'

'I didn't say he wasn't in the hospital,' Vaughan said. 'I said he didn't have cancer from smoking.'

She forked right, away from an I-25 on-ramp, and used a state four-lane that seemed way too wide for the traffic it was getting. She drove a mile between green hills and turned left through a grove of pines on a worn grey road that had no centre line. There was no wire and no painted sign, but Reacher was sure the land on both sides was owned by the army. He knew there were thousands of spare acres beyond the northern tip of Fort Carson, requisitioned decades ago at the height of hot or cold war fever, and never really used for much. And what he was seeing out the window looked exactly like Department of Defense property. It looked the same everywhere. Nature, made uniform. A little sullen, a little half-hearted, somewhat beaten down, neither raw nor developed.

Vaughan slowed after another mile and made a right into a half-hidden driveway. She passed between two squat brick pillars. The bricks were smooth tan items and the mortar was yellow. Standard army issue, back in the middle fifties. The pillars had hinges but no gates. Twenty yards farther on was a modern billboard on thin metal legs. The billboard had some kind of a corporate logo and the words *Olympic TBI Center* on it. Twenty yards later another billboard said: *Authorized Personnel Only*. Twenty yards after that the driveway's shoulders had been mowed, but not recently. The mown section ran on straight for a hundred yards and led to a carriage circle in front of a group of low brick buildings. Army buildings, long ago deemed surplus to requirements and sold off. Reacher recognized the architecture. Brick and tile, green metal window casements, green tubular handrails, radiused corners built back when

344

chamfered edges had looked like the future. In the centre of the carriage circle was a round patch of weedy dirt, where once a CO would have been proud of a rose garden. The change of ownership was confirmed by a repeat of the first billboard, next to the main entrance hall: the corporate logo, plus *Olympic TBI Center* again.

A section of lawn on the right had been hacked out and replaced by gravel. There were five cars on it, all of them with local plates, none of them new or clean. Vaughan parked the Crown Vic on the end of the line and shut it down, first the shifter, then the brake, then the key, a slow and deliberate sequence. She sat back in her seat and dropped her hands to her lap.

'Ready?' she asked.

'For what?' he said.

She didn't answer. Just opened her door and swivelled on the sticky mouse-fur seat and climbed out. Reacher did the same on his side. They walked together to the entrance. Three steps up, through the doors, on to the kind of mottled green tile floor Reacher had walked a thousand times before. The place was recognizably mid-fifties U.S. Army. It felt abandoned and run down and there were new mandated smoke detectors sloppily wired through exposed plastic conduits, but otherwise it couldn't have changed much. There was an oak hutch on the right, where once a busy sergeant would have sat. Now it was occupied by a mess of what looked like medical case notes and a civilian in a grey sweatshirt. He was a thin sullen man of about forty. He had unwashed black hair worn a little too long. He said, 'Hello, Mrs

Vaughan.' Nothing more. No warmth in his voice. No enthusiasm.

Vaughan nodded but didn't look at the guy or reply. She just walked to the back of the hall and turned left into a large room that in the old days might have served any one of a number of different purposes. It might have been a waiting room, or a reception lounge, or an officers' club. Now it was different. It was dirty and badly maintained. Stained walls, dull floor, dust all over it. Cobwebs on the ceiling. It smelled faintly of antiseptic and urine. It had big red waist-high panic buttons wired through more plastic conduit. It was completely empty, except for two men strapped into wheelchairs. Both men were young, both were entirely slack and still, both had open mouths, both had empty gazes focused a thousand miles in front of them.

Both had shaved heads, and misshapen skulls, and wicked scars.

Reacher stood still.

Looked at the panic buttons.

Thought back to the medical files.

He was in a clinic.

He looked at the guys in the wheelchairs.

He was in a residential home.

He looked at the dust and the dirt.

He was in a dumping ground.

He thought back to the initials on the billboard.

TBI.

Traumatic Brain Injury.

He moved on. Vaughan had moved on too, into a corridor. He caught up with her, halfway along its length.

'Your husband had an accident?' he said.

'Not exactly,' she said.

'Then what?'

'Figure it out.'

Reacher stopped again.

Both men were young.

An old army building, mothballed and then reused.

'War wounds,' he said. 'Your husband is military. He went to Iraq.'

Vaughan nodded as she walked.

'National Guard,' she said. 'His second tour. They extended his deployment. Didn't armour his Humvee. He was blown up by an IED in Ramadi.'

She turned into another corridor. It was dirty. Dust balls had collected against the baseboards. Some were peppered with mouse droppings. The light bulbs were dim, to save money on electricity. Some were out and had not been changed, to save money on labour.

Reacher asked, 'Is this a VA facility?'

Vaughan shook her head.

'Private contractor,' she said. 'Political connections. A sweetheart deal. Free real estate and big appropriations.'

She stopped at a dull green door. No doubt fifty years earlier it had been painted by a private soldier, in a colour and in a manner specified by the Pentagon, with materials drawn from a quartermaster's stores. Then the private soldier's workmanship had been inspected by an NCO, and the NCO's approval had been validated by an officer's. Since then the door had received no further attention. It had dulled and faded and gotten battered and scratched. Now it had a wax pencil scrawl on it: *D. R. Vaughan*, and a string of digits that might have been his service number, or his case number.

'Ready?' Vaughan asked.

'When you are,' Reacher said.

'I'm never ready,' she said.

She turned the handle and opened the door.

FIFTY

David Robert Vaughan's room was a twelve-foot cube, painted dark green below a narrow cream waist-high band, and light green above. It was warm. It had a small sooty window. It had a green metal cabinet and a green metal footlocker. The footlocker was open and held a single pair of clean pyjamas. The cabinet was stacked with file folders and oversize brown envelopes. The envelopes were old and torn and frayed and held X-ray films.

The room had a bed. It was a narrow hospital cot with locked wheels and a hand-wound tilting mechanism that raised the head at an angle. It was set to a forty-five degree slope. In it, under a tented sheet, leaning back in repose like he was relaxing, was a guy Reacher took to be David Robert Vaughan himself. He was a compact, narrow-shouldered man. The tented sheet made it hard to estimate his size. Maybe five ten, maybe a hundred and eighty pounds. His skin was pink. He had blond stubble on his chin and his cheeks. He had a straight nose and blue eyes. His eyes were wide open.

Part of his skull was missing.

A saucer-sized piece of bone wasn't there. It left a wide hole above his forehead. Like he had been wearing a small cap at a jaunty angle, and someone had cut all around the edge of it with a saw.

His brain was protruding.

It swelled out like an inflated balloon, dark and purple and corrugated. It looked dry and angry. It was draped with a thin man-made membrane that stuck to the shaved skin around the hole. Like cling film.

Vaughan said, 'Hello, David.'

There was no response from the guy in the bed. Four IV lines snaked down towards him and disappeared under the tented sheet. They were fed from four clear plastic bags hung high on chromium stands next to the bed. A colostomy line and a urinary catheter led away to bottles mounted on a low cart parked under the bed. A breathing tube was taped to his cheek. It curved neatly into his mouth. It was connected to a small respirator that hissed and blew with a slow, regular rhythm. There was a clock on the wall above the respirator. Original army issue, from way back. White Bakelite rim, white face, black hands, a firm, quiet, mechanical tick once a second.

Vaughan said, 'David, I brought a friend to see you.'

No response. And there never would be, Reacher guessed. The guy in the bed was completely inert. Not asleep, not awake. Not anything.

Vaughan bent and kissed her husband on the forehead.

Then she stepped over to the cabinet and tugged

an X-ray envelope out of the pile. It was marked *Vaughan D. R.* in faded ink. It was creased and furred. It had been handled many times. She pulled the film out of the envelope and held it up against the light from the window. It was a composite image that showed her husband's head from four different directions. Front, right side, back, left side. White skull, blurred grey brain matter, a matrix of bright pinpoints scattered all through it.

'Iraq's signature injury,' Vaughan said. 'Blast damage to the human brain. Severe physical trauma. Compression, decompression, twisting, shearing, tearing, impact with the wall of the skull, penetration by shrapnel. David got it all. His skull was shattered, and they cut the worst of it away. That was supposed to be a good thing. It relieves the pressure. They give them a plastic plate later, when the swelling goes down. But David's swelling never went down.'

She put the film back in the envelope, and shuffled the envelope back into the pile. She pulled another one out. It was a chest film. White ribs, grey organs, a blinding shape that was clearly someone else's wristwatch, and small bright pinpoints that looked like drops of liquid.

'That's why I don't wear my wedding band,' Vaughan said. 'He wanted to take it with him, on a chain around his neck. The heat melted it and the blast drove it into his lungs.'

She put the film back in the stack.

'He wore it for good luck,' she said.

She butted the paperwork into a neat pile and moved to the foot of the bed. Reacher asked, 'What was he?'

351

'Infantry, assigned to the First Armored Division.'

'And this was IED versus Humvee?'

She nodded. 'An improvised explosive device against a tin can. He might as well have been on foot in his bathrobe. I don't know why they call them *improvised*. They seem pretty damn professional to me.'

'When was this?'

'Almost two years ago.'

The respirator hissed on.

Reacher asked, 'What was his day job?'

'He was a mechanic. For farm equipment, mostly.'

The clock ticked, relentlessly.

Reacher asked, 'What's the prognosis?'

Vaughan said, 'At first it was reasonable, in theory. They thought he would be confused and uncoordinated, you know, and perhaps a little unstable and aggressive, and certainly lacking all his basic life and motor skills.'

'So you moved house,' Reacher said. 'You were thinking about a wheelchair. You bought a one-storey and took the door off the living room. You put three chairs in the kitchen, not four. To leave a space.'

She nodded. 'I wanted to be ready. But he never woke up. The swelling never went away.'

'Why not?'

'Make a fist.'

'A what?'

'Make a fist and hold it up.'

Reacher made a fist and held it up.

Vaughan said, 'OK, your forearm is your spinal

352

cord and your fist is a bump on the end called your brain stem. Some places in the animal kingdom, that's as good as it gets. But humans grew brains. Imagine I scooped out a pumpkin and fitted it over your fist. That's your brain. Imagine the pumpkin goo was kind of bonded with your skin. This is how it was explained to me. I could hit the pumpkin or you could shake it a little and you'd be OK. But imagine suddenly twisting your wrist, very violently. What's going to happen?'

'The bond is going to shear,' Reacher said. 'The pumpkin goo is going to unstick from my skin.'

Vaughan nodded again. 'That's what happened to David's head, apparently. A shearing injury. The very worst kind. His brain stem is OK but the rest of his brain doesn't even know it's there. It doesn't know there's a problem.'

'Will the bond reform?'

'Never. That just doesn't happen. Brains have spare capacity, but neuron cells can't regenerate. This is all he will ever be. He's like a brain-damaged lizard. He's got the IQ of a goldfish. He can't move and he can't see and he can't hear and he can't think.'

Reacher said nothing.

Vaughan said, 'Battlefield medicine is very good now. He was stable and in Germany within thirteen hours. In Korea or Vietnam he would have died at the scene, no question.'

She moved to the head of the bed and laid her hand on her husband's cheek, very gently, very tenderly. Said, 'We think his spinal cord is severed too, as far as we can tell. But that doesn't really matter now, does it?'

353

The respirator hissed and the clock ticked and the IV lines made tiny liquid sounds and Vaughan stood quietly for a spell and then she said, 'You don't shave very often, do you?'

'Sometimes,' Reacher said.

'But you know how?'

'I learned at my daddy's knee.'

'Will you shave David?'

'Don't the orderlies do that?'

'They should, but they don't. And I like him to look decent. It seems like the least I can do.' She took a supermarket carrier bag out of the green metal cabinet. It held men's toiletries. Shaving gel, a half-used pack of disposable razors, soap, a washcloth. Reacher found a bathroom across the hall and stepped back and forth with the wet cloth, soaping the guy's face, rinsing it, wetting it again. He smoothed blue gel over the guy's chin and cheeks and lathered it with his fingertips and then set about using the razor. It was difficult. A completely instinctive sequence of actions when applied to himself became awkward on a third party. Especially on a third party who had a breathing tube in his mouth and a large part of his skull missing.

While he worked with the razor, Vaughan cleaned the room. She had a second supermarket bag in the cabinet that held cloths and sprays and a dustpan and brush. She stretched high and bent low and went through the whole twelve-foot cube very thoroughly. Her husband stared on at a point miles beyond the ceiling and the respirator hissed and blew. Reacher finished up and Vaughan stopped a minute later and stood back and looked.

'Good work,' she said.

'You too. Although you shouldn't have to do that yourself.'

'I know.'

They repacked the supermarket bags and put them away in the cabinet. Reacher asked, 'How often do you come?'

'Not very often,' Vaughan said. 'It's a Zen thing, really. If I visit and he doesn't know I've visited, have I really visited at all? It's self-indulgent to come here just to make myself feel like a good wife. So I prefer to visit him in my memory. He's much more real there.'

'How long were you married?'

'We're still married.'

'I'm sorry. How long?'

'Twelve years. Eight together, then he spent two in Iraq, and the last two have been like this.'

'How old is he?'

'Thirty-four. He could live another sixty years. Me too.'

'Were you happy?'

'Yes and no, like everyone.'

'What are you going to do?'

'Now?'

'Long term.'

'I don't know. People say I should move on. And maybe I should. Maybe I should accept destiny, like Zeno. Like a true Stoic. I feel like that, sometimes. But then I panic and get defensive. I feel, first they do this to him, and now I should divorce him? But he wouldn't know,

355

anyway. So it's back to the Zen thing. What do you think I should do?'

'I think you should take a walk,' Reacher said. 'Right now. Alone. Walking by yourself is always good. Get some fresh air. See some trees. I'll bring the car and pick you up before you hit the four-lane.'

'What are you going to do?'

'I'll find some way to pass the time.'

FIFTY-ONE

Vaughan said goodbye to her husband and she and Reacher walked back along the dirty corridors and through the dismal lounge to the entrance hall. The guy in the grey sweatshirt said, 'Goodbye, Mrs Vaughan.' They walked out to the carriage circle and headed for the car. Reacher leaned against its flank and Vaughan kept on going. He waited until she was small in the distance and then he pushed off the car and headed back to the entrance. Up the steps, in the door. He crossed to the hutch and asked, 'Who's in charge here?'

The guy in the grey sweatshirt said, 'I am, I guess. I'm the shift supervisor.'

Reacher asked, 'How many patients here?'

'Seventeen,' the guy said.

'Who are they?'

'Just patients, man. Whatever they send us.'

'You run this place according to a manual?'

'Sure. It's a bureaucracy, like everywhere.'

'You got a copy of the manual available?'

'Somewhere.'

'You want to show me the part where it says it's

357

OK to keep the rooms dirty and have mouse shit in the corridors?'

The guy blinked and swallowed and said, 'There's no point *cleaning*, man. They wouldn't *know*. How could they? This is the vegetable patch.'

'Is that what you call it?'

'It's what it *is*, man.'

'Wrong answer,' Reacher said. 'This is not the vegetable patch. This is a veterans' clinic. And you're a piece of shit.'

'Hey, lighten up, dude. What's it to you?'

'David Robert Vaughan is my brother.'

'Really?'

'All veterans are my brothers.'

'He's brain dead, man.'

'Are you?'

'No.'

'Then listen up. And listen very carefully. A person less fortunate than yourself deserves the best you can give. Because of duty, and honour, and service. You understand those words? You should do your job right, and you should do it well, simply because you can, without looking for notice or reward. The people here deserve your best, and I'm damn sure their relatives deserve it.'

'Who are you, anyway?'

'I'm a concerned citizen,' Reacher said. 'With a number of options. I could embarrass your corporate parent, I could call the newspapers or the TV, I could come in here with a hidden camera, I could get you fired. But I don't do stuff like that. I offer personal choices instead, face to face. You want to know what your choice is?'

'What?'

'Do what I tell you, with a cheery smile.'

'Or?'

'Or become patient number eighteen.'

The guy said nothing.

Reacher said, 'Stand up.'

'What?'

'On your feet. Now.'

'What?'

Reacher said, 'Stand up, now, or I'll make it so you never stand up again.'

The guy hesitated a beat and got to his feet.

'At attention,' Reacher said. 'Feet together, shoulders back, head up, gaze level, arms straight, hands by your sides, thumbs in line with the seams of your pants.' Some officers of his acquaintance had barked and yelled and shouted. He had always found it more effective to speak low and quiet, enunciating clearly and precisely as if to an idiot child, bearing down with an icy stare. That way he had found the implied menace to be unmistakable. Calm, patient voice, huge physique. The dissonance was striking. It was a case of whatever worked. It had worked then, and it was working now. The guy in the sweatshirt was swallowing hard and blinking and standing in a rough approximation of parade ground order.

Reacher said. 'Your patients are not just whatever they send you. Your patients are people. They served their country with honour and distinction. They deserve your utmost care and respect.'

The guy said nothing.

Reacher said, 'This place is a disgrace. It's filthy and chaotic. So listen up. You're going to get off your skinny ass and you're going to organize your people and you're going to get it cleaned up. Starting right now. I'm going to come back, maybe tomorrow, maybe next week, maybe next month, and if I can't see my face in the floor I'm going to turn you upside down and use you like a mop. Then I'm going to kick your ass so hard your colon is going to get tangled up in your teeth. Are we clear?'

The guy paused and shuffled and blinked. There was silence for a long moment. Then he said, 'OK.'

'With a cheery smile,' Reacher said.

The guy forced a smile.

'Bigger,' Reacher said.

The guy forced dry lips over dry teeth.

'That's good,' Reacher said. 'And you're going to get a haircut, and every day you're going to shower, and every time Mrs Vaughan comes by you're going to stand up and welcome her warmly and you're going to personally escort her to her husband's room, and her husband's room is going to be clean, and her husband is going to be shaved, and the window is going to be sparkling, and the room is going to be full of sunbeams, and the floor is going to be so shiny Mrs Vaughan is going to be in serious danger of slipping over and hurting herself. Are we clear?'

'OK.'

'Are we clear?'

'Yes.'

'Completely?'

'Yes.'

'Crystal?'

360

'Yes.'

'Yes what?'

'Yes, sir.'

'You've got sixty seconds to get started, or I'll break your arm.'

The guy made a phone call while still standing and then used a walkie-talkie and fifty seconds later there were three guys in the hallway. Dead on sixty seconds a fourth guy joined them. A minute later they had buckets and mops out of a maintenance closet and a minute after that the buckets were full of water and all five guys were casting about, as if facing an immense and unfamiliar task. Reacher left them to it. He walked back to the car and set off in pursuit of Vaughan.

He drove slow and caught up with her a mile down the DoD road. She slid in next to him and he drove on, retracing their route, through the pines, through the hills. She said, 'Thank you for coming.'

'No problem,' he said.

'You know why I wanted you to?'

'Yes.'

'Tell me.'

'You wanted someone to understand why you live like you live and do what you do.'

'And?'

'You wanted someone to understand why it's OK to do what you're going to do next.'

'Which is what?'

'Which is entirely up to you. And either way is good with me.'

She said, 'I lied to you before.'

He said, 'I know.'

'Do you?'

He nodded at the wheel. 'You knew about Thurman's military contract. And the MP base. The Pentagon told you all about them, and the Halfway PD too. Makes sense that way. I bet it's right there in your department phone book, in your desk drawer, *M* for military police.'

'It is.'

'But you didn't want to talk about it, which means that it's not just any old military scrap getting recycled there.'

'Isn't it?'

Reacher shook his head. 'It's combat wrecks from Iraq. Has to be. Hence the New Jersey plates on some of the incoming trucks. From the port facilities there. Why would they bypass Pennsylvania and Indiana for regular scrap? And why would they put regular scrap in closed shipping containers? Because Thurman's place is a specialist operation. Secret, miles from nowhere.'

'I'm sorry.'

'Don't be. I understand. You didn't want to talk about it. You didn't even want to think about it. Hence trying to stop me from ever going there. Get over it, you said. Move on. There's nothing to see.'

'There are blown-up Humvees there,' she said. 'They're like monuments to me. Like shrines. To the people who died. Or nearly died.'

Then she said, 'And to the people who should have died.'

*　　*　　*

They drove on, north and east across the low slopes of the mountains, back to I-70, back towards the long loop near the Kansas line. Reacher said, 'It doesn't explain Thurman's taste for secrecy.'

Vaughan said, 'Maybe it's a respect thing with him. Maybe he sees them as shrines, too.'

'Did he ever serve?'

'I don't think so.'

'Did he lose a family member?'

'I don't think so.'

'Anyone sign up from Despair?'

'Not that I heard.'

'So it's not likely to be respect. And it doesn't explain the MPs, either. What's to steal? A Humvee is a car, basically. Armour is plain steel sheet, when it's fitted at all. An M60 wouldn't survive any kind of a blast.'

Vaughan said nothing.

Reacher said, 'And it doesn't explain the airplane.'

Vaughan didn't answer.

Reacher said, 'And nothing explains all these young guys.'

'So you're going to stick around?'

He nodded at the wheel.

'For a spell,' he said. 'Because I think something is about to happen. That crowd impressed me. Would they have that much passion for the beginning of something? Or the middle of something? I don't think so. I think they were all stirred up because they're heading for the end of something.'

FIFTY-TWO

Vaughan sat quiet and Reacher drove all the way back to Hope. He bypassed Despair and came in from the east, the long way around, on the same road the guy in the Grand Marquis had used, way back at the beginning. They hit town at five in the afternoon. The sun was low. Reacher pulled off First Street and headed down to Third, to the motel. He stopped outside the office. Vaughan looked at him enquiringly and he said, 'Something I should have done before.'

They went in together. The nosy clerk was at the counter. Behind her, three keys were missing from their hooks. Reacher's own, for room twelve, plus Maria's, room eight, plus one for the woman with the large underwear, room four.

Reacher said, 'Tell me about the woman in room four.'

The clerk looked at him and paused a second, like she was gathering her thoughts, like she was under pressure to assemble an accurate capsule biography. Like she was in court, on the witness stand.

'She's from California,' she said. 'She's been

here five days. She paid cash for a week.'

Reacher said, 'Anything else?'

'She's a fuller-figured person.'

'Age?'

'Young. Maybe twenty-five or six.'

'What's her name?'

The clerk said, 'Mrs Rogers.'

Back in the car Vaughan said, 'Another one. But a weird one. Her husband wasn't arrested until yesterday, but she's been here five whole days? What does that mean?'

Reacher said, 'It means our hypothesis is correct. My guess is they were on the road together up until five days ago, he found the right people in Despair and went into hiding, she came directly here to wait it out, then he got flushed out by the mass mobilization yesterday and bumped into the wrong people and got picked up. The whole town was turned upside down. Every rock was turned over. He was noticed.'

'So where is he now?'

'He wasn't in a cell. So maybe he got back with the right people again.'

Vaughan said, 'I knew I had heard the name. His wife came in with the supermarket delivery guy. He drives in from Topeka, Kansas, every few days. He gave her a ride. He mentioned it to me. He told me her name.'

'Truck drivers check in with you?'

'Small towns. No secrets. Maria came in the same way. That's how I knew about her.'

'How did Lucy Anderson come in?'

Vaughan paused a beat.

365

'I don't know,' she said. 'I never heard of her before the Despair PD dumped her at the line. She wasn't here before.'

'So she came in from the west.'

'I guess some of them do. Some from the east, some from the west.'

'Which raises a question, doesn't it? Maria came in from the east, from Kansas, but she asked the old guy in the green car to let her out at the MP base west of Despair. How did she even know it was there?'

'Maybe Lucy Anderson told her. She would have seen it.'

'I don't think they talked at all.'

'Then maybe Ramirez told her about it. Maybe on the phone to Topeka. He came in from the west and saw it.'

'But why would he notice it? Why would he care? Why would it be a topic of conversation with his girlfriend?'

'I don't know.'

Reacher asked, 'Is your watch commander a nice guy?'

'Why?'

'Because he better be. We need to borrow his car again.'

'When?'

'Later tonight.'

'Later than what?'

'Than whatever.'

'How much later?'

'Eight hours from now.'

Vaughan said, 'Eight hours is good.'

Reacher said, 'First we're going shopping.'

*   *   *

They got to the hardware store just as it was closing. The old guy in the brown coat was clearing his sidewalk display. He had wheeled the leaf blowers inside and was starting in on the barrows. The rest of the stuff was all still in position. Reacher went in and bought a slim flashlight and two batteries and a two-foot wrecking bar from the old guy's wife. Then he went back out and bought the trick stepladder that opened to eight different positions. For storage or transport it folded into a neat package about four feet long and a foot and a half wide. It was made of aluminum and plastic and was very light. It fit easily on the Crown Vic's rear bench.

Vaughan invited him over for dinner, at eight o'clock. She was very formal about it. She said she needed the intervening two hours to prepare. Reacher spent the time in his room. He took a nap, and then he shaved and showered and cleaned his teeth. And dressed. His clothes were new, but his underwear was past its prime, so he ditched it. He put on his pants and his shirt and raked his fingers through his hair and checked the result in the mirror and deemed it acceptable. He had no real opinion about his appearance. It was what it was. He couldn't change it. Some people liked it, and some people didn't.

He walked two blocks from Third to Fifth, and turned east. It was full dark. Fifty yards from Vaughan's house, he couldn't see the watch commander's car. Either it was on the driveway, or Vaughan had given it back. Or gotten an emergency call. Or changed her plans for the evening. Then from thirty yards away, he saw the car right there on the kerb. A hole in the darkness. Dull glass. Black paint, matte with age. Invisible in the gloom.

Perfect.

He walked through the plantings on her stepping-stone path and touched the bell. *The average delay at a suburban door in the middle of the evening, about twenty seconds*. Vaughan got there in nine flat. She was in a black knee-length sleeveless A-line dress, and black low-heel shoes, like ballet slippers. She was freshly showered. She looked young and full of energy.

She looked stunning.

He said, 'Hello.'

She said, 'Come in.'

The kitchen was full of candlelight. The table was set with two chairs and two places and an open bottle of wine and two glasses. Aromas were coming from the stove. Two appetizers were standing on the counter. Lobster meat, avocado, pink grapefruit segments, on a bed of lettuce.

She said, 'The main course isn't ready. I screwed up the timing. It's something I haven't made for a while.'

'Three years,' Reacher said.

'Longer,' she said.

'You look great,' he said.

'Do I?'

'The prettiest view in Colorado.'

'Better than Pikes Peak?'

'Considerably. You should be on the front of the guide book.'

368

'You're flattering me.'

'Not really.'

She said, 'You look good, too.'

'That's flattery for sure.'

'No, you clean up well.'

'I try my best.'

She asked, 'Should we be doing this?'

He said, 'I think so.'

'Is it fair to David?'

'David never came back. He never lived here. He doesn't know.'

'I want to see your scar again.'

'Because you're wishing David had come back with one. Instead of what he got.'

'I guess.'

Reacher said, 'We were both lucky. I know soldiers. I've been around them all my life. They fear grotesque wounds. That's all. Amputations, mutilations, burns. I'm lucky because I didn't get one, and David is lucky because he doesn't know he did.'

Vaughan said nothing.

Reacher said, 'And we're both lucky because we both met you.'

Vaughan said, 'Show me the scar.'

Reacher unbuttoned his shirt and slipped it off. Vaughan hesitated a second and then touched the ridged skin, very gently. Her fingertips were cool and smooth. They burned him, like electricity.

'What was it?' she asked.

'A truck bomb in Beirut.'

'Shrapnel?'

'Part of a man who was standing closer.'

'That's awful.'

'For him. Not for me. Metal might have killed me.'

'Was it worth it?'

Reacher said, 'No. Of course not. It hasn't been worth it for a long time.'

'How long a time?'

'Since nineteen forty-five.'

'Did David know that?'

'Yes,' Reacher said. 'He knew. I know soldiers. There's nothing more realistic than a soldier. You can try, but you can't bullshit them. Not even for a minute.'

'But they keep on showing up.'

'Yes, they do. They keep on showing up.'

'Why?'

'I don't know. Never have.'

'How long were you in the hospital?'

'A few weeks, that's all.'

'As bad a place as David is in?'

'Much worse.'

'Why are the hospitals so bad?'

'Because deep down to the army a wounded soldier who can't fight any more is garbage. So we depend on civilians, and civilians don't care either.'

Vaughan put her hand flat against his scar and then slid it around his back. She did the same with her other hand, on the other side. She hugged his waist and held the flat of her cheek against his chest. Then she raised her head and craned her neck and he bent down and kissed her. She tasted of warmth and wine and toothpaste. She smelled like soap and clean skin and delicate fragrance. Her hair was soft. Her eyes were closed. He ran his tongue along the row of unfamiliar teeth and found her tongue. He cradled her head with one hand and put the other low on her back.

A long, long kiss.

She came up for air.

'We should do this,' she said.

'We are doing it,' he said.

'I mean, it's OK to do this.'

'I think so,' he said again. He could feel the end of her zipper with the little finger of his right hand. The little finger of his left hand was down on the swell of her ass.

'Because you're moving on,' she said.

'Two days,' he said. 'Three, max.'

'No complications,' she said. 'Not like it might be permanent.'

'I can't do permanent,' he said.

He bent and kissed her again. Moved his hand and caught the tag of her zipper and pulled it down. She was naked under the dress. Warm, and soft, and smooth, and lithe, and fragrant. He stooped and scooped her up, one arm under her knees and the other under her shoulders. He carried her down the hallway, to where he imagined the bedrooms must be, kissing her all the way. Two doors. Two rooms. One smelled unused, one smelled like her. Her carried her in and put her down and her dress slipped from her shoulders and fell. They kissed some more and her hands tore at the button on his pants. A minute later they were in her bed.

Afterwards, they ate, first the appetizer, then pork cooked with apples and spices and brown sugar and white wine. For dessert, they went back to bed. At midnight, they showered together. Then they dressed, Reacher in his pants and shirt, Vaughan in black jeans and a black sweater and black sneakers and a slim black leather belt.

Nothing else.

'No gun?' Reacher asked.

'I don't carry my gun off duty,' she said.

'OK,' he said.

At one o'clock, they went out.

FIFTY-THREE

Vaughan drove. She insisted on it. It was her watch commander's car. Reacher was happy to let her. She was a better driver than him. Much better. Her panic 180 had impressed him. Backward to forward, at full speed. He doubted if he could have done it. He figured if he had been driving the mob would have caught them and torn them apart.

'Won't they be there again?' Vaughan asked.

'Possible,' he said. 'But I doubt it. It's late, on the second night. And I told Thurman I wouldn't be back. I don't think it will be like yesterday.'

'Why would Thurman believe you?'

'He's religious. He's accustomed to believing things that comfort him.'

'We should have planned to take the long way around.'

'I'm glad we didn't. It would have taken four hours. It wouldn't have left time for dinner.'

She smiled and they took off, north to First Street, west towards Despair. There was thick cloud in the sky. No moon. No stars. Pitch black. Perfect. They thumped over the line and a mile before the top of the rise Reacher said, 'It's time to go stealthy. Turn all the lights off.'

Vaughan clicked the headlights off and the world went dark and she braked hard.

'I can't see anything,' she said.

'Use the video camera,' he said. 'Use the night vision.'

'What?'

'Like a video game,' he said. 'Watch the computer screen, not the windshield.'

'Will that work?'

'It's how tank drivers do it.'

She tapped keys and the laptop screen lit up and then stabilized into a pale green picture of the landscape ahead. Green scrub on either side, vivid boulders, a bright ribbon of road spearing into the distance. She took her foot off the brake and crawled forward, her head turned, staring at the thermal image, not the reality. At first she steered uncertainly, her hand-eye coordination disrupted. She drifted left and right and over-corrected. Then she settled in and got the hang of the new technique. She did a quarter-mile perfectly straight, and then she speeded up and did the next quarter a little faster, somewhere between twenty and thirty.

'It's killing me not to glance ahead,' she said. 'It's so automatic.'

'This is good,' Reacher said. 'Stay slow.' He figured that at twenty or thirty there would be almost no engine noise. Just a low purr, and a soft burble from the pipes. There would be surface noise at any speed, from the tyres on the grit, but that would get better closer to town. He leaned left and put his head on her shoulder and watched the screen. The landscape reeled itself in, silent and green and ghostly. The camera had no human reactions. It was just a dumb unblinking eye. It didn't glance left or right or up or down or change focus. They came over the rise and the screen filled with blank cold sky for a second and then the nose of the car dipped down again and they saw the next nine miles laid out in front of them. Green scrub, scattered rocks glowing lighter, the ribbon of road, a tiny flare of heat on the horizon where the embers of the police station were still warm.

Reacher glanced ahead through the windshield a couple of times, but without headlights there was nothing to see. Nothing at all. Just darkness. Which meant that anyone waiting far ahead in the distance was seeing nothing either. Not yet, anyway. He recalled walking back to Hope, stepping over the line, not seeing Vaughan's cruiser at all. And that was a newer car, shinier, with white doors and polished reflectors in the light bar on the roof. He hadn't seen it. But she had seen him. *I saw you half a mile away*, she had said. *A little green speck*. He had seen himself on the screen afterwards, a luminous sliver in the dark, getting bigger, coming closer.

Very fancy, he had said.

Homeland Security money, she had replied. *Got to spend it on something*.

He stared at the screen, watching for little green specks. The car prowled onward, slow and steady, like a black submarine loose in deep water. Two miles. Four. Still nothing ahead. Six miles. Eight.

Nothing to see, nothing to hear, except the idling motor and the squelching tyres and Vaughan's tense breathing as she gripped the wheel and squinted sideways at the laptop screen.

'We must be getting close,' she whispered.

He nodded, on her shoulder. The screen showed buildings maybe a mile ahead. The gas station hut, slightly warmer than its surroundings. The dry goods store, with daytime heat trapped in its brick walls. A background glow from the downtown blocks. A pale blur in the air a little ways south and west, above where the police station had been.

No little green specks.

He said, 'This is where they were yesterday.'

She said, 'So where are they now?'

She slowed a little and drifted onward. The screen held steady. Geography and architecture, nothing more. Nothing moving.

'Human nature,' Reacher said. 'They got all pumped up yesterday and thought they'd gotten rid of us. They don't have the stamina to do it all again.'

'There could be one or two out and about.'

'Possible.'

'They'll call ahead and warn the plant.'

'That's OK,' Reacher said. 'We're not going to the plant. Not yet, anyway.'

They drifted on, slow and dark and silent. They passed the vacant lot and the abandoned motor court. Both barely showed up on the screen. Thermally they were just parts of the landscape. The gas station and the household goods store shone brighter. Beyond them the other blocks glowed mid-green. There were window-sized patches of brighter colour, and heat was leaking from roofs with imperfect insulation. But there were no pinpoints of light. No little green specks. No crowds, no small groups of shuffling people, no lone sentries.

Not dead ahead, anyway.

The camera's fixed angle was useless against the cross streets. It showed their mouths to a depth of about five feet. That was all. Reacher stared sideways into the darkness as they rolled past each opening. Saw nothing. No flashlights, no match flares, no lighter sparks, no cigarette coals glowing red. The tyre noise had dropped away to almost nothing. Main Street was worn down to the tar. No more pebbles. Vaughan was holding her breath. Her foot was feather light on the pedal. The car rolled onward, a little faster than walking, a lot slower than running.

Two green specks stepped out ahead.

They were maybe a quarter of a mile away, at the west end of Main Street. Two figures, emerging from a cross street. A foot patrol. Vaughan braked gently and came to a stop, halfway through town. Six blocks behind her, six ahead.

'Can they see us?' she whispered.

'I think they're facing away,' Reacher said.

'Suppose they're not?'

'They can't see us.'

'There are probably more behind us.'

Reacher turned and stared through the rear window. Saw nothing. Just pitch black night. He said, 'We can't see them, they can't see us. Laws of physics.'

The screen lit up with a white flare. Cone-shaped. Moving. Sweeping.

'Flashlight,' Reacher said.

'They'll see us.'

'We're too far away. And I think they're shining it west.'

Then they weren't. The screen showed the beam turning through a complete circle, flat and level, like a lighthouse. Its heat burned the screen dead white as it passed. Its light lit up the night mist like fog.

Vaughan asked, 'Did they see us?'

Reacher watched the screen. Thought about the reflectors in the Crown Vic's headlights. Polished metal, like cats' eyes. He said, 'Whoever they are, they're not moving. I don't think they have enough candlepower.'

'What do we do?'

'We wait.'

They waited two minutes, then three, then five. The idling engine whispered. The flashlight beam snapped off. The image on the laptop screen collapsed back to two narrow vertical specks, distant, green, barely moving. There was nothing to see through the rear window. Just empty darkness.

Vaughan said, 'We can't stay here.'

Reacher said, 'We have to.'

The green specks moved, from the centre of the screen to the left-hand edge. Slow, blurred, a ghost trail of luminescence following behind them. Then they disappeared, into a cross street. The screen stabilized. Geography, and architecture.

'Foot patrol,' Reacher said. 'Heading downtown. Maybe worried about fires.'

'Fires?' Vaughan said.

'Their police station burned down last night.'

'Did you have something to do with that?'

'Everything,' Reacher said.

'You're a maniac.'

'Their problem. They're messing with the wrong guy. We should get going.'

'Now?'

'Let's get past them while their backs are turned.'

Vaughan feathered the gas and the car rolled forward. One block. Two. The screen held steady. Geography, and architecture. Nothing more. The tyres were quiet on the battered surface.

'Faster,' Reacher said.

Vaughan speeded up. Twenty miles an hour. Thirty. At forty the car set up a generalized *whoosh* from the engine and the exhaust and the tyres and the air. It seemed painfully loud. But it generated no reaction. Reacher stared left and right into the downtown streets and saw nothing at all. Just black voids. Vaughan gripped the wheel and held her breath and stared at the laptop screen and ten seconds later they were through the town and in open country on the other side.

Four minutes after that, they were approaching the metal plant.

FIFTY-FOUR

They slowed again and kept the lights off. The thermal image showed the sky above the plant to be lurid with heat. It was coming off the dormant furnaces and crucibles in waves as big as solar flares. The metal wall was warm. It showed up as a continuous horizontal band of green. It was much brighter at the southern end. Much hotter, around the secret compound. It glowed like crazy, on the laptop screen.

'Some junkyard,' Reacher said.

'They've been working hard in there,' Vaughan said. 'Unfortunately.'

The acres of parking seemed to be all empty. The personnel gate seemed to be closed. Reacher didn't look at it directly. He was getting better information below the visible spectrum, down in the infra-red.

Vaughan said, 'No sentries?'

Reacher said, 'They trust the wall. As they should. It's a great wall.'

They drove on, slow and dark and silent, past the lot, past the north end of the plant, on to the truck route. Fifty yards later, they stopped. The

380

Tahoes' beaten tracks showed up on the screen, almost imperceptibly lighter than the surrounding scrub. Compacted dirt, no microscopic air holes, therefore no ventilation, therefore slightly slower to cool at the end of the day. Reacher pointed and Vaughan turned the wheel and bumped down off the blacktop. She stared at the screen and got lined up with the ruts and drove on, slower. The car bucked and bounced across the uneven ground. She followed the giant figure-eight. The camera's dumb eye showed nothing ahead except grey-green desert. Then it picked up the fieldstone wall. The residential compound. The stones had trapped some daytime heat. The wall showed up as a low speckled band, like a snake, fifty yards to the right, low and fluid and infinitely long.

Vaughan circled the compound in the Tahoes' tracks, almost all the way around, to a point Reacher judged to be directly behind the airplane barn. They parked and shut down and Reacher switched the interior light to the off position and they opened their doors and climbed out. It was pitch dark. The air felt fresh and cold. The clock in his head showed one thirty in the morning.

Perfect.

They walked fifty yards to the fieldstone wall. Reacher checked back periodically along the way. The black Crown Vic was hard to see after ten yards, very hard after twenty, and invisible after thirty. The wall was faintly warm to the touch. They climbed it easily and dropped down on the other side. The back of the airplane barn was directly ahead of them, huge, looming, darker than the sky. They headed straight for it, past cypress trees and over stony ground. They reached it and followed its perimeter counterclockwise to the front. The barn was standing dark and empty. The plane was out. Reacher waited at the corner and listened hard. Heard nothing. He signalled and Vaughan came up alongside him.

'Step one,' he whispered. 'We just verified that when they work by day, the plane flies by night.'

Vaughan asked, 'What's step two?'

'We verify whether they're bringing stuff in, or taking stuff out, or both.'

'By watching?'

'You bet.'

'How long have we got?'

'About half an hour.'

They stepped into the barn. It was vast and pitch dark. It smelled of oil and gasoline and wood treated with creosote. The floor was beaten dirt. Most of the space was completely empty, ready to receive the returning plane. They felt their way around the walls. Vaughan risked a peek with the flashlight. She clamped its head in her palm and reduced its light to a dull red glow. There were shelves on the walls, loaded with gas cans and quarts of oil and small components boxed up in cardboard. Oil filters, maybe, and air filters. Service items. In the centre of the back wall was a horizontal drum wrapped with thin steel cable. The drum was set in a complex floor-mounted bracket and had an electric motor bolted to its axle. A winch. To its right the walls were lined with more shelves. There were spare tyres. More components. The whole place felt halfway between tidy and chaotic. It was a workspace, nothing more. There were no obvious hiding places. And there were arc lights faintly visible, high above them in the rafters. If they were turned on, the space would be as bright as day.

Vaughan turned off the flashlight.

'No good,' she said.

Reacher nodded in the dark. Led the way back out of the barn, to the taxiway, which was a broad strip of dirt beaten and graded the same as the runway. Either side of it were patches of cultivated garden a hundred yards square, spiky silver bushes and tall slender trees set in gravel. Xeroscaping, near enough the barn for a reasonable view, far enough away that light spill would fall short. Reacher pointed and whispered, 'We'll take one each. Hunker down and don't move until I call you. The runway lights will come on behind you, but don't worry about them. They're set to shine flat, north and south.'

She nodded and he went left and she went right. She was invisible in the gloom after three paces. He made it to the left-hand cultivation and crawled his way to its centre and lay down on his front with bushes either side of him and a tree towering over him. Ahead at an angle he had a good oblique view into the barn. He guessed Vaughan would have a complementary view from the other direction. Together they had the whole thing covered. He pressed himself into the ground and waited.

He heard the plane at five after two in the morning. The single engine, distant, lonely, feathering and blipping. He pictured the landing light as he had seen it before, hanging in the sky, hopping a little, heading down. The sound grew closer but quieter, as Thurman found his glide path and backed off the power. The runway lights came on. They were brighter than Reacher had expected. He felt suddenly vulnerable. He could see his own shadow ahead of him, tangled up with the shadows of the leaves all around him. He craned his neck and looked for Vaughan. Couldn't see her. The engine noise grew louder. Then the hangar lights came on. They were very bright. They threw a hard edge of shadow from the barn's roof that came within six feet of him. He looked ahead and saw the giant from the metal plant standing in the barn, his hand on a light switch, a huge shadow thrown out beyond him, almost close enough for Reacher to touch. Nine hundred yards away to his right the plane's engine blipped and sputtered and he heard a rush of air and felt a tiny thump through the ground as the wheels touched down. The engine noise dropped to a rough idle as the plane coasted and then ramped back up to a roar as it taxied. Reacher heard it coming in behind him, unbearably loud. The ground shook and trembled. The plane came in between the two garden areas and the noise thundered and the propeller wash blasted dust off the ground. It slowed and darted right on its unstable wheelbase and the engine revved hard and it turned a tight circle and came to rest in front of its barn, facing outward. It rocked and shuddered for a second and then the engine shut down and the exhaust popped twice and the propeller jerked to a stop.

Silence came back, like a blanket.

The runway lights died.

Reacher watched.

The plane's right-hand door opened and Thurman eased himself out on to the wing step. Big, bulky, stiff, awkward. He was still in his wool suit. He climbed down and stood for a second and then walked away towards the house.

He was carrying nothing.

No bag, no valise, no briefcase, no kind of a package.

Nothing.

He stepped beyond the light spill and disappeared. The giant from the metal plant hauled the steel cable out of the barn and hooked it to an eye below the tail plane. He walked back to the winch and hit a button and the electric motor whined and the plane was pulled slowly backward into the barn. It stopped in its parked position and the giant unhooked the cable and rewound the winch all the way. Then he squeezed around the wing tip and killed the lights and walked away into the darkness.

Carrying nothing.

He had opened no compartments or cubbies, he had checked no holds or nacelles, and he had retrieved nothing from the cabin.

Reacher waited twenty long minutes, for safety's sake. He had never blundered into trouble through impatience, and he never planned to. When he was sure all was quiet he crawled out from the planted area and crossed the taxiway and called softly to Vaughan. He couldn't see her. She was well concealed. She came up from the darkness at his feet and hugged him briefly. They walked to the darkened barn and ducked under the Piper's wing and regrouped next to the fuselage.

Vaughan said, 'So now we know. They're taking stuff out, not in.'

Reacher said, 'But what, and to where? What kind of range does this thing have?'

'With full tanks? Around seven or eight hundred miles. The state cops had a plane like this, once. It's a question of how fast you fly and how hard you climb.'

'What would be normal?'

'A little over half power might get you eight hundred miles at a hundred and twenty-five knots.'

'He's gone seven hours every night. Give him an hour on the ground, call it six hours in the air, three there, three back, that's a radius of three hundred and seventy-five miles. That's a circle over four hundred thousand square miles in area.'

'That's a lot of real estate.'

'Can we tell anything from the vector he comes in on?'

Vaughan shook her head. 'He has to line up with the runway and land into the wind.'

'There's no big tank of gas here. Therefore he refuels at the other end. Therefore he goes where you can buy gas at ten or eleven at night.'

'Which is a lot of places,' Vaughan said. 'Municipal airfields, flying clubs.'

Reacher nodded. Pictured a map in his head and thought: *Wyoming, South Dakota, Nebraska, Kansas, part of Oklahoma, part of Texas, New*

Mexico, the northeast corner of Arizona, Utah.
Always assuming Thurman didn't just fly an hour
each way and spend five at dinner somewhere
close by in Colorado itself. He said, 'We're going
to have to ask him.'

'Think he'll tell us?'

'Eventually.'

They ducked back under the wing and retraced
their steps behind the barn to the wall. A minute
later they were back in the car, following the
ghostly green image of the Tahoes' ruts counterclockwise, all the way around the metal plant to
the place where Reacher had decided to break in.

FIFTY-FIVE

The white metal wall was blazing hot in the south
and cooler in the north. Vaughan followed it
around and stopped a quarter of the way along
its northern stretch. Then she pulled a tight left
and bounced out of the ruts and nosed slowly
head-on towards the wall and stopped with her
front bumper almost touching it. The front half of
the hood was directly below the wall's horizontal
cylinder. The base of the windshield was about
five feet down and two feet out from the cylinder's
maximum bulge.

Vaughan stayed in her seat and Reacher got
out and dragged the stepladder off the rear
bench. He laid it on the ground and unfolded
it and adjusted it into an upside down L-shape.
Then he estimated by eye and relaxed the angle
a little beyond ninety degrees and locked all the
joints. He lifted it high. He jammed the feet in the
gutter at the base of the Crown Vic's windshield,
where the hood's lip overlapped the wipers. He
let it fall forward, gently. It hit the wall with a
soft metallic noise, aluminum on painted steel.
The long leg of the L came to rest almost vertical.

The short leg lay on top of the cylinder, almost horizontal.

'Back up about a foot,' he whispered.

Vaughan moved the car and the base of the ladder pulled outward to a kinder angle and the top fell forward by a corresponding degree and ended up perfectly flat.

'I love hardware stores,' Reacher said.

Vaughan said, 'I thought this kind of wall was supposed to be impregnable.'

'We're not over it yet.'

'But we're close.'

'Normally they come with guard towers and searchlights, to make sure people don't bring cars and ladders.'

Vaughan shut the engine down and jammed the parking brake on tight. The laptop screen turned itself off and they were forced back to the visible spectrum, which didn't contain anything very visible. Just darkness. Vaughan carried the flashlight and Reacher took the wrecking bar from the trunk. He levered himself up on to the hood and turned and crouched under the swell of the cylinder. He stepped forward to the base of the windshield and turned again and started to climb the ladder. He carried the wrecking bar in his left hand and gripped the upper rungs with his right. The aluminum squirmed against the steel and set up a weird harmonic in the hollows of the wall. He slowed down to quiet the noise and made it to the angle and leaned forward and crawled along the short horizontal leg of the L on his hands and knees. He shuffled off sideways and lay like a starfish on the cylinder's top surface. Six feet in diameter, almost nineteen feet in circumference, effectively flat enough to be feasible, but still curved enough to be dangerous. And the white paint was slick and shiny. He raised his head cautiously and looked around.

He was six feet from where he wanted to be.

The pyramid of old oil drums was barely visible in the dark, two yards to the west. Its top tier was about eight feet south and eighteen inches down from the top of the wall. He swam forward and grabbed the ladder again. It shifted sideways towards him. No resistance. He called down, 'Get on the bottom rung.'

The ladder straightened under Vaughan's weight. He hauled himself towards it and clambered over it and turned around and lay down again on the other side. Now he was exactly where he wanted to be. He called, 'Come on up.'

He saw the ladder flex and sway and bounce a little and the strange harmonic keening started up again. Then Vaughan's head came into view. She paused and got her bearings and made it over the angle and climbed off and lay down in the place he had just vacated, uneasy and spread-eagled. He handed her the wrecking bar and hauled the ladder up sideways, awkwardly, crossing and uncrossing his hands until he had the thing approximately balanced on top of the curve. He glanced right, into the arena, and tugged the ladder a little closer to him and then fed it down on the other side of the wall until the feet of the short leg of the L came to rest on an oil drum two tiers down from the top. The long leg sloped gently between wall and pyramid, like a bridge.

'I love hardware stores,' he said again.

'I love solid ground,' Vaughan said.

He took the wrecking bar back from her and stretched forward and got both hands on the ladder. He jerked downward, hard, to make sure it was seated tight. Then he supported all his weight with his arms, like he was chinning a bar, and let his legs slide off the cylinder. He kicked and struggled until he was lying lengthways on the ladder. Then he got his feet on the rungs and climbed down, backward, his ass in the air where the slope was gentle, in a more normal position after the angle. He stepped off on to the oil drum and glanced around. Nothing to see. He held his end of the ladder steady and called up to Vaughan, 'Your turn.'

She came down the same way he had, backward, butt high like a monkey, then more or less vertically after the turn, ending up standing on the drum between his outstretched arms, which were still on the ladder. He left them there for a minute and then he moved and said, 'Now it's easy. Like stairs.'

They clambered down the pyramid. The empty drums boomed softly. They stepped off on to the sticky dirt and crunched out into the open. Reacher waited a beat and then set off south and west.

'This way,' he said.

They covered the quarter-mile to the vehicle gate in less than five minutes. The white Tahoes were parked close together near one end of it and there was a line of five flat-bed semis near the other. No tractor units attached. Just the trailers, jacked up at their fronts on their skinny parking legs. Four were facing outward, towards the gate. They were loaded with steel bars. Product, ready to go. The fifth was facing inward, towards the plant itself. It was loaded with a closed shipping container, dark in colour, maybe blue, with the words CHINA LINES stencilled on it. Scrap, incoming. Reacher glanced at it and passed it by and headed towards the line of offices. Vaughan walked with him. They ignored the security hut, and Thurman's own office, and Operations, and Purchasing, and Invoicing, and the first white-painted infirmary unit. They stopped outside the second. Vaughan said, 'Visiting the sick again?'

Reacher nodded. 'He might talk, without Thurman here.'

'The door might be locked.'

Reacher raised the wrecking bar.

'I have a key,' he said.

But the door wasn't locked. And the sick deputy wasn't talking. The sick deputy was dead.

The guy was still tucked tight under the sheet, but he had taken his last breath some hours previously. That was clear. And maybe he had taken it alone. He looked untended. His skin was cold and set and waxy. His eyes were clouded and open. His hair was thin and messy, like he had been tossing on the pillow, listlessly, looking for companionship or comfort. His chart had not been added to or amended since the last time Reacher had seen it. The long list of symptoms and complaints was still there, unresolved and apparently undiagnosed.

'TCE?' Vaughan said.

'Possible,' Reacher said.

We're doing the best we can, Thurman had said. *We're hoping he'll get better. I'll have him taken to the hospital in Halfway tomorrow.*

Bastard, Reacher thought.

'This could happen in Hope,' Vaughan said. 'We need the data for Colorado Springs. For the lab.'

'That's why we're here,' Reacher said.

They stood by the bedside for a moment longer and then they backed out. They closed the door gently, as if it would make a difference to the guy, and headed down the steps and then up the line to the office marked Purchasing. Its door was secured with a padlock through a hasp. The padlock was strong and the hasp was strong but the screws securing the hasp to the jamb were weak. They yielded to little more than the weight of the wrecking bar alone. They pulled out of the wood frame and fell to the ground and the door sagged open an inch. Vaughan turned the flashlight on and hid its beam in her palm. She led the way inside. Reacher followed and closed the door and propped a chair against it.

There were three desks inside and three phones and a whole wall of file cabinets, three drawers high, maybe forty inches tall. A hundred and forty cubic feet of purchase orders, according to Reacher's automatic calculation.

'Where do we start?' Vaughan whispered.

'Try T for TCE.'

The T drawers were about four-fifths of the way along the array, as common sense and the alphabet dictated they should be. They were crammed with papers. But none of the papers referred to trichloroethylene. Everything was filed according to supplier name. The T drawers were all about corporations called Tri-State and Thomas and Tomkins and Tribune. Tri-State had renewed a fire insurance policy eight months previously, Thomas was a telecommunications company that had supplied four new cell phones three months previously, Tomkins had put tyres on two front-loaders six months ago, and Tribune delivered binding wire on a two-week schedule. All essential activity for the metal plant's operation, no doubt, but none of it chemical in nature.

'I'll start at A,' Vaughan said.

'And I'll start at Z,' Reacher said. 'I'll see you at M or N, if not before.'

Vaughan was faster than Reacher. She had the flashlight. He had to rely on stray beams spilling from the other end of the array. Some things were obviously irrelevant. Anything potentially questionable, he had to haul it out and peer at it closely. It was slow work. The clock in his head ticked around, relentlessly. He started to worry about the dawn. It wasn't far away. At one point he found something ordered in the thousands of gallons, but on close inspection it was only gasoline and diesel fuel. The supplier was Western Energy of Wyoming and the purchaser was Thurman Metals of Despair, Colorado. He crammed the paper back in place and moved left to the V drawers. The first file he pulled was for medical supplies. Saline solution, IV bags, IV stands, miscellaneous requisites. Small quantities, enough for a small facility.

The supplier was Vernon Medical of Houston, Texas.

The purchaser was Olympic Medical of Despair, Colorado.

Reacher held the paper out to Vaughan. An official purchase order, on an official company letterhead, complete with the same corporate logo they had seen twice on the billboards south of Colorado Springs. Main office address, inside the metal plant, two cabins down.

'Thurman owns Olympic,' Reacher said. 'Where your husband is.'

Vaughan was quiet for a long moment. Then she said, 'I don't think I like that.'

Reacher said, 'I wouldn't, either.'

'I should get him out of there.'

'Or get Thurman out of there.'

'How?'

'Keep digging.'

They paused a second and then got back to work. Reacher got through V, and U, and skipped T because they had already checked it. He learned that Thurman's oxyacetylene supplier was Utah Gases and his kerosene supplier was Union City Fuels. He found no reference to trichloroethylene. He was opening the last of the S drawers when Vaughan said, 'Got it.' She had the first of the K drawers open.

'Kearny Chemical of New Jersey,' she said. 'TCE purchases going back seven years.'

She lifted the whole file cradle out of the drawer and shone the flashlight on it and riffled through the papers with her thumb. Reacher saw the word *trichloroethylene* repeated over and over, jumping around from line to line like a kid's badly drawn flip cartoon.

'Take the whole thing,' he said. 'We'll add up the quantities later.'

Vaughan jammed the file under her arm and pushed the drawer shut with her hip. Reacher moved the chair and opened the door and they stepped out together to the dark. Reacher stopped and used the flashlight and found the fallen screws and pushed them back into their holes with his thumb. They held loosely and made the lock look untouched. Then he followed Vaughan as she retraced their steps, past Operations, past Thurman's digs, past the security office. She waited for him and they dodged around the China Lines container together and headed out into open space.

Then Reacher stopped again.

Turned around.

'Flashlight,' he said.

Vaughan gave up the flashlight and he switched it on and played the beam across the side of the container. It loomed up, huge and unreal in the sudden light, high on its trailer like it was suspended in mid-air. It was forty feet long, corrugated, boxy, metal. Completely standard in every way. It had CHINA LINES painted on it in large letters, dirty white, and a vertical row of Chinese characters, plus a series of ID numbers and codes stencilled low in one corner.

Plus a word, handwritten in capitals, in chalk.

The chalk was faded, as if it had been applied long ago at the other end of a voyage of many thousands of miles.

The word looked like CARS.

Reacher stepped closer. The business end of the container had a double door, secured in the usual way with four foot-long levers that drove four sturdy bolts that ran the whole height of the container and socketed home in the box sections top and bottom. The levers were all in the closed position. Three were merely slotted into their brackets, but the fourth was secured with a padlock and guaranteed by a tell-tale plastic tag.

Reacher said, 'This is an incoming delivery.'

Vaughan said, 'I guess. It's facing inward.'

'I want to see what's inside.'

'Why?'

'I'm curious.'

'There are cars inside. Every junkyard has cars.'

He nodded in the dark. 'I've seen them come in. From neighbouring states, tied down on open flat-beds. Not locked in closed containers.'

Vaughan was quiet for a beat. 'You think this is army stuff from Iraq?'

'It's possible.'

'I don't want to see. It might be Humvees. They're basically cars. You said so yourself.'

He nodded again. 'They are basically cars. But no one ever calls them cars. Certainly not the people who loaded this thing.'

'If it's from Iraq.'

'Yes, if.'

'I don't want to see.'

'I do.'

'We need to get going. It's late. Or early.'

'I'll be quick,' he said. 'Don't watch, if you don't want to.'

She stepped away, into the darkness so that he

couldn't see her any more. He held the flashlight in his teeth and stretched up tall and jammed the tongue of the wrecking bar through the padlock's hoop. Counted *one, two,* and on *three* he jerked down with all his strength.

No result.

Working way above his head was reducing his leverage. He got his toes on the ledge where the box was reinforced at the bottom and grabbed the vertical bolt and hauled himself up to where he could tackle the problem face to face. He got the wrecking bar back in place and tried again. *One, two, jerk.*

No result.

Case-hardened steel, cold-rolled, thick and heavy. A fine padlock. He wished he had bought a three-foot bar. Or a six-foot pry bar. He thought about finding some chain and hooking a Tahoe up to it. The keys were probably in. But the chain would break before the padlock. He mused on it and let the frustration build. Then he jammed the wrecking bar home for a third try. *One. Two.* On *three* he jerked downward with all the force in his frame and jumped off his ledge so that his whole bodyweight reinforced the blow. A two-fisted punch, backed up by two hundred and fifty pounds of moving mass.

The padlock broke.

He ended up sprawled in the dirt. Curved fragments of metal hit him in the head and the shoulder. The wrecking bar clanged off the ledge and caught him in the foot. He didn't care. He climbed back up and broke the tag and smacked the levers out of their slots and opened the doors.

Metal squealed and graunched. He lit up the flashlight and took a look inside.

Cars.

The restlessness of a long sea voyage had shifted them neatly to the right side of the container. There were four of them, two piled on two, longitudinally. Strange makes, strange models. Dusty, sandblasted, pastel colours.

They were grievously damaged. They were opened like cans, ripped, peeled, smashed, twisted. They had holes through their sheet metal the size of telephone poles.

They had pale rectangular licence plates covered with neat Arabic numbers. Off-white backgrounds, delicate backward hooks and curls, black diamond-shaped dots.

Reacher turned in the doorway and called into the darkness, 'No Humvees.' He heard light footsteps and Vaughan appeared in the gloom. He leaned down and took her hand and pulled her up. She stood with him and followed the flashlight beam as he played it around.

'From Iraq?' she asked.

He nodded. 'Civilian vehicles.'

'Suicide bombers?' she asked.

'They'd be blown up worse than this. There wouldn't be anything left at all.'

'Insurgents, then,' she said. 'Maybe they didn't stop at the roadblocks.'

'Why bring them here?'

'I don't know.'

'Roadblocks are defended with machine guns. These things were hit by something else entirely. Just look at the damage.'

'What did it?'

'I'm not sure. Cannon fire, maybe. Some kind of big shells. Or wire-guided missiles.'

'Ground or air?'

'Ground, I think. The trajectories look like they were pretty flat.'

'Artillery versus sedans?' Vaughan said. 'That's kind of extreme.'

'You bet it is,' Reacher said. 'Exactly what the hell is going on over there?'

They closed the container and Reacher scratched around in the sand with the flashlight until he found the shattered padlock. He threw the separate pieces far into the distance and hoped they would get lost among the clutter. Then they hiked the quarter mile back to the oil drum pyramid and scaled the wall in the opposite direction. Out, not in. It was just as difficult. The construction was perfectly symmetrical. But they got over. They climbed down and stepped off on to the Crown Vic's hood and slid back to solid ground. Reacher folded the ladder and packed it in the rear seat. Vaughan put the captured Kearny Chemical file in the trunk, under the mat.

She asked, 'Can we take the long way home? I don't want to go through Despair again.'

Reacher said, 'We're not going home.'

FIFTY-SIX

They crossed the Tahoes' tracks and found Despair's old road and followed it west to the truck route. They turned their headlights on a mile later. Four miles after that they passed the MP base, close to four o'clock in the morning. There were two guys in the guard shack. The orange night light lit their faces from below. Vaughan didn't slow but Reacher waved anyway. The two guys didn't wave back.

Vaughan asked, 'Where to?'

'Where the old road forks. We're going to pull over there.'

'Why?'

'We're going to watch the traffic. I'm working on a theory.'

'What theory?'

'I can't tell you. I might be wrong, and then you wouldn't respect me any more. And I like it better when a woman respects me in the morning.'

Thirty minutes later Vaughan bumped down off the new blacktop and U-turned in the mouth of the old road and backed up on the shoulder.

When the sun came up they would have a view a mile both ways. They would be far from inconspicuous, but also far from suspicious. Crown Vics were parked on strategic bends all over America, all day every day.

They cracked their windows to let some air in and reclined their seats and went to sleep. Two hours, Reacher figured, before there would be anything to see.

Reacher woke up when the first rays of the morning sun hit the left-hand corner of the windshield. Vaughan stayed asleep. She was small enough to have turned in her seat. Her cheek was pressed against the mouse fur. Her knees were up and her hands were pressed together between them. She looked peaceful.

The first truck to pass them by was heading east towards Despair. It was a flat-bed semi with Nevada plates on both ends. It was loaded with a tangle of rusted-out junk. Washing machines, tumble dryers, bicycle frames, bent rebar, road sign posts all folded and looped out of shape by accidents. The truck thundered by with its exhaust cackling on the overrun as it coasted through the bend. Then it was gone, in a long tail of battered air and dancing dust.

Ten minutes later a second truck blew by, an identical flat-bed doing sixty, from Montana, heaped with wrecked cars. Its tyres whined loud and Vaughan woke up and glanced ahead at it and asked, 'How's your theory doing?'

Reacher said, 'Nothing to support it yet. But also nothing to disprove it.'

402

'Good morning.'

'To you, too.'

'Sleep long?'

'Long enough.'

The next truck was also heading east, an ugly ten-wheel army vehicle with two guys in the cab and a green box on the back, a standardized NATO payload hauler built in Oshkosh, Wisconsin, and about as pretty as an old pair of dungarees. It wasn't small, but it was smaller than the preceding semis. And it was slower. It barrelled through the curve at about fifty miles an hour and left less of a turbulent wake.

'Resupply,' Reacher said. 'For the MP base. Beans, bullets, and bandages, probably from Carson.'

'Does that help?'

'It helps the MPs. The beans, anyway. I don't suppose they're using many bullets or bandages.'

'I meant, does it help with your theory?'

'No.'

Next up was a semi coming west, out of Despair. The bed was loaded with steel bars. A dense, heavy load. The tractor unit's engine was roaring. The exhaust note was a deep bellow and black smoke was pouring from the stack.

Vaughan said, 'One of the four we saw last night.'

Reacher nodded. 'The other three will be right behind it. The business day has started.'

'By now they know we broke into that container.'

'They know somebody did.'

'What will they do about it?'

403

'Nothing.'

The second of the outgoing semis appeared on the horizon. Then the third. Before the fourth showed up another incoming truck blasted by. A container truck. A blue China Lines container on it. Heavy, by the way the tyres stressed and whined.

New Jersey plates.

Vaughan said, 'Combat wrecks.'

Reacher nodded and said nothing. The truck disappeared in the morning haze and the fourth outgoing load passed it. Then the dust settled and the world went quiet again. Vaughan arched her back and stretched, perfectly straight from her heels to her shoulders.

'I feel good,' she said.

'You deserve to.'

'I needed you to know about David.'

'You don't have to explain,' Reacher said. He was turned in his seat, watching the northern horizon a mile away. He could see a small shape, wobbling in the haze. A truck, far away. Small, because of the distance. Square, and rigid. A box truck, tan-coloured.

He said, 'Pay attention, now.'

The truck took a minute to cover the mile and then it roared past. Two axles, plain, boxy. Tan paint. No logo on it. No writing of any kind.

It had Canadian plates, from Ontario.

'Prediction,' Reacher said. 'We're going to see that truck heading out again within about ninety minutes.'

'Why wouldn't we? It'll unload and go home.'

'Unload what?'

'Whatever is in it.'

'Which would be what?'

'Scrap metal.'

'From where?'

'Ontario's biggest city is Toronto,' Vaughan said. 'So from Toronto, according to the law of averages.'

Reacher nodded. 'Route 401 in Canada, I-94 around Detroit, I-75 out of Toledo, I-70 all the way over here. That's a long distance.'

'Relatively.'

'Especially considering that Canada probably has steel mills all its own. I know for sure they're thick on the ground around Detroit and all over Indiana, which is practically next door. So why haul ass all the way out here?'

'Because Thurman's place is a specialist operation. You said so yourself.'

'Canada's army is three men and a dog. They probably keep their stuff for ever.'

Vaughan said, 'Combat wrecks.'

Reacher said, 'Canada isn't fighting in Iraq. They had more sense.'

'So what was in that truck?'

'My guess is nothing at all.'

They waited. Plenty more trucks passed by in both directions, but they were all uninteresting. Semi trailers from Nebraska, Wyoming, Utah, Washington state, and California, loaded with crushed cars and bales of crushed steel and rusted industrial hulks that might once have been boilers or locomotives or parts of ships. Reacher looked at them as they passed and then looked away. He kept his focus on the eastern horizon and the clock in his head. Vaughan got out and brought the captured file from under the mat in the trunk. She took the papers out of the cardboard cradle and turned them over and squared them on her knee. Licked her thumb and started with the oldest page first. It was dated a little less than seven years previously. It was a purchase order for five thousand gallons of trichloroethylene, to be delivered prepaid by Kearny Chemical to Thurman Metals. The second-oldest page was identical. As was the third. The fourth fell into the following calendar year.

Vaughan said, 'Fifteen thousand gallons in the first year. Is that a lot?'

'I don't know,' Reacher said. 'We'll have to let the state lab be the judge.'

The second year of orders came out the same. Fifteen thousand gallons. Then the third year jumped way up, to five separate orders for a total of twenty-five thousand gallons. A refill every seventy-some days. An increase in consumption of close to 67 per cent.

Vaughan said, 'The start of major combat operations. The first wrecks.'

The fourth year held steady at twenty-five thousand gallons.

The fifth year matched it exactly.

'David's year,' Vaughan said. 'His Humvee was rinsed with some of those gallons. What was left of it.'

The sixth year she looked at jumped again. Total of six orders. Total of thirty thousand gallons. Iraq, getting worse. A 20 per cent increase. And the current year looked set to exceed even that. There were already six orders in, and the year still had a whole quarter to run. Then Vaughan paused and looked at the six pages again, one by one, side by side, and she said, 'No, one of these is different.'

Reacher asked, 'Different how?'

'One of the orders isn't for trichloroethylene. And it isn't in gallons. It's in tons, for something called trinitrotoluene. Thurman bought twenty tons of it.'

'When?'

'Three months ago. Maybe they misfiled it.'

'From Kearny?'

'Yes.'

'Then it isn't misfiled.'

'Maybe it's another kind of de-greaser.'

'It isn't.'

'You heard of it?'

'Everyone has heard of it. It was invented in 1863 in Germany, for use as a yellow dye.'

'I never heard of it,' Vaughan said. 'I don't like yellow.'

'A few years later they realized it decomposes in an exothermic manner.'

'What does that mean?'

'It explodes.'

Vaughan said nothing.

'Trichloroethylene is called TCE,' Reacher said. 'Trinitrotoluene is called TNT.'

'I've heard of *that*.'

'Everyone has heard of it.'

'Thurman bought twenty tons of dynamite? Why?'

'Dynamite is different. It's nitroglycerine soaked

into wood pulp and moulded into cylinders wrapped in paper. TNT is a specific chemical compound. A yellow solid. Much more stable. Therefore much more useful.'

'OK, but why did he buy it?'

'I don't know. Maybe he busts things up with it. It melts easily, and pours. That's how they get it into shell casings and bombs and shaped charges. Maybe he uses it like a liquid and forces it between seams he can't cut. He was boasting to me about his advanced techniques.'

'I never heard any explosions.'

'You wouldn't. You're twenty miles from the plant. And maybe they're small and controlled.'

'Is it a solvent, when it's liquid?'

'I'm not sure. It's a reagent, that's all I know. Carbon, hydrogen, nitrogen and oxygen. Some complicated formula, lots of sixes and threes and twos.'

Vaughan riffled back through the pages she had already examined.

'Whatever, he never bought any before,' she said. 'It's a new departure.'

Reacher glanced ahead through the windshield. Saw the tan box truck heading back towards them. It was less than a mile away. He took the red bubble light off the dash and held it in his hand.

'Stand by,' he said. 'We're going to stop that truck.'

'We can't,' Vaughan said. 'We don't have jurisdiction here.'

'The driver doesn't know that. He's Canadian.'

FIFTY-SEVEN

Vaughan was a cop from a small quiet town, but she handled the traffic stop beautifully. She started the car when the truck was still a quarter-mile away and put it in gear. Then she waited for the truck to pass and pulled out of the old road on to the new and settled in its wake. She hung back a hundred yards, to be clearly visible in its mirrors. Reacher opened his window and clamped the bubble light on the roof. Vaughan hit a switch and the light started flashing. She hit another switch and her siren quacked twice.

Nothing happened for ten long seconds.

Vaughan smiled.

'Here it comes,' she said. 'The *Who, me?* moment.'

The truck started to slow. The driver lifted off and the cab pitched down a degree as weight and momentum settled on the front axle. Vaughan moved up fifty yards and drifted left to the crown of the road. The truck put its turn signal on. It rolled ahead and then braked hard and aimed for a spot where the shoulder was wide. Vaughan skipped past and tucked in again and the two vehicles came to a stop, nose to tail in the middle of nowhere, forty miles of empty road behind them and more than that ahead.

She said, 'A search would be illegal.'

Reacher said, 'I know. Just tell the guy to sit tight, five minutes. We'll wave him on when we're done.'

'With what?'

'We're going to take a photograph.'

Vaughan got out and cop-walked to the driver's window. She spoke for a moment and then walked back. Reacher said, 'Back up on the other shoulder, at right angles. We need to see the whole truck, side-on with the camera.'

Vaughan checked ahead and behind and jockeyed forward and back and then reversed across the blacktop in a wide curve and came to rest sideways on the opposite shoulder, with the front of her car pointed dead-centre at the side of the truck. It was a plain, simple vehicle. A stubby hood, a cab, twin rails running back from it with a box body bolted on. The box had alloy skin and was corrugated every foot for strength and rigidity. Tan paint, no writing.

Reacher said, 'Camera.'

Vaughan hit laptop keys and the screen lit up with a picture of the truck.

Reacher said, 'We need to see the thermal image.'

Vaughan said, 'I don't know if it works in the daytime.' She hit more keys and the screen blazed white. No detail, no definition. Everything was hot.

Reacher said, 'Turn down the sensitivity.'

410

She toggled keys and the screen dimmed. Ahead through the windshield the real-time view stayed unchanged but the image on the laptop screen faded to nothing and then came back ghostly green. Vaughan played around until the road surface and the background scrub showed up as a baseline grey, barely visible. The truck itself glowed a hundred shades of green. The hood was warm, with a bright centre where the engine was. The exhaust pipe was a vivid line, with green gases shimmering out the end in clouds. The rear differential was hot and the tyres were warm. The cab was warm, a generalized green block with a slight highlight where the driver was sitting and waiting.

The box body was cold at the rear. It stayed cold until it suddenly got warmer three-quarters of the way forward. A section five feet long directly behind the cab was glowing bright.

Reacher said, 'Take it down some more.'

Vaughan tapped a key until the tyres went grey and merged with the road. She kept on going until the greys went black and the picture simplified to just five disembodied elements in just two shades of green. The engine, hot. The exhaust system, hot. The differential case, warm. The cab, warm.

The first five feet of the box body, warm.

Vaughan said, 'It reminds me of the wall around the metal plant. Hotter at one end than the other.'

Reacher nodded. Stuck his arm out the window, waved the driver onward, and peeled the bubble light off the roof. The truck lurched as the gears

411

caught and it pulled across the rumble strip and got straight in the traffic lane and lumbered slowly away, first gear, then second, then third. The laptop screen showed a vivid plume of hot exhaust that swelled and swirled into a lime green cloud before cooling and dissipating and falling away into blackness.

Vaughan asked, 'What did we just see?'

'A truck on its way to Canada.'

'That's all?'

'You saw what I saw.'

'Is this part of your theory?'

'Pretty much all of it.'

'Want to tell me about it?'

'Later.'

'Than what?'

'When it's safely across the border.'

'Why then?'

'Because I don't want to put you in a difficult position.'

'Why would it?'

'Because you're a cop.'

'Now you're trying to keep *me* out of trouble?'

Reacher said, 'I'm trying to keep everybody out of trouble.'

They turned around and drove back to where the old road forked. They bumped down off the new blacktop and this time they kept on going, between the two ruined farms, all the way to Halfway township. They got there at ten o'clock in the morning. First stop was the coffee shop, for a late breakfast. Second stop was a Holiday Inn, where they rented a bland beige room and showered and made love and went to sleep. They woke up at four, and did all the same things in reverse order, like a film run backward. They made love again, showered again, checked out of the hotel, and headed back to the coffee shop for an early dinner. By five thirty they were on the road again, heading east, back towards Despair.

Vaughan drove. The setting sun was behind her, bright in her mirror. It put a glowing rectangle of light on her face. The truck route was reasonably busy in both directions. The metal plant ahead was still sucking stuff in and spitting it out again. Reacher watched the licence plates. He saw representatives from all of Colorado's neighbouring states, plus a container truck from New Jersey, heading outward, presumably empty, and a flat-bed semi from Idaho heading inward, groaning under a load of rusted steel sheet.

He thought: *Licence plates*.

He said, 'I was in the Gulf the first time around. I told you that, right?'

Vaughan nodded. 'You wore the same BDUs every day for eight months. In the heat. Which is a delightful image. I felt bad enough putting these clothes back on.'

'We spent most of the time in Saudi and Kuwait, of course. But there were a few covert trips into Iraq itself.'

'And?'

'I remember their licence plates being silver. But the ones we saw last night in the container were off-white.'

'Maybe they changed them since then.'

413

'Maybe. But maybe they didn't. Maybe they had other things to worry about.'

'You think those weren't Iraqi cars?'

'I think Iran uses off-white plates.'

'So what are you saying? We're fighting in Iran and nobody knows? That's not possible.'

'We were fighting in Cambodia and nobody knew. But I think it's more likely there's a bunch of Iranians heading west to Iraq to join in the fun every day. Maybe like commuting to a job. Maybe we're stopping them at the border crossings. With artillery.'

'That's very dangerous.'

'For the passengers, for sure.'

'For the world,' Vaughan said. 'We don't need any more trouble.'

They passed the MP base just before six fifteen. Neat, quiet, still, six parked Humvees, four guys in the guard shack. All in order, and recently resupplied.

For what?

They slowed for the last five miles and tried to time it right. Traffic had died away to nothing. The plant was closed. The lights were off. Presumably the last stragglers were heading home, to the east. Presumably the Tahoes were parked for the night. Vaughan made the left on to Despair's old road and then found the ruts in the gathering gloom and followed them like she had the night before, through the throat of the figure-eight and all the way around the residential compound to the spot behind the airplane barn. She parked there and went to pull the key but

Reacher put his hand on her wrist and said, 'I have to do this part alone.'

Vaughan said, 'Why?'

'Because this has to be face to face. It might be confrontational. And the whole deal here is that you're permanent and I'm not. You're a cop from the next town, with a lot of years ahead of you. You can't go trespassing and breaking and entering all over the neighbourhood.'

'I already have.'

'But nobody knew. Which made it OK. This time it won't be OK.'

'You're shutting me out?'

'Wait on the road. Any hassle, take off for home and I'll make my own way back.'

He left the ladder and the wrecking bar and the flashlight where they were, in the car. But he took the captured switchblades with him. He put one in each pocket, just in case.

Then he hiked the fifty yards through the scrub and climbed the fieldstone wall.

FIFTY-EIGHT

It was still too light to make any sense out of
hiding. Reacher just leaned against the barn's
board wall, near the front corner, outside, on the
blind side, away from the house. He could smell
the plane. Cold metal, oil, unburned hydrocarbons
from the tanks. The clock in his head showed one
minute before seven in the evening.

He heard footsteps at one minute past.

Long strides, a heavy tread. The big guy from
the plant, hustling. Lights came on in the barn.
A bright rectangle of glare spilled forward,
shadowed with wings and propeller blades.

Then nothing, for two minutes.

Then more footsteps. Slower. A shorter stride.
An older man with good shoes, overweight,
battling stiffness and limping with joint pain.

Reacher took a breath and stepped around the
corner of the barn, into the light.

The big guy from the plant was standing behind
the Piper's wing, just waiting, like some kind of a
servant or a butler. Thurman was on the path leading from the house. He was dressed in his wool
suit. He was wearing a white shirt and a blue tie.

He was carrying a small cardboard carton.

The carton was about the size of a six-pack of beer. There was no writing on it. It was entirely plain. The top flaps were folded shut, one under the other. It wasn't heavy. Thurman was carrying it two-handed, out in front of his body, reverentially, but without strain. He stopped dead on the path but didn't speak. Reacher watched him try to find something to say, and then watched him give up. So he filled the silence himself. He said, 'Good evening, folks.'

Thurman said, 'You told me you were leaving.'

'I changed my mind.'

'You're trespassing.'

'Probably.'

'You need to leave now.'

'I've heard that before.'

'I meant it before, and I mean it now.'

'I'll leave when I've seen what's in that box.'

'Why do you want to know?'

'Because I'm curious about what part of Uncle Sam's property you're smuggling out of here every night.'

The big guy from the plant squeezed around the tip of the Piper's wing and stepped out of the barn and put himself between Reacher and Thurman, closer to Thurman than Reacher. Two against one, explicitly. Thurman looked beyond the big guy's shoulder directly at Reacher and said, 'You're intruding.' Which struck Reacher as an odd choice of word. *Interfering*, *trespassing*, *butting in*, he would have expected.

'Intruding on what?' he asked.

417

The big guy asked his boss, 'You want me to throw him out?'

Reacher saw Thurman thinking about his answer. There was debate in his face, some kind of a long-range calculus that went far beyond the possible positive or negative outcome of a two-minute brawl in front of an airplane hangar. Like the old guy was playing a long game, and thinking eight moves ahead.

Reacher said, 'What's in the box?'

The big guy said, 'Shall I get rid of him?'

Thurman said, 'No, let him stay.'

Reacher said, 'What's in the box?'

Thurman said, 'Not Uncle Sam's property. God's property.'

'God brings you metal?'

'Not metal.'

Thurman stood still for a second. Then he stepped around his underling, still carrying the box two-handed out in front of him, like a wise man bearing a gift. He knelt and laid it at Reacher's feet, and then stood up and backed away again. Reacher looked down. Theoretically the box might be booby-trapped, or he might get hit on the head while he crouched down next to it. But he felt either thing was unlikely. The instructors at Rucker had said: *Be sceptical, but not too sceptical.* Too much scepticism led to paranoia and paralysis.

Reacher knelt next to the box.

Unlaced the criss-crossed flaps.

Raised them.

The box held crumpled newspaper, with a small plastic jar nested in it. The jar was a standard medical item, sterile, almost clear, with a screw lid. A sample jar, for urine or other bodily fluids. Reacher had seen many of them.

The jar was a quarter full with black powder.

The powder was coarser than talc, finer than salt.

Reacher asked, 'What is it?'

Thurman said, 'Ash.'

'From where?'

'Come with me and find out.'

'Come with you?'

'Fly with me tonight.'

'Are you serious?'

Thurman nodded. 'I have nothing to hide. And I'm a patient man. I don't mind proving my innocence, over and over and over again, if I have to.'

The big guy helped Thurman up on to the wing and watched as he folded himself in through the small door. Then he passed the box up. Thurman took it and laid it on a rear seat. The big guy stood back and let Reacher climb up by himself. Reacher ducked low and led with his legs and made it into the co-pilot's seat. He slammed the door and squirmed around until he was as comfortable as he was ever going to get, and then he buckled his harness. Beside him Thurman buckled his and hit a bunch of switches. Dials lit up and pumps whirred and the whole airframe tensed and hummed. Then Thurman hit the starter button and the exhaust coughed and the propeller blade jerked around a quarter of the way and then the engine caught with a roar and the prop spun up and the cabin filled with loud noise and furious vibration. Thurman released the brakes and hit the throttle and the plane lurched forward, uncertain, earthbound, darting slightly left and right. It waddled forward out of the hangar. Dust blew up all over the place. The plane moved on, down the taxiway, the prop turning fast, the wheels turning slow. Reacher watched Thurman's hands. He was operating the controls the same way an old guy drives a car, leaning back in his seat, casual, familiar, automatic, using the kind of short abbreviated movements born of long habitude.

The taxiway led through two clumsy turns to the north end of the runway. The lights were on. Thurman got centred on the graded strip and hit the power and the vibration leached forward out of the cabin into the engine and the wheels started thumping faster below. Reacher turned and saw the cardboard carton slide backward on the seat and nestle against the rear cushion. He glanced ahead and saw lit dirt below and rushing darkness above. Then the plane went light and the nose lifted and the far horizon slid away. The plane clawed its way into the night sky and climbed and turned and Reacher looked down and saw first the runway lights go off and then the hangar lights. Without them there was little to see. The wall around the metal plant was faintly visible, a huge white rectangle in the gloaming.

The plane climbed hard for a minute and then levelled off and Reacher was dumped forward in his seat against his harness straps. He looked over at the dash and saw the altimeter reading two thousand feet. Airspeed was a little over a hundred and twenty. The compass reading was southeast. Fuel was more than half full. Trim was good. The artificial horizon was level. There were plenty of green lights, and no reds.

Thurman saw him checking and asked, 'Are you afraid of flying, Mr Reacher?'

Reacher said, 'No.'

The engine was loud and the vibration was setting up a lot of buzzes and rattles. Wind was howling around the screens and whistling in through cracks. Altogether the little Piper reminded Reacher of the kind of old cars people used as taxis at suburban railroad stations. Sagging, worn out, clunky, but capable of making it through the ride. Probably.

He asked, 'Where are we going?'

'You'll see.'

Reacher watched the compass. It was holding steady on south and east. There was an LED window below the compass with two green numbers showing. A GPS readout, latitude and longitude. They were below the fortieth parallel and more than a hundred degrees west. Both numbers were ticking downward, slowly and in step. South and east, at a modest speed. He called up maps in his mind. Empty land ahead, the corner of Colorado, the corner of Kansas, the Oklahoma panhandle. Then the compass swung a little further south, and Reacher realized that Thurman had been skirting the airspace around Colorado Springs. An air force town, probably a little trigger-happy. Better to give it a wide berth.

Thurman kept the height at two thousand feet and the speed at a hundred and a quarter and the compass stayed a little south of southeast. Reacher consulted his mental maps again and figured that if they didn't land or change course they were going to exit Colorado just left of the state's bottom right-hand corner. The time readout on the dash showed seventeen minutes past seven in the evening, which was two minutes fast. Reacher thought about Vaughan, alone in her car. She would have heard the plane take off. She would be wondering why he hadn't come back over the wall.

Thurman said, 'You broke into a container last night.'

Reacher said, 'Did I?'

'It's a fair guess. Who else would have?'

Reacher said nothing.

Thurman said, 'You saw the cars.'

'Did I?'

'Let's assume so, like intelligent men.'

'Why do they bring them to you?'

'There are some things any government feels it politic to conceal.'

'What do you do with them?'

'The same thing we do with the wrecks towed off I-70. We recycle them. Steel is a wonderful thing, Mr Reacher. It goes around and around. Peugeots and Toyotas from the Gulf might once have been Fords and Chevrolets from Detroit, and they in turn might once have been Rolls-Royces from England or Holdens from Australia. Or bicycles or refrigerators. Some steel is new, of course, but surprisingly little of it. Recycling is where the action is.'

'And the bottom line.'

'Naturally.'

'So why don't you buy yourself a better plane?'

'You don't like this one?'

'Not much,' Reacher said.

They flew on. The compass held steady on south of southeast and the carton held steady on the rear seat. There was nothing but darkness ahead, relieved occasionally by tiny clusters of yellow light far below. Hamlets, farms, gas stations. At one point Reacher saw brighter lights in the distance to the left and the right. Lamar, probably, and La Junta. Small towns, made larger by comparison with the emptiness all around them. Sometimes cars were visible on roads, tiny cones of blue light crawling slowly.

Reacher asked, 'How is Underwood doing? The deputy?'

Thurman paused a moment. Then he said, 'He passed on.'

'In the hospital?'

'Before we could get him there.'

'Will there be an autopsy?'

'He has no next of kin to request one.'

'Did you call the coroner?'

'No need. He was old, he got sick, he died.'

'He was about forty.'

'That was old enough, evidently. Ashes to ashes, dust to dust. It's in store for all of us.'

'You don't sound very concerned.'

'A good Christian has nothing to fear in death. And I own a town, Mr Reacher. I see births and deaths all the time. One door closes, another opens.'

They flew on, steadily through the dark, south

of southeast. Thurman leaned back, his gut between him and the stick, his hands held low. The engine held fast on a mid-range roar and the whole plane shivered with vibration and bucked occasionally on rough air. The latitude number counted down slowly, and the longitude number slower still. Reacher closed his eyes. Flight time to the state line would be about seventy or eighty minutes. He figured they weren't going to land in Colorado itself. There wasn't much left of it. Just empty grassland. He figured they were going to Oklahoma, or Texas.

They flew on. The air got steadily worse. Reacher opened his eyes. Downdraughts dropped them into troughs like a stone. Then updraughts hurled them back up again. They were sideswiped by gusts of wind. Not like in a big commercial Boeing. No juddering vibration and bouncing wings. No implacable forward motion. Just violent physical displacement, like a pinball caught between bumpers. There was no storm outside. No rain, no lightning. No thunderheads. Just roiling evening thermals coming up off the plains in giant waves, invisible, compressing, decompressing, making solid walls and empty voids. Thurman held the stick loosely and let the plane buck and dive. Reacher moved in his seat and smoothed the harness straps over his shoulders.

Thurman said, 'You *are* afraid of flying.'

'Flying is fine,' Reacher said. 'Crashing is another story.'

'An old joke.'

'For a reason.'

Thurman started jerking the stick and hammering the rudder. The plane rose and fell sharply and smashed from side to side. At first Reacher thought they were seeking smoother air. Then he realized Thurman was deliberately making things worse. He was diving where the downdraughts were sucking anyway and climbing with the updraughts. He was turning into the side winds and taking them like roundhouse punches. The plane was hammering all over the sky. It was being tossed around like the insignificant piece of junk it was.

Thurman said, 'This is why you need to get your life in order. The end could come at any time. Maybe sooner than you expect.'

Reacher said nothing.

Thurman said, 'I could end it for you now. I could roll and stall and power dive. Two thousand feet, we'd hit the deck at three hundred miles an hour. The wings would come off first. The crater would be ten feet deep.'

Reacher said, 'Go right ahead.'

'You mean that?'

'I dare you.'

An updraught hit and the plane was thrown upward and then the decompression wave came in and the lift under the wings dropped away to a negative value and the plane fell again. Thurman dropped the nose and hit the throttle and the engine screamed and the Piper tilted into a forty-five degree power dive. The artificial horizon on the dash lit up red and a warning siren sounded, barely audible over the scream of the engine and the battering airflow. Then Thurman pulled out of the dive. He jerked the nose up and the airframe groaned as the main spar stressed and the plane curved level and then rose again through air that was momentarily calmer.

Reacher said, 'Chicken.'

Thurman said, 'I have nothing to fear.'

'So why pull out?'

'When I die, I'm going to a better place.'

'I thought the big guy got to make that decision, not you.'

'I've been a faithful servant.'

'So go for it. Go to a better place, right now. I dare you.'

Thurman said nothing. Just flew on, straight and level, through air that was calming down. Two thousand feet, a hundred and twenty-five knots, south of southeast.

'Chicken,' Reacher said again. 'Phoney.'

Thurman said, 'God wants me to complete my task.'

'What, he told you that in the last two minutes?'

'I think you're an atheist.'

'We're all atheists. You don't believe in Zeus or Thor or Neptune or Augustus Caesar or Mars or Venus or Sun Ra. You reject a thousand gods. Why should it bother you if someone else rejects a thousand and one?'

Thurman didn't answer.

Reacher said, 'Just remember, it was you who was afraid to die, not me.'

Thurman said, 'It was just a little sport, man to man. The thermals are always bad there. It's the same every night. Something to do with the wilderness.'

They flew on, twenty more minutes. The air went still and quiet. Reacher closed his eyes again. Then dead on an hour and a quarter total elapsed time Thurman moved in his seat. Reacher opened his eyes. Thurman hit a couple of switches and fired up his radio and held the stick with his knees and clamped a headset over his ears. The headset had a microphone on a boom that came off the left-hand earpiece. Thurman flicked it with his fingernail and said, 'It's me, on approach.' Reacher heard a muffled crackling reply and far below in the distance saw lights come on. Red and white runway lights, he assumed, but they were so far away they looked like a tiny pink pinpoint. Thurman moved the stick and backed off the gas a little and started a long slow descent. Not very smooth. The plane was too small and light for finesse. It jerked and dropped and levelled and dropped again. Laterally it was nervous. It darted left, darted right. The pink pinpoint jumped around below them and drew closer and resolved into twin lines of red and white. The lines looked short. The plane wobbled and stumbled in the air and dipped low and then settled on a shallow path all the way down. The runway lights rushed up to meet it and started blurring past, left and right. For a second Reacher thought Thurman had left it too late, but then the wheels touched down and bounced once and settled back and Thurman cut the power and the plane rolled to a walk with half the runway still ahead of it. The engine note changed to a deep roar and the walk picked up to taxiing speed and Thurman jerked left off the runway and drove a hundred yards to a deserted apron. Reacher could see the vague outlines of brick buildings in the middle distance. He saw a vehicle approaching, headlights on. Big, dark, bulky.

A Humvee.

Camouflage paint.

The Humvee parked twenty feet from the Piper and the doors opened and two guys climbed out.

Battledress uniform, woodland pattern.

Soldiers.

FIFTY-NINE

Reacher sat for a moment in the sudden silence with his ears ringing and then he opened the Piper's door and climbed out to the wing. Thurman passed him the cardboard carton from the rear seat. Reacher took it one-handed and slid down to the tarmac. The two soldiers stepped forward and snapped to attention and threw salutes and stood there like a ceremonial detail, expectantly. Thurman climbed down behind Reacher and took the box from him. One of the soldiers stepped forward. Thurman bowed slightly and offered the box. The soldier bowed slightly and took it and turned on his heel and slow-marched back to the Humvee. His partner fell in behind him, line astern. Thurman followed them. Reacher followed Thurman.

The soldiers stowed the box in the Humvee's load bed and then climbed in the front. Reacher and Thurman got in the back. Big vehicle, small seats, well separated by the massive transmission tunnel. A diesel engine. They turned a tight circle on the apron and drove towards a building that stood alone in a patch of lawn. Lights were on in two ground-floor windows. The Humvee parked and the soldiers retrieved the box from the load bed and slow-marched it into the building. A minute later they came back out again without it.

Thurman said, 'Job done, for tonight, at least.'

Reacher asked, 'What was in the jar?'

'People,' Thurman said. 'Men, maybe women. We scrape them off the metal. When there's been a fire, that's all that's left of them. Soot, baked on to steel. We scrape it off and collect it in twists of paper, and then we put the day's gleanings into jars. It's as close as we can get to giving them a proper burial.'

'Where are we?'

'Fort Shaw, Oklahoma. Up in the panhandle. They deal with recovered remains here. Among other things. They're associated with the identification laboratory in Hawaii.'

'You come here every night?'

'As often as necessary. Which is most nights, sadly.'

'What happens now?'

'They give me dinner, and they gas up my plane.'

The soldiers climbed back into the front seats and the Humvee turned again and drove a hundred yards to the main cluster of buildings. A fifties army base, one of thousands in the world. Brick, green paint, whitewashed kerbs, swept blacktop. Reacher had never been there before. Had never even heard of it. The Humvee parked by a side door that had a sign that said it led to the Officers' Club. Thurman turned to Reacher and said, 'I won't ask you to join me for dinner. They'll have set just one place, and it would embarrass them.'

Reacher nodded. He knew how to find food on post. Probably better food than Thurman would be eating in the O Club.

'I'll be OK,' he said. 'And thanks for asking.'

Thurman climbed out and disappeared through the O Club door. The grunts in the front of the Humvee craned around, unsure about what to do next. They were both privates first class, probably stationed permanently in the States. Maybe they had a little Germany time under their belts, but nothing else of significance. No Korea time. No desert time, certainly. They didn't have the look. Reacher said, 'Remember wearing diapers, when you were two years old?'

The driver said, 'Sir, not specifically, sir.'

'Back then I was a major in the MPs. So I'm going to take a stroll now, and you don't need to worry about it. If you want to worry about it, I'll dig out your CO and we'll do the brother officer thing, and he'll OK it and you'll look stupid. How does that sound?'

The guy wasn't totally derelict. Not totally dumb. He asked, 'Sir, what unit, and where?'

Reacher said, '110th MP. HQ was in Rock Creek, Virginia.'

The guy nodded. 'It still is. The 110th is still in business.'

'I certainly hope so.'

'Sir, you have a pleasant evening. Chow in the mess until ten, if you're interested.'

'Thanks, soldier,' Reacher said. He climbed out and the Humvee drove away and left him. He

431

stood still for a moment in the sharp night air and then set out walking to the stand-alone building. Its original purpose was unclear to him. No reason to have a physically separated building unless it held infectious patients or explosives, and it didn't look like either a hospital or an armoury. Hospitals were bigger and armouries were stronger.

He went in the front door and found himself in a small square hallway with stairs ahead of him and doors either side. The upstairs windows had been dark. The lit windows had been on the ground floor. *If in doubt, turn left*, was his motto. So he tried the left-hand door and came up empty. An administrative office, lights blazing, nobody in it. He stepped back to the hallway and tried the right-hand door. Found a medic with the rank of captain at a desk, with Thurman's jar in front of him. The guy was young for a captain, but medics got promoted fast. They were usually two steps ahead of everyone else.

'Help you?' the guy said.

'I flew in with Thurman. I was curious about his jar.'

'Curious how?'

'Is it what he says it is?'

'Are you authorized to know?'

'I used to be. I was an MP. I did some forensic medicine with Nash Newman, who was probably your ultimate boss back when you were a second lieutenant. Unless he had retired already. He's probably retired now.'

The guy nodded. 'He is retired now. But I heard of him.'

'So are there people in the jar?'

432

'Probably. Almost certainly, in fact.'

'Carbon?'

'No carbon,' the guy said. 'In a hot fire all the carbon is driven off as carbon dioxide. What's left of a person after cremation are oxides of potassium, sodium, iron, calcium, maybe a little magnesium, all inorganic.'

'And that's what's in the jar?'

The guy nodded again. 'Entirely consistent with burned human flesh and bone.'

'What do you do with it?'

'We send it to the central identification lab in Hawaii.'

'And what do they do with it?'

'Nothing,' the guy said. 'There's no DNA in it. It's just soot, basically. The whole thing is an embarrassment, really. But Thurman keeps on showing up. He's a sentimental old guy. We can't turn him away, obviously. So we stage a sweet little ceremony and accept whatever he brings. Can't trash it afterwards, either. Wouldn't be respectful. So we move it off our desks on to Hawaii's. I imagine they stick it in a closet and forget all about it.'

'I'm sure they do. Does Thurman tell you where it comes from?'

'Iraq, obviously.'

'But what kind of vehicles?'

'Does it matter?'

'I would say so.'

'We don't get those details.'

Reacher asked, 'What was this building originally?'

'A VD clinic,' the medic said.

'You got a phone I could use?'

The guy pointed to a console on his desk.

'Have at it,' he said.

Reacher dialled 411 upside down and got the number for David Robert Vaughan, Fifth Street, Hope, Colorado. He said the number once under his breath to memorize it and then dialled it.

No answer.

He put the phone back in the cradle and asked, 'Where's the mess?'

'Follow your nose,' the medic said. Which was good advice. Reacher walked back to the main cluster and circled it until he smelled the aroma of fried food coming out of a powerful extraction vent. The vent came through the wall of a low lean-to addition to a larger square one-storey building. The mess kitchen, and the mess. Reacher went in and got a few questioning looks but no direct challenges. He got in line and picked up a cheeseburger the size of a softball, plus fries, plus beans, plus a mug of coffee. He hauled it all away to a table and started eating. The burger was excellent, which was normal for the army. Mess cooks were in savage competition to produce the best patty. The coffee was excellent too. A unique standardized blend, in Reacher's opinion the best in the world. He had been drinking it all his life. The fries were fair and the beans were adequate. All in all, probably better than the limp piece of grilled fish the officers were getting.

He took more coffee and sat in an armchair and read the army papers. He figured the two PFCs would come get him when Thurman was ready to leave. They would drive their guests out to the flight line and salute smartly and finish their little show in style, just after midnight. Taxiing, takeoff, the climb, then ninety minutes in the air. That would get them back to Despair by two, which seemed to be the normal schedule. Three hours' worth of free aviation fuel, plus a free four-hour dinner. Not bad, in exchange for a quarter-full jar of soot. *A born-again Christian American and a businessman*, was how Thurman had described himself. Whatever kind of a Christian he was, he was a useful businessman. That was for damn sure.

The mess kitchen closed. Reacher finished the papers and dozed. The PFCs never showed. At twelve ten in the morning Reacher woke up and heard the Piper's engine in the distance and by the time the sound registered in his mind it was revving hard. By the time he made it outside the little white plane was on the runway. He stood and watched as it gathered speed and lifted off and disappeared into the darkness above.

SIXTY

The Humvee came back from the flight line and the two PFCs got out and nodded to Reacher like nothing was wrong. Reacher said, 'I was supposed to be on that plane.'

The driver said, 'No sir, Mr Thurman told us you had a one-way ticket tonight. He told us you were heading south from here, on business of your own. He told us you were all done in Colorado.'

Reacher said, 'Shit.' He thought back to Thurman, in front of the airplane barn. The deliberate pause. *Debate in his face, some kind of a long-range calculus, like he was playing a long game, thinking eight moves ahead.*

Fly with me tonight.

I won't ask you to join me for dinner.

Reacher shook his head. He was ninety minutes' flying time from where he needed to be, in the middle of the night, in the middle of nowhere, with no airplane.

Outwitted by a seventy-year-old preacher.

Dumb.

And tense.

I think they were all stirred up because they're heading for the end of something.

What, he had no idea.

When, he had no clue.

He checked the map in his head. There were no highways in the Oklahoma panhandle. None at all. Just a thin red tracery of state four-lanes and county two-lanes. He glanced at the Humvee and at the PFCs and said, 'You guys want to drive me out to a road?'

'Which road?'

'Any road that gets traffic more than once an hour.'

'You could try 287. That goes south.'

'I need to go north. Back to Colorado. Thurman wasn't entirely frank with you.'

'287 goes north, too. All the way up to I-70.'

'How far is that?'

'Sir, I believe it's dead on two hundred miles.'

Hitchhiking had gotten more and more difficult in the ten years since Reacher left the army. Drivers were less generous, more afraid. The west was sometimes better than the east, which helped. Day was always better than night, which didn't. The Humvee from Fort Shaw let him out at twelve forty-five, and it was a quarter past one in the morning before he saw his first northbound vehicle, a Ford F150 that didn't even slow down to take a look. It just blew past. Ten minutes later an old Chevy Blazer did the same thing. Reacher blamed the movies. They made people scared of strangers. Although in reality most movies had the passing strangers messed up by the locals, not the other way around. Weird inbred families, that hunted people for sport. But mostly Reacher blamed himself. He knew he was no kind of an attractive roadside proposition. *Look at yourself. What do you see?* Maria from San Diego was the kind of person that got rides easily. Sweet, small, unthreatening, needy. Vaughan would do OK, too. Wild men six-five in height were a riskier bet.

At ten of two a dark Toyota pick-up at least slowed and took a look before passing by, which was progress of a sort. Five after two, a twenty-year-old Cadillac swept past. It had an out of tune motor and a collapsed rear suspension and an old woman low down behind the wheel. White hair, thin neck. What Reacher privately called a Q-tip. Not a likely prospect. Then at a quarter past two an old Suburban hove into view. In Reacher's experience new Suburbans were driven by uptight assholes, but old models were plain utilitarian vehicles often driven by plain utilitarian people. Their bulk often implied a kind of no-nonsense self-confidence on the part of their owners. The kind of self-confidence that said strangers weren't necessarily a problem.

The best hope so far.

Reacher stepped off the shoulder and put one foot in the traffic lane. Cocked his thumb in a way that suggested need, but not desperation.

The Suburban's brights came on.

It slowed.

It stopped altogether fifteen feet short of where Reacher was standing. A smart move. It gave the guy behind the wheel a chance to look over his potential passenger without the kind of social pressure that face to face proximity would generate. Reacher couldn't see the driver. Too much dazzle from the headlights.

A decision was made. The headlights died back to low beam and the truck rolled forward and stopped again. The window came down. The driver was a fat red-faced man of about fifty. He was clinging to the wheel like he would fall out of his seat if he didn't. He said, 'Where are you headed?' His voice was slurred.

Reacher said, 'North into Colorado. I'm trying to get to a place called Hope.'

'Never heard of it.'

'Me neither, until a few days ago.'

'How far away?'

'Maybe four hours.'

'Is it on the way to Denver?'

'It would be a slight detour.'

'Are you an honest man?'

Reacher said, 'Usually.'

'Are you a good driver?'

'Not really.'

'Are you drunk?'

Reacher said, 'Not even a little bit.'

The guy said, 'Well, I am. A lot. So you drive to wherever it is you want to go, keep me out of trouble, let me sleep it off, and then point me towards Denver, OK?'

Reacher said, 'Deal.'

Hitchhiking usually carried with it the promise of random personal encounters and conversations made more intense by the certainty that their durations would necessarily be limited. Not this time. The florid guy heaved himself over into the passenger seat and collapsed its back against a worn mechanism and went straight to sleep without another word. He snored and bubbled far back in his throat and he moved restlessly. According to the smell of his breath he had been drinking bourbon all evening. A lot of bourbon, probably with bourbon chasers. He was still going to be illegal when he woke up in four hours' time and pressed on to Denver.

Not Reacher's problem.

The Suburban was old and worn and grimy. Its total elapsed mileage was displayed in a window below the centre of the speedometer in LED figures like a cheap watch. A lot of figures, starting with a two. The motor wasn't in great shape. It still had power but it had a lot of weight to haul and it didn't want to go much faster than sixty miles an hour. There was a cell phone on the centre console. It was switched off. Reacher glanced at his sleeping passenger and switched it on. It wouldn't spark up. No charge in the battery. There was a charger plugged into the cigarette lighter. Reacher steered with his knees and traced the free end of the wire and shoved it into a hole on the bottom of the phone. Tried the switch again. The phone came on with a tinkly little tune. The sleeping guy paid no attention to it. Just snored on.

The phone showed no service. The middle of nowhere.

The road narrowed from four lanes to two. Reacher drove on. Five miles ahead he could see a pair of red tail lights. Small lights, set low, widely spaced. Moving north a little slower than the Suburban. The speed differential was maybe five miles an hour, which meant it took sixty whole minutes to close the gap. The lights were on a U-Haul truck. It was cruising at about fifty-five. When Reacher came up behind it speeded up to a steady sixty. Reacher pulled out and tried to pass, but the Suburban wouldn't accelerate. It bogged down at about sixty-two, which would have put Reacher on the wrong side of the road for a long, long time. Maybe for ever. So he eased off and tucked in behind the truck and battled the frustration of having to drive just a little slower than he wanted to. The cell phone was still showing no service. There was nothing to see behind. Nothing to see to the sides. The world was dark and empty. Thirty feet ahead the U-Haul's back panel was lit up bright by the Suburban's headlights. It was like a rolling billboard. An advertisement. It had a picture of three trucks parked side by side at an angle, small, medium and large. Each was shown in U-Haul's distinctive red and white colours. Each had *U-Haul* painted on its front. Each promised an automatic transmission, a gentle ride, a low deck, air conditioning, and cloth seats. A price of nineteen dollars and ninety-five cents was advertised in large figures. Reacher eased the Suburban closer to check the fine print. The bargain price was for in-town use of a small truck for one day, mileage extra, subject to contract terms. Reacher eased off again and fell back.

U-Haul.

You haul. We don't. Independence, self-reliance, initiative.

In general Reacher didn't care for the corruption of written language. *U* for you, *EZ* for easy, *hi* for high, *lo* for low. He had spent many years in school learning to read and spell and he wanted to feel that there had been some point to it. But he couldn't get too worked up about *U-Haul*. What was the alternative? *Self-Drive-Trucks*? Too clunky. Too generic. No kind of a catchy business name. He followed thirty feet behind the bright rolling billboard and the triple U-Haul logos blurred together and filled his field of view.

U for you.

Then he thought: *You for U.*

You did this to me.

To assume makes an ass out of u and me.

He checked the phone again.

No signal. They were in the middle of the Comanche National Grassland. Like being way out at sea. The closest cell tower was probably in Lamar, which was about an hour ahead.

The drunk guy slept noisily and Reacher followed the wallowing U-Haul truck for sixty solid minutes. Lamar showed up ahead as a faint glow on the horizon. Probably not more than a couple of street lights, but in contrast to the black grassland all around it felt like a destination. There was a small municipal airfield to the west. And there was cell coverage. Reacher glanced down and saw two bars showing on the phone's signal strength meter. He dialled Vaughan's home number from memory.

No answer.

He clicked off and dialled information. Asked

for the Hope PD. Let the phone company connect him. He figured his sleeping passenger could spring for the convenience. He heard the ring tone and then there was a click and more ring tone. Automatic call forwarding, he guessed. The Hope PD building wasn't manned at night. Vaughan had mentioned a day guy, but no night guy. Incoming calls would be re-routed out straight to the night-time prowl car. To a cell provided by the department, or to a personal cell. Ten nights out of fourteen it would be Vaughan answering. But not tonight. She was off duty. It would be another officer out there chasing gum wrappers. Maybe a deputy.

A voice in his ear said, 'Hope PD.'

Reacher said, 'I need to talk to Officer Vaughan.'

The guy in the passenger seat stirred, but didn't wake up.

The voice in Reacher's ear said, 'Officer Vaughan is off duty tonight.'

Reacher said, 'I know. But I need her cell number.'

'I can't give that to you.'

'Then call it yourself and ask her to call me back on this number.'

'I might wake her.'

'You won't.'

Silence.

Reacher said, 'This is important. And be quick. I'll be heading out of range in a minute.'

He clicked off. The town of Lamar loomed up ahead. Low dark buildings, a tall water tower, a lit-up gas station. The U-Haul pulled off for fuel.

Reacher checked the Suburban's gauge. Half full. A big tank. But a thirsty motor and many miles to go. He followed the U-Haul to the pumps. Unplugged the phone. It showed decent battery and marginal reception. He put it in his shirt pocket.

The pumps were operational but the pay booth was closed up and dark. The guy from the U-Haul poked a credit card into a slot on the pump and pulled it out again. Reacher used his ATM card and did the same thing. The pump started up and Reacher selected regular unleaded and watched in horror as the numbers flicked around. Gas was expensive. That was for damn sure. More than three bucks for a gallon. The last time he had filled a car, the price had been a dollar. He nodded to the U-Haul guy, who nodded back. The U-Haul guy was a youngish well-built man with long hair. He was wearing a tight black short-sleeve shirt with a clerical collar. Some kind of a minister of religion. Probably played the guitar.

The phone rang in Reacher's pocket. He left the nozzle wedged in the filler neck and turned away and answered. The Hope cop said, 'Vaughan didn't pick up her cell.'

Reacher said, 'Try your radio. She's out in the watch commander's car.'

'Where?'

'I'm not sure.'

'Why is she out in the watch commander's car?'

'Long story.'

'You're the guy she's been hanging with?'

'Just call her.'

'She's married, you know.'

'I know. Now call her.'

The guy stayed on the line and Reacher heard him get on the radio. A call sign, a code, a request for an immediate response, all repeated once, and then again. Then the sound of dead air. Buzzing, crackling, the heterodyne whine of night-time interference from high in the ionosphere. Plenty of random noise.

But nothing else.

No reply from Vaughan.

SIXTY-ONE

Reacher got out of the gas station ahead of the minister in the U-Haul and headed north as fast as the old Suburban would go. The drunk guy slept on next to him. He was leaking alcohol through his pores. Reacher cracked a window. The night air kept him awake and sober and the whistle masked the snoring. Cell coverage died eight miles north of Lamar. Reacher guessed it wouldn't come back until they got close to the I-70 corridor, which was two hours ahead. It was four thirty in the morning. ETA in Hope, around dawn. A five-hour delay, which was an inconvenience, but maybe not a disaster.

Then the Suburban's engine blew.

Reacher was no kind of an automotive expert. He didn't see it coming. He saw the temperature needle nudge upward a tick, and thought nothing of it. Just stress and strain, he figured, because of the long fast cruise. But the needle didn't stop moving. It went all the way up into the red zone and didn't stop until it was hard against the peg. The motor lost power and a hot wet smell came in through the vents. Then there was a muffled thump under the hood and strings of tan emulsion blew out of the ventilation slots in front of the windshield and spattered all over the glass. The motor died altogether and the Suburban slowed hard. Reacher steered to the shoulder and coasted to a stop.

Not good, he thought.

The drunk guy slept on.

Reacher got out in the darkness and headed around to the front of the hood. He used the flats of his hands to bounce some glow from the headlight beams back on to the car. He saw steam. And sticky tan sludge leaking from every crevice. Thick, and foamy. A mixture of engine oil and cooling water. Blown head gaskets. Total breakdown. Repairable, but not without hundreds of dollars and a week in the shop.

Not good.

Half a mile south he could see the U-Haul's lights coming his way. He stepped around to the passenger door and leaned in over the sleeping guy and found a pen and an old service invoice in the glove compartment. He turned the invoice over and wrote: *You need to buy a new car. I borrowed your cell phone. Will mail it back.* He signed the note: *Your hitchhiker.* He took the Suburban's registration for the guy's address and folded it into his pocket. Then he ran fifty feet south and stepped into the traffic lane and held his arms high and waited to flag the U-Haul down. It picked him up in its headlights about fifty yards out. Reacher waved his arms above his head. The universal distress signal. The U-Haul's headlights flicked to bright. The truck slowed, like Reacher knew it would. A lonely road, and a disabled vehicle and a stranded driver, both of them at least fleetingly familiar to the Good Samaritan behind the wheel.

The U-Haul came to rest a yard in front of Reacher, halfway on the shoulder. The window came down and the guy in the dog collar stuck his head out.

'Need help?' he said. Then he smiled, wide and wholesome. 'Dumb question, I guess.'

'I need a ride,' Reacher said. 'The engine blew.'

'Want me to take a look?'

Reacher said, 'No.' He didn't want the minister to see the drunk guy. From a distance he was out of sight on the reclined seat, below the window line. Close up, he was big and obvious. Abandoning a broken-down truck in the middle of nowhere was one thing. Abandoning a comatose passenger was another. 'No point, believe me. I'll have to send a tow truck. Or set fire to the damn thing.'

'I'm headed north to Yuma. You're welcome to join me, for all or part of the way.'

Reacher nodded. Called up the map in his head. The Yuma road crossed the Hope road about two hours ahead. The same road he had come in on originally, with the old guy in the green Grand Marquis. He would need to find a third ride, for the final western leg. His ETA was now about ten in the morning, with luck. He said, 'Thanks. I'll jump out about halfway to Yuma.'

The guy in the dog collar smiled his wholesome smile again and said, 'Hop in.'

*　　*　　*

The U-Haul was a full-size pick-up frame overwhelmed by a box body a little longer and wider and a lot taller than a pick-up's load bed. It sagged and wallowed and the extra weight and aerodynamic resistance made it slow. It struggled up close to sixty miles an hour and stayed there. Wouldn't go any faster. Inside it smelled of warm exhaust fumes and hot oil and plastic. But the seat was cloth, as advertised, and reasonably comfortable. Reacher had to fight to stay awake. He wanted to be good company. He didn't want to replicate the drunk guy's manners.

He asked, 'What are you hauling?'

The guy in the collar said, 'Used furniture. Donations. We run a mission in Yuma.'

'We?'

'Our church.'

'What kind of a mission?'

'We help the homeless and the needy.'

'What kind of a church?'

'We're Anglicans, plain vanilla, middle of the road.'

'Do you play the guitar?'

The guy smiled again. 'We try to be inclusive.'

'Where I'm going, there's an End Times church.'

The minister shook his head. 'An End Times congregation, maybe. It's not a recognized de-nomination.'

'What do you know about them?'

'Have you read the Book of Revelation?'

Reacher said, 'I've heard of it.'

The minister said, 'Its correct title is the Revela-tion of Saint John the Divine. Most of the original

449

is lost, of course. It was written either in ancient Hebrew or Aramaic, and copied by hand many times, and then translated into Koine Greek, and copied by hand many times, and then translated into Latin, and copied by hand many times, and then translated into Elizabethan English and printed, with opportunities for error and confusion at every single stage. Now it reads like a bad acid trip. I suspect it always did. Possibly all the translations and all the copying actually improved it.'

'What does it say?'

'Your guess is as good as mine.'

'Are you serious?'

'Some of our homeless people make more sense.'

'What do people think it says?'

'Broadly, the righteous ascend to heaven, the unholy are left on earth and are visited by various colourful plagues and disasters, Christ returns to battle the Antichrist in an Armageddon scenario, and no one winds up very happy.'

'Is that the same as the Rapture?'

'The Rapture is the ascending part. The plagues and the fighting are separate. They come afterwards.'

'When is all this supposed to happen?'

'It's perpetually imminent, apparently.'

Reacher thought back to Thurman's smug little speech in the metal plant. *There are signs*, he had said. *And the possibility of precipitating events*.

Reacher asked, 'What would be the trigger?'

'I'm not sure there's a trigger, as such.

Presumably a large element of divine will would be involved. One would certainly hope so.'

'Pre-echoes, then? Ways to know it's coming?'

The minister shrugged at the wheel. 'End Times people read the bible like other people listen to Beatles records backward. There's something about a red calf being born in the Holy Land. End Times enthusiasts are very keen on that part. They comb through ranches, looking for cattle a little more auburn than usual. They ship pairs to Israel, hoping they'll breed a perfect redhead. They want to get things started. That's another key characteristic. They can't wait. Because they're all awfully sure they'll be among the righteous. Which makes them self-righteous, actually. Most people accept that who gets saved is God's decision, not man's. So it's a form of snobbery, really. They think they're better than the rest of us.'

'That's it? Red calves?'

'Most enthusiasts believe that a major war in the Middle East is absolutely necessary, which is why they've been so unhappy about Iraq. Apparently what's happening there isn't bad enough for them.'

'You sound sceptical.'

The guy smiled again.

'Of course I'm sceptical,' he said. 'I'm an Anglican.'

There was no more conversation after that, either theological or secular. Reacher was too tired and the guy behind the wheel was too deep into night-driving survival mode, where nothing existed except the part of the road ahead that his

451

headlights showed him. His eyes were wedged open and he was sitting forward, as if he knew that to relax would be fatal. Reacher stayed awake too, watching for the Hope road. He knew it wouldn't be signposted and it wasn't exactly a major highway. The guy behind the wheel wouldn't spot it on his own.

It arrived exactly two hours into the trip, a lumpy two-lane crossing their path at an exact right angle. It had stop signs, and the main north-south drag didn't. By the time Reacher called it and the minister reacted and the U-Haul's overmatched brakes did their job they were two hundred yards past it. Reacher got out and waved the truck off and waited until its lights and its noise were gone. Then he walked back through the dark empty vastness. Pre-dawn was happening way to the east, over Kansas or Missouri. Colorado was still pitch black. There was no cell phone signal.

No traffic, either.

Reacher took up station on the west side of the junction, standing on the shoulder close to the traffic lane. East-west drivers would have to pause at the stop sign opposite, and they would get a good look at him twenty yards ahead. But there were no east-west drivers. Not for the first ten minutes. Then the first fifteen, then the first twenty. A lone car came north, trailing the U-Haul by twenty miles, but it didn't turn off. It just blasted onward. An SUV came south, and slowed, ready to turn, but it turned east, away from Hope. Its lights grew small and faint and then they disappeared.

It was cold. There was a wind coming out of the east, and it was moving rain clouds into the sky. Reacher turned his collar up and crossed his arms over his chest and trapped his hands under his biceps for warmth. The world turned and cloudy diffused streaks of pink and purple lit up the far horizon. A new day, empty, innocent, as yet unsullied. Maybe a good day. Maybe a bad day. Maybe the last day. *The end is near*, Thurman's church had promised. Maybe a meteorite the size of a moon was hurtling closer. Maybe governments had suppressed the news. Maybe rebels were even then forcing the locks on an old Ukrainian silo. Maybe in a research lab somewhere a flask had cracked or a glove had torn or a mask had leaked.

Or maybe not. Reacher stamped his feet and ducked his face into his shoulder. His nose was cold. When he looked up again he saw headlights in the east. Bright, widely spaced, far enough away to seem to be static. A large vehicle. A truck. Possibly a semi trailer. Coming straight towards him, with the new dawn behind it.

Four possibilities. One, it would arrive at the junction and turn right and head north. Two, it would arrive at the junction and turn left and head south. Three, it would pause at the stop sign and then continue west without picking him up. Four, it would pause and cross the main drag and then pause again to let him climb aboard.

Chances of a happy ending, 25 per cent. Or less, if it was a corporate vehicle with a no-passenger policy because of insurance hassles.

Reacher waited.

When the truck was a quarter-mile away he saw that it was a big rigid panel van, painted white. When it was three hundred yards away he saw that it had a refrigerator unit mounted on top. Fresh food delivery, which would have reduced the odds of a happy outcome if it hadn't been for the stop signs. Food drivers usually didn't like to stop. They had schedules to keep, and stopping a big truck and then getting it back up to speed could rob a guy of measurable minutes. But the stop signs meant he had to slow anyway.

Reacher waited.

He heard the guy lift off two hundred yards short of the junction. Heard the hiss of brakes. He raised his hand high, thumb extended. *I need a ride*. Then he raised both arms and waved. The distress semaphore. I *really* need a ride.

The truck stopped at the line on the east side of the junction. Neither one of its direction indicators was flashing. A good sign. There was no traffic north or south, so it moved on again immediately, diesel roaring, gears grinding, heading west across the main drag, straight towards Reacher. It accelerated. The driver looked down. The truck kept on moving.

Then it slowed again.

The air brakes hissed loud and the springs squealed and the truck came to a stop with the cab forty feet west of the junction and the rear fender a yard out of the north-south traffic lane. Reacher turned and jogged west and climbed up on the step. The window came down and the driver peered out from seven feet south. He was a short, wiry man, incongruously small in the huge cab. He said, 'It's going to rain.'

Reacher said, 'That's the least of my problems. My car broke down.'

The guy at the wheel said, 'My first stop is Hope.'

Reacher said, 'You're the supermarket guy. From Topeka.'

'I left there at four this morning. You want to ride along?'

'Hope is where I'm headed.'

'So quit stalling and climb aboard.'

Dawn chased the truck all the way west, and overtook it inside thirty minutes. The world lit up cloudy and pale gold and the supermarket guy killed his headlights and sat back and relaxed. He drove the same way Thurman had flown his plane, with small efficient movements and his hands held low. Reacher asked him if he often carried passengers and he said that about one morning in five he found someone looking for a ride. Reacher said he had met a couple of women who had ridden with him.

'Tourists,' the guy said.

'More than that,' Reacher said.

'You think?'

'I know.'

'How much?'

'All of it.'

'How?'

'I figured it out.'

The guy nodded at the wheel.

'Wives and girlfriends,' he said. 'Looking to be

close by while their husbands and boyfriends pass through the state.'

'Understandable,' Reacher said. 'It's a tense time for them.'

'So you know what their husbands and boyfriends are?'

'Yes,' Reacher said. 'I do.'

'And?'

'And nothing. Not my business.'

'You're not going to tell anyone?'

'There's a cop called Vaughan,' Reacher said. 'I'm going to have to tell her. She has a right to know. She's involved, two ways around.'

'I know her. She's not going to be happy.'

Reacher said, 'Maybe she will be, maybe she won't be.'

'I'm not involved,' the guy said. 'I'm just a fellow traveller.'

'You are involved,' Reacher said. 'We're all involved.'

Then he checked his borrowed cell phone again. No signal.

There was nothing on the radio, either. The supermarket guy hit a button that scanned the whole AM spectrum from end to end, and he came up with nothing. Just static. A giant continent, mostly empty. The truck hammered on, bouncing and swaying on the rough surface. Reacher asked, 'Where does Despair get its food?'

'I don't know,' the guy said. 'And I don't care.'

'Ever been there?'

'Once. Just to take a look. And once was enough.'

'Why do people stay there?'

'I don't know. Inertia, maybe.'

'Are there jobs elsewhere?'

'Plenty. They could head west to Halfway. Lots of jobs there. Or Denver. That place is expanding, for sure. Hell, they could come east to Topeka. We're growing like crazy. Nice houses, great schools, good wages, right there for the taking. This is the land of opportunity.'

Reacher nodded and checked his cell phone again. No signal.

They made it to Hope just before ten in the morning. The place looked calm and quiet and unchanged. Clouds were massing overhead and it was cold. Reacher got out on First Street and stood for a moment. His cell phone showed good signal. But he didn't dial. He walked down to Fifth and turned east. From fifty yards away he saw that there was nothing parked on the kerb outside Vaughan's house. No cruiser, no black Crown Vic. Nothing at all. He walked on, to get an angle and check the driveway.

The old blue Chevy pick-up was on the driveway. It was parked nose-in, tight to the garage door. It had glass in its windows again. The glass was still labelled with paper bar codes and it was crisp and clear except where it was smeared in places with wax and handprints. It looked very new against the faded old paint. The ladder and the wrecking bar and the flashlight were in the load bed. Reacher walked up the stepping-stone path to the door and rang the bell. He heard it sound inside the house. The neighbourhood was still and silent. He stood on the step for thirty long seconds and then the door opened.

Vaughan looked out at him and said, 'Hello.'

SIXTY-TWO

Vaughan was dressed in the same black clothes she had worn the night before. She looked still and calm and composed. And a little distant. A little preoccupied. Reacher said, 'I was worried about you.'

Vaughan said, 'Were you?'

'I tried to call you twice. Here, and in the car. Where were you?'

'Here and there. You better come in.'

She led him through the hallway, to the kitchen. It looked just the same as before. Neat, clean, decorated, three chairs at the table. There was a glass of water on the counter and coffee in the machine.

Reacher said, 'I'm sorry I didn't get right back.'

'Don't apologize to me.'

'What's wrong?'

'You want coffee?'

'After you tell me what's wrong.'

'Nothing is wrong.'

'Like hell.'

'OK, we shouldn't have done what we did the night before last.'

'Which part?'

'You know which part. You took advantage. I started to feel bad about it. So when you didn't come back with the plane I switched off my phone and my radio and drove out to Colorado Springs and told David all about it.'

'In the middle of the night?'

Vaughan shrugged. 'They let me in. They were very nice about it, actually. They treated me very well.'

'And what did David say?'

'That's cruel.'

Reacher shook his head. 'It isn't cruel. It's a simple question.'

'What's your point?'

'That David no longer exists. Not as you knew him. Not in any meaningful sense. And that you've got a choice to make. And it's not a new choice. There have been mass casualties from the Civil War onward. There have been tens of thousands of men in David's position over more than a century. And therefore there have been tens of thousands of women in your position.'

'And?'

'They all made a choice.'

'David still exists.'

'In your memory. Not in the world.'

'He's not dead.'

'He's not alive, either.'

Vaughan said nothing. Just turned away and took a fine china mug from a cupboard and filled it with coffee from the machine. She handed the mug to Reacher and asked, 'What was in Thurman's little box?'

'You saw the box?'

'I was over the wall ten seconds after you. I was never going to wait in the car.'

'I didn't see you.'

'That was the plan. But I saw you. I saw the whole thing. Fly with me tonight? He ditched you somewhere, didn't he?'

Reacher nodded. 'Fort Shaw, Oklahoma. An army base.'

'You fell for it.'

'I sure did.'

'You're not as smart as you think.'

'I never claimed to be smart.'

'What was in the box?'

'A plastic jar.'

'What was in the jar?'

'Soot,' Reacher said. 'People, after a fire. They scrape it off the metal.'

Vaughan sat down at her table.

'That's terrible,' she said.

'Worse than terrible,' Reacher said. 'Complicated.'

'How?'

Reacher sat down opposite her.

'You can breathe easy,' he said. 'There are no wrecked Humvees at the plant. They go someplace else.'

'How do you know?'

'Because Humvees don't burn like that. Mostly they bust open and people spill out.'

Vaughan nodded. 'David wasn't burned.'

Reacher said, 'Only tanks burn like that. No way out of a burning tank. Soot is all that's left.'

'I see.'

461

Reacher said nothing.

'But how is that complicated?'

'It's the first in a series of conclusions. Like a logical chain reaction. We're using main battle tanks over there. Which isn't a huge surprise, I guess. But we're losing some, which *is* a huge surprise. We always expected to lose a few, to the Soviets. But we sure as hell didn't expect to lose any to a bunch of ragtag terrorists with improvised devices. In less than four years they've figured out how to make shaped charges good enough to take out main battle tanks belonging to the U.S. Army. That doesn't help our PR very much. I'm real glad the Cold War is over. The Red Army would be helpless with laughter. No wonder the Pentagon ships the wrecks in sealed containers to a secret location.'

Vaughan got up and walked over to her counter and picked up her glass of water. She emptied it in the sink and refilled it from a bottle in her refrigerator. Took a sip.

'I got a call this morning,' she said. 'From the state lab. My tap water sample was very close to five parts per billion TCE. Borderline acceptable, but it's going to get a lot worse if Thurman keeps on using as much of the stuff as he uses now.'

'He might stop,' Reacher said.

'Why would he?'

'That's the final conclusion in the chain. We're not there yet. And it's only tentative.'

'So what was the second conclusion?'

'What does Thurman do with the wrecked tanks?'

'He recycles the steel.'

'Why would the Pentagon deploy MPs to guard recycled steel?'

'I don't know.'

'The Pentagon wouldn't. Nobody cares about steel. The MPs are there to guard something else.'

'Like what?'

'Only one possibility. A main battle tank's front and side armour includes a thick layer of depleted uranium. It's a by-product from enriching natural uranium for nuclear reactors. It's an incredibly strong and dense metal. Absolutely ideal for armour plate. So the second conclusion is that Thurman is a uranium specialist. And that's what the MPs are there for. Because depleted uranium is toxic and somewhat radioactive. It's the kind of thing you want to keep track of.'

'How toxic? How radioactive?'

'Tank crews don't get sick from sitting behind it. But after a blast or an explosion, if it turns to dust or fragments or vapour, you can get very sick from breathing it, or from being hit by shrapnel made of it. That's why they bring the wrecks back to the States. And that's what the MPs are worried about, even here. Terrorists could steal it and break it up into small jagged pieces and pack them into an explosive device. It would make a perfect dirty bomb.'

'It's heavy.'

'Incredibly.'

'They'd need a truck to steal it. Like you said.'

'A big truck.'

Reacher sipped his coffee and Vaughan sipped her water and said, 'They're cutting it up at the plant. With hammers and torches. That must make dust and fragments and vapour. No wonder everyone looks sick.'

Reacher nodded.

'The deputy died from it,' he said. 'All those symptoms? Hair loss, nausea and vomiting, diarrhoea, blisters, sores, dehydration, organ failure? That wasn't old age or TCE. It was radiation poisoning.'

'Are you sure?'

Reacher nodded again. 'Very sure. Because he told me so. From his deathbed he said *The*, and then he stopped, and then he started again. He said, *You did this to me*. I thought it was a new sentence. I thought he was accusing me. But it was really all the same sentence. He was pausing for breath, that's all. He was saying, *The U did this to me*. Like some kind of a plea, or an explanation, or maybe a warning. He was using the chemical symbol for uranium. Metalworkers' slang, I guess. He was saying, the uranium did this to me.'

Vaughan said, 'The air at the plant must be thick with it. And we were right there.'

Reacher said, 'Remember the way the wall glowed? On the infrared camera? It wasn't hot. It was radioactive.'

464

SIXTY-THREE

Vaughan sipped her bottled water and stared into space, adjusting to a new situation that was in some ways better than she had imagined, and in some ways worse. She asked, 'Why do you say there are no Humvees there?'

Reacher said, 'Because the Pentagon specializes. Like I told you. It always has, and it always will. The plant in Despair is about uranium recycling. That's all. Humvees go somewhere else. Somewhere cheaper. Because they're easy. They're just cars.'

'They send cars to Despair too. We saw them. In the container. From Iraq or Iran.'

Reacher nodded.

'Exactly,' he said. 'Which is the third conclusion. They sent those cars to Despair for a reason.'

'Which was what?'

'Only one logical possibility. Depleted uranium isn't just for armour. They make artillery shells and tank shells out of it, too. Because it's incredibly hard and dense.'

'So?'

'So the third conclusion is that those cars

465

were hit with ammunition made from depleted uranium. They're tainted, so they have to be processed appropriately. And they have to be hidden away. Because we're using tanks and DU shells against thin-skinned civilian vehicles. That's overkill. That's *very* bad PR. Thurman said there are some things any government feels it politic to conceal, and he was right.'

'What the hell is happening over there?'

Reacher said, 'Your guess is as good as mine.'

Vaughan picked up her glass again. She raised it halfway and stopped and looked at it like she was having second thoughts about ingesting anything and put it back down on the table. She said, 'Tell me what you know about dirty bombs.'

'They're the same as clean bombs,' Reacher said. 'Except they're dirty. A bomb detonates and creates a massive spherical pressure wave that knocks things over and pulps anything soft, like people, and generally small fragments of the casing are flung outward on the wave like bullets, which does further damage. That effect can be enhanced by packing extra shrapnel inside the casing around the explosive charge, like nails or ball bearings. A dirty bomb uses contaminated metal for the extra shrapnel, usually radioactive waste.'

'How bad is the result?'

'That's debatable. With depleted uranium, the powdered oxides after a high-temperature explosion are certainly bad news. There are fertility issues, miscarriages, and birth defects. Most people think the radiation itself isn't really a huge problem. Except that, like I said, it's debatable. Nobody really knows for sure. Which is the exact problem. Because you can bet your ass everyone will err on the side of caution. Which multiplies the effect, psychologically. It's classic asymmetric warfare. If a dirty bomb goes off in a city, the city will be abandoned, whether it needs to be or not.'

'How big would the bomb need to be?'

'The bigger the better.'

'How much uranium would they need to steal?'

'The more the merrier.'

Vaughan said, 'I think they're already stealing it. That truck we photographed? The front of the load compartment was glowing just like the wall.'

Reacher shook his head.

'No,' he said. 'That was something else entirely.'

SIXTY-FOUR

Reacher said, 'Walk to town with me. To the motel.'

Vaughan said, 'I don't know if I want to be seen with you. Especially at the motel. People are talking.'

'But not in a bad way.'

'You think?'

'They're rooting for you.'

'I'm not so sure.'

'Whatever, I'll be gone tomorrow. So let them talk for one more day.'

'Tomorrow?'

'Maybe earlier. I might need to stick around to make a phone call. Apart from that, I'm done here.'

'Who do you need to call?'

'Just a number. I don't think anyone will answer.'

'What about all this other stuff going on?'

'So far all we've got is the Pentagon washing its dirty linen in private. That's not a crime.'

'What's at the motel?'

'I'm guessing we'll find room four is empty.'

*　　*　　*

They walked together through the damp late-morning air, two blocks north from Fifth Street to Third and then three blocks west to the motel. They bypassed the office and headed on down the row. Room four's door was standing open. There was a maid's cart parked outside. The bed was stripped and the bathroom towels were dumped in a pile on the floor. The closets were empty. The maid had a vacuum cleaner going.

Vaughan said, 'Mrs Rogers is gone.'

Reacher nodded. 'Now let's find out when and how.'

They backtracked to the office. The clerk was on her stool behind the counter. Room four's key was back on its hook. Now only two keys were missing. Reacher's own, for room twelve, and Maria's, for room eight.

The clerk slid off her stool and stood with her hands spread on the counter. Attentive, and helpful. Reacher glanced at the phone beside her and asked, 'Did Mrs Rogers get a call?'

The clerk nodded. 'Six o'clock last night.'

'Good news?'

'She seemed very happy.'

'What then?'

'She checked out.'

'And went where?'

'She called a cab to take her to Burlington.'

'What's in Burlington?'

'Mostly the airport bus to Denver.'

Reacher nodded. 'Thanks for your help.'

'Is anything wrong?'

'That depends on your point of view.'

469

*   *   *

Reacher was hungry and he needed more coffee, so he led Vaughan another block north and another block west to the diner. The place was practically empty. Too late for breakfast, too early for lunch. Reacher stood for a second and then slid into the booth that Lucy Anderson had used the night he had met her. Vaughan sat across from him, where Lucy had sat. The waitress delivered ice water and silverware. They ordered coffee, and then Vaughan asked, 'What exactly is going on?'

'All those young guys,' Reacher said. 'What did they have in common?'

'I don't know.'

'They were young, and they were guys.'

'And?'

'They were from California.'

'So?'

'And the only white one we saw had a hell of a tan.'

'So?'

Reacher said, 'I sat right here with Lucy Anderson. She was cautious and a little wary, but basically we were getting along. She asked to see my wallet, to check I wasn't an investigator. Then later I said I had been a cop, and she panicked. I put two and two together and figured her husband was a fugitive. The more she thought about it, the more worried she got. She was very hostile the next day.'

'Figures.'

'Then I caught a glimpse of her husband in Despair and went back to check the rooming

470

house where he was staying. It was empty, but it was very clean.'

'Is that important?'

'Crucial,' Reacher said. 'Then I saw Lucy again, after her husband had moved on. She said they have lawyers. She talked about people in her position. She sounded like she was part of something organized. I said I could follow her to her husband and she said it wouldn't do me any good.'

The waitress came over with the coffee. Two mugs, two spoons, a Bunn flask full of a brand new brew. She poured and walked away and Reacher sniffed the steam and took a sip.

'But I was misremembering all along,' he said. 'I didn't tell Lucy Anderson that I had been a cop. I told her I had been a *military* cop. That's why she panicked. And that's why the rooming house was so clean. It was like a barracks ready for inspection. Old habits die hard. The people passing through it were all soldiers. Lucy thought I was tracking them.'

Vaughan said, 'Deserters.'

Reacher nodded. 'That's why the Anderson guy had such a great tan. He had been in Iraq. But he didn't want to go back.'

'Where is he now?'

'Canada,' Reacher said. 'That's why Lucy wasn't worried about me following her. It wouldn't do me any good. No jurisdiction. It's a sovereign nation, and they're offering asylum up there.'

'The truck,' Vaughan said. 'It was from Ontario.'

Reacher nodded. 'Like a taxi service. The glow

on the camera wasn't stolen uranium. It was Mrs Rogers's husband in a hidden compartment. Body heat, like the driver. The shade of green was the same.'

SIXTY-FIVE

Vaughan sat still and quiet for a long time. The waitress came back and refilled Reacher's mug twice. Vaughan didn't touch hers.

She asked, 'What was the California connection?'

Reacher said, 'Some kind of an antiwar activist group out there must be running an escape line. Maybe local service families are involved. They figured out a system. They sent guys up here with legitimate metal deliveries, and then their Canadian friends took them north over the border. There was a couple at the Despair hotel seven months ago, from California. A buck gets ten they were the organizers, recruiting sympathizers. And the sympathizers policed the whole thing. They bust your truck's windows. They thought I was getting too nosy, and they were trying to move me on.'

Vaughan pushed her mug out of the way and moved the salt and the pepper and the sugar in front of her. She put them in a neat line. She straightened her index finger and jabbed at the pepper shaker. Moved it out of place. Jabbed at it again, and knocked it over.

473

'A small sub-group,' she said. 'The few left-hand people, working behind Thurman's back. Helping deserters.'

Reacher said nothing.

Vaughan asked, 'Do you know who they are?'

'No idea.'

'I want to find out.'

'Why?'

'Because I want to have them arrested. I want to call the FBI with a list of names.'

'OK.'

'Well, don't you want to?'

Reacher said, 'No, I don't.'

Vaughan was too civilized and too small-town to have the fight in the diner. She just threw money on the table and stalked out. Reacher followed her, like he knew he was supposed to. She turned right on Second Street and headed east. Towards the quieter area on the edge of town, or towards the motel again, or towards the police station. Reacher wasn't sure which. Either she wanted solitude, or to demand phone records from the motel clerk, or to be in front of her computer. She was walking fast, in a fury, but Reacher caught her easily. He fell in beside her and matched her pace for pace and waited for her to speak.

She said, 'You knew about this yesterday.'

He said, 'Since the day before.'

'How?'

'The same way I figured the patients in David's hospital were military. They were all young men.'

'You waited until that truck was over the border before you told me.'

474

'Yes, I did.'

'Why?'

'I didn't want you to have it stopped.'

'Why not?'

'I wanted Rogers to get away.'

Vaughan stopped walking. 'For God's sake, you were a military cop.'

Reacher nodded. 'Thirteen years.'

'You hunted guys like Rogers.'

'Yes, I did.'

'And now you've gone over to the dark side?'

Reacher said nothing.

Vaughan said, 'Did you know Rogers?'

'Never heard of him. But I knew ten thousand just like him.'

Vaughan started walking again. Reacher kept pace. She stopped fifty yards short of the motel. Outside the police station. The brick façade looked cold in the grey light. The neat aluminum letters looked colder.

'They had a duty,' Vaughan said. 'You had a duty. David *did* his duty. They should do theirs, and you should do yours.'

Reacher said nothing.

'Soldiers should go where they're told,' she said. 'They should follow orders. They don't get to choose. And you swore an oath. You should obey it. They're traitors to their country. They're cowards. And you are too. I can't believe I slept with you. You're *nothing*. You're disgusting. You make my skin crawl.'

Reacher said, 'Duty is a house of cards.'

'What the hell does that mean?'

'I went where they told me. I followed orders.

I did everything they asked, and I watched ten thousand guys do the same. And we were happy to, deep down. I mean, we bitched and pissed and moaned, like soldiers always do. But we bought the deal. Because duty is a transaction, Vaughan. It's a two-way street. We owe them, they owe us. And what they owe us is a solemn promise to risk our lives and limbs if and only if there's a damn good reason. Most of the time they're wrong anyway, but we like to feel some kind of good faith somewhere. At least a little bit. And that's all gone now. Now it's all about political vanity and electioneering. That's all. And guys know that. You can try, but you can't bullshit a soldier. *They* blew it, not us. They pulled out the big card at the bottom of the house and the whole thing fell down. And guys like Anderson and Rogers are over there watching their friends getting killed and maimed and they're thinking, why? Why should we do this shit?'

'And you think going AWOL is the answer?'

'Not really. I think the answer is for civilians to get off their fat asses and vote the bums out. They should exercise control. That's *their* duty. That's the next-biggest card at the bottom of the house. But that's gone, too. So don't talk to me about AWOL. Why should the grunts on the ground be the only ones who *don't* go AWOL? What kind of a two-way street is that?'

'You served thirteen years and you support the deserters?'

'Under the circumstances I understand their decision. Precisely because I served those thirteen years. I had the good times. I wish they could have had them, too. I loved the army. And I hate what happened to it. I feel the same as I would if I had a sister and she married a creep. Should she keep her marriage vows? To a point, sure, but no further.'

'If you were in now, would you have deserted?'

Reacher shook his head. 'I don't think I would have been brave enough.'

'It takes courage?'

'For most guys, more than you would think.'

'People don't want to hear that their loved ones died for no good reason.'

'I know. But that doesn't change the truth.'

'I hate you.'

'No, you don't,' Reacher said. 'You hate the politicians, and the commanders, and the voters, and the Pentagon.' Then he said, 'And you hate that David didn't go AWOL after his first tour.'

Vaughan turned and faced the street. Held still. Closed her eyes. She stood like that for a long time, pale, a small tremble in her lower lip. Then she spoke. Just a whisper. She said, 'I asked him to. I begged him. I said we could start again anywhere he wanted, anywhere in the world. I said we could change our names, anything. But he wouldn't agree. Stupid, stupid man.'

Then she cried, right there on the street, outside her place of work. Her knees buckled and she staggered a step and Reacher caught her and held her tight. Her tears soaked his shirt. Her back heaved. She wrapped her arms around him. She crushed her face into his chest. She wailed and cried for her shattered life, her broken dreams, the telephone call two years before, the chaplain's visit to her door, the X-rays, the filthy hospitals, the unstoppable hiss of the respirator.

Afterwards they walked up and down the block together, aimlessly, just to be moving. The sky was grey with low cloud and the air smelled like rain was on the way. Vaughan wiped her face on Reacher's shirt tail and ran her fingers through her hair. She blinked her eyes clear and swallowed and took deep breaths. They ended up outside the police station again and Reacher saw her gaze trace the line of twenty aluminum letters fixed to the brick. *Hope Police Department*. She said, 'Why didn't Raphael Ramirez make it?'

Reacher said, 'Ramirez was different.'

SIXTY-SIX

Reacher said, 'One phone call from your desk will explain it. We might as well go ahead and make it. Since we're right here anyway. Maria has waited long enough.'

Vaughan said, 'One call to who?'

'The MPs west of Despair. You were briefed about them, they'll have been briefed about you. Therefore they'll cooperate.'

'What do I ask them?'

'Ask them to fax Ramirez's summary file. They'll say, who? You'll tell them, bullshit, you know Maria was just there, so you know they know who he is. And tell them we know Maria was there for twenty-one hours, which is enough time for them to have gotten all the paperwork in the world.'

'What are we going to find?'

'My guess is Ramirez was in prison two weeks ago.'

The Hope Police Department's fax machine was a boxy old product standing alone on a rolling cart. It had been square and graceless to start with,

479

and now it was grubby and worn. But it worked. Eleven minutes after Vaughan finished her call it sparked up and started whirring and sucked a blank page out of the feeder tray and fed it back out with writing on it.

Not much writing. It was a bare-bones summary. Very little result for twenty-one hours of bureaucratic pestering. But that was explained by the fact that it had been the army doing the asking and the Marines doing the answering. Inter-service cooperation wasn't usually very cooperative.

Raphael Ramirez had been a private in the Marine Corps. At the age of eighteen he had been deployed to Iraq. At the age of nineteen he had served a second deployment. At the age of twenty he had gone AWOL ahead of a third deployment. He had gone on the run but had been arrested five days later in Los Angeles and locked up awaiting court martial back at Pendleton.

Date of arrest, three weeks previously.

Reacher said, 'Let's go find Maria.'

They found her in her motel room. Her bed had a dent where she had been sitting, staying warm, saving energy, passing time, enduring. She answered the door tentatively, as if she was certain that all news would be bad. There was nothing in Reacher's face to change her mind. He and Vaughan led her outside and sat her in the plastic lawn chair under her bathroom window. Reacher took room nine's chair and Vaughan took room seven's. They dragged them over and positioned them and made a tight little triangle on the concrete apron.

Reacher said, 'Raphael was a Marine.'

Maria nodded. Said nothing.

Reacher said, 'He had been to Iraq twice and didn't want to go back a third time. So nearly four weeks ago he went on the run. He headed up to LA. Maybe he had friends there. Did he call you?'

Maria said nothing.

Vaughan said, 'You're not in trouble, Maria. Nobody's going to get you for anything.'

Maria said, 'He called most days.'

Reacher asked, 'How was he?'

'Scared. Scared to death. Scared of being AWOL, scared of going back.'

'What happened in Iraq?'

'To him? Not much, really. But he saw things. He said the people we were supposed to be helping were killing us, and we were killing the people we were supposed to be helping. Everybody was killing everybody else. In bad ways. It was driving him crazy.'

'So he ran. And he called most days.'

Maria nodded.

Reacher said, 'But then he didn't call, for two or three days. Is that right?'

'He lost his cell phone. He was moving a lot. To stay safe. Then he got a new phone.'

'How did he sound on the new phone?'

'Still scared. Very worried. Even worse.'

'Then what?'

'He called to say he had found some people. Or some people had found him. They were going to get him to Canada. Through a place called Despair, in Colorado. He said I should come here,

481

to Hope, and wait for his call. Then I should join him in Canada.'

'Did he call from Despair?'

'No.'

'Why did you go to the MPs?'

'To ask if they had found him and arrested him. I was worried. But they said they had never heard of him. They were army, he was Marine Corps.'

'And so you came back here to wait some more.'

Maria nodded.

Reacher said, 'It wasn't exactly like that. He was arrested in LA. The Marines caught up with him. He didn't lose his phone. He was in jail for two or three days.'

'He didn't tell me that.'

'He wasn't allowed to.'

'Did he break out again?'

Reacher shook his head. 'My guess is he made a deal. The Marine Corps offered him a choice. Five years in Leavenworth, or go undercover to bust the escape line that ran from California all the way to Canada. Names, addresses, descriptions, techniques, routes, all that kind of stuff. He agreed, and they drove him back to LA and turned him loose. That's why the MPs didn't respond. They found out what was going on and were told to stonewall you.'

'So where is Raphael now? Why doesn't he call?'

Reacher said, 'My father was a Marine. Marines have a code. Did Raphael tell you about it?'

Maria said, 'Unit, corps, God, country.'

Reacher nodded. 'It's a list of their loyalties, in

482

priority order. Raphael's primary loyalty was to his unit. His company, in fact. Really just a handful of guys. Guys like him.'

'I don't understand.'

'I think he agreed to the deal but couldn't carry it through. He couldn't betray guys just like him. I think he rode up to Despair but didn't call in to the Marines. I think he hung around on the edge of town and stayed out of sight, because he was conflicted. He didn't want to know who was involved, because he was afraid he might have to give them away later. He hung out for days, agonizing. He got thirsty and hungry. He started hallucinating and decided to walk over to Hope, and find you, and get out some other way.'

'So where is he?'

'He didn't make it, Maria. He collapsed half-way. He died.'

'But where is his body?'

'The people in Despair took care of it.'

'I see.'

Then for the second time in an hour Reacher watched a woman cry. Vaughan held her and Reacher said, 'He was a good man, Maria. He was just a kid who couldn't take any more. And in the end he didn't betray what he believed in.' He said those things over and over again, in different orders, and with different emphases, but they didn't help.

Maria was all cried out after twenty minutes and Vaughan led her back inside. Then she joined Reacher again and they walked away together. She asked, 'How did you know?'

Reacher said, 'No other rational explanation.'

'Did he really do what you said? Agonized and sacrificed himself?'

'Marines are good at self-sacrifice. On the other hand maybe he double-crossed the Corps from the get-go. Maybe he planned all along to head straight to Hope and grab Maria and disappear.'

'It doesn't take four days to walk from Despair to Hope.'

'No,' Reacher said. 'It doesn't.'

'So he probably did the right thing.'

'I hope that was Maria's impression.'

'Do you think he told them about the people in California?'

'I don't know.'

'This will carry on if he didn't.'

'You say that like it's a bad thing.'

'It could get out of hand.'

'You could make a couple of calls. They're in the hotel register in Despair, name and address. You could check and see who they are, and whether they're still around, or whether they've disappeared into federal custody.'

'I'm sorry about what I said before.'

'Don't worry about it.'

They walked on, and then Reacher said, 'And you weren't wrong, when you did what you did the night before last. Otherwise whoever killed David killed you too. You want to give them that? Because I don't. I want you to have a life.'

'That sounds like the beginnings of a farewell speech.'

'Does it?'

'Why stay? The Pentagon is washing its dirty

linen in private, which isn't a crime. And we seem to have decided this other thing isn't a crime either.'

'There's one more thing on my mind,' Reacher said.

SIXTY-SEVEN

Reacher and Vaughan walked back to the diner, where Reacher ate for the first time since the burger he had scored in the Fort Shaw mess the night before. He topped up his caffeine level with four mugs of coffee and when he had finished he said, 'We need to go see those MPs. Now you've established contact we might get away with a face to face meeting.'

Vaughan said, 'We're going to drive through Despair again?'

Reacher shook his head. 'Let's take your truck and go cross-country.'

They peeled the paper bar codes off the new glass and Vaughan fetched paper towels and Windex from her kitchen and they wiped the wax and the handprints off the screen. Then they set off, early in the afternoon. Vaughan took the wheel. They drove five miles west on Hope's road and risked another nine on Despair's. The air was clear and the mountains were visible ahead, first invitingly close and then impossibly distant. Three miles before Despair's first vacant lot they slowed and bumped down off the road, on to the scrub, and started a long loop to the north. They kept the town on their left, on a three-mile radius. It was just a blur in the distance. Not possible to tell if it was guarded by mobs or sentries, or abandoned altogether.

It was slow going across the open land. They steered around rocks and bushes and drove over anything small enough not to present a major obstacle. Undergrowth scraped along the underside and low bushes slapped at their flanks. The ladder and the wrecking bar in the load bed bounced and rattled. The flashlight rolled from side to side. Occasionally they found dry washes and followed them through looping meanders at a higher speed. Then it was back to picking their way around table rocks bigger than the Chevy itself and keeping the sun centred on the top rail of the windshield. Four times they drove into natural corrals and had to back up and start over. After an hour the town fell away behind them and the plant showed up ahead on the left. The wall glowed white in the sun. The parking lot looked to be empty. No cars. There was no smoke rising from the plant. No sparks, no noise. No activity at all.

Reacher said, 'What day is it?'

Vaughan said, 'It's a regular work day.'

'Not a holiday?'

'No.'

'So where is everybody?'

They steered left and narrowed the gap between themselves and the plant. The Chevy was raising a healthy dust plume in the air behind it. It would be visible to a casual observer. But there were no casual observers. They slowed and stopped two miles out and waited. Five minutes. Ten. Then fifteen. No circulating Tahoes came around.

Vaughan asked, 'What exactly is on your mind?'

'I like to be able to explain things to myself,' Reacher said.

'What can't you explain?'

'The way they were so desperate to keep people out. The way they shut down the secret compound for the day just because I was barging around within half a mile of it. The way they found Ramirez's body and dealt with it so fast and efficiently. It was no surprise to them. It's like they set themselves up to be constantly vigilant for intruders. To expect them, even. And they worked out procedures for dealing with them in advance. And everyone in town is involved. The first day I showed up, even the waitress in the restaurant knew exactly what to do. Why would they go to those lengths?'

'They're playing ball with the Pentagon. Keeping private things private.'

'Maybe. But I'm not sure. Certainly the Pentagon wouldn't ask for that. Despair is already in the middle of nowhere and the plant is three miles out of town and the bad stuff happens in a walled-off compound inside it. That's good enough for the Pentagon. They wouldn't ask local people to go to bat for them. Because they trust walls and distance and geography, not people.'

'Maybe Thurman asked the people himself.'

'I'm sure he did. I'm certain of it. But why? On

behalf of the Pentagon, or for some other reason of his own?'

'Like what?'

'Only one logical possibility. Actually, an illogical possibility. Or a logical impossibility. One word from the MPs will decide it. If they talk to us at all.'

'What word?'

'Either yes or no.'

They got going again and drove due west in as direct a line as the landscape allowed. They hit the truck route two miles west of the plant and drove across the sand shoulder and bumped up on to the blacktop. Vaughan got straight in her lane and hit the gas. Two minutes later they could see the MP base in the distance. A minute after that, they arrived at it.

There were four guys in the guard shack, which seemed to be their usual daytime deployment. Overkill, in Reacher's opinion, which meant the post was most likely commanded by a lieutenant, not a sergeant. A sergeant would have had two in the shack and the other two either resting up with the others or out on mobile patrol in a Humvee, depending on the perceived threat assessment. But officers had to sign off on fuel requisitions, which would nix the mobile Humvee, and officers didn't like men sitting around with nothing to do, which is why the shack was overcrowded. But Reacher didn't expect the grunts to be unhappy about it. Or about anything. They had been in Iraq, and now they weren't. The only question in his mind was whether their officer had been in

489

Iraq with them. If he had, he might be reasonable. If he hadn't, he might be a royal pain in the ass.

Vaughan drove past the base and U-turned and came back and parked facing the right way, tight on the shoulder, close to but not blocking the gate. Like she would outside a fire station. Respectful. Unwilling to put a foot wrong in the dance that had to be coming.

Two guys came out of the guard shack immediately. They were the same two Reacher had seen before. Morgan, the bespectacled specialist with the squint lines, and his partner, the silent private first class. Reacher kept his hands clearly visible and slid out of the truck. Vaughan did the same thing on her side. She introduced herself by name, and as an officer with the Hope PD. Morgan saluted her, in a way Reacher knew meant the MPs had run her plate the first time around, despite his best efforts, and that they had found out what her husband had been, and what he was now.

Which will help, he thought.

Then Morgan turned and looked straight at him.

'Sir?' he said.

'I was an MP myself,' Reacher said. 'I did your lieutenant's job about a million years ago.'

'Sir, which unit?'

'The 110th.'

'Rock Creek, Virginia,' Morgan said. A statement, not a question.

Reacher said, 'I went there a couple of times, to get my ass kicked. The rest of the time, I was on the road.'

'On the road where?'

'Everywhere you've ever been, and about a hundred other places.'

'Sir, that's interesting, but I'm going to have to ask you to move your vehicle.'

'At ease, corporal. We'll move it as soon as we've talked to your lieutenant.'

'On what subject, sir?'

'That's between him and us,' Reacher said.

'Sir, I can't justify disturbing him on that basis.'

'Move along, soldier. I've read the manual too. Let's skip a few pages, to where you've already determined that this is important.'

'Is this about the missing Marine private?'

'Much more interesting.'

'Sir, it would help me to have fuller particulars.'

'It would help you to have a million dollars and a date with Miss America, too. But what are the chances, soldier?'

Five minutes later Reacher and Vaughan were inside the wire, inside one of the six green metal buildings, face to face across a desk with a one-striper called Connor. He was a small lean man. He was maybe twenty-six years old. He had been to Iraq. That was for sure. His BDUs were beat up and sandblasted and his cheekbones were burned shiny. He looked competent, and probably was. He was still alive, and he wasn't in disgrace. In fact he was probably headed for a captain's rank, pending paperwork. Medals, too, maybe. He asked, 'Is this an official visit from the Hope PD?'

Vaughan said, 'Yes.'

'You're both members of the department?'

491

Vaughan said, 'Mr Reacher is a civilian adviser.'

'So how can I help?'

Reacher said, 'Long story short, we know about the DU salvage at Thurman's plant.'

Connor said, 'That bothers me a little.'

Reacher said, 'It bothers us a little too. Homeland Security rules require us to maintain a register of chemically sensitive sites within twenty miles.' He said it as if it was true, which it might have been. Anything was possible, with Homeland Security. 'We should have been told.'

'You're more than twenty miles from the plant.'

'Twenty exactly to downtown,' Reacher said. 'Only fifteen to the town limit.'

'It's classified,' Connor said. 'You can't put it in a register.'

Reacher nodded. 'We understand that. But we should have been made aware of it, privately.'

'Sounds like you are aware of it.'

'But now we want to verify some details. Once bitten, twice shy.'

'Then you need to speak to the Department of Defense.'

'Better if we don't. They'll wonder how we got wind of it. Your guys talking will be their first guess.'

'My guys don't talk.'

'I believe you. But do you want to take a chance on the Pentagon believing you?'

Connor said, 'What details?'

'We think we're entitled to know when and how the scrap DU gets transported out, and what route is used.'

'Worried about it rolling down First Street?'

'You bet.'

'Well, it doesn't.'

'It all goes west?'

Connor said, 'It goes nowhere.'

Vaughan said, 'What do you mean?'

'You guys aren't the only ones with your panties in a wad. The state itself is pretty uptight. They want to close the Interstate and use an armed convoy. Which they can't contemplate on a regular basis. Once every five years is what they're thinking.'

'How long ago did the first convoy leave?'

'It didn't. The first convoy will happen about two years from now.'

Reacher said, 'So right now they're stockpiling the stuff at the plant?'

Connor nodded. 'The steel moves out, the DU stays.'

'How much have they got there?'

'As of right now, maybe twenty tons.'

'Have you seen it?'

Connor shook his head. 'Thurman reports monthly by mail.'

'You like that?'

'What's not to like?'

'The guy is sitting on a mountain of dangerous stuff.'

'And? What could he possibly do with it?'

SIXTY-EIGHT

Reacher and Vaughan got back in the truck and Vaughan said, 'Was that answer a yes or a no?'

'Both,' Reacher said. 'No, it doesn't get moved out, yes, it's all still there.'

'Is that a good both or a bad both?'

Reacher ducked his head and looked up through the screen. Four o'clock in the afternoon. The sun was a dull glow behind the cloud, but it was still way above the horizon.

'Four hours until dark,' he said. 'We've got time for a considered decision.'

'It's going to rain.'

'Probably.'

'Which will wash more TCE into the aquifer.'

'Probably.'

'We're not going to sit here until dark, in the rain.'

'No, we're not. We're going to the Holiday Inn in Halfway again.'

'Only if we get separate rooms.'

'Shut up, Vaughan. We're going to get the same room we got before, and we're going to do all the same things.'

494

*   *   *

The same room was not available, but they got one
just like it. Same size, same décor, same colours.
Indistinguishable. They did all the same things in
it. Showered, went to bed, made love. Vaughan
was a little reserved at first, but got into it later.
Afterwards she said that David had been better
in bed. Reacher wasn't offended. She needed to
believe it. And it was probably true.

They lay in the rucked sheets and Vaughan
explored Reacher's scars. She had small hands.
The bullet hole in his chest was too big for the
tip of her little finger. Her ring finger fitted it
better. Every woman he had been naked with was
fascinated by it, except the woman he had gotten
it for. She had preferred to forget. The rain started
after an hour. It was heavy. It drummed on the
hotel's roof and sheeted against the window. A
cosy feeling, in Reacher's opinion. He liked being
inside, in bed, listening to rain. After an hour
Vaughan got up and went to shower. Reacher
stayed in bed and leafed through the bible that
the Gideons had left in the night stand.

Vaughan came back and asked, 'Why does it
matter?'

'Why does what matter?'

'That Thurman is stockpiling depleted uranium?'

Reacher said, 'I don't like the combination. He's
got twenty tons of radioactive waste and twenty
tons of TNT. He's an End Times enthusiast. I
spoke to a vicar last night. He said that End Times
people can't wait to get things started. Thurman
himself said there might be precipitating events on

495

the way. He said it kind of smugly, like he secretly knew it was true. And the whole town seems to be waiting for something to happen.'

'Thurman can't start the End Times. They'll happen when they happen.'

'These people are fanatics. They seem to think they can nudge things along. They're trying to breed red cows in Israel.'

'How would that help?'

'Don't ask me.'

'Cows aren't dangerous.'

'Another requirement seems to be a major war in the Middle East.'

'We've already got one.'

'Not major enough.'

'How could it be worse?'

'Lots of ways.'

'Personally I don't see any.'

'Suppose another country joined in?'

'They'd be crazy to.'

'Suppose someone fired the first shot for them?'

'How would they?'

Reacher said, 'Suppose a dirty bomb went off in Manhattan or D.C. or Chicago. What would we do?'

'According to you, we'd evacuate the city.'

'And then?'

'We'd investigate.'

Reacher nodded. 'We'd have people in hazmat suits crawling all over the wreckage. What would they find?'

'Evidence.'

'For sure. They'd identify the materials involved. Suppose they found TNT and depleted uranium?'

'They'd make a list of possible sources.'

'Correct. Everyone in the world can buy TNT, but DU is rarer. It's a by-product of an enrichment process that occurs in maybe twenty places.'

'Nuclear powers.'

'Exactly.'

'A list of twenty suspects wouldn't help.'

'Exactly,' Reacher said again. 'And the intended victim isn't going to stand up and take responsibility, because the intended victim didn't know anything about anything in the first place. But suppose we were nudged in the preferred direction?'

'How?'

'Remember Oklahoma City? The Federal Building? That was a big explosion, but they knew it was a Ryder truck. Within hours. They're great at putting tiny fragments together.'

'But presumably one uranium fragment is like another.'

'But suppose you were a state-sponsored terrorist from overseas. You'd want maximum bang for the buck. So if you didn't have quite enough uranium when you were building your bomb, you might use other stuff to pack it out.'

'What other stuff?'

'Maybe pieces of wrecked cars,' Reacher said.

Vaughan said nothing.

Reacher said, 'Suppose the guys in the hazmat suits found fragments of Peugeots and Toyotas sold only in certain markets. Suppose they found fragments of Iranian licence plates.'

Vaughan was quiet for a moment. Then she said, 'Iran is working with uranium. They're boasting about it.'

'There you go,' Reacher said. 'What would happen next?'

'We'd make certain assumptions.'

'And?'

'We'd attack Iran.'

'And after that?'

'Iran would attack Israel, Israel would retaliate, everyone would be fighting.'

'Precipitating events,' Reacher said.

'That's insane.'

'These are people that believe red cows could signal the end of the world.'

'These are people who care enough to make sure ash gets a proper burial.'

'Exactly. Because by anyone's standards that's a meaningless gesture. Maybe it's just camouflage. To make sure no one looks at them too closely.'

'We have no evidence.'

'We have an End Times nutcase with technical expertise and twenty tons of TNT and twenty tons of DU and four Iranian cars and a limitless supply of shipping containers, some of which were last seen in the Middle East.'

Vaughan said, 'You think it's possible?'

'Anything is possible.'

'But no judge in America would sign off on a search warrant. Not with what we've got. It's not even circumstantial. It's just a crazy theory.'

Reacher said, 'I'm not looking for a search warrant. I'm waiting for dark.'

* * *

Darkness came two hours later. With it came doubts from Vaughan. She said, 'If you're really serious about this, you should call the State Police. Or the FBI.'

Reacher said, 'I would have to give my name. I don't like to do that.'

'Then talk to that MP lieutenant. He already knows your name. And it's his bag, after all.'

'He's looking at medals and a promotion. He won't want to rock the boat.'

It was still raining. A steady, hard downpour.

Vaughan said, 'You're not a one-man justice department.'

'What's on your mind?'

'Apart from legalities?'

'Yes, apart from those.'

'I don't want you to go there. Because of the radiation.'

'It won't hurt me.'

'OK, *I* don't want to go there. You said there were fertility issues and birth defects.'

'You're not pregnant.'

'I hope.'

'Me too.'

'But these things can linger. I might want children one day.'

That's progress, Reacher thought. He said, 'It's the dust that's the problem. And this rain will damp it down. And you don't have to come in. Just drive me there.'

They left thirty minutes later. Halfway was a small place but it took a long time to get out of it. Traffic was slow. People were driving cautiously, like they usually did in storms in places that were normally dry. The roads were running with water, like rivers. Vaughan put her wipers on high. They batted back and forth, furiously. She found the turn east and took it. Within a minute the old Chevy was the only car on the road. The only car for miles around. Rain battered the windshield and drummed on the roof.

'This is good,' Reacher said.

'You think?'

'Everyone will be indoors. We'll have the place to ourselves.'

They passed the MP post thirty minutes later. There were still four guys in the guard shack. They were dressed in rain capes. Their orange night light was on. It made a thousand dull jewels from the raindrops on the windows.

Vaughan asked, 'Will Thurman fly in this weather?'

Reacher said, 'He doesn't need to. They weren't working today.'

They drove on. Up ahead they saw a horizontal sliver of blue light. The plant, lit up. Much smaller than before. Like it had moved ten miles south, towards the horizon. But as they got closer they saw that it hadn't moved. The glow was smaller because only the farthest quarter was illuminated. The secret compound.

Vaughan said, 'Well, they're working now.'

'Good,' Reacher said. 'Maybe they left the gates open.'

They hadn't. The personnel gate and the main vehicle gate were both closed. The bulk of the plant was dark. Nearly a mile away the secret compound was bright and distant and tempting.

Vaughan said, 'Are you sure about this?'

Reacher said, 'Absolutely.'

'OK, where?'

'Same place as before.'

The Tahoes' beaten ruts were soft and full of water. The little Chevy spun its wheels and fishtailed and clawed its way forward. Vaughan found the right place. Reacher said, 'Back it in.' The wheels spun and the truck bumped up out of the ruts and Vaughan stopped it with its tailgate well under the curve of the metal cylinder, which put its rear window about where the base of the Crown Vic's windshield had been.

'Good luck,' she said. 'Take care.'

'Don't worry,' Reacher said. 'My biggest risk will be pneumonia.'

He got out into the rain and was soaked to the skin even before he got his stuff out of the load bed. He knelt in the mud beside the truck and adjusted the ladder to the relaxed L-shape that had worked before. He put the flashlight in one pocket and hooked the crook of the wrecking bar in the other. Then he lifted the ladder vertically into the back of the pick-up and jammed its feet into the right angle between the load bed floor and the back wall of the cab. He let it fall forward and the short leg of the L came down flat on top of the cylinder, aluminum against steel, a strange harmonic *clonk* that sounded twice, once immediately and then once again whole seconds later, as if the impact had raced all around the miles of hollow wall and come back stronger.

Reacher climbed into the load bed. Rain

lashed the metal and bounced up to his knees. It drummed on the steel cylinder above his head and sheeted down off the bulge of its maximum curvature like a thin waterfall. Reacher stepped sideways and up and started climbing. Rain hammered his shoulders. Gravity pulled the wrecking bar vertical and it hit every tread on the ladder. Steel against aluminum against steel. The harmonics came back, a weird metallic keening modulated by the thrash of the rain. He made it over the angle of the L and stopped. The cylinder was covered in shiny paint and the paint was slick with running water. Manoeuvring had been hard before. Now it was going to be very difficult.

He fumbled the flashlight out of his pocket and switched it on. He held it between his teeth and watched the water and picked the spot where half of it was sluicing one way and half the other. The geometric dead centre of the cylinder. The continental divide. He lined up with it and eased off the ladder and sat down. An uneasy feeling. Wet cotton on wet paint. Insecure. No friction. Water was dripping off him and threatening to float him away like an aquaplaning tyre.

He sat still for a long moment. He needed to twist from the waist and lift the ladder and reverse it. But he couldn't move. The slightest turn would unstick him. Newton's law of motion. Every action has an equal and opposite reaction. If he twisted his upper body to the left, the torque would spin his lower body to the right, and he would slide right off the cylinder. *An effective design, derived from prison research.*

Fourteen feet to the ground. He could survive

a controlled fall, if he didn't land on a tangle of jagged scrap. But without the ladder on the inside it wasn't clear how he would ever get out again.

Perhaps the gates had simpler switches on the inside. No combination locks.

Perhaps he could improvise a ladder out of scrap metal. Perhaps he could learn to weld, and build one.

Or perhaps not.

He thought: *I'll worry about all that later*.

He sat for a moment more in the rain and then nudged himself forward and rolled over on to his stomach as he slid and his palms squealed against the wet metal and the wrecking bar thumped and banged and then ninety degrees past top dead centre he was free-falling through empty air, one split second, and two, and three.

He hit the ground a whole lot later than he thought he would. But there was no scrap metal under him and his knees were bent and he went down in a heap and rolled one way and the wrecking bar went the other. The flashlight spun away. The breath was knocked out of him. But that was all. He sat up and a fast mental inventory revealed no physical damage, beyond mud and grease and oil all over his clothes, from the sticky earth.

He got to his feet and wiped his hands on his pants. Found the flashlight. It was a yard away, still burning bright. He carried it in one hand and the wrecking bar in the other and stood for a moment behind the pyramid of old oil drums. Then he stepped out and set off walking, south and west. Dark shapes loomed up at him. Cranes, gantries, crushers, crucibles, piles of metal. Beyond them the distant inner compound was still lit up.

The lights made a *T* shape.

A very shallow *T*. The crossbar was a blazing blue line half a mile long. Above it light spill haloed in the wet air. Below it the *T* shape's vertical stroke was very short. Maybe fourteen feet tall. That was all. Maybe thirty feet wide. A very squat foundation for such a long horizontal line.

But it was there.

The inner gate was open.

An invitation. A trap, almost certainly. *Like moths to a flame.* Reacher looked at it for a long moment and then slogged onward. The flashlight beam showed rainbow puddles everywhere. Oil and grease, floating. Rain was washing down through the sand and capillary action was pulling waste back to the surface. Walking was difficult. Within ten paces Reacher's shoes were carrying pounds of sticky mud. He was getting taller with every step. Every time the flashlight showed him a pile of old I-beams or a tangle of old rebar he stopped and scraped his soles. He was wetter than if he had fallen into a swimming pool. His hair was plastered to his head and water was running into his eyes.

Ahead he could see the white security Tahoes, blurred and ghostly in the darkness. They were parked side by side to the left of the main vehicle gate. Three hundred yards away. He headed straight for them. The trip took him seven minutes. Half speed, because of the soft ground. When he got there, he turned right and checked the vehicle gate. No luck. On the inside it had the same grey box as on the outside. The same keypad. The same three-million-plus combinations. He turned away from it and tracked along the wall and walked past the security office, and Thurman's office, and the operations office. He stopped outside Purchasing. Scraped his shoes and climbed the steps and used his fingernails to pull the screws out of the padlock hasp. The door sagged open. He went inside.

He headed straight for the row of file cabinets. Aimed towards the right-hand end. Opened the T drawer. Pulled the Thomas file. The telecoms company. The cell phone supplier. Clipped to the back of the original purchase order was a thick wad of paper. The contracts, the details, the anytime minutes, the taxes, the fees, the rebates, the makes, the models. And the numbers. He tore off the sheet with the numbers and folded it into his pants pocket. Then he headed back out to the rain.

Close to one mile and forty minutes later he was approaching the inner gate.

SIXTY-NINE

The inner gate was still open. The inner compound was still blazing with light. Up close, the light was painfully bright. It spilled out in a solid bar the width of the opening and spread and widened like a lighthouse beam that reached a hundred yards.

Reacher hugged the wall and approached from the right. He stopped in the last foot of shadow and listened hard. Heard nothing over the pelting rain. He waited one slow minute and then stepped into the light. His shadow moved behind him, fifty feet long.

No reaction.

He walked in, fast and casual. No alternative. He was as lit up and vulnerable as a stripper on a stage. The ground under his feet was rutted with deep grooves. He was up to his ankles in water. Ahead on the left was the first artful pile of shipping containers. They were stacked in an open V, point outward. To their right and thirty feet further away was a second V. He aimed for the gap between them. Stepped through, and found himself alone in an arena within an arena within an arena.

Altogether there were eight stacks of shipping containers arranged in a giant circle. They hid an area of maybe thirty acres. The thirty acres held cranes and gantries and crushers, and parked backhoes and bulldozers, and carts and dollies and trailers loaded with smaller pieces of equipment. Coils of baling wire, cutting torches, gas bottles, air hammers, high pressure spray hoses, hand tools. All grimy and battered and well used. Here and there leather welders' aprons and dark goggles were dumped in piles.

Apart from the industrial infrastructure, there were two items of interest.

The first, on the right, was a mountain of wrecked main battle tanks.

The mountain was maybe thirty feet high and fifty across at the base. It looked like an elephants' graveyard, from a grotesque prehistoric nightmare. Bent gun barrels reared up, like giant tusks or ribs. Turret assemblies were dumped and stacked haphazardly, characteristically low and wide and flat, peeled open like cans. Humped engine covers were stacked on their ends, like plates in a rack, some of them torn and shattered. Side skirts were everywhere, some of them ripped like foil. Parts of stripped hulls were tangled in the wreckage. Some of them had been taken apart by Thurman's men. Most of them had been taken apart much farther away, by different people using different methods. That was clear. There were traces of desert camouflage paint in some places. But not many. Most of the metal was scorched dull black. It looked cold in the blue light and it glistened in the rain, but Reacher felt he could see smoke still rising off it, and hear men still screaming under it.

He turned away. Looked left.

The second item of interest was a hundred yards east.

It was an eighteen-wheel semi truck.

A big rig. Ready to roll. A tractor, a trailer, a blue forty-foot China Lines container on the trailer. The tractor was a huge square Peterbilt. Old, but well maintained. The trailer was a skeletal flat-bed. The container looked like every container Reacher had ever seen. He walked towards it, a hundred yards, two minutes through mud and water. He circled the rig. The Peterbilt tractor was impressive. A fine paint job, an air filter the size of an oil drum, bunk beds behind the front seats, twin chrome smokestacks, a forest of antennas, a dozen mirrors the size of dinner plates. The container looked mundane and shabby in comparison. Dull paint, faded lettering, a few dings and dents. It was clamped tight to the trailer. It had a double door, secured with the same four foot-long levers and the same four sturdy bolts that he had seen before. The levers were all in the closed position.

There were no padlocks.

No plastic tell-tale tags.

Reacher put the wrecking bar in one hand and pulled himself up with the other and got a precarious slippery foothold on the container's bottom ledge. Got his free hand on the nearest lever and pushed it up.

It wouldn't move.

It was welded to its bracket. An inch-long worm

of metal had been melted into the gap. The three other levers were the same. And the doors had been welded to each other and to their frames. A neat patient sequence of spot welds had been applied, six inches apart, their bright newness hidden by a flick of dirty blue paint. Reacher juggled the wrecking bar and jammed the flat of the tongue into the space between two welds and pushed hard.

No result. Impossible. Like trying to lift a car with a nail file.

He climbed down, and looked again at the trailer clamps. They were turned tight. And welded.

He dropped the wrecking bar and walked away. He covered the whole of the hidden area, and the whole of the no-man's-land that lay beyond the stacks of piled containers, and the whole length of the perimeter track inside the wall. A long walk. It took him more than an hour. He came back to the inner circle the other way. From the side opposite the inner gates. They were two hundred yards away.

And they were closing.

SEVENTY

The gates were motorized. Driven by electricity. That was Reacher's first absurd conclusion. They were moving slowly, but smoothly. A consistent speed. Too smooth and too consistent for manual operation. Relentless, at about a foot a second. They were already at a right angle to the wall. Each gate was fifteen feet wide. Five yards. The total remaining arc of travel for each of them was therefore about eight yards.

Twenty-four seconds.

They were two hundred yards away. No problem for a college sprinter on a track. Debatable for a college sprinter in six inches of mud. Completely impossible for Reacher. But still he started forward involuntarily, and then slowed as the arithmetical reality hit him.

He stopped altogether when he saw four figures walk in through the closing gap.

He recognized them immediately, by their size and shape and posture and movement. On the right was Thurman. On the left was the giant with the wrench. In the middle was the plant foreman. He was pushing Vaughan in front of him. The

510

three men were walking easily. They were dressed in yellow slickers and sou'wester hats and rubber boots. Vaughan had no protection against the weather. She was soaked to the skin. Her hair was plastered against her head. She was stumbling, as if every few paces she was getting a shove in the back.

They all kept on coming.

Reacher started walking again.

The gates closed, with a metallic clang that sounded twice, first in real time and then again as an echo. The echo died, and Reacher heard a solenoid open and a bolt shoot home, a loud precise sound like a single shot from a distant rifle.

The four figures kept on coming.

Reacher kept on walking.

They met in the centre of the hidden space. Thurman and his men stopped and stood still five feet short of an imaginary line that ran between the pile of wrecked tanks and the eighteen-wheeler. Reacher stopped five feet on the other side. Vaughan kept on going. She picked her way through the mud and made it to Reacher's side and turned around. Put a hand on his arm.

Two against three.

Thurman called, 'What are you doing here?'

Reacher could hear the rain beating against the slickers. Three guys, three sets of shoulders, three hats, stiff plastic material.

He said, 'I'm looking around.'

'At what?'

'At what you've got here.'

Thurman said, 'I'm losing patience.'

Reacher said, 'What's in the truck?'

'What kind of incredible arrogance makes you think you're entitled to an answer to that question?'

'No kind of arrogance,' Reacher said. 'Just the law of the jungle. You answer, I leave. You don't, I don't.'

Thurman said, 'My tolerance for you is nearly exhausted.'

'What's in the truck?'

Thurman breathed in, breathed out. Glanced to his right, at his foreman, and then beyond the foreman at the giant with the wrench. He looked at Vaughan, and then back at Reacher. Reacher said, 'What's in the truck?'

Thurman said, 'There are gifts in the truck.'

'What kind?'

'Clothes, blankets, medical supplies, eyeglasses, prosthetic limbs, dried and powdered foodstuffs, purified water, antibiotics, vitamins, sheets of construction-grade plywood. Things like that.'

'Where from?'

'They were bought with tithes from the people of Despair.'

'Why?'

'Because Jesus said, it is more blessed to give than to receive.'

'Who are the gifts for?'

'Afghanistan. For refugees and displaced persons and those living in poverty.'

'Why is the container welded shut?'

'Because it has a long and perilous journey ahead of it, through many countries and many tribal areas where warlords routinely steal. And

512

padlocks on shipping containers can be broken. As you well know.'

'Why put it all together here? In secret?'

'Because Jesus said, when you give alms, do not let your left hand know what your right hand is doing, so that your alms may be in secret. We follow scripture here, Mr Reacher. As should you.'

'Why turn out the whole town in defence of a truck full of gifts?'

'Because we believe that charity should know neither race nor creed. We give to Muslims. And not everyone in America is happy with that policy. Some feel that we should give only to fellow Christians. An element of militancy has entered the debate. Although in fact it was the prophet Muhammad himself who said a man's first charity should be to his own family. Not Jesus. Jesus said, whatever you wish that men would do to you, do so to them. He said, love your enemies and pray for those who persecute you, so that you may be sons of your father who is in heaven.'

Reacher said, 'Where are the cars from Iran?'

'The what?'

'The cars from Iran.'

Thurman said, 'Melted down and shipped out.'

'Where is the TNT?'

'The what?'

'You bought twenty tons of TNT from Kearny Chemical. Three months ago.'

Thurman smiled.

'Oh, that,' he said. 'It was a mistake. A typo. A coding error. A new girl in the office was one number off, on Kearny's order form. We got TNT instead of TCE. They're adjacent in Kearny's inventory. If you were a chemist, you'd understand why. We sent it back immediately, on the same truck. Didn't even unload. If you had troubled yourself to break into Invoicing as well as Purchasing, you would have seen our application for a credit.'

'Where is the uranium?'

'The what?'

'You pulled twenty tons of depleted uranium out of these tanks. And I just walked all over this compound and I didn't see it.'

'You're standing on it.'

Vaughan looked down. Reacher looked down.

Thurman said, 'It's buried. I take security very seriously. It could be stolen and used in a dirty bomb. The state is reluctant to let the army move it. So I keep it in the ground.'

Reacher said, 'I don't see signs of digging.'

'It's the rain. Everything is churned up.'

Reacher said nothing.

Thurman said, 'Satisfied?'

Reacher said nothing. He glanced right, at the eighteen-wheeler. Left, at the parked backhoe. Down, at the ground. The rain splashed in puddles all around and thrashed against the slickers ten feet away.

'Satisfied?' Thurman asked again.

Reacher said, 'I might be. After I've made a phone call.'

'What phone call?'

'I think you know.'

'I don't, actually.'

Reacher said nothing.

Thurman said, 'But anyway, this is not the right time for phone calls.'

Reacher said, 'Not the right place, either. I'll wait until I get back to town. Or back to Hope. Or Kansas.'

Thurman turned and glanced at the gate. Turned back. Reacher nodded. Said, 'Suddenly you want to check on what numbers I know.'

'I don't know what you're talking about.'

'I think you do.'

'Tell me.'

'No.'

'I want some courtesy and respect.'

'And I want to hit a grand slam at Yankee Stadium. I think both of us are going to be disappointed.'

Thurman said, 'Turn out your pockets.'

Reacher said, 'Worried about those numbers? Maybe I memorized them.'

'Turn out your pockets.'

'Make me.'

Thurman went still and his eyes narrowed and debate crossed his face, the same kind of long-range calculus that Reacher had seen before, in front of the airplane hangar. The long game, eight moves ahead. Thurman spent a second or two on it and then he stepped back, abruptly, and raised his right arm. His plastic sleeve came out into the downpour and made noise. He waved his two employees forward. They took two long strides and stopped again. The plant foreman kept his hands loose at his sides and the big guy slapped the wrench in and out of his palm, wet metal on wet skin.

Reacher said, 'Not a fair fight.'

Thurman said, 'You should have thought about that before.'

Reacher said, 'Not fair to them. They've been cutting uranium. They're sick.'

'They'll take their chances.'

'Like Underwood did?'

'Underwood was a fool. I give them respirators. Underwood wouldn't put his on. Too lazy.'

'Did these guys wear theirs?'

'They don't work in here. They're perfectly healthy.'

Reacher glanced at the foreman, and then at the giant. Asked, 'Is that right? You don't work in here?'

Both guys shook their heads.

Reacher asked, 'Are you healthy?'

Both guys nodded.

Reacher asked, 'You want that state of affairs to last more than the next two minutes?'

Both guys smiled, and moved a step closer.

Vaughan said, 'Just do it, Reacher. Turn out your pockets.'

'Still looking out for me?'

'It's two against one. And one of them is the same size as you and the other one is bigger.'

'Two against two,' Reacher said. 'You're here.'

'I'm no use. Let's just suck it up and move on.'

Reacher shook his head and said, 'What's in my pockets is my business.'

The two guys took another step. The foreman was on Reacher's right and the big guy was on his left. Both of them close, but not within touching distance. The rain on their clothing was loud.

Water was running out of Reacher's hair into his eyes.

He said, 'You know we don't have to do this. We could walk out of here friends.'

The foreman said, 'I don't think so.'

'Then you won't walk out of here at all.'

'Big talk.'

Reacher said nothing.

The foreman glanced across at the big guy.

He said, 'Let's do it.'

Get your retaliation in first.

Reacher feinted left, towards the giant. The big guy rocked back, surprised, and the foreman rocked forward, towards the action. Momentum, moving west. A perfect little ballet. Reacher planted his heel very carefully in the mud and jerked the other way, to his right, to the east, and smashed the foreman in the stomach with his elbow. A five-hundred-pound collision. One guy moving left, one guy moving right, an elbow the size of a pineapple moving fast. The stomach is high in the midsection. Behind it lies the coeliac plexus, the largest autonomic nerve centre in the abdominal cavity. Sometimes called the solar plexus. A heavy blow can shut the whole thing down. Result, great pain and diaphragm spasms. Consequence, a fall to the ground and a desperate struggle to breathe.

The foreman went down.

He fell face first into a foot-wide rut filled with water. Reacher kicked him in the side to roll him out of it. He didn't want the guy to drown. He stepped over the writhing form into clear air and glanced around through the bright blue light.

Thurman had backed off twenty feet. Vaughan was rooted to thc spot. The big guy was crouched eight feet away, holding his wrench like a clean-up hitter waiting on a high fastball.

Reacher kept his eyes on the big guy's eyes and said, 'Vaughan, step away. This guy is going to start swinging. He could hit you by mistake.' But he sensed Vaughan wasn't moving. So he danced away east, dragging the fight with him. The big guy followed, big feet in rubber boots splashing awkwardly through standing water. Reacher dodged north, towards Thurman. Thurman backed off, keeping his distance. Reacher stopped. The big guy wound up for a swing. The huge wrench slashed horizontal, at shoulder height. Reacher stepped back a pace and the wrench missed and its wild momentum carried the big guy through a complete circle.

Reacher backed off another pace.

The big guy followed.

Reacher stopped.

The big guy swung.

Reacher stepped back.

Thirty acres. Reacher wasn't fast and he wasn't nimble but he was a lot more mobile than anyone who outweighed him by a hundred pounds. And he had the kind of natural stamina that came from being exactly what he was born to be. He wasn't on the downside of twenty years of weight rooms and steroids. Unlike his opponent. The big guy was breathing hard and every missed swing was jacking his fury and his adrenalin rush all the way up to carelessness. Reacher kept on moving and stopping and dodging and stopping again. Eventually the big guy learned. With his fifth swing he aimed for a spot three feet behind Reacher's back. Reacher saw it coming in the guy's crazed eyes and dodged the other way. Forward. The wrench hissed through empty air and Reacher rolled around the guy's spinning back and bent his knees and smashed his elbow up into the guy's kidney. Then he stepped away, two paces, three, and stood still and shook his arms loose and rolled his shoulders. The big guy turned. His back looked stiff and his knees were weakening. He charged and swung and missed and Reacher dodged away.

Like a bullfight. Except the big guy's IQ was marginally higher than a bull's. After a dozen fruitless swings he recognized that his tactics were futile. He sent the wrench spinning away into the marshy ground and got ready to charge. Reacher smiled. Because by then the damage was done. The guy was panting and staggering a little. The violent exertions and the adrenalin overload had spent him. He was going to lose. He didn't know it. But Reacher knew it.

And Thurman knew it.

Thurman was hurrying back towards the gate. Hurrying, but slowly. An old man, a heavy coat, awkward footwear, mud on the ground. Reacher called, 'Vaughan, don't let him leave. He has to stay here.' He saw her move in the corner of his eye. A small soaked figure, darting north. Then he saw the giant launch himself. A crazed lunge, across fifteen feet of distance. Three hundred and fifty pounds, coming on like a train. Reacher felt small and static by comparison. The guy might have been fast on a football field but he was slow now. His boots churned in the liquid mud. No grip. No traction. He came in on a flailing run and Reacher feinted left and stepped right and tripped him. He splashed down in the water and slid a full yard and Reacher turned away and was hit in the back by what felt like a truck. He went down hard and got a mouthful of mud and reflexively rolled away and jacked himself back up and dodged and missed a punch from the plant foreman by about an inch and a half.

Two against one again.

Inefficient.

The foreman launched another big roundhouse swing and Reacher swatted it away and saw the giant struggling to get up. His hands and knees were scrabbling and sliding in the mud. Fifty feet north Vaughan had hold of Thurman's collar. He was struggling to get free. Maybe winning. Then the foreman swung again and Reacher moved and the foreman's fist glanced off his shoulder. But not before stinging a bruise from where he had been hit before, in the bar.

Which hurt.

OK, no more Mr Nice Guy.

Reacher planted his back heel in the mud and leaned in and launched a flurry of heavy punches, a fast deadly rhythm, four blows, right, left, right, left, *one* to the gut, *two* to the jaw, *three* to the head, and *four*, a crushing uppercut under the chin, like he was his demented five-year-old self all over again, but five times heavier and eight times more experienced. The foreman was already on his way down when the uppercut landed. It lifted

520

him back up and then dropped him like the earth had opened up. Reacher spun away and lined up and kicked the scrabbling giant in the head, like he was punting a football, instep against ear. The impact pin-wheeled the guy's body a whole two feet and dropped him back in the mud.

The foreman lay still.

The giant lay still.

Game over.

Reacher checked his hands for broken bones and found none. He stood still and got his breathing under control and glanced north through the light. Thurman had broken free of Vaughan's grasp and was heading for the gate again, slipping and sliding and twisting and turning to fend her off. His hat was gone. His hair was wet and wild. Reacher set off in their direction. Paused to collect the giant wrench from where it had fallen. He hefted it up and carried it on his shoulder like an axe. He trudged onward, heavily. A slow-motion chase. He caught Vaughan ten yards from the gate and passed her and clamped a hand on Thurman's shoulder and pressed downward. The old guy folded up and went down on his knees. Reacher moved onward, to the gate. He found the little grey box. Flipped the lid. Saw the keypad. Swung the wrench and smashed it to splinters. Hit it again. And again. It fell out of its housing in small broken pieces. A small metal chassis hung up on thin trailing wires. Reacher chopped downward with the wrench until the wires tore and ruptured and the chassis fell to the ground.

Thurman was still on his knees. He said, 'What are you doing? Now we can't get out of here.'

'Wrong,' Reacher said. 'You can't, but we can.'

'How?'

'Wait and see.'

'It's not possible.'

'Would you have given me the combination?'

'Never.'

'So what's the difference?'

Vaughan said, 'Reacher, what the hell is in your pockets?'

'Lots of things,' Reacher said. 'Things we're going to need.'

SEVENTY-ONE

Reacher trudged through the mud and rolled Thurman's men into what medics called the recovery position. On their sides, arms splayed, necks at a natural angle, one leg straight and the other knee drawn up. No danger of choking. A slight danger of drowning, if the puddles didn't stop filling. The rain was still hard. It thrashed against their slickers and drummed on the sides of their boots.

Thurman made his way to the gate and poked and prodded at the shattered box where the keypad had been. No result. The gates stayed closed. He gave up and slipped and slid back to the centre of the hidden area. The lights were still on. Reacher and Vaughan fought their way across to the eighteen-wheeler. It was just standing there, shut-down and silent and oblivious.

Vaughan said, 'You really think this is a bomb?'

Reacher said, 'Don't you?'

'Thurman was mighty plausible. About the gifts for Afghanistan.'

'He's a preacher. It's his job to be plausible.'

'What if you're wrong?'

'What if I'm right?'

'How much damage could it do?'

'If they built it right I wouldn't want to be within three miles of it when it goes off.'

'Three *miles*?'

'Twenty tons of TNT, twenty tons of shrapnel. It won't be pretty.'

'How do we get out of here?'

'Where's your truck?'

'Where we left it. They ambushed me. Opened the outer gate and drove me through the plant in Thurman's SUV. It's parked the other side of the inner gate. Which you just made sure will never open again.'

'No big deal.'

'You can't climb the wall.'

'But you can,' Reacher said.

They talked for five fast minutes about what to do and how to do it. Knives, welds, the average size and thickness of a car's roof panel, canvas straps, knots, trailer hitches, four wheel drive, low-range gearing. Thurman was pacing aimlessly a hundred yards away. They left him there and headed through the mud to the wall. They picked a spot ten feet left of the gate. Reacher took the two switchblades out of his pocket and handed them to Vaughan. Then he stood with his back to the wall, directly underneath the maximum radius of the horizontal cylinder above. Rain sheeted off it and soaked his head and shoulders. He bent down and curled his left palm and made a stirrup. Vaughan lined up directly in front of him, facing him, and put her right foot in the stirrup. He took her weight and she balanced with her wrists on his shoulders and straightened her leg and boosted herself up. He cupped his right hand under her left foot. She stood upright in his palms and her weight fell forward and her belt buckle hit him in the forehead.

'Sorry,' she said.

'Nothing we haven't done before,' he said, muffled.

'I'm ready,' she said.

Reacher was six feet five inches tall and had long arms. In modest motel rooms he could put his palms flat on an eight-foot ceiling. Vaughan was about five feet four. Arms raised, she could probably stretch just shy of seven feet. Total, nearly fifteen feet. And the wall was only fourteen feet high.

He lifted. Like starting a bicep curl with a free weights bar loaded with a hundred and twenty pounds. Easy, except that his hands were turned in at an unnatural angle. And his footing was insecure, and Vaughan wasn't a free weights bar. She wasn't rigid and she was wobbling and struggling to balance.

'Ready?' he called.

'Wait one,' she said.

He felt her weight move in his hands, left to right, right to left, shifting, equalizing, preparing.

'Now go,' she said.

He did four things. He boosted her sharply upward, used her momentary weightlessness to shift his hands flat under her shoes, stepped forward half a pace, and locked his arms straight.

She fell forward through a slight angle and met the bulge of the cylinder with the flats of her forearms. The hollow metal construction boomed once, then again, much delayed.

'OK?' he called.

'I'm there,' she said.

He felt her go up on tiptoes in his palms. Felt her reach up and straighten her arms. According to his best guess her hands should right then have been all the way up on the cylinder's top dead centre. He heard the first switchblade pop open. He swivelled his hands a little and gripped her toes. For stability. She was going to need it. He moved out another few inches. By then she should have been resting with her belly against the metal curve. Rain was streaming down all over him. He heard her stab downward with the knife. The wall clanged and boomed.

'Won't go through,' she called.

'Harder,' he called back.

She stabbed again. Her whole body jerked and he dodged and danced underneath her, keeping her balanced. Like acrobats in a circus. The wall boomed.

'No good,' she called.

'Harder,' he called.

She stabbed again. No boom. Just a little metallic clatter, then nothing.

'The blade broke,' she called.

Reacher's arms were starting to ache.

'Try the other one,' he called. 'Be precise with the angle. Straight downward, OK?'

'The metal is too thick.'

'It's not. It's from an old piece-of-shit Buick,

probably. It's like aluminum foil. And that's a good Japanese blade. Hit it hard. Who do you hate?'

'The guy that pulled the trigger on David.'

'He's inside the wall. His heart is the other side of the metal.'

He heard the second switchblade open. Then there was silence for a second. Then a convulsive jerk through her legs and another dull boom through the metal.

A different boom.

'It's in,' she called. 'All the way.'

'Pull on it,' he called back.

He felt her take her weight on the wooden handle. He felt her twist as she wrapped both fists around it. He felt her feet pull up out of his hands. Then he felt them come back.

'It's slicing through,' she called. 'It's cutting the metal.'

'It will,' he called back. 'It'll stop when it hits a weld.'

He felt it stabilize a second later. Called, 'Where is it?'

'Right at the top.'

'Ready?'

'On three,' she called. 'One, two, *three*.'

She jerked herself upward and he helped as much as he could, fingertips and tiptoes, and then her weight was gone. He came down in a heap and rolled away in case she was coming down on top of him. But she wasn't. He got to his feet and walked away to get a better angle and saw her lying longitudinally on top of the cylinder, legs spread, both hands wrapped tight around the knife

527

handle. She rested like that for a second and then shifted her weight and slid down the far side of the bulge, slowly at first, then faster, swinging around, still holding tight to the knife handle. He saw her clasped hands at the top of the curve, and then her weight started pulling the blade through the metal, fast at first where a track was already sliced and then slower as the blade bit through new metal. It would jam again at the next weld, which he figured was maybe five feet down the far side, allowing for the size of a typical car's roof panel, minus a folded flange at both sides for assembly purposes, which would be about a quarter of the way around the cylinder's circumference, which would mean she would be hanging off the wall at full stretch with about four feet of clear air under the soles of her shoes.

A survivable fall.

Probably.

He waited what seemed like an awful long time, and then he heard two hard thumps on the outside of the wall. They each sounded twice, once immediately and then again as the sound raced around the hollow circle and came back. He closed his eyes and smiled. Their agreed signal. Out, on her feet, no broken bones.

'Impressive,' Thurman said, from ten yards away.

Reacher turned. The old guy was still hatless. His blow-dried waves were ruined. Ninety yards beyond him his two men were still down and inert.

Four minutes, Reacher thought.

Thurman said, 'I could do what she did.'

'In your dreams,' Reacher said. 'She's fit and agile. You're a fat old man. And who's going to boost you up? Real life is not like the movies. Your guys aren't going to wake up and shake their heads and get right to it. They're going to be puking and falling down for a week.'

'Are you proud of that?'

'I gave them a choice.'

'Your lady friend can't open the gate, you know. She doesn't have the combination.'

'Have faith, Mr Thurman. A few minutes from now you're going to see me ascend.'

Reacher strained to hear sounds from the main compound, but the rain was too loud. It hissed in the puddles and pattered on the mud and clanged hard against the metal of the wall. So he just waited. He took up station six feet from the wall and a yard left of where Vaughan had gone over. Thurman backed off and watched.

Three minutes passed. Then four. Then without warning a long canvas strap snaked up and over the wall and the free end landed four feet to Reacher's right. The kind of thing used for tying down scrap cars to a flat-bed trailer. Vaughan had driven Thurman's Tahoe up to the security office and had found a strap of the right length in the pile near the door and had weighted its end by tying it around a scrap of pipe. He pictured her after the drive back, twenty feet away through the metal, swinging the strap like a cowgirl with a rope, building momentum, letting it go, watching it sail over.

Reacher grabbed the strap and freed the pipe

and re-tied the end into a generous two-foot loop. He wrapped the canvas around his right hand and walked towards the wall. Kicked it twice and backed off a step and put his foot in the loop and waited. He pictured Vaughan securing the other end to the trailer hitch on Thurman's Tahoe, climbing into the driver's seat, selecting four wheel drive for maximum traction across the mud, selecting the low-range transfer case for delicate throttle control. He had been insistent about that. He didn't want his arms torn off at the shoulders when she hit the gas.

He waited. Then the strap went tight above him and started to quiver. The canvas around his hand wrapped tight. He pushed down into the loop with his sole. He saw the strap pull across the girth of the cylinder. No friction. Wet canvas on painted metal, slick with rain. The canvas stretched a little. Then he felt serious pressure under his foot and he lifted smoothly into the air. Slowly, maybe twelve inches a second. Less than a mile an hour. Idle speed, for the Tahoe's big V-8. He pictured Vaughan behind the wheel, concentrating hard, her foot like a feather on the pedal.

'Goodbye, Thurman,' he said. 'Looks like it's you that's getting left behind this time.'

Then he looked up and got his left hand on the bulge of the cylinder and pushed back and hauled with his right to stop his wrapped knuckles crushing against the metal. His hips hit the maximum curve and he unwrapped his hand and hung on and let himself be pulled up to top dead centre. Then he dropped the strap and let the loop around his foot pull his legs up sideways

530

and then he kicked free of the loop and came to rest spread-eagled on his stomach along the top of the wall. He jerked his hips and sent his legs down the far side and squealed his palms across ninety degrees of wet metal and pushed off and fell, two long split seconds. He hit the ground and fell on his back and knocked the wind out of himself. He rolled over and forced some air into his lungs and crawled up on his knees.

Vaughan had stopped Thurman's Tahoe twenty feet away. Reacher got to his feet and walked over to it and unhooked the strap from the trailer hitch. Then he climbed into the passenger seat and slammed the door.

'Thanks,' he said.

'You OK?' she asked.

'Fine. You?'

'I feel like I did when I was a kid and I fell out of an apple tree. Scared, but a good scared.' She changed to high-range gearing and took off fast. Two minutes later they were at the main vehicle gate. It was standing wide open.

'We should close it,' Reacher said.

'Why?'

'To help contain the damage. If I'm right.'

'Suppose you're not?'

'Maximum of five phone calls will prove it one way or the other.'

'How do we close it? They don't seem to have any manual override.'

They stopped just outside the gate and got out and walked over to the grey metal box on the wall. Reacher flipped the lid. One through nine, plus zero.

'Try six-six-one-three,' he said.

Vaughan looked blank but stepped up and raised her index finger. Pressed six, six, one, three, neat and rapid. There was silence for a second and then motors whined and the gates started closing. A foot a second, wheels rumbling along tracks. Vaughan asked, 'How did you know?'

'Most codes are four figures,' Reacher said. 'ATM cards, things like that. People are used to four figure codes.'

'Why those four figures?'

'Lucky guess,' Reacher said. 'Revelation is the sixty-sixth book in the King James bible. Chapter one verse three says the time is at hand. Which seems to be Thurman's favourite part.'

'So we could have gotten out without climbing.'

'If we had, they could have, too. I want them in there. So I had to smash the lock.'

'Where to now?'

'The hotel in Despair. The first phone call is one that you get to make.'

SEVENTY-TWO

They drove around the perimeter and abandoned
Thurman's Tahoe next to where Vaughan's old
Chevy was waiting. They transferred between
vehicles and bumped through the deserted parking lot and found the road. Three miles later they
were in downtown Despair. It was still raining.
The streets and the sidewalks were dark and wet
and completely deserted. The middle of the night,
in the middle of nowhere. They threaded through
the cross streets and pulled up outside the hotel.
The façade was as blank and gloomy as before.
The street door was closed but not locked. Inside
the place looked just the same. The empty dining
room on the left, the deserted bar on the right, the
untended reception desk dead ahead. The register
on the desk, the large square leather book. Easy
to grab, easy to swivel around, easy to open, easy
to read. Reacher put his fingertip under the last
registered guests, the couple from California,
from seven months previously. He tilted the book,
so that Vaughan had a clear view of their names
and addresses.

'Call them in,' he said. 'And if they're helping

the deserters, do whatever your conscience tells you to.'

'If?'

'I think they might be into something else.'

Vaughan made the call from her cell and they sat in faded armchairs and waited for the call back. Vaughan said, 'Gifts are a perfectly plausible explanation. Churches send foreign aid all the time. Volunteers, too. They're usually good people.'

'No argument from me,' Reacher said. 'But my whole life has been about the people that aren't usual. The exceptions.'

'Why are you so convinced?'

'The welding.'

'Locks can be broken.'

'The container was welded to the trailer. And that's not how containers get shipped. They get lifted off and put on boats. By cranes. That's the whole point of containers. The welding suggests they don't mean for that container to leave the country.'

Vaughan's phone rang. A three-minute wait. From a cop's perspective, the upside of all the Homeland Security hoopla. Agencies talked, computers were linked, databases were shared. She answered and listened, four long minutes. Then she thanked her caller and clicked off.

'Can't rule out the AWOL involvement,' she said.

'Because?' Reacher asked.

'They're listed as activists. And activists can be into all kinds of things.'

'What kind of activists?'

'Religious conservatives.'

'What kind?'

'They run something called the Church of the Apocalypse in LA.'

'The Apocalypse is a part of the End Times story,' Reacher said.

Vaughan said nothing.

Reacher said, 'Maybe they came here to recruit Thurman as a brother activist. Maybe they recognized his special potential.'

'They wouldn't have stayed in this hotel. They'd have been guests in his house.'

'Not the first time. He didn't know them yet. The second time, maybe. And the third and the fourth, maybe the fifth and the sixth. Depends how hard they had to work to convince him. There's a four month gap between their first visit and when he ordered the TNT from Kearny.'

'He said that was a bureaucratic error.'

'Did you believe him?'

Vaughan didn't answer.

'Four phone calls,' Reacher said. 'That's all it's going to take.'

They left the hotel and got back in the Chevy and drove west to the edge of town. Three miles away through the rainy darkness they could see the plant's lights, faint and blue and distant, blurred by the rain on the windshield, a fragmented sepulchral glow way out in the middle of nowhere. Empty space all around it. They parked on a kerb facing out of town, level with the last of the buildings. Reacher eased his butt off the seat and took the cell phone he had borrowed out of his pocket. Then he took out the sheet of paper he had taken from the purchasing office. The new cell phone numbers. The paper was wet and soggy and he had to peel apart the folds very carefully.

'Ready?' he asked.

Vaughan said, 'I don't understand.'

He dialled the third number down. Heard ring tone in his ear, twice, four times, six times, eight. Then the call was answered. A muttered greeting, in a voice he recognized. A man's voice, fairly normal in tone and timbre, but a little dazed, and muffled twice, first by coming from a huge chest cavity, and again by the cellular circuitry.

The big guy, from the plant.

Reacher said, 'How are you? Been awake long?'

The guy said, 'Go to hell.'

Reacher said, 'Maybe I will, maybe I won't. I'm not sure about the likelihood of things like that. You guys are the theologians, not me.'

No reply.

Reacher asked, 'Is your buddy awake too?'

No reply.

Reacher said, 'I'll call him and see for myself.'

He clicked off and dialled the second number on the list. It rang eight times and the plant foreman answered.

Reacher said, 'Sorry, wrong number.'

He clicked off.

Vaughan asked, 'What exactly are you doing?'

'How did the insurgents hurt David?'

'With a roadside bomb.'

'Detonated how?'

'Remotely, I assume.'

Reacher nodded. 'Probably by radio, from the

nearest ridge line. So if Thurman *has* built a bomb, how will he detonate it?'

'The same way.'

'But not from the nearest hill. He'll probably want a lot more distance than that. He'll probably want to be out of state somewhere. Maybe at home here in Colorado, or in his damn church. Which would take a very powerful radio. In fact, he'd probably have to build one himself, to be sure of reliability. Which is a lot of work. So my guess is he decided to use one that someone else already built. Someone like Verizon or T-Mobile or Cingular.'

'Cell phone?'

Reacher nodded again. 'It's the best way. The phone companies spend a lot of time and money building reliable networks. You can see their commercials on TV. They're proud of the fact that you can call anywhere from anywhere. Some of them even give you free long distance.'

'And the number is on that list?'

'It would make sense,' Reacher said. 'Two things happened at the same time, three months ago. Thurman ordered twenty tons of TNT, and four new cell phones. Sounds like a plan to me. He already had everything else he needed. My guess is he kept one phone for himself, and gave two to his inner circle, so they could have secure communications between themselves, separate from anything else they were doing. And my guess is the fourth phone is buried in the heart of that container, with the ringer wired to a primer circuit. The ringer on a cell phone puts out a decent little voltage. Maybe they fitted a standby battery, and maybe they connected an external antenna. Maybe one of those antennas on the Peterbilt was a cell antenna from Radio Shack, wired back to the trailer.'

'And you're going to call that number?'

Reacher said, 'Soon.'

He dialled the first number on the list. It rang, and then Thurman answered, fast and impatient, like he had been waiting for the call. Reacher asked, 'You guys over the wall yet? Or are you still in there?'

Thurman said, 'We're still here. Why are you calling us?'

'You starting to see a pattern?'

'The other phone was Underwood's. He's dead, so he won't answer. So there's no point calling it.'

Reacher said, 'OK.'

'How long are you going to keep us here?'

'Just a minute more,' Reacher said. He clicked off and laid the phone on the Chevy's dash. Stared out through the windshield.

Vaughan said, 'You can't do this. It would be murder.'

Reacher said, 'Live by the sword, die by the sword. Thurman should know that quotation better than anyone. It's from the bible. Matthew, chapter twenty-six, verse fifty-two. Slightly paraphrased. Also, they have sown the wind, and they shall reap the whirlwind. Hosea, chapter eight, verse seven. I'm sick of people who claim to live by the scriptures cherry-picking the parts they find convenient, and ignoring all the rest.'

'You could be completely wrong about him.'

'Then there's no problem. Gifts don't explode. We've got nothing to lose.'

'But you might be right.'

'In which case he shouldn't have lied to me. He should have confessed. I would have let him take his chance in court.'

'I don't believe you.'

'We'll never know now.'

'He doesn't seem worried enough.'

'He's used to saying things and having people believe him.'

'Even so.'

'He told me he's not afraid of dying. He told me he's going to a better place.'

'You're not a one-man justice department.'

'He's no better than whoever blew up David's Humvee. Worse, even. David was a combatant, at least. And out on the open road. Thurman is going to have that thing driven to a city somewhere. With children and old people all around. Thousands of them. And more thousands maybe not quite close enough. He's going to put thousands more people in your situation.'

Vaughan said nothing.

'And for what?' Reacher said. 'For some stupid, deluded fantasy.'

Vaughan said nothing.

Reacher checked the final number. Entered it into his phone. Held the phone flat on his palm and held it out to Vaughan.

'Your choice,' he said. 'Green button to make the call, red button to cancel it.'

Vaughan didn't move for a moment. Then she took her hand off the wheel. Folded three fingers and her thumb. Held her index finger out straight. It was small, neat, elegant, and damp, and it had a trimmed nail. She held it still, close to the phone's LED window.

Then she moved it.

She pressed the green button.

Nothing happened. Not at first. Reacher wasn't surprised. He knew a little about cell phone technology. He had read a long article, in a trade publication abandoned on an airplane. Press the green button, and the phone in your hand sends a request by radio to the nearest cell tower, called a base transceiver station by the people who put it there. The phone says: *Hey, I want to make a call.* The base transceiver station forwards the plea to the nearest base station controller, by microwave if the bean counters got their way during the planning phase, or by fibre optic cable if the engineers got theirs. The base station controller bundles all the near-simultaneous requests it can find and moves them on to the closest mobile switching centre, where the serious action starts.

Maybe at this point a ring tone starts up in your earpiece. But it means nothing. It's a placebo. It's there to reassure you. So far you're not even close to connected.

The mobile switching centre identifies the destination phone. Checks if it's switched on, that it's not busy, that it's not set to call divert. Speech channels are limited in number, and therefore expensive to operate. You don't get near one unless there's a viable chance of an answer.

If all is well, a speech channel clicks in. It extends first from your local mobile switching centre to its distant opposite number. Maybe by fibre optics, maybe by microwave, maybe by satellite if the distance is great. Then the distant mobile switching centre hits up its closest base station controller, which hits up its closest base transceiver station, which emits a radio blast to the phone you're looking for, an 850 megahertz or a 1.9 gigahertz pulse surfing on a perfect spherical wavefront close to the speed of light. A nanosecond later, the circuit is complete and the tone in your ear morphs from phoney to real and the target phone starts its urgent ringing.

Total time lag, an average of seven whole seconds.

Vaughan took her finger back and stared forward out the windshield. The Chevy's engine was still running and the wipers were still beating back and forth. The windshield smeared in perfect arcs. There was still a little protective wax on the glass.

Two seconds.

'Nothing,' Vaughan said.

Reacher said, 'Wait.'

Four seconds.

Five.

They stared into the distance. The blue arena lights hung and shimmered in the wet air, pale and misty, fractured by intervening raindrops like twinkling starlight.

Six seconds.

Seven.

Then: the silent horizon lit up with an immense

white flash that filled the windshield and bloomed instantly higher and wider. The rain all around turned to steam as the air superheated and jets of white vapour speared up and out in every direction like a hundred thousand rockets had launched simultaneously. The vapour was followed by a halo of black soot that punched instantly from a tight cap to a raging black hemisphere a mile high and a mile wide. It rolled and tore and folded back on itself and was pierced by violent trails of steam as supersonic white-hot shrapnel was flung through it at more than fifteen thousand miles an hour.

No sound. Not then. Just blinding light and silence.

In still air the sound would have taken fourteen seconds to arrive from three miles away. But the air wasn't still. It was moving fast in a massive compression wave. The wave carried the sound with it. It arrived three seconds after the light. The truck rocked back against the brake and the air roared with the rolling violence of the explosion, first a crisp deafening *crump* and then a banshee screaming from the shrapnel in the air and an otherworldly pelting sound as a million blasted fragments obliterated everything in their path and fell to earth and tore up the scrub and boiled and hissed where they lay. Then the decompression wave blew in the other way as air rushed back to fill the vacuum, and the truck rocked again, and the black cloud was pulverized to nothing by the violent wind, and then there was nothing to see except tongues of random flame and spouts of drifting steam, and nothing to hear except the steady patter of shrapnel falling back to earth from three miles up, and after ten long seconds there was not even that, just the patient rain on the Chevy's roof.

SEVENTY-THREE

Vaughan called out the whole of the Hope PD for crowd control. Within thirty minutes she had all four of her deputies and her brother officer and her watch commander and the desk guy all lined up on the western edge of Despair's last block. Nobody was allowed through. The state cops showed up next. Within an hour they had three cars there. Five more showed up within the next four hours. They had taken the long way around. Everyone knew there had been uranium at the plant. The state cops confirmed that the MPs had the road blocked to the west, on a five-mile perimeter. It was close to dawn and they were already stopping incoming trucks.

Dawn came and the rain finally stopped and the sky went hard blue and the air went crystal clear. *Like nerves after pain*, Reacher had read once, in a poem. The morning was too cool to raise steam off the soaked ground. The mountains looked a thousand miles away, but every detail was visible. Their rocky outcrops, their pine forests, their tree lines, their snow channels. Reacher borrowed a pair of binoculars from Vaughan's watch commander and climbed to the third floor of the last building to the west. He struggled with a jammed window and crouched and put his elbows on the sill and focused into the distance.

Not much to see.

The white metal wall was gone. Just a few rags and tatters of shredded metal remained, blown and tumbled hundreds of yards in every direction. The plant itself was mostly a black smoking pit, with cranes and gantries knocked over and smashed and bent. Crushers had been toppled off their concrete pads. Anything smaller had been smashed to pieces too small to reliably identify. The office buildings were gone entirely. Thurman's residential compound had been obliterated. The house had been smashed to matchwood. The fieldstone wall was a horizontal rock field spread south and west like grains of spilled salt on a table. The plantings were all gone. Occasional foot-high stumps were all that was left of the trees. The airplane barn had been demolished. No sign of the Piper.

Immense damage.

Better here than somewhere else, Reacher thought.

He came downstairs to a changed situation. Federal agencies had arrived. Gossip was flowing. Air force radar in Colorado Springs had detected metal fifteen thousand feet up. It had hung there for a long second before falling back to earth. Radiation-sniffing drone planes had been dispatched and were closing in on wide circular paths. The rain was seen as a mercy. DU dust was held to be strongly hygroscopic. Nothing bad would drift. Every contractor within a hundred miles, in Colorado and Nebraska and Kansas, had been contacted. A hurricane fence nearly nineteen miles long was needed. The site was going to be fenced off for ever, on a three-mile radius. The fence was going to be hung with biohazard signs every six feet. The agencies already owned the signs, but not the wire.

No hard information was volunteered by the townsfolk. No hard questions were asked by the agencies. The word on everyone's lips was *accident*. *An accident at the plant.* It was second nature, a part of the hardscrabble culture. An accident at the mill, an accident at the mine. Consistent with history. If the agencies had doubts, they knew better than to voice them. The Pentagon had begun to stonewall even before the last fragments had cooled.

State officials arrived, with contingency plans. Food and water was to be trucked in. Buses were to be laid on, for job searches in neighbouring towns. Special welfare would be provided, for the first six months. Transitional help of every kind would be afforded. After that, any stragglers would be strictly on their own.

First Reacher and then Vaughan were pushed steadily east by the official activity. By the middle of the afternoon they were sitting together in the Chevy outside the dry goods store, with nothing more to do. They took one last look to the west and then set off down the road towards Hope.

*   *   *

They went to Vaughan's house, and showered, and dressed again. Vaughan said, 'David's hospital is going to fold.'

'Someone else will step in,' Reacher said. 'Someone better.'

'I'm not going to abandon him.'

'I don't think you should.'

'Even though he won't know.'

'He knew beforehand. And it was important to him.'

'You think so?'

'I know so. I know soldiers.'

Reacher took the borrowed phone out of his pocket and dropped it on the bed. Followed it with the registration, from the old Suburban's glove box. Asked Vaughan to mail both things back, with no return address on the package. She said, 'That sounds like the start of a farewell speech.'

'It is,' Reacher said. 'And the middle, and the end.'

They hugged, a little formally, like two strangers who shared many secrets. Then Reacher left. He walked down her winding path, and walked four blocks north to First Street. He got a ride very easily. A stream of vehicles was heading east, emergency workers, journalists, men in suits in plain sedans, contractors. The excitement had made them friendly. There was a real community spirit. Reacher rode with a post hole digger from Kansas who had signed up to dig some of the sixteen thousand holes deemed necessary for the new fence. The guy was cheerful. He was looking at months of steady work.

Reacher got out in Sharon Springs, where there was a good road south. He figured San Diego was about a thousand miles away, or more, if he followed some detours.

THE END

A HISTORY
OF
PAGAN
EUROPE

PRUDENCE JONES & NIGEL PENNICK

BARNES
&NOBLE
BOOKS
NEW YORK

CONTENTS

v

ILLUSTRATIONS

MAPS

PLATES

vii

PREFACE AND ACKNOWLEDGEMENTS

This book has been in the making for twenty years, since one of the authors lived in Canada, a European culture made intangibly different by the absence of encrusted layers of European history. Part of the reason for this intangible difference is made clear in the present volume. The European Pagan heritage is one that is generally overlooked, but here we bring it to light.

Over the years many people have helped with ideas and research. For the present volume, two people in particular have given of their time and expertise and our manuscript would be much the poorer without them. One is Mr Phil Line, who kindly offered his considerable knowledge of Finnic and Baltic religion in reading our chapters 9 and 10. The other, and principal helper, is Dr Ronald Hutton, who valiantly read through the whole manuscript, making many observations on matters of fact, restraining any impulse to comment on points of interpretation, but keeping us up to date with current scholarship on the subject. Any errors that remain are ours and not theirs.

We are acutely aware that worthwhile research is impossible without easy access to literary sources and commentaries. The open bookstacks of the Cambridge University Library are a blessing to the serious investigator, and its friendly and helpful staff turn research into a pleasure.

All references are credited in the footnotes, but we are grateful to the following for permission to reprint longer passages of copyright material:

Viking Penguin, Inc., Laurence Pollinger Ltd and the Estate of Frieda Lawrence Ravagli for the quotation from D.H. Lawrence on p. 2; Thomas Kinsella for the quotation from his edition of *The Táin* on p. 91; Chatto & Windus for the quotations from the *Orkneyinga Saga* on p. 150; Basil Blackwell Ltd and Harper Collins USA for the quotation from J.M. Wallace-Hadrill's *The Barbarian West* on p. 152; and Macmillan Ltd for the quotation from Eric Christiansen's translation of the *Galician-Livonian Chronicle* on p. 172. All attempts at tracing the copyright holder of the quotations from John Holland Smith's *Death of Classical Paganism* in chapter 4 have been unsuccessful, but we are grateful to Cassell plc, present owners of the Geoffrey Chapman imprint, for their help in the matter.

Prudence Jones
Nigel Pennick
Lammas 1994

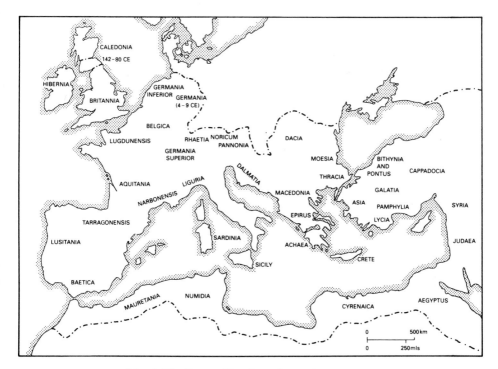

Map 1 The Roman Empire at its maximum extent
(dates in brackets denote short-term occupations).

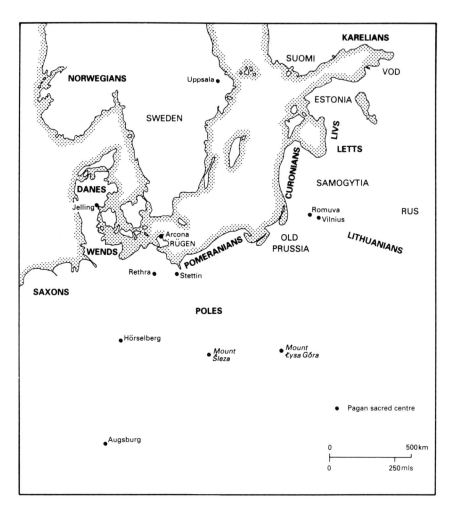

Map 2 The Baltic and East–Central Europe, tenth to twelfth century.

1

INTRODUCTION: PAGANISM OLD AND NEW

In this book we describe the hidden history of Europe, the persistence of its native religion in various forms from ancient times right up to the present day. Most people today are more familiar with native traditions from outside Europe than with their own spiritual heritage. The Native American tradition, the tribal religions of Africa, the sophistication of Hindu belief and practice and the more recently revived Japanese tradition, Shinto, are widely acknowledged as the authentic native animistic traditions of their respective areas. In marked contrast, the European native tradition, from the massive civilisations of Greece and Rome to the barely documented tribal systems of the Picts, the Finns and others on the northern margins of the continent, has been seen as having been obliterated totally. This tradition is presented as having been superseded first by Christianity and Islam and, more recently, by post-Christian humanism. In this book we argue that, on the contrary, it has continued to exist and even to flourish more or less openly up to the present day, when it is undergoing a new restoration.

But first to define our terms. The word 'pagan' (small 'p') is often used pejoratively to mean simply 'uncivilised', or even 'un-Christian' (the two generally being assumed to be identical), in the same way that 'heathen' is used. Its literal meaning is 'rural', 'from the countryside (*pagus*)'. As a religious designation it was used first by early Christians in the Roman Empire to describe followers of the other (non-Jewish) religions, not, as was once thought, because it was mainly country bumpkins rather than sophisticated urban freethinkers who followed the Old Ways, but because Roman soldiers of the time used the word *paganus*, contemptuously, for civilians or non-combatants. The early Christians, thinking of themselves as 'soldiers of Christ', looked down on those who did not follow their religion as mere stay-at-homes, *pagani*. This usage does not seem to have lasted long outside the Christian community. By the fourth century, 'Pagan' had returned closer to its root meaning and was being used non-polemically to describe anyone who worshipped the spirit of a given locality or *pagus*.[1]

The name stuck long after its origin had been forgotten, and developed a new overlay of usage, referring to the great Classical civilisations of Greece

1

and Rome, Persia, Carthage, etc. Early Christian writers composed diatribes 'against the Pagans', by which they meant philosophers and theologians such as Plato, Porphyry, Plutarch, Celsus and other predecessors or contemporaries. Much later, when Classical literature resurfaced in the European Renaissance, the literati of the time composed essays on Pagan philosophy, and by the nineteenth century the use of the word as a near-synonym for 'Classical' had become established. At the beginning of the twentieth century, D.H. Lawrence's literary group 'The Pagans' drew its inspiration from Greece and what he later called its 'big, old Pagan vision, before the *idea* and the concept of personality made everything so small and tight as it is now'.[2]

Lawrence's terminology has overtones of more recent contemporary usage, where 'Pagan' is employed once more in its root meaning to describe a Nature-venerating religion which endeavours to set human life in harmony with the great cycles embodied in the rhythms of the seasons. In what follows we adhere broadly to this convention, using the word 'Paganism' (capital 'P') to refer to Nature-venerating indigenous spiritual traditions generally, and in particular to that of Europe, which has been specifically reaffirmed by its contemporary adherents under that name. Pagan religions, in this sense, have the following characteristics in common:

- They are polytheistic, recognising a plurality of divine beings, which may or may not be avatars or other aspects of an underlying unity/duality/trinity etc.
- They view Nature as a theophany, a manifestation of divinity, not as a 'fallen' creation of the latter.
- They recognise the female divine principle, called the Goddess (with a capital 'G', to distinguish her from the many particular goddesses), as well as, or instead of, the male divine principle, the God. (Throughout this book we use the word 'god' exclusively to refer to male divinities, not to the divine source or godhead itself.)

In this sense all native animistic religions worldwide are Pagan, fulfilling all three characteristics. A religion such as Hinduism is Pagan, but Judaism, Islam and Christianity are obviously not, since they all deny the Goddess as well as one or both of the other characteristics. Buddhism, which grew out of the native Hindu tradition, is a highly abstract belief system, dealing with that which is beyond time and manifestation rather than with the interventions of deities in the world. In its pure form it retains little in common with its Pagan parent. All three characteristics listed above are, however, shared by modern Paganism in its various forms with the ancient religions of the peoples of Europe, as this book will show.

In recent years many people of European origin have been drawing on the ancient indigenous tradition as the basis of a new religion for the twenty-first century. This new religion, called neo-Paganism or simply Paganism, is most broadly a form of Nature-mysticism. It is a belief which views the Earth

2

and all material things as a theophany, an outpouring of the divine presence, which itself is usually personified in the figure of the Great Goddess and her consort, the God or masculine principle of Nature. Between them, these two principles are thought to encompass all existence and all development. In some ways this is a new religion for the New Age. Modern thought is represented in these two basic divinities whose influence is complementary rather than hierarchical or antagonistic. Present-day Pagans tend to see all gods and goddesses as being personifications of these two, in contrast to the situation in antiquity, when the many gods and goddesses of the time were usually thought of as truly independent entities. In its most widely publicised form, neo-Paganism is a theology of polarity, rather than the polytheism of ancient European culture.

But modern Paganism is also an outgrowth from the old European tradition. It has reclaimed the latter's sacred sites, festivals and deities from obscurity and reinterpreted them in a form which is intended to be a living continuation of their original function. Followers of specific paths within it such as Druidry, Wicca and Ásatrú aim to live a contemporary form of those older religions which are described or hinted at in ancient writings, as in Iceland, where Ásatrú is a legally established religion, drawing its guidelines directly from the Old Norse sagas and shaping their outlook into a form which is continuous with the past but appropriate for the twentieth century. At the opposite extreme, many neo-Pagans, in Anglo-Saxon countries in particular, follow no structured path but adhere to a generally Nature-venerating, polytheistic, Goddess-centred outlook which is of a piece with the general religious attitude chronicled here.

Why has Paganism arisen again in modern Europe and America? We deal with the historical process in the final chapter, but the underlying impetus seems to have been first, the search for a religion which venerated the Goddess and so gave women as well as men the dignity of beings who bear the 'lineaments of divinity'. This has been thought necessary by women whose political emancipation has not been paralleled by an equivalent development in their religious status. (Even in Pagan, polytheistic Hinduism the cult of Kali, the Great Mother, is one of the most rapidly growing popular religions at the present time.[3]) Secondly, in Europe and America a greater respect for the Earth has come into prominence. The ecological 'green' movement has gone hand in hand with a willingness to pay attention to the intrinsic pattern of the physical world, its rhythm and its 'spirit of place'. This has led to a renewed recognition of the value of understanding traditional skills and beliefs and their underlying philosophy, which is generally Pagan. And finally, the influence of Pagan philosophies from the Orient has gone hand in hand with this development, providing a sophisticated rationale for practices which might in former times have been dismissed as superstitious and unfounded. The Pagan resurgence thus seems to be part of a general process of putting humanity, long seen by both the monotheistic religions and by secular materialism in abstraction from its surroundings, back into a more general context. This context is both physical, by reference to the material world understood as an essential part of life, and chronological, as shown in the search for modern continuity with ancient philosophies. The ancient religions are often not well known outside their areas of academic specialisation, and the evidence for their continuation is often misunderstood or misrepresented as 'accident' or 'superstition'. It is the evidence for such continuity which this book investigates.

The area of our study covers the whole of Europe, beginning with Greece and the eastern Mediterranean, home of the earliest written records; continuing west by way of Rome and its Empire; then through the so-called 'Celtic fringe' of France, Britain and parts of the Low Countries; then to what are now Germany and Scandinavia; and finally to eastern and central Europe, the Baltic states and Russia, which (apart from Russia and the South Slav states) emerged most recently into historical record. Europe in this sense is a geographical entity divided roughly into north and south by the Alps, and into east and west by the Prague meridian. After the Holy Roman Empire in the west and the Byzantine Empire in the east defined Christendom between them, Europe became a cultural unity, and its native religious tradition disappeared area by area into relative obscurity. This vital, yet half-hidden, European tradition is what we put on record here.

The centuries covered run from the dawn of recorded history to the present day: different timescales in different areas. The process of interpreting Stone-age remains is too extensive and currently too embattled to be capable of fair handling in the context of this book. It is enough to describe what people believed and what they did, at what times and in what places. In this lies a fascinating story, and we shall begin with the earliest records.

2

THE GREEKS AND THE EASTERN MEDITERRANEAN

The earliest written records in Europe come from Crete. This civilisation, flourishing without a break from about 2800 to the beginning of the 300-year-long Dark Age in about 1100 BCE, provides a unique link between archaeology and written history. From later Greek legend (written down after 800 BCE) we hear that Crete was well populated and prosperous, that its navy ruled the seas, and that one of its kings, Minos, exacted tribute of seven boys and seven girls every seven years from Athens. These victims were said to be sacrificed to the Minotaur, a monster half man, half bull, which lived at the centre of a labyrinth built by the great technician Daedalus.[1] The Greeks spoke of the main deity of the island as Poseidon, their own god of the sea, earthquakes and storms, and of his cult animal as the bull. Archaeology shows evidence of high culture and prosperity, of a lack of fortifications indicating protection by the sea rather than by a garrison. It shows an extensive bull-cult, and in the deciphered Cretan writings (the so-called Linear B script, dating from around 1500 BCE) Poseidon himself is named. His name means simply 'Lord'.

However, Poseidon is never depicted, at least in human form, in the art of the Cretans themselves. The only anthropomorphic divinity which is pictured throughout Cretan iconography is, in fact, a goddess, or several goddesses, which in style resemble one from nearby Asia Minor who was later known as the Great Mother. This goddess was worshipped continuously in Asia Minor from the seventh millennium before our era until the fall of the Roman Empire.[2] Her worship was brought to Athens and later to Rome. Nevertheless, the Cretan inscriptions do not name a Great Mother. They mention various goddesses, some known from Greek times, such as Hera and Athene, and others who are unknown from later writings.

At this time many peoples in the Near East, an area with which Crete had trading links, worshipped goddesses similar to the later Great Mother, each accompanied by a male consort who was named but never portrayed, a sky-god of lightning and storms. Examples are the Syrian Atargatis and Ramman, and, of course, the Canaanite Asherah and Baal, against whose worship the Israelite prophets of the rival god Jahweh campaigned.[3] A double

5

axe like that of the Near Eastern sky-gods also appears in Cretan art, but in Crete it is almost always found in the hands of a woman, a goddess, presumably, or her priestess. Its Cretan name is *labrys*, and it apparently gave its name to the labyrinth, home of the monstrous Minotaur, half man, half bull. In ninth-century Canaan, Asherah, represented not by a human image but by a tree or a pillar, had a bull as her cult animal, the bull that is criticised by the prophets of Jaweh in the Old Testament as the golden calf. It is heir to a long tradition of bull images reaching back to Çatal Hüyük in the seventh millennium BCE, which itself no doubt had another legacy in the bull-cult of Egypt, likewise an active participant in the political and trading network of the eastern Mediterranean. It is against this background of deity-forms and sacred images that the bull horns, bull sacrifices and bull-god of legendary Crete must be seen.

The Greek goddess Hera's epithet, 'ox-eyed', may also recall the Cretan goddess and her contemporaries in the Near East. Her original cult image at Samos was a plank, and at Argos a pillar, later decorated with garlands and jewels, but in its original form recalling the wooden pillar of Asherah. The oldest temples in Greek culture (dating from about 800 BCE) were built to house cult images of this goddess, which may be because she was the most important deity of the time, or perhaps because her image was thought of as most in need of protection.[4] As late as the first century of our era, Lucian, describing the worship of the Great Mother Atargatis in Syria, calls the goddess Hera, and her consort, the sky-god Ramman, he calls Zeus. Such persistent accounts and images of the Queen of the Immortals, her pillar, her ox and her consort, the aniconic god of storms and (in Greece and Asia) lightning or (in Crete) sea and earthquakes, are difficult to ignore. This storm-god – Baal, Ramman, Poseidon, Zeus – is no boyish son of the Great Mother, he is not Tammuz or Attis, but an independent principle, worshipped in his own right alongside the goddess and sometimes described as her brother (as Zeus is of Hera, and Baal is of Ana't). In using gender to symbolise a complementary duality the early culture of Greece, through Crete, appears to be continuous with that of the Near East.

Many sanctuaries in later Greek culture centred on a sacred tree, and the Cretan icons reveal a similar practice. The single tree, fenced or walled off, with or without an altar beside it, is a universal feature of European sacred culture, and indeed it appears throughout Eurasia and Africa. In Minoan Crete the icons show people dancing in the walled-off area around a single fig or olive tree. Sometimes a goddess appears hovering in the air above the dancers, perhaps seen by them in a visionary state brought on by their activity. Once more, Greek legend (e.g. the *Iliad* XVIII.591) tells how King Minos built a dancing-floor for his daughter Ariadne. Some of the early tombs also have what appear to be dancing-floors next to them. Were the dances a solemn celebration of the ritual event, as in later Greek choral practice? Or did the dancers dance themselves into ecstasy in order to see

Plate 2.1 Cretan seal showing female figures, perhaps goddesses or priestesses, with the familiar symbol of the double axe and the Sun and Moon. The waning Moon and shield-bearing warrior (a god?) on the left may indicate death and diminishment; the Sun and the berries or grapes on the right may indicate life and abundance, 1500 BCE.

their deities, as did the later Greek worshippers of Dionysos? We do not know.

Another Cretan goddess we know of (from the *Odyssey* XIX.188) is Eileithyia, whose cave is found at Amnisos near Knossos. In this cave are found shards of pottery dating from neolithic to Roman times. Eileithyia was the Greek goddess of childbirth and her cave is a remarkable site. At the entrance is a rock formation similar to a recumbent belly with a noticeable navel. At the back is what appears to be a seated figure, and near it is a pool of mineral water, a healing spring. In the middle of the cave is a stalagmite which unmistakably resembles a female figure, although the top of it (the head) has been broken off. It is surrounded by a low wall, with a stone block in front which may have served as an altar. The goddess-like stalagmite was worn smooth by constant touching. Here is a Goddess site at which worship seems to have been continuous throughout human habitation in the area.[5]

The deities were also worshipped on mountain tops, where we have the only archaeological evidence of sacrifice by fire. The charred remains both of votive terracottas and of animals have been found, but otherwise there is no evidence, literary or pictorial, of what was done there or which deities were worshipped. In the cities, however, many houses had a sanctuary or temple room, with a low altar on which stood the well-known figurines of bare-breasted women – goddesses? – in flounced skirts, often holding snakes or other animals such as cats. There were temples, too, and the Linear B inscriptions mention priestesses (but only in one case a priest). No trace has been found, however, of the sort of lifesize or larger cult statues which existed in later Greek temples. We can speculate once more about the pillar-goddess of the Near East. Plato, in the *Critias* (IX c), describes the sacred pillar, made of orichalcum, in the temple of Poseidon in Atlantis, on which bulls were sacrificed and which was lustrated with their blood afterwards. However, no such pillar has been found on Crete.[6]

In Crete, then, we see the population, protected by the sea and their fleet, pursuing an artistic, creative celebration of the forces of Nature, expressed through dance and through athletic rituals such as bull-leaping. Since the majority of Crete's inhabitants did not have to be perpetually ready for war, and since, according to Greek legend, a king of the island, Minos, instituted the first laws in the world, a ceremonial culture emerged. The icons of that culture did not depict Poseidon, the raging storm-god, but an impressive, even inspirational goddess (or goddesses) whose names are unknown.

But Cretan culture was not simply an outpost of Middle Eastern Goddess-worship. On the mainland of Greece, a civilisation grew up which from the second millennium intermingled with it. This was initially characterised, in the third millennium, by walled settlements with large central buildings. In contrast to the Cretans, who mostly sacrificed by gifts to their deities, placed on the altar and left whole, the mainland settlements show traces of animal sacrifice by fire. The few statues which have been found include ithyphallic male figures, and masks,[7] both of which are used worldwide as symbols of defence, warnings of the reality which the settlement walls embodied. On the mainland, all settlements had to be ready to defend themselves in hand-to-hand combat, and warriors had a high status. This early culture matured by the middle of the second millennium BCE into the Mycenean civilisation which is the subject of the *Iliad*.

In Mycenae itself, the contents of the shaft-graves dating from the seventeenth and sixteenth centuries make it clear that this was a warrior society, not simply a self-protective community which fortified its settlements. The tall, strong skeletons and the large quantities of weapons contained in the graves argue for a warrior elite whose members were given sumptuous burials. The style of Mycenean artwork, seal-stones, frescoes and metalwork is Minoan, but the scenes depicted are scenes of warfare and of hunting, not the dances and rituals of Minoan art. Beginning with the Cretan earthquake of 1730 BCE, which flattened the buildings of early Minoan culture, the Mycenean and Minoan communities became more strongly interconnected, perhaps through trading, perhaps through conquest, perhaps through migration. Cretan colonies sprang up on the other Aegean islands, but the Myceneans ruled the mainland of Greece from their citadel cities, and after the eruption of Mount Thera (Santorini) around 1500 they conquered Crete itself and became the undisputed rulers of the whole Mediterranean.

The Myceneans spoke Greek, an Indo-European language, and probably introduced it to the islands if not to the mainland. Linear B, the script which appears on Crete after their conquest, as well as in Pylos, Thebes and Mycenae, is a form of Greek. It gives us invaluable information about the deities worshipped at the time. There are references to Zeus (Diwija) and Hera, Athene (Atana), Poseidon (Posedaon), Paeon (Pajawo – the Greek form is an epithet of Apollo) and to Dionysos (Diwonusojo), who never became an Olympian and who had previously been assumed to be a new god, imported from Thessaly or from Asia Minor. As Crete was reported to be, the Greek ports which traded with Crete are indubitably sites of Poseidon worship.[8] We do not know, however, whether the Cretans also worshipped these other deities who later became the Olympians, or whether the Myceneans brought them with them from the mainland.

THE GREEKS

After the fall of the Myceneans around 1150, history is silent for nearly four hundred years until the poems of Hesiod and of Homer were committed to writing and fixed the names and natures of the Olympian deities. The names of these twelve deities and the stories of their family squabbles as told by Homer and the other poets have become common knowledge in European culture. Scholars once assumed that this was all there was to Greek religion: the imposition of a model of the patriarchal extended family upon the more 'primitive' indigenous cults of a conquered land. In fact, the dichotomy is not so simple.

There was no one clear conquest. The sixth-century historian Herodotus claims that another Greek-speaking people, the Dorians, invaded Mycenean land from the north-west of Greece and took over almost all the peninsula (except Attica). The gods and goddesses in the ensuing Greek literature, beginning with the poems attributed to Homer and to Hesiod, were said to live on Mount Olympus, a peak in the north of Thessaly, near Macedonia. Under economic as well as military pressure, many of the previous inhabitants, now calling themselves Ionians, dispersed eastward to Asia Minor and the Aegean islands, southward to Libya, Egypt and Ethiopia, and westward to found such colonies as Gades (Cadiz) in what is now Spain, Massilia (Marseilles) in France, and the extensive Italian settlements of Magna Graecia. In Italy, the Greek colony later shaped early Roman culture.

The distinction between the old deities and those of the newcomers is not clear cut. As we have seen, several of the deities of Olympus, long thought to have been introduced by the Dorian invaders, were known in Minoan-Mycenean Crete as early as 1500 BCE. On the mainland, the new Greeks took over many of the old sanctuaries dating back to pre-Mycenean times.

They erected fire altars and later temples to house the divine images. The cults set up by the conquerors, immigrants and traders became continuous with the existing cults based on the personified spirit of place. In Athens, for example, the ruling family had traced its descent to a snake-ancestor, Erechtheus, whose tomb stood on the Acropolis. An oracle spoke and also allowed sacrifices to be made to Poseidon in the temple of Erechtheus. Poseidon, as we have already seen, was already worshipped in the Aegean and was not a new deity imported by the Dorians. As a gift to the city he gave a salt-water spring which gushed from the rocks of the citadel.[9] Later Poseidon is said to have 'quarrelled' with the goddess Athene over which one of them was to become the guardian deity of the enlarged city. Now Athene, under her byname, Pallas, may have been the goddess of the earlier ruling clan, the Pallantidae, and so the quarrel would have been a human quarrel of succession. In a vote between the two deities, Athene won. Her gift to the city was the olive tree. A sacred spring and a sacred tree: these totems are typical of indigenous religion the world over, they embody the spirit of place. Early icons of Athene show her with a cloak fringed by snakes, with snakes in her hands, perhaps in continuity with the local ancestor-cult, perhaps in continuity with the snake-goddesses of Crete. In the contest with Poseidon, interestingly, she won because of the women's votes, which outnumbered the men's and as a result of which the Athenian women supposedly lost their voting rights and citizenship. This story reads like a justification for the change in women's status, which again suggests that Athene presided over an earlier state of social organisation. Perhaps among the Pallantidae women did have full citizenship. Athene's name also indicates that she was the personification of Athens, itself the citadel of the state of Attica. Yet both she and Poseidon are fitted by Hesiod and by Homer, writing in the eighth century, into the genealogy of Olympus.

Similar stories can be told from cities all over Greece and the Aegean. Pagan religions always interact creatively with their neighbours, their deities developing or being assimilated under such influence. Yet something new came into Greek religious culture at the time of the Dorian migrations. A mobile, nomadic lifestyle produced a religion which valued abstraction and self-reliance at least as much as clan obligations and affiliation with the spirit of place. Like the god of the Israelites by contrast with the gods and goddesses of the settled Canaanites, the deities of the incoming Dorians stayed with their people wherever they were, and gave them help in dire need. Unlike the One God of the Israelites, however, the various Olympian deities favoured particular individuals and had an affinity with such individuals' characters, thus emphasising the distinguishing traits of personality which had affiliated the person with that deity in the first place.

Thus in the *Hippolytos* of Euripides the chaste and self-contained hero worships the virgin huntress, patroness of wild untamed things, Artemis. Artemis is, of course, the tutelary deity of Hippolytos' mother, the queen of the Amazons. However, his worship of Artemis proves to be excessive, and for his insulting indifference to the goddess of love and enjoyment, Aphrodite, he is cursed. Interestingly, Hippolytos dies through the intervention of the god of the place, Poseidon, rather than through Aphrodite's direct intervention. The abstract, internationalised deities Artemis and Aphrodite (themselves originally local goddesses from elsewhere) battle it out through the medium of the spirit of place. Poseidon was, of course, an earlier 'portable' god from the international Minoan-Mycenean seafaring culture, being the patron of many cities around the Aegean including Athens, as we have seen. In this tale, however (his followers having presumably settled in Athens some time ago), he is presented as the 'father' of Theseus the king, i.e. the latter's mythical ancestor and justification of his kingship according to the ancient tenets of ancestor-worship – soon to be challenged, as we have already seen, by Pallas Athene and her followers, hearkening back to an even older ancestor clan.

Like the Myceneans, the Dorian Greeks offered burnt sacrifices to their deities as well as what were said to be the older 'bloodless' and 'wineless' offerings of milk, wool, oil and honey. Athenaeus (I.46) tells us how gluttonously the heroes of Homer ate meat by contrast with the fruit, fish and vegetable diet of the coastal people, and this distinction is embodied in the different foods brought to sacrifice. Only about half of the Mycenean deities were recognised by the new culture, perhaps because writing effectively died out during the Dark Age, or perhaps because their worship seemed irrelevant to the new ways. Two new deities, Apollo and Aphrodite, are named by Homer and have cult sites going back to the eighth century and the twelfth century respectively. They again were originally local deities, both of them apparently introduced from the Near East via Cyprus. The culture of the eastern Mediterranean was one large interrelated continuum. Its deities interacted, many of its religious practices remained constant, but the cultural attitude to them changed.

The Greeks, like the Myceneans, lived in fortified hilltop cities. The acropolis, the citadel of each settlement, seems originally to have been simply a fortified burgh which was a refuge for the inhabitants of the surrounding villages.[10] An Athenian called Hipparchos is said to have instituted stone pillars in about 520 to mark the halfway point between each of the Attic villages and the Acropolis at Athens. Normally the temple, home of the city's protective deities, was housed in the acropolis, but many exceptions occur. In particular the temples of Hera at Argos, Samos and Olympia, and that of Aphrodite at Paphos, are well outside the Greek cities, a pattern which argues for continuity with pre-Mycenean times. The Greek cities stood on the same fortified hilltops as those of the Myceneans before them, but these sanctuaries of goddesses had been sited independently.

SACRIFICE AND SANCTIFICATION

The basic site for the honouring of a deity was the open-air altar. Early sanctuaries had included the hearth-house, a roofed building with a circular hearth inside it, as found at a few places (Dreros and Pinias) on Crete and at the oracle of Apollo at Delphi. The domestic hearth remained sacred, dedicated to Hestia, and the head of the household would make ritual offerings at it as part of domestic life. Plutarch, in his *Quaestiones Graecae* 296 F, describes how in Argos the hearth of a house in which someone has died is ritually extinguished and then, after the prescribed period of mourning, is rekindled, with a sacrifice, by fire from the state hearth. At some time during the Dark Age, however, the hearth-house was superseded by the raised altar in the open, around which all the celebrants stood while the sacrifice was offered.

At the mountain-top sanctuaries in Crete, dating from before 1700 BCE, there are deposits of layers of ash with animal bones as well as terracotta votive objects and occasional metal objects. There is no way of knowing whether the presumed burnt sacrifices at these places were of the nature of a ritual meal with the gods in the later Greek fashion, or were a holocaust, as were the rituals of Artemis at Patrae in Greek times, described by Pausanias (VII.18.12), where the altar was encircled by green logs of wood with an earthen ramp leading up to it, up which the virgin priestess would advance in a car drawn by deer:

Plate 2.2 The Lady of the Wild Things, painting on a Boeotian amphora, 750–700 BCE. Female figures, thought to be goddesses, flanked by wolves or lions, were depicted in Greece, Asia Minor, Crete and the Aegean islands throughout the prehistoric and archaic periods.

They throw animals onto the altar, including edible birds and all kinds of victims, wild boar, deer and gazelles, and some bring wolf and bear cubs, others fully grown animals . . . I saw there a bear and other beasts that had been thrown on, struggling to escape the first rush of the flames and escaping by brute force. But those who threw them on put them back on the fire. I cannot recall anyone being harmed by the wild beasts.

A similar story is repeated at the beginning of the Common Era by Lucian in his quasi-antique account of the worship of Atargatis ('Hera') in Syria (*De Dea Syria* 49):

Of all the festivals, the greatest that I know of is held at the beginning of spring. Some people call it the Pyre, and others the Torch. At this feast the sacrificing is done as follows. Having cut down large trees and set them up in the courtyard, they also bring goats and sheep and other herd animals and hang them from the trees. They also bring birds and garments and artefacts of gold and silver. When all is prepared, they bear the victims round the trees and set fire to them and then all are consumed.

Here the Asiatic sacrifice is a ceremonial dedication of total combustion which anticipates Adam of Bremen's account, over 1,000 years later, of the festival at Uppsala in Sweden. We do not know whether the mountain-top bonfires in Minoan Crete followed the same pattern, but the bulk of sacrifices among the later Greeks did not. Both Pausanias (IV.32.6) and Lucian also say that all kinds of tame animals were kept in the court of the sanctuary. This recalls the sacred animals and birds kept in Egyptian and northern European temple-complexes. Birds and fish are present in Roman-age depictions of the temple of Aphrodite at Kouklia (Old Paphos), Cyprus, and there were sacred horses kept in the fanes of the Prussians and Lithuanians.

The deities which Homer calls the Olympians – Zeus, Hera, Athene, Artemis, Apollo, Hermes, Poseidon, Aphrodite, Ares, Demeter, Hestia, Hephaistos – were honoured mainly with sacrifices which were of the nature of a ritual meal: 'more a feast for the honoured lord', as Lucian observes in the second century of our era. One thousand years before, Homer described Odysseus telling Telemachus to 'Sacrifice the best of the pigs so that we can eat soon' (*Odyssey* XXIV.215). The formula had not changed. In a time far distant from modern deep freezes and supermarkets, when the store cupboard was the grazing herd and a beast had to be killed whenever meat was to be eaten, the ritual slaughter of an animal before the altar, its ceremonial roasting or boiling and the offering of certain parts – conveniently the inedible ones – to the presiding deity, was at times merely the sanctification of a feast. On most occasions, however, it was indeed an offering which caused some financial hardship to the supplicant. But the slaughter would always be followed by a roast meal, even if several of the choice cuts were handed over to the temple-priest. The Olympian 'fragrant' burnt sacrifice, unlike the holocaust of the Anatolians, was not an orgy of destruction but a convivial meal. Greek society, despite its cult of individual prowess, had a strong sense of community and of public duty.

Other sacrifices were, however, holocausts. Sometimes a small animal such as a piglet or a cock would be burnt before the main sacrifice[11] and in the cult of the ancestors and of the underworld deities total combustion was common. The ancestors in particular demanded blood sacrifice: the blood of the sacrificed animal would be poured into a trench dug beside the tomb towards the west, which was the direction of endings in sacred cosmology[12]. As in many societies today, the ancestors were seen as continuing the vengeful motives of the living from beyond the grave, and were thought to need placating. In modern Rajasthan many villagers fear the *bhootha*, the unquiet spirit which may haunt burial grounds and secluded places, ready to possess and injure unsuspecting humans. Here the spirit can be exorcised by the local *bhopa* (the shaman or mantis, as the Greeks would have called him), and if its identity is known it can be placated. Sometimes family spirits remain benevolently active towards the living and will have a shrine built for them. Local heroes and heroines – people who have saved the community in some case of need – are also venerated in modern Rajasthan, and some of these give oracles. The family and community spirits are presented with offerings of perfume, strong liquor, tobacco and sweets, as in the 'fireless and bloodless' sacrifice of the Greeks. However, the local protector god, Bhairon (who complements the local mother goddess, Mata), has two forms. His bright form, Gora Bhairon, is worshipped with gifts of sweetmeats, but his dark form, Kala Bhairon, demands liquor and animal sacrifices. This recalls the two forms of sacrifice in ancient Greece: bloodless offerings of first-fruits for the earth-deities, but blood sacrifice and holocaust for the ancestors and the spirits of the Underworld.[13]

The local shrines of modern Rajasthan are, like the historical Greek shrines of ancestors, those of local heroes and heroines and of local deities, essentially independent of the central Hindu pantheon. In Greece local deities were however sometimes given the names of Olympian equivalents, perhaps as a justification of their continuance. One example is Zeus Meilichios, who seems to have absorbed the attributes of an ancestral snake-cult from the area and to have functioned as an avenger of blood-guilt.[14]

The 'pure' bloodless and fireless sacrifices which were offered at various altars and sanctuaries even to gods who were elsewhere served by burnt offerings, were thought by the later Greeks themselves to be the practice of an earlier, simpler world.[15] When fruit and honeycombs and wool were laid on the altar of the Black Demeter in Arcadia, and olive oil poured over, or when wheat and barley and cakes were offered without fire to Apollo the Sire in Delos, both the celebrants themselves and their later commentators saw the conservative retention of practices from before the discovery of fermentation, before the invasion of meat-eating immigrants from the plains of Middle Europe, i.e. from the third millennium BCE. Certainly in Minoan Crete, as we have seen, burnt sacrifices were far and away the exception in all but the mountain-top sanctuaries, whereas for the Myceneans and for the Dorian Greeks they were the rule.

Libation, the pouring of drink into the ground or onto a special libation-table or onto an altar for the use of the presiding deity, can perhaps be seen in the context of the fireless sacrifice of milk, oil and honey, perhaps also in the context of sharing a meal with the gods, since the first cup of an evening's drinking-party was always poured as a libation, and since in other contexts a deity was asked to accept the libation and enter into companionship with the human being who was pouring it. At blood sacrifices, too, the blood from the slaughtered animal had to spill onto the altar. Plato tells us in the *Critias* that in ancient Atlantis (which may have been Minoan Crete) the blood from bulls sacrificed in the temple was made to gush over the pillar on which was inscribed the laws which governed the island, given by Poseidon to its founders.

The emphasis that comes through the main practice of sacrifice is one of social responsibility: of sharing what one has with other people and with the originators of all bounty, the Immortals. The ceremonial pouring of liquids in addition sanctifies a place, whether the ground itself, its altar or its omphalos. The other kind of sacrifice is a re-sanctification, the redressing of a wrong, an alternative to the punishment which the Fates would otherwise inflict. We invoke this kind of retributive justice even today when we swear an oath by some sacred object, inviting the divine powers to strike us down if we perjure ourselves. The ancient Greek when swearing an oath simply stood on the dismembered carcass of his sacrificial animal and dedicated himself to the same sort of destruction as the victim if he broke his word. Such ceremonies have a powerful psychological effect, just as the ancestors – our parents and family – have imprinted us strongly with their thoughts, both conscious and unconscious. Perhaps the ancient ceremonies of riddance were effective in 'dis-spelling' such internalised curses. Aeschylus, of course, tells us in his *Oresteia* (458 BCE) how the Athenians eventually replaced the burden of blood-guilt, which no riddance had lifted from Orestes and which drove him fruitlessly from place to place, by the rule of law, in which the lawful punisher is absolved from revenge, the criminal is purified by punishment, and so the cycle of vendetta is broken. The old rituals were thus capable of modification.

THE SITE AND THE GODDESS

As we have seen, the sanctuary itself could be marked by a built altar, by a sacred tree, by a spring (as at several of the oracle sites – see below), or by a stone called the omphalos, or navel. We have already seen the navel-stone

Plate 2.3 The *Oresteia*. Vase from Magna Graeca showing the judgement of Athene on Orestes, 350–340 BCE. © British Museum.

at the Cave of Eileithyia on Crete, but the classic Greek omphalos was a much more elaborate object. It was a dome-shaped stone about one metre high, often elaborately carved, and was the regular site of libations and other offerings. The original omphalos at Delphi, which still exists, was an unworked stone bearing the inscription *Ge*, probably an aniconic image of the earth-goddess Ge-Themis (Gaia). Vase paintings show omphaloi draped with fillets – knotted strands – of wool, which were the routine form of sacrifice of first-fruits of sheeprearing, but which later became the adornment of the sacrificial victim and, indeed, of the seer or anybody else 'given up' to the will of the Immortals. The omphalos is often shown on vase paintings with a gigantic female figure arising from the earth beside it. It is an attribute of the earth-goddess. Sometimes the figure is called Ge (Earth),

16

sometimes Pandora (All-giving) or Aneisidora (Giver of Earth's Bounty), and sometimes Meter (Mother).

In many sanctuaries before sacrificing to other deities a preliminary sacrifice had to be made to Earth. Aeschylus, in the *Eumenides*, has the priestess at Apollo's shrine at Delphi begin her address with the words:

> First in my prayer before all other gods
> I call on Earth, primeval prophetess.

The next lines explain Apollo's rulership of the sanctuary as a gift from the goddess:

> Next Themis on her mother's oracular seat
> Sat, so men say. Third by unforced consent
> Another Titan, daughter too of Earth,
> Phoebe. She gave it as a birthday gift
> To Phoebus, and giving called it by her name.

In the *Choephori* 127, Aeschylus adds:

> Yea, summon Earth, who brings all things to life
> And rears and takes again into her womb.

The Athenians also called the dead 'Demeter's people'. We know that in the myth of the rape of Persephone it is Demeter's daughter, not Demeter herself, who becomes Queen of the Underworld, but popular culture preserved or conflated the identity of the two. The underworld goddess was thus the dark Earth, bringer of fruitfulness as well as ruler and holder of the dead. Aneisidora too was a bountiful earth/underworld goddess, mentioned by Aristophanes (*The Birds* 971, and schol. ad loc.) both as a goddess to whom white-fleeced lambs were sacrificed, and as the Earth, bestowing all things necessary for life. She was connected with Pandora, who has come down to us mainly in the death-dealing aspect of the Underworld. Her positive aspect appears, however, when in the first century of our era the sage Apollonius of Tyana, helping a man who wanted a dowry for his daughter, prayed successfully to Pandora.

A more differentiated theme, the marriage of heaven and Earth, appears in the cult of Zeus at Dodona. His priestesses declaim:

> Zeus was, Zeus is, Zeus will be: O great Zeus!
> Earth sends up fruits: so praise we Earth the Mother.

Zeus is described in an ancient children's rhyme from Athens as the bringer of rain. At the Eleusinian Mysteries, sacred to Demeter and her daughter, the worshippers at the conclusion of the ceremonies would look up to heaven and cry 'Rain!' then to Earth and cry 'Be fruitful!'. At Olympia, the sanctuary of Hera and Zeus, a cleft in the ground was sacred to Earth and a libation was poured into this before any other sacrifices.[16]

17

Plate 2.4 The goddess of the Underworld: Persephone enthroned.

There seems, then, to have been a basic and apparently ancient veneration of the Earth itself, which continued alongside the newer cults and which was differentiated into the cults of particular goddesses such as Demeter and Kore (Persephone), Pandora and Aneisidora. The symbol of the Earth was the cleft, the underground chamber or megaron (at Eleusis), and the omphalos, all representations of the female anatomy. It is worth pointing out, however, that not all goddesses are earth-goddesses. The earth-goddesses in Greece were quite specific underworld deities of prosperity and destruction. In the same way, not all gods are sky-gods.

ORACLES

The Greek goddesses and gods spoke through their followers by means of trance and inspiration. At one time it was thought that Classical religion was a matter of outward observance only, of going to the festivals and performing the prescribed sacrifices,[17] but this is manifestly false. Gods and goddesses appeared to individual people in dreams and on shamanistic flights of inner vision; they appeared to whole armies and crowds in visions; and from earliest times there were established oracles at permanent sanctuaries, staffed by professional seers, as we have seen is still the case in a modern Pagan country like India. The deities in the ancient world also were active in people's inner lives. The shrine of Zeus at Dodona, in the heartland of the mythical Dorians and styling itself the oldest oracle, was a tree sanctuary of the classic sort. It was founded in an ancient oak forest around the eighth century BCE by an Egyptian missionary priestess from Thebes.[18] In a clearing stood a single oak tree which she had identified as sacred. At its foot was an intermittent spring, and in its branches lived three doves (according to Hesiod) or three priestesses called doves, who entered a state of ecstasy and prophesied without remembering what they said.[19] We have already seen dancers receiving a vision of a goddess at the Cretan tree-shrines, so this practice is familiar.

Oracles sometimes grew up around springs. At the oracle of Apollo in Miletus the priestess sat with her feet in the waters of the spring and breathed its vapours in order to go into trance. At the same god's oracle in Klaros the priest drank the water and so became entranced. At Delphi the priestess bathed in the spring before prophesying. The Oracle of the Dead at Ephyra had two rivers, called Acheron (Sorrow) and Kokytos (Lamentation) after two of the rivers of Hades. A blood sacrifice at a local ancestor shrine, for example Odysseus' sacrifice at the grave of Teiresias described in the *Odyssey* XI.23 ff., could also attract the spirits of the dead so that they could be consulted. Here it was not the seer but the spirits who were entranced by the liquid, and so in this case it could be that the two procedures are entirely unconnected.

At Miletus Apollo's prophetess sat on an *axon* beside the sacred spring. An *axon* is literally an axle, but the word was used at the time to refer to the axis of the heavens. Thus the prophetess sat, symbolically, at the centre of the world. Similarly, at Delphi the seeress sat on a tripod beside the omphalos, in the sunken area at the end of the temple interior. The omphalos too was seen as the centre of the world, as Plato tells us ('Apollo sits in the centre on the navel of the earth'),[20] but unlike the *axon* at Miletus, which was open to the sky and presumably pointed to the Pole Star, the omphalos was placed in an underworld setting. Delphi, according to Aeschylus (see above), was originally a shrine of the earth-goddess, and so the tradition of prophecy must have continued in the time-honoured manner, by reference to the Underworld, not to the axis of the heavens. The tradition of seership by consulting the underworld spirits at the centre of the universe was carried on by the Etruscans (see chapter 3), who are thought to have migrated to Italy from the eastern Mediterranean and laid the foundations of Roman culture.

The tree, by contrast, is an image of the celestial axis: the pole of the heavens marked by the North Star, around which the constellations appear to revolve. The trees which marked certain shrines – the oak of Zeus at Dodona, the willow of Hera at Samos, the olive of Athene at Athens – are likely to have been seen as the local axis, linking the mundane world with the celestial world, just as the omphalos linked the mundane world with the hidden riches and terrors of the Underworld. It is just as appropriate to see the Cretan goddess appearing from above to the dancers at her tree-shrine as it is to see Demeter arising from the Earth at her omphalos. The model of the celestial, mundane and nether worlds linked by the cosmic axis and extended to the plane of the ecliptic is one which had been developed in detail, both symbolically and mathematically, by the Mesopotamians and the Egyptians. When we come to the northern tradition we will see its image as the tree developed to an unprecedented extent. Meanwhile, it seems that the same symbolism was alive in ancient Greece. Prophecy, for the Greeks, became objective by being integrated with the co-ordinates of the cosmos itself. The true seer was the one who sat at the centre of the visible world.

TEMPLES AND IMAGES

The scholiast of Aristophanes states that the olive tree was Athene's temple and her image before the times of built temples and images.[21] Each deity had her or his own holy tree, e.g. Zeus, the oak; Aphrodite, the myrtle; Hera, the willow; and Dionysos, the vine. Sacred trees were often considered more holy than the altars associated with them.[22] According to tradition, the Greeks started religion by fencing off groves of trees. Pausanias asserts (X.5.9) that the first temple of Apollo at Delphi was a hut made of laurel trees. No temple was dedicated unless there was a holy tree associated with it.[23] Hera's tree at Samos was incorporated into the altar itself. In a relief of Amphion and Zethos in the Palazzo Spada in Rome, an image of Artemis stands before a sacred tree at the centre of a temple.

Temple buildings came after the open-air altars at Greek sanctuaries. The oak tree of Zeus at Dodona was replaced by a temple only in the fourth century. The oldest temples which have been found so far are all dedicated to Hera, from the ninth-century Heraion on Samos with its tenth-century altar, through Argos to Olympia, where her temple predates that of Zeus.[24] This might mean that Hera was the most important deity in the Dark Age, or it might mean simply that her image was the first to be thought of as being in need of shelter. The temples were used to house the images of the deities, and are patterned after the Mycenean megaron or throne room. The original cult image of Hera at Samos was, according to Phoronis (fr. 4), simply a plank. In Argos it was a pillar. These were later decorated with pectorals and chains of fruit. We see the same simple iconography on vase paintings showing the worship of the 'womanish' Dionysos (but not in the worship of other deities). Here the cult image is a plank with a mask hung on it and a robe and woollen fillets draped over it. This may be another aspect of tree-worship, since stone pillars, the other obvious image-bearers, do not seem to have been used in this role. (But for images of Hermes, see below.)

Votive offerings brought to the sacred place were left there after the ceremonies. Animal skins, skulls, bones, horns and antlers, eggs, garlands of flowers, sheaves of corn, flowers and fruit, ropes, nets, tools and weapons are all recorded. These are the fabric of the ornament reproduced in stone on temples: almost every design component of the Classical temple derives from one or other of these elements.[25] Fully developed temples preserved and revered the original sacred objects. The original rock where rites were celebrated was left exposed (as can be seen today at the Dome of the Rock mosque in Jerusalem and the chapel in the Christian monastery of Mont-Sainte Odile, Alsace, France, both built on the sites of earlier Pagan sanctuaries). Temples were erected around stones that contained sacred virtue. The most famed of these is the aniconic image of Aphrodite, a baetyl (a meteorite which still exists in the Cyprus Museum, Nicosia) revered in the shrine at Paphos, Cyprus.

Certain deities, in particular Zeus and Poseidon, were never depicted by images during the Archaic period (c.800–c.530 BCE). Zeus was the daytime sky, its rain and its lightning. We have already seen this symbolism expressed in verse and ritual. So Zeus, like Ge, the Earth, and Poseidon, spontaneous natural force, was thought of as an abstract principle, without an image. Similarly, the primary image of Aphrodite was aniconic. It was the *baetylos* mentioned above, a black meteoric stone kept in her temple at Kouklia (Old Paphos), Cyprus, which dated from around 1200 BCE, predating Greek temples of Hera. Hermes, on the other hand, appears from earliest times as one of several sorts of boundary-marker. The earliest herms are cairns, piles of stones as used all over the world to mark boundaries and way-stations. From the sixth century on we find the characteristic stone pillar, which was reputedly instituted by Hipparchos of Athens in the year 520 to mark the halfway points between the Attic villages and the agora at Athens. Walter Burkert has convincingly observed[26] that ithyphallic male figures such as Hermes in Greece and Frey in Scandinavia are probably apotropaic figures, warning interlopers, like the baboons who sit in the same attitude guarding

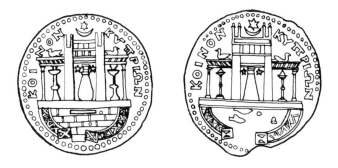

Plate 2.5 Roman coins with representations of the temple of Aphrodite at Kouklia (Old Paphos), Cyprus, showing sacred fence, enclosure with offerings, aniconic image of the goddess, crescent and star symbols on the roof. The modern aniconic image at Costarainera (1992) (plate 3.2) reflects the archaic Aphrodite. Nigel Pennick.

their band, that fit adult males are at hand to defend the territory. Also, in the case of Priapus, the phallus is invoked for the fertility as well as the protection of horticulture.

Until the fifth century Hermes was always depicted (on vase paintings and elsewhere) as an adult male with a beard. The winged boy who appears in later art is an expression of his rulership of adolescence. Hermes is the god of intermediate states, and so serves to establish boundaries as well as to cross them. Similarly, in modern Rajasthan, there is a god of boundaries, an aspect of Bhairon, 'the powerful male principle'.[27] He protects the Indian village against intruders and is an aniconic presence in the no-man's-land around it. Visitors usually make an offering to him when they cross this no-man's-land. In Greece, local versions of Hermes could also have additional attributes. Pausanias (VII.22.2) saw an image of Hermes, the Market god, at Pharae in Achaea. This was a smallish square pillar surmounted by a bearded head. In front of it was a stone hearth with bronze lamps clamped to it with lead. Beside it was an oracle: the enquirer would arrive at evening, burn incense on the hearth, light the lamps, lay a coin on the altar to the right of the image and whisper his question into the ear of the image. Then the enquirer would stop up his ears and leave the market place. After a while, the enquirer would uncover his ears and take whatever word was first heard for an oracle.

LATER DEVELOPMENTS

The deities of Olympus, then, were assimilated to and usually descended from a host of local gods and goddesses who had practical functions in the everyday life of their human communities. The Greek genius for storytelling and classification was overlaid onto religious practices which were concerned with the veneration of the spirits of place, the ancestors and other more abstract beings. The Classical period, dating from the realistic, non-symbolic style of Athenian red-figure vase painting which began c.535 BCE, saw a systematic development of speculative thought. The law became more impersonal, and so did the deities, as in the conversion of the Furies to the Kindly Ones and their installation in a temple, a change fancifully clothed with great antiquity by Aeschylus in his *Oresteia*. Thales' discovery of the method of predicting eclipses (585 BCE) had no doubt already contributed to humanity's sense of objective distance from the natural world. People in the eastern Mediterranean began to work out how to anticipate, rather than simply to react. (The transcendental religions, such as Buddhism and Zoroastrianism, date from this time.) Tremendous advances in astronomy were made, the laws of mathematics and of reasoning itself were investigated, and eventually Athens acquired its own school of philosophy with the advent of Socrates (d. 399) and his pupil Plato (428–347).

Socrates was put to death for corrupting the youth of Athens by teaching them to question the traditions which everyone had held unthinkingly, or at least not questioned so effectively, until then. But the demon of free thought (Socrates' *daimon*, his inspiring spirit) was out of the bag. The western intellectual tradition follows in a direct line from the methods of reasoning developed in the eastern Mediterranean during the sixth to the fourth centuries BCE and crystallised so notably in the schools at Athens. The contemporaries of Socrates thought that the intellect offended the divine powers, and so they found him guilty of corruption. In the long run, however, his school of thought produced a mystical philosophy, Neoplatonism, which coexisted with and (in the eyes of its adherents) even justified the Pagan religions of the time as well as the later monotheisms, and it has persisted to the present day. The methods of reasoning developed by Socrates, his contemporaries and his predecessors, as well as the parallel discoveries in mathematics and in astronomy, have been even more influential, but do not concern us here.

Plato's pupil Aristotle was tutor to the young Alexander of Macedon (356–323), who, as Alexander the Great, later conquered not only mainland Greece but its old enemy the Persian Empire, and much of Asia besides, thus introducing Greek philosophers and priests to Babylonians, Zoroastrians and Brahmins. Alexander's short reign had the result of binding together what became known as the Hellenistic cultural sphere. This not only had a common Greek language and administrative system in its various independent countries, but also a syncretistic religion, developed by Ptolemy I of Egypt in around 331. Based on the Nile cult of Isis and Osiris, this religion included Greek elements and was, in the normal Pagan fashion, hospitable to other local cults. Isis was a mistress of magic and a saviour goddess (*soteria*), who initiated human beings into the mysteries of everlasting life. Her cult generally eclipsed that of her consort, who was the judge of the dead in the Underworld, but in theory the two were worshipped together, and in whatever fashion their cult was widely followed throughout the Hellenistic and later Roman Empires.

Alexander set up his new Hellenistic states on the democratic pattern of ancient Athens, with magistrates, a council and a popular assembly. But each city also had a king, and these kings rapidly became the focus of a ruler-cult. The monarch and his consort were worshipped as deities in their lifetime, rather than being posthumously heroised as demigods. The existing protective divinities of the city-state concerned did, however, retain their own cult. So for example at Teos in Ionia, statues of the conquering king and his queen were placed in the temple alongside that of the city's god, Dionysos, and every year an offering of first-fruits was placed beside the statue of the king in the council chamber. The cult of the monarch, which was perhaps introduced from Oriental sources, or perhaps grew up in the wake of Alexander's own claim to be the divinely begotten son of Zeus, was generally thought to preserve the wellbeing of the kingdom itself.[28] It introduced a new element

Plate 2.6 Goddess building a trophy, fourth century BCE. The tradition of commemorating notable events and dedicating them to a divinity is an integral part of the Pagan tradition. The assembling of trophies was practised also by the Celts, and in modern times by European nation-states. © British Museum.

into Mediterranean Paganism. During the third century, the Greek colonies in the western Mediterranean were gradually invaded by the rising power of Rome, and so it is to this area that we now turn.

3

ROME AND THE WESTERN MEDITERRANEAN

THE ETRUSCANS

In the eighth century, the time when Greek society was emerging after the post-Mycenean Dark Age, an elaborate civilisation grew up in western and central Italy. For three hundred years the Etruscans dominated the western Mediterranean. They mined copper, made weapons, utensils and jewellery, developed agriculture, practised engineering, including agricultural irrigation, and traded with the Greeks, Carthaginians, Phoenicians and other members of the international community of the time. Overland, their merchants travelled to Gaul, Germany and the Baltic, trading wine and copper for amber and salt. It is thought that they introduced the two-wheeled war chariot to the Celts of central Europe. Around 545 BCE their formidable navy joined that of the Carthaginians to limit Greek power in the western Mediterranean. Their engineering and organisational skills produced the city of Rome in the late seventh century, and two if not three of Rome's early kings were Etruscan.[1]

The Etruscans were experts in divination and the mantic arts, and as the frescoes from their tombs show, their culture included the arts of music, dancing, banquets, athletics and writing. The sixth century, the period of the last three semi-legendary Roman kings, marks the height of Etruscan power. Afterwards, the Etruscan cities, civilised but disorganised, fell before the single-minded militarism of Republican Rome. History was rewritten by the victors, and the remnants of Etruscan civilisation can now only be glimpsed from archaeology, from reports by the ancient historians, and from a few inscriptions which have been only partly deciphered. The twelve-volume history of this people, written by the Emperor Claudius in the first century CE, is lost.

Scholarly opinion is divided about where the Etruscans originated. Most ancient commentators thought that they arrived in Italy from the eastern Mediterranean, but Dionysius of Halicarnassus, in the first century BCE, thought that they were native Italians who had learned quickly from foreign traders and invaders, particularly the Greeks in the south of Italy. Modern archaeological evidence is inconclusive. Etruscan artwork, however, was Greek or Phoenician in style, their hydraulic engineering was typical of that

25

of Egypt and the Fertile Crescent rather than of anything in Italy beforehand or contemporaneously, and their political organisation is more reminiscent of the centralised theocratic kingdoms of the Middle East than of the loosely organised Greek city-states, in which no one would have seen a king as an incarnate god. Each Etruscan city was independent, but in the original Etruscan settlement area, modern Tuscany, the main cities formed a League of Twelve. This centred on a common shrine at Tarquinii, where there was a pan-Etruscan gathering and sacrifice once a year.

The earliest Etruscan remains date from around 750 BCE. During the seventh century, Etruscan cities grew up in north and central Italy as farming, trading, mining and manufacturing centres. Their complex urban civilisation contrasted starkly with the simple village settlements of the native (Villanovan) culture. During the sixth century, the Etruscans expanded north into the Po Valley and south into Campania, also colonising parts of Latium, including Rome, between about 625 and 509. Etruscan trade extended north as far as the Black Sea and the Baltic, and their naval alliance with Carthage around 545 gave them mastery over the western Mediterranean. In the late sixth century, many Etruscan cities replaced the kingship by an oligarchy, and during the next two centuries Etruria gradually lost her power, through naval defeats in the Mediterranean, through Celtic incursions into the Po Valley and the Apennines, and through the expansionist tendencies of Republican Rome. Nevertheless, Etruscan cultural influence remained active in central Italy until as late as the fifth century CE, when, under attack by Alaric the Goth, the Christian city of Rome accepted the offer of some Etruscan visitors to perform a ritual to bring a thunderstorm which would turn back the invader. But the ritual had to be performed in public, with the whole Senate attending, and this the Pope would not allow, so the plan was abandoned.[2]

The earliest Etruscan remains are elaborate stone tombs dating from about 750 BCE, square and later cupola-shaped, in marked contrast to the simple urn burials and trench-graves which continued around them. The cult of the dead remained important throughout Etruscan culture, as in many Pagan societies, and the frescoes in the tombs show a wealth of divine beings which awaited the soul beyond death. The remains of the dead were elaborately honoured and they were housed in elaborate necropolises, but we do not know whether this amounted to an actual cult of the ancestors, including Greek-style hero-shrines and appeasement rituals, or whether the dead were thought of merely as subjects of the underworld deities.

The latter is more likely, for Etruscan religion was not simply a religion of practice and precedent, in the more usual Pagan style, but also a revealed religion, whose sacred writings gave detailed instructions for the practice of ceremonies and concerning the nature of the divine powers. In a field near Marta belonging to a farmer called Tarchon, so Cicero tells us,[3] a child mysteriously arose from a newly ploughed furrow. Tarchon summoned the priests, to whom the child (calling himself Tages, son of Genius, son of

Tinia, the chief god) dictated the sacred doctrine, upon finishing which he fell down dead. Following the instructions given by Tages, Tarchon founded a sacred city on the spot. It was called Tarquinii, and was to become the holy city of the League of Twelve. The doctrine of Tages was preserved in sacred books, which like many Etruscan *sacra* were divided into three groups. These were the books of divination (by entrails), the books of interpretation of omens (especially lightning) and the books of rituals. These last were themselves divided into three: the books of the allotment of time, the books on the afterlife, and the rules for interpretation, expiation and placation of spirits.

Etruscan priests and augurs were professionals trained for many years in their colleges, reminiscent of the learned Babylonian *baru*-priests. (Interestingly, the Etruscan word *maru* similarly means a priest or magistrate rather than the part-time priests and priestesses of the Hellenic world, or even of their full-time but untrained seers and seeresses.[4]) It appears that, for the Etruscans, all science had a sacred function (there was little or no 'secular' study, by contrast with Greece), and equally that the sacred world was carefully analysed and measured by means of precise divination to an extent which we moderns, and even the Romans, who coexisted with the Etruscans for some centuries, would call superstitious. The elaborate Etruscan techniques of divination were rejected on those grounds by many Romans (e.g. Cicero, Cato), who preferred to obtain a simple yes–no sign of approval from the gods, rather than the detailed prediction and analysis which Etruscan methods offered them.

The king of each city was also the high priest, the *lucumo*. The style of his diadem, his sceptre, his purple robe, his *lituus* or staff of office, and his ivory throne were adopted by the Roman magistrates, later by the emperors, and eventually by the Roman Catholic Pope and cardinals. The king's symbols of executive power, the *fasces*, or rods for scourging, and the double-headed axe, were also adopted by the Romans (but using a single-headed axe) and restored in the twentieth century by the Fascist dictator Mussolini.

The *lucumo* and his deputies were responsible for carrying out the public ceremonies of Etruscan religion, but they were advised by a college of scholars who are now chiefly remembered for their skill in divination, the *haruspices*. However, the *haruspices* were also astronomers, mathematicians and engineers. Even after Etruscan political power had been crushed by Rome, a college of *haruspices* was maintained in that city as part of the administrative establishment. It was a *haruspex* who warned Caesar against the Ides of March. The sacred offices of the *lucumones* were carried out after the overthrow of the Etruscan kings in Rome by a ceremonial 'king', the *rex sacrorum*.

The layout of the Etruscan cities and countryside conformed to sacred measure. It was foursquare, oriented to the cardinal points of the compass. Four roads (or, more usually, three, omitting the northern quarter) ran out from a central point to the four gates, one in the middle of each city wall. This layout probably dates from the Bronze Age, since a bronze plough was used in the ceremony of drawing the city boundaries, but it may have developed from an indigenous original, since the same foursquare pattern is also visible in the settlements of the north Italian lake dwellers of the Bronze Age, the *terramaricoli*. The Etruscan version may, however, come from a Middle Eastern sacred pattern reflecting the perceived layout of the cosmos, the annual path of the Sun quartered by the solstices and equinoxes, with which we are familiar from Mesopotamian sacred astronomy,[5] since the Etruscans are known to have quartered the sky as well as the Earth for purposes of divination. Varro describes the quartered pattern of an Etruscan settlement, and tells us that it is exactly reproduced in the ancient citadel of Rome, the ancient *Roma quadrata* on the Palatine. The Romans believed that they had inherited their pattern of city planning from the Etruscans, and the Roman foursquare city with its central shaft sealed by a stone (not an omphalos as in Greece), its three gates and its three roads survives in the modern streetplans of Turin, of Timgad in Algeria (founded by Trajan in 100 CE) and of Colchester in England, founded by the Tyrrhenophile Emperor Claudius in 49 CE. According to Polybius, Roman military camps, too, were laid out as specified in the *disciplina etrusca*, and Roman fields were also designed as grids of a specified size oriented to the cardinal points. The Romans acknowledged that their concern with land law was derived from that of the Etruscans. The outward form of Etruscan land discipline has persisted into the modern age, for the same foursquare, cardinal-oriented pattern was adhered to, in both town and country planning, by the founders of the modern USA. But in ancient Etruria, naturally enough, the purpose of the foursquare planning and its attendant ceremonial was not simply ease of organisation, but the thoroughgoing magical protection of the settlement and its inhabitants from all threats originating in the unseen world.

The earliest known temples date from about 600 BCE, and so may have been preceded, as in other cultures from Greece to (as we shall see) Norway, by open-air altars enclosed by a wall. One such altar still exists at Marzabotto. The typical Etruscan temple, however, was almost square, slightly deeper than it was wide, with an elaborately colonnaded front, plain sides and back (unlike the Greek temples, which were open, with columns, to all four sides), and inside it had three compartments, or *cellae*, for a triad of deities. Sometimes there was only one *cella*, with a wing on either side. The walls and roof were usually made of wood rather than stone, with overhanging eaves decorated with brightly painted terracotta images. In front of the temple stood an altar, and the whole precinct was enclosed by a wall.

Some of the Etruscan deities seem to have been specific to their culture, but many were borrowed from Greece. Three important Etruscan deities were Tinia, the god of boundaries and land law (claimed as ancestor by the legendary Tages), Uni, the goddess of dominion, who carried a sceptre, and Menrva, goddess of the skilled intellect, patroness of craft workers. The name 'Tinia' is Etruscan, but the Romans identified this god with Jupiter, their version of the Indo-European sky-god. Tinia was said to have instituted the sacred land law. Uni is an Italic goddess, sharing her name and nature with the Roman Juno, and Menrva is another Italic deity, known in Rome as Minerva. These three deities filled the three *cellae* in the central temple of the Roman Republic, the Temple of Jupiter, supposedly vowed by the Etruscan king Tarquinius Priscus in around 600, built on the Capitoline Hill at the foundation of the Republic in 509, and surviving until its wooden superstructure burnt down in 83 BCE.

According to Varro,[6] the Etruscans' chief god was not Tinia but Voltumna or Veltune, whose shrine was near Volsinii, at which the members of the original League of Twelve met annually to conduct the traditional ceremonies, including games and a fair, and to settle matters of law and policy. This celebration fell into disuse in the days of Etruria's decline, but was later revived, probably by the Emperor Claudius, and it continued into the fourth century CE, the reign of the Christian Emperor Constantine. The goddess Nortia, called Arthrpa after the Greek Atropos, also had a temple at Volsinii. In its wall the highest-ranking Etruscan official would hammer one nail at each annual festival. The accumulation of these nails, one per year, showed the passing of the aeons, and when the wall was covered it was thought that the lifetime of the Etruscan civilisation would be over. There was a goddess of implacable fate, called Vanth, who in the frescoes seems modelled on the Greek Artemis, with short skirt and hunting boots. The god of death was Mantus, after whom some ancient authors said the city of Mantua was named, and the god of the Underworld was Aita. After death, it was thought, souls were met in the Underworld by Charun, a monstrous figure with wings and a beaked nose, who brandished a mallet, and other winged deities were met in the infernal regions. Such terrors were not absorbed into Roman religion as such, but they did become part of its public pageantry. The Roman gladiatorial games, first recorded in 264 BCE, may have descended from the Etruscan funeral custom of staging a fight to the death between three pairs of warriors, and certainly the dead bodies of the losers in the Roman spectacle would be dragged out of the circus by an attendant gruesomely dressed as Charun.

Etruscan society seems to have acknowledged a fatalism which was not shared by the other cultures of the northern Mediterranean. Individuals did not always fight against death and endings, but by contrast saw themselves as powerless to oppose these. During the Roman seige of Veii, Livy tells us, the soldiers tricked a soothsayer into revealing the secret of the defences: that if ever the Alban Lake beside the city was drained, Veii would fall. When he discovered the trick, far from dissembling his error, the expert lamented the fact that the gods had led him to reveal the prophecy, and went on to give detailed instructions for draining the lake. The idea that everything had its fixed term has already been mentioned in relation to the temple at Volsinii, where the nails driven into the wall every year predicted the lifespan of Etruscan civilisation. We learn from Censorinus, writing in 238 CE,[7] that the civilisation was in fact thought to have a lifetime of ten *saecula* of unknown length. Portents, to be interpreted by the *haruspices*, would announce the end of each *saeculum*. The fifth *saeculum* began in 568 BCE, when Etruria was at the height of its power. Previous *saecula* had been one hundred years long, which takes us back to 968, a time before there was any evidence of Etruscan culture anywhere. The sixth *saeculum* began in 445, the seventh in 326 and the eighth in 207. In 88, when Etruscan political power had long been eclipsed by that of Rome, the *haruspices* announced the beginning of the ninth *saeculum*, and at the death of Caesar, when, as Shakespeare has it, 'the sheeted dead / Did squeak and gibber in the streets', Vulcatius the *haruspex* proclaimed the beginning of the tenth *saeculum*, which ended at the death of Claudius in 54 CE, when a comet, and lightning which struck the tomb of the dead emperor's father, provided the necessary portents.

Plate 3.1 Medieval wall-painting of the black Sibyl of Europe in the Madonna shrine at Piani, Liguria, Italy. The sibylline tradition, important in Roman Paganism, was absorbed into Christian mythology. © 1992 Rosemarie Kirschmann.

THE TRANSITION TO ROME

Near the mouth of the Tiber, on the opposite bank from the Etruscan Veii, was a ford surrounded by swamps, and on the hills above this a group of villages amalgamated to form a township. The tradition recorded by Livy would have it that Rome was founded in 753 BCE by Romulus, a descendant of Aeneas of Troy, himself the son of the goddess Aphrodite. Rome calculated its calendar from that date (*ab urbe condita* – AUC), and, at the time of Livy (the last years BCE), the imperial ruling family of Rome, the Julians, took their own divine ancestress, a local goddess called Venus, assimilated long before to the Greek Aphrodite, as the city's protectress. But archaeology shows that before about 625 BCE only a collection of wattle and daub huts existed on the site of the future city. If Romulus ever existed, he was the tribal chief of a group of villagers. Early images show the older tradition of Romulus being suckled by a wolf, the animal of Rome's original protector, Mars. The city itself was probably called after the Etruscan name of the Tiber, Rumlua. The three kings who are said by Livy to have followed Romulus – Numa Pompilius, Tullus Hostilius and Ancus Marcius – would similarly have been local chiefs, not kings on the sophisticated scale of the urban Etruscans. Each of these kings is said to have reigned thirty-five years, which brings us to 613 BCE and the reign of the Etruscan Lucius Tarquinius Priscus. As his Latin name shows, the Romans remembered him as the venerable priest-king (Roman *lucumo* for Etruscan *lauchme*) from Tarquinii (the shrine of Voltumnus, central city of the Etruscan League). Archaeology confirms that it was in the last quarter of the seventh century that the floodplain of the Tiber was settled, presumably by Etruscan engineers who drained the swamps around the Tiber ford. Typical Etruscan potsherds bear witness to their presence, and Etruscan engineering skill was thenceforth devoted to the establishment of the new city.

The huts in the valley were demolished at the beginning of the sixth century and an open space, the Forum, built. Roads were laid out in the grid plan of the Etruscan discipline, houses made of stone and brick with tiled roofs were built, the foundations of the later Temple of Jupiter on the Capitoline Hill were laid, and, finally, the Circus Maximus was built, all before about 575 BCE. The *pagus* (countryside) was now an *urbs* (city) in the eastern Mediterranean style, like the cities of Etruria itself.

The next king of Rome, Servius Tullius, was said by Roman tradition to have reigned from 578 to 535 and to have been a Latin of humble birth. Etruscan tradition, however, identified him with the leader of a faction among the Etruscan nobility who deposed the first Tarquin. Independent evidence is slight on either count. Servius is credited with instituting the first known democratic system of government in the city, which did not, however, last beyond his lifetime. This included property bands of taxation and the principle of an armed citizenry, grouped into what the Romans later called *centuriae*. It was under Servius' rulership that the fortifications of Rome were extended by the Servian Wall to include all seven hills, and the temple of Diana, patroness of the Latin League, was built jointly by Romans and other Latin tribes. Rome had become head of the League. The last king, L. Tarquinius Superbus (534–510), restored the old patrician order and completed the temple on the Capitoline, built according to the Etruscan sacred measure. Tarquinius Superbus is also credited with the donation of the Sibylline Books of augury, offered to him at vast expense by a seeress, and (on the practical level) with the construction of the Cloaca Maxima, the main sewer, which is still operative today. By the end of his reign, Rome was a functioning city with craftsmen, temples, stone houses, mains drainage and a system of government which, however patrician, accustomed all the free inhabitants to civic responsibility and to organised corporate action.

After the overthrow of Tarquinius Superbus in 510, Etruscan names gradually disappeared from the lists of city dignitaries and Etruscan craftsmanship – jewellery, music, dance and banquets – disappeared from the newly constituted Republic of armed farmers. Simplicity and utility became the rule and luxury was frowned on, as the archaeological evidence and the romantic puritanism of later writers such as the elder Cato indicate. The localised religion of the Roman *pagus* (see next section) replaced the deities and ceremonies of Etruscan religion, but the Capitoline Triad of deities remained and was eventually to be reproduced in cities all over the later Empire. The Sibylline Books, which whether genuine or not were sanctified by antiquity, were used as a deciding authority in questions of religion, and the Etruscan augurs were consulted as acknowledged experts in matters of seership. As we have seen, the ceremonial regalia of the Etruscan kings, the sceptre, diadem, purple robe and ivory throne, were taken over for religious and ceremonial occasions by the new Republic, and have continued to this day, together with the *lituus*, or crooked staff of office, as the insignia of the Roman Catholic Papacy. It is even tempting to see the Etruscan demons, which had no part in Roman religion, surviving in the iconography of later Catholicism (though if Etruscan culture, like Christianity, originated in the Middle East, this shared origin would be enough to explain the coincidence).

The Etruscan cities failed to appreciate the Roman urge for the possession and control of territory, or at any rate they failed to respond effectively to the military threat which Rome soon posed. During the fourth and third centuries, Rome conquered first Veii, then Tarquinii, Vulci and Volsinii. Several tutelary deities were brought to Rome, so that the cities were spiritually as well as materially disempowered. Other Etruscan cities were shackled by truces, and the Roman road network cut through Etruscan territory. The Greeks were pressing on Etruria from the sea, and the Celts overland from the north. During the third century the Etruscans made alliances against Rome with the Celts and with the Italic tribes, and then with Hannibal (225–203), but after the latter's defeat, Roman colonisation and control of Etruria, Campania and the Po Valley increased. During the events leading up to the civil war in Rome (83–82), Etruria again sided with the future loser, and Etruscan territory was promptly devastated by the victorious Sulla in 82. (We notice the ninth *saeculum* beginning in 88, the time of the Social War between Rome and her Italian client states, including Etruria.) By now the Etruscan cities were effectively Romanised and Rome had regained her Etruscan engineering skills, but curiously enough, Etruscan mantic skills (disastrous though these had obviously been in advising Etruscan generals from the fourth century on), were much in demand in Rome. They were seen as indigenous practices, by contrast with the 'depraved and foreign' (i.e. Oriental) mantic and religious cults which were flooding Roman popular culture through the city's new international links.

Etruscan culture was re-established in Rome by the Emperor Claudius (41–54 CE), a college of *haruspices* was reinstated, and the old League of Twelve became a League of Fifteen and resumed its celebrations at the shrine of Voltumnus near Volsinii. The Etruscan cities seem to have defined themselves as what we would call a cultural grouping rather than as what we (and the Romans) would call a properly political grouping, and it is in the cultural sphere that their achievements have persisted, from the foursquare layout of town and countryside through to the ceremonial practices of ancient Rome and of the Roman Catholic Church.

REPUBLICAN ROME

The earliest written history which remains from Rome, the Greek prose work of Fabius Pictor, dates from around 202 BCE. Our picture of the early Republic (from 509), the Etruscan kings (supposedly from 613) and their predecessors (supposedly from 753), and of the tribal settlement before that, has to be pieced together from the sketchy accounts of contemporary Greek travellers, the imaginative accounts of later Roman apologists, and the evidence of epigraphy, anthropology and archaeology. Incomplete as this picture is, some of its outlines are still remarkably clear.

Rome's deities were originally guardians of the land. Both the fledgling city, reputedly laid out by Romulus in the mid-eighth century, and the farming localities or *pagi* of which it was the focus, were laid out in a foursquare pattern according, so Plutarch tells us, to the *disciplina etrusca*.[8] The *agrimensor*, or land-surveyor, would indicate the north–south and east–west orientations running from his position and use these to quarter a unit of land. In Classical times such units were twenty *actus* square: 2,400 Roman feet, with an area of one *centuria*: 200 *iugera*. The basic quartered square could be subdivided indefinitely, until each farmer had a square or a strip of land bordered by three or four identical ones. Each district with its various farmsteads was known as a *pagus*, and the spirits of the *pagi* were the original deities of ancient Rome.[9]

Plate 3.2 'Goddess' image in niche on a house at Costarainera, Liguria, Italy, 1992. Aniconic images such as this natural stone are a direct link with archaic representations of divinity. © 1992 Nigel Pennick.

Varro tells us that the early Romans worshipped their deities without images. Indeed, they seem to have worshipped them without personification of any kind. The basic Roman belief seems to have been in *numen* or supernatural power rather than in personified spirits.[10] An early ceremony for clearing a piece of ground for farming is addressed to 'Thee, whether god or goddess, to whom this place is sacred'. A sacred spot, *locum sacrum*, was one which had been ritually cleansed and ceremonially set aside for religious activities. There were also uncanny spots, *loca religiosa*, at which some portent such as a lightning strike had occurred. These were fenced off and set aside as numinous, as still happens more or less spontaneously nowadays, for example when flowers or children's toys or, notoriously in the case of a football crowd disaster in the 1980s, scarves and rosettes are left at the sites of accidents. Such modern shrines are ephemeral, but in earlier times memorial stones were laid. At Quy Fen in Cambridgeshire there is a stone commemorating the death of a local youth who was struck by lightning on the spot in the eighteenth century.

In Rome the spirits of the fields were known as Lares. They were not, as far as we know, given any personality or even an individual name. At each crossroads where four properties met was a shrine to the joint Lares, the *compitales*. Each of the four individual shrines looked out over its allotment, and fifteen feet in front of each one was a sacrificial altar. Ovid, in the *Fasti*

II.639ff., tells us that in December each locality would honour its various divinities at the crossroads. The farmers would celebrate at the shrine of the joint Lares. They would garland the boundary stone and sprinkle it with the blood of the animals sacrificed at their individual altars. (That is, the boundary stone would be honoured with gifts in the way already described from ancient Greece and modern India.) Fire had been brought from the family hearth by the mistress of the household, and a basket of produce was carried by one of the sons of the family and its contents tipped into the fire by one of his sisters. Then there would be feasting and jollity in the traditional Pagan way.

At first, there was a single *Lar familiaris*, but from the early first century BCE, there were two, represented as youthful, dancing images. In the houses of the poor, they were kept in a niche by the hearth, whilst in more prosperous households they had their own shrine, the *lararium*.[11] Their worship remained virtually unchanged through the regal, Republican and Imperial periods. In later times, the deity became known as *Monacello* (Little Monk) or *Aguriellu* (Little Augur), the *genius* of the household. Later, Christian images of the infant Jesus were direct continuations, in size, style and attributes, of Lares. The Isle of Capri is especially noted for them.[12]

In historical times the Lares were worshipped indoors (as *Lares familiares*), and were seen as the unseen masters of the household. Houses in Imperial times (after 27 BCE) contained shrines with statues of the family Lares, and the city itself had a shrine of the *Lares compitales*. The indoor *numina*, however, were originally the Penates, the rulers of the store cupboard or *penus*. Once again, these were known collectively and not given individual names. The table was never left empty, and at the main meal of the day, the midday *cena*, one of the sons of the family would get up and ceremoniously throw on the fire a piece of bread which had been baked according to an archaic recipe by the daughters of the family and placed on a small dish, a *patella*. As the flames blazed up to take it the boy would announce that the gods were favourable: *di propitii*. Vesta, the goddess of the hearth, is an Indo-European deity, identical with the Greek Hestia. Vesta was the flame in the hearth and was tended with all due reverence. The mistress of the household had to leave the hearth swept at the end of every evening.

The doorway (*ianus, ianua*) of the house, too, was sacred. Like Vesta, the flame on the hearth, it was itself a deity, the god Janus. As the transition point between the uncontrolled outer world and the safe territory indoors, the doorway was hedged about with taboos. When a new bride was brought to the household she had to smear the doorposts with wolf's fat and bind them about with woollen fillets, before being carried over the threshold. When a child was born to the household, the doorway became the object of a triple ritual. One person chopped at the threshold with an axe, another pounded it with a pestle, and a third swept it with a besom. These rituals were explained as protecting the household from ill luck: we would say, from ill luck being brought in. Outside the household were the ambivalent gods Mars, whose animal was the wolf, Faunus, the god of wild beasts generally, and Silvanus, the god of the woods. The Roman farmer would have been wise to propitiate these deities but extremely foolish to invite their influence indoors.

URBAN RELIGION

Janus is, of course, better known as a god of the Roman state religion, which is thus revealed as the Romans' domestic religion carried out on a collective scale. Janus had no temple until 260 BCE but a huge freestanding double door, the *ianus geminus*, in the north-east corner of the Forum, through which the Roman armies marched out on their way to war. The door was left open when the Republic was at war and only closed in time of peace. On the opposite side of the Forum was the hearth of Vesta, and so the Forum reproduced the design of the individual house, with Janus as the taboo-ridden boundary between it and the outside world and Vesta as the sacred centre, the source of life within. Vesta's hearth was tended by the six Vestal Virgins, who were chosen at the age of ten from aristocratic families and who served for thirty years, carrying out elaborate forms of the archaic rituals which unmarried daughters had performed in the original homesteads of early Rome. By Republican times, in any full-length invocation of all the deities, the god Janus was to be addressed first and the goddess Vesta last. These two deities encompassed the extremes of existence, from the outermost to the innermost points of the Roman dominion, and their worship illustrates the fundamental Roman preoccupation with the possession and administration of territory.

From the early Republican calendar, which has been pieced together from the inscriptions on a series of tablets dating from Imperial times, we have the names of the thirty-three original deities of Rome. Twelve of these had permanent priests, individuals of aristocratic origin, i.e. descendants of the original founders of Rome, whose job it was to perform (later, to administer) the sacrifices and carry out the other rituals of their deity which were needed to ensure the peace between the divine world and the human world which the Romans sought to keep at all costs. This sacred peace, the *pax deorum*, was later embodied across the ever-expanding Republic as the *Pax Romana*, and finally, in Imperial times, found its expression in the *Pax Augusta*. Cicero, writing at the end of the Republic, stated bluntly: 'This whole empire is created and increased and maintained by the power of the gods.'[13]

Three of the sacrificing priesthoods were the major ones of Jupiter, Mars and Quirinus, and a fourth was the priesthood of Janus, which was administered by an official known as the *rex sacrorum*, the king of the sacred things, who oversaw the state celebrations. This official's wife, the *regina sacrorum*, sacrificed to Juno on the first of every month (see below), which was also sacred to Janus, the deity served by the *rex*. It may be that the *rex sacrorum* took over the functions once carried out by the Etruscan priest-king, but his name and function also remind us of the Mycenean office of *basileus*, the sacred king who was distinct from the secular king or *anax*, a distinction which goes back 1,000 years before Republican Rome. The headquarters of the Roman 'king' was known as the Regia, or Palace, a building which in fact dates from the beginning of the Republic (c.509), not from the time of the monarchy, and which, despite its name, is clearly designed as a temple, not a residence.

Jupiter's priest was the *flamen Dialis*, whose office was restricted by many taboos. He could not engage in such ordinary activities as riding a horse, seeing an army in battle array (a familiar sight in Rome), wearing a ring or knots on his clothing, or doing any secular work. Needless to say, in Republican times this office was not easy to fill. It has been suggested[14] that Jupiter was the original god of Alba Longa, the nearby city and head of the Latin League, which Rome is said to have conquered before the period of the Etruscan monarchy. Jupiter presided over the period of the full moon (which later became the Ides of each calendar month), over lightning and oak trees and hilltops. In Rome his earliest sanctuary was that of Jupiter Feretrius on the Capitoline Hill, where there was an oak tree on which Romulus was said to have hung the spoils of his battles, and where (so Dionysius of Halicarnassus tells us) there was in the first century BCE a small temple, fifteen feet wide, which contained a sacred stone used by the Fetiales, one of the guilds of priests, to sanctify oaths. These oaths were sworn 'by Jupiter the stone', indicating that the god was thought to be immanent in the object itself, just as Vesta was thought of as immanent in the hearth flame. The *flamen Dialis* also administered the archaic rite of aristocratic marriage, in which a cake made of *far*, a form of wheat, was solemnly broken and eaten by the bride and groom, perhaps as a sacrament to the marriage vows.

The priest of Mars must have been an important official in early Rome. In the archaic ritual of the homesteads, Mars was an outsider god whose animal was the wolf. He was invoked in the ancient boundary ritual of the farmsteads, preserved for us by Cato,[15] but in Rome he did not have a temple within the city boundary until the reign of Augustus, beginning in 27 BCE. The altar of Mars was of course in the Campus Martius, the army training ground outside the city, but his rites were also carried on by two colleges of twelve priests each within the city. These were called the Salii, or 'leapers'. Every year in March, the month named after the god, they collected the sacred weapons, or *ancilia*, which had been stored in the Regia over the winter, and performed a sacred dance, sung to archaic words, which invoked the fruitfulness of the fields and announced the start of the military campaigning season. A similar rite the following October involved a horserace and sacrifice, the singing of another hymn which ended the campaigning season, and the replacement of the ceremonial weapons in the Regia. Here, then, we see Mars as the god of youthful male vigour, perhaps symbolised by the growing shoots of vegetation, perhaps associated with the protection of the fields, but certainly presiding over warfare. In historical times, at the declaration of war, the consul responsible would go to the Regia and rattle the sacred weapons, shouting 'Mars, awake!'.

Mars was a god of central importance in Rome, probably the original protective deity of the city. His priest, as we have seen, was the second in importance after the priest of Jupiter, and his nature may indeed have been echoed by the last of the three major deities, the god Quirinus. Almost nothing is known about Quirinus. The hill named after him, the Quirinal, was the home of one of the two Martial guilds, the Salii. These were called simply the Salii of the Hill, by contrast with the Salii of the Palatine, whose home was the hill on which the original settlement of Rome was said to have been founded by Romulus. Thus it seems that the Quirinal Salii predated the Palatine Salii, and perhaps that the god Quirinus was the battle-god of the township on the Quirinal, whilst Mars served the same function in early Rome, the township on the Palatine. In formal orations the Roman people are also known as the 'Roman Quiritian' people, which again argues for an early identification of the two settlements under their two gods.

These were the major sacrificing priesthoods, administered by the principal *flamines* or 'flame-kindlers'. Among the remaining priesthoods, only one was for a deity whom the general public knows well, i.e. Ceres. The remainder were for long-forgotten and presumably ancient deities such as Furrina, Falacer, Portunus etc., whose origins were unknown even to the commentators of the later Republic. But even among the familiar deities who do not appear among the sacrificial priesthoods, their original functions, before their later assimilation to the Olympians of Greece, are not always what we would expect. There is no evidence, for example, that the deities came in married pairs. We certainly see pairs of deities, for example Saturn and Lua Mater, Mars and Nerio, but these seem to have been independent deities with related functions, not husband-wife teams. Juno, in particular, was not originally the wife of Jupiter, but a deity whose name meant 'youth' and who was thought to preserve the vigour and fertility of men and women from puberty until age forty-five (the end of junior status and of its associated liability for military service) for men, and presumably until the menopause for women. As a goddess of vigour and strength, Juno appears as the presiding deity of many towns and as a goddess of battle, in her chariot and with her spear.[16] As we have seen, she ruled over the beginning of each calendar (originally lunar) month: the Calends. She was a goddess of increase, and her many shrines in Rome and elsewhere in Italy identify her area of influence. Juno Rumina protected the city of Rome, Juno Populona the Roman people, Juno Lucina the sacred grove (*lucus*), etc. Each woman also had her individual Juno, her protective spirit of youthful vigour, just as a man also had his *genius* (from the same root as 'engender'), his power of procreation and of originality. In Imperial times the *genius* or *numen* of the emperor became the object of religious cult, and in all households from archaic times the *genius* of the *paterfamilias* was celebrated on the latter's birthday; but from the very beginning of the Republic we also see the king's Juno, Juno Regina, venerated in the temple on the Capitol.

Juno, then, has roots quite distinct from the Greek Hera. So, too, with the other deities. Venus, a goddess of fruit trees and market gardens, was the presiding deity of Ardea and Lavinium. She was later assimilated to the Greek Aphrodite, the legendary mother of Aeneas of Troy, and was claimed as the ancestress of Rome, which, according to this account, current in the Greek settlements of south Italy and popularised in Rome by Virgil in the first century BCE, had originally been founded by Aeneas. But the original Venus had never been worshipped as the guardian deity of Rome; on the contrary, as we have seen, Rome's guardian seems to have been Mars or Quirinus.

By contrast, Diana was assimilated early on to the Greek Artemis. Diana presided over several towns in Latium, in particular one which seems to have been an early shrine of the Latin League, Aricia. Her priest at Aricia was the notorious Rex Nemorensis (another priestly 'king', the King of the Grove). Each holder of this office had seized it by challenging and slaying the previous incumbent, and each was destined to be slain in his turn. During the early sixth century, under the traditional kingship of Servius Tullius, a temple to Diana was built outside the walls of Rome on the Aventine Hill, marking Rome's treaty with the towns of the Latin League. The statue in this temple was in fact a copy of the Artemis of Massilia (Marseilles), itself a copy of the great Artemis of Ephesus. Here the links between the Greek and Roman deities go back to early times. Servius Tullius was also credited with building the temple of Fortuna, who became notorious in Imperial times as the goddess of blind chance. She was, however, originally a goddess of plenty, ruling childbirth and later the fate of children. Fortuna had an oracle at Praeneste, which operated not through seership but through the drawing of lots. It is easy to see how, once her agricultural roots were forgotten, she could develop into the goddess of blind fate which she later became.[17]

The god of the winter sowing was Saturn. His name was derived by the Romans from *saeta*, seed, and he was associated with the legendary Golden Age of plenty, celebrated at the Saturnalia of the winter solstice. Modern research, however, sees his name as an Etruscan word of unknown meaning.[18] Saturn presided over many archaic ceremonies of cleansing and purification, and so it can be conjectured that this was his original function. His cult partner, Lua Mater, apparently derives her name from the verb for ritual purification or expiation, *luere*. The verb for the purification ceremonies over which Saturn presided, *lustrare*, gives us our modern word 'lustration'. It was

Plate 3.3 Wire caducei, symbols of Mercury, from a sacred well at Finthen, Mainz, Germany, first century CE. Votive offerings for good luck at wells and fountains continue today, with coins as the usual sacrifices. Nigel Pennick.

only after the reforms of the Second Punic War (in 217 BCE) that Saturn became identified with the Greek Kronos, who also had a festival at midwinter. Lua was then replaced as his cult partner (in the new style, his wife) by Ops, who had originally been the cult partner of Consus. Both these last two deities are obscure, but Ops was apparently identified with the Greek Rhea and so was assigned to the Hellenised Kronos-Saturn.

These individual cults with their altars and temples seem to have been the oldest forms of worship in Republican, if not in regal, Rome. When the Romans moved into the city from the countryside, they continued worshipping individual deities who presided over places and functions, and seem to have made no attempt to relate them to one another, either through legend or through theology in the sense of a rational arrangement of functions. The individual cults of family and farmstead were generalised to national cults without losing their essential nature. We have seen the state doorway and the state hearth with their cults in the Forum. In addition, the perambulation of the farm boundaries was echoed by the perambulation of the city, the Ambarvalia, superintended by a special guild of priests, the Arval Brethren. The annual ceremony of the Lupercalia (from *lupus*, wolf), in which two young patrician men sacrificed a dog (a wolf might have been difficult) and a goat in a cave on the Palatine, smeared themselves with the blood, laughed, wiped themselves clean with fillets of wool dipped in milk and then, naked except for a loincloth, ran around the boundary of the old city, striking at people with strips of goat's hide, recalls the new bride's apotropaic ritual of anointing the doorposts with wolf's fat. Each individual family's All Souls' Day, the Parentalia, on the anniversary of the relevant ancestor's death, was gradually replaced by the national Parentalia each February.

One final cult was specific to city life, and (despite its origin at the time of the monarchy) essentially to the Republic. When Rome became a city in the late seventh century, the Capitoline Hill was levelled and over the next century an Etruscan-style temple was built on it. This was finally dedicated on the Ides of September, 509, at the inauguration of the Republic. The temple was of the typical Etruscan tricellar type, with an image each of Tinia (Jupiter), Uni (Juno) and Menrva (Minerva). The two goddesses faded into comparative insignificance at that particular shrine, but its presiding god, Jupiter Optimus Maximus (Jupiter Best and Greatest) became the presiding deity of the Roman Republic. It was to him that the victorious generals came and dedicated their spoils in the Etruscan-style triumphs which became the custom after a successful campaign. The cult of Jupiter Optimus Maximus was quite separate from the older cult of Jupiter Feretrius, whose temple was elsewhere on the same hill, and of Jupiter Latiaris, the original god of the Latin League, on the Alban hill. Nor did the ancient priest of Jupiter, the *flamen Dialis*, have anything to do with the Capitoline cult. The latter was national and international, and its epithets were eventually even applied to the name of the supreme god in Christian times, for in 1582 we read Johannes Lasicius, a Polish bishop, praising the cult of 'Deus optimus maximus', i.e. the Christian God.[19] In the Capitoline temple, too, the Sibylline Books were deposited. These were the books of Sibylline prophecies, which were resorted to as oracles in times of confusion, and were interpreted by the two Commissars for the Sacred Rites (*duoviri ad sacris faciendis*), whose number later increased to ten, then to fifteen, following the increase in importance of the Greek rites which they administered.

FOREIGN DIVINITIES

The Romans allowed incomers to worship their ancestral deities, but the outsiders (*di novensiles*) were kept if possible beyond the *pomoerium*, the inviolate strip of land bordering the old Servian Walls. This reinforced the distinction between the patricians, who claimed to be descendants of the founding families of Rome, and the plebeians, who were not. We have already seen the temple of Diana set up in about 570 to serve the visitors from Latium, and likewise before the inauguration of the Republic the merchants and traders who settled around the Cattle Market had acquired their own temples to Hercules and to Castor and Pollux within Rome itself. Minerva had arrived from Falerii as a patroness of artists and craft workers and been given her temple on the Aventine, dedicated on 19 March. The Aventine became the centre of the plebeian religion, but with no one overriding cult. It seemed obvious to the Romans that different peoples were protected by different divine beings. They did not ask, at this stage in their intellectual history, how the various divine beings interrelated, or rather, they seem to have assumed that they were like human beings, each concerned

41

with their own interests and making alliances mainly for the sake of expediency. When the Romans beseiged a foreign city, they would ritually beseech its protective deity to change sides and come to Rome, where a worthy cult would be set up in the deity's honour. In this way the famous statue of Juno from Veii, the Etruscan city across the Tiber which was captured in 396, arrived in Rome.

PONTIFFS AND AUGURS

Priests and priestesses were not allowed to hold any secular office of state, although in most cases (with the notable exceptions of the *flamen Dialis* and the Vestal Virgins) they could carry on a normal life as private citizens. They were, so to speak, the executive arm of the divine order. Members of the legislative arm, by contrast, the group of men (no women here) who were empowered to interpret the will of the gods, to write rituals and to determine forms of worship, were also able to hold civil office. They were the colleges of pontiffs and of augurs, and in the later Republic they included such powerful individuals as Julius Caesar, Pontifex Maximus in 63 BCE, and Cicero, who was an augur soon afterwards.

The pontiffs, whose name means literally 'bridge-builders' and is of unknown significance, are said to have been installed by the legendary king Numa Pompilius at some time during the seventh century. They originally numbered five (nine after the democratic reforms of 300 BCE) and were credited with the formulation of the earliest laws and oaths. They arbitrated on matters of divine law and on the relationship between religion and state, including the religious calendar, of which more below. The Romans attached the greatest importance to preserving the 'peace of the gods' (*pax deorum*). This was an arrangement which supposedly assured that the actions of human beings were always in accord with the will of the divine beings, whose intentions, though obscure, were seen as far more influential than the puny impulses of mere humans. These intentions were known as the *lex divina*, the divine law, and they were ascertained in two ways: rationally, by the pontiffs, and non-rationally, by the augurs and the lesser colleges of omen-readers who interpreted the portents of the gods. The defining quality of a human being who acted deliberately in accordance with both the divine will and the civil law was *pietas*, a central Roman virtue which included obedience to all duly appointed authority figures. The English derivative 'piety' became more trivial in meaning, but the Latin *pietas* passed into Roman Catholic Christianity as the virtue of Jesus, the son of God who willingly allowed his father to slay him for the good of the universe, the *civitas Dei* or City of God.

The pontiffs, then, had the important task of guarding the right relationship between humans and deities. The earliest laws lay down the correct times for sacrifice, the forms of ceremony, what to do if a ceremony is carried out wrongly, and how a transgressor against the divine law should expiate his or her crime. One memorable law stipulated that a woman who had sexual relations outside wedlock should not touch the altar of Juno. If she did, she should sacrifice a ewe lamb with her hair unbound. A son who struck his father, however, had offended mortally against the gods and was condemned to death. The father, the *paterfamilias*, was the representative of the divine order to the whole of his family, both blood relations and slaves, and demanded absolute obedience from them. The standard formula for death under the divine law was *sacrum facere*, to be made sacred, or devoted to the deity who had been offended, and thus no longer one of the living. Normally, though, a minor misdemeanour could be rectified by a *piaculum* or expiatory sacrifice, a sort of fine, usually a piglet. For instance, the boundary ceremonies of the Arval Brethren, carried out in their grove at the fifth milestone along the Via Capena between Rome and Ostia, included a taboo against iron. However, the Arvales would sometimes deliberately use this convenient metal, with the wise precaution of two piacular sacrifices, one before and one afterwards.

These, then, were the ceremonies that the pontiffs regulated. They also prescribed the form of words for celebration, for expiation and for 'evoking' (calling out) a tutelary deity from the town it was guarding. They supervised the often archaic rituals of the sacrificing priesthoods and integrated these into the increasingly sophisticated life of the expanding city. They prescribed the forms and occasions of the rituals of the increasing number of foreign deities, and they advised individuals on how to harmonise their daily life with the regulations of the divine law. As guardians of the calendar, which was not published until 304 BCE, the pontiffs alone knew which days were fit (*fas*) for carrying out mundane business, and which were unfit (*nefas*) and had to be devoted to sacred activities. They knew when the feast days of the various deities were, and they announced the beginning of each month. All this information was kept secret until the middle of the fifth century, when the so-called Twelve Tables of the laws published a part of it. Fifty years later, the Lex Ogulnia opened the college to plebeians (non-members of the founding families of Rome), and at around this time the pontiffs' number was increased from five to nine, of whom five had to be plebeians. The pontiffs, like the augurs (see below) nevertheless remained a secretive and self-selecting body until the Lex Domitia in 104 BCE introduced elections.

The college of augurs or diviners had the duty of interpreting omens, which revealed the will of the gods. The chief magistrate or consul would ceremonially observe the omens from a special area, the *templum*, quartered and laid out for the purpose according to the sacred fourfold pattern. As the name 'augury' indicates, the flight of birds (*aves*) was particularly important in this procedure, but other omens could also be asked for by the secular official who was observing them. These omens were consulted before any important state action, such as going to war, to see whether the proposed human change in the *status quo* was acceptable to the deities. Augury was also taken from interpretation of the entrails of a sacrificial victim. Armies would take along whole herds of oxen and sheep for this purpose. During the famines and general civil unrest of the fifth century BCE, Etruscan sooth-sayers, the *haruspices*, were also consulted, and their elaborate techniques of divination from the liver and other entrails were held in high regard. The detailed interpretation of lightning flashes which fell in the quartered field of observation possibly dates from Etruscan times. During the life of the Republic (509–527 BCE), the official practice of augury became more or less a formality, rather like the announcement of *di propitii* by the young son of each family who threw the cake of spelt on the fire at the midday meal. It was the magistrate, rather than the augur, who was held responsible for maintaining the peace of the gods, and accordingly, the augurs had more prestige than power. Cicero, himself an augur, wrote forcefully against what he considered to be superstition in his *De Divinatione*. It was nevertheless thought correct, in a more or less ceremonial way, to consult the will of the gods before undertaking any action, and no doubt individual Romans, like individual citizens when faced with a public ceremony in the modern world, differed in the nature of the importance they granted to such actions.

THE CALENDAR

The original calendar seems to have been a lunar one. Each month began with the first sight of the sickle moon, which a junior priest would call out (*calare*) to the chief pontiff. When the calendar was eventually based on the solar year (before written records began) the first day of each month was still called the 'Calends', and it was made sacred to Juno and to Janus. The full moon, later the thirteenth or fifteenth day after the Calends, was the Ides, sacred to Jupiter, and between these, the ninth day before the Ides was called the Nones. Since the Romans counted inclusively, the Nones fell at the end of the week before the Ides, thus referring in the original lunar calendar to the first quarter moon. This was supposedly the date on which the king of ancient Rome used to meet with villagers from the surrounding countryside, the *pagus Romanus*, and give out his edicts. In the early Republic it was the day on which the pontiffs announced the holidays for that month. This, then, was the calendar whose inaccuracies Caesar corrected in 45 BCE, giving us the system of months now used throughout the western world.

The major festivals in the calendar were dedicated to the native deities, the *di indigetes*, already mentioned. These festivals described the progress of the natural year. There were springtime festivals of cleansing, riddance and invocation, which cleared the way for a prosperous summer; there were harvest festivals themselves, the October festivals marking the end of the military campaigning season; and there were winter festivals of sowing and purification, the Saturnalia, Sementivae and Lupercalia. Ovid, in the *Fasti* I.163ff., evokes the festival of the Sementivae:

Stand garlanded, o bullocks, beside the full manger:
With the warm spring your labour will return.
The countryman hangs his deserving plough upon the pole:
The cold soil shrinks from every wound.
Steward, let the earth rest now the seed is sown;
Let your men rest, tillers of the soil.
Let the district [*pagus*] have a feast: purify the district, settlers,
And offer the year-cakes on the district hearths.
May the mothers of corn be pleased, both Tellus and Ceres,
With due [offerings of] spelt and the entrails of a pregnant victim
Ceres and the Earth share a single function:
The one gives the grain its origin, the other its location.[20]

The original calendar began with the spring equinox (or with the new or full moon after the spring equinox) in March. It seems to have been a ten-month calendar with what later became the winter months of January and February as a fallow period.[21] From the winter solstice to the spring equinox, time was suspended. (There was a similar feature in Delphi, where, according to Plutarch, Apollo, the god of order, ruled nine months of the year, but the dissolute Dionysos ruled the winter quarter, the season of 'craving'.) The king who introduced the months January and February to Rome must have intended the year to begin with the god of the gateway, the two-faced Janus, and not with the month of Mars as hitherto. Until 153 BCE, the consuls were, however, appointed according to the 'traditional' year beginning in March, rather as the modern British fiscal year begins according to the old 'Annunciation-style' Church New Year, 25 March (corrected by eleven days to 5 April following the calendar reforms of 1752), although the start of the secular calendar year is 1 January. Likewise in Republican Rome, many public festivities still followed the old New Year of 1 March, although the 'hieratic' calendar[22] as regulated by the pontiffs seems to have taken 1 January as its start from an earlier date.[23]

THE SIBYLLINE BOOKS

Alongside the apparently indigenous priestly system of the pontiffs, augurs and lesser colleges, there was an oracular system derived from the Greek shrine at Cumae, in south Italy. In the basement of the Capitoline temple were housed the Sibylline oracles, a collection of verses supposedly bought from a prophetess by Tarquinius Superbus. These were interpreted by a college of two men (increased to ten in 367, then to fifteen in 81), and resorted to for questions which the officials of the main state religion were not competent to answer. The Sibylline oracles advised the foundation of several Greek temples in the early years of the Republic, all outside the *pomoerium*, or sacred city boundary. As the Republic expanded, the duties of the Sibylline officials became more important. They were responsible for administering all the ceremonies of the Greek rite in the city and presided over public rituals which were not of Roman origin (see next section). What is remarkable about Rome is not that there was from the beginning of the Republic a strong Greek influence in religious affairs, since the international trading links and Hellenised culture of the city's Etruscan developers would have guaranteed that, but that the indigenous, non-Etruscan, non-Greek religion persisted so strongly and centrally alongside these more sophisticated influences.

ROME EXPANDS

The urban religion of Rome, then, seems to have grown out of the family religion of the individual farmsteads and their *pagi*. Roman religion was essentially a religion of the spirits of the locality, who were seen as the latter's unseen inhabitants. The state was the farmstead writ large. Its routines and ceremonies were similar to those of the family. But as the Roman state expanded, new deities had to be included in the life of the city, and new opportunities had to be found for the vastly expanding 'congregation' to take an active part in religious rituals.

During the last years of the kingship and the first century of the Republic, Rome became a major economic and military power in central Italy, attracting visitors and settlers from the rest of the peninsula and from elsewhere in the Mediterranean. Pressure from the *plebs*, those citizens who could not trace their descent from the original founding clans of Rome, forced the patricians step by step to extend their privileges to the wider population. The laws once guarded by the pontiffs were published in about 450 as the Twelve Tables, and both the pontificate and the augural college were opened to plebeians some fifty years later. The office of praetor was created in 366, so that ordinary citizens could gain advice on the law, and the dates of the Fasti, or festival calendar, were published at the beginning of the third century. Practical power was passing into the hands of the ordinary citizen, and in this way the civil law, or *ius humana*, became more and more clearly distinguished from the divine law, the *ius divina*. Secular life was beginning to detach itself from religious life.[24]

Throughout the fifth century, Rome had been finding its administrative and economic feet without Etruscan guidance, and as a result suffered from continual war, plague and famine. Clearly, so it would seem to the average Roman citizen, the ancient peace of the gods was not being upheld by existing religious practices. Many new temples to foreign and minor indigenous deities were dedicated during that century, including one to Saturn in the Forum in 496, one to Mercury in 495, to Ceres, Liber and Libera (Demeter,

Dionysos and Persephone) on the Aventine in 493, to Castor and Pollux in 484, to the Dius Fidius (Jupiter) in 466, and to Apollo in 431. The Sibylline Books were regularly consulted and were responsible for the introduction both of Greek-style rites and of the worship of Greek divinities into Republican practice. In 399, during a severe plague, the Sibylline Books prescribed a new form of worship, the *supplicatio*. Unlike the old rituals, where the priest or priestess offered a sacrifice or made a vow to the relevant deity, using the prescribed form of words, with the non-participants watching in reverent silence, the *supplicatio* was a colourful procession of ordinary men, women and children, crowned and bearing laurel branches, to the temple of a deity. There they prostrated themselves before the image of the deity, the women with hair unbound, and begged for that deity's favour. For eight days there was also a *lectisternia* (literally, a spreading before the couches), in which food was offered to images of paired deities (Apollo and Latona, Diana and Hercules, Mercurius and Neptunus), which reclined on couches before the tables. The whole citizenry kept open house, and hospitality was the order of the time. It was these Greek-style rites which offered the ordinary people a chance to take part in religious ceremonies, and perhaps for this reason they became increasingly important in the city.

During the following century, the Romans instituted a more open style of government, open to plebeians as well as patricians. They beat back the Celtic threat (the Gauls had sacked the city itself in 390, destroying its Etruscan street planning) and achieved mastery of most of Italy by 330. In 312 the Via Appia was opened, linking Rome with the newly conquered Greek and Etruscan colonies in Campania (southern Italy), and also opening her to increasing Hellenistic influence. During the third century Rome then consolidated her gains, expanded into the western Mediterranean, and of necessity assimilated the knowledge and worship of more foreign deities.[25] Religious life was passing out of the pontiffs' control. The first gladiatorial games (perhaps based on Etruscan funeral games, which included ritual fights to the death) were recorded in 264, and an equally grisly innovation, the human sacrifice of Greek and Celtic victims, was recorded in 216, with the chief of the *decemviri*, the interpreters of the Sibylline Books, conducting the religious part of the ceremony. (To prevent this happening again, in 196 BCE the Senate passed a law forbidding human sacrifice.) In the latter half of the third century Rome battled with Carthage for economic control of the western Mediterranean, and the Carthaginian Hannibal's arrival in Italy during the Second Punic War (218–201) posed a terrifying threat. In 212 an order went out for the registration of all religions. No-one was to sacrifice in public with a strange or foreign rite unless their form of worship had been authorised by the praetor. The praetor, of course, was responsible to the chief pontiff. The tension between the indigenous Roman religion, regulated by the pontiffs, and the multiplicity of cults from outside, under the broad control of the *decemviri*, had come to a head.

In fact, an important point of contact had already been made. In 217 the Sibylline Books prescribed another *lectisternia*, which was organised according to the Greek pantheon in a Roman disguise. Images of Jupiter and Juno, Neptune and Minerva, Mars and Venus, Apollo and Diana, Volcanus and Vesta, and Ceres and Mercury presided at the feast. The deities, with their Roman names, were in fact Greek cult pairs. Mars and Venus, for example, had nothing to do with each other in Roman worship, but in Greek myth Ares and Aphrodite were lovers. The informal assimilation of Roman deities to Greek deities who had a similar function, which had been going on for some time, was thus given official authorisation. From then on the original nature of the Roman deities would fade into obscurity, and their now familiar equivalence to Greek deities become established.

The last foreign deity introduced to Rome by order of the Sibylline Books was the Great Mother of Asia Minor, who has already been mentioned in connection with Greek religion. Although the Romans venerated Vesta, the goddess of the hearth, and Tellus, or Mother Earth, as well as a variety of individual goddesses such as Ceres, it is difficult to find a trace of any worship, however archaic, of a Supreme Mother as recognised in Asia Minor and the Levant. When the Great Mother, in her form as a black meteorite given by permission of the king of Pessinonte, arrived in Rome, scandal ensued. Her priests were castrati, and they practised orgiastic rites of delirium and self-laceration. This was not at all Roman, and although the arrival of the image, in 203, was followed by the successful conclusion of the Punic War, Roman citizens were nevertheless not allowed to become priests of this goddess. In addition, rites of the goddess had to be conducted in private, within the temple precinct. Every effort was made to contain this alien form of worship.

MYSTICAL SECTS

During the second century Rome expanded eastward, consolidating the gains of the Punic Wars, and more Oriental cults came within her ambit. Given the practical, unimaginative and externally directed nature of the Roman character, these cults were impossible to assimilate. Greek society had developed a greater emphasis on individual experience, both intellectual and mystical, than Rome, and in Greece the eastern cults, though initially resisted and inevitably modified, eventually found their place alongside the native practices of the various city-states. (Compare two Athenian plays from the late fifth century: the *Bacchae* of Euripides, which describes a worst-case scenario of the perceived threat, and the *Clouds* of Aristophanes, which satirises the excesses of contemporary religious and philosophical cults.) Rome simply could not find a place for ecstatic religious experience. Like Greek art and Greek literature, it was seen by the authorities as a decadent and enfeebling influence. The Bacchic rites were banned in 186, and the requirement of 212 for registration of new cults remained. It is a sign of the pluralistic nature of ancient Paganism, however, that even a banned cult like that of Dionysos could be practised in private, within strict limits, if a practitioner succeeded in obtaining special dispensation from the Senate. At the ceremonies of such 'unlicensed' religions (*religiones illicitae*), no more than five people might be present, no permanent priest or priestess could be appointed, and no temple funds were allowed to exist. These restrictions, intended to deprive small sects of any practical power, later determined the much-vaunted form of the early Christian gatherings: small, informal, without permanent officials, and vowed to poverty.

The practically functioning religious cults, then, in an increasingly multi-cultural Rome, were *religiones lictae*, or registered religions.[26] Interestingly, the Latin word *superstitio* simply meant religious practice which was outside the state rituals: private religion, which could well be duly registered. For the modern meaning of superstition, the excessive fear of spirits, we have to look to the Greek word *deisidaimonia*, which meant just that. The Romans regulated people's actions; the Greeks, with finer sophistication, also judged people's attitudes.

PHILOSOPHY

In the aftermath of the Punic War, as a result of subduing the eastern Mediterranean countries and the Celts of the Po Valley who had supported Carthage, Rome had effectively achieved mastery of the whole civilised world by the year 160. Roman brutality in maintaining and exploiting her conquests became legendary, but the cultural influence of the newly conquered territories began to provide a counterbalance. Curiously enough, the eastern Mediterranean had become culturally united during the same decade, the 330s, in which Rome had conquered the bulk of Italy. In 336 Alexander the Great began his career, and the following year the philosopher Aristotle, Alexander's teacher, founded his school, the Lyceum in Athens. Aristotle was the last of the scientific philosophers, and by the third century scientists were pursuing their research separately from philosophers, who had become students of the arts of living (ethics) and of understanding (epistemology). Epicureanism and Stoicism developed at the same period, and in the following century the contemplative side of Platonism as well as the teachings of Pythagoras were revived with the addition of a strong ethical component. The much older civilisations with which Rome came into contact began to have their effect. The upper classes began to educate their sons in grammar, rhetoric, gymnastics and eventually philosophy, rather than leaving them to absorb the arts of war and leadership from their elders as hitherto.

In 155 the philosopher Carneades, head of the Academy in Athens, arrived in Rome as part of an embassy. His teaching, carried out as a side-line, put philosophy on the intellectual map. At a time when the cult of the old Roman deities seemed increasingly unsophisticated and irrelevant to personal spiritual needs, but the imported religions of the eastern Mediterranean were chaotic and confusing, the sceptical method of Carneades, intellectually stimulating though it must have been, was thought to be hastening the progress of moral relativism rather than providing any new standard of conduct, and the philosopher was expelled from Italy. But over the next few decades, three ordered systems of thought were seized on by the increasingly well-educated upper classes of Rome. These were the recently founded schools of Epicureanism, Stoicism and, eventually, Neoplatonism.

These systems offered people two main things. First, they offered a description of the nature of the universe, replacing the tacit assumption of the indigenous religion that each locality had its invisible inhabitants, some wiser and all more powerful than human beings, who demanded from their human neighbours a particular way of life, including particular rituals, in order to preserve the peace between them. Second, the philosophical systems offered an ethical account which described a model of human excellence which could be achieved by understanding rather than by obedience, replacing the old Roman *pietas* with a different model, more suitable for people in contact with the differing social norms of an international community.

The first system, Epicureanism, named after its founder Epicurus, was a radical individualism. The universe was thought to be made up of atoms moving in a void, collections of which went to make up physical objects. The prime motive of all beings was to seek pleasure, but the wise human should choose his or her pleasures rationally. Divine beings existed, to be sure, but they took no part in human affairs and were of use to humans primarily as objects of contemplation, inspiring presences which might flash across the mind's eye during meditation and so impel the soul to act more nobly and more wisely. This system never really took root during the second century. In the first century it inspired the wonderful poem of Lucretius (*De Rerum Natura*, published after his death in 55 BCE), and was taken up by people of a contemplative bent, but as a practical philosophy for people of a more active disposition its advocacy of pleasure seemed like a sanction for irresponsibility and hedonism, as recognised by our modern popular use of the name.

Stoicism, named after the porch or stoa at Athens in which it was developed, took hold in Rome immediately. This was probably because of its advocacy at the time by the successful general Scipio Aemilianus Africanus. Scipio was a soldier in the old Roman fashion, whose troops had wiped the resurgent state of Carthage off the face of the earth in 149–146. But he was also an intellectual who was looking for a more abstract guide to life, and he became convinced of Stoicism by his friend and teacher Panaetius of Rhodes. The Stoics saw Nature as an intermingling of mind and matter, with different beings tending more to one than to the other. Thus a rock is predominantly material, a disembodied spirit is predominantly psychic, but no being is devoid of either principle. The Stoics were monists, believing that the divine Being was the hidden intelligence of the universe, the ordering principle of Nature which was nevertheless contained within the latter. This outlook, seeing Nature as an active theophany, was much closer to the traditional religion of the *pagus* than that of the abstract divinities in Epicureanism. The Stoics also understood the different deities of traditional religion to be manifestations of the One divine power, which should be worshipped accordingly. Thus their monism allowed pantheism and polytheism, and so permitted the practice of traditional theistic religion. It generalised the indigenous local cults, even the city-cult of Rome, which was by now itself too parochial for the whole Mediterranean world, into an overarching religion which could in fact serve an international community. Ethically, the Stoics sought conformity with Nature, or rather with what we call 'the nature of things', which is Reason (*ratio*, a translation of the Greek *logos*). If all beings behaved according to their true nature (*logos*), then justice would prevail, according to the orator Cicero (106–43), the second great exponent of Stoicism in Rome. In practice a dichotomy grew up between reason and emotion in the Stoics' minds, as our popular use of the name implies, and the snobbish anti-emotionalism of Stoic doctrine guaranteed that it would not appeal to the followers of the ecstatic cults already in Rome. Nevertheless, it remained influential among the upper classes for a further two centuries, its last great exponent in public life being the Emperor Marcus Aurelius (d. 180 CE), the author of the *Meditations*, who was admired in his lifetime as a wise and just ruler.

In 88 BCE, Plato's Academy in Athens had been taken over by Antiochus of Ascalon, who retreated from the sceptical method of Carneades which had brought a similar questioning outlook to that of modern philosophy. Antiochus favoured a contemplative, some said dogmatic, analysis of the immaterial Forms or Ideas which were thought to exist in the world of thought as invisible patterns underlying material objects. This line of research became the foundation of Neoplatonism, the belief in the progressive emanation of being from the unified spiritual Source through successive layers of increasingly material and dissimilar types of being. Neoplatonism eventually found an expression in Jewish mysticism, via Philo of Megara (25 BCE–45 CE) to the four Worlds of the Cabbala; in Christian mysticism, via pseudo-Dionysius the Areopagite, *c.*500, with his Celestial Hierarchies of Thrones, Powers, Dominions, Angels, Archangels, etc.; and eventually in the cultured humanist thought of the Renaissance with its Great Chain of Being. In the Rome of the late Republic, the birth of Middle Platonism brought an increased interest in the possible divinity and immortality of the soul and of the unified nature of the divine Source. Thus, for example, Cicero[27] argues that death is not to be feared if we accept that the soul is immortal and by its very nature must rise into the ether rather than sink with the body into the

51

earth. This doctrine is far removed, as Cicero points out, from the original Roman assumption that the spirits of the dead lived at ground level or in the family tomb. Under the influence of Greek philosophy, the Romans were beginning to speculate and to reach some un-Roman conclusions.

Another influence was neo-Pythagoreanism, associated with Cicero's friend Nigidius Figulus (praetor in 58) and in the early years of the Common Era with the famous prophet and teacher Apollonius of Tyana. In 181 BCE some documents had been forged to prove that Numa, the legendary king who was supposedly responsible for Roman religion, was in fact a disciple of Pythagoras. One hundred years later the Pythagorean current had reached maturity. A belief in reincarnation and the superiority of the immaterial world (the world of thought, the Pythagoreans being investigators of number-theory) to the material world, led to an ascetic, humanitarian outlook. Because of their belief in reincarnation, neo-Pythagoreans were among the first Romans to be vegetarians, and their reluctance to take part in animal sacrifice caused them some trouble in a world where loyalty to the state implied active loyalty to its deities.

4

THE ROMAN EMPIRE

THE AUGUSTAN REVOLUTION: 30 BCE–14 CE

Nevertheless, these philosophical movements touched only a handful of people, and the effect of intellectual elitism, though profound, is always delayed. The 173 years from the defeat of Hannibal to the accession of Augustus, in 30 BCE, were years of political and intellectual turmoil. Carthage, Rome's great rival in the western Mediterranean, was finally destroyed in 146 and Africa became a province of Rome. Greek literary, artistic and behavioural influences had already flooded in since the conquest of Hannibal's allies in the eastern Mediterranean, leaving the Romans confused about standards of good conduct. Pressure from the urban poor and from Rome's Italian allies increasingly forced further democratic concessions, but the system of government was not strong enough to withstand the accompanying threats of anarchy and serial tyranny. The Social War with the Italians (91–88) and the Civil War of 83–82 brought the conflict to a head. After the great reformer Julius Caesar was assassinated in the year 44 for having taken too much power to himself too fast (albeit, in his own opinion, on behalf of the Roman people), constitutional reform was essential.

Caesar was succeeded by the Second Triumvirate of Marcus Antonius, Lepidus and Octavian, the dictator's nephew and adopted son. Fifteen years of jockeying for power eventually brought Octavian to the position of supreme authority. In the year 29 he returned from defeating Antony at the Battle of Actium and reigned supreme.[1] He closed the gates of Janus in the Forum, thus beginning what later became known as the *Pax Augusta*, and installed an altar to Victory in the Senate. (In ancient Rome, religious and secular life remained intimately intertwined, even in a cynical age, and public buildings, from assembly halls through baths to circuses, were well provided with statues, altars and small shrines.) Augustus – literally, The Blessed One – as Octavian later became, set about far-reaching constitutional and religious reforms, based on restoring the ancient Republic, the focus of Roman idealism, in an appropriate form for his time. He restored eighty-two temples which had fallen into disrepair during the previous century, and authorised the state to build another thirteen.[2] Over the previous seventy years the state had founded only four new temples (the normal rate since the start of the Republic had been at least two per decade), but the trend was about to be reversed. The forty-four years of Augustus' rule saw the ancient priesthoods renewed and religion incorporated into a focus of national identity and pride.

Augustus seems to have been extremely careful to let his considerable personal power be seen as dedicated to, and exercised only by permission of, the political collective. A state religion, of whatever kind, was a means of strengthening this collective. The genius of Augustus was that he was able to reanimate an ancient and politically significant religion, which gave its followers a sense of ancient justification and of manifest destiny, in a form which also took account of the later religious influences which had almost destroyed it. His revived religion was able to satisfy almost everyone.

The climax of Augustus' restoration took place with the Secular Games in 17 BCE. These were sacrifices and games in honour of Dis (Pluto) and Proserpina, which took place every *saeculum*. The last of the Pagan historians, Zosimus, writing in the early fifth century CE, describes a *saeculum* as the lifespan of the longest-lived human being born at a given time. Although the word later passed into Church Latin as meaning one hundred years, the canonical reckoning in Classical times was 110 years, a reckoning more honoured in the breach than in the observance. Each Secular Games marked an epoch, as an event which no one living had seen before and no one living would see again. Augustus used the Games of 17 BCE to inaugurate his new order. The first three days, 26–28th May, saw a general purification of the Roman people. This was presumably intended as a ritual cleansing from the chaos of the past. On the following three nights, Augustus himself sacrificed black lambs and she-goats to the Greek Fates, then incense to Eileithyia, the goddess of childbirth, and finally a black sow to Tellus Mater, Mother Earth, while praying for the security and prosperity of himself, his household and the Republic. By day, Augustus offered white bulls to Jupiter and white heifers to Juno, who are described in the Sibylline oracle given by Zosimus as the celestial deities. Augustus himself was a devotee of Apollo, a god seen both as the bringer of civilisation to barbarous lands and also as the Sun. On the third and last day, white victims were sacrificed to Apollo at his new temple on the Palatine while two choirs, one of boys, the other of girls, sang a paean in honour of all the divinities, while at Juno's altar Roman matrons prayed to that goddess. The paean of praise had been written for the occasion by the great poet Horace, and after being sung at Apollo's temple it was then sung outside the original temple of the Republic, the scene of the previous two days' sacrifices, on the Capitol.[3] In this way the ceremonies cleansed and unified the Roman people, then placed them under the protection of three sets of divinities: those of the Underworld, whose rites resembled the ancient protective rituals of the farmsteads; the celestial deities of the old Republic; and the new international god who ruled the peace and civilisation of the newly extended Roman world. It was a masterly ceremony, welding what was to become the Empire into a cohesive whole for the next two hundred years, and it was to provide the backbone of the old order during the disintegration of the two centuries after that.

EMPEROR WORSHIP

Other factors were, however, at work in the religion of the future Empire. Julius Caesar had been posthumously deified after his death in 44 BCE, the first Roman leader to receive this honour, and Augustus openly referred to himself as the 'son of [the] god', presumably to justify his claims to power. Deification is probably best seen as an imported Greek tradition of hero-

Plate 4.1 Roman tombstone from Spain with swastikas.

55

worship: Augustus, too, was deified after his death, as were his successors Tiberius and Caligula (who deified himself during his own lifetime). The fourth emperor, Claudius, conqueror of Britain, received a colonial temple during his lifetime, in place of the usual temple to the Capitoline Triad, at Colchester (Camulodunum) in that country, but was deified only post-humously in Rome itself. Thereafter, however, divine pretensions spread according to the taste of the current emperor.

During Augustus' lifetime the emperor was declared 'father of the father-land' (in 2 BCE) and sacrifices were offered to his *genius*, the progenitive spirit by the favour of which he held his office, just as we have seen the ancient households venerated the *genius* of their own *paterfamilias*. Since from the Secular Games of 17 BCE onwards the prince was effectively iden-tified with the state, his *genius* was also seen as a *numen*, a more general divine power. Whatever the fantasies of the later emperors, in practice it was to the Imperial *numen* and to the deities of the Empire that loyal citizens sacrificed in the centuries to come. Following the usual Pagan tradition of free thought, citizens were free to put on this whatever interpretation they wished, and in the eastern parts of the Empire particularly he was often taken quite literally as a god, in accordance with the practice which had arisen when Alexander the Great set up his Hellenistic kingdoms in the 330s and 320s. The Roman emperor, however, held divine status only by virtue of his office. If he were deposed or if he abdicated, his divinity would leave him, just as a modern military officer, however talented, receives formal obedience not as an individual but as the holder of a given rank.

UNIFYING RELIGIONS – THE CULT OF ISIS

So we see at the start of the Empire three contenders for the new role of unifying divine principle. First, there was the One of the philosophers, iden-tified in practice with Jupiter in Rome and with Zeus in the eastern provinces. Then there was the civilising and, by now, predominantly solar deity Apollo, instituted by Augustus. And finally, there was the Imperial *numen*, the *genius* of the emperor, which was seen as the invisible protector of the state. A proposed religion for the whole civilised world had, of course, already been set up by the Egyptian Pharaoh Ptolemy I, following the conquest of Egypt by Alexander the Great in 331 BCE. It is outside our scope to describe Egyptian religion, its rites and practices, in detail here, but in outline the religion of Isis and Serapis (originally Osiris) had been created, rather like Augustus' revived ancient religion, out of the original pantheon of Egypt. Its central legend gave the new Graeco-Egyptian religion its primary image of the Mother, Son and Consort. Osiris, identified by some Greek commen-tators with the dismembered Dionysos and by others with the dying and resurrected vegetation-god Attis of Asia Minor, was in fact too complex a figure to assimilate completely, and so was replaced in the new religion by a personification of the divine Bull, Apis, into which Osiris was said to have passed after death. The new god, Serapis, could be identified with Zeus, Poseidon, and indeed, Dionysos, all of whom were associated with bulls. Isis, initially identified by Herodotus in the fifth century BCE with Demeter, was later seen as the mistress of magic and the bringer of civilisation to the world. Although in 3,000 years of Egyptian state religion Isis (her name means 'throne') had been only one of the central figures in the pantheon, in the Hellenistic version of the last three centuries BCE her significance far outweighed that of her new consort, Serapis. Identified with many other goddesses of the eastern Mediterranean through the natural process of comparison and assimilation, she had temples throughout the Hellenistic world.

Rome, however, was more suspicious. Isis was a saviour-goddess, and the Romans had no conception of *metanoia* – spiritual transformation or, as Christians call it, repentance. A College of the Servants of Isis was founded in Rome around the year 80 BCE,[4] after the victorious Roman troops under Sulla had returned from subduing Greece and Asia Minor, but Roman citizens looked askance at the wailing penitents beating their heads against the door of the temple and begging for transformation.[5] During the 50s the altar of Isis on the Capitol was destroyed as superstitious by order of Aemilius Paulus, but in 43 the ruling triumvirate authorised the building of further temples to the goddess and her consort. After being banned again following the defeat of Egypt in 31 by Octavian, the cult of Isis and Serapis again became established in Rome, and by the late 30s CE had its own state-funded temple in the Campus Martius. The annual festival of Isis in Rome ran from 28 October to 1 November, followed by that of Osiris, which involved a public ceremony of lamentation for the dying god.[6]

The Isian religion, in most un-Roman fashion, was also one of Mystery initiation. In the mid-second century CE, the African barrister Lucius Apuleius, himself an initiate of the Mysteries of Isis, wrote *The Golden Ass*, an entertaining allegorical tale of one man's conversion from materialistic desire, symbolised by his metamorphosis into an ass and accompanying bawdy adventures, to the state of pure service of the sublime Goddess, who is known by many names in many places, but whose true name is Queen Isis. Isis seems likely to be a prototype of the modern Pagans' Great Goddess, who is known by many names (likewise a goddess for a syncretistic, multinational world). Surprisingly for us and for the hero of the novel, the hero's initiation is followed by one into the Mysteries of Osiris in Rome, 'the great god and supreme father of the gods, the invincible', whose nature is 'linked and even united' with that of Isis, but whose initiation rites, according to Lucius, differ greatly from those of the goddess. Here once more we have a universal religion, one which does not tend towards monotheism, as did those of the philosophers' Jupiter and of Apollo, but one which aims to amalgamate all other pantheons within itself. Syncretism is a natural reaction to the confusions of a multi-ethnic community, and for some time the 'Roman interpretation' of foreign, especially barbarian, deities in terms of the Graeco-Roman Republican pantheon had been carried out in the west. Thus, for example, we have Tacitus identifying the Germanic Woden with Mercury. With the introduction of the religion of Isis into the western Empire the *interpretatio Romana* met what might be called an *interpretatio Aegyptia*, and any tidy-minded soul would have reason to feel uneasy. But somehow neither a clash nor an amalgamation ever occurred. The religion of Isis and Serapis/Osiris was not intimately tied up with the state as its original had been in Egypt and as the Republican religion was in Rome. It flourished as a private cult, with state recognition and support, but Isis, it seems, was never viewed as a contender for recognition as the *numen* which holds the Empire together.

MITHRAISM

Another cult which arose at the time the Empire was founded, and which became widespread and popular, was Mithraism, an outgrowth of the Zoroastrian religion of Persia. The Emperor Commodus (180–192) was initiated into its mysteries, and the Stoic Emperor Marcus Aurelius founded a Mithraic temple on the Vatican Hill whose eventual desecration by the Christian Prefect of Rome in 376 was later to herald the destruction of Pagan civilisation. Mithraic shrines and inscriptions first appear among Syrian mercenaries in the Danube provinces around 60 CE. At one point there were two dozen shrines in Rome alone, but the inscriptions become far less numerous after the second century CE and the religion is not mentioned by other writers after this time. Brought in by soldiers, Mithraism remained a religion of soldiers, and as far as we know it had no place for women in its rites. Perhaps for this reason it was seen as a private religion, an individual commitment which could find no place in the broader life of the community. The Mithraic shrines were small, capable of accommodating only about one hundred people, and situated underground, either in caves, in the cellars of houses, or in buildings specially constructed for the purpose. Most of what we know about the religion has to be deduced from inscriptions and brief, mostly hostile, allusions in the writings of outsiders.[7]

All social classes were admitted to the rites of Mithras, but a painful and terrifying initiation seems to have been required of them, as suits a soldiers' religion. The god Mithras, originally in Persian the mediator between the god of light and order, Ahura-Mazda, and the god of darkness and chaos, Ahriman, is depicted in Roman iconography as a young man wearing a Phrygian cap, usually in the act of slaying a bull (whether as a sacrifice or as a conquest we have no idea), and surrounded by Zodiacal symbols. One notable image shows the god emerging out of a rock, naked except for his Phrygian cap, carrying a knife in one hand and a burning torch in the other.

This was thought by ancient commentators to represent the sunrise seen over the mountains. Mithras is often described in ancient inscriptions as a solar god, and so seems to have lost his original role as mediator between light and darkness. Altars of the principle of darkness, Ahriman, are, however, also found in Mithraeums, although we do not know their purpose.

The followers of the religion were called *sacrati*, 'Consecrated Ones'. There were seven grades of initiation, the first four of which – the Raven, the Hidden One, the Warrior and the Lion – led to full membership of the cult, and the last three of which – the Persian, the Sun Runner and the Father – were higher grades. The rites seem to have included a communion meal rather than the simple feasting which was normal after ordinary Pagan sacrifices, and other features led the early Christians to see the Mithraic cult as a blasphemous parody of their own. It is more likely, however, that the two cults simply developed along different lines from a similar background. There is no evidence that the Mithraists ever preached a morality of love, rather the opposite; nor is there any that the Christian cult was ever all-male from the outset, as the Mithraic one was, nor that the Mithraic cult ever admitted women, as the Christian cult did. Mithraic dualism sprang directly from its Zoroastrian parent, but Christian dualism was a temporary feature of Jewish thought in the Apocalyptic period, the time of Christianity's origin. Christians called themselves soldiers in virtue of their faith, but many if not most Mithraists actually were soldiers, and their faith was simply suited to their calling. The bull sacrifice of Mithraism can hardly be seen as a parody of the Christian communion, since it stands fully in the tradition of the religions of antiquity.

DUALISM AND CHRISTIANITY

Mithraism does, however, introduce the Persian dualistic idea of the battle between light and darkness, which are seen as good and evil in a strong sense that is unique to the religions of the Middle East at this time. In most religions, harmful spirits are seen as having their place in the order of things, their influence giving way in time to that of spirits which are helpful to human beings. Many spirits are themselves seen as ambivalent, with the power to blast or to bless. The very strong strain of dualism derived from sixth-century Persia, however, saw a perpetual battle between two eternal principles of good and evil, in which the good had to strive to overcome the evil, which would otherwise win by default. This deeply pessimistic view of the nature of the world contrasts strongly with that of the Pagan religions, which see the rule of nature as either good (e.g. Stoicism) or neutral. It affected some strains of Egyptian and Hellenistic religion, through which the god of the desert, Seth, became magnified into a more threatening adversarial principle, forever pitted against his brother Horus the Elder in a battle of which the outcome was uncertain. Dualism also affected the Jewish religion during the period after the rebellion of Judas Maccabeus (167 BCE). The overwhelmingly hostile social climate of the time led to an accentuated religious emphasis on Satan, the servant of Jahweh and tempter of humanity, in which dualistic tendencies are apparent. Smaller dualistic cults, offshoots of the main Middle Eastern religions, also grew up in the deserts of Syria, Palestine and Persia. The Essenes, many Gnostic sects, and later the followers of the prophet Mani (d. 276 CE) were dualists in varying degrees. Most of them had no lasting effect; Judaism and the religion of Isis eventually returned to a less polarised or more holistic outlook. One small sect, however, did. This was Christianity, whose dualistic tendencies were present from an early stage in its drive to stamp out 'sin'.

The Christians, followers of the early reform rabbi Jesus of Nazareth, had grown invisibly during the first century CE by appealing to a wide range of people. Many of their followers were insignificant in political terms and so we hear nothing of their early growth, but by the year 64 they must have had the necessary combination of a high public profile and a low level of influence in order to be selected as scapegoats by the Emperor Nero for the fire which ravaged Rome for nine days. In the year 90, twenty years after the destruction of the Temple at Jerusalem during the Jewish Revolt of 66–73, the Jewish community reorganised itself, abolishing the Temple priesthood and its sacrifices, replacing it by the rabbinical structure and, along the way, excommunicating the Christians. Christianity then became a separate religion in its own right.

It introduced several attitudes which were not shared by the many cults of the Pagan world.[8] The first of these was charity, the idea of the spiritual worth of the poor. Pagan society was deeply stratified and snobbish, and both rich and poor knew their place. Families could advance over several generations, and individuals could be respected beyond their economic class for good manners and learning, but there was no idea that people were intrinsically equal simply as they were. Christianity was from the start a socially revolutionary movement. Second, its notion of sin was foreign to Paganism. Pagans could do unworthy deeds, or make mistakes, or be unenlightened (in terms of the Mysteries), but sin and guilt were meaningless concepts, as was the Christians' third concept, heresy. 'Heresy', in the original Greek, simply means a choice, and in the Pagan world the choice of cults multiplied almost daily. People could serve many cults at once, and they took it for granted that these were not incompatible with the deities of the Empire or with the supreme source of divine Being (if they thought there was one). Pagan religions have guidelines and precedents but no dogma, and the idea of a Devil, a subverter of the One Truth, is not found in Paganism. The Christians also based their salvific story on history rather than myth; they sought revelation rather than Mystery; and where the Pagans honoured and prayed to the dead, the Christians prayed for them.

Conceptual innovations apart, the Christians also had one rule of conduct which even the broadest Pagan tolerance could not stomach. Like their parent body, the Jews, they refused the obligatory sacrifice to the deities of the Empire, who, as we have seen, were regarded as guarantors of the material and spiritual stability of all of Rome's dominions. Sacrificing to the emperor's *numen* was understood in much the same way as the American custom of saluting the flag or the British custom of standing when the national anthem is played. The Jews were strict monotheists and iconoclasts, but they did not impose their religious tastes on those around them, they sought no converts, and so (especially after losing their home base in Palestine) they were generally tolerated as visiting aliens. Christianity, however, rapidly developed into an otherworldly religion, not only democratically ignoring, but ascetically eschewing, the benefits of material existence, and Christians sought both converts and martyrdom on the slightest of pretexts. The records are full of accounts of Pagan magistrates desperately offering Christian non-sacrificers the chance to make the most nominal of offerings to the Imperial *numen* so as to save their skin. To the Pagans' utter incomprehension, the Christians generally refused. Despite their political disruptiveness, in the early years the Christians seem to have had little impact on Pagan thought, and their theories were not discussed in Pagan circles until the end of the second century.

POLITICAL INSTABILITY: THE THIRD CENTURY

By this time, the scope of the Empire had widened far beyond Rome and its traditions. Trajan, 'the best of princes' (98–117), was the first emperor not born in Rome, and his successor Hadrian (117–138), also successful and also a Spaniard, travelled far and wide throughout the Empire inspecting the state of the provinces. Hadrian, a keen amateur architect, was responsible for the building of the Pantheon, the temple to all the deities. The second century continued the comparative stability and civilised way of life inaugurated by Augustus. Cults and philosophies came and went, political turmoil arose and was dissolved, and what later citizens looked back on as the Golden Age of the Empire lasted until the death of the Stoic Emperor Marcus Aurelius in the year 180. By then, signs of instability were showing. A trade recession was beginning and the birth-rate was falling. To the north-east of the Empire, the Goths were pressing forward and seeking entry into the Danube provinces. In 165–167 the legions had brought back a plague from the eastern provinces, and for all these reasons the Empire was finding difficulty in mustering the internal resources to meet its external challenges. Rome had survived similar periods of disintegration before, but it had never previously had so much territory to administer.

At times of economic stress, religious innovations often occur. The *Meditations* of Marcus Aurelius had demonstrated the persistence of Stoicism, the cults of the various deities and the increasingly philosophical pronouncements of oracles continued to flourish,[9] and a biography of the Pythagorean teacher Apollonius of Tyana was compiled by the philosopher Philostratus for the Empress Julia Domna, the wife of Septimius Severus (193–211). In 178 the Platonist Celsus wrote *True Reason*, a refutation of Christianity, and around the year 200 the Christian Tertullian wrote extensive criticisms of the Pagans as well as of Gnostics and other Christian schismatics. Christianity had reached intellectual maturity and was now considered worth disputing with by the intellectual establishment.

Meanwhile, on the political scene migrating tribespeople were beginning to infiltrate the Empire. Population movements had forced the nomads of the Asian steppes to press on Rome's northern frontiers, and from the beginning of the third century they were invited not only to serve in the legions as mercenaries, but actually to settle within the Imperial boundary in exchange for military service. Control of the military soon passed to able barbarians, and the troops developed the habit of electing emperors. Nobody could quarrel with the soldiers' choice except another body of soldiers, and of the twenty emperors between 235 and 284, all but three died by the assassin's hand.

In Rome itself, however, a new growth of philosophy and literature was taking place. Ammonius of Alexandria (*fl.* 235), Plotinus (204–275) and Porphyry (*fl.* 270) brought Neoplatonism from Alexandria to Rome. Plotinus was a contemplative mystic, asserting the ultimate unity of all religions, teaching the doctrine of emanation from the spiritual Unity to the material multiplicity, but denying any evil or 'fallen' quality of the material world, because, as he said, he had seen no evidence of it. His disciple Porphyry was to become one of the most bitter enemies of Christianity, and his works were banned by the later Christian administration in 333. By contrast with Plotinus, the Persian teacher Mani (d. 276), also a visionary, taught the evil of the material world and the necessity for human beings to 'purify' themselves in order to approach the eternal Light. Mani's doctrines led to many Christian sectarian movements, even as late as the thirteenth century, when Waldenses, Cathars and other Christian schismatics came to the notice of the Papal authority. In Mani and Plotinus we see the contrast between Middle Eastern dualism and the broader Pagan holism against which it stood out.

From 222 to 226 the Empire was ruled by Elagabalus, scion of a family of Syrian sun-worshippers. The Syrian religion was not dualistic, was of great antiquity and had doubtless influenced the attribution of solar qualities to the Greek Apollo in the fifth century BCE. Now it met its distant heir in the Roman Imperial cult of Apollo, but when Elagabalus, Hellenistically renaming himself Heliogabalus, instituted the religion of his solar deity El Gabel, the culture shock was too much to bear. After his death the cult was erased and the Imperial cult went back to its old pragmatic ways. But in 274 the troops of the Emperor Aurelian (270–275) were inspired in battle by 'a divine form',[10] which turned out to be the Syrian El Gabel. Honouring the god who had given him victory, Aurelian modified the cult to suit the established outlook of the Empire and instituted the worship of *sol invictus deus* – The Sun, the Unconquered God – whose temple on the Campus Agrippa was dedicated on the winter solstice, the feast day of Mithras, 25 December, 274. Aurelian was a successful emperor, attacking corruption in the civil service, reclaiming the ravaged eastern frontier and describing himself on his coins as 'Recreator of the World'. The Unconquered Sun was clearly intended to be a unifying factor in the Empire, coexisting with other divinities but taking into himself elements of the solar deities who already existed in Rome and her provinces. Aurelian's successors, Tacitus, Probus and Carus, continued to revere the sun-god.

Between these two solar cults, however, came the first systematic persecution of the Christians. In 249–251, Decius used his short reign to institute an absolute requirement for all citizens to swear allegiance to the state and its deities in order to receive the coveted certificate of loyalty. The aim was to restore unified central government, and the means chosen was the old Roman appeal to conservatism and continuity. Clearly, by this time those foreign cults which devalued practical duties in favour of spiritual duties were seen as a real threat to the Empire. The Christians themselves later admitted that this campaign nearly wiped them out.[11] But the Emperor Gallienus (260–268), who himself invoked the protection of Mithras, suspended the persecution and so the dualists and semi-dualists could regroup while the unifying religion of the Empire reverted to solar worship.

DIOCLETIAN: STATE PAGANISM RESTORED

Around the year 275, Porphyry wrote *Against the Christians*, an attack against which, like that of Celsus one hundred years earlier, the newcomers felt obliged to defend themselves. The political chaos of fifty years was then reversed by the accession of Diocletian (284–305), a Dalmatian provincial, in no way a noble, a professional soldier and an organising genius. Like Augustus three hundred years before him he radically reorganised the administrative hierarchy and reasserted the old religion of Republican Rome in a form adapted to contemporary circumstances. He disestablished the cult of the Unconquered Sun and reinstituted the traditional cult of the Empire, with Jupiter, Hercules and Victory at its head. His edict of 287, 'On Malefactors and Manichees', was an ideological attack on dualist believers, who were to be burned 'along with their abominable writings' for 'futile, evil and superstitious teaching' which was 'contrary to human nature'.[12] This is the first instance of censorship of thought rather than simply of practice (as when the Bacchic rites were banned as a 'depraved foreign superstition' in 186 BCE) that we have from the Roman world. It shows that the fashion for dogmatic religion was beginning to infect Paganism itself. Diocletian was not as successful against the Manichees as Pope Innocent II was to be against the (more geographically localised) Cathars more than nine hundred years later. Manichaeanism went underground and persisted, and Christianity grew by leaps and bounds.

In 298 the emperor instituted a disciplinary purge of the army by making the statutory oath of allegiance to the Imperial cult an individual rather than a collective obligation. This made it impossible for Christians and Manichaeans to continue their military service, and their presumably subversive influence was thereby eradicated. In September 303, following continued inflation and natural disasters, the emperor instituted the 'Great Persecution' of the Christians, ordering the destruction of their churches and sacred writings. Perhaps this was the normal cynical Imperial scapegoating of the handiest minority group, but to judge from Diocletian's edicts he believed, as his more easy-going Pagan subjects did not, that the dogmatism of the dualists and semi-dualists could not be accommodated within the open-minded polytheism of the Pagan consensus. It would be natural for Pagans to assume that the monotheistic and dualistic cults would take their place among the multiplicity of other cults in the Empire. Diocletian clearly perceived that the dualists 'set their own beliefs against the old cults',[13] actively trying to undermine them, and he obviously did not trust that time and revelation and rational debate would bring about eventual integration.

Diocletian also moved the capital of the western Empire from Rome to Milan and eventually to Ravenna. As a provincial, he felt uncomfortable with, and was loftily ignored by, the old aristocracy of Rome, and when the time for the twentieth anniversary of his rule came in 303–304 he ill-advisedly cut short the celebrations, including the all-important Secular Games, which he was attending in the old capital, and fled to Ravenna, where he contracted a fever and became so ill that he eventually abdicated. This insult to the city and its ancestral divinities was bound to strike a blow at the morale of the whole Empire. The Pagan historian Zosimus attributes the whole decline of Rome to this act of sacrilege. Even if we do not take such divine intervention literally, it could be said that Diocletian's action, incongruous in such a master strategist, knocked the heart out of the Empire and the self-confidence out of its people. At any rate, over the next century Rome itself became increasingly marginal and ineffective. Pagan arts and letters flourished there as if in a backwater, but had no practical effect on day-to-day government.

Diocletian was followed in 305 by his Caesar in the east, Galerius, such a rough man he was nicknamed 'the Drover' even by his own soldiers, who intensified the persecution of Christians and other un-Roman sects. But, strangely enough, on his deathbed in 311 he issued an edict of toleration, and this was a turning-point in religious history. From this time on the Christians grew stronger and intensified their own campaign against the old polytheism. The years 313–314 saw the building of the first Christian basilica in Rome. Meanwhile, the rulership of the Empire went through several coups and changes during which the temple of Fortune burned down in 309. However, the new eastern emperor, Maximin Daia, responded to petitions from cities such as Nicomedia and Aricanda in Lycia to reinstitute anti-Christian legislation throughout his area of jurisdiction. He founded the shrine of Zeus Friend of Humanity in Antioch, and set up an organised Pagan priesthood in every town in the area. This was imposed from above rather than growing up organically from local shrines as in the past, just as the Christian Church organisation was delegated from above on the model of the secular Imperial administration. Daia also introduced anti-Christian schoolbooks which described Jesus of Nazareth as a slave and a criminal rather than as one inspired prophet among many, which is how the liberal Pagans of the time saw him.

Daia's edicts caused tremendous hardship among the Christians who were driven out of their homes and countries, but aroused great enthusiasm among local Pagans, not so much for the persecutions but for the restored opportunity of serving their communities and representing their divine protectors in the age-old tradition, which by conventional reckoning was by now over 1,000 years old. It was at this time too that Hierocles, governor of Bithynia, added some imaginative reconstructions of miracles to Philostratus' *Life of Apollonius* and presented it as a Pagan alternative to the Christian Gospels. Once more this shows that in terms of organisation the Pagans were on the defensive, trying to match the miracles as well as the teachings of Jesus with similar prodigies by Apollonius. It is interesting that at a time when politically so much power depended on the whim of the chief emperor of the time, in the religious sphere what seems to have been sought were miracles showing the inspirational power of a single great leader, and a priestly hierarchy with autocratic power delegated from above rather than one developing organically from tradition in the manner of the old Republican religion. The cult of the individual had arrived.

CONSTANTINE: PAGANISM DISESTABLISHED

The reforms of Daia were to last only three years. The power struggle among the would-be emperors continued and in 312 Constantine, the son of Galerian's western Emperor Constantius Chlorus, seized power in Rome. By 313 Daia was dead, having succumbed to cholera after his army had been routed by Constantine's future co-emperor, Licinius. The victorious army had marched under the battle-cry *Summe sancte deus* – 'O Supreme and Holy God' – although its general was notoriously irreligious.[14] Daia's partisans were massacred and his new administration dismantled.

Constantine's father, a devotee of the Unconquered Sun, had been lax in implementing Diocletian's acts of persecution in his territory. Constantine himself had no obvious religious allegiance, but (as John Holland Smith explains in detail[15]) he seemed keen to appear inspired in a general way. The triumphal arch erected after his victory over the western Emperor Maxentius at Mulvian Bridge reads:

> To the Emperor Caesar Flavius Constantine who being instinct with divinity and by the greatness of his spirit with his forces avenged the commonwealth in a just cause on both the tyrant and all his party.

The panegyric read before the new emperor at a celebration several months after his victory includes the question:

> What god was it that made you feel that the time had come for the liberation of the city against the advice of men and even against the warning of the auspices? Assuredly, O Constantine, there is in you some secret communication from the divine mind which delegating the care of us to lesser gods, deigns to reveal itself to you alone.
>
> (*Paneg. Lat.* XI.3.4–5)

In a series of later accounts, the first one published about a year after the event, an answer is constructed. Constantine was variously directed in a dream on the eve of battle to mark the Christian chi-rho sign on his soldiers' shields (Lactantius), or thus directed in a vision on the march before the campaign, or directed to add to the monogram the words 'Conquer in this sign', according to subsequent versions. At any rate, with each new telling the original intimation of a divine mission became more specifically Christian, and like Aurelian before him Constantine was able to present himself before the people as a man divinely guided. But unlike Aurelian, he did not immediately offer his saving god to the people as a unifying symbol for the commonwealth.

What Constantine actually did was to grant freedom of religion to all within the Empire, under the Edict of Milan of 313. He did not especially favour the Christians, but as we have seen he was personally inclined to the worship of a supreme and nameless deity, as the philosophers had been before him. His mother, however, was a Christian. At his tenth anniversary in 315 (he had declared himself emperor during the power struggle with Galerius in 305), he insulted the ancient divinities by refusing to take part in sacrifices and allowing only prayers of thanks without flames and smoke. From then on there was an increasingly tight partnership between the emperor and the extremely well-organised Christians, who had begun their career as 'soldiers of Christ', dying for their cause in the arena, and who had modelled their organisation on the lines of the Imperial administration itself, with terms such as 'vicar' and 'diocese' taken directly from Diocletian's administrative remodelling. The otherworldly Manichees had no such organisation, and neither, apparently, did the various priests of the Unconquered Sun, which may have been Constantine's original deity. The 'Sunday Observance' laws of 321 forbade all but essential work on that day, not described as the Sabbath, as in Jewish usage, nor as the day of the resurrection of Jesus, as Christian understanding now has it, but simply as the 'Venerable Day of the Sun'. In 326 Constantine gave the shrine of Helios Apollo in Nero's circus to the Christians for the foundation of their new church of St Peter.

To direct the emotional sympathies of his many subjects, Constantine used the superb administrative network of the Christian Church. By 318 the bishops had been given all the civil rights and privileges of the Pagan high priests, and the Christian ministry had become a career rather than a vocation. In 323, under the chi-rho sign and the battle-cry of *Deus summus salvator!* – 'God the Highest, Saviour!' – Constantine had attacked and defeated his co-emperor, Licinius, who according to Eusebius was now fighting under the Republican deities and was accompanied by a corps of augurs working from a shrine in a sacred grove. Three explanations are possible for this. The first is that Licinius had simply transferred his allegiance to a different set of deities under the free-market regime of polytheism. The second is that he had experienced a conversion (or an apostasy) in the Christian sense, turning bitterly against the Supreme and Holy God who had once given him victory over his eastern rival. And the third is that Eusebius was simply inventing the story in order for Constantine's victory to

Plate 4.2 Roman altar with swastikas, lunar horns and Daeg rune. Inscription reads: 'I, T. Licinius Valerianus, tribune, make this for the genius and colours of 1st Cohort of Varduli.

be presented as a religious one, just as that of Licinius had been described to be when he was fighting against an emperor who happened to be Pagan.

In order to organise the Christian Church still further, Constantine convened the Council of Nicaea in May 325, instituting the famous Nicene Creed which laid down a clear set of beliefs for Christians to subscribe to, and effectively making the bishops a branch of the Imperial civil service. In 328 the emperor transformed the town of Byzantium, once protected by the goddess Hecate, into the city of Constantinople, which was to be the capital of the new unified Empire. Constantine looted Pagan shrines in the Aegean to enrich his newly founded city. The temple of Asclepius in Agis in Cicilia and Venus Ourania near Mount Lebanon were ransacked.[16] On 4 November, Constantine himself cut the furrow defining the walls of the new city. The whole ceremony was conducted according to the 'ancestral rites', with the help of the high priest and the Neoplatonist Sopater, who presumably drew up the horoscope for the occasion – Sun in Sagittarius and Cancer rising, indicating a religious city which would be a home to the Empire. The temple on the acropolis (actually and symbolically the strong-point) of the new city was a Christian church, but elsewhere there were four other religious shrines. Three of these were Pagan: shrines to Castor and Pollux (gods of the cavalry), Holy Peace, and the Fortune of the city. The last was a shrine to Constantine himself, constructed with the utmost symbolic care.

It consisted of a huge statue containing in its base the sacred Palladium which Constantine had reputedly removed from the house of the Vestals in Rome two years before. The Palladium, the 'attribute of Pallas', was a relic whose appearance is now unknown, which had supposedly been brought from Troy by Aeneas and which therefore, placed in the sacred hearth of the city, guaranteed the lineage of Rome from the most ancient Mediterranean civilisation known to its mythographers. By removing the Palladium, Constantine had symbolically destroyed the power of Rome. By placing it in the foundation of his own statue, he had placed himself at the head of the spiritual and political lineage which it represented. The whole foundation of the new Empire was a careful piece of symbolic and spiritual engineering, conducted according to the age-old techniques of Pagan magical technology.

On the practical level, the capital of the Empire had to move east, since it was the eastern frontier that needed securing. Practically also, this put the western Roman religion into close contact with eastern practices and philosophies which had hitherto been contained within private devotions rather than public ceremonial. The rituals of public life were going to have to change to take account of this. Syrian sun-worship had already been Romanised and presented as a framework for such a change, and would have fitted seamlessly into the pantheon of the Roman ancestral deities, but it lacked the bureaucratic structure which Christianity offered. Likewise, the religion of Isis had no political organisation worth mentioning, and although massively popular among the citizens of the Empire, it seems not to have appealed to the more action-minded, military emperors, who offered their personal devotions to Sol, Mithras or Jupiter. Constantine, then, was looking for a religion which would unify the eastern and western provinces of the Empire. In the orb which his statue carried, symbol of world dominion (Pagan scientists had already demonstrated that the Earth was round) was embedded a fragment of what was claimed to be the True Cross of the Christians, discovered by the emperor's mother. Symbolically, according to the 'ancestral rites', this would be seen as representing not simply Christianity, but also the cross of the four quarters of the Earth and heavens, the ancient *templum* of the augurs and land-surveyors. Alexandria, Rome, Constantinople and Jerusalem were the cities which quartered the Mediterranean, at least according to ancient symbolism, and according to that same tradition, their axes crossed at the site of Troy, the mythical source of Roman civilisation and the home of the Palladium, which Constantine had adopted as the foundation of his rule. Through both Christian and Pagan spirituality, the new emperor was mastering the world. He seems in fact to have been a normal polytheist and he both permitted and founded shrines to other divinities. In 320 he passed a law authorising augury to interpret lightning strikes on public buildings. Pagans did not understand the exclusive nature of Christianity and would naturally see it as one cult among the many to which they could subscribe, under the philosophical aegis of the Supreme Divine Principle – whatever It is.

In the 320s, a new form of Christianity was developing. Arius, a teacher in Egypt, had begun teaching a form of Neoplatonism which denied the absolute identity of the Supreme God and the prophet Jesus (the 'consubstantiality' doctrine). This allowed all kinds of philosophical and mystical Pagan teachings to coexist with the thoughtful sort of Christianity, but ironically, the Arian missionaries were also successful at converting northern 'barbarian' tribes. It was not a Catholic Christian but an Arian, Alaric the Goth, who was eventually to bring about the fall of Rome.

THE PAGANS FIGHT BACK

Constantine was baptised into Christianity by an Arian bishop on his deathbed, on Whitsunday 337. Constantine never followed the Christian sectarians in persecuting non-Christians, but his three sons did. In 340 a ban was put on Pagan sacrifices, 'superstition' and 'unsoundness of thinking' in the east, and in 342 this edict was extended to the whole Empire. In 346 public sacrifices were banned and Pagan observance was made a capital offence. The Pagans kept their heads down and waited for the tide of history to sweep the new sect away. Never before had a new cult tried to stamp out the established religion of the state. The dualism of Christian thought was completely unprecedented and presumably incomprehensible to Pagans.

In 349, Pagan sectarians backed the political rebellion of one Count Magnentius, commanding officer of the elite Jovian and Herculean legions set up by Diocletian. He was bought off by the youngest emperor, Constans, but renewed his efforts the following year, taking the whole of the western Empire. His Pagan regime was received with great rejoicing by the majority of the population, who obviously only needed a champion in order to reassert their own beliefs. Yet at the same time Christian conversions were multiplying rapidly, especially in the cities. It is at this time that the word 'pagan' ceased to be used by the Christians simply to refer to a cowardly non-combatant in the army of Christ, and regained its literal meaning: a country person, a rustic, a yokel who was too slow-witted to take up the religion of the modern age. Magnentius was defeated after some diplomatic realignment of forces by the eastern emperor, Constantius, in September 351 and committed suicide two years later in Gaul or Britain, to which he had retreated. In the campaign against Magnentius, however, Constantius had had to give power to the only male relatives (apart from his brothers) whom he had not butchered on his accession, his cousins Gallus and Julian. It was Julian who was to lead the next Pagan restoration.

Julian was a thoughtful young man, prickly and defensive, who eventually developed the eccentric habit of dressing like a Hellenistic philosopher, with an unkempt beard and wearing a rough robe. He and his brother had been brought up in seclusion as Arian Christians. Julian completely lacked the courtly manners of a gentleman of whatever faith, but when called to military command distinguished himself as a brave leader, a fair disciplinarian and a just victor.[17] When his duties took him to Greece the young prince reconverted to Paganism at the shrine of Athena of Ilium – once more the purported site of ancient Troy, the symbolic home of the mysterious Palladium. The following year he experienced an ecstatic vision during his initiation into the Mithraic Mysteries at Ephesus (the site of Maximin Daia's shrine of Zeus Friend of Humanity), and became a committed Pagan missionary for the rest of his life. Clearly, private Pagan worship including the Mysteries was still going on, but Julian noted with bitterness the decay of the public temples.

Julian's military appointment under Constantius took him as Caesar to Gaul, where the Germanic tribes, pressed by Gothic invasions from the east, had been ravaging the province. The new Caesar restored order and, it would seem, prosperity there, then duly rose against the emperor in what had become the time-honoured way of taking power. After more diplomatic intrigue, Constantius died on 3 November, 361, naming Julian as his successor, and the new emperor marched into Constantinople on 11 December, 361. He did not institute a massacre of the Christians, which led them to complain that they had been cheated of martyrdom.[18] He reduced corruption in the administration, repealed the laws of religious persecution, but prevented Christians from serving in the army (because their law forbade killing), from receiving grants and gifts (because their religion preached poverty) and from using Pagan texts in schoolbooks (because Pagan myths demonstrated Pagan ethics, which could only mislead Christian children). It is unclear whether these rulings were superbly cynical or naively sincere.

Under Julian the temples were reopened and the marauding bands of Christians who had become used to pillaging and destroying Pagan shrines became subject to the usual penalties of the law. Julian himself seems to have been a philosopher at heart, and this may have been the climate of the times, with people fighting over ideas, whether rational or revelatory, and seeking to put into practice an ethical rule of life. There is some evidence that Julian intended to set up a Pagan 'church' preaching Pagan 'doctrines', with authority imposed from above by himself as supreme pontiff. This is the religion of a Follower of the Word, whereas for the bulk of Julian's subjects the many divinities of what we can now see as the Pagan religion were simply unseen presences whose existence was proved by their effects, *numina* whose presence people would be mad to deny. The climate of thought was changing, whether because of the dogmatic preaching of the Christians and Manichees or as the precondition of this. Julian's version of 'Hellenism' reflected the change in the times.

In 363 the emperor went to secure the eastern frontier against the Persians and died in battle. Christianity became the official religion once more, but Paganism was tolerated until the accession of Theodosius in 379. Meanwhile, Pagan art and literature had taken heart again in Rome and the so-called 'Aristocracy of Letters' flourished in that backwater until the Pagan rebellion against Theodosius in 394. After Theodosius declared Catholic Christianity the only permissible faith in 381, the western emperor, Gratian, snubbed the Pagans of Rome by declining the title of Pontifex Maximus and then enacting a series of deadly laws against the cults of the old Republic. State funding was to be withdrawn from Pagan shrines and ceremonies, the Altar of Victory was to be removed from the Senate, and, perhaps worst of all, the Vestals were to lose their privileges and immunities and their sacred fire was to be put out. The Roman establishment was stunned. By the end of the year, however, Gratian was murdered by his barbarian Master of Cavalry at Lyons.

After Gratian's assassination, a patrician called Symmachus became Prefect of Rome in 384. He fronted the Pagan party in the argument over the Altar of Victory, arguing that ancestral usage ought to be maintained, for different nations have different faiths. Rome should be allowed to live in her own way.

We ask peace for the gods of our fathers, peace for our nature divinities. It is only just to assume that the object of all people's worship is the same. We look up to the same stars, one sky covers us all and the same universe surrounds us. Do the means by which a man seeks the truth really matter? There is no single road by which we may arrive at so great a mystery.

(Symmachus, *Relatio* 3, in Smith (1976), p. 152)

The Christian emperor, under the guidance of Bishop Ambrose, refused to restore the Altar, Symmachus was assailed by a whispering campaign and resigned as chief magistrate in 385, just before Emperor Valentinian held his ten-year jubilee in Rome. That year, 386, saw Libanius publish his *Defence of the Temples*, but it also saw the fanatical ex-monk John Chrysostom appointed as archbishop of Constantinople. In 392, thoroughgoing laws against Pagans and non-Catholic Christians made Pagan wills invalid when contested by Christian heirs, banned all celebratory games and Pagan holy days, and forbade even the worship of the household deities in private. In the west, however, Valentinian was assassinated in 392 and Eugenius (392–394) restored the image of Victory in the Senate and payments to Pagan priests began again. Pagan shrines were restored ceremonially by senior officials, including that of Hercules at Ostia.

Theodosius had been principal emperor since 379 and in his eastern area of jurisdiction anti-Pagan legislation had been continuous. Given the unstable nature of the times, he had a horror of secret societies and of magic, so private Pagan rituals were forbidden from the start of his reign. Monasteries and nunneries had been founded in the east, and gangs of black-robed monks would roam the cities and countryside desecrating temples and inciting mobs to destroy them, while the civil authorities turned a blind eye. In 390 a mob burned down the library of Alexandria, an irreplaceable collection of documents dating back to remotest antiquity, and in the following year the Serapeium (temple of Isis and Serapis) was destroyed by order of Archbishop Theophilus of Alexandria. After decades of expecting the Christians to go away, the Pagans finally fought back. The old Roman habit of obedience to authority was perhaps weaker in the east, and there were battles in the streets. One Bishop Marcellus, having sent a party of soldiers and gladiators to destroy a temple, was seized by the local populace and burned alive.[19] At Alexandria, some of the wreckers were crucified. But the Pagan cults were disunified, there was no concept of a general Pagan religion (Julian's 'Hellenism' had not been tested for long enough), and Libanius' 'men in black, who show their piety by dressing in the clothes of mourning' ultimately had their way, destroying most of the artwork and the learning of the ancient world in their zeal to discover and eradicate 'sin'.

In 394, Theodosius took over the whole Empire and announced that the state could not afford to pay for Pagan rites, as the money was needed for the army. Official Paganism was forced underground, and Pagans were persecuted. The civil rights of Pagans continued to be suppressed, culminating in 416, when Pagans were barred from the Imperial Service. But by then, the Empire was divided, ravaged by Goths, Vandals and Huns, moving west under pressure from the Huns who had recently been expelled from China. Many of these were Arian Christians. The Roman troops who defeated Eugenius, the Pagan emperor in the west, in 394 were under the control of an Arian, a Vandal named Stilicho, and included Gothic Arian mercenaries under one Alaric. Alaric next appears the following year pillaging and largely destroying the Pagan shrines of Greece. Some Pagan commentators of the time[20] were convinced that this was a religious crusade. The Mystery shrine, still functioning at Eleusis, was destroyed then, and the Erechtheum, the shrine of Poseidon on the Acropolis, became the first Pagan site on the peninsula to be converted into a Christian church.

Stilicho the Vandal, a naturalised Roman, was now chief of staff under the western Emperor Honorius (395–423), who instituted the long-feared decree to destroy the temples in 398. The law attacking the temples was, however, repealed, and the Empire relapsed into its previous state of confusion. At some time after 402 Stilicho burned the Sibylline Books, perhaps to demonstrate his contempt for the Pagans' explanation of the chaos as a consequence of abandoning the ancestral deities. In 405 more than 200,000 Goths, under a Scythian Pagan called Radegais, flooded into Italy from the north-east. They were defeated, but only just, by Alaric. More pretenders to the throne arose and were defeated, Stilicho was executed on a pretext by Honorius, and then in 409 Alaric found himself on the receiving end of a new persecution. The administration was to be purged of 'barbarians'. Briefly, Alaric, although Christian, set up a new Pagan Imperial administration in Rome, but the experiment failed to impress Honorius, and in a fit of frustration on 24 August, 410 Alaric sacked the city.

As a Christian, Alaric allowed one sanctuary to be spared, the church of St Peter on Vatican Hill. In it were kept the valuables of as many Christians as could get them there, and their girl children. The new city was set up as a Christian foundation. Further edicts referred to Pagan practices as an error on the part of Christian believers, rather than as part of a separate and independent religion. One thousand years of Pagan tradition had come to an end.

THE LEGACY

However, the common people remained Pagan in fact if not in theory, as decrees and the writings of observers show. The writings of Church fathers from Augustine (354–430) through to the antiquarians of the nineteenth century (e.g. J.B. Andrews' observations of the Italian *streghe* reported in the journal *Folk-Lore*, vol. VIII, no. I, March, 1897) variously condemn, bewail or simply observe the remnants of ancient belief and practice among unlettered folk. The temple of the Mother of Heaven (i.e. Isis) at Carthage, disused and overgrown by the early fifth century, was made into a church. But in the year 440, bishops noticed that worshippers there were continuing to worship the old goddess, and had the temple demolished.[21]

A few Pagan intellectuals managed to salvage and transmit the learning and values of the past during that first bleak century. We have already mentioned Zosimus the historian, writing at the end of the fourth century, whose account of Roman civilisation fills out with its own bias the biased record of his Christian contemporaries. In addition, the lawyer Martianus Capella, a contemporary of Augustine at Hippo, compiled *The Marriage of Philology and Mercury*, a great compendium of what became known as the seven liberal arts, including long quotations from Classical authors. Platonic teaching continued in Alexandria, a hotbed of Christian missionary zeal, but in 415 the head of the school, Hypatia, was torn apart by a Christian mob on her way to the lecture theatre. In 432–433 a young visionary called Proclus studied in Athens under the Pagan philosophers Syrianus and Plutarch. After further wandering under the guidance of his goddess Hecate, the divine patroness of his birthplace, Byzantium, Proclus himself became head of the Academy in around 450. He wrote and taught voluminously, and when in 529 the eastern Emperor Justinian closed down the Pagan schools in Athens, the remaining philosophers, rather than recanting, fled to Persia and taught at the university of Jundishapur.[22] Greek learning was thus preserved and built upon by the Persians and also by the Arabs, who had received it through centuries of interaction with the Graeco-Roman Empire. It was eventually returned to the western world when the Christian Frankish Empire clashed with the Islamic Moorish Empire in Spain in the ninth century.

Cultured Christians such as Boethius (480–524) and Cassiodorus (*c.*477–*c.*565) were rare but invaluable in the transmission of learning. Boethius translated Aristotle into Latin, wrote several treatises on logic, music and arithmetic, and used quotations from Classical authors freely in his work *The Consolation of Philosophy*. By applying philosophical categories to questions of Christian theology, he prepared the way for the later re-admission of intellectual speculation into the theological fold. Cassiodorus was a pupil of Boethius, who extended Capella's work on the seven liberal arts and eventually founded a house of contemplatives which included a well-stocked library of many ancient texts. Boethius and Cassiodorus gave medieval philosophy the intellectual nicety for which we respect it today, much of which is derived from Pagan thought.

After the death of Emperor Theodosius in 395, the old Roman Empire with its two Christian capitals split once more into east and west. This time there was to be no co-ordinating authority. In 381 Theodosius had declared the eastern patriarchate in Constantinople equal in authority to the western patriarchate in Rome, and after that the two Christian dominions went their increasingly separate ways, as the political strength of the western Empire diminished following the sack of Rome. Despite localised fanaticism, such as that of the Christian mobs in Egypt, the Byzantine Empire retained the Greek respect for intellectual and visionary information, and preserved many ancient documents as well as incorporating some mystical teachings into its form of Christianity. By contrast, as Neoplatonism grew during the second century, the Christians in Rome had abandoned Greek, their original liturgical language, and began to distrust it as sophistical and dangerous to honest minds. Western Christianity based on Rome was politically active, considering itself a moral counterbalance to the ignorance of its new political rulers, the one-time warrior nomads who knew little of urban civilisation, but in its initial years it also set itself against speculative thought, both intellectual and mystical.

Divided by conflicts between Catholics and Arians, the western Empire grew increasingly weak, its last emperor being deposed in 476 in favour of a barbarian king of Italy. The Goths and Vandals who held Italy and Spain, however, saw themselves as custodians of an ancient civilisation which they, as newcomers, did not share. This civilisation was, of course, Pagan. The Catholic Church in these countries adopted many of the outward forms of Pagan ceremonial. For example, the Goths wore their hair long and their tunics short, but Christian priests retained the short hair and long robe of a Roman gentleman. A shaven head had been characteristic of a priest of Egyptian religion, so much so that St Jerome (b. 348) stated that Christian priests should not appear with shorn head lest they be confounded with priests of Isis and Serapis.[23] Yet by 663, the Synod of Whitby included an argument not over whether priests should be tonsured, but over what style of tonsure to adopt. Christianity was vehemently opposed to the worship of goddesses. Yet one of the earliest churches dedicated to Mary Mother of God was on the site of the temple of Diana at Ephesus. A synod held at Ephesus in 431 first designated Mary as Mother of God.[24] The procession celebrating the beatification of Mary used smoking censers and flaring torches, as were once used in the processions of Diana. The use of holy water and incense, solemn processions (the old lustrations), religious rites of passage marking the turning-points of human life, the veneration of local saints, and the great feast of the dead, the annual Christian Parentalia on All Souls' Day, can all be seen as direct imitations of Pagan tradition.

St Augustine proposed the 'christening' of Pagan objects as well as of Pagan people, to convert them to Christian use. Notoriously, in 601 Pope Gregory I advised his missionaries in northern Europe to do the same thing with holy places. We have already seen the unexpected result of an early attempt to do this (the temple of the Mother of Heaven at Carthage, above). In Rome, the Litania Major of the Catholic Church was held on St Mark's Day (25 April), the day of the Roman Robigalia. In that city, it included a procession that took the same route as the Pagan procession.[25] During the following centuries, Church directives become full of orders to Christian priests not to allow, for example, 'carols' of dancing and singing, especially by young women, in their churches.[26] Priests even took part in the rites of the Calends of May.[27] The orders were mixed and *ad hoc*, because they were fighting against the inevitable. The Roman midwinter feast of Saturnalia (17 December), the winter solstice or Brumalia on 25 December and the New Year feast on the Calends of January persisted in their Pagan form through an accident of Church doctrine. In theory they were Pagan holidays, not Christian ones. New Year celebrations had been inveighed against by Bishop Martin of Braga in 575:

> You shall not perform the wicked celebration of the Calends and observe the holiday of the Gentiles, nor shall you decorate your houses with laurel and green branches. This whole celebration is Pagan.
> (*Acta Conciliarum* V.iii.399, quoted in Tille (1899), p. 103 n. 2)

In 742 the Northumbrian missionary Bishop Boniface warned his German converts against celebrating the solstice. However, they said they had seen the same done in Rome outside St Peter's Church and not forbidden. In fact, the winter solstice or Brumalia, by now the feast of Mithras and the Unconquered Sun, had been associated with the birth of Jesus in 354 by Bishop Liberius of Rome.[28] This move had been made in order to accommodate the new doctrine, one move in the continuing battle against Arianism, that Jesus had been divine from his birth rather than receiving divinity when he was baptised by John, which latter occasion was celebrated as the Epiphany on 6 January. ('Epiphany', of course, is the old word for a Pagan god or goddess showing themselves to their worshippers in a vision.) The new feast of Christ's mass at the winter solstice was exported to Constantinople in 379, and in 506 the Law Book of Alarich designated it as a public holiday. As we have seen, in the time of Constantine, the new faith of Christianity was taken to be similar to that of the Unconquered Sun, whose feast day, together with that of Mithras, was also at the winter solstice. Why Bishop Liberius chose the winter solstice as the birth of Christ we do not know, but we can assume that his choice took account of the historical conflation of Christ, Mithras and Sol.

What is certain is that once the choice was made the old Pagan celebrations were almost bound to attach themselves to the new date. The name of Saturnalia died out, but its celebrations, such as decking houses with evergreens, giving presents and feasting, were attached to Christmas. Some features of the New Year, such as the keeping of a perpetual fire in the hearth and the laying of a table for the goddess Fortuna (later for local spirits or for Father Christmas), were transferred to the new feast. But New Year, which corresponded to a genuine turning-point in civic life each year, also remained as a (heretical) feast in its own right and was never assimilated by the Church. It is not generally true to say that the Church adopted Pagan feast days as its own feast days, but it did adopt the celebrations of adjacent ones, such as the Saturnalia, into its own liturgical year, and it did lend its blessing to local events which would have been celebrated anyway, such as Plough Monday, St George's Day, beating the village bounds, and May Eve, as we shall see.

The western Empire was broken up eventually by the continuing rivalry between Catholics and Arians. In 534, the eastern Emperor Justinian reclaimed Africa from the (mostly Arian) Vandals and was hailed as a liberator by the Catholic Church there, and between 535 and 555 he took Italy back from the (Arian) Goths, all in the name of religion. The wealth and infrastructure of the country were almost destroyed in the process,[29] and it did not have time to recover before the next wave of barbarian invasions, led by the Lombards in 568. Any pretence at a western Empire was now over, and yet the ideal remained, to be revived as the Holy Roman Empire by Charlemagne the Frank (741–814). The eastern Empire remained politically and liturgically intact (though held by the Franks on behalf of Rome for fifty years until 1261), until it fell to the Islamic Turks in 1453. After that the self-appointed championship of the Holy Roman Empire of the east, with its Orthodox rite, differing from that of the Catholics, was taken on by Russia.

ISLAM

Between 580 and 632, the prophet Mohammed lived, worked as a merchant and taught his new monotheistic faith, a reworking of Jewish, New Testament, Parsee and Gnostic influences current in the Levantine countries at the far end of his caravan journeys. The new religion, Islam ('obedience'), swept away the old Paganism of southern Arabia, with its aniconic shrines including that of the Caba at Mecca, which Mohammed later declared to be the temple of Abraham, and its moon-god Sin, who had already subsumed the worship of the three goddesses Al'lat, Al-Uzzah and Manat, later mentioned by Mohammed in the famous 'Satanic verses' of the Koran. The crescent and star motif of Islam recalls the emblems of the moon-god Sin and the evening-star god Attar, and, indeed, Mohammed changed the original luni-solar calendar of the Arabs to the purely lunar one which is still used today. Mohammed's inspired reworking of a moon-god monotheism which was already in progress led to a conquering religion which was as successful as that of ancient Rome or those of Catholic and Orthodox Christianity. It was following the Arab conquest in 637 that the Parsees, followers of Persian solar dualism, fled to India and Persia became Islamic. Arab rulers, fanatically anti-Pagan, were on the whole tolerant of the other monotheisms, Judaism and Christianity, and many parts of Europe came under their control in the following centuries.

The Christian kingdom of Spain was taken over by the Arabs under Islam, with Berber troops, in 711, so linking this western peninsula with eastern art and scholarship in a generally tolerant, multicultural society under Islamic control. In 870, the library of Al Hakem at Cordoba boasted books from all over the world. Classified and catalogued in order were 600,000 volumes.[30] The few tiny Christian kingdoms, huddled up against the Pyrenees, began their reconquest of the south in 1085 and finished it in 1266, with Portugal founded in 1147. Strangely enough, it was not only the Christians who fought against the Arabs. Sardinia, itself Islamic from 720–740, sent Pagan missions to Spain in about the year 1000. In the late sixth century, Pope Gregory the Great had found Sardinia to be a stronghold of Paganism, with the people bribing the governor to turn a blind eye.[31] In the eleventh century, Paganism was strong in Sardinia, and 'many professors of it'[32] went into Spain, where they attempted to spread their belief, but were driven out by the Catholics and also, presumably, the Arabs. Crete was Islamic from 823 to 961, Sicily from 832 to 878, Corsica from 852 to 1077 and Malta from 870 to 1090. Southern France was invaded by Arab forces in 720, but after a decisive defeat by the northern French at Poitiers in 732, the raiders made no more serious attempts at settlement and were eventually beaten back over the Pyrenees.

Islam spread north from its home to Egypt, Persia and Syria, where it inherited the intellectual legacy of the Classical world, which it retransmitted to the Roman kingdoms in the west. Spain and southern France became centres of learning under their Islamic overlords, and this learning was disseminated further north after the Berber invasion of Castile in 1195, which forced many Christian and Jewish intellectuals to flee north into the Christian kingdoms, taking with them logic, astronomy and other aspects of Greek learning which had been nurtured by the Arabs. (In 1492 Ferdinand and Isabella expelled these same intellectual classes as actual or potential heretics, and Spain became a doctrinaire outpost of militant Catholicism.) By the eleventh century Islam had spread far north in the old Hellenistic world and was the antagonistic neighbour of the eastern Roman Empire, where we shall meet it again in the penultimate chapter. Meanwhile, the Celto-Roman west was becoming Germanic.

5

THE CELTIC WORLD

The Greeks gave the name *Keltoi* to the barbarian peoples of central Europe, who came down in their raiding parties from the fifth century BCE and terrorised the settled city-states of the Mediterranean. During the late fifth century these tribes expanded westwards into Gaul, Britain and Ireland, southwest into Iberia, southwards into northern Italy and eastwards through the Balkans and into Asia Minor. Tribes now considered 'Celtic' include the Helvetii in the area of what is now Switzerland, the Boii in what is now Italy, the Averni in what is now France, and the Scordisci in what is now Serbia. Nineteenth-century historians set great store by the supposed difference between 'Celtic' and 'Germanic' root-stocks, but modern research indicates that these were originally part of a common north European tradition, already differentiating into separate linguistic groups when they were geographically split apart by the Romans. We use the word 'Celtic' as shorthand for the indigenous peoples of north-west Europe who, apart from the Irish, were colonised by Rome and in all cases were cut off by the boundary of the Roman Empire from the 'German' tribes east of the Rhine and north of the Danube.[1]

Celtic civilisation emerged around 700 BCE in Austria: the so-called Hallstatt culture. The wealth of Hallstatt was based on salt, which was traded for goods from Greece and Etruria. A development took place around 500 BCE in north-east France and the middle Rhine, the early La Tène period, after which the Celts became noticeably mobile. When they swept down into the Italian peninsula, they won the Po Valley from the Etruscans, founded Milan in the fifth century and sacked Rome in 390. They reached their widest area of influence in about 260, and were seen, together with the Persians and the Scythians, as one of the three great nations of barbarian Europe. During the seventh century the Celts arrived in Gaul, where from the third century onwards, under Roman influence, they took up a semi-sedentary life in towns, and began to act as merchants, travelling across Europe to buy, sell and often plunder goods. They had settled Britain in the sixth century BCE and at intervals thereafter, parts of Spain during the third century, and during the same century they colonised the Dalmatian coast (part of what was until recently Yugoslavia), Thrace (modern Bulgaria) and parts of Asia Minor, where they became known as the Galatians. Strabo reported that the Celts were quarrelsome, brave, quick to fight, but otherwise not uncouth.[2] Under the name of Gaesatae, they often worked as mercenaries, e.g. for Dionysius of Syracuse (Sicily) in the early fifth century, for the Macedonians, including Alexander the Great (336–323), and later for Hannibal (247–182).

During the third century, the Mediterranean nations developed an effective resistance against them. In 225 a Celtic invasion of Italy was defeated by the inhabitants under Roman leadership, and in 201, after defeating Hannibal's Carthaginian invasion, Rome reclaimed the Po Valley from its Celtic settlers and began to enslave or exterminate Celtic tribes including the Cenomani, the Insubres and the Boii. Spain and Gaul were conquered by the Romans over some two hundred years, beginning with the second Punic War, when the strongholds of Carthage in Spain and southern France were captured, and ending with the final conquest of north-west Spain in the reign of Augustus. During the early third century the Celts had attacked Macedonia and Greece but were routed at Delphi in 279, with the result that the deity of that shrine, Apollo, was taken for ever afterwards as the champion of civilisation against barbarism.

Nevertheless, the nomadic Celts and the settled cultures of the south did interact. Cultural interchange with the Mediterranean civilisations seems initially to have been one-way. Around 650, through contact with the Greek and Etruscan civilisations, the Celts began to absorb elements of Mediterranean culture. Through these contacts, the characteristically Celtic style of art came into being as the development of the central European Hallstatt style with modified Greek (Etruscan) elements. The figurative art of Greece and Etruria seems to have had less impact than the more abstract elements, which were transmuted by the Celts into their unique style. Despite contact with the alphabet-using Greeks and Etruscans, there was no written Celtic language. Thus, names of deities and religious meanings of artefacts come down to us only from a later period, after the Roman conquests. The Celts were renowned for their reverence of the spoken word: Bards were respected members of society, and Druids maintained their knowledge through highly developed memory. In the first century BCE, when the Roman conquest of the Po Valley had settled down, the old Celtic lands produced many outstanding men of letters, among them Catullus, Cato, Varro, Virgil and others. Much later, after the fall of the Empire in the fifth century CE, the provinces of Spain and what is now southern France likewise became tenacious strongholds of Roman social, artistic and literary culture under the rulership of their new Visigothic overlords.

To the Greeks and Romans, the Celts were barbarians (people whose language sounded like 'ba ba ba'). They were nomads who lacked the arts of civilisation and they were thoroughly despised by their settled neighbours.

But in religious matters, to the modern eye they were part of the same broad Pagan grouping: Nature-venerating, polytheistic and recognisant of female divinities. Their deities were easily, if not accurately, Romanised (just as those of the Romans had been easily Graecised), in a way which the Jewish and then Christian divinities never were. They venerated both local and general deities, usually in natural sanctuaries, especially shrines at springs, rivers, lakes and in woodland. The water-spring goddess Sirona was revered at Pforzheim, Germany, and continuity of water-cults is known at hundreds of holy wells in Britain and Ireland, for example the hot springs at Buxton in Derbyshire, known in Roman times as Aquae Arnemetiae (the waters of the goddess of the sacred grove). Certain rivers have their own deities, many recalled by their still-Celtic names, e.g. Axona (Aisne), Nechtan (Neckar, Neckinger), Sequana (Seine), Sinend (Shannon), Deva (Dee) and Belisama (Mersey). Important shrines of water-deities existed at the sources of rivers, such as that at the source of the Seine. Here, healing shrines developed. Major British examples are Sul, divinity of the hot springs at Bath, identified by the Romans with Minerva, and Nodens, who was perhaps equivalent to the Irish god Nuada Argetlám, revered in the forest sanctuary at Lydney, Gloucestershire. In the late fourth century CE this site expanded and became a pilgrimage sanctuary of healing, equipped with rich temples, baths and accommodation for visitors.

RELIGIOUS PRACTICES

Like the Mediterranean civilisations, the Celts worshipped in sacred groves or *Nemetona*, but unlike them they did not have elaborate temples to house the images of their deities. In his *Pharsalia*, Lucan refers to the Gaulish Druids who live in deep groves and sequestered uninhabited woods. The Scholiast's comment on this passage is 'They worship the gods in the woods without using temples'.[3] Dio Cassius wrote that the Britons had sanctuaries in which they offered sacrifice to Andraste, goddess of victory.[4] These groves were dread places, held in great awe and approached only by the priesthood. The place-name *nemet-* indicates the site of a sacred grove. They may also have been administrative meeting places: Strabo reports that the main meet-ing place of the Galatae, the Celts who had settled in Asia Minor, was called Drunemeton, or Oak Grove.[5] As centres of native loyalty, they were some-times destroyed by conquerors. Julius Caesar cut down a sacred grove near Marseilles, which had tree trunks carved into the likeness of gods, and Suetonius Paulinus destroyed the Druidic groves on Anglesey during his sack of the island in 61.[6] The Celtic practice of tree veneration continued into Christian times, when priests like St Martin and St Patrick also found groves to desecrate.

The *Temenos* (ditched enclosure, literally 'place set apart') was the major place of worship, the temple inside it being a secondary consideration, as it

Plate 5.1 Image of the goddess Sequana, deity of the river Seine, France, from the Romano-Gallic shrine at the river's source. Nigel Pennick.

had been in the early days of Greece and Rome. The enclosure was usually square or rectangular; if irregular, it still had straight sides. Sometimes, the enclosure contained a sacred tree or pillar, perhaps carved or adorned like modern Maypoles. A circular ditched enclosure at Goloring (near Koblenz, Germany; sixth century BCE) had a post hole at the centre. There is archaeological evidence for the perambulation of shrines, perhaps in circle dancing, as in Maypole traditions. Inside a wide ditch at the late La Tène II barrow at Normée (Marne, France) is a 20-metre-square floor, compressed hard as if people had walked or danced in large numbers around a central point.[7] In Roman Imperial times, there was continuity of shrine-sites in England. At Frilford, near Abingdon, Oxfordshire, two Roman shrines were erected on the site of an earlier wooden structure, whilst at Gosbecks Farm near Colchester, Essex, a Roman temple of Celtic style was erected in an earlier ditched sanctuary. A bronze image of Mercury was found there.

Wells were also sacred, often associated with healing, as we shall see below. Each well was associated with a particular deity, as, for example, Coventina at Carrawburgh. In the north of England, the ancient territory of the Brigantes, and in Ireland, well-worship continues in a modern form, sometimes as a local folk-observance but more often by adoption into Christianity

Plate 5.2 Well-offering in the form of a 'dolly' from Kilmacrenan, Donegal, Ireland, 1894. Those visiting the well for its healing properties would leave a 'dolly' in acknowledgement and thanksgiving, continuing ancient Celtic Pagan practice. © 1992 Nigel Pennick.

in the form of 'well-dressing'. Pictures made of flower petals are carefully constructed the night before and then carried to the well in a procession, sometimes with floats and dancing children, sometimes more soberly, where the vicar blesses the well as a source of water for the community. Originally, a local saint was associated with the well, the successor of the original Celtic deity, but this feature has sometimes been lost in Protestant times.

Although the Celts had been in contact with the Mediterranean world since at least the seventh century BCE (through trading) and had become settled agrarians since occupying the Po Valley in the fifth, Caesar, writing in 53 BCE, can still report that the Celts in the main part of Gaul beyond the Alps practised human sacrifice. The Celts were 'slaves to superstition', he says, and believed that in order to preserve their own lives in battle they must sacrifice an equal number of others.[8] The Druids presided over these regular public sacrifices, which among some tribes were accomplished by burning the victims in huge wickerwork effigies. By the Imperial age, some fifty years later, travellers no longer report human sacrifice, and so it may be that Caesar was recording the last evidence of an earlier phase of Celtic culture. Strabo, writing at the beginning of the Common Era, says as much:

> The heads of enemies held in high repute they used to embalm in cedar oil and exhibit to strangers, and they would not deign to give them back even for a ransom of an equal weight of gold. But the Romans put a stop to these customs, as well as to all those connected with the sacrifices and divinations that are opposed to our usages. They used to strike a human being, whom they had devoted to death, in the back with a sabre, and then divine from his death-struggle. But they would not sacrifice without the Druids. We are told of still other kinds of human sacrifices; for example, they would shoot victims to death with arrows, or impale them in the temples, or having devised a colossus of straw and wood, throw into the colossus cattle and wild animals of all sorts and human beings, and make a burnt-offering of the whole thing.[9]

Similarly, Homer described the Greek leader Agamemnon's sacrifice of his daughter in the Trojan War of 1180 BCE, likewise the sacrifice of Trojan prisoners of war before the pyre of Patroclus, but there is no evidence that Homer's Greek contemporaries three hundred years later practised or even countenanced human sacrifice. On the contrary, nations who called themselves civilised rejected it as an abomination, and as we have seen, the Romans passed a law explicitly forbidding it.

We do not hear of women as priestesses or as seeresses among the earliest reports of the Celts. The Druids and their associated male colleges, the Vates and the Bards, seem to have monopolised the field. According to Pliny (IV.4), the Bards were singers and poets, the Vates were seers and scientists, and the Druids were both scientists and moral philosophers, the judges and arbitrators of both private and public disputes. Pliny mentions that the Druids and 'others', presumably the Vates, taught the immortality of the soul; Caesar had mentioned that they taught that the soul would pass into another body after death. In the Mediterranean world, such beliefs were only held among the Pythagoreans, and so the Druids were sometimes described as such. Pliny echoes Caesar's earlier report (which he may simply be repeating) that the Druids also used to decide matters of public policy such as the decision to go to war. We have already seen that the main political meeting place of the Celts in Asia Minor was a sacred oak grove. In Caesar's time, the main centre of Druidism was in the area of the Carnutes, after whom Chartres is named. There, Druids met annually at a shrine believed to be the site of Chartres Cathedral. This was the omphalos of Gaul, the sacred though not the geographical centre of the country.

It seems, then, that the Celtic priesthood had much more direct political power than that of Greece or Rome, where magistracies were a secular appointment, augurs had only the power to advise, not to direct, and secular officials, however many priestly obligations they might have in virtue of their office, were chosen for their rationality, good judgement and perhaps good luck, rather than for any direct line they had to the gods. After the Roman conquest of Spain, Gaul and Britain, reports of the Druid priesthood are few, presumably since the political structure of decision-making had changed. Both Claudius and Tiberius attempted to stamp out the 'religion of the Druids',[10] and the altars for the 'savage superstition' of human sacrifice were destroyed,[11] but we do not hear details of a general persecution. Occasional reports of single Druids and Druidesses surface in the later Empire, and in Ireland, which was never Romanised, the traditional tales mention Druids and *fili*, poets or seers whose pronouncements were highly valued and often feared by their communities. In historical times too the Irish *fili* and Druids travelled around and were known as 'hedge-preachers', like the wandering *sadhus* of India, passing on their teaching to anyone who would have it.

Tacitus, towards the end of the first century CE, also reported that the Celts made no distinction between male and female rulers. In Britain, the famous revolt led by Boudicca (60 CE) seems to have inspired unhesitating loyalty throughout the province. Queen Cartimandua, leader of the neighbouring Brigantes in the north-east, clearly enjoyed absolute authority over her tribe. She handed over Caratacus, the leader of an earlier rebellion, to the Romans in the year 47, and in the year 53 we hear of her again, having divorced her husband in favour of his presumably younger and more virile charioteer. But the ancient authors tell us little of priestesses. Strabo[12] repeats a report by Poseidonius of an island off the coast of Gaul, on which the women of the Samnitae lived without men, devoted to the ecstatic worship of Dionysos, to whom they devoted mystic initiations as well as other rites. This would be a female college similar to the Vates, the Celtic seers. There is also a report by Artemidorus, as saying that on an island near Britain women perform sacrifices like those in Samothrace, devoted to the (all-female) worship of Demeter and Kore. Unfortunately, these reports were never confirmed by later travellers and are sometimes dismissed as apocryphal. Tacitus, however, mentions black-robed women rushing between the ranks of British warriors, waving firebrands, before the battle of Anglesey, but it is not clear whether these are Druidesses or laity. These are tantalising hints, but there is little more. In medieval and modern times, the Celtic countries have boasted of many female well-guardians, often seeresses who presumably follow in direct line from the ancient healing and prophetic sanctuaries evidenced by archaeology and the ancient authors. But in between the line is obscure.

THE CELTIC DIVINITIES

The Celts seem to have been devoted to individual achievement and prowess, rather than to collective pursuits such as nationalism. Tribal warfare, which was frequent, seems to have been as much an occasion for individual heroism as for national prestige (as among the Germans and Romans) or even for booty. Celtic gods later identified with Mars appear in inscriptions to hybrids such as Mars Rigisamus (West Coker, Somerset), Mars Corotiacus (Martlesham, Suffolk) and Mars Loucetius (Bath). In the north of Britain the gods Belatucadrus and Cocidius were invoked and occasionally depicted, with helmet, a spear and a shield. In particular there were many battle-goddesses, for example Nemetona. The Irish myths, written down by monks in the ninth century, name a triple goddess called the Macha, one called the Morrigan and one called Badb, but both from these later tales and from ancient artefacts it seems that almost any goddess has at least a subsidiary role as a deity of battle.[13] The ancient writers report that the Celtic women were tall, fierce and strong, and as terrible in battle as their men, and Celtic coins often depict a naked woman on horseback triumphantly brandishing a spear or a sword. Being naked, perhaps she is a deity of battle or a personification of victory rather than an actual warrior. The Gaulish goddess Epona, whose name means 'Divine Horse', was adopted by many soldiers in the Roman cavalry and her cult spread across the Empire.

Romano-Celtic shrines, like later Celtic myths, tell of triple goddesses such as the Proximae (kinswomen), Dervonnae (oak-sprites) and Niskai (water-goddesses). These are often known as the three Mothers and are particularly numerous in the Rhineland. Some of these have nurturing attributes, such as baskets of fruit or flowers; others are more enigmatic, as in the triads of goddesses carrying two discs and a chain, provisionally identified by one writer[14] with goddesses of Earth, Sun and Moon. These triple goddesses are usually named as guardians of place: the Mothers of Britain and the Mothers of Nîmes, the Mothers of the Homeland and the Mothers of the Celts.[15] In

Wales, the fairies, who were considered to be the source of esoteric knowledge, especially foretelling the future, are known still as 'The Mothers' (Y Mamau). They are not necessarily called 'Mothers' on account of their childbearing capacity, however. 'Mother' and 'Father' in the ancient world were often honorific titles, referring to a mature and authoritative person of the relevant sex, as in ecclesiastical titles today. Irish myths, however, tell of a father god, the Daghda, who has a cauldron of plenty and of the renewal of life, and (in the tenth-century *Cormac's Glossary*) of a mother of the gods, Dana, whose name also appears in the Irish tales as the mother of her human tribe the People of Dana, or Tuatha de Danaan. An inscription of the mid-third century CE from Lanchester invokes the *numen* of the emperor and the goddess Garmangabis, together with a carving of a knife, a jug, a patera or ritual plate, and a disc. This goddess was presumably a deity of prosperity and plenty.

There were many local gods and goddesses, the 'spirits of place' which we have already seen in local cults around the Mediterranean. Herodian, writing in the early third century CE, tells that Belenus, the god of Noricum, was venerated greatly at Aquileia, where he was considered the same as Apollo.[16] Penninus or Poeninus, god of mountain ranges, was revered at the Alpine pass now called the Little St Bernhard. A shrine containing numerous offerings of Celtic and Roman coins was excavated when the modern road was driven through its site. In Roman times, Poeninus was assimilated to Jupiter Dolichenus. Also in the Alps, Brigantia, later Christianised as St Brigida, was guardian of mountain passes. Both names appear in northern England, where

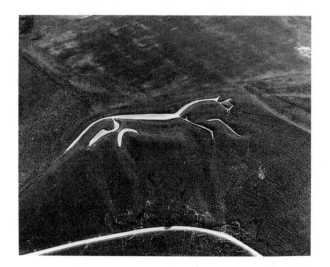

Plate 5.3 First-century BCE hill-figure at Uffington, Berkshire, England, marking a sacred hill, and perhaps serving as a tribal totem, visible from afar. Ministry of Defence, Crown Copyright reserved.

a similar cult appears to have existed among the Brigantes, who lived on and to the east of the Pennines. Possibly this tribe once controlled the passes which cross those inhospitable hills. Esus, the totemic god of the Essuvii, was worshipped in that region of Gaul, and several cities including Lyons in Gaul, Leiden in Frisia and Carlisle in Britain were named after the god Lugh, as was Mainz (Maguntiacum) after Mogounus. Lugh is one of the few truly international Celtic deities, but he is thought to be a late import into some countries. Caesar speaks of Dis, the lord of the Underworld, as the ancestral god of the Gauls. For this reason, Caesar says, the Gauls count each day as beginning with the preceding night.[17]

Sul was goddess of the hot springs at Bath. Her name means 'Sun': the underground Sun which heats the waters. In Celtic lands the Sun was thought to sink under water each evening, according to the brothers Grimm, and 'Sun springs' are commonplace names, e.g. Sunnebrunno near Düsseldorf. Sometimes these springs were thought to cure eye diseases, bringing the light of the Sun to the eye of the sufferer. A similar complex of associations can be seen in the case of the solar god Apollo: healing, prophecy (clear-sightedness), a spring (at Delphi) and the Sun. Apollo presided over many healing springs in Iberia and Gaul, but the Celtic sun-deities, however, were often (perhaps originally) feminine. The Matres Suleviae are found in Hungary, Rome, Gaul, Germany and Britain, linked with healing and the Sun,[18] and large numbers of female figurines decorated with solar discs are found at Celtic healing springs throughout France and Germany, with a single example in Britain.[19] The Gaelic for 'Sun' is *grian*, a feminine noun, and the modern Irish *grian na maighdean*, meaning the fairest of maidens, is literally 'the Sun among maidens'. J.F. Campbell, the nineteenth-century folklorist, reported that 'Dia Greine' was the old Scottish name of the sun-goddess.[20] The Megalithic sites now known as Newgrange (in Ireland), Granja de Toniñuelo (in Spain) and Bois-de-la-neuve-Grange (in France) may also carry this element in their names. Where the Sun strikes into the heart of the tomb at the winter solstice at Newgrange, we are reminded of the Baltic (and Japanese) stories of the sun-goddess hiding in a cave at midwinter, a theme which is echoed in the later legend of Grainne (the name means 'hateful' but could be derived from *grian*) and her lover Diarmat. This tells of the lovers fleeing from Grainne's husband and travelling around Ireland in a year and a day (one 'circuit' of sunrises and sunsets moving along the horizon), sleeping in a different cave every night. In the same way the Persian solar god Mithras was associated with a cave. The god Apollo bears the Celtic solar title at the shrine of Apollo Grannus near modern Grand in France and that of Grannus Phoebus in Trier. According to Dio Cassius the Emperor Caracalla paid an unsuccessful visit to the healing shrine of Grannus in 215 CE.

In Romano-Celtic iconography, under the *interpretatio Romana*, the sky-god Jupiter also appears with the spoked solar or sky disc of north European palaeolithic art. Gods identified with Jupiter under the *interpretatio Romana* included Ambisagrus (the persistent) as well as Taranucus (the thunderer), Taranis and Uxellimus (the highest one). Many inscriptions and place-names are dedicated to the worship of Minerva and Mercury, deities of civilisation and commerce. Minerva was most famously commemorated as Sulis Minerva at Bath. The gods identified with Mercury include the people's god, Teutates, Atesmiius, Caletos and Moccos. Those identified with Mars include Albiorix (king of the world), Caturix (battle-king), Dunatis (god of fortresses), Leucetius (lightning-god), Vintius (wind-god) and Vitucadrus (brilliant in energy). Surviving sacred objects bear images of the more important deities of the pantheon. The Gundestrup Cauldron, which has Thracian and Celtic elements, the result, it is thought, of cooperation between Triballian (Thracian) and Scordiscian (Celtic) silversmiths, bears images of the Lord of Animals (Dionysos), the war-god (Perun-Ares), the Great Mother (Kybele), and the antlered god (Cernunnos).[21] An altar found at Notre Dame in Paris bears an image of the axe-god Esus, a bull and three cranes, with the inscription 'Tarvos Trigaranus'.

Animal deities and animal totems continued throughout the Romano-Celtic period: the horses of Epona and 'Jupiter'; the dog of Nehalennia; Arduina, the mistress of the wild boars of the Ardennes; Artio, the bear-goddess of Berne and Berlin; the ram-headed serpents which are never named; and, of course, the Gaulish antlered god named on one inscription as [C]ernunnos, the Horned One, who is paralleled by bull-horned deities in Britain. There appears to have been a belief that members of certain clans were magically descended from totemic beasts.[22] They are reflected in the names of animal-linked deities such as Tarvos (the bull), Mullo (ass), Moccos (the god of swine), and Epona, Artio and Damona, goddesses of horses, bears and cattle respectively. Gallic Celtic names such as Brannogenos (son of the raven) and Artogenos (son of the bear) parallel the comparable totemic warrior-cults of Scandinavia (the Berserkers etc.). According to Caesar, the Britons kept hares, chickens and geese, but did not kill them. They were held in supreme respect. Before her final battle against the Roman troops, Boudicca is said to have released a hare which she had carried under her cloak, presumably to propitiate the deities or perhaps to consult the omens. Later, the cat, too, joined these respected beasts. The Helvetii, who migrated from the area of modern Bavaria south into Switzerland, seem to have placed themselves under the protection of the bear-goddess Artio. An image of this goddess was found at Muri near Berne in Switzerland. In the thirteenth century, a revelation of a bear to a knight led to the foundation of the city, where bears are kept to this day as totems of the city.

THE SACRED YEAR OF THE CELTS

In Gaul and Ireland, the year was divided basically into two halves: winter and summer. The winter half was the beginning of the year, starting at

Samhain (1 November). This was the most important festival of the year, showing the pastoralist, rather than agricultural, origin of the calendar. Samhain was the end of the grazing season, when flocks and herds were collected together, and only the breeding stock set aside from slaughter. It was a time of gathering-together of the tribe at their ritual centre for rituals of death and renewal, dedicated to the union of the tribal god (in Ireland, the Daghda) with a goddess of sovereignty, the Morrigan, or, more localised, Boann, deity of the River Boyne.

The second great festival of the year was Beltane or Cétshamhain (1 May, May Day). This was the beginning of the summer half of the year, also a pastoralist festival. As at Samhain, the lighting of bonfires was an important rite. Cattle were driven through the smoke to protect them in the coming season. Beltane may be connected with the Austrian deity Belenos, who was particularly associated with pastoralism,[23] or it may simply take its name from the bright (*bel*) fires which were part of its celebration. Beltane is the only festival recorded in the ninth-century Welsh tales, a time when the Otherworld communicates with the world of humans, either through portents such as the dragon fight in the tale of Lludd and Llevelys, or through apparitions such as the hero Pwyll's sighting of the goddess Rhiannon. The Romanesque church at Belsen, on an old Celtic holy hill

Plate 5.4 Samhain Cake, Cambridgeshire, England, 1987. Private ceremonies continue to use traditional designs knowingly. © 1987 Nigel Pennick.

near Tübingen, Germany, has contemporary images of Béél, with ox- and sheeps' heads.

In Ireland, the year was further subdivided by two more festivals. (The solstices and equinoxes do not have corresponding Celtic festivals.) In the story of the wooing of Emer by the Irish hero Cú Chulainn, the maiden asks her suitor to go sleepless from 'Samhain, when the summer goes to its rest, until Imbolc, when the ewes are milked at spring's beginning; from Imbolc until Beltine at the summer's beginning and from Beltine to Bron Trogain, earth's sorrowing autumn'.[24] Like Samhain and Beltine, Imbolc (1 February) was a pastoralist festival, celebrating the lambing, the first lactation of the ewes. It was sacred to the goddess of healing, poetry and smithcraft, Brigit, who was assimilated by the church into St Brigit, still fêted on the same day. It is possible that Imbolc was a festival specific originally to a single cultural or occupational group, later being absorbed into general recognition.

Lughnasadh (1 August, also called Bron Trograin) appears to have been imported into Ireland at a later date, perhaps by continental devotees of Lugh, who in the Irish pantheon is a latecomer, the *ildánach*, master of all skills, more modern in character than the other goddesses and gods. Correspondingly, Lughnasadh differs from the other three festivals in being agrarian in character, marking the harvest, and baking of the first loaf from the new grain. The deity honoured at Lughnasadh was Lugh, who was said to have instituted the games in honour of his foster-mother, Táiltiu. 'Táiltiu' (Teltown) is in fact the name of the site of the festival in Tara. It is an ancient burial ground, and its name is thought to mean 'fair' or 'lovely',[25] so if it ever was associated with a presiding goddess of that name, like Demeter in Greece she would have ruled both the Underworld and the fruits which sprang from it.

The most complex known Celtic calendar is from Roman Gaul, recorded on a bronze tablet, from Coligny, Ain, France. Dating from the first century BCE, it is fragmentary, but enough survives to indicate that it was divided into sixteen columns showing sixty-two consecutive lunar months, each divided into a bright and a dark half, the changeover-point being marked ATENOVX. There are also two intercalary months, used to realign the lunar year with the solar one. All months are named; good months are marked MAT and inauspicious ones ANM. The days are numbered from I to XV in the light half of each month, and from I to XIV (or XV) in the dark half. Certain significant days are marked by abbreviations, but festivals are not marked.[26]

THE CELTS BECOME ROMANISED

The Phoenicians had set up a trading post at Gades (modern Cadiz in Spain) and one at Massilia (modern Marseilles, France) before the eighth century BCE, but otherwise the hinterland of the western Mediterranean was untouched by the old eastern civilisations and the Celts swept down towards the coast in the seventh century. Iberia (modern Spain and Portugal) seems to have had a mixture of inhabitants; writing in the fifth century BCE, Himilco the Carthaginian reports seeing Ethiopians living there.[27] Strabo, at the beginning of the Common Era, says that there were no indigenous altars in the south of the country, but only stones 'lying in groups of three or four, which in accordance with a native custom are turned round by those who visit the place, and then, after the pouring of a libation, are moved back again'.[28] It looks as if the inhabitants were using megalithic sites for contemporary worship, a practice which continued into historical times and was forbidden by the seventh-century Edict of Nantes. Strabo adds that the inhabitants forbid people to offer sacrifice there or even to go there at night, because the gods occupy the place at that time. Modern Westerners in such a situation would say that the place was haunted, or that the Little People were there. For the ancients, however, full Olympian sacrifice (*thuein*) was debarred, yet the spirits there were seen as *theoi*, divine and deserving of libation. This gives us an interesting insight into the nature of ancient Pagan thought and also into our own assumptions, whether we accept modern folkloric practices as 'survivals' or, alternatively, dismiss them as 'superstitions'.

In northern central Iberia lived the Celtiberians, who apparently were once the most savage of all the inhabitants, but who by the time of Strabo spoke Latin, wore the toga and were thoroughly Romanised.[29] However, they retained at least one non-Roman custom, that of sacrificing before the doors of their houses to an unnamed deity on the night of the full moon every month, then dancing the whole night through. Strabo unfortunately had never been to Iberia and was only reporting other travellers' tales, but at least his is an early record and his story, if true, forms an engaging parallel with modern Pagan full moon celebrations. He also gives details of sacrifice and of divination similar to the unpleasant rites described by Caesar fifty years before and repeated by Tacitus more than fifty years afterwards.

The Carthaginians had occupied Iberia from about 240 BCE, followed by the Romans beginning some twenty years later. Roman expansion into the north-west of the province took another two hundred years, but by then Celtic culture was almost invisible; the Iberians were becoming Romans. (Iberia later produced not only the writers Seneca and Lucan, but also the Emperors Trajan and Hadrian.) Indeed, it seems that Roman Paganism survived there into the sixth century CE, for the Bishop of Braga, St Martin, who was appointed in 560 to convert the Arian inhabitants of the north-west, the Galicians, to Catholicism, describes the old practices as still extant:

> Observing the Vulcanalia and the kalends, decorating tables, wearing laurels, taking omens from footsteps, putting fruit and wine on the log in the hearth, and bread in the well, what are these but worship of the

devil? For women to call upon Minerva when they spin, and to observe the day of Venus at weddings and to call upon her whenever they go out upon the public highway, what is that but worship of the devil?[30]

Southern Gaul was invaded by Rome at the beginning of the second century BCE, after the defeat of Hannibal, and effectively annexed one hundred years later. It was the first 'province' outside Italy and the eastern part of it still bears that name: Provence. During the century of Roman occupation, the Celts settled and developed commercial towns throughout the whole of what is now France. The conquest of 'long-haired Gaul' (*Gallia comata*), the area north of *Gallia togata*, the modern Provence and Languedoc, was carried out by Caesar in 57–55 BCE. His description of it in the *Gallic Wars* has given us our only first-hand account of tribal Celtic life. After Caesar, there were regular revolts in northern Gaul until Augustus annexed the province and saved it from a German invasion. After this, the Druids fade from view, and during the first fifty years CE Tiberius and Claudius tried to suppress their remnants; but otherwise there was no interference with the worship of the Celtic divinities. The Gauls, as several ancient writers mention, soon became accustomed to Roman ease and were rather despised for it by their conquerors. Nevertheless, five centuries later they were to become the guardians of Roman organisation and culture, which they, like their kins-people and neighbours the Iberians, managed to impose on their conquerors when overrun by the Goths, the Alemanni and the Franks in the fifth century CE. The system of Roman law as codified by Theodosius and Justinian has survived to form the basis of European Union law today.

Britain, conquered by Claudius in 43 BCE and initially milked for taxes, slaves and auxiliary troops, attempted to expel the Romans in Boudicca's rebellion of 60 CE. The rebellion nearly succeeded, but after it was put down and the punitive victor, Suetonius Paulinus, discreetly removed to another command, a series of new governors and their financial directors set about a systematic process of Romanisation. As Tacitus observed with some acerbity, 'Among the conquered it is called culture, when in fact it is part of their slavery'.[31] Britain, in contrast to Gaul and Iberia, is known for two great queens: Boudicca and Cartimandua. Once more in Tacitus' words, 'They do not distinguish among their rulers by sex'.[32] Boudicca, the widow of King Praesutagus of the Iceni, devoted the spoils of her battles to the goddess Andraste,[33] and as already mentioned, ceremonially released a hare onto the battlefield before her final standoff with the Romans under Paulinus. Cartimandua's decisive role has already been described.

The Romano-Celtic phase in both Gaul and Britain was characterised by three main features. First, there is the comparative absence of the Druids, and the total absence of their bloodthirsty sacrifices and divinations. They may possibly have become the temple-priests of the newly expanded religion, but if so it is strange that we have no records of this, nor hear of them as official augurs, perhaps in a college in their own right, like the Etruscan *haruspices*. In Gaul there was a rebellion in 69–70 in which Druids are mentioned,[34] but thereafter both Druids and Druidesses appear only occasionally, as freelance seers. One Druidess is said to have been an innkeeper, who prophesied to the soldier Diocles that he would one day become emperor – which indeed he did, as Diocletian.[35] Next there is the appearance of native monuments and images, which had been more or less absent in the pre-Roman phase. There is some evidence that the pre-Roman Celts had images made of wood, but only after the Romans came did they start carving in stone. Celtic square temples have already been described, and so

Plate 5.5 2,000-year-old Celtic images kept at Newhouse Farm, Stretton Grandison, Herefordshire, England. ©1991 Nigel Pennick.

have some of the native divinities. Images of triple goddesses are specifically Celtic, as are gods carrying or adorned with wheels. Other wheel-gods are identified with Jupiter (see below). The Roman Jupiter ruled the sky, thunder and lightning, but the Celts, especially the Gauls, had a specific god of thunder, Taranis. He is often shown carrying a hammer, like Thor in later Germanic art. Sucellus, 'the Good Striker', is specifically a hammer-god, and he is sometimes shown with an elaborate headdress of thin-handled hammers radiating out from his head in what could equally well be a solar motif. The Celtic deities often remain obscure to us, since the Romans did not comment on them in any detail but preferred to assimilate them to Roman ones.

The third feature of Romano-Celtic religion is that of assimilation. Many dual deities are depicted and also mentioned in dedications. These range from ill-assorted hybrids like Sulis Minerva and Mars Loucetius to genuinely new departures in syncretic religion such as the famous Jupiter columns which are found all over the northern provinces of the Empire, especially in the east. Maximus of Tyre stated that the representation of Zeus to the Celts was a high oak,[36] and Celtic columns are often decorated with tree imagery, for example with oak leaves and acorns at Hausen-an-der-Zaber. Often, the figure at the top of the column is a mounted god trampling a snake-limbed monster. The Celtic sky-god here is given the name of his Roman equivalent, but his horse, spoked wheel, celestial column, sacred tree imagery and fight with the underworld snake look forward to the Germanic sky-god Odin, fully described only as late as the thirteenth century by Icelandic writers, using identical celestial symbolism. Here an enduring north European tradition has found expression within a Classical framework. Some 150 Jupiter columns have been documented, and it would be interesting to know whether they served, in true sky-pillar fashion, as the omphaloi of their settlements, the symbolic and practical centre of the built environment.

6

THE LATER CELTS

The north-west provinces, the 'Celtic' lands, developed an identity of their own and declared independence several times in the late Empire. During the third century, seaborne pirates from Saxony and from Ireland started to harass Britain and northern Gaul. Since the eastern Imperial frontier was already being attacked by the Goths, troops could seldom be spared to defend the northern provinces. Around the year 260, the Rhine commander Marcus Postumus declared Spain, Gaul, Britain and the Rhineland to be the Empire of the Gallic Provinces. This Empire lasted until 274, during which time the Alemanni, a confederation from east of the Rhine, invaded and devastated northern Gaul. The towns were unwalled and fifty to sixty of them were captured. British towns, meanwhile, expanded, perhaps taking refugees from the continent. Country villas in Britain also show signs of building, since the rich landowners would be the first to be able to retreat to the comparative safety of the island, and some superb mosaics, including the Orphic pavement at Littlecote House in Oxfordshire, date from this time. In Gaul, the years 284–286 saw another secession by the unemployed and homeless whom the Alemanni had dispossessed, and in 287 Britain seceded from the Empire under Carausius and then Allectus.[1]

This outer threat coincided with the inner turmoil caused by (or addressed by?) Christianity, as the Roman body politic struggled to formulate a unifying religious system. The turn of the century, the time of Diocletian's persecution of the Christians followed by Constantine's toleration of them, saw many new temples built in Britain. The Gallic provinces must also have been a comparative haven for Christians during Diocletian's reign, because their Caesar, Constantius, husband of the Christian Helena and father of the future Christian Constantine, was lax in implementing the anti-Christian edicts. The new administration following the reconquest of Britain by the Empire in 306 in fact expedited Christian rule. Britain, Frisia, the Rhineland, Gaul and Spain were formed into a new prefecture with its capital in Trier (the site of a healing shrine of Apollo on the modern French–German border). This had its own civilian administration independent of the central power based in the western capital, and under the rule of Constantine, this bureaucracy became dominated by Christians. As Constantine's favour for Christianity grew, the Pagan temples were starved of funds. In Britain, which had not suffered as Gaul and Spain had from the Gothic invasions, this had the curious result of a general increase in civic prosperity as the funds of the temples were recycled into the Christian-controlled community.

The western Empire as a whole, including Italy and Illyricum (Dalmatia) as well as the Gallic provinces, was also involved in the battles of the Imperial succession: when the Pagan Count Maxentius opposed Constantine from 306 to 312, and when Magnentius, who tolerated Paganism as well as endorsing official Christianity, battled with the last of Constantine's sons from 350 to 353. The short-lived revolt of Magnentius (see above, p. 70) was a time of great hope for Pagans, who by now were losing their property through fines and their income through exclusion from office in the newly confident Christian Empire of Constantine's sons. In Britain the revolt was put down with great savagery by a tidy-minded bureaucrat, an Imperial notary who earned the nickname of 'Paul the Chain' from the paranoid link-age of associations he constructed so as to acquire new victims for his reprisal tribunals. Luckily for Pagans, two years later Emperor Julian came to the throne, and although his influence was as short as his reign on the continent, on the island of Britain there are signs of a new-found Pagan confidence. The healing sanctuary of Mars Nodens in Gloucestershire was expanded and became an enormous centre, and at around this time the Pagan temple at Verulamium was rebuilt. The Mithraeum in London was dismantled and then rebuilt, indicating that an expected attack either did not happen or had been survived (although the dating here is uncertain), and it was perhaps at this time that the governor of southern Britain restored the Jupiter column at Cirencester. This had either crumbled through neglect or had been destroyed by Christians. His inscription reads:

> To Jupiter, Best and Greatest, His Perfection Lucius Septimius . . .
> governor of Britannia Prima, restored [this monument], being a
> citizen of Rheims.
> This statue and column erected under the ancient religion Septimius
> restores, ruler of Britannia Prima.[2]

Whether this temporary revival extended for long, had any deep-reaching effect, or even existed at all, is a matter of dispute among scholars. Inscriptions by Roman soldiers are mostly Pagan, but probably the civilian administration was Christian. Certainly, when a continental bishop, Germanicus, was called to Britain in 429 to dispute on matters of Christian heresy, he described a ruling class which was entirely Christian.

On the continent, militant Christianity began again. This was not a time of multifaith tolerance, at least among adherents of the new religion. From 380 to 385, St Martin of Tours inspected northern Gaul, destroying Pagan shrines and particularly trees. One story has it that the Pagans in one town challenged him to perform a miracle. He could cut their sacred tree down if he would stand under it as it fell. St Martin declined their challenge and went elsewhere.[3]

The Emperor Theodosius (379–395) extended the draconian laws against Paganism which had lapsed since Julian, but fortunately for Pagans in the north-west prefecture, they were largely ignored by the praetorian prefect in charge of the area, a Pagan Frankish barbarian named Arbogast. The Franks, who had crossed into Gaul from the eastern bank of the Rhine at the time of Carausius' Empire, had already been Romanised by their conqueror Constantius, and we can assume that Arbogast was defending Roman rather than Germanic Paganism. When Theodosius passed his famous law forbidding even household Pagan worship in private, Arbogast installed a puppet western emperor, Eugenius, who immediately rescinded the anti-Pagan legislation and ordered the restoration of the Altar of Victory to the Senate (see chapter 4) as well as the revival of some very odd and recondite Pagan cults. But Theodosius fought back, and Eugenius and Arbogast died in the battle of Flavia Frigida on 6 September, 394. Iberia and Gaul were swept into the chaos of Christian infighting that was to lead to Alaric's sack of Rome in 410, the Rhineland did battle with invading Germans (see chapter 7), who followed the basic tribal form of north European Paganism, and of Britain we know little apart from monumental inscriptions.

In 409–410, Britain and Armorica (modern Brittany) seceded for the last time from the Empire, taking responsibility for their own defence against the marauding Saxons and Irish who had been harassing the coast for the last century. The Irish had never been part of the Roman Empire, and so what we know about them has had to be deduced from archaeology and the careful interpretation of ballads and stories written down by monks centuries after the world they described had disappeared. The Irish tales describe the same proud, superstitious warrior-aristocracy as Roman observers saw in Britain and on the mainland. They also add a tradition of powerful, autonomous women and battle-goddesses which is absent from Romanised areas after the initial decades during which such rulers as Cartimandua and Boudicca played a decisive role. Like the Galatians in Asia Minor, the Irish regularly met in cult centres which were huge earthworks, the most famous being that of Tara in County Meath. Like the Gaulish Druids, whose meeting place at Chartres was thought to be the centre of their country, the Irish saw Meath as the centre of their island, with the four provinces of Ulster, Leinster, Connaught and Munster encircling it. Ulster in the north was seen as the odd one out, being at one time opposed by a coalition of the other provinces led by Queen Maedb. Whether the north was symbolically the unlucky quarter (it is the quarter of the gods in Germanic tradition), or whether the story is less overtly symbolic, we cannot tell. An echo of this tradition was preserved in the Celtic outpost of Cornwall. Medieval Cornish miracle plays, performed at permanent circular earthworks (the Plen an

Gwary), retained the tradition of the north as the direction of the Pagan gods. 'Bad or Pagan characters in the Cornish Plans are grouped near the North, and in Meryasek we find this confirmed as the only proper arrangement, for a demon and Jupiter are each called there "our patron saint on the North Side."'[4]

Nodens, the healing god of the Gloucestershire spring sanctuary, has a name cognate with 'Nuada', the name of a legendary Irish king who lost his arm, had it replaced by a silver one, and later was miraculously healed. It is interesting that the shrine of Nodens only came into prominence at the time of the Irish sea-raids, although it seems unlikely that the people of the area would adopt one of the heroes of their enemies as a god. In the late fourth century, a king known as Niall of the Nine Hostages was raiding Britain. There is a symbolic tale told about him, too, to the effect that he went into the forest on a survival test with his brothers, and was the only one of them to recognise the disguised maiden who was the Sovereignty of Ireland, only by union with whom a man could be pronounced High King. It was quite possibly Niall who kidnapped the future Saint Patrick, Christian converter of Ireland, and kept him in slavery for seven years in Ireland. Patrick had returned to Britain and was living with his family around the year 418, so he is broadly contemporary with Niall.

Irish Paganism was very tolerant to Christianity. In 438, the High King, Laighaire, held a folk-moot at Tara on the question of faith. To accommodate Christianity, he called together a committee to draft new laws for Ireland. The committee comprised three kings, three *Brehona* (Pagan law-speakers) and three Christian missionaries. The laws they drew up became the *Seanchus Mór*, which contained elements from Pagan and Christian law. This remained valid until superseded by English law in the seventeenth century. In 448, St Patrick arrived and established Christianity as the official religion of Ireland, and we hear no more of the country for the next century.

Plate 6.1 Sheela-na-gig and beastie on mid-twelfth-century church at Kilpeck, Herefordshire, England. © 1990 Nigel Pennick.

99

Meanwhile, in Gaul and Spain the ruling classes were becoming absorbed into the new Christian administration. Church officials, like the old temple-priests and priestesses, were exempt from many taxes as well as from the swingeing burden of public finance, much of which came out of the pockets of the city notables. For this reason as well as because the effective power was now in the hands of avowed Christians, the Romano-Celtic aristocracy became Catholic and, on the continent, relied on Gothic Arian mercenaries to run their armies. In Britain the troops are likely to have been Saxon mercenaries, Pagans rather than Christians, and when after 430 King Vortigern's foreign troops turned against him the island degenerated into chaos. The traditional date for the Saxon invasion of Britain is 449, under Hengist and Horsa, whose names are totemic: they mean 'stallion' and 'mare' respectively.

In 460 many Britons migrated to Gaul, where they moved into Armorica, a part of the country which had never been properly reabsorbed after the secession of 409, and, being pugnacious and dominant according to Gildas, took it over and founded Brittany. It is at this time that the semi-legendary Ambrosius Aurelianus appears in British history, fighting against the Saxons and routing them at Mount Badon at the turn of the sixth century. This is the historical basis for the King Arthur legends. After Ambrosius' victory there was said to be peace for two generations. Gildas, writing in the mid-sixth century, speaks of 'our present serenity' and mentions a generation which had no experience of 'the great storm'.[5] However, this peace is likely to have been kept by small-scale warrior-chieftains on the old tribal Celtic model, not by a national government based in cities. Gaul, by contrast, was settled under the old Roman civic bureaucracy by the Frankish monarchs, the fabled Merovingians or descendants of Meroveus, the 'sea-fighter' who had captured Tournai in 446. Their Germanic Pagan tradition forbade them to cut their hair, and they retained this tradition even after converting to Christianity in 503 or thereabouts.[6] They eventually became ceremonial monarchs in the style of the late Empire, rather than Germanic fighting kings, until they were deposed by their chief minister Pepin in 751 when he founded the Carolingian dynasty. So, by the sixth century, the north of modern France then was ruled by the western Germans, the (Catholic) Franks, and the south, the old Roman Provincia, together with Spain, by the eastern Germans, the (Arian) Goths. However, Paganism remained in vernacular practice. In 589 the third Council of Toledo thundered that 'the sacrilege of idolatry is rooted in almost the whole of Gaul and Spain'. Ireland, too, swayed back and forwards between official Christianity and official Paganism. In 554, the geomantic centre of Ireland, Tara, was cursed by the Christian monk Ruadhan of Lothra, presumably because people still venerated its sacred nature. Five years later, the king Diarmat McCerbaill celebrated the *feis* or ceremonial marriage with the goddess of the land, part of the traditional inauguration of Irish kings, at the last Assembly of Tara.

Plate 6.2 Chalk graffito of labyrinth and 'Celtic Rose' pattern (*c.*1600) in the abandoned medieval stone mines at Chaldon, Surrey, England. Believed to be the relic of Pagan miners' rites. © Jeff Saward, Caerdroia Archives.

But Diarmat died in 565, probably the last Pagan king of Ireland, and we hear no more of official Paganism. Diarmat must have been part of a Pagan restoration, for the next High King, Ainmire (565–571), was so concerned at the decline of the Christian religion that he invited Gildas and other monks from Britain to revive it.

There were no more sacred marriages in Ireland, but the cult of St Bridget retained its vitality. Bridget is generally agreed to be a Christianisation of the goddess known as Brighde in Ireland, Bride in Scotland and possibly Brigantia in the north of Britain. She had to do with warmth, fire, summer and possibly the Sun, since an Irish legend tells that in winter she was imprisoned in an icy mountain by a one-eyed hag.[7] In some places she presided over thermal springs, presumably as the underground Sun, and in Scotland until the mid-twentieth century she was welcomed in at Imbolc (1 February) by the symbolic rekindling of the hearth fire after the house had been spring-cleaned from top to bottom. In County Kildare Brighde had a shrine with a sacred flame, which was tended by a college of women rather like the Vestal Virgins in Rome. This is not simply a Roman story, since the flame was kept burning into historical times after the purported temple became a Christian nunnery. In 1220 Archbishop Henry of Dublin ordered the flame to be extinguished. In 722 St Bridget, as she now was, appeared to the Irish army of Leinster, hovering in the sky before they routed the forces of Tara, rather as the sun-god El Gabel had appeared to Aurelian in 273 and as the Christian chi-rho sign had appeared to Constantine in 312.

In Britain the Saxons invaded again after the peace of Ambrosius, probably in about 570. History then is silent until the mission of Augustine in 597, when the Roman monk found a country which was entirely Germanic, ruled by Saxon kings who traced their ancestry to Woden, who lived in townships or villages rather than cities, who spoke Anglo-Saxon rather than Celtic or Latin, and who followed German laws which were almost identical with those noted five hundred years before by Tacitus. The Saxons had obviously been impervious to the blandishments of Romanisation, unlike their continental neighbours the Franks and the Goths. Pockets of resistance held out in the north of Britain. In Strathclyde a struggle for supremacy broke out. There were four British kings in Strathclyde; the Angles had invaded and conquered the Lothians. Under Anglian influence, the Picts and the Welsh returned to Paganism, and around the year 550 the missionary Kentigern undertook a crusade to extirpate it.[8] This was a spectacular failure, however, as a great part of the British population in the south of Strathclyde restored their ancestral faith 'fostered by their bards, who recalled the old traditions of the race before they had been Christianized under the Roman dominion',[9] or at any rate adopting a different form of Paganism under the influence of the invaders. (It should, however, be noted that the Cumbrian language was used in the area until the fourteenth century, and so the traditional Pagan tales carried in its ballads would be accessible until that time.) In 573, the four kings fought for supremacy over the area. Three of them (one Christian, Uriens, one anti-Christian, Morcant, and one unknown, Gwenddoleu) claimed descent through Coil Hên, the 'Ancient One' of Wales, from Beli and Anna, the divine ancestors of Celtic myth.[10] The other king, Rhydderch Hael, was a keen Christian, descended, according to the Four Books of Wales,[11] from the Emperor Magnus Maximus (383–388), the Christian Roman commander who had been raised to western emperor by the troops while serving in Britain. At the Battle of Arderyd, on the River Esk eight miles north of Carlisle, the Christian Rhydderch won the victory, the Welsh Gwenddoleu was slain, and Kentigern and his priests were invited back into Cumbria to extirpate native tradition.[12] The tradition of kings who claimed descent from divine ancestors, which we shall see more clearly among the Germanic tribes, in this part of Britain had come to an end.

We are now moving away from official Paganism into the time of folklore and Christianised practices. Finding that it could not stamp out the small rituals of life, once presided over by the ancient divinities, the Church took many of these on board. May Day processions were blessed, helpful deities like Brighde were adopted as saints, together with the trappings of their old cult, and troublesome deities like Woden were anathematised as devils. The *Capitularia Regum Francorum*, published at Paris in 1677, lists rural practices then in use, but forbidden in France by the Church. Among them were

Plate 6.3 May Garland, Northampton, England, 1826. Nideck Picture Collection.

103

ceremonies for the deceased, known as *Dadsissas*, and ceremonies at their tombs. The ceremonies of Mercury and Jupiter were forbidden, along with sacrifices made to any other divinity. This included the observance of the festivals of Mercury or Jupiter and *Vince Luna* (eclipses of the moon). The Church condemned 'those believing that because women worship the moon, they can draw the hearts of men towards the Pagans'. In true dual faith manner, the Mother Goddess was petitioned in the form 'of that which good people call St Mary'. Doubtless, she still is. French Pagans worshipped at 'the irregular places which they cherish for their ceremonies', which included 'water-springs as the sites of sacrifice', also moats around houses and stones. As in England, they also processed through churches and along 'the Pagan trackway, which they name *Yries*', which was 'marked with rags or with shoes'. Certain ceremonies involved the construction of small huts known as sanctuaries, connected with 'the ceremonies of the woodland, known as *Nimidas*'. Seventeenth-century French Pagans made images of flour sprinkled on the ground (step patterns and the like); images made from rags; 'the image which they carry through the fields', and 'the wooden feet or hands used in Heathen ritual'. Pagan amulets included horns and snail-shells, phylacteries and 'things bound'.

Pagan deities were also venerated into historical times as folk-spirits, not simply as Christian saints, as will be described below. This is entirely of a piece with a properly Pagan outlook which recognises many sorts of spirits, each having their place and function, and which in the early days of the Church, of Islam and of Judaism (if the Book of Kings is to be believed) would simply take the monotheistic deity as one among many, perhaps the supreme among many, pre-existing deities. This is a Pagan outlook and it has continued in Europe up to the present day.

VERNACULAR PAGANISM

In Wales, Scotland, Ireland and Brittany, the old gods, worshipped sometimes under the guise of Celtic saints (i.e. those not canonised by the Pope), were revered in truly Pagan fashion. For example, at Llanderfel, Merionethshire, Wales, Darvel Gadarn was revered in an image 'in which the people have so greate confidence, hope and trust, that they come dayly a pilgrimage unto hym, some with kyne, other with oxen and horses'.[13] Taken to London, the image was burnt at Smithfield in the same year. In 1589, John Ansters reported that bullocks were sacrificed 'the half to God and to Beino' in the churchyard at Clynog, Lleyn, Wales.[14] Cattle born with 'the mark of Beyno' were literally earmarked for later sacrifice. Such cattle were later sold for slaughter by the churchwarden on Trinity Sunday. The custom fell into disuse in the nineteenth century.

Worship of goddesses continued under several names. Until the seventeenth century in Brittany, there were shrines kept by old women known as Fatuae or Fatidicae, who taught 'the rites of Venus' to young women, instructing them in shamanistic practices.[15] In Wales, the Goddess of Heaven or Mother of all human beings was known as Brenhines-y-nef.[16] In Brittany, the cult of St Anne 'stepped into the place of one of the Bonæ Deæ, tutelary earth goddesses . . . themselves representing the Celtic or pre-Celtic Ane, mother of the gods'.[17] Sometimes actual Pagan images were revered:

> In 1625, whilst ploughing a field at Keranna, in the parish of Plunevet, in Morbihan, a farmer named Yves Nicolayic turned up out of the ground a statue, probably a Bona Dea of the pagan Armoricans, numbers of which have been found of late years . . . the Carmelites, who had been zealous advocates of the cult of the Mother of Our Lady . . . constructed a chapel for the image, and . . . organized pilgrimages to it, which met with great success. The image was destroyed at the Revolution, but the pilgrimages continue.[18]

Gwen Teirbron, three-breasted patroness of nursing mothers, was also revered in Brittany. Nursing mothers offered Gwen Teirbron a distaff and flax to secure a proper quantity of milk for their babies. A major shrine was at the chapel of St Venec between Quimper and Châteaulin. In the 1870s, most images of Gwen Teirbron were got rid of by the priests, 'who have buried them, regarding them as somewhat outrageous and not conducive to devotion'. In Britain, churches of St Candida, St White and St Wita are sites of the devotion of Gwen Teirbron.[19]

Paganism flourished in Scotland after the break-up of the Catholic Church. In the region of Gaerloch, Wester Ross, the 'old rites' of the divinity Mhor-Ri, the Great King, transformed into St Maree, Mourie or Maelrubha, were observed until the nineteenth century. In 1656, the Dingwall Presbytery, 'findeing, amongst uther abhominable and heathenishe practices, that the people in that place were accustomed to sacrifice bulls at a certaine tyme upon the 25 of August, which day is dedicate, as they conceive, to St Mourie, as they call him . . . and withall their adoring of wells and uther superstitious monuments and stones', attempted to suppress the observances of Mhor-Ri, which, according to the Presbytery Records, Dingwall, included 'sacrificing at certain times at the Loch of Mourie . . . quherein ar monuments of Idolatrie', also 'pouring of milk upon hills as oblationes'. Strangers and 'thease that comes from forren countreyes' participated in the 'old rites' of Mhor-Ri.

The attempted suppression failed. Twenty years later, in 1678, members of the Mackenzie clan were summoned by the Church at Dingwall for 'sacrificing a bull in ane heathenish manner in the island of St Ruffus . . . for the recovering of the health of Cirstaine Mackenzie'.[20] In 1699, a man was arraigned before the Kirk Sessions at Elgin, Morayshire, charged with idolatry. He had set up a standing stone and raised his cap to it.[21] In 1774, Thomas Pennant wrote of the sacred places of Mhor-Ri: 'if a traveller passes any of his resting-places, they never neglect to leave an offering . . . a stone, a stick, a bit of rag'.

During the nineteenth century, sacred places, such as standing stones, hills and holy wells, were spoken of generally as shrines of goddesses and gods, for example: 'In the north end of the island of Calligray there are faint traces of a very ancient building called Teampull-na-H'Annait, the temple of Annat, a goddess . . . having for her particular province the care of young maidens. Near the temple is a well of water called Tobar-na-H'Annait'.[22] On the Isle of Man, Odin's Cross at Kirk Andreas, Thor Cross at Kirkbride and the Heimdall stone at Jurby maintained their Pagan identity.[23]

Hills continued to be used as the *loci* of Pagan observances. The Fairy Goddesses, Aine and Fennel, were honoured at two hills near Lough Gur, County Limerick, Ireland, 'upon whose summits sacrifices and sacred rites used to be celebrated according to living tradition'.[24] Sir A. Mitchell, writing in 1860 of the sacred places in the landscape around Loch Maree, stated: 'The people of the place often speak of the god Mourie.'[25] A hill called Claodh Maree was sacred to the cult. Dr Reeves, writing in 1861, observed: 'it is believed . . . that no-one can commit suicide or otherwise injure himself within view of this spot.'[26]

On the island of Maelrubha in Loch Maree, the sacred oak tree of Mhor-

Plate 6.4 Thirteenth-century graffito of a dancer wearing the Pagan 'Celtic Rose' pattern, in the church at Sutton, Bedfordshire, England. This design, known as far back as a Bronze-age stone carving at Tossene, Sweden, always had a Pagan connotation, and was rarely if ever used officially in ecclesiastical buildings. Nigel Pennick.

Ri was studded with nails to which ribbons were tied. Buttons and buckles were also nailed to the tree.[27] This tree was associated with a healing well, reputed to cure insanity. The Dingwall Presbytery Records tell of the *derilans* who appear to have been officiating priests on the island. Dixon suggests that this title comes from the Gaelic *deireoil*, 'afflicted', inferring that the priesthood was composed of people enthused by 'divine madness', in the manner of shamans the world over.[28] In 1774 Thomas Pennant[29] visited Loch Maree and witnessed the rites. A person suffering from insanity was brought to the 'sacred island' and 'made to kneel before the altar, where his attendants leave an offering of money. He is then brought to the well, and sips some of the holy water. A second offering is made; that done, he is thrice dipped in the lake'. The shrine was profaned in 1830 by a man who attempted to cure a mad dog there.[30] Then its healing virtue was lost for a time, until around 1840, when visits resumed.

Holy wells are revered all over Europe. There are myriad examples, whose customs show continuity both from antiquity and across the continent. In the nineteenth century, a famous dripping well at Kotzanes in Macedonia had curative water 'said to issue from the Nereids' breasts, and to cure all human ills'.[31] In Vinnitsa, Ukraine, there was a holy well where sick people, after bathing, hung handkerchiefs and shirts on the branches as votive offerings.[32] The holy well Ffynnon Cae Moch, near Bridgend, Glamorgan, Wales, was visited by supplicants who then tied a rag to a tree or bush growing next to it. The rags were tied to the bush by strands of wool in the natural state.[33] At Ffynnon Elian, at Llanylian yn Rhos, near Abergele, Denbigh, Wales, corks studded with pins floated in the water of the well.[34]

Many holy wells had guardians who looked after them and oversaw observances there. In the early part of the nineteenth century, the hereditary well-guardian of Ffynnon Elian, Jac Ffynnon Elian (John Evans), was imprisoned twice for reopening Ffynnon Elian after it had been sealed by the local Christian priest.[35] The holy well 'stood in the corner of a field, embosomed in a grove . . . Sometimes, and that during its most flourishing period latterly, it had a "priestess", one named Mrs Hughes'.[36] Speaking in 1893 at a joint meeting of the Cymmrodorion and Folk-Lore societies in London, Professor John Rhys made the following telling statement about the famous Ffynnon Elian:

> Here there is, I think, very little doubt that the owner or guardian of this well was, so to say, the representative of an ancient priesthood of the well. His function as a pagan . . . was analogous to that of a parson or preacher who lets for rent the sittings in his church. We have, however, no sufficient data in this case to show how the right to the priesthood of a sacred well was acquired; but we know that a woman might have charge of St Elian's Well.

The well was finally destroyed in January, 1829.[37]

Plate 6.5 Scouring the White Horse hill-figure at Uffington, Berkshire, England, 1889. This was a regular event, the 'pastime', which included traditional country sports, feasting and drinking. Nideck Picture Collection.

Sacred fish were kept in some holy wells. St Bean's Well at Kilmore, Argyll, Scotland, held two black 'mystical or sanctified fishes' known as *Easg Siant* (The Holy Fishes).[38] Ffynnon Wenog in Cardigan, Wales, held a trout with a golden chain, as did the Golden Well at Peterchurch, Herefordshire, England.[39] The fish at Ffynnon Bryn Fendigaid, at Aberffraw on Anglesey, were used in rites of divination. The *Liverpool Mercury* (18 November, 1896) reported the placing of two new fish in Ffynnon y Sant at Tyn y Ffynnon, Nant Peris, Llanberis, Wales. They replaced two others which had died. In the early part of the nineteenth century, Garland Sunday observances at the sacred lake called Loughharrow, in County Mayo, Ireland, continued ancient practice:

> The people . . . swim their horses in the lake on that day to defend them against incidental ills during the year and throw spancels and halters into it which they leave there . . . they are also accustomed to throw butter into it that their cows may be sufficiently productive.[40]

Throwing offerings into lakes or rivers was known in ancient Ireland, Britain and Denmark. It continues today.

Pagan observances continue in the twentieth century in Celtic countries.

A Pagan prayer, collected around 1910 by W.Y. Evans-Wentz from an old Manx woman, invokes the Celtic god of the sea:

> Manannan beg mac y Leirr, fer vannee yn Ellan
> Bannee shin as nyn maatey, mie goll magh
> As cheet stiagh ny share lesh bio as marroo 'sy vaatey'.
> [Little Manannan, son of Leirr, who blessed our land,
> Bless us and our boat, well going out
> And better coming in with living and dead in the boat.]

This prayer had been used by the woman's father and grandfather. Her grandfather had addressed the Celtic sea-god Manannan, but her father had substituted St Patrick's name for Manannan.[41]

In the Scottish Highlands, libations of milk are poured on a special hollowed stone, the Leac na Gruagach (Dobby Stane), in honour of the Gruagach, a goddess who watches over the cows.[42] At Samhain, it is a Breton custom to pour libations over the tombs of the dead. On the island of Lewis, ale was sacrificed at Hallowtide to the sea-god Shony.

> After coming to the church of St Mulvay at night a man was sent to wade into the sea, saying: 'Shony, I give you this cup of ale hoping that you will be so kind as to give us plenty of sea-ware for enriching our ground the ensuing year.'[43]

Evans-Wentz records (1911) that in his day, Lewis people poured libations to Shony for seaweed.[44] Also, 'Until modern times in Iona similar libations were poured to a god corresponding to Neptune'.[45] In Brittany, the equivalent deity Yann-An-Ôd appears sometimes on the seashore, lurking among the sand dunes. He has the habit of shape-shifting, changing from a giant to a dwarf at will. Sometimes he is seen wearing an oil-cloth seaman's hat, and at other times a broad-brimmed black felt hat. Similar apparitions of Odin are known in Northumbria.

James Anderson, writing in the *Journal* of the Society of Antiquaries of Scotland in 1792 about customs in the Lothians thirty years earlier, stated:

> The celebration of the Lammas Festival was most remarkable. Each community agreed to build a tower in some conspicuous place, near the centre of their district . . . This tower was usually built of sods . . . In building it, a hole was left in the centre for a flag staff, on which was displayed the colours on the great day of the festival.

On Lammas Day, the participants danced and sang, took part in sports and banqueting, 'drinking pure water from a well, which they always took care should be near the scene of their banquet'. In Ireland, the Pagan celebration of Lammas continued into the twentieth century. Sometimes, the festivities were held on the nearest Sunday to Lammas Day, known as Garland Sunday. The ceremonies centred on a girl, seated in a chair on the hilltop, who was

Plate 6.6 Eighteenth-century milkmaids' dance with silver plate, London. May Morning dances continued until the end of the century.

garlanded with flowers. In some places, a female effigy was set up, decorated with ribbons and likewise garlanded with flowers. Round this, dancers circled, the girls picking flowers or ribbons off the figure as they danced.[46] Research conducted in Ireland in 1942 by the Irish Folklore Commission identified 195 assembly sites.[47] Most were hilltop sites; of the 195, only seventeen had any connection with the Christian Church.[48]

Thus Pagan ceremonies have continued until the present time. A few of them have continued directly, others have been amalgamated with Christianity, and yet more have turned into folklore and undeciphered tradition.

7

THE GERMANIC PEOPLES

Between the Rhine and what is now Lithuania, northern Europe was inhabited by peoples whom the Romans called Germani. In Latin, the name means simply 'related', and might refer to the Germans' kinship with the Celts, but Tacitus tells us that it was originally the name of one tribe and was later generalised to the whole people (*Germania* 2). Whatever the origin of the name, the tribes living east of the Rhine did not seem to think of themselves as a collective, and modern scholarship is equally disinclined to speak of any deep distinction between the peoples living east and west of the Rhine at the beginning of the Common Era.[1] Their differences, linguistic and cultural, seem to have been intensified by Julius Caesar's creation of an artificial boundary between them. In what follows we trace the religious history of the people who lived, or at least originated, east of the Rhine in Roman times.

The culture which grew up in the region of modern Copenhagen was rather simpler than the 'Celtic' cultures of Hallstatt and La Tène to the south. There were no large metal deposits on the German plains,[2] and perhaps for this reason the western Germanic tribes did not develop sophisticated weaponry until their meagre resources were exploited in the third and fourth centuries CE.[3] At that time the peoples of the Baltic peninsula stayed in their homeland and became the Scandinavians, but some had earlier migrated and set up home on the eastern mainland. One of these eastern tribes, the Bastarnae from the Carpathian Mountains, menaced the Greek cities of the Black Sea around 200 BCE, and in the following century the western Germans were pressing on the Rhine frontier and southward into the Alps. Here they forced the Celtic Helvetii into Switzerland and the Celtic Boii, whose original home, Bohemia, is still called after them, down to the Po Valley. The western Germans of the Rhineland skirmished with the Celts of Roman Gaul and eventually confederated to become the Franks and the Saxons. In 9 CE these westerners had beaten back a Roman invasion force with the massacre of three legions, but they did not attempt to advance beyond the Rhine frontier. They stayed, with their primitive weapons technology, east of the river until weapons-grade iron became available four centuries later and the smith-god gained a heroic place in their mythology.

The eastern Germans, who in Tacitus' time were called Suebi and later Goths, seem to have had access to better technology. Tacitus describes them as carrying round shields and short swords (*Germania* 43.6), and the ritual hoard found in Pietroasse, Romania, dated to the third century CE, consists of elaborately worked and inlaid gold vases, cups, necklaces etc. in Germanic, Greek and Iranian styles.[4] Their origin myth, reported by their historian Jordanes in the seventh century, claims that they originated in south Scandinavia (the Suebi share their name with the Swedes) and crossed in three ships to the Baltic shore of what is now Prussia, where they defeated the Vandals and others. It was their fifth king who took them south to the Black Sea, where, however, Graeco-Roman armies contained them until the time of Aurelian (270–275 CE). Then they invaded Dacia, pushing out the Celtic inhabitants who had settled there in the fifth century, and became known as the Visigoths. The tribes who stayed in the Ukraine became the Ostrogoths, who built an enormous empire from the Don to the Dniester, from the Black Sea to Belarus. However, in 370 they themselves were conquered by the invading Huns (although the Gothic language continued to be spoken in the Crimea until at least 1554), and the great Gothic migration began. We have already seen how Italy was conquered by the Ostrogoths, southern Gaul and Iberia by the Visigoths and Africa by the Vandals, another east Germanic people. In 568 Italy, only recently reconquered from the Goths by the Emperor Justinian, was again captured by the Lombards, a Gothic people who had originally lived near modern Hamburg at the mouth of the Elbe.[5] Even when they were Christian, the Goths still enacted laws based on Germanic customs, which were eventually codified when they settled in Spain. As for the western Germans, by 487, when Clovis defeated the last of the independent Gallo-Roman leaders, the Franks had effectively founded France. In Italy, France and Spain, the Goths became somewhat Romanised, and so 'Latin' culture prevailed, whilst Latin-derived languages took over from Gothic. In Germany and Britain, this did not occur and the languages and initial culture remained Germanic, with Celtic enclaves persisting on the western fringes. By 550, the Angles and then the Saxons were taking control of what was to become England, and the ruling classes of Europe, whether Latinised or not, had become German.

EARLY GERMANIC RELIGION

Tacitus, writing in the last decade of the first century CE, says that the Germanic peoples committed their history only to songs. Theirs was an oral culture like that of the Celts, but they did have a kind of sacred script, which was carved on strips of wood in the drawing of lots.[6] Their origin myth was one of patrilineal descent: the story of the god Tuisto, a son of Earth, who sired three sons who gave their names to the three groups of German tribes. Tuisto is the tribal god (Gothic *thiudisko*, like the Celtic *Teutates*), and his epithet 'Son of Earth' is echoed in a Norse legend written down much later. *The Deluding of Gylfi*, recorded in the mid-thirteenth century, describes how the Earth was made from the body of a giant and the human race sprang from two ancestors made out of tree trunks: Ash and Elm. Here, too, human beings are described as springing from the life force of Earth. In the earlier myth, Tuisto's three sons gave their names to three peoples: the Ingaevones, those nearest the sea; the Herminones, those of the interior; and the Istaevones, 'the rest' according to Tacitus, but according to Pliny the dwellers near the Rhine. Two of these race-names emerge later in the names of tribal gods. The Swedish kings of the *Ynglingasaga*, rulers of some of the 'peoples nearest the sea', traced their ancestry to the god Ingvi, and the inhabitants of central Germany were conquered in the ninth century by the Frankish King Charlemagne at the sacred grove whose image was the Irminsul, or 'Pillar of Heaven', a tall wooden post reminiscent of the Jupiter columns of the Romano-Celtic Rhineland. The name of the Istaevones does not recall any Germanic god, but Pliny might have been wrong about the river. From the time of Herodotus (II.33) and

Plate 7.1 Maypole at Winterbach, near Esslingen, Baden-Württemberg, Germany, May 1992, showing symbols of the village trades, spiral bindings, garland, ribbons and uncut branches at the top.
© 1992 Nigel Pennick.

for centuries afterwards it was not the Rhine but the Danube which was known as the Hister or Istar. The Istaevones could have been the eastern Germans and Ista the deity of their river.

All the Germans, according to Tacitus, were extremely strong and hardy, but unlike the Celts they dressed plainly and in some cases hardly at all, the men going naked except for a cloak. Their tribal loyalty was strong, and it was seen as a disgrace for a man to outlive his leader in battle. Unlike the Celts, they did not live in fortified towns but in villages with widely spaced huts, and they hunted, fished and cultivated grain. Their national drink was beer, and as the Celts did with Mediterranean wine, they drank a great deal of it. The western Germans were democratic (or practical), electing their leaders by merit, but civil order and punishment were in the hands of their priests – 'not as a punishment or by their leader's command, but as if by order of the god whom they believe to be with them in battle'.[7] This would seem to indicate a cult of symbolic atonement rather than of individual responsibility, rather as the Druids were said to offer innocent victims to the gods if enough criminals were not available. Images and signs or perhaps banners (*signa*), normally kept in the Germans' sacred groves, were carried with them into battle, and their special gods were, in the *interpretatio Romana*, Mercury (Woden?), Hercules (Thunor?) and Mars (Tiw?). Tacitus mentions that one of the eastern confederations, the Suebi, also sacrificed to Isis, whose sign was a ship, a Liburnian galley, showing that the religion was imported (*Germania* 9.2). However, the image of Sequana, goddess of the Seine, was also a ship, and with modern hindsight we can allow that the cult of 'Isis' was possibly indigenous. The form of the ship nevertheless suggests that the Suebi had once had contact with the goods of the eastern Mediterranean. In Tacitus' time, the river Oder was known as the Suebus, so a water-deity might well have ruled that confederation, and as we shall see, the eastern Germans were better known for their goddesses than those of the west.

All the Germans believed in women's prophetic power, as both Tacitus and Caesar agree, and the prophetesses were sometimes seen as divine. Veleda, who sang the Germans into battle during the reign of Vespasian (69–79 CE) and was taken to Rome in 78 CE,[8] was one such, and an earlier prophetess Aurinia and other women were similarly revered. Deification of an inspired sibyl paralleled Roman Pagan practice and the modern Shinto tradition where a departed worthy becomes *kami*. Another famed sibyl was the Alemannic-Frankish wise woman, Thiota. The seeress of the Semnones who went to Rome with King Masyas in 91 CE was called Ganna (the old German magic was called *gandno*). Waluburg (after *walus*, a magic staff) was in Egypt with Germanic troops during the second century.[9] The wise women called Haliarunnos, who consulted the shades of the dead, were expelled from the lands of the Goths by King Filimer in the fifth century. Later, the famous Icelandic sibyl Thordis Spákona is known from the *Biskupa*, *Heiðarviga* and *Vatnsdoela* sagas. There is some evidence of rapport with animals. In Sweden there lived the Vargamors, wise women who inhabited the forests, communing with wolves. The sagas also describe ordinary women routinely foretelling the future and working protective and healing spells for their men. This seems to have been part of the normal business of the household for Germanic wives.

Divination, according to Tacitus, was also carried out by the father of the family or, in cases of tribal augury, by the priest of the people, by means of strips of wood cut from a nut-bearing tree and carved with sigils,[10] which were then spread out at random on a white cloth and selected by the diviner whilst looking up at the heavens. A similar procedure is reported in medieval times as divination by runestaves: strips of wood with runes carved on them. The phonetic runic alphabet was, however, not introduced until the fourth century; these earlier sigils were probably ideograms. Divination by means of the flight of birds and the movements of horses was also practised. The sacred white horses were taken from the groves where they were kept and then yoked to a ceremonial chariot, after which their neighing and snorting were observed.

Plate 7.2 Early runestone with horseman, dog and wend-runes (runes written from right to left with magical intention), Moybro Stenen, Uppland, Sweden. Nigel Pennick.

Public meetings were held at the new and full moon, which were said to be auspicious times for conducting business. Crime and responsibility obviously were recognised in some areas of life, because punishments varied for different kinds of offence. Traitors and deserters were hanged from a tree, but cowards and practitioners of 'bodily abominations' were plunged into marshes and held down by a hurdle. Several such bog burials have been excavated in recent years, although they do not all seem to have been punitive. Once more there is a similarity between Celtic and Germanic practice. According to Tacitus morality was strict, by contrast with the dissolute Romans and the soft-living Celts of Gaul. The Germans were fit, law-abiding and monogamous. But days spent lying around the fire in idleness were not counted as degenerate, and all the Germans drank heavily. Burial customs were simple: men were burned on a pyre with their arms and perhaps their horse, then a turf mound was raised above them. We do not hear how women were buried.

These were the warlike western German peoples. The eastern Germans, whom Tacitus calls the Suebi, were rather different. They, too, were warlike and unsophisticated, but one characteristic of theirs was their elaborate hair-styling. The men drew their hair back and knotted it, either at the nape of the neck or at the crown, in order to make themselves look taller and more terrifying. Their religion seems to have been shamanistic – involving trance and possession – and devoted to goddesses as much as to gods. The Semnones, who in Tacitus' time lived in Brandenburg, near modern Berlin, but who later migrated south and became the confederation of the Alemanni, would meet at regular intervals in an ancient forest, long hallowed by time, and would sacrifice a human life before beginning their rituals. The meeting place included a grove which no one could enter unless they were bound and thus 'had diminished themselves so they could openly carry the power of the deity'.[11] This reads like an account of trance possession, as in the Santeria concept of being 'ridden' by a deity. At the very least they would be personating the deity, as in modern Wiccan practice. If the person in the grove fell down by accident (again, another likelihood in a trance situation), they were not allowed to get to their feet but had to squirm out of the place along the ground. Tacitus dismisses this as a 'superstition' in the modern sense, and mentions that it arose from the Semnones' belief that the grove was the home of the god who was the origin of their race and who ruled over all things, everything else being subject to him and part of his household. As holders of the grove, the Semnones considered themselves to be the chief clan of the Suebi.

This Suebic outlook sounds rather similar to that of the Romans, whose sense of manifest dominion over all other peoples and whose ever-expanding household religion it echoes. But unlike any of the other peoples we have encountered so far, the German tribes all traced their human ancestry back to a god. Jordanes, the historian of the Visigoths, reports that these peoples worshipped their ancestors under the name of the Anses, as well as a god who was equivalent to Mars. To this god they gave the first-fruits of their battle-spoils, hanging the booty on tree trunks. The northern Pagan tradition of sacrificing booty to the gods is also reported by Orosius in his account[12] of the defeat of a Roman military force by the Cimbri in the lower Rhône valley in 105 BCE. The Cimbri captured two Roman military camps, and proceeded to sacrifice everything in fulfilment of a vow to the gods.

> Garments were torn apart and thrown away, gold and silver hurled into the river, the soldiers' armour was chopped in pieces, the horses' harness destroyed, the horses themselves thrown in the river, and the men hanged from trees, so that there was neither booty for the victor nor mercy for the vanquished.

Similarly, Caesar reports that the Celts dedicated the spoils of war likewise,[13] though the loot was piled up in heaps on consecrated ground rather than hung on trees or in temples. Jordanes mentions that the Visigoths too used to practise human sacrifice, but that this custom had ended by the time they reached the Black Sea.

It is not clear whether the goddesses worshipped by the eastern tribes were also seen as divine ancestresses or simply as divine protectresses. The tribes

Plate 7.3 Romano-Frisian altar-shrine of the goddess Nehalennia from her shrine on the sacred island of Walcharen, the Netherlands. Nideck Picture Collection.

around the mouth of the Elbe and in the south of modern Denmark are the ones who, as is now well known, worshipped Nerthus, Mother Earth. They saw her as intervening in human affairs and riding among her people in a wagon drawn by cows. The priest of Nerthus would sense when she was ready to leave her island shrine, and then with deep reverence would follow the wagon on its tour through the lands of her people, which would be the occasion for a general holiday, the only time when these warlike people put down their arms. At the end of the perambulation, the wagon and its contents would be washed in a lake by slaves who were then drowned. No-one was allowed to see the goddess on pain of death. We have seen images being paraded and then ritually washed by the Greeks and Romans, but the gruesome sequel is an archaic touch which they did not share.

The Naharvali, who lived nearer the source of the Oder, on the Riesengebirge, practised an ancient religion which involved a priest in women's clothes presiding over the rituals of twin gods, the Alci (which probably means simply 'gods'), who were equated by the *interpretatio Romana* with Castor and Pollux. The priest in female clothes is typical of trance religion. We have already seen the *Galli*, the castrati priests of the ecstatic cult of the Great Mother of Asia Minor, who according to Apuleius dressed as women, and in eastern shamanism the male shaman also cross-dresses as a sign of his separateness from normal life. However, Tacitus does not let us know the details of the worship of the Alci. Even further east, in what is now Lithuania, Tacitus tells us the tribe of the Aestii (whose name survives in that of the Estonians), spoke a language like that of the Britons, worshipped the mother of the gods and took her emblem, the figure of a wild boar, as a protection even where arms would normally be needed. It would seem that those devoted to the service of this goddess were considered taboo, protected from the rough-and-tumble of normal life. The boar was a sacred animal to the Celts also, and in later Germanic religion it was sacred to Freya and Frey, the bringers of success and of plenty. The Aestii were also harvesters of amber, another emblem of Freya in later mythology, and Tacitus tells us that they were unaware of its value to the Roman traders. This seems unlikely, because the amber routes had operated between the Baltic and the Mediterranean since the time of the Etruscans.

Finally, Tacitus mentions the Sitones, who were like the other tribes in all respects except that they were matriarchal. It seems that among the eastern Germanic tribes a female figure, a goddess or even an actual woman, carried greater authority than among the western Germans, whose deities are all described as gods and among whom we never hear that, like the Britons, they 'do not discriminate among their rulers by gender'. The ancient Germanic tribes of the east overlap with the Slavic peoples of that area, who are described in chapter 8. When the Ostrogoths and Visigoths emerge from ethnography into history, however, we hear little of their religion. The story of the martyrdom of St Saba in the late fourth century by the Visigoths describes death by drowning, which might have been a ritual method of death, as in the case of the slaves of Nerthus. In addition, the tribes around the Black Sea, including the Goths, are described by several writers as honouring a god of the sword. According to Ammianus Marcellinus, the Alans (a Mongolian people, but typical of this area) 'thrust a drawn sword into the ground which they honour as the god of war and protector of their homes'.[14] An identical emblem of a war-god who is also a god of justice is found in accounts of the Norse god Tyr, whose attribute is the sword and whose rune, which shares his name, is in the shape of an upwards-pointing arrow or stylised sword. Records from the time of the Gothic incursions, however, tell us nothing of their goddesses.

SHRINES AND SANCTUARIES

Germanic and Nordic sacred places show the same evolution recorded in the other areas considered so far. The most basic were natural features. In tenth-century Iceland, the *Landvættir* (land-wights, earth-spirits) had fields or fells hallowed for them. *Landnámabók* (5.6), the record of the settlement of Iceland, describes worship at waterfalls, caves and sacred hills into which souls passed at death. Helgafell was so sacred that no person was allowed to look at it unwashed.[15] On these sacred lands, no person should urinate, no fetid smell should be made and no living thing might be destroyed there.[16]

Sacred places in the landscape were marked by hill-figures, Maypoles, cairns and labyrinths. Cairns were built where important offering ceremonies, known as *blóts*, had been celebrated. (The word *blót* means a blood sacrifice. It is cognate not only with modern English 'blood', but also with 'blessing'.) Each cairn had a commemorative name (e.g. Flokavarda, *Landnámabók* 1.2). Often, they were at important boundaries. Weland's Stock, a boundary-marker near Whiteleaf, Buckinghamshire, mentioned in a charter of 903,[17] was a 'Maypole' or phallic image sacred to the smith-god Wayland. The most celebrated of these poles was that called Irminsul, which existed at the Eresburg (now Ober-Marsberg, Westphalia, Germany). The *Translatio S. Alexandri* (ch. 3) states that the Saxons worshipped 'a large wooden column set up in the open. In their language it is called *Irminsul*, which in Latin is "a universal column"'. Labyrinths were used in spring rites, weather-magic and ceremonies of the dead (as at Rösaring, Laåsa, Uppland, Sweden, where a straight 'road of the dead' and a stone labyrinth adjoined a grave-field).[18]

The Anglo-Saxon *Wih* was an unsheltered image standing in the open. An important example of this class of site, where worship was out of doors, is the Norse *Vé*: a sacred enclosure, rectangular, lenticular or triangular, surrounded by standing stones or a consecrated fence of hazel poles (and ropes) known as the *Vébond*. These could be set up temporarily, as when the community gathered to witness the paying of a debt or the swearing of an

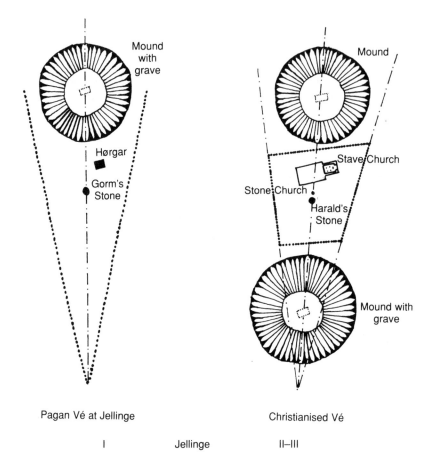

Pagan Vé at Jellinge

Christianised Vé

| I | Jellinge | II–III |

Plate 7.4 Plan of the royal Vé (sacred enclosure) at Jellinge, Denmark, in Pagan (left) and Christian (right) forms. The boundaries of the sacred enclosure remained almost unchanged, whilst the holy centre-line was used to define the positioning of the later church. Thus the advent of the church altered little the Pagan traditions of geomancy and the use of sacred places. Nigel Pennick.

oath. Ritual combat also took place in the *Vébond,* and the modern boxing 'ring' (in fact a square) is a survival of this practice. More developed is the *Træf* (Anglo-Saxon), the Scandinavian *Hørgr* or *Hörgr* (literally, 'rocky out-crop'), which was a tented shrine, tabernacle or pavilion sheltering an altar or a sacred image. An enclosed sacred building was the *Hof,* an ordinary farm hall, where regular festivals such as those to mark the seasons were observed. The *Hof* was divided into two areas: the *skáli,* or hall proper, and the *afhús,* a sanctuary, where the sacred objects and images were kept.

Although most religious observances took place in a *Hof,* there were also

120

fully enclosed wooden temples (the Anglo-Saxon *Ealh*). Important temples to deities of the Nordic pantheon stood at Jellinge in Denmark, Sigtuna and Uppsala in Sweden, Trondenes, Lade, Skiringssal and Mæri in Norway, and Dublin in Ireland. The temple at Uppsala had a square plan, like that of the Prussian god Svantovit at Arcona on the Baltic holy island of Rügen. In Iceland, every farmer in the locality paid dues to a temple, though it was the temple-priest's duty to maintain the temple at his own expense. *Erbyggja Saga* records a temple built by Thórólf Mostrarskegg at Thórsness on Snæfellsness. Thórólf brought with him the high-seat pillars of his original temple in Norway, and cast them overboard from his ship, so that, where they came ashore, the new temple would be built. This seems to have been a common practice, for when Thorhadd the Old, temple-priest at Thrandheim in Mæri, emigrated to Iceland, he took the earth beneath the temple and the pillars with him (*Landnámabók* 4.6). After the earth upon which they stand, trees, poles and posts are the most hallowed features of sacred enclosures, including the holy grove, *Vé* and temple. Pilgrimage to ancestral sites was not unknown in the north: the Icelander Lopt made a pilgrimage to his grandfather's temple in Norway every third year to worship (*Landnámabók* 5.8).

The entrance to Thórólf's temple was in a side wall, near the gable. Immediately inside the door were the high-seat pillars, studded with the 'divine nails'. They marked the boundary of the sanctuary. Inside the temple was a chancel containing an altar, around which were images of the gods. On this altar was a sacred ring, worn by the temple-priest at all public gatherings and upon which oaths were sworn. The altar also held a sacrificial bowl, with a blood-sprinkler. The temple at Uppsala was described around 1200, perhaps one hundred years after its destruction, by Adam of Bremen: 'In this temple, ornamented entirely with gold, the people worship images of three gods . . . Priests are assigned to all their gods, to offer sacrifices for the people.' The temple of the Black Thor at Dublin, called 'the golden castle', was sacked by the Irish King Mæl Seachlainn in 994, who looted it of its sacred treasures, including the golden ring.[19]

When Christianity was imposed, the most important Pagan sacred sites were occupied and churches built upon them. The *Vé* at Jellinge, Denmark, is a prime example. Similarly, at Gamla Uppsala in Sweden, a great wooden temple existed until around 1100. It is thought that this site originated as a sacred grove, then evolved into a *Hørgr* and then a temple. A cathedral was built upon the temple site. On the other hand, during Anglo-Saxon, and later, Viking times, Pagan burials were made in sacred enclosures that had been re-Paganised. Peel Cathedral in the Isle of Man had Norse Pagan interments after earlier Christian burials. The Viking-age runic-inscribed Pagan tombstone found in 1852 in the churchyard of St Paul's Cathedral in London, which may have been carved by a Swedish rune-master, is a notable example.[20]

THE GERMANIC FESTIVAL CALENDAR

Tacitus, in *Germania* 26, tells us that the Germans had only three seasons: spring, summer and winter. Some 1,000 years later, the Law Book of Iceland described the year as divided into two: winter and summer. In fact, it seems that the ancient Germans had a sixfold year made up of sixty-day tides, or double months as we should call them. In the Viking Age (post-eighth century) there were two Roman-style months called Litha in summer, and the sixth-century Gothic Church calendar calls the Roman month of November 'the first Yule', indicating that there was once a second Yule, i.e. December. The Venerable Bede, an Anglo-Saxon monk writing in about 730, likewise records a double Litha in June and July, plus a 'Giuli' tide in the months of December and January. Thus we have the names of two of the presumed old sixty-day tides, but unfortunately none of the others. The sixfold Germanic year, apparently divided by three major festivals, has given us the year of the legal and university terms.[21]

Like the Celtic year, the Germanic year started at the beginning of winter with a feast equivalent to the Celtic Samhain. In Germany and France this feast was eventually absorbed into the Christian Martinmas (11 November), and in England into All Hallows (1 November). It was the beginning of the financial year: church-scot (tax) had to be paid then, as had other dues such as the first of three annual instalments of the wages of female servants and the first instalment on a lease. Appointments were made from Martinmas to Martinmas, and accounts ran over the same period. In Scandinavia, where the winter sets in earlier, the festival was known as 'Winter Nights' and began on the Thursday between 9 and 15 October.

The second term began in mid-March, later equated to Easter, mid-Lent or St Gertrude's Day (17 March). Pagan festivities at this time have been included in Easter, such as Easter eggs, taken from Baltic Paganism (see chapter 8) and the Easter rabbit or hare, which recalls the sacred hares of the British tribes. March or Easter was the second of three instalments in the paying of dues, in the inspection and culling of livestock, and in the three terms of the ploughing year. In Holland, the four months from 15 March to 15 July were called May.[22] In Scandinavia, where neither Roman nor Christian influence was strong until about the year 1000, the year began one month earlier, in October, and its second festival, four months later, is recorded in the *Saga of Olaf the Holy* (ch. 77) as 'the principal blood-offering of Sweden . . . at Uppsala, in the month of Gói [February]'. A market and a fair were held then for a week, but with the coming of Christianity there the market was moved to Candlemas (2 February) and held for only three days.

The final term began in mid-July, later equated to Lammas (1 August). In Germany, France and England it survives as a legal and farming date. Sheep were not to be shorn before Lammas, and in the weeks leading up to Lammas

HOROLOGII ICONISMUS.

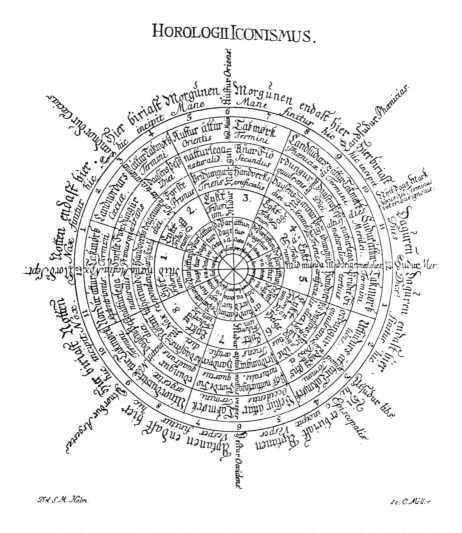

Plate 7.5 Northern tradition eightfold time-space wheel from *Rímbegla* by Stephán Björnssen, Copenhagen, 1780. Nideck Picture Collection.

the weaklings were to be put out to fatten for an early sale.[23] Summer grazing for sheep and cattle often finished at Lammas, and 'Lammas Land' denotes a pasture leased until this date each year. In Scandinavia, the third division took place a month earlier and was known as 'in summer', a sacrifice 'for peace and the plenty of the year' (*Saga of Olaf Tryggvason*, ch. 74). It began on the Thursday between 9 and 15 June. In Iceland this feast became the date of the annual General Assembly, or Althing.

123

The Germanic half-year division is better known, as its Scandinavian version has been preserved in the twelfth-century Icelandic Law Book. Summer's Day, the beginning of the summer half-year, was on the Thursday between 9 and 15 April, opposite to Winter's Day, which fell between 9 and 15 October. In England, Germany, the Low Countries and northern France, half a year after the beginning of winter brought the beginning of summer to mid-May. This was later assimilated to Whitsunday or the Rogation Days, and in France and England it took on some of the characteristics of the Celtic Beltane. Throughout medieval Europe, the two divisions of Martinmas (November) and Whitsun (May) dated the half-yearly accounts of boroughs until the sixteenth century, when Easter and Michaelmas superseded them. Whitsun was celebrated in the normal Pagan fashion with games, processions, horseraces and feasting.[24] The Whitsun games continued into the High Medieval period as the tourneys familiar to all readers of the Arthurian romances, and in modern times in the north of England they survived as local carnivals including bands, floats and dancing flower-maidens.[25]

In the Viking Age, the year seems to have been quartered, and references to the dates of the three and four festivals are ambiguous. Scandinavian sources describe a midwinter feast between 9 and 15 January, halfway through the winter half-year. In Norway, the Christian King Håkon the Good (940–963) 'made a law that Yule should be held at the same time that Christian men hold it. But previously Yule had been held on *höku* night, that is midwinter night, and it was held for three nights'. Now in the original Germanic year, Yule was not the name of a feast, but of a two-month tide. According to Tille,[26] the *Ynglingasaga* makes no mention of a Yule feast before 840: the main feast is that of the 'Winter Nights' in mid-October. From 840 to 1000 Winter Nights and Yule are mentioned with equal frequency, and after the year 1000 Yule becomes the main feast. Since Scandinavia adopted official Christianity around this time, the change is not surprising. Was there, however, a Pagan festival at the winter solstice?

The English monk Bede, writing around 730, states that the ancient Angles began their year on 24–25 December. He calls this not Yule (for him, that is the name of the months December and January), but 'Mothers' Night'.[27] In the eighth century the Church started its year at Christmas, but the Roman calendar, from which that of the Church was derived, began its year at the Calends of January. All other evidence shows the north European year starting with Winter Nights or Samhain. Was Bede reporting an otherwise unknown Anglian custom, perhaps sacred to the three goddesses known as the Mothers? Possibly, but as Tille argues, he could equally likely be describing a Pagan adaptation of the imported feast of Christmas. During the eighth century at least one Church decree (from the Council of Trullus, 706) had forbidden some rather crude ceremonies carried out by the faithful honouring the confinement of the Mother of God. The round, flat cakes or *placentae*, once used at the Roman domestic festivals, were baked in honour of the afterbirth of the Divine Mother. Christmas Eve was her night. Even in the nineteenth century a symbolic lying-in was enacted by households in country districts in Scotland. One member of the family would get up early on Christmas morning and bake 'care cakes', which would be eaten in bed by the other family members.[28] Bede's assertion that the Germanic year began at the winter solstice remains an isolated claim, contradicted by other sources.

The midwinter customs which became attached to the birth of Christ were, as we have seen, northern adaptations of the Roman Saturnalia. But the summer solstice, under its statutory date of 25 June, became a popular festivity early in Germanic history. The German word *Sonnenwende* always refers, in medieval texts, to the summer solstice, not to the winter solstice. At the end of the first century CE some German troops in the Roman army at Chesterholme listed their supplies for the celebration in a record which has come down to us. In the early seventh century, Bishop Eligius of Noyon in Flanders criticised the chants, carols and leaping practised by his flock on 24 June.[29] In medieval Germany this same date, adopted into Christianity

Plate 7.6 Eighteenth-century Yule pastry mould from Frisia, showing the spinning, horned goddess. Like the traditional cake designs, pastries and biscuits are remarkably conservative in design, retaining Pagan motifs. Nigel Pennick.

as St John's Eve, was a night of revelry, when apprentice boys in particular ran wild. In some Scandinavian settlements the solstice replaced the summer offering-tide of 9–15 June. The Isle of Man in Britain retains its Viking-founded parliament, held at an artificial hill called Tynwald (assembly plain) on 25 June every year. Christianisation has ensured that each delegate wears a sprig of St John's Wort on the day. In modern Scandinavia, midsummer bonfires are lit to this day, and the custom of rolling flaming wheels down hills at midsummer still persists in northern Europe.

THE FRANKS AND SAXONS

By the mid-third century, the tribes nearest to the Rhine had grouped together and called themselves the Franks, meaning the bold or spirited ones. In the south, some of the Suebians had reformed themselves into the 'All-men' or Alemanni, and began to harass Italy and southern Gaul. Towards the end of the century, the central tribes had confederated as the Saxons and were beginning to expand. They forced the Franks westwards and also began sea-raids on southern Britain and northern Gaul, causing devastation, as we have seen in chapter 6. The Saxons remained Pagan for another half-millennium. In Britain, their arrival was seen as a clash of faiths as well as a battle between civilisation and barbarism, and it was the barbarians who won. The bloodiness of the confrontation is attested by its only historian, Gildas, writing about a century after the invasion. Britain became a Germanic Pagan confederation ruled by kings who traced their divine ancestry not to Beli and to Anna, but to Woden.

In Britain the conversion to official Christianity took place in the seventh century more by argument and petty legal constraints than by massacre and the demolition of temples. The Christian mission sent from Rome to Britain under Augustine in 597 visited the king of Kent, who agreed that it would be politically valuable to have continental support, and so became Christian. The Church authorities in Rome decided that Britain should be converted (ignoring the existing sect of Celtic Christianity which existed in non-Saxon parts, but which itself had ignored the opportunity to convert the incomers). Following Roman practice, the missionaries divided Britain into a southern province ruled by London, and a northern one ruled by York. Mellitus, one of Augustine's assistants, visited London in 603 and convinced Sebert, king of Essex, that he should become Christian, as his powerful neighbour and potential enemy in Kent had done. The Pagan temple in London was taken over and became Paul's Cathedral. But this did not last long, as on the death of Sebert in 614, his three sons, Saxred, Sigebert I and Seward, who were Pagan, expelled the Christians, who fled back to Canterbury and even considered quitting England altogether. Paul's Cathedral was reconverted to a Pagan temple, and the Elder Faith flourished in London for another forty-one years. During this time, the ecclesiastical system became established in its temporary headquarters, and so Canterbury instead of London remained as the centre of the new religion.

The politico-religious wars of Europe have been elevated into heroic struggles between good and evil, following Christian authors, when in reality, religion and politics were intertwined. For example, the Celtic Christian king of Wales, Caedwal II, fought on the side of Penda, the Pagan king of Mercia, against the Roman Christian King Edwin of Northumbria, killing him at the Battle of Hatfield on 12 October, 633. When Caedwal II died, he was buried in Pagan London at the place which is now Martin's Church in Ludgate. Following the downfall of Romano-Celtic society, there was no good-and-evil Christian versus Pagan battle which apologists often portray. Kings converted to the god who brought them victory and prosperity, and for many kings the Christian god was successful. In England the perceived good-versus-evil conflict dates from the Anglo-Saxon wars against the Danes in the eighth and ninth centuries.

In Saxony itself, by contrast, the Pagan inhabitants were persecuted from outside by their old tribal enemies the Franks, who had meanwhile become fanatical Christians. Once more religion was used to rationalise old political hatreds. At the end of the eighth century, the Frankish monarch Charlemagne led a religious as well as a territorial crusade against the Saxons. In 782 he slaughtered 4,500 Pagan prisoners who refused to convert at a grove which has given its name to the modern town nearby, Sachsenhain-bei-Verden. Frankish troops cut down the sacred icon of the Saxons, Irminsul, the Pillar of Heaven, and in 785 the Pagan leader Widukind was baptised. Charlemagne instituted the death penalty for refusing baptism and for other aspects of continued adherence to the Pagan faith.[30] 'With respect to trees, stones, and fountains, where certain foolish people light torches or practise other superstitions, we earnestly ordain that that most evil custom detestable to God, wherever it be found, should be removed and destroyed.'[31] Despite this repression, the Saxons rebelled in 793. Mass deportations followed, when one in three of the inhabitants of Saxony was expelled on the orders of Charlemagne.[32] There was a second, more successful, rebellion of Saxony in 870, when Paganism was restored for a while.

Despite the long existence of official Paganism among the Saxons, we know unfortunately little about their religion. We know that some of those who invaded Britain worshipped a divine ancestor Seaxnot, a totemic sword-god called after the single-edged cutting sword used by these people. The others traced their ancestry back to Woden, the storm-god. We can speculate that Irmin, the holy being of the continental Saxons, was a god of heaven whose name had developed from that of the mythical ancestor of the first-century Herminones. The German leader who beat back the Romans in the year 9 was also called Hermann (in Latin: Arminius). He might have been this same mythical ancestor, or he might have been named after the latter, as the Yngling dynasty of Scandinavia was named after the god Ingvi.

William A. Chaney has presented a closely argued case for the Anglo-Saxon kings being the mediators between heaven and earth, the bringers of 'luck' to their people.[33] When the kingdom's 'luck' disappeared, the king would be deposed or killed. One feature of this system is that any abuse of royal power would be extremely difficult, which recalls Tacitus' comment about the frankness and ingenuousness of the German tribes (*Germania* 22.4). The Anglo-Saxon kings also made a habit of marrying, on their accession, their predecessor's widow. Even the newly Christian King Canute did this as late as 1018. Since the Angles and Frisians who colonised what was to become England were originally among the worshippers of the goddess Nerthus, it has been suggested that this might be a matrilineal feature. Through such marriages the new kings might have been identifying themselves with a female power-holder, a representative of the kingdom's sovereignty like the goddesses of Ireland.[34]

Charlemagne's Franks were the Germans of the Low Countries and the Rhine. They had come into contact with Gallo-Roman civilisation in the first century BCE, and they occupied an uneasy border country which nevertheless contained the capital of all the Gallic provinces, Trèves or Trier. Their history as a nation begins in 446, when they captured Tournai, probably under the leadership of the semi-legendary (and semi-divine) Meroveus, literally, the 'sea-fighter'. Meroveus gave his name to the Merovingian dynasty, the so-called 'long-haired kings', who in the fashion of the late Roman Empire eventually became titular monarchs only, while their chief minister, the 'mayor of the Palace', had

Plate 7.7 Wildberg image, possibly of a priest in ceremonial dress. Nigel Pennick.

executive power. Wearing long hair and a beard seems to have been a liturgical characteristic of the Pagan priesthood. An image of this exists in the Württembergische Landesmuseum at Stuttgart. It is a statue of a bearded Swabian Pagan priest, his vestments still bearing traces of red coloration, hair braided in ten waist-length pigtails. Found in a wall in Wildberg (near Calw, Baden-Württemberg) in 1698, the Wildberger Mann has been dated to the thirteenth century on stylistic grounds. A comparable figure from Ekaterinoslav, south Russia, exists in the Pitt-Rivers Museum in Oxford, the Kamene Baba. It, too, has the characteristic pigtailed hair, but lacks the beard of the Wildberger Mann, and so, despite lacking breasts, is described as female.

In 487 the Merovingian kings of the Franks were still leaders of their people. In that year Clovis conquered Syagrius, the last Gallo-Roman leader, at Soissons, and took over northern Gaul. At some time, traditionally in 496 but possibly as late as 503, Clovis converted to Catholic Christianity and so enlisted the support of the (Catholic) Roman Empire for his military ambitions. In 496 he defeated the Alemanni in the south-west of his territory and moved his capital to Paris. Then, with the Church's blessing, he took on the Arian Goths. In 507 he defeated Alaric II at Vouillé and confined the Goths to the French Pyrenees and to Spain. Clovis's battle with the Burgundians, who had settled in the Rhône valley, was won in 534, when they were incorporated in the Frankish Empire. One hundred years earlier, when this Baltic people had reached the city of Worms in their westerly migration, they had

Plate 7.8 Images on the Gallehus Horn. Nigel Pennick.

been attacked by the marauding Huns and driven out in 436. The exiles settled in the Rhône valley and gave their name to the area, but after the victory of Clovis they disappeared as a nation. Their songs, however, did not. The story of the battle between the Burgundian king, Gundahar, and the Hunnish leader, Attila, together with various other historical figures such as Queen Brynhild, was commemorated in an epic which became the *Nibelungenlied*, the basis of Wagner's opera cycle *The Ring of the Nibelung*. The songs of the Germans, which had so distressed one Gallo-Roman poet living in Toulouse that he complained that his visitors' epic carousing put him off composing his hexameters, now survived to help form the new French language through the magnificent *chansons de geste*.[35]

The Germanic worship of the divine ancestor, living through his present representative, the king, was transformed into obedience to the Lord's anointed following the eclipse of the Merovingians during the early eighth century by their chief ministers. The latter, the Arnulfings and then the Carolingians, retained a hereditary hold on the rulership, and on taking power they were anointed by their bishops. At the coronation of Charlemagne in 800, the significance of this was extended. Just as in the eastern Church the Patriarch of Constantinople consecrated the emperor by acclaiming him at his coronation, so Charlemagne acquiesced in a similar procedure carried out by the Pope in Rome. During Mass on Christmas Day, the Pope placed a crown on Charlemagne's head, knelt before him and pronounced him *imperator et augustus*, the ancient titles of the victorious Roman emperor. Charlemagne's army was now an arm of the Roman Church, invaluable in the latter's territorial disputes with the eastern Empire. It also meant that Charlemagne was no longer merely the leader of a people or even of a territory, as the Anglo-Saxon kings were. He was the leader of western Christendom, and as such he could lead religious crusades. The myth of the Roman Empire, fighting for civilisation against barbarism, had now been amplified by the myth of the One True Faith which was coterminous with the Empire. This would later be used to justify all kinds of territorial crusades. The Norman Conquest of England in 1066 was rationalised partly as an extension of the Roman Church to the semi-independent Church in England. The Norman invasion of Ireland a century later was presented as the bringing of Christian civilisation to people who were 'Christians only in name, Pagans in fact'.[36] And the Frankish crusades against the Pagans of eastern Europe, which we will consider in detail in chapter 9, were seen as the self-evidently justified colonisation of people whose religion made them barely human. However, Charlemagne's crusade was merely a dry run for these future developments, which did not crystallise fully until the accession of Otto I in 936 created the Holy Roman Empire.

In Britain, more than a century had passed since the 'dual faith' period, when King Rædwald of East Anglia (d. 625) had been able to have 'one altar to sacrifice to Christ, another to sacrifice to demons,'[37] and had later been buried, if it was he, in the magnificent Pagan burial mound at Sutton Hoo. The Synod of Whitby in 663 had amalgamated the Church in Britain with the hierarchy based in Rome, replacing the Irish pattern of individual hermits, travelling preachers, independent bishoprics and monastic communities which had been brought to northern Britain during the sixth and seventh centuries. Suddenly, Britain was once more part of an international community, and the kings and bishops played power politics accordingly. In 677 Bishop Wilfrid of York, on his way to appeal to Rome against a decision by King Ecgfrith of Northumbria, was shipwrecked on the coast of Frisia and took advantage of the opportunity to preach to the inhabitants. He was helped in his endeavours by the then chief minister of the Franks, Pippin the Arnulfing, and political and ecclesiastical ambition once more joined hands in an anti-Pagan crusade. Ironically, it was the Pagan Frisians who had been among the first 'Saxons' to invade Britain in the fifth century. They were still Pagan, and resolutely so. They fought back, regained the city of Utrecht from the Franks and expelled the new bishop. In 716 King Rêdbod led a Pagan campaign against the interlopers, but in 719 Wilfrid's successor, Boniface, returned and began to destroy Pagan sanctuaries and suppress Pagan teaching. In the year 722, the Frisian chieftains Detdic and Dierolf, 'although professing Christianity, were worshippers of idols',[38] and in Hessia and Thuringia in the 730s, 'the belief and practice of the converts [to Christianity] were still largely mixed with paganism'. In a letter to Pope Zacharias, Boniface even speaks of dual faith presbyters who offered sacrifices to the heathen gods as well as the Christian.[39]

Various Church councils held in Germany called for the suppression of heathen practices, including divination, the use of amulets, the need-fire and the offering of sacrifices, both to the old Pagan deities and to the saints who had taken their place.[40] But these had much less effect than the Church wanted, for there was continued resistance on a large scale. In 732, for example, it was reported to Pope Stephen that thirty churches had been burnt or demolished by Pagans in the Frankish territories.[41]

Boniface, no doubt rendering one favour for another, had in 731 consecrated Pippin as king of the Franks and thereby deposed the Merovingian dynasty with its strange Pagan taboos. But the Pagan rebellion the following year which destroyed thirty churches led to a further resurgence, and on 5 June 754 Boniface and fifty colleagues were killed in West Frisia by Pagans opposing conversion. Meanwhile, however, the Franks were attacking the Pagans in Saxony (see above p. 127), and in 785 the shrines of the god Fosite, including that on 'Holy Island' – Heligoland – were destroyed by the Christians. It looked as if the religious conflict in western Europe was over, until a new player arrived on the scene. The Viking Age had begun.

THE VIKINGS

Scandinavia had played no part in western politics for 1,000 years, since the ancestors of the Goths had sailed over to the Vistula and set their course for the Crimea. Norwegian, Swedish and even Danish society was still based on small tribal groupings rather than on a larger national identity, and the ethics of cattle-raiding and clan warfare still prevailed over any possibility of advancement within a static social hierarchy. Unlike the Irish, who had a similar social structure but who also saw themselves as part of the international community of Christendom, the Scandinavians retained an outlook which western Europe had discarded some centuries before, and when their raiding parties arrived they appeared to mainstream Europe like uncanny visitors from another world. When Charlemagne's conquest of Frisia left the North Sea routes undefended (the Franks were no great sailors), the Norwegians and Danes set out in search of booty. Their tactics and attitudes were similar to those of the Celts who had swept down to plunder the Mediterranean lands 1,000 years before, and of the German raiding parties which had ventured across the Rhine five hundred years later to seize Romano-Celtic slaves and horses. But by the late eighth century most of Europe had forgotten these tactics and for a while was unable to fight back. The Vikings' nastiness was blamed on their religion rather than on their expansionism or their primitive social organisation, and the northern coasts of Europe quailed before the raids of 'the heathen'. Even modern commentators write of the Vikings as if the latter were conducting an unwarranted campaign against Christianity, having 'no respect for the sanctity of religious houses and the pacifism of their inmates'.[42] But there is no reason why they should have had. Churches and monasteries were full of rich pickings, and in the eyes of a warrior society, if their communities did not care for these enough to defend them, then why should strangers? In the ancient warrior

Plate 7.9 Viking-age hogsback tombstone from Brampton, Yorkshire, England, with bear-cult and house of the dead imagery. Nigel Pennick.

societies, an attack on the deities of one's enemy was an attack on the enemy himself. The Goths destroyed the temple of Artemis at Ephesus in 250 BCE, the Romans destroyed the sacred groves of recalcitrant tribes, the rebellious Britons burned down the temple of the deified Claudius in Colchester, without these being specifically religious attacks. The eighth-century Christians and their modern apologists forget that their god was not the god of the Norsemen, and so he should expect no quarter. The two sides were playing by different rules.

Some earlier commentators argued that there might have been reason for specific religious bitterness.

> Many [of the raiders] were men who had suffered from the forcible means employed by Charlemagne for the conversion of pagans, or were the offspring of such men. Their enmity against Christianity was therefore fierce and unsparing; there was religious hatred, as well as the lust of spoil, in the rage which selected churches and monasteries as especial objects.[43]

Some or even many individuals might have found especial joy in revenging themselves against the god who himself had ordered atrocities against their shrines and their families. These Christian atrocities are, however, not condemned in the same tones that are used for Viking atrocities against Christian shrines and their guardians. Nevertheless, as the sagas record, religious hatred was not the main or even an important motive in the wave of invasions. The Vikings came for plunder.

They also became settlers. The last decade of the eighth century saw Norwegian Vikings colonising the Scottish islands, the Isle of Man and Ireland. On the islands, Christianity was tolerated but gradually died out, and Ireland became dual faith, although its literary culture, once fostered by the monasteries, collapsed into a fragmented vernacular form. Over the next three centuries the north-west fringe of Europe became one vast dynasty. The Scottish Lords of the Isles were Vikings. In the ninth century a Hebridean, a Christian lady called Aud the Deep-Minded, married the king of Dublin, was widowed, ruled with her son Thorstein the Red, and after his death sailed around the northern seas, 'with a crew of twenty free-born men', forging dynastic alliances and eventually settling in Iceland.[44] Further south, where political systems were more firmly established, things moved more slowly. The eastern half of England, from the Thames to the Tyne, was captured and re-Paganised in the 860s by the sons of the famous Viking, Ragnar Lodbrok. But Wessex was being stabilised under Alfred the Great (871–901), who had been taken to Rome as a boy and made an honorary consul by the Pope. Alfred united the south of England in one large and officially Christian confederation. He established a law code, he used the learning of the monks to bring literacy to his people, and he fostered the literary development of Anglo-Saxon. He also conquered and made treaties with the Danish earls who had settled to the east of him, most notably founding the initially Christian kingdom of East Anglia with its capital at Godmanchester (Guthrum's Camp), after defeating Earl Guthrum at the Battle of Wedmore and forcing him to convert. Northumbria, with its capital in York, was Scandinavian and dual faith for nearly a century (865–954) under Danish and Irish-Norse kings, with the connivance of various archbishops. Sometimes the kings were Pagan, sometimes Christian, but no religious persecutions took place. Eventually, King Canute (1016–1035), the Danish conqueror of Wessex and its English dependencies, adopted Christianity and brought England, Denmark, Norway and the Hebrides together in one empire.

Following Charlemagne's death in 814 Danish and then Norse Vikings sacked vast areas of France, including Bordeaux, Paris, Nantes, Toulouse and Orléans, and occupied Chartres (the old Druidic 'centre' of the country). They used French ports as bases for raids into the Mediterranean, including Spain, Morocco and perhaps Alexandria. Eventually, the French fought back, but in 911 King Charles the Simple bowed to necessity and invited one of the raiding parties to settle. One of the conditions was that the settlers should become Christian. The condition was accepted, the newcomers adopted Roman customs as the Franks had done before them, and in 1066 they invaded and conquered England.

Although the Normans – the 'men of the north' – were officially Christian, in the usual way dual faith practices prevailed. A resurgence of Thor worship in the tenth century turned the Christians into a minority within their own country,[45] and later the father of William the Conqueror became known as Robert the Devil because of his adherence to the old ways. Nevertheless, it was in Normandy that the future Christianiser of Norway, Olaf the Saint, was baptised in 1013, and it was with the approval of the Pope that Duke William invaded England in 1066.[46] The Normans had adopted centralised Roman-style administration from its contemporary guardian, the Church of Rome, and once more religion and politics went hand in hand.

In the homelands of the Vikings, dual faith was barely considered. Whereas in other communities, from Constantine's Rome to Alfred's Wessex, the Christian god had brought success to his followers, for the Scandinavians the opposite was the case. Their own gods had brought them success, and they were not going to turn their backs on these divine helpers to take a gamble with a new religion. Kings often tolerated Christian missionaries, but their earls tended to speak against them. In 963 King Håkon the Good attempted to Christianise Norway, but had to give up in the face of stiff opposition from his earls, who determined 'to make an end of the Christian faith in Norway . . . and compel the king to blood-offering', which they did.[47] When Håkon died, he was given a Pagan funeral in a howe at Sein, North Hordaland. His *skald*, Eyvind Scaldaspiller, composed a Pagan eulogy about how well the king, 'who had upheld the temples', was received with gladness in Valhalla by 'the high gods'.[48]

Later, the Christian sons of King Erik of Denmark came to Norway, smashed down the temples and abolished Pagan sacrifices, but they were deposed and executed by the nobles and the sacrifices restored. It was only in 998 that King Olaf Tryggvason, followed by Olaf Haraldson, canonised on his death in 1033, made Norway Christian by armed force, looting and burning Pagan temples and compelling community after community to be baptised or die, taking hostages to enforce continued Christian observance.[49] Nevertheless, many Pagans were willing to be tortured and to die a martyr's death rather than give up their beliefs. Olaf Tryggvason ordered that the Pagan seer, Thorleif the Wise, was to be blinded. He was captured by Olaf's agent, and bore his torture with such heroic composure that his attackers fled after tearing out one eye. Eyvind Kelde (drowned along with his comrades), Iron Skegge (killed defending the temple at Mæri), Eyvind Kinnrifi (tortured to death with hot coals), and Raud the Strong (tortured with a poisonous snake and red-hot iron), among others, died for the old faith. Also the Viking leader Ragnar Lodbrok, killed by Christians in Northumbria, was seen as a martyr, and is celebrated as such by contemporary followers of Ásatrú.

Norwegians had settled Iceland in the ninth century, escaping political unrest at home. Although some of the early settlers were Christian, the organisation of the island was basically Pagan, with the ritual hallowing of land, setting up of temples and regular attendance at the legal assembly held at the offering-tides. When Iceland adopted Christianity as the state religion in the year 1,000, it was not through persuasion or conversion but a substantial bribe that made the law-speaker Thorgeirr come down on the side of the Church against the faith of his forebears.[50] Surviving documents show that in the north, as elsewhere, Christian evangelists used every method available: trickery, bribery and armed force.

Following Biblical Jewish precedent, Christian writings report magic contests between Christian and Pagan priests, which the Christians win (e.g. the sanctified fires in *Njál's Saga*). But sometimes this ploy backfired. Writing about the twelfth-century Swedes, a contemporary English cleric stated:

> Swedes and Goths seem certainly, as long as everything goes well for them, to hold in name the Christian faith in honour. But when the storms of misfortune come over them, if the earth denies them her crops or heaven her rain, storms rage, or fire destroys, then they condemn (Christianity) . . . this happens not only in words but in actions, through pursuit of believing Christians whom they seek to drive from the country.[51]

Denmark likewise resisted Christianisation. In the early ninth century there were battles for and against Christianity, under Frankish pressure from the south. In Church architecture the northerly orientation, home of the deities in Scandinavian religion, clashed with the easterly orientation, which Christianity had adopted since the time of Constantine, the one-time sun-worshipper. 'In the east–west churches of the Frisians, who had recently been Christianized by Charlemagne, the Danish King Gotrik (c.800) had northern doors cut out and forced people to crawl through them.'[52] By the middle of the ninth century, Denmark collapsed into anarchy and Viking expansion began in earnest, leading to the creation of the English Danelaw and the Duchy of Normandy in what is now France. The Danish communities were united into one kingdom in about 950 under the formidable Harald Gormsson, who instituted the famous Jómsvíking community at the mouth of the Oder, brought Norway under his rule, and ruthlessly imposed Christianity on Denmark. This was enormously resented by the inhabitants, and in 988 Harald's son Swein drove his father from Denmark and reinstated the old religion. However, the pressures of international alliances proved too strong, and Swein ended as a reluctant patron of Christianity. His younger son Canute, who conquered England and established the Danish Empire, was, as we have seen, a keen Christian, but even so, in Denmark Pagan worship was carried out openly.

Sweden took little part in the Viking raids. Its ambitions lay eastwards. Swedish raiders and merchants travelled east to the Volga. They established trading posts at Riga, Novgorod and Kiev, and there, known as the Rus or Red Ones, gave their name to the country which they founded, Russia. They maintained their ancestral faith, and the report of an Arab traveller in 921 has left us an invaluable account of a northern ship-burial, providing details about which we could otherwise only conjecture (see below pp. 138–9). The Swedes of Kiev looked southwards to Constantinople, and in 860, 880, 907 and 914 they attacked the city. Eventually the authorities, in the time-honoured manner, employed their attackers as bodyguards and so a rich flow of commerce and diplomacy was set up between Russia and Byzantium. On the steppes, the Swedes also seem to have come into contact with the remnants of the Alans, who had arrived around 100 BCE and controlled the steppe from the Don to the Volga and southwards over the valley of the Kuban. The Greeks called the Alans As or Asii, from whom come both the name of Asia and the ruling dynasty of Norse gods, the Æsir. The area ruled by the Alans was a hub of trade and business, a centre of prosperity. This flourishing area seems to have been the Åsaheim of the later Norse writer Snorri Sturluson (1179–1241). It lay east of the Tanakvisl (River Don). Its capital city was Åsagarth (Asgard). It appears that certain elements of northern mythology, which we will describe in the next chapter, originate in the history of the Alan people in this period.

Sweden itself resisted Christianity, despite forced conversion. As a trading nation it was prosperous and comparatively settled, and the temple at Uppsala was famous throughout the northern world. Between 1000 and 1024, Olave Scotkonung imposed official Christianity on part of the country,

Plate 7.10 The temple at Uppsala, Sweden, sixteenth-century engraving by Olaus Magnus. Nideck Picture Collection.

but there was a mass reversion to Paganism around 1060, when the bishops of Sigtuna and Skara were expelled. In 1080, King Inge the Elder was exiled from Uppsala for refusing to sacrifice at the temple there. Even after the destruction of the Uppsala temple in around 1100, Paganism continued openly until the 1120s, when the Christian Norwegian King Sigurd the Jerusalem-Traveller declared a crusade against the Pagans in Småland, south Sweden, and laid the country waste. The Swedes were the last Germanic people to adopt official Christianity.

8

LATE GERMANIC RELIGION

Since the Scandinavian and Baltic countries remained for so long independent of the Roman organisation and Christian beliefs of the rest of Europe, their ancient religious practices contained many features from an earlier age. In the year 921 an Arab traveller, Ibn Fadlan, reported a full-scale ship-burial among the Rus of the Volga. His account gives the most remarkable insight into what might lie behind the great howe and barrow burials which litter the European landscape. First, the chieftain's body was buried for ten days in the semi-frozen ground while the preparations were made. Then the body was exhumed, blackened with the cold but otherwise not decayed, and dressed in the sumptuous clothes which had been made for it. It was laid on Byzantine silken cushions on a bench in the ship, and surrounded with food, drink and herbs before animals, including horses, cows, a dog, a cock and a hen, were cut to pieces and thrown onto the ship. One of the dead man's retainers, a slave girl, had volunteered to die with him. She had been treated like royalty meanwhile, as well as becoming thoroughly intoxicated through drinking, singing and having sex with as many men as she liked, 'for love of her master'. Before she went onto the ship she was lifted up three times to look over a structure that resembled a doorframe. She was looking into the Otherworld, where she said she saw first her parents, then her dead relatives, and finally her master, whom she wanted to join there. She then went onto the ship, singing two ceremonial farewell songs, and was led into the tent where the chieftain's body lay. A group of men banged their shields with sticks, to drown any screams, as she underwent a double death by simultaneous strangling and stabbing. Her executioner was the old woman in charge of the whole proceedings, a Hun known as the Angel of Death. Afterwards the chieftain's nearest kinsman approached the ship on its pyre of brushwood. He was naked, and walked backwards with one hand on his anus. He picked up a brand, set fire to it and set the pyre alight. Other people added sticks and timber, and the whole structure went up in flames. In the opinion of the Rus, the Arabs and other inhumers were mad to bury their dead. 'We burn them up in an instant, so that they go to Paradise in that very hour.'[1]

It is impossible to imagine that this ceremony was exactly the same as those of the Bronze Age, or, indeed, that such ceremonies were ever identical throughout all of Europe. But it does show how at least one community interpreted barrow burials. It tells us that among them death was seen as the doorway into another world which could be seen from the present one by a person in a trance. It tells us that the funeral sacrifice was entered into willingly and was the occasion of a certain grim rejoicing. The double death of the chieftain's retainer recalls the double or triple deaths of the prehistoric bog-burials (stunning, strangling and stabbing or drowning) and the ceremonial triple deaths described in the Irish tales. Unfortunately, Ibn Fadlan had to speak to the Rus through an interpreter, so he did not pick up the meaning of other details such as the nature of the deities invoked, the reason for the carcasses of animals being thrown on the ship, the ritual sex of the followers and the slave girl, the reason for her manner of death, and the reason why the lighter of the pyre should be naked, walk backwards and have his hand on his anus.

The two horses that were sacrificed are part of a tradition which is one of the many that continued into modern times. Ceremonial horse slaughter for a sacral meal of horseflesh was part of northern European Paganism. The horse was the totemic beast of Woden/Odin, and part of the ceremonies used

Plate 8.1 Reconstruction of a seventh-century horse sacrifice at Lejre, Denmark.
Nigel Pennick.

139

the stallion's penis (Volsi). Because of its sacral connotations, Pope Gregory III (731–741) forbade eating horseflesh as an 'unclean and execrable act'.[2] The Council of Celchyth (787) condemned the consumption of horseflesh as a stain on the character of British people.[3] This appears to be the origin of the continuing taboo on eating horseflesh in Britain. But the tradition did not die immediately. The monks of the Abbey of St Gall ate horse, and they gave thanks for it in a metrical grace written by the monk Ekkehard III (d. 1036).[4] Eating horseflesh was also banned at Paris in 1739.[5]

Pagan horse sacrifice continued in Denmark until the early eleventh century,[6] and it continued as a funeral rite of kings and knights. Horses were slaughtered at the funerals of King John of England,[7] the Emperor Karl IV in 1378 and Bertrand Duguesclin in 1389.[8] In 1499, the *Landsknechte* sacrificed a horse to celebrate the end of the Swabian Wars (*Schwabenkrieg*).[9] During the funeral of Cavalry General Friedrich Kasimir at Trier in the Rhineland in 1781, his horse was killed and thrown into his grave.[10] The archaic practice of divination by unbroken horses was used to honour the burial of an early saint. At the death of St Gall in Switzerland (seventh century), unbroken horses carried the coffin, and decided his burial place.[11]

Foundation-sacrifices continued to use horses. Just as burning a body allowed its spirit to escape quickly, so burying it may have imprisoned the spirit on the site. The *Saga of Olaf Tryggvason* (I, ch. 322) tells that the death of Frey, mythical ancestor of the Swedish kings, was kept secret for a while. When people found out that he was dead and buried in his howe, but that his kingly luck still protected the kingdom, 'they believed that it would be so as long as [he] remained in Sweden, and they would not burn him'. The animals sacrificed at the funeral of the chieftain of the Rus are therefore likely to have been seen as guardians of his grave. The practice continued into Christian times. When the monastery at Königsfelden in Germany was founded in 1318, a horse was sacrificed.[12] There are numerous examples of horse-skull burials in churches and special buildings. The church of St Botolph at Boston, Lincolnshire, had horse bones in the floor,[13] and that at Elsdon, Northumberland, in the belfry.[14] Eight horse skulls were found embedded in the pulpit at the Bristol Street Meeting House, Edinburgh, demolished in 1883,[15] and others at Llandaff Cathedral, Wales, where they were inside the choir stalls.[16] As late as 1897, a horse's head was buried in the foundations of a new Primitive Methodist chapel at Black Horse Drove, near Littleport in the Cambridgeshire Fens. A libation of beer was poured over it before bricks and mortar were shovelled on top. A workman described it as 'an old heathen custom to drive evil and witchcraft away'.[17] At Hahnenkan near Eichstadt, a horse was offered to St Willibald in the nineteenth century.[18] A minimal horse sacrifice is recorded from Holland in the eighteenth century, when Henrik Cannegeiter of Arnhem stated that the Dutch peasants drove away the Moirae (fates = bad luck) by throwing a horse skull upon the roof.[19]

The barrows of the dead were a link with the past and the ghosts of the ancestors in the same way that we have seen in all Pagan societies so far. They were seen as houses of the dead, and their inhabitants are often described as looking out of their houses or welcoming new inhabitants or even feasting within the mounds. In both Viking and Saxon barrows there are later interments of bodies and of ashes, and secondary interments of this sort also appear in Bronze-age barrows. In Iceland, the hill Helgafell (Holy Mountain), which looks like an enormous howe, was adopted as a symbolic burial place by the family of Thórólf Mosturbeard. These men were said to go 'into the mountains' when they died. In the Viking Age, we hear mostly of male burials, but barrows in Scandinavia include burials of women with rich grave-goods. In England one of the Sutton Hoo burials is of a middle-aged woman who has, among other ornaments, a small crystal ball suspended from her belt and what seems to be a libation spoon, with five holes pierced in it. We can guess that these implements were needed for priestly duties. When the Vikings captured Dublin in the 930s, Ota, the wife of the leader Turgeis, is said to have taken the Christian altar at Clonmacnoise as the altar of her own prophecies. In Germanic Europe as in Greece and Rome, it seems there was no full-time professional priesthood, and the political leaders also had religious duties to perform.

Continuity of site was practised. The moot hill, the meeting place of the tribal assembly, was sometimes a barrow, either that of a known ancestor or a prehistoric construction. Tynwald Hill on the Isle of Man is an artificial hill built specifically as a meeting place on the site of a Bronze-age barrow. The action of Ota in Dublin is usually presented as a desecration of a Christian holy place, but it might equally have been part of the reverent tradition of continuity. In Denmark the reverse happened. The Pagan burial site at Jellinge was taken over by the Christian religion at the time of Harald Gormsson (who was later expelled from Denmark by his Pagan subjects in 988). The stone of King Gorm, Harald's father and an assiduous worshipper of the old gods, was replaced by that of King Harald, and the Pagan *Hörgr* by a Christian stave church. Nevertheless, the layout of the site was kept intact and even added to by Harald, rather as Constantine used the old Etruscan discipline in laying out his Christian city of Constantinople. Similarly, the seventh-century Saxon palace of Yeavering in Northumberland was built on the site of a Bronze-age barrow, which was retained intact at the eastern end of the new enclosure. On top of it was put a tall post – a procedure identical with that carried out at the ship-burial on the Volga – and there were other ancient cremations and inhumations.[20] The Anglo-Saxon temple was built at the western end of the enclosure, beside a Bronze-age knoll which had been used for cremations. All the Anglo-Saxon buildings were aligned with the post on the barrow. Later, the barrow was to be enclosed in a Christian churchyard.

Part of the reason for using barrows as moot hills may have been that the

Plate 8.2 Foundation-offering of a cat and rat, found in 1811 and preserved in W. Eaden Lilley's department store, Cambridge. The practice of making ceremonial offerings, usually of coins, papers and 'time capsules' under buildings continues all over Europe. © 1985 Nigel Pennick.

dead were supposed to be able to inspire the living at these sites, thus giving them wise counsel. The *Flateyjarbók* tells of a man who was inspired with the gift of poetry by a dead *skald* on whose howe he slept. The tradition of inspiration has persisted into modern times. The nineteenth-century mystic Richard Jeffries experienced a series of remarkable visions and transcendental states while lying on a tumulus on the Wiltshire Downs, which he recorded in his autobiography, *The Story of My Heart*. Barrows, then, were consecrated places, like the *loca sacra* and *loca religiosa* of the Romans, seen as gateways to the Otherworld under the guardianship of those who were buried there. This is the same situation as in Celtic myth, where, however, the deities and ancestors are disguised for a later age as the Little Folk.

THE LATE GERMANIC DEITIES

Fortunately, we have a record of the Vikings' deities and their manner of worship. In the thirteenth century, the Icelandic diplomat and landowner Snorri Sturluson recorded many of the old sagas and poems and composed some of his own, including a thinly disguised introduction to Norse Pagan mythology, *The Deluding of Gylfi*. These stories, recorded after at least two centuries of official Christianity, were influenced by Classical as well as by Biblical models and so cannot be taken entirely at face value. But even allowing for the distortion of time and outlook, modern scholars generally agree that they offer us an invaluable record of a vanished world. The characters of Snorri's chief gods and goddesses are well known nowadays: Odin, the

Plate 8.3 The Norse Pagan trinity of Frigg, Thor and Odin, sixteenth-century engraving by Olaus Magnus. Nideck Picture Collection.

leader of the gods and the god of battle; Thor, the thunder-god with his hammer; Freya, the radiant goddess and first chooser of the noble dead; her brother, Frey, the fertility god; Loki, the trickster; Odin's wife, Frigga; these and many others are familiar to today's schoolchildren. We tend to see them as a well-knit group defined by myth, like Homer's Olympians, but investigation of the deities' origins yields a more complex story, some outlines of which can be sketched here.

Snorri's introduction to the *Gylfaginning*, his account of the Norse-Icelandic pantheon of ancient times, gives these divinities a justified place within the world-view of his times. He traces the development of human-kind from Noah, in accordance with Christian teaching; he attributes different cosmologies to human beings' natural 'wisdom', exercised, however, 'without spiritual understanding'; and then he elaborates the Classical origin myth of Troy as the centre of the tripartite world, with its geomantic twelve-fold division, its chieftains and its population of monsters, dragons and a prophetess, the Sibyl of Europe. One of the twelve chieftains of Troy was, according to Snorri, the father of Thor, and Thor became duke of Thrace and married the Sibyl, one of their descendants being 'Vóden whom we call Odin', who, having the gift of prophecy, travelled north through Germany, Denmark, Sweden and Norway, where in accordance with the prophecy he founded the various Germanic races with their quasi-divine ancestors. Because of their origin Odin and his sons were called the Æsir, or 'race of Asia'.

The cult of Woden (in Norse: Odin) appears to have supplanted those of Tîwaz, the god of the sword and of justice described above (pp. 116–7, 119), and of Thunor, the god of thunder and of the protection of property. In the main part of the *Edda* the god Tyr (Tîwaz) loses his hand through a

143

necessary bargain, and the god Thor is described as Odin's son, although in the introduction he was described as the latter's ancestor. These occurrences could be seen as disempowerment and takeover myths. As the god of battle, Odin is a fickle master, and he was known as a deceitful god. He was the ruler of the invisible world, of poetic inspiration, of battle-madness and of the written script – the runes – which we know were derived from North Italic script and which had reached Denmark by the third century CE. Odin is the god of trade, of living by one's wits, commemorated in the *interpretatio Romana* by inscriptions to Mercury. He is a suitable god for migrants, and by taking up residence (according to Snorri's introduction) in Sigtuna, Sweden, he may have supplanted the cult of Freya and Frey.

The kings of Sweden (Pliny's Ingaevones) derived their ancestry, according to Snorri in his introduction to the *Heimskringla*, from Yngvi, sometimes known as Yngvi-Frey. Yngvi shares his name with the rune Ing, signifying ancestry, but the name 'Frey' means simply 'lord'. Nobility based on aristocratic stock and 'good breeding' is here directly linked with the Germanic cult of the divine ancestor. Frey was a god of breeding. He was portrayed as ithyphallic, or if clothed, with some other token of his virility. He was invoked at weddings, and was thought to bring prosperity as well as many children. He had several descriptive bynames, one of which was *enn fróði*, the luxuriant. His sacred animals were the horse and the pig, itself a fertile creature, and he was said to travel around the Swedish countryside in a wagon, bringing prosperity to his worshippers.

Frey's sister Freya and Woden were the Pagan divinities most frequently alluded to in medieval German references to Paganism, and in the *Gylfaginning* Snorri tells us that Freya was the most renowned of the goddesses and that her worship survived to his own day. Indeed, during the twelfth century there had been a resurgence of Freya worship, and Schleswig cathedral has on its wall a mural from that time depicting Freya riding naked on a giant cat (in the sagas we are told that she rode in a chariot pulled by cats), alongside Frigga (Odin's wife), similarly unclad, riding on a distaff. It was an insult to Freya at the Althing (Parliament) which opened the final round in the battle over the Christianisation of Iceland. A Christian partisan called Freya a 'bitch goddess',[21] and the contest began. Freya seems once to have been an extremely important figure. The *Gylfaginning* tells us that each day after battle she chose half the slain, while Odin had the remainder. The story of how her golden necklace was stolen by Loki for Odin, like the story of Tyr's maiming by the wolf, also bears the classic hallmarks of a takeover myth. The golden necklace itself, like the tears of gold which Freya is said to weep, may link her with the sun-goddesses of the Baltic. Her brother Frey was connected with another solar figure, perhaps the spirit of the midnight Sun, the giantess Gerd. The *Gylfaginning* tells us that when Gerd went into her house on the northern horizon, she raised her arms to open the door, and 'they illumined the sky and sea, and the whole world grew bright from her'.

Plate 8.4 Twelfth-century mural of the goddess Frigga riding a distaff, in the cathedral at Schleswig, Schleswig-Holstein, Germany. Nigel Pennick.

Freya and Frey were said to be the children of Njörd, a god of the sea whose home is known as the 'Boatyard', and his unnamed sister. Frey was said in the sagas to have a magic ship, *Skíðblaðnir* (Skate-blade), which could be folded up and kept in a pouch when not needed. Freya was not connected with a ship in the literature of the Viking Age, although from Roman times we know of the ship as an attribute of Sequana, goddess of the Seine, and of the unnamed goddess of the Suebi reported by Tacitus. Modern commentators have been quick to see Njörd as a later form, perhaps the brother, of Nerthus, the goddess of Tacitus' Danish tribes. Nerthus, like Frey, travelled in a wagon, bringing happiness and prosperity to her worshippers. Prosperity, good harvests and peace are what are said in the prologue to the *Gylfaginning* to have been brought by Odin and the Æsir when they reached Sweden: another indication of their taking over an earlier cult of the Vanir there. Nerthus was connected with water: her home was on an island and her slave attendants were drowned after seeing her. We do not know of ritual drowning associated with Frey, but *Víga-Glúm's Saga* tells us that Frey's sanctuary was defiled by having blood shed in it. Weapons were not allowed in Frey's temple, which recalls the cult of Nerthus, when all weapons had to be put away. Freya and Frey, Njörd and the other deities called by Snorri the Vanir seem originally to have been bringers of peace, prosperity and continuity, and their worship seems to have included a ban on weapons. The association of Freya with battle is said in the fourteenth-century *Flateyjarbók* to have been the price she paid for the return of her necklace from Odin. A complex set of origins is indicated here.

Deities in wagons seem to have been an ancient part of north European religion, perhaps to do with the migratory habits of the Celts and, especially, the Germans. Pliny (IV.80) includes among his Sarmatians the Aorsi, or Wagon-Dwellers. The various *Lives* of St Martin of Tours indicate that in fourth-century CE Gaul, images said to be of Kybele, shielded by white curtains, were carried around the fields. Gregory of Tours records that at Autun the image of the goddess Berencyntia was carried on a wagon for the protection of the vines and other crops.[22] When the Gothic King Athaneric decided to reimpose Paganism on his subjects he sent the image of a god around in a covered wagon and demanded that the inhabitants of each village sacrifice to it. Much later, the *Flateyjarbók* (I.467) tells of the Swedish King Erik consulting the god Lytir, whose presence came into a wagon. The presence was felt by the additional weight of the wagon, which was drawn then into the king's hall. In the same way, Tacitus tells us, the priest of Nerthus 'felt' when the goddess was present and led her wagon forth amid great rejoicing.

Archaeological finds of sacred wagons include small models and full-size vehicles, covering a 2,000-year period. These include several small wagons which may be models of full-size vehicles that were drawn along sacred roadways. Many of them include representations of horses. The best known is the vehicle found in a peat bog at Trundholm, Denmark, deposited around 1200 BCE, which carries a bronze horse and what is thought to be a solar disc. (Much later *The Deluding of Gylfi* tells us that the Sun and Moon are drawn across the sky on chariots.) A 12-cm-high late Bronze-age (*c*.1000 BCE) vehicle from a burial at Alcolshausen, Landkreis Würzburg, Germany, now in the Mainfränkisches Museum at Würzburg, carries a cauldron-like vessel. A seventh-century BCE Celtic bronze sacred wagon from Strettweg, near Graz, Austria, depicts a goddess surrounded by male and female attendants holding stags.[23] She holds a vessel above her head. A similar cauldron-holding female figure on a wheeled vehicle surrounded by animal and human attendants was among the Etruscan exhibits at the Franco-German exhibition held in Paris and Berlin in 1992. A boar-hunting horseman is depicted on a small Celtic wagon from Merida in Spain (second–first century BCE). Full-sized wagons include that from the Celtic tumulus-burial at Hochdorf, Baden-Württemberg, Germany (sixth century BCE); two found at Dejbjerg Mose, Ringkøbing, West Jutland, Denmark; and the ninth-century CE wagon buried with a ship at Oseberg, Norway, which accompanied the body of a noblewoman. We can only assume that the cult of the Vanir had some connection with this ancient symbolism, whatever it meant.

Another important god in the sagas was Thor. He is thought to be a later form of the god known to Tacitus and equated with Hercules, who was said to have appeared to some of the Rhineland tribes.[24] Hercules with his club was also a common equivalent of Taranis the Gaulish thunder-god. Later, the Saxon thunder-god Thunor was equated with Jupiter and gave his name to Jupiter's day: Thursday. Many settlements throughout Scandinavia, Germany and Britain are named after Thor, but we do not know of any royal houses who traced their lineage from him. According to the *Edda* he was not a god of the nobility. The Norse Vikings who settled Ireland were his worshippers, and their temple of the Black Thor in Dublin was renowned throughout the Viking world. When in 994 the Irish King Mæl Seachlainn conquered Dublin and took the Sword of Charles (said to have been owned by Charlemagne) and the holy ring of Thor from the great temple, it must have seemed that the end had come for the Norsemen. Thor was a god of great vitality and zest for life: strong, greedy, bombastic and lacking in subtlety, he was no mysterious god of the shadow realm. The thunder was said to be Thor's hammer striking in heaven, and lightning the sparks as the hammer hit the ground. His sacred tree was the oak, his animal was the goat – greedy, determined and unsubtle – and two goats pulled his chariot across the sky. In Snorri's *Edda* he is a figure of some ridicule, but in everyday worship two hundred years before he was clearly seen as honourable and highly venerated.

Thor seems to have had a connection with the land, because his worshippers in Iceland would often take the soil from beneath their temple pillars with them when they settled. They also took the high-seat pillars themselves, which were sometimes carved with an image of the god and with the 'god's nail'. Thor was connected with the oaks of the forest, which the pillars may have represented,[25] as well as with the axis of the heavens, the source of thunderstorms, which was also represented by a tree.[26] In this the cult of his predecessor in the Rhineland may have been signalled by the Jupiter columns described in the previous chapter. A newcomer to Iceland would cast his high-seat pillars overboard within sight of land and would then settle wherever the pillars were washed up. Helgi the Lean, a descendant of Froði (Frey), by contrast, cast a boar and a sow overboard to determine where he should settle. Thor, like Jupiter, also held the guardianship of oaths, which were sworn on his temple-ring, usually an arm-ring. The priest of Thor wore this ring only and always during temple ceremonies. The three Danish kings of East Anglia whom King Alfred forced to terms in 876 likewise took their oath on 'the holy armlet of Thor'. Thursday – Thor's Day in the seven-day week as used by the Scandinavians – was the first day of the week and a holy day. The Althing of Iceland always began on a Thursday, and both Summer's Day and Winter's Day were Thursdays, of variable date. By contrast with the *Edda*, the historical records show Thor as an honourable figure, an enforcer of law and of oaths. He not only protected the community, but in a sense he held it together, a paradoxical achievement for such a violent, irascible figure.

RELIGIOUS ORGANISATION

History, by contrast with Snorri's *Edda*, indicates that the polytheistic pantheon was held together not so much by a chief deity, as in official Graeco-Roman religion, nor even by a deity of place, as in archaic Graeco-Roman religion, but by the cult of the divine ancestor. In the early tribal days the divine ancestor of the king was the deity of the tribe, and we see the last appearance of this among the Anglo-Saxons. (It is not clear whether the mainland Saxons, Pliny's Herminones, defeated by Charlemagne in 772, worshipped a divine ancestor or a more abstract sky-god.) The temples had many altars, however, from that of King Rædwald of East Anglia with his altar for Christ and his altar for 'demons', to that of the great temple at Uppsala with its images of Thor, Odin and Frey, and individuals were free, as in all Pagan societies, to offer their special allegiance to whichever deity suited them best. If one deity seriously failed them, they would transfer their allegiance to another, as, for example, the Icelander Víga-Glúm, who transferred from Frey to Odin.

Iceland, colonised from Scandinavia in the ninth century, showed Pagan democratic principles in action. Uniquely among the Scandinavian lands, it was governed by a kind of theocratic oligarchy, ruled by hereditary Goðar. Originally, the Goði was a priest of a tribe or clan which had the same temple in common. In the settlement times, there was no full-time priesthood (if there ever had been), and the chieftain or landowner had the duty of upkeep of his temple. Temples could be private or public. *Vápnfirðinga Saga* records that a public temple (*Höfuð-hof*) was owned by a woman named Steinvör.[27] The Icelandic Law Book states that a woman who inherited a chieftaincy had to delegate her authority to a man in the district. The testimony of *Vápnfirðinga Saga* indicates that she may have been able to retain its priestly duties for herself.[28] Sometimes, whole wooden temples were transported from Norway. *Erbyggja Saga* tells how Thórólf Mostrarskegg dismantled his temple of Thor in Norway and transported it, including the sacred soil beneath the god's image, to Iceland. Other temples were built new in Iceland. As tribalism declined, the office of Goði became progressively more secularised. In Iceland, the Goði became an official of the commonwealth, with sovereign power over his liegemen, hallowing and presiding over courts. The Goði of the temple at Kialarnes, descendant of the first settler of Iceland, Ingulf Arnarson, bore the title *alsherjargoði*. His temple was the oldest in the land, and its priest had precedence over the others. Hence he would hallow the Althing each year.

The Goðar were the nucleus of the law-making assembly (*lögrétta*). The Goðar also settled prices of goods. Iceland was divided geomantically into four quarters, which contained three jurisdictions (Things). Each Thing was divided into three Goðorð, each presided over by a Goði. There were thus thirty-six Goðar in all. Later, another jurisdiction was added to the northern quarter, bringing the total to thirty-nine. The original thirty-six Goðorð were called *full oc forn*, 'full and ancient'. The Althing contained other men: nine elected Lögrettamaðr, making forty-eight. Each member was accompanied by two assessors or counsellors, making the whole body number 144. In 1056 and 1106 respectively, the bishops of Skalholt and Holar were added to the *ex officio* members of the Althing.[29]

Northern Paganism included the regular use of seership, both to discover the present or future state of things and the will of the spiritual beings, the goddesses and gods. Runic techniques are well attested, and in the tenth chapter of Tacitus' *Germania*, as we have already seen, he describes the German diviners making lots using twigs marked with sigils: proto-runes. According to legend, the runes had been given to humankind by Odin, and they were empowered with sacred magic, enabling the user to gain access to other levels of consciousness. It is clear from the sagas and the Icelandic Settlement Book that it was common for people to have second sight or to work magic to see into the future. Even the Christian Queen Dowager Aud of Dublin, a late settler in Iceland, knew when she was going to die. She held a feast, which she declared would be her funeral feast, correctly predicting

Plate 8.5 Shepherd saluting the setting moon, from a German shepherds' calendar of 1560. Nigel Pennick.

her death three days later.[30] Seership seems to have become desacralised with the growth of Christianity. Originally, the Pagan offering-tides were also occasions of foretelling the future, as is made clear in the sagas. The *Orkneyinga Saga* shows this progression clearly.[31] The mythical ancestor of the Norwegians, Thorri, is described in chapter 1 as holding a feast after the main midwinter sacrifice 'with the aim of finding out what had happened to' his missing daughter Goa. By Christian times, in the late eleventh century (ch. 36), the earl's heir Håkon was in Sweden when he 'got to hear of a certain wise man who could see into the future, though it is not known whether he used sorcery or other means'. Håkon consults the seer, who places himself ironically outside Christianity by saying: 'I'm glad you feel you can place so much trust in me, more than you and your kin give to your professed faith.' By the mid-twelfth century (ch. 77), we have the merely laconic description of one of the earl's followers as 'a shrewd man [with] a talent for seeing into the future, but . . . ruthless and violent'.

Norse mythology, as recorded by Snorri, has its three spirits of Fate, the Norns. It is quite likely that these figures were influenced by the literary tradition of the three Fates from Classical sources, but we must also remember the native tradition of the three goddesses, the Matres, from the Rhineland. In Snorri's account the first Norn is Urd, 'that which was', who parallels Clotho from Greek tradition. Verdandi, 'that which is becoming', is the equivalent of Lachesis; and Skuld, 'that which is to come', is identified with Atropos. Like the three Greek Fates, the first Norn spins the thread of existence. She passes the spun thread on to Verdandi, who weaves it into the present pattern of existence. In Anglo-Saxon this fabric was known as the Web of Wyrd. The woven web then passes to Skuld, who tears it apart and disperses it. The Norns' Web of Wyrd was envisaged as a woven fabric composed of myriad strands or threads. This concept occurs in an Old English expression, 'woven by the decrees of fate'. Saxo Grammaticus, describing Denmark around the year 1200, stated that in his time, it was customary for the Pagans, wishing to know their children's future, to consult the threefold goddess. 'Three maidens sitting on three seats', three priestesses (their setting reminiscent of that of the three Matres), served as oracles for the three Fates. In medieval England, they were called The Weird Sisters. Writing around 1385, in *The Legend of Good Women*, Geoffrey Chaucer spoke of 'the Werdys that we clepen Destiné' (the Wyrds that we call destiny). Later, the three Fates reappear as the three witches in William Shakespeare's *Macbeth*. The story of Macbeth came from Holinshed's *Chronicles* of 1577, which tells of 'three women in wild apparel resembling creatures from an elder world'. Further on in the work, Holinshed states that these were none other than the 'Weird Sisters, that is . . . the goddesses of destinie'.

In Scandinavia and Iceland, women performed ceremonies of trance seership known as *seiðr*. As far as is known, this was not used for healing, as in

Plate 8.6 The Weird Sisters, from the story of Macbeth in Holinshed's *Chronicles,* 1577. This is the sixteenth-century manifestation of the three goddesses of time that are acknowledged throughout European Paganism. Nideck Picture Collection.

Lappish shamanism, but served an oracular function. It was ruled by the goddess Freya, who is also said to have taught it to Odin, but men in general did not practise this technique as for them it was considered shameful. The Nordic sibyl was called *spákonr* or *Vǫlva*. The reverence felt for sibyls is implicit in the Icelandic text *Vǫluspá* (The Sibyl's Vision), believed to date from the tenth century. The poem describes northern cosmology and beliefs in the form of a question-and-answer session with a seeress. The characteristic practice of the sibyl was *útiseta*, 'sitting out', where she would sit on a raised seat or platform, upon which she would go into a trance. Often, she had a considerable congregation, and was accompanied by helpers. *Orvar-Odds Saga* (2), for example, records that a sibyl was accompanied by a choir of fifteen maidens and fifteen youths. The *Saga of Erik the Red* tells of *seiðr* being practised in the nominally Christianised Westviking community of Greenland. The practice of sitting out continued with the Dutch Witta Wijven of Drenthe Province until the mid-seventeenth century.[32] In earlier times, the Dutch wise women were called Hagadissae. They gave their name to the capital city of the Netherlands, Den Haag.

The practice of magic was also widespread in the Norse settlements. *Seiðr* had its magical applications, apparently including the raising of corpses and the 'hag-riding' of unfortunate living beings through the 'night-mare'. Male sorcerers, too, are included in the *Landnámabók*. One was Lodmund, who, failing to find his high-seat pillars after they had been cast overboard, settled in a place of his own choice. When the news reached him that the high-seat pillars had been discovered, Lodmund hurriedly loaded all his possessions into his ship, set sail and, instructing his crew not to speak to him or even to say his name, lay motionless, wrapped in his cloak. As the ship drew away a huge landslide engulfed the house, and Lodmund then pronounced a formal curse on all seagoing vessels which attempted to put into its harbour. Later in life, when blind in old age, Lodmund was magically attacked by a neighbour. The neighbour, also a sorcerer, diverted a stream to overrun Lodmund's property, saying it was the sea, but when his servant came to tell him, Lodmund dipped his staff in the water, pronounced it fresh, and magically diverted it back. Eventually, the two neighbours directed the stream to form a boundary between their properties.[33]

In battle, followers of Odin not only aroused themselves into battle-madness, but attempted to affect their enemies by placing the 'war-fetter' on them. This was an unaccountable paralysis which made the enemy unable to fight back. It might have been a sonic technique as practised nowadays in the Japanese martial art of kiai-jitsu, stunning the nervous system into paralysis. The Roman writers report a more psychological technique by waiting troops: for example the Germans who shouted into their shields to create an echo, and not only terrified the enemy but divined the outcome of the battle from the quality of sound produced.[34] The Celtic army opposing Suetonius Paulinus on Anglesey used similar tactics to reduce the Roman troops to shocked immobility.[35] On the other hand, the war-fetter might simply have been magic of the normal kind, affecting its victim without any identifiable cause.

The Icelandic pattern of freelance magic is probably unusual, a by-product of the individualism and self-sufficiency of the early settlers. In organised Pagan societies magic, like any other source of individual power, has always been strictly regulated. It is accepted in that its effectiveness is taken for granted, but any hint of its abuse is generally severely punished, and scapegoating with its usual misogyny is rife. The Haliarunnos, the Gothic women necromancers expelled by King Filimer in the fifth century, were blamed for the arrival of the Huns. The Goths thought that these women had mated with monsters in the desert and given birth to this terrifyingly warlike race – thereby neatly shifting the blame for King Ermenrich's inability to withstand the Hunnish invasion. The early Christian laws actually lift some of the threats against magicians, e.g. the Edict of Rothari, the Lombard king of Italy, published in 643. Chapter 376 enjoins: 'Let no man presume to kill another man's slave-woman or servant on the ground that she is a witch (or *masca* as we say); for Christian minds refuse to believe it possible that a woman could eat a living man from inside him.'[36] Organised magic, contained within the communally sanctioned limitations of the cult, was, however, normal, and this also was denied as a 'delusion' by the laws of the newly Christian Germanic kings. The Pagan view of nature as a theophany, a showing-forth of the divine essence, leads naturally to a belief in magic and foreknowledge. Interestingly, under both Pagan and Christian regimes, seers and seeresses, those with passive foreknowledge of the future, were generally respected and exempt from persecution, whereas sorcerers with their active use of the unseen powers were feared and often persecuted.

Viking society seems to have been a relatively egalitarian place for women, who could own and administer their own property and are often described in the sagas as independent agents rather than simply as junior members of someone else's household. In 845 the Arab scholar and diplomat Al-Ghazali visited the stronghold of the Vikings, who had been raiding his territory. There he met the queen, called Noud, who talked to him freely and informed him that among her people husbands were not jealous and their wives were free to change them if they wished.[37] One queen did exactly that in the late tenth century. Sigrid the Proud, the wife of King Erik of Sweden, left him and married Swein of Denmark because she did not want to die with Erik as the price of joining him in Valhalla.[38]

Women owned and commanded ships, as we know from the example of Aud. In the *Song of Atli* we read that King Hniflungr courted Gudrun because she was 'a woman of deeds', and later in the poem she tells how she, her brothers and her husband went a-viking, each commanding their own ship.[39] A documented example of a woman warrior occurs in chapter 9 of *Sögubrot*, which recounts the battle fought at Bravoll in eastern Jutland around the year 700 between the army of Harald Hilditonn (king of Denmark, Sweden and part of England) and that of the pretender, Sigurd Hring. One of Harald's champions was a woman, Vébjorg:

> The Shield-Maiden Vébjorg, made fierce attacks on the Swedes and the Goths; she attacked the champion Soknarskoti; she had trained herself so well to use the helmet, mail-shirt and sword, that she was one of the foremost in knighthood [*Riddarskap*], as Storkold the Old says: she dealt the champion heavy blows and attacked him for a long time, and with a heavy blow at his cheek cut through his jaw and chin; he put his beard into his mouth and bit it, thus holding up his chin. She performed many great feats of arms. Later, Thorkel the Stubborn, a champion of Hring, met her and they attacked each other fiercely. Finally, with great courage, she fell, covered with wounds.

The lays and sagas also describe women as using the runic script. Although brought by Odin, this was evidently not seen as a male mystery. In chapter 3 of the *Song of Atli*, Gudrun sends a runic message to Kostbera, wife of Hogni, who recognises that the message has been tampered with by the messenger. A fragment of wood, part of a loom found at Neudingen in Germany in 1979, shows unequivocally the existence of rune-mistresses in ancient times. There, incised in runes on a woman's tool, are the words 'Blithgund wrait runa' – 'Blithgund [a woman's name] wrote these runes'.

NORTHERN MARTIAL ARTS

The northern warrior tradition appears to have originated in hunting magic.[40] In the heroic period, it had developed into a form of physical-spiritual martial arts activity comparable to the later Japanese Samurai Shinto code of *Bushido*. At all times, warriors had to exercise self-reliance and always be willing to die selflessly for family and comrades. In order to be capable of feats of arms, a strict training in self-control was necessary, and this was essentially religious. Later, the religious element seems to have been taken over by Christianity, transforming the northern martial arts into the knightly arts of chivalry, and the totemic animals into heraldic devices.

There were three main animal-cults in the northern martial arts: those of the bear, wolf and boar. The wearing of a bearskin shirt was the mark of the Berserker, a practitioner of the martial arts who went without normal chain-mail armour, yet who was so strong and ferocious that he was feared by his opponents. Bear-warriors 'went without mail byrnies, as ferocious as dogs or wolves', records the *Ynglingasaga*, 'they bit their shields and were as strong as bears or boars; they killed men, but neither fire nor iron could hurt them. This is called "running berserk"'.

The bearskin shirt was a totemic sign that, in battle, the Berserker could draw upon the strength of the bear. The Berserkers were devotees of the cult of the bear, widespread throughout the northern hemisphere.[41] The power of the bear was gained at the Berserker's initiation. *Hrolfs Saga Kraki* tells us that, among the tests, the would-be Berserker had to kill the image of a beast set up in *Hof*, then to drink its blood, when the power of the beast would be assimilated with the warrior's power. The power of the bear was also called upon in times of trouble. When he was marooned with his crew on an island in the Baltic, Orvar-Odd set up the head and skin of a bear, supported on a staff, as an offering (*Orvar-Odd's Saga* 5). In the *Færeyinga Saga*, a dead bear is propped up with a piece of wood between its jaws. The bodies of dead Berserkers were laid on a bearskin prior to the funeral rites.[42]

Because of their renowned martial prowess, tested in battle, Berserkers were valued fighting men in the armies of Pagan kings. Harald Fairhair, Norwegian king in the ninth century, had Berserkers as his personal body-guard, as did Hrolf, king of Denmark. The bear-warrior symbolism survives in the present day in the bearskin hats worn by the guards of the Danish and British monarchs. But despite their fighting prowess, their religious duties were still observed. For example, *Svarfdoela Saga* (12) records that a Berserker postponed a single combat until three days after Yule so that he would not violate the sanctity of the gods.

The Úlfheðnar wore wolf-skins instead of mail byrnies (*Vatnsdoela Saga* 9). Unlike the Berserkers, who fought in squads, the Úlfheðnar entered combat singly as guerrilla fighters. A wolf-warrior is shown on a helmet-maker's die from Torslinda on the Baltic island of Öland. In Britain, there

154

NP.88.

Plate 8.7 Sixth-century helmet panels from Torslinda, Öland, Sweden, with scenes showing Berserkers, Úlfheðnar and Svínfylking warriors from the northern martial arts tradition, and the binding of the Fenris-Wolf by Tíwaz/Tyr. Nigel Pennick.

is a carving on the eleventh-century church at Kilpeck in Herefordshire showing a wolf-mask with a human head looking out from beneath it. This may be a stone copy of the usable masks hung up on Pagan temples, worn in time of ceremony or war. Similar masks, used by shamans, serve as spirit receptacles when they are not being worn. In his *Life* of Caius Marius, Plutarch describes the helmets of the Cimbri as the open jaws of terrible predatory beasts and strange animal masks.

The boar was a sacred animal in the cult of the Vanir. 'The Lady', Freya, had a wild pig called Hildisvín (battle-swine), and her brother Frey owned the golden-bristled boar Gullinbursti, which could outrun any horse. Hilda Ellis Davidson speculates that priests of the Vanir may have worn swine-masks, claiming protection from Frey and Freya.[43] In Vendel-period Sweden and early Anglo-Saxon England, the image of the boar appears on many

155

ceremonial items, such as the Benty Grange (Derbyshire) helmet. The Swedish King Athils had a helmet named Hildigoltr (battle-pig). He captured another boar helmet, Hildisvín, from his enemy, King Ali.[44] The Boar-Warriors fought in the battle-formation known as Svínfylking, the Boar's Head. This was in the shape of a wedge, led by two champions known as the Rani (snout). Boar-Warriors were masters of disguise and escape, having an intimate knowledge of terrain. Like the Berserkers and Úlfheðnar, the Boar-Warriors used the strength of their animal the boar as the basis of their martial arts.[45]

'DUAL FAITH' AND VERNACULAR PAGANISM

The arrival of official Christianity was marked in Germanic communities as elsewhere by the usual prohibitions of continuing Pagan practices. These give us some idea of what everyday Pagan worship was like. For example, the *Punishments for Pagans and Others who turn from the Church of God*, ordained around the year 690, lists:

2: If anyone eats or drinks unknowingly at a heathen shrine,
5: If any keep feasts at the abominable places of the heathen,
15: If any burn grain where a man has died for the wellbeing of the living or for the house . . . [46]

It would appear that at the end of the seventh century, there were still 'heathen shrines' in England, recognised as such. Another prohibition, from half a century later, states:

Anyone who practises divination or evocation at a spring or a stone or a tree, except in the name of God . . . [47]

The prohibitions were intensified at the time of the Viking invasions. We have already seen how the Scandinavian countries adopted Christianity unwillingly, under bloodthirsty coercion. Countries such as England which had already taken Christianity as their official religion adopted a missionary zeal against the resurgence of Paganism under the influence of the invaders. The English King Edgar (959–975) explicitly forbade toleration or assimilation:

[We enjoin] that every priest zealously promote Christianity, and totally extinguish every heathendom; and forbid well worshippings and necromancies, and divinations, and enchantments, and man worshippings, and the vain practices which are carried on with various spells, and with frith-splots [sanctuaries], and with elders and with various other trees, and with stones, and with many various delusions, with which men do much of what they should not . . . And we enjoin, that on feast days there be complete abstinence from heathen songs and devil's games.[48]

Later, the newly Christian King Canute, the Danish ruler of an England which had been officially Christian for nearly four hundred years, added (1020–1023):

> Heathendom is, that men worship idols; that is, that they worship heathen gods, and the sun or moon, fire or rivers, water-wells or stones, or forest-trees of any kind; or love witch-craft, or promote morth-work [death spells] in any wise; either by sacrifice, or divining, or perform anything pertaining to such delusions.[49]

Julius Caesar had said that the Germanic tribes worshipped the Sun and Moon. Although we can assign solar and lunar attributes to various deities mentioned by later observers and practitioners, we have no evidence for the worship of those two celestial bodies as such. Canute's decrees were drawn up by Archbishop Wulfstan of York, but presumably the king, of Danish upbringing and the son of a Pagan father, would be unlikely to legislate about practices which he knew to be fictitious. His decree leaves us with a tantalising hint of unrecorded practice.

Following the official conversion of the Scandinavian lands and their raiders, within the Germanic European states many Pagan practices were assimilated into Christianity or persisted as folk-

Plate 8.8 The Saxon lunar god, from R. Verstigan, *A Restitution of Decayed Intelligence*, Antwerp, 1605. Nideck Picture Collection. This follows the Germanic tradition of the 'Man in the Moon' and Celto-Germanic-Baltic hare totemism.

traditions alongside the new religion in the usual way. At Cologne in 1333, Petrarch saw women conjuring the Rhine as a rite of the people.[50] Cologne was the site of an important Pagan temple.[51] When 'three great fires in the air' came down to rest on the Horselberg, a holy mountain in Thuringia (better known as the Venusberg of *Tannhäuser*), in 1398, the phenomenon was interpreted as an apparition of the goddess Horsel.[52] Sometimes priests took part in adapted Pagan rituals which were part and parcel of community life. The ritual perambulation of parish boundaries ('beating the bounds'), the 'wassailing' of cider apple trees by pouring a libation over them and firing shotguns into the air, the annual blessing of a plough in the parish on a day specially named after the occasion (Plough Monday, the first Monday after Twelfth Night), are all ceremonies which persist to this day in Britain. In Germany and Scandinavia, where the urbanisation of the population at the time of the Industrial Revolution was not so drastic, even more ceremonies for honouring the land and the seasons have remained. Midsummer bonfires and sunwheels persist in Denmark and Norway, midsummer fairs throughout northern Europe. In Germany and the Netherlands, the fourth Sunday in Lent is known as 'Rejoicing Day' and attributed to the Biblical Book of Isaiah 66.10, but in fact it seems to be the old Summer's Day, when mummers and marchers celebrate the victory of summer over winter.[53] Most towns and villages still have their Maypoles or May trees, and local festivals such as the Shepherds' Race in Markgröningen, Baden-Württemberg, are well attended. What Caesar of Arles, in the sixth century, called 'devilish, erotic and wicked songs' (*cantica diabolica, amatoria et turpia*), or 'obscene and wicked songs *with choruses of women*' developed into carols as we know them: songs to celebrate midwinter and spring in their Christianised form. In his book, *The Anatomie of Abuses* (1583), the English Christian fundamentalist Stubbes recorded the Pagan ceremonies of his time:

> Then march these heathen company towards the church and church-yard, their pipers piping, their drummers thundering, their stumps

Plate 8.9 Horn Dancers at Abbots Bromley, Staffordshire, England, 1897. The horns are said to date from Anglo-Saxon times, a direct continuity of Pagan ceremonial. From the *Strand Magazine*, 1897. Nideck Picture Collection.

dancing, their bells jingling, their handkerchiefs swinging about their heads like madmen, their hobby-horses and other monsters skirmishing amongst the throng; and in this sort they go to the church (I say) and into the church (though the minister be at prayer or preaching) dancing and swinging their handkerchiefs, over their heads in the church . . . Then, after this, about the church they go again and again, and so forth into the church-yard, where they have commonly their summer halls, their bowers, arbours, and banqueting-houses set up, wherein they feast, banquet and dance all that day and (peradventure) all the night too.

Dancing no longer takes place in the churchyard or in the choir, but at Abbots Bromley, Staffordshire, the reindeer antlers for the traditional 'Horn Dance' are ceremoniously kept in the church. The antlers have been carbon-dated to the eleventh century, a time when reindeer were already extinct in the British Isles, and it is thought that they were brought in by Norwegian settlers.[54]

Plate 8.10 Serpent-labyrinth village dance at Ostmarsum, the Netherlands, 1939. Collective ceremonies assert and maintain the continuity of village life, commemorating local deities, the ancestors and the cycle of the year. Nideck Picture Collection.

Some of the deities of the old pantheon persisted under the new order. Jacob Grimm reports that in seventeenth-century Scandinavia, offerings were made to Thor against toothache.[55] Until 1814, when it was destroyed by a farmer, the Odin Stone, a holed stone at Croft Odin, Orkney, was used for oath-taking.[56] In 1791, a young man was arraigned by the Elders of Orkney for 'breaking the promise to Odin', an oath sworn on this stone.[57] When visiting the stone, it was customary to leave an offering of bread, cheese, a piece of cloth or a stone. An 1823 woodcut of standing stones in Orkney shows the Ring of Stenness, known as The Temple of the Moon, where a woman is invoking Odin to hallow her promise of betrothal.[58] Even in the twentieth century the Swiss psychiatrist C.J. Jung explained a dream of his own by reference to the still-current imagery of the Wild Hunt led by the Green-Hatted One, Wotan.[59] O.S. Reuter identified what seems to be an early reference to the Wild Hunt in a passage from the (Christian) Old Norse visionary poem *Draumakvädi*: 'The horde of demons arrives from the north with splendour and ornament, and old Greybeard [Odin] at their head.'[60] In medieval and modern folklore, the Wild Hunt was a supposed troop of spirits which rode the storm, sometimes thought, as Jung reports, to carry souls away to somewhere other than the Christian heaven. In Germanic culture, it was often thought to be led by Woden, although churchmen elsewhere seem to have envisioned it as led by a goddess, Herodias or Diana, as for example in the tenth-century *Canon Episcopi*.

Quite apart from direct survivals, over a long period Christian images were added to Pagan shrines, or Pagan images actually renamed as those of saints or prophets. Many of the Pagan deities were simply renamed by Christian priests. Beneficial deities became saints: Freya became Maria; Baldur, St Michael; Thor, St Olaf; Tónn, St Antonius, etc., whilst demons and destructive deities were identified with the Christian Devil. We have already seen the polytheistic outlook of King Rædwald of East Anglia, with his personal shrine in which he worshipped both Pagan and Christian deities. It was sacred places in the landscape, such as holy wells, hills and caves, which suffered the least alteration. Certain churches on old Pagan sites in German-speaking lands, dedicated to Verena and Walburga, were known as *Heidenkirchen* (Pagan churches).[61] A hill in Alsace bearing a church of St Maternus was known as *Heidenkanzel* (Pagan pulpit).[62] In Saarland, there was the *Heidenkirche* on the Halberg.[63] In the Tyrol there is a sacred hill called *Heidenbühel*. It was surmounted by a chapel inside a cemetery called *Heidenfriedhof* (Pagan cemetery). Elsewhere there were churches called *Heidentempel*.[64]

Sometimes the local deity was simply called a saint, e.g. Thor's holy well at Thorsås in Sweden was known as Saint Thor's Spring.[65] Other Pagan places were revered well into the medieval period: among the more notable examples are the fane of the Swabian goddess Zisa at the Zisenburg in Augsburg; the sacred places of Jutta at Heidelberg; the prophetic holy well of Mons Noricus,

Plate 8.11 Twelfth-century carving of Woden, his ravens Hugin and Munin, and swastikas, symbol of Thunor, in the church at Great Canfield, Essex, England. © 1992 Nigel Pennick.

Nuremberg; and the labyrinth dance-place of Libussa at Prague. The tenth-century stone cross at Gosforth, Cumbria, has images from both Norse and Christian mythology. Thirteenth-century murals in Schleswig Cathedral, Germany, depict the goddesses Frigga and Freya.[66] There is an image of Woden, complete with ravens and fylfots, in the church at Great Canfield, Essex, England. The church at Belsen, Kreis Tübingen, Baden-Württemberg, Germany, has two images of the god Béél. A fifteenth-century wall-painting of the Goddess in the Labyrinth exists in the church at Sibbo, Nyland, Finland.[67] At the time of the conversions, images could serve both Christian and Pagan worshippers. Axe-carrying statues of King Olaf the Saint, slain at the Battle of Stiklastad in 1030, were set up in Norwegian churches, where they were worshipped as images of Thor by Pagans.[68] In more recent times, an ancient Buryat sacred image in a monastery at Lake Baikal was transformed into an image of St Nicholas and worshipped with equal zeal by Pagan and Christian devotees.[69] Pagan pillars were erected in north Germany under the name *Rolandseulen*, and in the fifteenth century, there was a temple of Jupiter Christus at Istein, Germany.[70]

In the Pagan tradition, where each deity has its place, the Christian deities took their place in the Pagan pantheon. The Icelandic settler Helgi the Lean is said to have believed in Christ, calling upon Thor for seafaring and adventurous acts.[71] Pagan prayers and invocations were modified by the addition (and sometimes the substitution) of the names of Christian divinities. The second *Merseburg Charm*, dating from the tenth century, mentions Phol, Woden, Frigga and Volla. The *Canterbury Charm* against sickness (1073) contains the words 'Thor hallow you'. An Icelandic leechbook from the late thirteenth century contains the names of Odin, Fjölnir, Thor, Frigg and Freya along with Judaeo-Christian names of power.[72] The runic Healing Stick from Ribe in Denmark (*c.*1300) is a classic example of a dual faith holy object. This 30-cm-long pine stave bears a runic spell to exorcise pain in the shape of *The Trembler* (probably malaria): 'I pray, guard Earth and High Heaven; Sól and St Maria; and God the King; that he grant me healing hand, and words of remedy, for healing of pain when relief is needed'.[73]

Following the Norman conquest in 1066, official Christianity in England retained a separatist outlook. The king reserved the right to appoint bishops, and the Pope campaigned against this. The tension surfaced during the reign of the particularly separatist King Henry II (1154–1189) with the popularity of the Grail myth, which told of Joseph of Arimathea, the uncle of Jesus, setting up an independent church in England at Glastonbury. The myth of the English apostolic succession served a convenient political purpose, but the vehicle which carried it incidentally perpetuated an older Celtic Pagan tradition in the stories of the miraculous food-producing vessel, the Grail, and its female priestess or guardian. The popularity of the Grail stories, which were favoured in England, Wales, Germany and France, arose at a time when the importance of the Christian communion (a miraculous meal) was growing, as was the cult of the Virgin Mary. Pagan stories were used here to carry the symbolism of a development within Christianity.

England remained at odds with the Roman Church. In 1208, the Pope put an interdict on the country because King John refused to submit to him. All consecration was stopped: churches closed, bells were not rung, weddings celebrated without clergy, and the dead buried in ground not consecrated by the Church. In 1209, things were taken further, and England as a whole was excommunicated. King John ordered all priests to leave the country, and expropriated the property of the Church. Then came a period of remarkable prosperity and vitality. John's Yule court at Windsor was particularly sumptuous, attended by all the nobles of the realm. At this time, Richard of Devizes was amazed to visit London, where he found a vibrant pluralism of lifestyles: 'Actors, jesters, smooth-skinned youths, Moors, flatterers, pretty boys, effeminates, pederasts, singing-girls, quack doctors, belly-dancers, sorceresses, extortioners, night-wanderers, magicians, mimes, beggars, buffoons: all this tribe fill all the houses.'

Some curious relics of indigenous tradition remained or were renewed in medieval England. In her *English Society in the Middle Ages*, Lady Stenton describes how, in 1255, a company of thirteen people hunted all day illegally in Rockingham Forest. They cut off the head of a buck and put it on a stake in the middle of a certain clearing. They put a spindle in its mouth, making

Plate 8.12 Decorated poplar tree at Aston-on-Clun, Shropshire, England, the last surviving commemorative tree in memory of King Charles II, whose 'Royal Oak' traditions continued the Pagan belief in the Lord of the Forest. © 1991 Nigel Pennick.

it gape towards the Sun, 'in great contempt of the King and his foresters'. The symbolism of this is obscure. Over one hundred years later, following the death of Queen Philippa in 1369, King Edward III's lady friend Alice Piers appears to have had great influence. She sat herself with the judges, and directed justice. In 1374, she appeared in the guise of 'The Lady of the Sun', the personification of the goddess Sól. She sat by the king's side in a chariot, attended by a train of nobles and knights, each of which was led by a richly dressed damsel. They rode from the Tower of London to Smithfield, where a week-long tournament was held in honour of the Lady of the Sun. Being very unpopular at court, she was forced to leave, but the king recalled her. Significantly, Alice attended him on his deathbed, where she refused the priests access to him. When he died, he had no last rites of the Church. She took the rings from his hands, and left.

In Germany, anti-Pagan activities were fostered. The custom of *Heidenwerfen* was encouraged by the Church. An image representing a Pagan deity was set up, stoned, smashed and burnt. *Heidenwerfen* are recorded from Hildesheim (from the thirteenth century), Halberstadt (sixteenth century) and Trier. At Hildesheim, a wooden post was set up in front of the church. A crown and mantle were put on it, and it was called Jupiter. Then it was stoned and burnt.[74] Until 1811, a torso of a Roman Venus Victrix was kept at the monastic church of St Matthias near Trier. Occasionally it was set up, and the parishioners were encouraged to stone it.[75] Here it was Roman rather than German deities which were attacked, just as the temple of Jupiter Christus at Istein honoured a Roman deity. Classical texts had been trickling into northern Europe since the reconquest of Spain which began in 1086, and monastic teaching was also full of examples couched in the language of the New Testament, with its image of embattled Christians pitted against the deities of the ancient world. Classical names and attributes were thus available to the clergy of the Middle Ages, and it would seem that these were used freely. The people, however, clung to the traditional names of their indigenous deities.

9

THE BALTIC LANDS

The area between the Elbe and the Gulf of Finland emerged from prehistory and travellers' tales comparatively recently. It was never part of the ancient Roman Empire, and it joined the Holy Roman Empire only between the tenth and fourteenth centuries. Hence information from ancient chronicles and from the day-to-day observations of letter-writers, diarists and satirists is lacking until late in the history of the area. Until recently, historical accounts have tended to be biased. The imperial powers – Church, Germans, Scandinavians, Russians – who fought to control the area overlooked the independent history of its inhabitants, and later nationalistic movements among the once-colonised peoples tended to exaggerate their own achievements. With the weakening and collapse of the Soviet empire in the 1980s, independent historical investigation has once more become possible, and we write at an early stage in that process.

The ancient history of the area is sketchy but uncontroversial. In the fifth century BCE Herodotus reported the existence of 'Scythians' who lived around the rivers Dnieper and Don, nomads and hunters (IV.17ff.). He describes a tribe called the Geloni, originally Greeks, who were driven out of their cities on the Black Sea and travelled north to the Don, where they built a wooden city, supported by an agrarian economy and containing temples to the Greek divinities, and spoke a language that was half Scythian, half Greek (277). Six hundred years later, Tacitus reported the existence of the mysterious Aestii on the eastern shore of the Baltic, who spoke a language akin to British, and who gathered amber, worshipped the mother of the gods and took as her emblem the wild boar. The geographer Ptolemy, writing in the middle of the second century CE, described the Venedi (Wends), the Finni, the Ossi (Osilians) and other dwellers on the Baltic shore.[1] The Lithuanian tribes of the Galindae and Sudini lived inland, 'to the east' of the Finnic peoples on the shore. In the sixth century CE the Gothic historians Procopius and Jordanes added to the picture. When the Rus arrived from Sweden in the ninth century and settled on the Volga, dominating the Slavic tribes, they seem to have employed the Estonian Chud as mercenaries.[2] The Rus (the Swedish Vikings described in chapter 8) carved out an empire corresponding to the modern states of Belarus and the Ukraine, dominating the Slavic-speaking inhabitants of the area, and extended their influence down the eastern boundary of Europe to the Black Sea and Constantinople. The lands around the Baltic seaboard were, however, left alone.

It seems that the Balts had been seafaring, piratical people. Johannes (1488–1544), the brother of the famous Bishop Olaus Magnus, wrote the *History of All the Kings of Gotland and Sweden*. He gives several examples of eastern Baltic naval warfare, dating from the fifth century CE. For instance, in the year 410, Tordo, the thirty-third king of Sweden, armed his country against a mighty fleet of Estonians, Curonians and Ulmigeri (Prussians), whom he forced to retreat.[3] Meanwhile, the Saxons took their turn to ravage Gotland, Holstein, Denmark, Pomerania, Curonia and Estonia.[4] The migration of the Goths from Gautland (southern Sweden) and the island of Gotland began, according to Johannes Magnus, after a series of particularly severe raids by the peoples of the eastern Baltic.[5] The future Visigoths under Götrijk landed in Rügen and Pomerania. One group of them then migrated south to the Alps. A second group set off under the leadership of their king to conquer the Prussians, Curonians, Samogytians and Estonians, after which Götrijk handed over command to his son, Filimer, and returned to Gautland where he re-established his kingdom. The third group, under Ermanerik, conquered the Vandals and then the Estonians.[6] Much later, the Swedish King Erik the Victorious (940–944) beat off an invasion of Estonians and invaded them in his turn, forcing them to become his vassals. However, the victory does not seem to have outlasted its author. Adam of Bremen[7] records the existence of pirates called the Ascomanni or Wichingi (Vikings) who ravaged the coast of Frisia in the year 994 and sailed up the Elbe. Their name suggests that they came from the Estonian province of Askala, the 'land of wizards'.[8] The famous Norwegian King Olaf Tryggvason was captured by Estonian Vikings and enslaved when he was a boy, in about 970.[9] Saxo Grammaticus, writing in the late twelfth century, and Henry of Livonia, writing in 1227, both describe Estonian pirate ships and tactics.[10]

Most of the Baltic lands in the first millennium CE seem to have been inhabited by people who were neither nomads nor settled agriculturalists, but raiders. The ethics of a raiding society are an extension of the hunter-gatherer outlook. Just as animals are there to be killed and eaten, so other human settlements are there to raid and pillage. The successful raider would bring home piles of loot and defend his settlement against other human predators. Raiding here is not an outbreak of lawlessness, but a normal and, indeed, central occupation of adult male life. This was also the outlook of the ancient Irish (sc. *The Cattle Raid of Cooley*), the Norse and Danish Vikings, and the people of the mainland of eastern Europe in early medieval times. In the Treaty of Christburg (1249) it was reported that the Prussians had a special class of priest who attended funerals, 'praising the dead for their thefts and

Plate 9.1 Wooden images of Baltic divinities, late medieval. Nigel Pennick.

predations, the filthiness, robbery and other vices and sins they committed while alive'.[11] Anyone who reads the Viking sagas will recognise a similar glorification going on. The Viking *skaldar*, the epic poets, were never described as priests, but in Ireland the *fili* and before that the bards certainly were. In these pre-literate societies an individual's fame had to be reaffirmed and re-earned at regular intervals. Acts of what we (and the ancient civilisations) would call boastfulness and self-exhibition were normal, and a warrior's good name would simply die without the efforts of his bard.

At the end of the tenth century the Holy Roman Empire cast its crusading eyes eastwards. Following the missionary activities of Willibrord and his Northumbrian monks in Frisia in the 690s, Christian campaigners in the Frankish Empire had treated the Elbe as the eastern limit of their activity. In 831–834, however, a see was established at Hamburg by Pepin I of Aquitaine, grandson of Charlemagne, and a century later (946–949) the Holy Roman Emperor Otto I used it and other new foundations as outposts in his sustained campaign to conquer for Christendom the West Slavs, the inhabitants of the Pagan lands of the east. His only success in the north was in Poland. Poland was set up as a Catholic state between 962 and 992 by Prince Mieszco I. But between it and the Catholic rulers of Saxony lay Pagan territory, the land of the ancient Venedi or, as they were now called, the Wends. The Wends ejected the missionaries and their land-hungry followers in 1018 and 1066, and the Holy Roman Empire waited fifty years before trying again.

'The Slavs', so runs a proclamation [of 1108] of the leading bishops and princes of Saxony, 'are an abominable people, but their land is very rich in flesh, honey, grain, birds, and abounding in all produce of fertility of the earth when cultivated so that none can be compared with it. So say they who know. Wherefore O Saxons, Franks, Lotharingians, men of Flanders most famous, here you can both save your souls and if it please you acquire the best of land to live in.'[12]

This was an incitement to a crusade, following the spirit aroused in the western empire by the first Crusade of 1096. The peoples east of the Elbe did not submit easily, and some in the far eastern corner of Europe never did. In 983 the great Slav uprising in Brandenburg ejected the Ottonian conquerors, but in 1047 the kingdom of Wends was established by the Christian Gottschalk, stretching from the Elbe to the Oder. In 1066 both Gottschalk and the bishop of Mecklenburg were killed by the Pagan resistance.[13]

Reconquest began with the Wendish Crusade in 1147. The western part of Wendland, between the Oder and the Vistula, was known as Pomerania (the land of the 'dwellers on the shore'), and was the first target of the eastern crusade, but as late as 1153 the god Triglav was being worshipped by Slavs and Saxons at Brandenburg. One thousand years previously this area had been the centre of Germanic Paganism, where the Semnones worshipped their supreme god in their sacred grove.[14] In the High Middle Ages, Svantovit, revered by Balts and Slavs alike, still had his main cult-centre at the north of this area, on the holy island of Rügen in the Baltic. The island itself was sacred to the god Rugevit, whose sacred rowan trees grew there in abundance. At Karentia (Garz), at the southern end of the island, there was a shrine containing the multi-headed images of Porevit and Rugevit. In the temple of Svantovit, on the northernmost promontory of Rügen, there was a carved pillar depicting the four aspects of Svantovit. One aspect held a horn of precious metal which was filled with wine annually as an oracle, when the whole nation assembled at the harvest festival and the high priest decided whether the nation should go to war or not. The high priest was the only Wendish man allowed to grow his hair long. He was given his own estates and all the bullion taken in war; in addition, he had his own army of three hundred cavalry.[15] The temple itself was a square building, like many Celto-Roman temples and that at Uppsala.[16] The images of the deities were considered so sacred that only the priests were allowed to see them in the inner sanctum where they were kept. Other sacred objects were kept in the temples. At Arcona were a holy saddle and bridle of Svantovit, used on the sacred horses during ceremonies. A major cult-object was Svantovit's sword. At Wolgast, the temple held the sacred shield of Gerovit, and at Stettin were aurochs horns decorated with gold and jewels. A sacred white horse was kept in the *Temenos* at Arcona. Others were kept at the shrine of Zuarasiz (Radegost) at Rethra. Triglav's shrine at Stettin, which included an oak tree and a holy well, had black horses. Stettin itself contained four temples as well as halls where the nobles met for sacred feasts using gold and silver dishes.[17]

At Rethra, during a rebellion, the bishop was executed and his head offered to Radegost. Triglav was being worshipped at Brandenburg by Slavs and Saxons around 1153, at a time when Duke Nyklot of the Abotrites (who lived near Mecklenburg in Pomerania) was reasserting Paganism in the wake of the official conversion in 1128. Svantovit's temple was destroyed by Archbishop Absolom and King Valdemar I of Denmark in 1168, and the temple at Karentia in 1169. But a granite slab built into the wall of the church at Altenkirchen bears a carving of a beardless man holding horns.[18] It is still known as Svantovit.[19]

The Pomeranians converted to Christianity in 1128 under the influence of the missionary Bishop Otto of Bamberg. Amid great debate and organised Pagan resistance, the upper classes of Pomerania were persuaded by the advantages of a culture shared with their trading partners. An active Pagan faction remained after the conversion, as we have seen, and the temples on

Plate 9.2 Shoemakers' Guild labyrinth dancing-place at Stolp, Pomerania (Słupsk, Poland), from the *Pommeranische Archive* III, 1784. Nideck Picture Collection.

169

Rügen remained active until 1168–1169, after the death of their defender Duke Nyklot in 1160. The peasants, as usual, remained Pagan for a great deal longer than the aristocracy, and nowhere did they accept Christianity without coercion and often armed resistance.[20] Pomerania was absorbed into Poland in 1294, and here, too, the old traditions have lingered. When the ashes of a Polish freedom fighter and his wife were reinterred in their native village in 1993, two young birch trees, sacred trees in Baltic Paganism, had been planted by the grave. An observer noted that this seemed to be a uniquely Polish mixture of 'Christian faith, militant patriotism and ancestor worship'. The remains of the general, he thought, were reinterred as if to guard the village and remind its inhabitants of their identity, as ancestral burials always do.[21]

OLD PRUSSIA AND THE BALTIC SHORE

East of the Gulf of Gdansk was Old Prussia, and on the eastern shore of the Baltic were Lithuania, Livonia and Estonia. The languages of Old Prussia, Lithuania and the southern part of Livonia (modern Latvia) are an archaic branch of Indo-European, on a par with such old languages as Sanskrit, Ancient Greek and Gothic. Until the twentieth century the Baltic languages were seen as a branch of Slavic, but nowadays they are placed in their own category. Most scholars think that the people of this linguistic group arrived in their present home some 4,000 years ago, although it may be that the Finno-Ugric speakers who are now confined to Estonia and points north lived further south than they do now.[22] As documents from the first 1,300 years of the Common Era make quite clear, all of these Finnic peoples were known to themselves, to the ancient world and to Germanic speakers as the Aestii, to the Scandinavians as Sembi, and to the Slavs (Wends and Poles) as Pruzi (Prussians).[23] The Highland Lithuanians, who lived inland,[24] moved in, according to this view, to settle in the coastal areas between the Vistula and the Dvina after incursions of Christian crusaders had destabilised the area.[25]

The identities of the Baltic states and their boundaries, unclear from prehistory, also shifted radically following the Frankish incursions of the tenth century, but their attitude to religion did not. These countries retained official Paganism well into the medieval period. The tribes of Old Prussia were devoutly Pagan. It was only through wars of extermination at the behest of Christian prelates that official Paganism was ended. The genocide of the Old Prussians was not accomplished easily. They took part with the Wends in the Baltic rebellion of 983, considering Christianity to be the worship of the *Teutonicus deus*.[26] In 997, Adalbert, bishop of Prague, was killed in his attempt to Christianise Old Prussia. He was followed by Bruno of Magdeburg, who was killed by the Yatvegians (southern Lithuanians/East Prussians, around the river Niemen) in 1009, when Christianity was extirpated from the country.

Because of these failures, Bishop Bertold asserted that only the conquest of Old Prussia and the Baltic lands would end Paganism. He died in battle in 1198, but his call was taken up by the founding of Christian military orders. In 1200, the Livs were subdued by Bishop Albert of Bremen, which led to the foundation of Riga, and in 1202, the establishment of the Fratres Militiae Christi, the 'Order of the Sword'. These knights attempted to impose Christianity by force, but they were resisted strongly. In 1225, the Teutonic Order (The Order of St Mary's Hospital of the Germans at Jerusalem, founded at Acre in 1190) were expelled from their feudal lands in Transylvania by the Pagan Kumans, and went to Prussia to take Baltic lands for their order.[27] Then began a sixty-year war, which was by no means a one-sided affair. The Knights of the Sword were defeated in battle by a Pagan army of Lithuanians at Saule near Bauska in 1236. In 1260 the 'Great Apostasy' in Old Prussia led the Teutonic Knights to institute the same test of loyalty as the Romans had when faced with the Christian menace twelve hundred years before. All inhabitants of the country were made to swear allegiance to the national deity, in this case the Christian god. Those who did so were rewarded with civil privileges.[28] Between 1270 and 1273, an official campaign of extermination was waged by the Christian military orders – the Teutonic Knights, the Knights of the Cross and the Knights of the Sword – against the Pagan Sambian nation of Old Prussia. A few years later (1280–1283), the crusade reached Sudovia, east of Old Prussia. The country was reduced to desolation, its inhabitants massacred or expelled. Until 1525, Prussia was an *Ordenstaat*, a country owned by a Christian military order, and it gave its name and its militaristic reputation to its successor state, Brandenburg.

Lithuania, by contrast, actually came into being as a Pagan state to counteract the dual threat from the Christianising military orders to the west and the Tartar invaders from the east. By the mid-fourteenth century it had become the largest state in Europe, fully modern, fully bureaucratic and possessed of a flourishing Pagan religion which was organised with all the political advantages that the Christian religion offered its own host states.[29] The fragmentation of the old local deities and allegiances was overcome by national celebrations of victory and the state funerals of heroes, in which the deities common to all the Lithuanians were invoked. Like the Scandinavians in the Viking Age, the Lithuanians had nothing tangible to gain by adopting Christianity, but unlike them, they were able to transform local Paganism, the worship of the spirits of place, into state Paganism, the worship of the tutelary spirits of the nation, in the same way as the Romans and other Mediterranean civilisations had done. In 1251, the Lithuanian King Mindaugas, the architect of this reconstruction, actually became Christian, but this did not lead to compulsory conversion for all his subjects, and Paganism remained during his reign and afterwards. In fact, it was thought that Mindaugas' conversion was only nominal. The *Galician-Livonian Chronicle* states that:

Plate 9.3 The Lithuanian deities Perkūnas and Perkūnatele (Zemyna), as envisioned in the sixteenth century. Nigel Pennick.

> Secretly he made sacrifices to the gods – to Nenadey [god of ill fortune], Telyavel [protector of the dead], Diveriks the hare-god [sky-god], and Meidein [forest-goddess]. When Mindaugas rode out into the field, and a hare ran across his path, then he would not go into the grove, nor dared he break a twig. He made sacrifices to his god, burnt corpses and conducted pagan rites in public.[30]

The Samogytians nevertheless warned Mindaugas against the political yoke which accompanied Christianity. They resisted the new religion to the end. Attempts by the Knights of the Sword to Christianise Samogytia (Lowland Lithuania) had met with a decisive defeat in 1259, and the Samogytians continued to offer their support to the Livonian tribes fighting against the Knights of the Sword based in Riga. Meanwhile, the main government in Vilnius was following an expansionist path. In 1315, Lithuania under Gudimin formally annexed Little Russia, the original home of the Rus, into which it had been expanding since Kiev was sacked by the Tartars in 1240. This move re-Paganised Little Russia. The inhabitants soon called themselves Lithuanians, but the official language was Belorussian.[31] Pagan Lithuania displayed religious tolerance: religion was a matter of individual conscience. After 1312, when Christian priests entered Lithuania, official Pagan shrines and monasteries of the Catholic and Orthodox sects existed side by side in the capital, Vilnius, whilst Muslim scribes were employed in the Royal-Ducal Chancery.[32] Highland Lithuania was officially Christianised in 1387, in return for the crown of Poland. Samogytia, a district which had tirelessly battled against the Frankish crusaders, did not accept official

Christianity until 1414. After the union of Poland and Lithuania had been made permanent in 1569, Poland began to be seen as the dominant partner in the relationship, and the state language became Polish. The political importance of Lithuania from the thirteenth to the sixteenth centuries has thus remained one of the best-kept secrets of European history. The ruling classes of Lithuania became Polonised, but the peasants kept their language and folk-customs, even under persecution after Lithuania passed to Russia in 1795. The movement in favour of popular culture, which grew in all the Baltic countries during the late nineteenth century, encouraged the collection and reaffirmation of the old practices, and a Lithuanian Pagan movement has grown steadily throughout the twentieth century.[33]

The Lithuanian temples, like those in the other parts of Pagan Europe, were originally funded and maintained independently, not as part of a larger national or transnational religious organisation. Medieval stories of centralised Paganism, based on a central temple, Romowe (Romuva), under the jurisdiction of a High Priest, *Kriwe Kriwejto*, were considered fanciful by some researchers,[34] but more recent commentators have tended to give them credence,[35] and modern Lithuanian Paganism, formally restored in 1967, repressed by the Soviets in 1971, and tolerated since 1988, has taken the name Romuva. Since 1988, the shrine-site at Romuva, in the Russian enclave of Kaliningrad (formerly in East Prussia), has been restored as a place of pilgrimage and celebration. According to a legend reported by Maciej Styjokowski,[36] the site of the present capital, Vilnius, was chosen by one Duke Sventaragis, who, when out hunting, came across an oak grove. Its beauty so enchanted him that he gave orders for his body to be cremated there, in the fashion of the Germans and Scandinavians which we have already seen:

> According to the custom of his forebears, the duke was cremated wearing his finest armor, arms, and his most beautiful raiment. Consumed by fire together with the remains of the duke were his beloved hunting dogs, hawk, falcon, steed, and manservant.

Afterwards the spot became the cremation ground of the Lithuanian dukes, and today it is the site of the cathedral square.

Although official Baltic Paganism was abolished in the fifteenth century, as in other parts of Europe popular Paganism continued. Largely, the medieval Estonian and Latvian peasantry did not accept Christianity. The language of the Church was Latin or German, and the Latvians preserved their own Pagan culture in their folk-songs and home religious practices. The oral tradition of Latvian Paganism, the *Latviju Dainas*, was published in six volumes between 1894 and 1915 by the Imperial Academy of Sciences in St Petersburg. The restoration of Dievturi came from Brastinu Ernests, who collected and commentated on traditional Latvian sacred folk-songs (1928).[37] It is fortunate that these have been preserved, because they contain an invaluable legacy of folk-culture and popular religion dating from the eleventh to the nineteenth century.[38] The more southerly lands, Curonia and Old Prussia, had their languages stamped out by the colonial powers and so much of their oral tradition was lost.

DEITIES OF THE BALTIC PANTHEON

Despite the differences in language, many deities of the Baltic pantheon are shared by the Slavs. Saule, the sun-goddess (otherwise Saule Motul, Mother Sun) and her daughters reside in a castle beyond *dausos*, the hill of heaven, abode of the dead. She is depicted riding across the hill of the sky in a copper-wheeled chariot; at eventide, she stops to wash her horses in the sea. The Sun itself is a jug or spoon from which light is poured. Saule is another example of the deity in the wagon. Her festival, Kaledos, is held at mid-winter; images of the Sun are carried through fields and villages to bring prosperity in the coming year. The Scandinavian–British festival of Yule is paralleled at Kaledos by guising in the form of cranes, goats, horses, bears and bulls, burning the *Blukis* (Yule log) and feasting on pork. Saule also has a festival at midsummer, Ligo, at which a bonfire is lit at the top of a pole in a high place. (The pole or tree as a symbol of the World Tree, the celestial axis of the Earth's rotation, is well attested in Baltic tradition.) The site is decorated with wreaths of flowers, there are dances and hymns, and a special meal of cheese and mead is prepared. In the Baltic lands there are wayside shrines on poles which are sometimes topped with a solar emblem, and Saule is described in colloquial speech as perching on top of a tree, especially a birch or rowan. She is symbolised by wheels, eggs and golden apples, and the flax is sacred to her.[39] Saule is also the hearth fire, and the house-snake, Zaltys, which lives by the fire, is said to be beloved of her.[40] Latvia, too, enjoys midsummer festivities and lyrical poetry. The Soviet authorities banned the ligo songs and abolished Midsummer Day as a national holiday as late as 1960.[41] The folklore tradition with its record of Pagan deities was being used for nationalistic purposes, and now in the post-Soviet era a renewal of national interest in indigenous practices is taking place for the same reason.

Mehnesis (Lithuanian: Mènuo) the moon-god, travels the sky in a chariot drawn by grey horses. He was married to Saule, but later fell in love with Auseklis (Lithuanian: Ausrinè), the morning/evening-star goddess, and was punished by Perkunas, who broke him into halves. The god of light is Svaixtix ('Star'). Perkunas (Pehrkons, Perun, Varpulis) is the axe-carrying thunder-god (like the Thracian Lycurgos and the West African Yoruba god Shango). He is the opponent of evil spirits, riding, like Thor, in a goat-drawn chariot. Other weather-deities include Lytuvonis, the rain-god. The sea is ruled by the goddess Juras Mate. Metalworking and construction is under the tutelage of Kalvaitis, the divine smith, whilst destruction is personified in Jods, the spirit of wrongdoing.

Plate 9.4 German greeting card, *c*.1925, showing the Pagan sun-tree. Spilkammaret, K. Frank Jensen.

Zemyna (otherwise Zemlja or Perkunatelé) is the earth-goddess and psychopomp of the dead. Her name is the linguistic equivalent of that of Semele, mother of Dionysos, in the Greek and Thracian traditions. She has a brother, Majas Kungs (Lithuanian: Zemepatis, Zeminkas), ruler of the home, except for the hearth, which is guarded by the fire-goddess Gabija. The sky-god is Dievs (Lithuanian: Dievas). Dievs is depicted as a handsome king, wearing a belted silver robe and cap, and carrying a sword. His domain is beyond the sky's hill, *dausos*, the realm of the dead, a country entered by three silver gates. Modern Latvian Paganism is called Dievturi, after Dievs, and the movement, Dievturiba. 'To live in harmony with Nature and other

175

members of society and to follow the will of the Gods' is the stated objective.[42] In association with Laima, goddess of life, Dievs determines the fate of humans. Mara, the goddess of the material world, giver, preserver and, finally, taker of life, was worshipped in southern Poland as Marzanna, whose special area is fruit.[43]

SHRINES AND TEMPLES

Temples existed in the large settlements, but as elsewhere in Europe, much worship was conducted out of doors at sacred places in the countryside. Pigs were sacrificed at rivers to Upinis, god of clean water. In Prussia, Antrimpas, god of lakes and the sea, was revered similarly. In Lithuania, specific sacred places were called *Alkas*: they included groves which could not be cut; holy wells that could not be fished; and sacred fields that could not be ploughed. Cremations took place in or beside them, and offerings were made there on altars (*Aukuras*). Dittmar, bishop of Merseburg (976–1018), wrote of the sacred wood at Zutibure (Svantibor), containing images of the gods. A mountain near the river Nawassa was sacred to the Samogytians (Lowland Lithuanians). There, a perpetual sacred fire was kept, attended by a priest.

In Baltic Paganism, it is believed that there is a component of the human being, the *Siela*, that does not depart with the *Vele* (soul), but becomes reincarnate on Earth in animals and plants, especially trees. In Pagan times, no abuse of tree or animal was tolerated. Individual sacred trees were revered also: Laima was venerated aniconically in linden trees, and Puskaitis, god who rules over the spirits of the Underworld (the *barstukai* – elves or fairies), was honoured by offerings left at elder trees. As in the west, the last sheaf of the corn harvest is venerated as the Rugiu Boba (The Old One of the Rye). Thirteenth-century texts refer to Medeine, goddess of the forest, whilst in the eighteenth century there are references to Giraitis, god of forests, and Silniets.

Lasicius (Bishop Ján Lasicki, 1534–1602), writing in his *De Diis Samagitarum* (Basle, 1580, 1615), and *Religio Borussorum* (1582), tells of the Pagan religion practised among the Borussians, Samogytians, Lithuanians, Ruthenians and Livonians of his day. He recounts the gods worshipped and the agricultural festivals officiated over by Vurschayten (priests). These include Pergrubius, god of flowers, plants and all growing things, whose festival was on 23 April. This is, of course, St George's Day in the Church calendar, and the Baltic festival of Pergrubius echoes the Green Man festivities of England on that day, and may also indicate a religious significance in the date of the 1343 St George's Night Rebellion in Estonia (see below, p. 178). In Poland, the cult of Pergrubius was assimilated with St Florian, guardian of 'St George's Flower Month'. Other festivals were Zazinck, the beginning of harvest, and O Zinck, the harvest home, when a goat was sacrificed. A later festival, Waizganthos (Vaizgautis), was held to augur well for the crop of flax and hemp in the forthcoming year, and this, as we know from other sources, was sacred to the Sun.

Patriarchally, Lasicius assumed that all of these deities were male, latinising them with masculine endings. However, from other sources we know that some of these 'gods' were goddesses, for he ascribes the harvest thanksgiving among the Samogytians to the earth-god Zemiennik, who is clearly the earth-goddess Zemyna. Among the Prussians, he tells of the worship in 1582 of Occopirnus, god of heaven and earth, and his counterpart Pocclus, god of the Underworld and death; Pilvitis (Pluto), god of riches; Pargnus, the thunder-god; Ausceutus (Asklepios), god of health; Potrympus, god of rivers and springs; Antrimpus, god of the sea; and Marcoppolus, god of the noble class. In addition to gods, he tells of lesser demigods and sprites, including the air-spirits, under the rulership of Pacollus, and the Barstuccae (*Erdmännchen*), Elves. Lasicius also tells of a custom which has persisted, deprived of its guardian-deity, until the present day.

> In addition these same people have amongst themselves seers, who in the Rutenican [Belorussian] language are called Burty, who invoking Potrimpus cast wax into water and from the signs or the images described in the molten wax, describe and foretell the nature of any situation which has been enquired about. I myself met one little woman who, having waited in vain for a long time for news of the return of her son, who had left Prussia for Denmark, consulted the seer, from whom she learned that her son had perished in a shipwreck. For the wax had melted in the water to form the shape of a broken ship and the effigy of a man on his back, floating next to the ship.

In the 1990s in the English Midlands, a visitor to an expatriate Latvian household on New Year's Eve was invited with great delight to take part in 'our ancient traditional custom'. Each guest heated up a small nugget of lead in an old pan on the stove, then poured the lead into a bucket of cold water, where it solidified, so allowing the lady of the house to read the guest's fortune for the coming year.

In the late seventeenth century, Matthäus Praetorius tells us in his *Delictae Prussicae oder Preussische Schaubühne* that at the harvest feast, black sucking-pigs were offered by priestesses to Zemyna, goddess of the Earth. The meat was made into sandwiches with the first bread of the harvest, and a portion of meat was taken to a barn, where the goddess was invoked in private. Rites of Zemyna also accompanied the planting of crops: for example, a loaf from the previous year would be ploughed into the Earth at the commencement of ploughing. As with trees and animals, Baltic Pagans revered the Earth, often kissing her on starting work or going to bed. It was considered sacrilegious to hit the Earth, spit on her or otherwise abuse her. The grass-snake, Zaltys, was revered and kept as a living guardian at sacred places and around the stoves of farmhouses. Lasicius had reported that in his day once a year

Plate 9.5 Lithuanian Pagan worship, showing fire altar and sacred snake (Zaltys), sixteenth-century engraving by Olaus Magnus. Nideck Picture Collection.

the domestic snakes were charmed out of their hiding places by the Pagan priests and offered the best of human food to eat, in order to ensure a prosperous year ahead.

FINNO-UGRIAN PAGANISM

Most of the languages of Europe, including Slavic, form one vast family, the Indo-European, with a common basic vocabulary and grammatical structure. The northernmost countries of the Baltic region, however, fall into a completely different linguistic grouping, that of the Finno-Ugrian languages. These include Finnish, Lappish (Saami), Estonian, Livonian and Karelian. In addition, there are some smaller groupings in Russia west of the Urals: the Erza, Komi, Mari, Moksha and Udmurt peoples, some of whom remain Pagan to this day. In Russia, the Mari and some Udmurt resisted both Islamicisation and Christianisation. During the 1870s, the Kugu Sorta (Great Candle) movement successfully resisted Church attempts to convert the Mari.[44] In Lapland, repeated attempts by the Church between 1389 and 1603 to suppress Paganism resulted in dual faith practices. When Saami were forcibly baptised, they washed off the effects of baptism with chewed alder-bark, sacred to Leib-Olmai, the reindeer-god. Johannes Schefferus, who recorded Pagan practices in seventeenth-century Lapland, wrote that it was an 'alloy of heathenism and Christianity, visible to all, seemingly condemned by none'.[45] His picture of an altar to Thor reveals a lively Paganism which was still actively practised. But there were also Pagan martyrs, like a *noid* (shaman) burnt alive along with his drum at Arjeplog in 1693.[46] In Estonia during the battle against Danish colonisation, the Pagan rebels of the 1343 Jüriöö Mäss (St George's Night) Rebellion destroyed all churches and

178

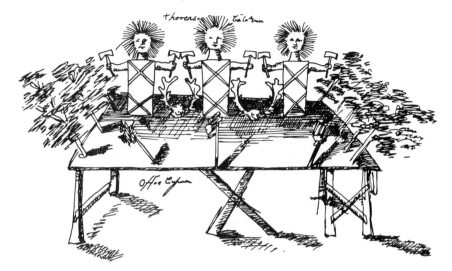

Plate 9.6 Lappish altar with images of Thor, offerings of reindeer skulls and vegetation, from Johannes Schefferus, 1671. Nideck Picture Collection.

manors, and drowned or otherwise killed all priests and lay brothers, but the Teutonic Knights were called in to slaughter many thousands of rebels in revenge.[47]

The Estonians, according to the fifth-century Roman historian Cassiodorus (*Variae* 546), were the people known to Tacitus as the Aestii. The extent of their territory in early medieval times is disputed, as we have seen, but the nature of their religion is not. Their religion was individualistic and included magical practices. They were known to the Scandinavians as experts in wind-magic, as were the Lapps (known at the time as Finns) on the north of the peninsula. The *Saga of Olaf Tryggvason* includes the story of Raud, 'a man much given to making sacrifices and a great sorcerer, [whom] a great number of Finns followed whenever he needed them'. Raud, whose name is the Finnish for 'iron', 'red' and 'strong',[48] prevented the Christianising King Olaf from entering the fjord in which he lived by raising squalls and a storm. The king arranged for his bishop to perform Christian counter-magic to calm the storm, and then sailed into the bay and killed Raud and his followers.[49] One northern province of Estonia was known as Askala: 'land of wizards'. In 1070, reports Adam of Bremen, the land of Curonia (on the south side of the Dvina basin) was inhabited by 'a primitive race, shunned by all because of its great cult of idols . . . Every house is full of diviners, augurs and magicians. People from all over the world come to ask questions of them, especially the Spaniards and the Greeks'.[50] Between the Baltic and the Mediterranean stretched the so-called 'amber routes', along which this valuable fossilised resin was transported. Some sources even say that the amber was transported by maidens to the shrine of Apollo at Delphi. The maidens were originally given safe passage, but after they had been attacked they used to deposit their amber at the border and it was taken in relays to the temple.[51] Amber, as a gold-coloured jewel, would presumably be sacred to Apollo in his capacity as sun-god. Diodorus Siculus reported that in about 500 BCE, beyond the land of the Celts there was an island containing a circular temple of Apollo, whose people spoke a unique language of their own and who had enjoyed friendly relations with the Greeks from 'most ancient times'.[52] The island might have been Rügen, or it might have been Samland on the east coast, which at the time was cut off by the sea from the mainland. The respect shown to the holy maidens in Pliny's account recalls Tacitus' observation that the Aestii worshipped the mother of the gods, and that the people beyond them were even ruled by women. As we shall see, the cult of the sun-goddess was also honoured north of the Dvina.

A traveller called Wulfstan reported to the court of King Alfred the Great (871–901) about the situation on the eastern Baltic. He said that the Wends held the country up to the Vistula, and beyond that were the 'Estum' or Estonians, who had a large country with a king in every town. The poor drank mead rather than ale, and the nobles drank mares' milk mixed with blood. Their burial customs, according to Wulfstan, included leaving the dead uncremated in the house of their relatives and friends, who then had a wake with drinking and sports until the day of the cremation. The richer the deceased, the longer the wake. The dead did not putrefy, however, because the Estonians had a way of making ice to preserve them. On the day of the funeral, the wealth that remained was divided into five or six piles which were deposited in increasing order of size at increasing distances from the property to a distance of about one mile. The local men with the fastest horses then assembled together and raced towards the dead man's house. The swiftest rider would reach the largest pile of property first, which he would claim, and so on in decreasing order of success. After the contest, the dead man was taken out and burned with his clothes and weapons. This story not only indicates the pugnacious nature and the horse-based economy of eastern Baltic society, but also recalls the tenth-century Rus funeral described by Ibn Fadlan (above, chapter 8). Just as a Rus warrior mocked the Arab for leaving his dead unburned, so, according to Wulfstan, the Estonians insisted that 'the people of every language' should be cremated, and anyone who left a bone unburnt should pay a large fine.[53]

Presumably the rite of cremation speeded the dead person's journey to join the dead beyond the 'hill of heaven', as it did for the Rus merchant interviewed by Ibn Fadlan. The dead would then not become earthbound spirits, which are usually thought to be dangerous to the living. The importance of burning even corpses of foreigners might have come from a fear of such spirits. Henry of Livonia records that as late as 1222 the Estonians disinterred

Christian dead and burned them.[54] By contrast with the Pagans of the time, the Christians thought it was important to preserve dead bodies because these would be resurrected at the end of time, and so it is tempting to see the action of the victorious Estonians as a deliberate attack on their enemy's sacred places. But in the light of what we now know, it is equally likely that this was primarily an act of psychic hygiene, ridding the place of ghouls. Interestingly, when conquered, the Estonians gleefully adopted the Christian feast day of All Saints (1 November). Syncretistically, they saw it as a continuation of their own veneration of the dead and the deities in the sky.

Like much of Pagan northern and eastern Europe, there was no written scripture among the Finno-Ugrian peoples, religious traditions being transmitted orally. Much later, they were written down as the Finnish poems of the *Kalevala*, and the Estonian *Kalevipoeg*. Runes were in use for calendars until much later than in Sweden. In Estonia, they were still being made at the end of the eighteenth century (one from Hiiumaa is dated 1796).[55] Thursday was the holy day, upon which the food was better than during the rest of the week – meat and butter were eaten then. The Pagan calendar divided the year into four quarters: Künnipäev (Plough Day, 14 April, equivalent to the Nordic Summer's Day); Karuspäev (Bear's Day, 13 July); Kolletamisepäev (Withering Day, 14 October, equivalent to the Nordic Winter's Day); and Korjusep (Collection Day, 14 January, the late Nordic midwinter feast).

Finno-Ugrian Pagan deities include a sky-god known by local names, e.g. Jumala in Finnish, Taevataat ('Sky Grandfather') in Estonian, Jumo (Mari), Inmar (Udmurt) and Ibmel (Saami). In Lapland, Pieve, the (feminine) Sun and Mano (Aske) the (masculine) Moon were deities who were never anthropomorphised. Pieve appears as a lozenge or circle with four rays, and Mano appears as a crescent.[56] Akko became the chief god of the Finns. His consort Akka guarded the harvest and fertility. Akka was known as Maan-Emo (Earth Mother) among the Estonians, and Muzem-mumi by the Udmurts. The thunder-god appears to the Saami under the name Horagalles (Old Man Thor), Tooru/Taara in Estonia, and as Torym to the Ostyaks. Rota, the national god of the Saami, is identified with Odin. Trade and settlement contacts between Scandinavia and these northern Finno-Ugric lands seem to have led to a partial assimilation of names and attributes. The Scandinavians of the Viking Age also saw the Lapps and Finns as miracle-workers, experts in the craft of magic. Living in small bands following a hunter-gatherer culture, the Lapps and, to a lesser extent, the more settled Finns preserved the role of the shaman, the expert who journeys in trance between the everyday world and the Otherworld, returning with information to benefit the tribe. Two Lapps were sent on a shamanic astral journey, a 'magic ride to Iceland', by the Norwegian Viking Ingimund the Old. He had lost a silver image of Frey, and the Lapps returned from their 'magic journey' to describe where it was to be found in Iceland. According to the story, told in the

Plate 9.7 Lappish shaman in trance, from Johannes Schefferus, 1673. Nideck Picture Collection.

Landnámabók (179), their description was entirely accurate, and when he went there Ingimund found his silver image exactly where the Lapps had predicted.

As in other parts of Europe, Finno-Ugrian religion honours the ancestors, the spirits of the land and elements, which are important in shamanic practices. The Saami venerate Radien-ahttje, their ancestral deity, accompanied by his consort Radien-akka, and the son and daughter, Radien-pardne and Rana-neida (patroness of springtime). Consecrated spindles were set up to Rana-neida at sacred places.[57] The cults of the guardian-spirits Metsik and Tónn were powerful in Estonia. Among a myriad of beings are the Estonian Ukus (house-spirit), the Saami Biegg-Olbmai (the wind-master), Väralden-Olmai (the man of the world, god of reindeer and hunting), the Udmurt spirits of the water, Obin-murt (rain-man), Vu-Murt (water-man) and Vu-nuna (water-uncle). The bear-cult, too, played an important role in many tribes.[58] Bronze amulets depicting a human figure with the head of a moose have also been found in the graves of the Chud (Estonians) at Lake Ladoga, and the Saami god Radien Kiedde is portrayed with antlers.

As with the Celts and Baltic peoples, sacred groves play an important role in Finno-Ugrian religion. The Mari *Jumon oto* was used for services in honour of the beneficial deities, whilst dangerous deities were propitiated in the *keremet*, a grove surrounded by a fence, equivalent to the Norse *Vébond*. At the end of the nineteenth century, at least sixty-four groves were in use by the Mari. The Udmurts also had groves (*lud*), and built sacred structures (*kvala*), basic windowless wooden buildings that were shrines of the family and clan gods. Inside was kept a wooden vessel containing images of the family or tribal ancestor. In common with European Paganism in general, sacred trees were decked with images and symbolic ornament.

Plate 9.8 The Norse god Ulli (Ullr), deity of winter hunting. Seventeenth-century Swedish print. Nideck Picture Collection.

One Finno-Ugrian people, the On-Ugri, migrated south and set up home in the Crimea. They became the Hungarians, and will be described in the next chapter.

10

RUSSIA AND THE BALKANS

The lands north of the Black Sea were settled around 700 BCE by the Scythians from central Asia. They were a mixed horde of people whose ruling element was Iranian. Eventually, their Empire encompassed the entire steppe, from the Volga and Kuban on the east to the Dniester in the west. Between the Don and Danube, thousands of burial mounds have been excavated. Among the most impressive are the royal burials containing, in addition to the deceased ruler, slaves and wives, horses, harness, weapons, utensils and wheeled vehicles. The Scythians' chief deity was Tabiti (Hestia in the *interpretatio graeca*), consort of Papaeus (Zeus). Other deities were Api (Mother Earth), Argimpasa (the Celestial Aphrodite) and Oetosyrus (Apollo). Thagimasadas (Poseidon) was the god of the Royal dynasty, which was said to be descended from Targitaus, son of Papaeus. The Scythian Empire lasted around four hundred years, but pressure from the Persian Empire late in the fourth century BCE, Celtic advances from the west and Sarmatian advances from the east fatally weakened it. During the third century, the Celts advanced eastwards from Galicia into the Dnieper Valley, but were forced to retreat. The first Sarmatians to reach the steppe from the east were the Iazygians, who settled on the north-west shore of the Black Sea. Later, the Roxalans, another Sarmatian tribe, settled the land east of the Iazygians. The Sarmatians finally gained complete control of the steppe during the second century. Around 100 BCE, the Alans, the last Sarmatian tribe to arrive, controlled the steppe from the Don to the Volga and southwards over the valley of the Kuban. Meanwhile, the Scythians had fled northwards, as their burial mounds show, and pressed the Slavs north into what is now Russia.[1]

There were Greek colonies on the Black Sea from 400 BCE. The shores of what are now Bulgaria, Romania and the Crimea were richly populated and integrated with the great Asian and Levantine civilisations of the time. The Greeks called the Alans As or Asii, from whom come both the name of Asia and the ruling dynasty of Norse gods, the Æsir, as already described in chapter 8. The area of the Alans was a flourishing hub of trade and business. It lay east of the Tanakvisl (River Don). The Alans were such excellent warriors that they served as mercenaries with other tribal armies. During the second half of the second century CE, Sarmatian and Teutonic forces crossed the Danube and attacked Dacia (modern Romania). Later, around 450, Alan forces served in the Hunnish army under Attila. Finally, the Alans were overrun by the migrating Goths, who after being overrun by the Huns in 376 left their language in the area, where it was last recorded in the sixteenth century.

This western shore of the Black Sea was held by Constantinople as part of the Roman Empire and will be discussed below. The north-east of our area, roughly 30° east from Greenwich, was contacted (as we have already seen) by Swedish Vikings in 859, when they imposed tribute on the inhabitants of the area around what was to become Novgorod. In 862 they were invited back by the inhabitants to impose order amongst them. Ruric and his Swedish warriors were to protect the trading cities on the Neva and the Dnieper. They and their descendants set up bases at Novgorod and Kiev, established a trading empire, attacked the Byzantine Empire several times as well as serving as mercenaries in the Varangian (Swedish) Guard in the imperial capital, and attempted to conquer Bulgaria. The Vikings retained close contact with their Scandinavian homeland, and although they intermarried with the indigenous ruling families, the latter and their peoples remained essentially Slavic.

In 988 Prince Vladimir (980–1015) imposed Christianity on the Russians. He summoned a council of boyars to discuss the possible adoption of Judaism, Islam, Christianity or some other politically aligned religion, which would gain him useful political and trading contacts with the wider world of adherents to that faith.[2] The council was attended by priests and missionaries of various faiths. It was decided that Russia should become Orthodox Christian, but in a form based on a nationalist Russian Church. The union of Church and state in the eastern Roman Empire was so strong that a nation which adopted Christianity was also expected to accept the emperor as overlord. Political parties in Russia followed religious lines: the nationalist party was Pagan, whilst the Imperial party was Christian. Vladimir blackmailed the Byzantine emperor into giving him his sister in marriage as the price of mercenary help in the Byzantine civil war, then returned to Kiev and began the work of Christianisation. Pagan temples were demolished, and churches built on their sites. The Kievan great image of Perun was first flogged by twelve strong men and then thrown into the river, to which the entire population of the city was then marched to be forcibly baptised. Byzantine influence gave the Russians a developed system of law, art and literature, which made up for its comparative dormancy during the centuries when its western allies had been part of the Roman Empire.

In 1169, Kiev was sacked and the capital removed to Vladimir by Prince Andrew Bogliouski. Next, external politics intervened. In 1224, the Tartar invasion began. The Russian defences were routed, as were those of Moravia,

Silesia, Cracow and Pest. The Tartar forces failed to take Vienna but set up the khanate of the Golden Horde with its capital Sarai on the Lower Volga. The Russians among others were reduced to tributaries, paying a heavy poll tax from which monks and priests were, however, exempt. As a result the Russian Orthodox Church became wealthy and influential. The Tartars converted to Islam and ruled the area for two hundred years, from 1264 until the rise of Muscovy and the Turkish Empire. In 1328, the Russian Ivan Kalita (Moneybag), Grand Prince of the township of Moscow, began to act as a tax-farmer for the Tartars. He acquired a monopoly and Moscow grew strong. Kiev lost importance and the main power passed to Moscow. However, from 1315 to 1377, Kiev became Pagan again, under the Baltic pantheon. The Lithuanian leaders Gudimin and his son Olgerd conquered the area and ruled from Vilnius.[3] When in 1386 Jagellon I of Lithuania converted to Catholic Christianity in order to unite Lithuania with Poland, Lithuanian Russia, centred on what is now the Ukraine, became known as Little Russia, Baltic Russia, or White Russia.[4] Moscow saw the Poles and Lithuanians, like the Muslim Tartars, as heretics. The Tartars remained an influential power in Russia, exacting tribute well into the sixteenth century. Bishop Ján Lasicius reported attending a Tartar prayer meeting near Vilnius in 1582.[5] When Constantinople fell to the Islamic Turks in 1453, Moscow took on the role of Imperial Holy City. Ivan the Great (1462–1505) later adopted the title of Caesar (Tsar) and added the two-headed eagle of the Roman Empire to the Russian national arms.[6]

The Slavonic deities are related closely to the Baltic ones. The sky-god is Svarog. His son is the fire-deity Svarozhitsch (Svarogitch) (the holy light), sometimes identified with the sun-deity, Khors or Dazhdbog, consort of the moon-deity Myesyats and father of the stars. To the Russians, Myesyats is a goddess, but in the Ukraine (as in the Baltic), he is a god, husband of the sun-goddess. Svarog was also known as Svantovit, and was later worshipped under the guise of St Vitus. Bielbog (Byelobog), the white, bright god, is opposed by Tschernobog (Chernobog), the black god of evil. In addition, there is a god of war, Jarovit, and Domovoi (Domovik), the god of the ancestors. Perun was assimilated with the Jewish prophet Elijah. He was associated with the weather-god, Erisvorsh, and the wind-gods Stribog, Varpulis (the storm-wind) and Dogoda (the gentle west wind). In the Ukraine and Belarus, Perun is the deity of summer, contrasted with Kolyada, the god of wintertime. Krukis is the patronal deity of blacksmiths and domestic animals, whilst judgement of wrongdoing is overseen by Proven.

Janet McCrickard lists evidence for a lost solar goddess in Russian and South Slavic folklore.[7] In Russian, the name for the Sun is neuter but verbs associated with it are always conjugated in the feminine form. In traditional songs the Sun appears as a bride or maiden, the Moon as a youth, father or grandfather. McCrickard also tells a Russian story which is exactly like that of the Scandinavian god Frey and the giantess Gerd, described above in chapter 8. A young man wanders to the world's end, where there is a cottage. A young girl of dazzling radiance comes to the cottage, takes off her dress and covers herself with a sheet. Darkness falls. In the morning she gets up, puts on her shining dress and flies into the sky. Her mother calls her 'Solntse': Sun.

The three Fates (Norns, Weird Sisters) are represented in Slav religion by the Zorya: Utrennyaya, goddess of dawn; Zorya Verchernyaya, warrior-goddess of dusk; and the Goddess of Midnight. They watch the demonic god chained to the wagon of the polar night; when he escapes, the world will end. The goddess of the dead is Baba-Yaga, who resides in a hut surrounded by a bone fence with skulls on top. This reflects the bone-strewn earth-lodges of the wise women in Drenthe province, Holland, which existed until the seventeenth century, and Siberian shamanic buildings made from mammoth tusks and bones. The Russian *volkhv* (shaman) dealt with other spirits, including the Domovoi (house-sprites), Leshy (wood-spirits who lead travellers astray) and Vodanyoi, malevolent water-sprites.

The fertility goddess Kupala was revered at midsummer by ritual bathing in sacred rivers, offerings of garlands to the waters, jumping through bon-fires and the erection of a birch pole decked with ribbons. Until well into the eighteenth century, Yarilo, god of erotic sexuality, was revered. Cattle were guarded by the god Walgino. The Slav and Czech goddess Devana (Serbian Diiwica, Polish Dziewona) is, like Diana, the goddess of the hunt. The natural world is recognised in the south Russian goddess Polevoi (Polevik), the field-spirit, whose hair is green; and the related Poludnitsa, a white-clad goddess of the fields. In Poland, three gods, Datan, Lawkapatim and Tawals, guard the fields. Ovinnik, the spirit of the barn, is worshipped as a black cat.[8]

In Slovakia, the chief god was Praboh, closely associated with the goddess of life, Zivena. She was counterposed with a death-goddess, Morena. Agriculture was the realm of Uroda, goddess of the fields, and Lada, goddess of beauty. As in the rest of Europe, the thunder-god Parom was revered universally. The Bieloknazi (White Priests) served and invoked the white gods, whilst the Black Priests practised magic.[9] The Slovaks have their imagery of light and darkness in common with the Russians, whose white god and black god have already been mentioned. A similar opposition of light and darkness occurs in the contrast of the light elves and dark elves in late Scandinavian mythology, although such a stark contrast is generally foreign to Pagan pantheons, which see all forces as having their place in the natural order. The imagery of light and darkness might well be one remnant of Iranian influences which were current among the Scythian inhabitants of Russia during the last five hundred years BCE.

One branch of Finno-Ugrian speakers drove a wedge between the South Slavs of the Balkans and their kinsfolk in the north. These were the Magyars, who had been driven from their home in the Volga area to the Black Sea

Plate 10.1 Guising animal heads (*Perchtenmasken*) for midwinter ceremonies, eighteenth century, Salzburg, Austria (cf. medieval English guising). Nigel Pennick.

steppes, where they mingled with the Turks. Between the fifth and the ninth centuries they confederated as the On-Ugri (the People of the Ten Arrows), and eventually became known as the Hungarians. Boundary disputes in the Byzantine Empire in the ninth century forced them west across the steppe to the Danube provinces which had once been Dacia and Pannonia. (The old provinces of Noricum and west Pannonia had been conquered by Charlemagne from the Avars and Lombards in 799 and made into the Ostmark: Austria, the eastern boundary of the Roman Catholic dominion.) In 890 the Magyars invaded the area under their king, Arpad. Holding fast to their tribal shamanism, they made incursions into the Western Empire as far as Alsace. They were repulsed by Henry the Fowler (919–936) at Merseburg in 933 and by Otto I at Augsburg in 955, and then fell back to settle in what is now Hungary, which under them returned to Paganism.

The official conversion of the Hungarians by Frankish missionaries occurred in 997, with the first bishopric being set up in 1001 at Estergom. In 1236 King Béla IV re-established contact with the ethnic Hungarians who lived in Bashkira, near the Udmurts and Mari. Their territory was known as Greater Hungary and they were still Pagan, eating horse- and wolfmeat. The Kumans (or Pechenegs), Turkic nomads who had settled in western Siberia, arrived in Hungary in the late tenth century, after ejecting the Magyars from the latter's earlier home on the north-west shore of the Black Sea. They formed a Pagan ethnic enclave known as Little Kumania, and were taken up by the Hungarian King Ladislas IV (1272–1290) to such an extent that the Pope preached a crusade against him for favouring Paganism. Shamanic practices persisted among the Hungarians, and the traditions of the *táltos* (shaman) are recorded until the 1940s.[10] Hungary, too, is the home of a highly sophisticated Pagan art revival, far removed from the tribal shamanism of the nomads. In the year 188 an Iseum was built at Szombathely, on what was then the Norican–Pannonian border. It was enlarged in the third century, and then rebuilt in the 1950s, complete with a frieze of Isis riding on Sothis. An annual Mozart festival is held there at which *The Magic Flute* is performed. This opera, as is well known, is based on Masonic symbolism, but more generally it includes the light-and-darkness imagery of Iranian dualism, the source of the Mithraism which was so popular in this area during the last years of official Roman Paganism. Zoroastrian dualism and Egyptian syncretism lie at opposite ends of the Pagan spectrum, and yet here there is a continuity of practice, if not exactly of belief, in the preservation of a Pagan Mystery-cult.

THE BALKAN STATES

The countries south of the Danube had been part of the Hellenistic Empire of Alexander the Great and his successors. The Thracians, for example, were viewed by the Greeks rather as the late Scandinavians viewed the Lapps: as experts in atavistic magic. According to Herodotus (V.7), the only deities worshipped by the Thracians were Artemis, Dionysos and Ares. With the epithet *basilea* (queen), Artemis was worshipped by Thracian and Paionian women who brought offerings wrapped in wheat straw.[11] In fact, the Thracians worshipped other goddesses as well. Bendis was shown dressed like Artemis, as a hunting-goddess. She was honoured at Athens in the Bendideia, being described by Aristophanes as the Great Goddess, *Megalē Thea*, the Thracian Bendis, related to Artemis Brauronia, whose female devotees performed her ritual bear-dance. Devotees of the Thracian goddess Kotyto were received into her fold through baptism. Tereia, another mother-goddess, was associated with the Phrygian Kybele, and Kabyle in Thrace was one of the cult-places of Kybele.

Thracia, Moesia, Macedonia and part of Dalmatia, later to become Illyria and Dacia Ripiensis, were the Balkan provinces of the Roman Empire. As the buffer zone of the vulnerable Danube frontier they were from the third century subject to invasion by migrating Goths, Huns and others. The depredations of Alaric, the Christian Gothic leader who sacked Rome in 410, devastated the economy of northern Greece and destroyed many of its old Pagan shrines, but the Balkans proper suffered even more than Greece from nomadic invaders, both Christian and Pagan. In the sixth or seventh century this area, together with a large part of Greece, was settled by the Slavonic-speaking peoples described above, most of whom were converted to Greek Orthodox Christianity in the ninth century. Between the pressures of nomadic invasions, political machinations by the eastern and western Empires, and the subsequent occupation by the Islamic Turks, which lasted from the fifteenth to the nineteenth centuries, the Balkan states had little chance to evolve organically as nation-states. The Turks were, however, tolerant of other religions, while the leaders of these lacked the political power to enforce systematic orthodoxy among their followers, and so a varied mixture of Christian and Slavic Pagan practices has continued throughout the area until the present, as we describe below. Dual faith practices were also observed before the Turkish conquest. In 1331, in the upper Isonzo valley, on the borders of modern Slovenia and Italy, around Caporetto, the Christian Church mounted a crusade against the Slavs who retained their Paganism.[12] Later, the pan-Slavic movement in the nineteenth century, promoted by Russia in order to extend her influence in the eastern Mediterranean, actually encouraged the retrieval of the folk-practices and Pagan survivals described above.

Romania, north of the eastern Danube, was resettled after the Slavic invasion by the old Roman colonists who had fled across the river centuries before to form the province of Dacia Ripiensis. To this day Romania retains a Latin-based language. Its Pagan tradition is, however, similar to that of the West Slavs. Before communism attempted to stamp out all rural traditions during the twentieth century, the moon was venerated in Romania as the goddess Ileana Sânziana, 'queen of flowers', 'sister of the Sun'. There were spells addressed to the moon, and each new moon was hailed with the prayer:

> Moon, new moon,
> Cut the bread in two,
> And give us
> half to Thee,
> Health to me.

At certain times of year, troupes of ceremonial dancers undertook a nine-day ceremony. They visited nine boundary-points, filled a ceremonial vessel with water from nine springs, and prayed to their patron goddess Irodeasa. (Her name is presumably not original but a version of 'Herodias', the name of the wickedest woman in the Bible, often used for Pagan goddesses by Christian prelates who preached against them.) The dancers carried swords and clubs, some wore masks or blacked their faces, and they were accompanied by a hobby-horse. At the close of the ceremony on the ninth day, a sacred pole made for the duration of the rite was cast into a river.[13] The lyrical folk-songs of Romania are called *doinas*, like the Latvian *dainas*, although the bulk of Romanian language is descended from Latin.

Bulgaria, too, followed a different path from its Slavic neighbours. It had been settled after the fall of Rome by the Huns, but later invaded by Slavic migrants, who intermingled with the Hunnic inhabitants and created an aggressive, expansionist nation-state which challenged the eastern Empire based on Constantinople. In 613 Kurt, king of the Bulgars, became Christian, but the bulk of his people remained Pagan. At the beginning of the ninth century, when the Greeks were recapturing their peninsula from the Arabs, the Bulgarian King Krum, a Slavic Pagan, played one side off against the other. Eventually, in 811, he killed the eastern Emperor Nicophorus in battle, displayed the latter's head in the usual fashion, and then had the skull plated with silver and used as a drinking vessel. Krum died in 814, and the Bulgarians adopted Christianity some fifty years later, after a naval blockade by the Greeks. Between 889 and 893, King Vladimir of Bulgaria returned to Paganism, but afterwards his brother Simeon the Great restored Christianity as part of his programme to establish Bulgaria as an up-to-date civilised state which could (and did) challenge Constantinople. It was due to Simeon's machinations that the Magyars were driven westwards to found Hungary.

Initially, the Balkan states had adopted official Christianity in the seventh century, at the same time as the other barbarian-invaded extremities of the Roman Empire. Bulgaria was joined in 640 by Serbia which adopted the Orthodox rite, but Slavonia (part of what is now Croatia) was only converted in 864, after the Slavs had replaced the Avar conquerors of the sixth century. In that year the missionaries Cyril and Methodius arrived from Constantinople and created an alphabet that was adequate to the Slavonic languages in order to translate the Bible. This became known as the Cyrillic script and spread throughout the Slavonic Orthodox churches. Moravia was converted by Cyril and Methodius in 863 and Bulgaria once again in 864. Cyril and Methodius had arrived in Constantinople as emissaries of Rome to the eastern Empire, since the schism between the two was foreshadowed in that decade. They were sent initially to convert the Turkic Khazars of the Crimea, so that religious ties would bind these more closely to the Empire than the political ties of pure self-interest which were at the time being undermined by their newly arrived neighbours, the Pagan Rus of Kiev. Once more, religious change was a by-product of political manoeuvring. The conversion of Little Russia in 988 can likewise be seen as a move in the game between Kiev and Constantinople for influence over Bulgaria and the mouth of the Hellespont.

THE BYZANTINE EMPIRE

In Constantinople itself, the process of Christianisation had from the start been heavily influenced by Pagan philosophical thought. Among the governing classes, Pagan ideals of human virtue and public duty remained operative, and among the educated classes, open Paganism continued in places until the end of the sixth century.[14] The Greek *paideia* (education) was as essential a part of a young person's upbringing as education is today, and rather as, say, the modern Icelandic literary corpus contains the ancient tales of the Norse divinities and their Pagan followers, so the *paideia* of early Christian society contained the myths, history and philosophy of a Pagan age. At the same time, uneducated working people still believed in wonder-workers and demigods, and the cult of saints was easily grafted onto this outlook.[15] A transcendental, mystical outlook which had much in common with Neoplatonism was adopted into Christian theology, and the doctrine of theosis, 'that God was made man so that man might become God [by mystical contemplation]', became a central part of Orthodox belief and practice. In the fourth century, Saints Basil and Gregory rejected the conception of (what they rather unfairly called) 'a narrow Jewish godhead' and allowed the divine presence to be celebrated in a wealth of art and ceremony. Mystical schemata such as the *Celestial Hierarchies*, attributed to St Paul's disciple Dionysius the Areopagite but actually written in the early sixth century, became part of official doctrine at a time when the analogous system of Jewish Cabbala, itself probably derived from Neoplatonism (see above, p.51), was still the pursuit of a heretical minority.[16]

Indeed, some Pagan ceremonies seem to have been retained in Greece with little or no alteration. The ninth-century patriarch Photius described one such at Thebes, the Daphnephoria:

> They wreathe a pole of live wood with laurel and various flowers. On the top is fitted a bronze globe, from which they suspend smaller ones. Midway down the pole they place a smaller globe, binding it with purple fillets – but the end of the pole is decked with saffron. By the topmost globe they mean the sun, which they actually compare with Apollo. The globe beneath is the moon: the smaller globes hung on are the stars and constellations, and the fillets are the course of the year – for they make them 365 in number ... The *Daphnephorus* himself holds onto the laurel, he has his hair hanging loose, he wears a golden wreath and is dressed out in a splendid robe to his feet and he wears light shoes. There follow him a chorus of maidens, holding out boughs before them to enforce the supplication of the hymns.[17]

At the time of the attacks by Islamic invaders, however, the Christian Church in Constantinople went through an iconoclastic period. From 726 to 787 and from 813 to 843, the eastern Empire was officially without graven images, and some orgies of puritanical destruction followed. The images, together with the cults of the saints and the Virgin, had previously been accepted rather ambivalently by the Church authorities as the ill-fitting relic of Paganism which, of course, they were. During the iconoclastic controversies, the opposing camps were renamed and the iconoclasts, the one-time party of Christian orthodoxy, became dismissed as 'Saracen-minded', those in favour of icons being known as 'Hellenophiles'. The restoration of the images in 843 was accompanied by great Christian rejoicing and was marked by an annual celebration, the Feast of Orthodoxy. Thus, ironically, Pagan practices were reintroduced in order to distinguish Christianity from Islam.

J.C. Robertson, in volume V of his *A History of the Christian Church*, reported an actual Pagan reconversion by a professor at the court of the Emperor Alexius Comnenus (acc. 1081). An Italian called John, a professor of Classical literature at Constantinople, began to teach the transmigration of souls, and the Platonic doctrine of Ideas. One of his disciples, according to Robertson, is said to have thrown himself into the sea, exclaiming 'Receive me, O Poseidon!'. The professor himself was eventually persuaded to 'renounce his errors', and Christian order was restored.

The Byzantine Empire reached its widest extent in 1023. It encompassed all of Asia Minor, Cyprus, Crete, half of the Levant, the southern Crimea, Greece and the mainland from the rivers Danube to Drava, plus eastern Sicily and southern Italy, that is, the old Magna Graecia. Shortly afterwards the western Church separated itself doctrinally from the eastern Church, and the two Empires should have gone their separate ways. However, the first Crusade, in 1096, reunited them against the Arabic conquerors of the old Roman province of Palestine. Nevertheless, the fourth Crusade of 1204, which was diverted by the western forces to conquer Constantinople, conveniently for Venetian trading interests, eventually consolidated the breach between the two halves of the old Empire. Meanwhile, a new enemy had arisen in the east. In the last decade of the tenth century, the Turks moved out from Turkestan in search of conquest. They embraced Islam and so added a religious crusade to their territorial ambitions. By 1360 they had north-west Asia Minor, or Turkey as it now became, and a toehold on the mainland at Gallipoli. They consolidated, expanded and, in 1453, captured Constantinople itself. The eastern Christian Empire passed to Moscow, and by 1648 Turkey had all of North Africa, the Levant, Mesopotamia, Asia Minor, Greece and the Balkans, part of Austria, Hungary, Romania and the Crimea. The old eastern Roman Empire had been captured and even extended (north of the Danube) by the new Ottoman Empire. The Crimean territories were eventually lost to Muscovite Russia in the late eighteenth century, and Greece became independent in 1832. In the late nineteenth century, with the pan-Slavic movement, the territories either side of the Danube were lost, followed by north Africa and the southern Balkans. After the First World War, Mesopotamia and the Levant became independent, leaving Turkey in possession only of Asia Minor, Constantinople and the latter's hinterland.

The centuries of Turkish rule had frozen south-eastern Europe in a pre-industrial but ideologically neutral state, where Pagan traditions were preserved in Christian belief and accommodated to the *realpolitik* of a tolerant but officially Islamic state. In 1892, when Greece and the Balkans were independent, a British officer in Greece, Renell Rodd, described many Pagan survivals which were actively continued at the time. He described how each household in even the rudest peasant village had its icon shrine, often with a perpetual flame burning before it: 'It will be solemnly borne away to the new dwelling if the family change quarters, like the household gods of the olden time; and should the little lamp go out upon the road, it would be held to forbode some grave misfortune.'[18] The renaming of ancient deities as saints has continued in Greece as elsewhere in Europe. Cults of St Eleutherios replace that of Eileithyia, goddess of childbirth, and at least one church of the

193

Virgin of Fecundity is built on the site of an ancient temple of this goddess.[19] Shrines of Demeter are replaced by churches of St Demetrios, and the twelve Apostles are invoked in ancient temples of the Twelve Gods. It was St Dionysios to whom the nineteenth-century Cretans ascribed the introduction of the grape, and St Paul who was credited with Herakles' ancient achievement of expelling the snakes from Crete. Votive offerings are given to the Christian icons of the domestic shrines as they were once given to the ancient deities in their public temples, and as late as the 1890s, the sacrifice of a lamb or a fowl would be blessed by the local Christian priest at the foundation ceremony of any new building.[20]

The local saint's day in each Greek village or city was called a *paneguris*, the same word as the ancient *panegyria*, a solemn coming together of all the people. In Athens the ancient Anthestereia, the so-called 'flower festival' which was actually a feast of the dead, was replaced by the medieval and modern 'feast of roses', the Rousalia, held on Easter Tuesday. Rodd reports that the modern Rousalia was also celebrated elsewhere in Greece at the feast of All Souls, this time explicitly in memory of the dead.[21] At the ancient Anthestereia, the casks of new wine were broached; interestingly, the Greek word *anthos* (flower), like the modern Spanish word *flor*, also refers to the yeast that forms on the top of weak or old wine. The feast could thus be seen as a celebration of the flowering of new life from the detritus of decay. In the modern rose festival, Renell Rodd reports, a song was sung, wishing goodwill to the community's children, and the male children were then lifted three times into the air with prayers that, in the words of another flower metaphor, they should flourish. This strange continuation of an ancient festival, itself apparently a garbled form of an even earlier original, was already dying out by Renell Rodd's time.[22]

In ancient times, the sky-god Zeus was seen as the cause of rain. In modern times, '[The] god is raining' is still a common turn of phrase. Old Poseidon, known as 'Earth-shaker', a principal god of the Minoan-Mycenean pantheon, seems to survive in the saying on the island of Zante, describing an earthquake: '[The] god is shaking his hair'. In ancient times the Furies were propitiated as the Eumenides, the Kindly Ones; in the nineteenth century it was smallpox which was personified as 'Eulogia': 'the kindly spoken one'. Charon, the mythical boatman who in ancient times was thought to carry souls across the River Styx, metamorphosed in modern Greece into Charos, an ill-wishing herald of death similar in function to the Etruscan Charun. But, unlike the latter, Charos appears as a grave and dignified old man dressed in black, and even, in a fresco on Mount Athos, as a skeleton with a scythe over his shoulder, like the Anglo-Saxon Old Father Time.[23] A widespread fear of vampires and the unquiet dead in modern popular culture might be attributed to Slavic influences, but as we saw in chapter 1, such a belief and the expiatory sacrifices which went with it were also present in ancient times. In the nineteenth century, most places still had their *stoikheion* or *genius loci* (such as the one that was propitiated by foundation-sacrifice). In particular, large or ancient trees had their spirit-guardian, which would be ceremonially shunned at the moment of felling the tree. And as in other parts of Europe, household snakes were venerated until modern times. In present-day Istanbul, the ancient Constantinople, Pierre Chuvin reports continuing widespread veneration of the spirit of place. Holy spots such as tombs and trees are surreptitiously decorated with ribbons or honoured with candles; springs have coins thrown into them and votive plaques are attached to structures above ground, despite notices at the sites explicitly forbidding these practices in the name of Islam.[24]

Many archaic Greek folk-beliefs and domestic practices thus seem to have survived in surprisingly unchanged form into the modern age. Public religion, too, has persisted by translation into the cult of saints, the persistence of festival dates and practices, and the continuity of sacred sites. Some of the ancient beliefs themselves passed at an early stage into the form of Christianity which took root in the eastern Empire, and the mystical inheritance of Neoplatonism in particular distinguishes Orthodox belief from its Catholic neighbour. But quite apart from the unacknowledged or discreetly assimilated survivals of Paganism which we have now seen from all over Europe, the articulated and explicit legacy of the ancient civilisations has also passed into mainstream European culture. It is to this reawakening that we now turn in the final chapter.

11

PAGANISM REAFFIRMED

The High Medieval period (950–1350), as we have seen in the earlier chapters, saw the militant monotheistic religions, Christianity and Islam, imposing their influence on the rulers of Europe, so that the official religions of the emerging kingdoms and empires became monotheistic and in practice androtheistic, referring to their supreme deity only in the masculine gender. We have also seen Pagan practices and beliefs continuing here and there, unnoticed by official sanctions, and also being incorporated into Christian practice as this developed. In that sense the Pagan outlook and deities remained, shaped the form of Christian society which overlay them, and were available as a living tradition to be recognised and reclaimed by later investigators in an age of independent thought. In Islamic areas of Europe, the situation was different. Islamic doctrine did not compromise with Pagan values (indeed, the famous 'Satanic verses' of the Koran were almost immediately repudiated by Mohammed as an attempt by the Devil to incorporate the three goddesses of Mecca in the celestial hierarchy), and Islam remained militantly anti-polytheist.

In Christian lands, the High Middle Ages were the crusading years. Christian dualism, never far beneath the surface of its official monotheism, was first turned against the Islamic conquerors of Palestine, then against its Pagan neighbours in the Baltic, and then against alleged heretics, infidels and apostates within its own jurisdiction. The persecution of the Jews in Europe intensified noticeably in extent after the eleventh century,[1] but its origins stem from the formative age of the Christian religion, in which early Church leaders regularly defamed Jews, Pagans and Christians of other sects. The prototypical defamer is St John the Divine, who wrote of Jesus telling those Jews who did not believe in him: 'Ye are of your father the devil' (John 8.44). In his *Expository Treatise against the Jews*, Hippolytus (170–236) wrote that the Jews were 'darkened, unable to see the true light'. Origen (185–254) called the Jews 'a most wicked nation', and said that they had suffered rightly through rejecting Jesus of Nazareth. Gregory of Nyssa (331–396) called Jews 'slayers of the Lord', 'advocates of the Devil' and 'haters of righteousness'. Chrysostom's *Eight Homilies against the Jews* claimed that 'The Jews sacrifice

Plate 11.1 Medieval dancers in animal guise. Folk-dance all over Europe continues this and similar traditions of Pagan sacred dance. Victorian engraving after MS. Bodl. 264, Fl. 21 V. Nideck Picture Collection.

their children to Satan . . . they are worse than wild beasts . . . The synagogue is a curse'. His most notorious piece of anti-Semitism continued: 'I hate the Jews, because they violate the Law. I hate the synagogue, because it has the Law and the Prophets. It is a duty of all Christians to hate the Jews.' In the year 414, the Patriarch Cyril instigated religious riots in Alexandria which led to the murder of all Jews who could not escape. The defamatory propaganda of those early times was institutionalised in the Church, periodically being brought out to attack Jews and Pagans. The purpose of this book is not to detail the history of the Witch-, Jew- and Gypsy-hunts, but their contemporary justification was given in these doctrines promulgated by the polemicists of late antiquity.

By the mid-fourteenth century, a small but significant Pagan influence was entering Europe from abroad. The modern Gypsies appear to be the descendants of people who migrated westwards from India at some time in the twelfth century. In 1322, two Franciscan priests on pilgrimage to Palestine reported cave-dwelling Gypsies near Candia, Crete. By 1348, *Cingarije* were in Serbia. Gypsies entered central Europe in the early fifteenth century; they were in Hildesheim, Germany, in 1407, at Zürich in 1419, and in France in 1421. Like the Jews, the Gypsies suffered appalling persecution for racial–religious reasons. They were persecuted wherever they went in Europe, often being killed, or sold into slavery. In 1370, forty Gypsy families in Wallachia, Romania, were taken prisoner and given as slaves to the monastery of St Anthony at Voditza.[2] In 1530, it was a capital offence to be a Gypsy in England, and in 1665 Gypsies were deported from Edinburgh to be slaves in the West Indies.[3] In Romania, they suffered slavery until 1856.

In addition to the racist fear of their dark skins, their Pagan beliefs and practices made the Gypsies the butt of persecution. Signs were erected on the roads into Bohemia, showing Gypsies being tortured and hanged, with the slogan, *Straff die Heiden* ('Punish the Pagans'). In Holland, Gypsies were also called *Heiden*, and *Heidenjachten* (Pagan-hunts) were instituted to exterminate them. Until the eighteenth century, periodic *Heidenjachten* were conducted as joint operations using infantry, cavalry and police. In sixteenth- and seventeenth-century Switzerland, laws sought to exterminate the Gypsies. They were made outlaws, so that anyone encountering them should kill them. Gypsy-hunts were instituted, and a 1646 Ordinance of the city of Berne gave anyone the right to 'personally kill or liquidate by bastinado or firearms' Gypsies and *Heiden*. In 1661, the Elector Georg II passed the death penalty on all Gypsies in Saxony, and hunted them with cavalry. Later, in 1721 the Emperor Charles VI ordered the extermination of the Gypsies, and in 1725 Frederick William I condemned any Gypsy over eighteen caught in his lands to be hanged. Gypsy-hunting continued in Denmark until 1835. The twentieth century has seen no end to their persecution. Early in the Second World War, all Gypsies in England and France were arrested and put into prison camps,[4] where they remained until 1948. All Gypsies in the Third Reich were taken to Auschwitz in 1943, where, it is estimated, between 250,000 and 300,000 of them died. Internal passports for Gypsies were compulsory in France until 1970.[5]

Many internal crusades were preached and practised within Christendom, some of which we have already seen, but one other deserves mention here. In 1208 Pope Innocent III, a ruthless and efficient systematiser, preached a crusade against the Cathars of southern France, a group of Christians who held overtly dualist beliefs and who were more influential in the politics of the area than the officials of the Roman Church. As a result of the crusade, the economic and cultural infrastructure of this prosperous and civilised area, which had preserved a version of the Roman way of life from five hundred years before despite the alternation of Catholic, Arian and eventually Saracen rulers, was destroyed. At the same time, the Inquisition was created. In 1233, one Dominic Guzman was given charge of an order of monks to inquire into the remnants of heretical belief in the area. His order, the Dominicans, soon took over all the other 'inquisitions' in the Papal jurisdiction, and the perennial search for doctrinal correctness found itself with teeth. Over the next two centuries, the Inquisition gradually gained the power to suspend many of the normal processes of law, with the result that it became difficult for a suspect, once accused, to be acquitted. At this time, the beginning of the modern age, the western Church was desperately trying to standardise belief against the background of an increasing influx of information from different cultures and from the processes of rational thought itself. People who, to modern eyes, are as varied as scientists, sorcerers and freethinking reformers of Christianity itself, all fell under suspicion as opponents of true belief.

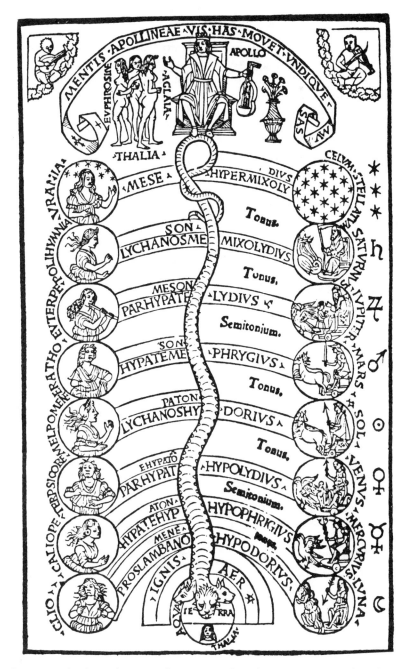

Plate 11.2 The divine harmony, from Luc Gafurius' *Practica musice*, 1496, showing Pagan divinities and cosmology in a Renaissance context. Nideck Picture Collection.

RENAISSANCE REASSERTION OF PAGAN VALUES

At the same time that doctrinaire Christianity was being enforced, however patchily, in the west, a resurgence of humanist classicism began to reinstate the Pagan goddesses and gods of European antiquity. The influx of Greek philosophy from Arab sources in Spain had already revolutionised academic thought in the universities, and many clerics were overawed by the art as well as the learning of the ancient world. Most notoriously, the pursuit of 'reason', argument from first principles, was opposed to that of 'authority', the literal adherence to the writings of the Church fathers, by the twelfth century. A different application of independent thought, the development of experimental method, was pursued by Roger Bacon and the Franciscans of Oxford a century later, although it became a casualty of the reimposition of theological dogma at Oxford following the anathematisation of Lollardy (John Wyclif, 1324–1384). In Italy, however, the rich laity had wealth and peace enough to take up the pursuit of letters, and Classical texts began to be re-examined in abundance. Symbolic goddesses and gods reasserted their place, for example Minerva, the goddess of crafts and learning, who replaced the medieval abstraction Sapientia. Christine de Pizan (1365–c.1430), the feminist author, began her heraldic treatise with an invocation to Minerva:

> O Minerva, goddess of arms and chivalry, who by virtue of understanding far surpassing other women discovered and established the use of forging iron and steel among other noble arts . . . Adored lady and high goddess, do not be displeased that I, a simple little woman, who am as nothing compared to the greatness of your famed learning, should undertake now to speak of such a magnificent enterprise as that of arms.[6]

The Tempietto Malatestiano at Rimini was designed by Leon Battista Alberti, and built in 1450 as a temple of victory for Sigismondo Malatesta, soldier, patron of the arts and enemy of the Pope. At the court of Rimini, 'recourse to Pagan gods', quite openly, was noted.[7] The Pagan iconography, probably devised by Basinio da Parma and Roberto Valturio, and executed by Agostino di Duccio and others, is expressed in several thematic chapels inspired by 'the most hidden secrets of philosophy'.[8] The Cappella dei Pianeti contains the planetary deities and the signs of the zodiac. The Cappella delle Arti Liberali enshrines Greek divinities, whilst in the Cappella degli Antenati, Jewish and Sibylline forerunners of Christianity are presented. Finally, in the Cappella di Sigismondo, the radiant Sun is thematic, representing the Apollo/Christ concept. It was condemned by Pope Pius II as full of Pagan images, and for this, Malatesta was excommunicated.[9] At Pienza, town improvements by Federico de Montefelto after the year 1455 included a church and a temple. This temple, the Tempietto delle Muse (Chapel of the Muses) reflected the church, providing equal veneration for the Christian and Pagan world-views.

In 1453 the capital of the eastern Roman Empire, Constantinople, fell to the Ottoman Turks, who then placed Greece, the Balkans and the Danube area under Islamic rule. (Internal strife within Christianity had ensured that the Catholics in the west refused to support their Orthodox co-religionists in the east.) Fleeing scholars brought Classical texts to the west, and later on the Ottomans set up a trade in these manuscripts with western scholars. One cardinal is said to have returned from a trip with nine hundred codices. The philosophical thought of the ancient world began to exert an influence on western ethics, with Ciceronian *humanitas*, civilised, humane behaviour, competing with Christian humility as a personal ideal, and the Pagan appreciation of beauty and excellence in the manifest world challenging the Christian contempt for the flesh. Lorenzo de Medici, ruler of Florence, even set up a Platonic Academy with philosophical discussion, art and music. The Renaissance ideal of the gentleman as a cultivated person, skilled in the arts and in letters, grew up in Italy at this time, as a deliberate continuation of the outlook of antiquity. It had nothing to do with Christianity, and it was seen by most people as something independent of and transcending religious affiliation. Hence atheism and humanism were also fruits of the Renaissance, although in antiquity, as we have seen, the corresponding outlooks were understood simply as philosophical refinements of the religion followed more crudely by the masses.

Representations of Classical antiquity referred to the accumulated wisdom of the ancient Pagan world, of which the Renaissance was the heir. Pagan themes appeared in art. Raphael's *The School of Athens* (1508–1511) in the Vatican is a prime example. Images of Pagan gods and goddesses began to reappear in public, especially as bronzes on fountains. Between 1567 and 1570, the doyen of bronze-masters, Giovanni de Bologna, created several fine Pagan deities, including the Hercules fountain at Bologna, Oceanus at the Boboli gardens and a fine Neptune in Florence. Soon, images of Pagan divinities spread outside Italy. An early example is the Hercules fountain in Augsburg made in 1602 by Bologna's disciple Adriaen de Vries. In central Europe, Pagan deities replaced the earlier popular figures of St George as a presiding spirit of fountains. The re-emergence of goddesses and, less emphatically, gods, was universal, in areas both under Catholic and Protestant rule. For example, at the restoration of King Charles II in 1660, the new coinage bore images of Britannia, goddess of Britain, as had not been done since Roman times. Later, the patriotic hymn, *Rule, Britannia*, was written, invoking goddess/nation. Elsewhere, other images of national goddesses emerged. A statue of the goddess of the land, Virtembergia, stood on top of Schloss Solitude, near Stuttgart, built in 1767 as a residence of the rulers of Württemberg.

In addition to their reappearance on a national level, Pagan deities began to adorn the gardens of private palaces and mansions. Some owners even added overtly Pagan temples, which often are ignored by students

Plate 11.3 Poseidon-fountain, Heidelberg, Germany. © 1993 Nigel Pennick.

of religion. The prime example of this is at Schwetzingen near Worms in Germany. Whenever a Christian chapel was erected by a landowner, then it is assumed to be authentic. Yet comparable Pagan temples are not. Space does not allow an analysis of the literature of this period, yet from it we can be certain that the ancient Pagan spirit of temple-in-landscape was understood and used properly by the landscape gardeners of the period. In his *Ichnographica Rustica* (1718–1742), the gardener Stephen Switzer (*c.*1682–1745) gave the rules for the location of images of the Pagan deities in gardens:

> *Jupiter* and *Mars* should possess the largest Open Centres and Lawns of a grand Design, elevated upon Pedestal Columnial, and other Architectonical Works . . . *Neptune* should possess the Centre of the greatest Body of Water . . . *Venus* ought to be placed among the *Graces, Cupid, &c.* And in all the lesser Centres of a Polygonar Circumscription, it would be proper to place *Apollo* with the *Muses* in the Niches . . . Then *Vulcan* with the *Cyclops* in a Centre of less note, and all the Deities dispers'd in their particular Places and Order.

Often, as at Stuttgart, the divinity was envisioned as guardian of the landscape. An enormous Hercules stands on top of a hill near Kassel, approached by a straight road that serves as the axis for the palace of the Elector, and one of the main streets of the city. The re-emergence of Pagan deities was not confined to those of the Classical pantheon. John Michael Rysbrack carved a set of the seven Saxon deities of the days of the week, commissioned by Lord Cobham in the late 1720s for his gardens at Stowe.

THE REFORMATION AND ITS EFFECTS

The reform movements within Catholicism which crystallised into the Protestant Reformation in the early sixteenth century brought about a desire for simplicity of ritual and belief which rejected many of the compromises which the Church had made with Pagan practice. The veneration of the Virgin Mary and of the saints, the use of images and of incense, and the marking of holy sites (cf. the Roman *loca sacra* and *loca religiosa*) with crosses and

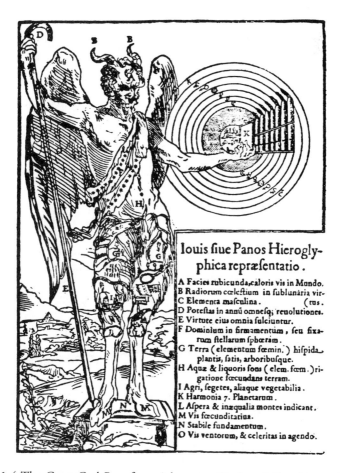

Iouis fiue Panos Hierogly-
phica repræfentatio.

A Facies rubicunda, caloris vis in Mundo.
B Radiorum cœleftium in fublunaria vir-
C Elementa mafculina.   (tus.
D Poteftas in annū omnefq; reuolutiones.
E Virtute eius omnia fulciuntur.
F Dominium in firmamentum, feu fixa-
   rum ftellarum fphæram.
G Terra (elementum fœmin.) hifpida
   plantis, fatis, arboribufque.
H Aquæ & liquoris fons (elem. fœm.) ri-
   gatione fœcundans terram.
I Agri, fegetes, aliaque vegetabilia.
K Harmonia 7. Planetarum.
L Afpera & inæqualia montes indicant.
M Vis fœcunditaria.
N Stabile fundamentum.
O Vis ventorum, & celeritas in agendo.

Plate 11.4 The Great God Pan, from Athanasius Kircher. A Renaissance image of Pan as the embodiment of Nature. Nideck Picture Collection.

wayside shrines, disappeared under Protestant influence. Traditional practices such as Maying, carolling, wassailing, and the many Pagan practices incorporated into Christmas celebrations, were also attacked. Under the Puritan rule of the Long Parliament in England and Wales (1642–1653), most of the permanent Maypoles in the towns and villages were destroyed. Not all of these sites and practices were restored when a more tolerant attitude returned towards the end of the seventeenth century.

The Reformation did, however, have one unexpectedly helpful effect on the preservation of Pagan continuity. By insisting on the use of the vernacular language in religious practice, Protestant missionaries preserved languages which had been on the verge of dying out, especially in the Baltic lands, and so unintentionally allowed the preservation of traditional tales and songs, which remained alive as part of the corpus of vernacular usage. These were reclaimed from time to time as part of nationalist movements, and the great nineteenth-century movement of nationalist revival saw them collected and recited by educated people in an effort to arouse a spirit of national identity. If the native languages had not been revivified by Protestant reformers in the sixteenth century, most of the information in their oral traditions would have been lost for ever.

A FALSE TRAIL: THE GREAT WITCH-HUNT

It has become a commonplace in modern Paganism that the hunting of alleged witches, which became widespread between about 1480 and about 1650, was a deliberate persecution of surviving Pagans and that it claimed some eight or nine million victims. The figure of nine million appears to have been suggested in the 1950s by Cecil Williamson, proprietor of the witchcraft museum on the Isle of Man, who erected a monument to that effect.[10] Modern estimates from careful archival research put the number at a maximum of 100,000 executions,[11] and some estimates are considerably lower.[12] The accused witches were victims of a new belief about a satanic conspiracy to subvert Christendom, prevalent among the intellectuals of the time. When unsophisticated folk accused their neighbours, as they occasionally did, of harmful magic and ill-wishing, the lawyers and clerics were all too ready to step in and transform the proceedings into an investigation into the supposed satanic conspiracy. Confessions and accusations were obtained by torture, and at times scores of people were executed. 'The place of execution looked like a small wood from the number of the stakes', wrote one observer of a trial at Wolfenbüttel in Brunswick in 1590.[13] Yet the trials were unevenly distributed both in time and in location. Communities could go for years without disturbance and then suddenly succumb to a bout of witch mania. Some countries were barely touched by the persecution at all, but others, such as Scotland and Germany, executed thousands of presumably innocent victims. The research so far indicates that few of the accused witches were practising harmful magic and that none of them at all were practising diabolic anti-Christianity.[14] However, in some of the cases in Scandinavia and in the eastern German territories, where magical Pagan religion had continued, such magical practices may well have been the cause of the initial accusations. In Iceland this was certainly the case. The use of runes was defined as witchcraft and made illegal in 1639,[15] and the surviving Icelandic grimoires show a mixture of Pagan and Christian terminologies, used with the classical magical intention of commanding the spirits invoked rather than of becoming the servant of the Devil in the way imagined by the Inquisitorial theorists of the mainland.[16] Cases on the mainland, however, involved accusations of diabolic pact and were generally levelled against innocent people. Only on the fringes of Europe did the Great Witch-hunt attack Pagan magic as such.

As we have already seen, the western Church stepped up its attacks on unorthodox thought by increasing the powers of the Inquisition. Until 1480, everyday magic of the sort we have seen prohibited by the early Christian bishops and the Anglo-Saxon kings, and described in the Norse sagas, was seen as outside the remit of the Inquisition. It was seen as foolishness, not heresy. But in 1480, a papal bull specifically stated that harmful magic, *maleficium* or witchcraft, was now to be seen as heresy and thus to come under the scrutiny of the Inquisition. This was because it was now said to involve a pact with the Devil. The increased practice of learned magic among the intelligentsia, sparked off by texts coming from the eastern Mediterranean via the Arabs in Spain, in Palestine and on the Mediterranean islands, had alerted the attention of the western Church hierarchy to what seemed to be deliberate commerce with demons. The image of magic as a diabolic pact spread down the social scale, until even the simplest peasant curse or baleful glance could be interpreted as an expression of satanic power.[17] The nature of the pact changed, too, in the eyes of the accusers. The Christian ceremonial magicians of the thirteenth century claimed (and were perceived) to be compelling fallen and inferior spirits by the power of their magical art. But by the fifteenth century they were deemed to have sold their souls to the Devil in exchange for material benefits and latterly for none at all: that is, to have sold themselves into slavery.[18] The diabolic witch, as imagined by the inquisitors, had sold herself into the Devil's power for no particular benefit. This may give a clue as to why it was women more than men who were accused of the new-style diabolic conspiracy. Not only are women more often accused (in all communities, worldwide) of spontaneous harmful magic, but in the misogynistic view of the early modern Church, only women would be stupid or weak or naturally slavish enough to give their power away to a malign spirit in exchange for no benefit to themselves. The fact that the Great Witch-hunt was primarily a hunting of women seems not to have been an expression but a result of the misogyny of the time. It was not a deliberate attack on women as such, but an attack on devils, with the assumption that the only human beings stupid enough to be taken in by these enemies of humankind were, naturally, women.

So much for the conclusions of modern research. The modern Pagan myth which is challenged by them stems from the romantic perceptions of the nineteenth century. This is when the arts and crafts movement began, together with the collection of folk-tales, traditional songs and dances, as well as nationalistic political movements fuelled by images of ethnic purity. The educated, newly emancipated middle classes saw the old vernacular ways disappearing around them and romanticised their significance, filled with nostalgia for a certainty (previously seen, pejoratively, as simplicity) which was rapidly fading. For some reason which has not been satisfactorily explained, some commentators saw the indigenous European religion as persisting among those accused of witchcraft three hundred years before. 'The witches' sabbath may be explained as an esoteric form of those pagan fertility rites which survived in Western Europe centuries after the official introduction of Christianity', wrote Arno Runeberg in 1947.[19] Runeberg, like two of the nineteenth-century theorists, in fact came from the north-east of Europe, where, as we have seen, the local religion took a more overtly magical form than elsewhere and was influential long after it had been assimilated into Christianity, relegated to folk-tradition, or reasserted as an aristocratic enthusiasm in the rest of Europe. Karl-Ernst Jarcke, professor of criminal law at the University of Berlin, argued in 1828 that the people accused in a local witch-trial had actually been followers of the old Germanic religion. In 1839, the archivist Franz-Joseph Mone of Baden proposed that the orgiastic features of the alleged witch-cult had in fact been part of an underground religion derived from Dionysiac worship in the Greek colonies on the Black Sea and brought back to Germany by the returning Goths. A version of the theory even reached popular culture. Mendelssohn's choral work *Die Erste Walpurgisnacht* (1832) described a traditional May Eve (30 April) celebration, where the village folk, under attack from local Christians, pretended to be witches in order to frighten their opponents away. And Runeberg, of Helsinki, produced in the twentieth century a wonderfully detailed study of Norse, Finnic and more distant magical religions, arguing that the supposed witch-cult was in fact a mutation of heretical Catharism and indigenous folk-magic. These thinkers drew attention to their regional heritage, but unfortunately failed to demonstrate by reference to contemporary records that any of the people accused had actually taken part in either 'witchcraft' ceremonies or ceremonies of a continuing Pagan religion. As we have seen, modern research tends to argue against these conclusions.

The most famous interpreter of diabolic witchcraft as a Pagan survival was, however, Professor Margaret Murray (1863–1963), an Egyptologist who first became interested in the European witch-trials when she was over sixty. Her conclusions, published in *The Witch Cult in Western Europe* (1921) and *The God of the Witches* (1933), were criticised at the time by archivists such as

C. L'Estrange Ewen, who had actually looked at the evidence of the trials, but it was not until Norman Cohn's definitive study, published in 1975 as *Europe's Inner Demons*, that the soundness of her arguments was generally questioned. Murray had quoted from evidence taken from defendants at the witch-trials, cutting out what she presumably thought was the irrelevant accreta, invented under torture, and leaving in what she thought was the bare bones of truthful evidence, the description of ritual celebrations and feasts presided over by a man known as the Devil. But as Cohn demonstrates, the passages omitted contain fantastic details such as shape-shifting, flying through the air, making rideable horses out of straw and so on, which cast doubt on the truth of anything else claimed in those confessions. Now these are the sort of feats which were and are claimed by sorcerers in shamanic Pagan communities, e.g. the Lapps' 'magic ride to Iceland' on behalf of the Norwegian, Ingimund, and it is quite possible that people who really followed a magical religion might have confessed to such apparent impossibilities and thought they were telling the truth. Arno Runeberg, for example, takes such 'fantasticall detailes' in his stride. Why did Margaret Murray leave them out? The most plausible answer is that she deliberately distorted her evidence.

Why should she have done so? Norman Cohn argues that Murray, together with the other authors mentioned, was driven simply by a deep personal need to believe in the continuation of Pagan religion, or perhaps more in its persecution by representatives of a hated modernity, and so created 'evidence' to prove their case. But in fact, no more evidence was needed to prove the continuation of Pagan customs and attitudes. The work of Sir James Frazer, which influenced Margaret Murray and Arno Runeberg deeply, as well as that of the many other nineteenth-century researchers, had already provided that. What Runeberg wrongly assumed and what Murray seems to have selected her evidence to 'prove', was the existence of a priesthood, a Pagan ministry which actively opposed the official religion of Christianity. And this the alleged witches never were. After the Baltic crusades, there was no organised Pagan resistance to Christianity in the west. What did remain was a continuation of Pagan attitudes and of local objects of veneration, and what arose independently was an affirmation among educated people of ancient Pagan civilisation and, among some, of its presiding deities. The witch-hunt was succeeded by the age of rationality, and during that intellectually secure period, the Pagan priesthoods began to be reinstated.

THE AGE OF REASON AND THE RE-EMERGENCE OF THE PRIESTHOODS

The witch persecution nevertheless marked a watershed in western European history. It coincided with the Reformation and has been seen as a side-effect of the latter, but perhaps more significantly it coincided with the emergence of rationalism, the freeing of the human spirit from the 'uncanny bonds' of superstition which, so it was thought, had held it in check. The freethinking of the Reformation can itself be seen as an expression of the independence of rational thought. The witch-hunt was seen by rationalist thinkers, probably correctly, as a last outburst of irrationality, both on the part of Protestant-inclined zealots who wanted to abolish the second component of the 'popery-and-superstition' complex, and also of Catholic-inclined ones who wanted to affirm its first component. The ordinary people who habitually accused their neighbours of ill-wishing were simply freed by changes in the law from the swingeing penalties which until the late fifteenth century had threatened accusers who failed to prove their case,[20] and so denunciation was able to proceed unhindered. The persecution died down at the end of the seventeenth century because rational society no longer believed in witchcraft, and many countries passed laws which declared as much.

The rise of the mathematical sciences in the sixteenth and seventeenth centuries led to a new and self-confident belief in humankind's power over Nature. No longer did gamblers have to doff their caps to the caprices of Dame Fortune. They could now calculate their chances through the mathematical calculus of probability. Astronomers could calculate eclipses and planetary positions, ballistics experts could predict the fall of shot, physicists could demonstrate that colour was merely a 'spectre' (i.e. spectrum) caused by the refraction of light. The old belief in a symbolic universe, ordained by divine providence (for the Christians), or expressing the nature of the indwelling divinity (for the Neoplatonists), gave way to a new belief in a meaningless, mechanical universe which was deterministically ruled by

Plate 11.5 The goddess Luna. A Renaissance drawing of the Roman goddess.

mathematical laws. These produced exact and predictable results which both prayer and magic were unable to match. The universe became less animated, but human self-confidence grew enormously.

These changes were most marked in the old western Empire. In the east, the Muscovite state used these same technical developments when Ivan the Terrible (1533–1584) set his sights on the Baltic coast, claiming for Muscovy the name of the original Kievan state: Russia. In the last years of the seventeenth century, Peter the Great succeeded in extending the Empire to the coast, where he founded a new capital, a centre of culture and commerce, in St Petersburg, near the old Ladoga trading station. The Kievan Russians had in fact been amalgamated into Lithuania-Poland in 1386, but rebelled and joined Moscow in 1648. Their territory became known as the Ukraine, or 'outermost area', in a neat reversal of its historical primacy. In 1795 ethnic Lithuania itself was ceded to Russia, following Estonia and Livonia (1721). The countries whose state religion was Eastern Orthodox did not suffer from the Great Witch-hunt, although there were accusations of simple ill-wishing (without diabolic overtones) in Russia in the eighteenth century, in which ninety-nine people, only one-third of whom were women, were accused.[21] In all of these countries the native languages were encouraged by Protestant reformers, who used them to preach the gospel in the vernacular, and they were later kept alive or even revived under the various colonising empires by nationalistic movements.

In the territory of the South Slavs the Empire of the Ottoman Turks expanded until, in 1683, they were beaten back from the gates of Vienna. In 1699 the Turkish portion of Hungary as well as Transylvania was ceded to the Austrians, and the Ukraine and Podolia to Poland. In 1774 Catherine the Great extended the Russian domain south to the Black Sea, annexing the Crimea. Thereafter, the Ottoman Empire in Europe remained fairly stable until the mid-nineteenth century, when Russia's pan-Slavic policies encouraged insurrections which gradually turned the Balkans from the world of official Islam to the world of official Christianity. Architecture, art and literature drew their inspiration from national folklore traditions, and when Paganism re-emerged in such places as Lithuania it was linked to nationalistic awareness.

In north-west Europe, antiquarian studies of megalithic sites became popular in the late seventeenth century, leading to a new awareness of Paganism among the learned. In 1676, in his *Britannia Antiqua Illustrata*, Aylett Sammes wrote that the Druids believed in 'the Immortality of the Soul, to which they added the Transmigration of it, according to the opinion of Pythagoras' (p. 101). In his *The Description of the Western Islands of Scotland* (1703), Martin Martin wrote of the Orkney stone circles at Stenness and Brodgar as: 'believed to have been Places design'd to offer Sacrifice in time of Pagan Idolatry; and for this reason the People called them the Ancient temples of the Gods' (p. 365). In Germany, Johann G. Keysler wrote *Antiquitates Selectae Septentrionales et Celticae* (Hanover, 1720), describing the remains of ancient Paganism at places in Germany and the Netherlands as well as Britain.

During the eighteenth century, there was a growing awareness of Britain's ancestral heritage, which was seen as Druidic. According to the architect John Wood the Elder (1704–1754), his native Bath was the Metropolitan Seat of the Druids, where Apollo was worshipped. Wood made a close study of megalithic sites, including Stonehenge, whose sacred geometry he reproduced in the Circus at Bath, in order to restore to it its antique Pagan grandeur. In his *Choir Gaure*, published in 1747, he wrote that Stonehenge was 'a temple erected by the British Druids'. In the eighteenth century, Druidic awareness penetrated many areas. A statue of a Druid was erected at the entrance of Penicuik House, Midlothian, Scotland, by Sir James Clerk in 1763. Copper penny tokens issued by the Parys Mine Company on the island of Anglesey in 1787 depicted the head of a Druid surrounded by a garland of oak leaves. It alluded to Anglesey's sacred heritage of the Druidic holy island.[22]

In Wales, there arose a renewed national awareness of the Druidic heritage, resulting in several influential books. The Reverend Henry Rowlands of Anglesey published *Mona Antiqua Restaurata* in 1723. Druidic Paganism was viewed not as harmful, but as a benign awareness of harmony with Nature. For example, in 1733, Pope wrote:

> Nor think in Nature's state they blindly trod;
> The State of Nature was the Reign of God.

The Druid John Toland's *Christianity not Mysterious* denied the necessity for believing in the uniqueness of Judaeo-Christian revelation, and later William Blake wrote: 'The antiquities of every Nation under Heaven is no less sacred than that of the Jews. They are the same thing.'

Druidism became nationally known in 1792, when a Bardic assembly was held in London. In October that year, *The Gentleman's Magazine* reported: 'This being the day on which the autumnal equinox occurred, some Welsh Bards, resident in London, assembled in congress on Primrose Hill, according to ancient usage.' The instigator of this Druidic event was Iolo Morgannwg (Edward Williams). A circle of stones was formed, surrounding the *Maen Gorsedd*, an altar stone, on which lay a sword. Iolo Morgannwg was an inspired mystic whose contributions to Druidism cannot be underestimated. The romantic interpretations of ancient Druidism are no more or less valid than the equivalent mythologies of other hagiographies. Materialist critics of Druidism who criticise Iolo fail to apply the same criteria of criticism to the prophets of other religions, all of whom have worked in more or less similar ways.

During the second half of the eighteenth century, and the beginning of the nineteenth, several significant books were published on Druidism. They include William Cooke's *An Enquiry into the Druidical and Patriarchal Religion* (1754); Edward Davies' *Celtic Researches* (1804), and *The Mythology and Rites of the British Druids* (1809); Jacques Cambry's *Monuments Celtiques* (1805); and Samuel Rush Meyrick and Charles Hamilton Smith's *Costume of the Original Inhabitants of the British Islands* (1815). Druidism found its way into opera, too: Bellini's *Norma*, produced in 1831 at La Scala, Milan, has a Druidic theme, the action being set at Stonehenge. It was popular in England for the next few years, eclipsed eventually by a change in musical fashion rather than one in subject matter.

Legendary histories of esoteric movements like Wicca and Freemasonry often claim unbroken continuity from ancient times. Without the documentation, which remains secret or non-existent, it is impossible to verify or refute these claims. However, in 1979, Colin Murray of the Golden Section Order published a document containing research by Michel Raoult on the history of Druidry in the British Isles and France. According to Raoult, English Druids claim their descent from the Mount Haemus Grove of Oxford under the Bard Philip Bryddod, 1245. Whether or not this is genuine, later Druidry is intimately connected with the rise of Freemasonry. In 1670, John Aubrey set up a new Mount Haemus Grove. Later, John Toland, his successor, set up The Ancient Druid Order, which met first in 1717, the year that modern Freemasonry was formalised. In 1781, another group, The Ancient Order of Druids, was set up in London by Henry Hurle as an esoteric society patterned on Masonic lines. In 1833, a split between the mystics and those who wanted a friendly society led to the majority forming The United Ancient Order of Druids, which still flourishes today. The mystical side continued as the Albion Lodge of the Ancient Order of Druids of Oxford, claiming descent from the Mount Haemus Grove. In 1908, Winston Churchill was an initiate of this sect.

Welsh Bardism, from which another strand of Druidism can be traced, is documented from 1176, when the first historical Eisteddfod at Cardigan was attended by Lord Rhys ap Grufydd. In 1594, an unsuccessful Eisteddfod was called, but it was at the end of the eighteenth century that a significant revival occurred, in parallel with developments in England. In 1789, an Eisteddfod was held at Corwen; in 1790, at St Asaph; in 1791, at Llanwrst; and in 1792, at Denbigh. Also in 1792, and more significantly for later developments, Iolo Morgannwg held a Gorsedd of Welsh Bards in London at Primrose Hill on the autumnal equinox. Later Eisteddfodau were sporadic, but at Carmarthen in 1819, Iolo Morgannwg set up his Gorsedd stone circle, integrating his ideas with the traditional Eisteddfod. In 1838, H. de la Villemarque held an Eisteddfod at Abergavenny. The first official Welsh National Eisteddfod was held at Llangollen in 1860, and it has been a central part of Welsh culture since then. The Druids' robes were designed by Sir Hubert Herkomer, RA, and the regalia (sceptre, crown, sword and Hirlas Horn) by Sir Goscombe John. Welsh Druidism of this period was very eclectic, drawing from historical European Paganism, byways of gnosticism and non-European Paganism from the British Empire. At the Eisteddfod at Pontypridd in 1878, the archdruid offered prayers to the Hindu goddess, Kali. The Eisteddfod flourishes today in a rather secularised form. Continental Druidism was strongly influenced by Welsh practice. In 1869, Nicolas Dimmer instituted the United Ancient Order of Druids at Paris, reinstating French Druidism. Thirty years later, M. Le Fustec was invested as a Druid at the Welsh Eisteddfod. In 1900, he proclaimed himself to be the first Grand Druid of Brittany, founding an organisation which still exists.

For many centuries, cremation of the dead was illegal in Britain because it was a Pagan practice. But in 1873, Sir Henry Thompson brought the idea forward from a utilitarian point of view. He was strongly opposed by churchmen. The test-case which altered the legal status was that of the Druid Dr William Price of Llantrisant (1800–1893). He was tried at Cardiff Assizes for cremating his infant son, who died at the age of five months in 1884. He was acquitted and, when he died in 1893, he, too, was cremated in Pagan fashion.[23] Cremation has since become a normal practice in Britain, but it was a Druid who re-established it, on specifically religious grounds.

ROMANTIC PAGANISM

Parallel with the restoration of Druidism, Classical Paganism underwent a new phase in northern Europe. It was through Thomas Taylor's translation of the *Orphic Hymn to Pan* (1787) that the Romantic poets rediscovered the soul of all things. The Romantic poets developed a nostalgia for lost ages, as in Schiller's *Götter Griechenlands*. In England, they had a mutually shared esteem for Paganism. After the death and destruction of the French Revolution and the Napoleonic Wars came the 'year without a summer' (1816), when famine swept Europe, accompanied by food riots. After the disintegration of the Old Order, the Romantic poets saw Paganism as the only remedy for the 'wrong turnings' of Christianity and industrialisation. In a letter to Thomas Jefferson Hogg (22 January, 1818), Leigh Hunt wrote:

> I hope you paid your devotions as usual to the Religio Loci, and hung up an evergreen. If you all go on so, there will be a hope some day ... a voice will be heard along the water saying 'The Great God Pan is alive again', – upon which the villagers will leave off starving, and singing profane hymns, and fall to dancing again.[24]

In his letters, Thomas Love Peacock signed himself 'In the name of Pan, yours most sincerely'.[25] In October 1821, Percy Bysshe Shelley wrote to Thomas J. Hogg:

> I am glad to hear that you do not neglect the rites of the true religion.

Plate 11.6 Woden depicted on a stained-glass window at Cardiff Castle, Wales, mid-nineteenth century. Nigel Pennick.

Your letter awoke my sleeping devotions, and the same evening I ascended alone the high mountain behind my house, and suspended a garland, and raised a small turf-altar to the mountain-walking Pan.[26]

Later in the nineteenth century, Edward Carpenter (1844–1929) was influential in the Pagan movement. He was a member of several socialist groups, including William Morris' Socialist League and the Fellowship of the New Life, from which came the Fabian Society.[27] Giving up his Anglican ministry in 1874, he promoted neo-Paganism as a return to the essentials of life. In 1883, he set up a self-sufficient community at Millthorpe between Sheffield and Chesterfield. In *Civilisation: Its Cause and Cure* he wrote:

The meanings of the old religions will come back . . . On the high tops once more gathering he will celebrate with naked dances the glory of the human form and the great processions of the stars, or greet the bright horn of the young moon which now after a hundred centuries comes back laden with such wondrous associations – all the yearnings and the dreams and the wonderment of the generations of mankind – the worship of Astarte and of Diana, of Isis and the Virgin Mary; once more in sacred groves will he reunite the passion and the delight of human love with his deepest feelings of the sanctity and beauty of Nature; or in the open, standing uncovered to the Sun, will adore the emblem of the everlasting splendour which shines within.[28]

Oscar Wilde echoed the sentiments of Carpenter, when he wrote:

> O goat-foot god of Arcady!
> The modern world hath need of thee!

Other idealistic Nature movements such as the Social Credit Party (which held seats in the Canadian legislature until 1980), and its offshoot the Woodcraft Folk (a young people's movement which is still active today) have their origin in this time. In Germany the *Wandervögel* ('wanderers') expressed an equivalent initiative.

In his *Pagan Papers* (1904), Kenneth Grahame called himself one of the 'faithful pagans' continuing the Old Religion: 'one's blood danced to imagined pipings of Pan from happy fields far distant'. Chapter 7 of *The Wind in the Willows*, titled 'The Piper At the Gates of Dawn', describes a vision of the Great God Pan. Grahame's biographer, Peter Green, called this vision 'the supreme example of nineteenth-century neo-pagan mysticism',[29] possibly the result of an intense visionary experience by Grahame.[30] At this time in this intellectual milieu, there was a feeling that a New Religion was about to be created: 'A religion so splendid and all-embracing that the hierarchy to which it will give birth, uniting within itself the artist and the priest, will supplant and utterly destroy our present commercial age'.[31] This was none other than 'the creative Pagan acceptance of life' promoted by playwright Eugene O'Neill.[32]

During the nineteenth century, the Germanic legends were collected by the Grimm brothers, and crafted into a powerful mythos by Richard Wagner. As Wagner himself wrote in his essay, 'What is German?': 'In rugged forests, in the long winter, in the warmth of the fire upon the hearth of his castle-chamber towering aloft into the air, he indulges long in the memories of his forefathers, he transmutes his home-bred myths of the gods in legends manifold and inexhaustible.' Wagner's commitment to building a national identity for the Germans through native myth was sincere, and another constant theme in his art was the tension between the Christian asceticism which he inherited and the Pagan affirmation of life to which as an artist he was committed. The reconciliation between 'Parnassus and Paradise' in the concluding Prize Song of *The Mastersingers* is one of the happier moments in this search. Wagner's commitment to recreating the spiritual-emotional

Plate 11.7 The Walhalla at Regensburg, Bavaria, Germany. A temple of national achievement, in the style of Classical Paganism. Modern 'halls of fame' are a direct continuation of the ancient worship of heroes. 1851 print. Nideck Picture Collection.

catharsis of Greek tragedy in his temple of music drama at Bayreuth was encouraged and partly shaped by his friend, the classicist Friedrich Nietzsche. Nietzsche split away from Wagner, however, when the latter also encompassed the Christian mythos in his final music drama, *Parsifal.*

Antiquarian study of the runes, especially in German-speaking countries, led to a reawakening of runic use, including their spiritual dimension. The runic inscription carved by William Kermode, the Manx antiquarian, on the tombstone of his family dog, is part of the re-emerging awareness.[33] On a more mystical level, the pan-Germanic mystic Guido von List dedicated himself to the service of Wotan and in 1904 devised a new system of runes based on the scriptural authority of the rune-song in the Eddic lay, *Hávamál.* In Germany, mystical elements from the northern tradition were used in architecture, most notably by Bernhard Hoetger (1874–1949). Hoetger respected the *genius loci* of the places where he built. In 1925, he used north German Pagan elements in the Worpswede Café and at the Große Kunstschau held at Worpswede in 1927. His most important work was the Böttcherstrasse development in Bremen (1923–1931), patronised by Ludwig Roselius. Called the Haus Atlantis, it was a 'high-tech' building, the first to use rolled steel in its construction. One façade had a sculpture of Odin on the tree, amid a wheel of runes. Elsewhere were northern tradition trees of life, solar imagery and a Hall of Heaven, reflecting Valhalla. Sadly, although the street was reconstructed in the 1950s after war damage, the image of Odin was the only part left out of the restoration.

In Britain, James Frazer (1854–1941), a Fellow of Trinity College, Cambridge, embarked on a programme of demonstrating that the Christian

215

myth of the dying and resurrected god was simply one example of a universal Pagan story: the dying and reborn Nature god as exemplified in the Babylonian myth of Tammuz. *The Golden Bough*, published in two editions between 1890 and 1915, was the massively influential result of this search. It was not, in fact, successful in its search for a universal dying-and-resurrected god, but it documented a wealth of surviving folklore practices which in Pagan times would have been sanctified by a deity, it provided a programme of interpretation, of looking for the hidden religious significance of such practices, and it inspired both a programme of research (the 'Cambridge School' of anthropology) and a popular following which treated the former's hypotheses as proven.

NEO-PAGANISM

The term 'neo-Paganism' is often applied to all contemporary Pagan practitioners, especially by American commentators. But it was applied first, in a rather pejorative way, to the artists of the Pre-Raphaelite movement. Later, there was actually a group that called itself the Neo-Pagans. Founded in Cambridge in 1908, it included the artist Gwen Raverat and the poet Rupert Brooke. But the Neo-Pagans seem to have had no real spiritual direction. The members went on long country walks and slept under canvas, but they made no serious attempt to restore the Pagan religion. After 1911, Francis Cornford continued neo-Paganism in Cambridge, but, by the 1920s, it had faded away.

Cornford was, however, one of the 'Cambridge School', a disciple of Jane Ellen Harrison (1850–1928), whose programme of demonstrating the 'primitive' substrate of Olympian religion, the folk-practices underlying the sophisticated art and rationality of Greek civilisation, showed how an elaborate intellectual structure could develop out of vernacular practice. She described this process as 'purging religion of fear'. She had a particular interest in Orphic mysticism, which she saw as the purification and consummation of the earlier, bloodthirsty rites of Dionysos. The sacramental idea of the higher Mystery religions such as Orphism, whereby the worshipper for a short time became the deity as he or she was shamanistically possessed by the latter, was in her opinion an ennobling influence on the human race. Her original inspirer was Sir James Frazer, and some of her work (e.g. *Themis*) and that of her followers is vitiated by an insistence on the universality of the dying-and-resurrected god. Other parts of her work, however, demonstrate the actual path of development between extremely primitive rites and the extremely sophisticated philosophies of the Mystery religions.

The search for a Frazerian-style fertility religion, if possible with signs of an 'esoteric core', led not only to the 'Cambridge School' of anthropology, but also to other initiatives which flourished in the early twentieth century.

Plate 11.8 Hermes, patron of trade. Stone carving and shrine by Hildo Krop, on the Wendingen-style Schipvaarthuis, Amsterdam, 1911. ©1968 Nigel Pennick.

The theory of the Egyptologist Margaret Murray has already been criticised. It was, however, accepted by many scholars outside the narrow field of Reformation studies until the 1970s. Hence the modern 'witches' who emerged in Britain after the repeal of the Witchcraft Act in 1951 were strongly influenced by it. They saw themselves as well-meaning rustic Pagans, following the inner Mysteries of a simple Nature religion which had been cruelly distorted by the black propaganda of the Church. In 1921 Jessie Weston, a specialist in Romance literature at the University of Paris, published an influential study of the Grail romances, claiming that they recorded a higher Mystery initiation which used the symbolism of the old Celtic fertility religion as it was still dimly remembered in Europe at the time. Weston relied heavily on inside information about ritual and the esoteric interpretation of ancient mythology from modern ceremonial magic (the Order of the Golden Dawn, of which her informant was a member, had been founded in 1888), also on the Orphic and Gnostic fragments which were just then being collated by scholars. Clearly, at that point in the twentieth century, some civilised westerners were looking for an esoteric religion which would both exalt them spiritually and ground them in vernacular peasant practice. One of the schools which fulfilled those criteria was Wicca.

Wicca, which emerged in 1951 after the repeal of the last Witchcraft Act in Britain, took its early self-image from Margaret Murray's interpretation of the north European medieval tradition as rendered by the religion's founder, Gerald Gardner, in his second novel *High Magic's Aid* (1948). It was leavened by an admixture of Classical Greek religion, particularly in the importance it placed on the Goddess, the female principle of divinity, who was modelled initially on the Greek goddess Aphrodite as described in Gardner's first novel, *A Goddess Arrives* (1941). This interpretation was perhaps derived from the description of the goddess Isis as given in Apuleius' *Golden Ass*, and was apparently influenced by a visionary experience of Gardner's own.[34] Later hands added more Classical touches. Part of an ode by Pindar is quoted to reveal the hidden nature of humanity, which initiation reveals. A Hellenised version of Ishtar's descent to the Underworld is a regular part of some later initiation rites; and a Sumerian hymn is used to pray for the return of the crops in spring. The hidden hand of Sir James Frazer has shaped this modern reinterpretation of ancient myth.

REAFFIRMATION OF THE GERMANIC DEITIES

It is often written that Hitler's regime in Germany (1933–1945) was Pagan in inspiration, but this is untrue. Hitler's rise to power came when the Catholic party supported the Nazis in the Reichstag in 1933, enabling Nazi seizure of power. Many churchmen of both Protestant and Catholic persuasion were committed supporters of the Nazi regime. The belief that it was Pagan in outlook comes from propaganda during the Second World War. As anti-German propaganda, the occultist Lewis Spence wrote:

> The ancient faith of Germany and Scandinavia, popularly known as 'the religion of Odin and Thor', has been the subject of many a literary encomium. To myself, as a student of Folklore and Mythology, it makes an appeal no more gracious or stimulating than any other religion of the lower cultus, and very much less so than those even of Polynesia or old Peru.
>
> It is, indeed, only the fact that it is being resuscitated by extreme Nazi fanatics which makes it important at all, and, even so, it is worthy of notice only in a temporary sense, for with the downfall of Hitler and his caucus it will go the way of all artificially revived heterodoxies.[35]

Himmler and Hess, two 'extreme Nazi fanatics', seem to have been active followers of an Ariosophical mysticism, promoting the future rule of the super-race. But Hitler himself said, in 1941: 'It seems to me that nothing would be more foolish than to re-establish the worship of Wotan. Our old mythology ceased to be viable when Christianity implanted itself.'[36]

Spence wrongly connected National Socialist ritual, derived from Prussian and Austrian military custom, with Paganism, as 'The Nazi Pagan Church'. Recent research by John Yeowell[37] has shown that, far from being influential in Nazi Germany, Pagans were persecuted. Leading Pagans were harassed or arrested by the Nazi regime. For example, in 1936, the noted runemaster Friedrich Bernhard Marby was arrested and spent the next nine years in concentration camps. He was not alone. In 1941, on orders from Heinrich Himmler, many Pagan and esoteric groups were banned (including the followers of Rudolf Steiner, the Ariosophists and followers of the religion of Wotan). Like other victims of Hitlerism, many Pagans subsequently died in concentration camps.

Around 1930, one of the earliest Odinist books in the English language, *The Call of Our Ancient Nordic Religion*, by the Australian Tasman Forth (A.R. Mills), was published in the United States by the League of Cultural Dynamics.[38] In Iceland the indigenous religion, or rather, that imported to the uninhabited land by Norse settlers in the tenth century, has always been known from literature. The sagas have always been read as part of the Icelandic literary heritage. In 1973, Ásatrú ('allegiance to the Æsir') was officially recognised as an established religion with the right to conduct, for example, legally binding weddings and child namings. Its members include high-ranking business people and diplomats, unusually for a religion which had been revived by enthusiasts only a few years before.[39] In Great Britain the Odinist Committee was founded in 1973, becoming the Odinic Rite in 1980. In 1988, it was registered as a religious charity with the British Charity Commissioners. Previous to this registration, it was considered generally by legal opinion that British law allowed only monotheistic beliefs to gain charitable status under the rubric of promotion of religion. Thus the Odinic Rite became, in its own words, 'the first heathen polytheistic body to be accorded recognition'.[40] It was followed in 1989 by the Odinshof, another Ásatrú organisation.

THE PRESENT DAY

At the end of the twentieth century, then, the indigenous religions of Europe, Nature-venerating, polytheistic and recognising deities of both genders, have re-emerged and are being reintegrated into the modern world. Some rely directly on surviving folk-practice, as in the Baltic countries; further west, the Germanic religions seek to adapt the myths recorded in the Viking Age for modern use. Celtic Druidry was influenced from the time of its re-emergence by Pythagorean (Masonic) and later Tibetan (Theosophical) traditions from oriental Paganism; and the latest form of resurgent Paganism, Wicca, derives its philosophy from the programme of the Cambridge School of anthropology as well as from the Goddess-venerating inspiration of its founder. A more broadly based, forward-looking Paganism has sprung from Wicca, dedicated to reaffirming what are seen as feminine values, embodied in the figure of an (often unnamed) Great Goddess, and the sanctity of the Earth, which is seen as being destroyed by unbridled technology. A nature-god, an image of unspoiled masculinity, is usually taken as the partner of the goddess in this more loosely defined pantheon, and both of these figures are seen as presiding over the surviving folk-rituals which we have described in the earlier chapters. Other goddesses and gods are seen as 'aspects' of these two. Their interaction is seen as offering an image of equal and complementary polarity rather than one of hierarchy and domination. This kind of Paganism looks ahead, offering a new philosophy, more strongly than it looks to its roots in the past.

It remains to be seen whether the various branches of re-emergent Paganism become a significant religious influence in the world of the future. Paganism is a possible religious philosophy for a pluralistic, multicultural society, but we are not concerned to debate its usefulness here. What we have attempted to do in the present volume is to show the extent of the modern resurgence's continuity with the Paganism of earlier ages. A new growth needs roots as well as blossoms, and we hope to have cut away some of the undergrowth which has entangled the current rejuvenation of an old and honourable stock.

NOTES

1 INTRODUCTION: PAGANISM OLD AND NEW

1 Chuvin (1990), p. 17.
2 D. H. Lawrence, letter to Frederick Carter, 1 October 1929, from the *Collected Letters of D. H. Lawrence*, intro. and edited by Harry Moore, London: Heinemann (1962), p. 1205. © 1962 by Angelo Ravagli and C. Montague Weekley, Executors of the Estate of Frieda Lawrence Ravagli.
3 Mookerjee (1988), pp. 47, 71.

2 THE GREEKS AND THE EASTERN MEDITERRANEAN

1 There are accounts in several ancient sources, including *Odyssey* XIX.172 ff.; *Iliad* XVIII.591; Ovid, *Metamorphoses* VII.159.
2 See Burkert (1985), Introduction.
3 Patai (1967), ch. 1.
4 Burkert (1985), p. 89.
5 Ibid., pp. 25–26.
6 See, e.g., *Cambridge Ancient History*, 3rd edn, vol. II, pt 2 (1975), p. 161.
7 Burkert (1985), p. 15.
8 Ibid., pp. 136–139.
9 Harrison (1906), ch. 2.
10 See *Cambridge Ancient History*, 3rd edn, vol. II, pt 2 (1975), ch. xxii, a, iii(a), p. 172.
11 Burkert (1985), pp. 63–64.
12 Athenaeus IX.78.
13 Details of practices in Rajasthan can be found in Kothari (1982). See also Harrison (1903), chs 1 and 2, and Burkert (1985), pt II, on Olympian altars, earth-god escharas and underworld megaras.
14 Harrison (1903), pp. 16ff.
15 Porphyry, *De Abst.* II.56.
16 Burkert (1985), p. 73.
17 See the extensive investigation of this claim in Lane Fox (1986).
18 Herodotus II.54–58.
19 Pausanius X.12.10; Strabo VII.329; Aristeides, *Or.* XLV.11.
20 Plato, cited without source in W.R. Lethaby (1969, 1892), p. 79.
21 Bötticher (1856), p. 486.
22 Rutkowski (1986), p. 101.
23 Bötticher (1856), p. 14.
24 Hersey (1988).
25 Ibid.

26 Burkert (1979), p. 40.
27 Kothari (1982).
28 Boardman *et al.* (1991), p. 336.

3   ROME AND THE WESTERN MEDITERRANEAN

 1 Accounts of Etruscan society can be found in Scullard (1967), Keller (1975) and Ogilvie (1976).
 2 Zosimus, *Historia Nova* V.41.
 3 Cicero, *De Divinatione*, XXIII.50.
 4 Scullard (1967), p. 228.
 5 Accounts are given in Santillana and Dechend (1969, 1977), Jones (1989).
 6 *De Lingua Latina*, V.46.
 7 *De Die Natali*, paraphrasing a lost work of Varro.
 8 *Life of Romulus* XI.
 9 Boardman *et al.* (1991), p. 400.
10 Warde-Fowler (1911), lecture VI, pp. 118ff.
11 Laing (1931), p. 16.
12 Trede (1901), vol. II, p. 210.
13 *Harusp. Resp.* 19.
14 Warde-Fowler (1911), p. 237.
15 *De agri cultura* 137.
16 See Palmer (1974), ch. 1.
17 C. Bailey in *Cambridge Ancient History*, 2nd edn, vol. VIII, ch. xiv (1970), p. 446.
18 Rose (1948), p. 77.
19 *De Russorum, Muscovitorum et Tartarorum Religione, Sacrificiis, Nuptiarum, Funerum ritu* (1582).
20 The translation is essentially Frazer's (Loeb, 1931). We have modified a few words.
21 Rose (1948), p. 51.
22 Lydus, *De Mensibus* III.22.
23 Cf. the *Fasti* of Fulvius Nobilior, *c.*189 BCE.
24 See Warde-Fowler (1911), ch. XII.
25 Accounts of the expansion of Rome can be found in the *Cambridge Ancient History*, 2nd edn, vols VII (1969) and VIII (1970), and in condensed form in Boardman *et al.* (1991), chs 16–18.
26 Rose (1948), pp. 120–121.
27 *Tusc. Disp.* I.16.36ff.

4   THE ROMAN EMPIRE

 1 A detailed account of Octavian's influence can be found in Syme (1939, 1971).
 2 Wissowa (1912), App. II.
 3 Warde-Fowler (1911), pp. 439–447.
 4 Baring and Cashford (1993), p. 270.
 5 Rose (1948), pp. 134–135; Wissowa (1912), p. 356.
 6 Wissowa (1912), p. 353.
 7 See Wissowa (1912), § 59; Cumont (1910).
 8 These six points are taken from the Introduction to Lane Fox (1986).
 9 See Lane Fox (1986) for a detailed account of their persistence.

10 Aurelian, *Historia Augusta* 25.
11 Cyprian, *De Lapsis*, 7–9.
12 *Codex Gregorianus*, XV.13.1, quoted in Smith (1976), p. 26.
13 Ibid.
14 Lactantius, *De Mortibus Persecutorum* 46.
15 Quoted in Smith (1976), p. 48. The details of how accounts of Constantine's conversion developed are taken from Holland Smith's version, as are many details in what follows.
16 Frend (1984), p. 554.
17 Smith (1976), p. 99, citing Socrates, *Ecclesiastical History*, II.47.
18 Gregory of Nazianus, *Invective against Julian* I.58.61.
19 Sozomen, *Ecclesiastical History*, VII.15, quoted in Trombley (1993), pp. 126–127.
20 E.g. Eunapius, *Lives of the Philosophers*, pp. 475–476, Claudius Claudianus, *De Bello Gothico*, pp. 173ff., *De Raptu Proserpine* I.1ff., quoted in Smith (1976), pp. 189–190.
21 Smith (1976), p. 229.
22 Ibid, pp. 321–323.
23 Laing (1931), p. 217.
24 Ibid, p. 93.
25 Duchesne (1904), p. 288.
26 E.g. Council of Autun, ch. ix; Statutes of Boniface, xxi.
27 Nelli (1963), pp. 29–30.
28 Tille (1899), p. 120.
29 Wallace-Hadrill (1952), p. 41.
30 Petrie (1912), p. 112.
31 Salway (1981), p. 736.
32 J.C. Robertson (1874–1875), vol. IV, p. 118.

5   THE CELTIC WORLD

1 See any general account of Celtic history, such as Cunliffe (1992).
2 Strabo, IV.4.1–2.
3 Lucan, I.453–454; H. Usener, *Scholia in Lucanem*, Leipzig, 1869, p. 33.
4 Dio Cassius LXII.6.7.
5 Strabo, XII.5.1.
6 Tacitus, *Annales* XIV.30.
7 *Revue Archéologique*, vol. 2, 1959, p. 55.
8 *De Bello Gallico* VI.16.
9 Strabo IV.4.5.
10 Suetonius, *Divus Claudius* XXV.5; Pliny, *N.H.* XXX.4.
11 E.g. Tacitus, *Annales* XIV.30.
12 Strabo IV.4.6.
13 Ross (1974), p. 267.
14 Scholl (1929).
15 M. Green (1986), pp.78–79.
16 Herodian VIII.3.8.
17 *De Bello Gallico* VII.18.
18 M. Green (1986), p. 79.
19 M. Green (1991), pp. 126–128.
20 Campbell (1890), vol. 2, p. 373.
21 Kaul *et al.* (1991), *passim*.
22 Reinach, Salomon, *Cultes, Mythes et Religion*, quoted in Anwyl (1906), pp. 24–25.

23 Powell (1980), p. 148.
24 Kinsella, Thomas (ed.), *The Tain*, London, Oxford Paperbacks, 1970, p. 27.
25 Binchy (1959).
26 Kendrick (1927), pp. 116–119.
27 Dinan, W., *Monumenta Historica Celtica*, London, David Nutt, 1911.
28 Strabo, III.1.4.
29 Ibid. II.15.
30 Quoted in Smith (1976), p. 242.
31 *Agricola* 21.
32 Ibid. 16.
33 Dio Cassius LXXII.2.
34 Tacitus, *Hist.* IV. 54.
35 Ross (1986a), p. 116.
36 *Logoi* VIII.8.

6 THE LATER CELTS

1 Salway (1981), chs 10, 11.
2 *Inscriptions from Roman Britain*, London Association of Classical Teachers Original Records no. 4, ed. M.C. Greenstock, London, LACT Publications, 1972, 1987, p. 129.
3 Canon Mahé, 'Essai', pp. 333–334, quotation from *Histoire du Maine* I.17, cited in Evans-Wentz (1911), p. 435.
4 Nance (1935), pp. 190–211.
5 Gildas (1938), p. 152.
6 Wallace-Hadrill (1967), p. 69.
7 McCrickard (1986), p. 27.
8 Jocelin MS ch. 23, p. 227, in Pinkerton, *Lives of the Scottish Saints*, vol. ii, 1889, pp. 1–96.
9 Skene (1876), p. 156.
10 Nennius, *Genealogy* X.
11 Four Books of Wales II.455.
12 Baring-Gould and Fisher (1907–1914), vol. II, p. 237.
13 Dr Ellis Prys, Thomas Cromwell's Commissary-General for the Diocese of St Asaph, letter dated 6 April, 1538, in Baring-Gould and Fisher (1907–1914), vol. I, p. 333.
14 Leland, *Collecteana*, cited in Baring-Gould and Fisher (1907–1914), vol. I, p. 217.
15 Wedeck (1975), p. 157.
16 The Reverend T.M. Morgan, cited in Evans-Wentz (1911), p. 390.
17 Baring-Gould and Fisher (1907–1914), vol. I, p. 164.
18 Ibid., p. 165.
19 Ibid., vol. III, p. 169.
20 Dixon (1886), App. F.
21 Hadingham (1976), p. 183.
22 Walker (1883), p. 186.
23 Kermode and Herdmans (1914).
24 Reverend F.J. Lynch, cited in Evans-Wentz (1911), p. 79.
25 Mitchell (1862), pp. 6, 14.
26 Reeves (1861).
27 Mitchell (1862), p. 253.
28 Dixon (1886), p. 411.

29 *A Tour in Scotland and Voyage to the Hebrides, 1772–4*, pt II, p. 330.
30 Dixon (1886), p. 157.
31 Rodd (1892), pp. 165, 176, cited in E.S. Hartland, 'Pin wells and rag bushes', *Folk-Lore*, vol. 4, 1893, pp. 457–458.
32 Hartland, 'Pin wells and rag bushes', p. 458.
33 Ibid., p. 452.
34 Ibid.
35 Bord and Bord (1985), p. 66.
36 Baring-Gould and Fisher (1907–1914), vol. II, p. 440.
37 Rhys, J., 'Holy wells in Wales', *Folk Lore*, vol. 4, 1893, p. 74.
38 Walker (1883), p. 207.
39 Bord and Bord, p. 119.
40 O'Connor, *Ordnance Survey Letters*, p. 368, cited in Bord and Bord (1985), p. 39.
41 Evans-Wentz (1911), p. 118.
42 Ibid., pp. 92–93; authors' personal observation.
43 Henderson (1910), p. 101.
44 Evans-Wentz (1911), p. 200.
45 Ibid., p. 93.
46 MacNeill (1962), pp. 223–224.
47 Ibid., p. 68.
48 Ibid.

7   THE GERMANIC PEOPLES

1 E.g. Davidson (1987).
2 Schutz (1983), pp. 135–136, and *Cambridge Ancient History*, vol. IX (1966), ch. III, *Cambridge Medieval History*, vol. I (1967), ch. vii.
3 See Tacitus, *Germania* 6, for the simple weaponry of the early Germans.
4 Thompson (1966), p. 29.
5 Tacitus, *Germania* 40, and n. 5 in Loeb edition.
6 Ibid. 10.1–3.
7 Ibid. 7.2.
8 Statius, *Silvae* I.iv.89.
9 Rosenberg (1988), p. 51.
10 '*notae*': *Germania* 10.1–3.
11 '*ut minor et potestatem numinis prae se ferens*': *Germania* 39.3.
12 *Historiae Contra Paganos* V.16.4.
13 *De Bello Gallico* VI.
14 Ammianus Marcellinus XXXI.2, quoted in Diesner (1978), p. 71.
15 *Landnámabók* 2.12.
16 Magnússon (1901), pp. 348ff.
17 Buck, *Cartularium Saxonicum* 603.
18 Gamell, David, 'Rösaring and the Viking Age cult road', *Archaeology and Environment*, vol. 4, 1985, pp.171–185, University of Umea, Sweden.
19 Marstrander, C., 'Thor en Irlande', *Revue Celtique*, vol. 36, 1915–1916, p. 241.
20 Wilson and Klindt-Jensen (1966), pp. 135–136.
21 Tille (1899), p. 2; see also Chaney (1970), pp. 57ff. Translations of Bede and the *Heimskringla* in what follows are from Tille.
22 Tille (1899), p. 45.
23 Walter of Henley, *Husbandry*, ed. E. Lamond, London, 1890, p. 97.
24 Cf. Council of Cloveshou, 747, can. xvi.

25 Authors' personal observation.
26 Tille (1899), p. 194.
27 Bede, *De Mensibus Anglorum.*
28 Jamieson, J., *An Etymological Dictionary of the Scottish Language*, Yule, no. VII, 1879, Paisley, Gardner.
29 Goulstone (1985), p. 7.
30 J.C. Robertson (1874–1875), vol. III, p. 112.
31 Boretius, *Capitularia Regum Francorum* I.59.
32 J.C. Robertson (1874–1875), vol. III, p. 114.
33 Chaney (1970).
34 Ibid., pp. 25–28.
35 Wolfram (1988), p. 210.
36 St Bernard, *Vita Sancti Malachiae* 8.16, quoted in Bartlett (1993), p. 22.
37 Bede, *Hist. Eccl.* II.15.
38 J.C. Robertson (1874–1875), vol. III, p. 64.
39 Ibid., vol. III, p. 66.
40 *Conc. Germ*, I, c. 5; *Conc. Liptin*, c. 4; *Conc. Suession*, c. 6, cited in J.C. Robertson (1874–1875), vol. III, p. 72.
41 Zach., Ep. 10, col. 940, cited in J.C. Robertson (1874–1875), vol. III, p. 80.
42 G.R. Owen (1981), p.165.
43 J.C. Robertson (1874–1875), 330–331.
44 *Landnámabók* 95, 97.
45 Brent (1975), p. 63.
46 Stenton (1971), p. 586.
47 *Saga of Håkon the Good,* ch. 19.
48 Ibid., ch. 32.
49 *Saga of Olaf Tryggvason*, ch. 59; *Saga of St Olaf, Heimskringla*, ch. 113ff.
50 Strömbäck (1975), pp. 15, 31.
51 Quoted by Adolf Schück, *Den äldre medertiden*, Sveriges historia genom tiderna, vol. I, p. 169.
52 Reuter (1987), p. 8.

8 LATE GERMANIC RELIGION

1 Quoted in G.R. Owen (1981), p. 101.
2 Keysler (1720), p. 339.
3 Johnson (1912), p. 437.
4 Ibid., p. 438.
5 Ibid.
6 Ibid., p. 435.
7 Sepp (1890), p. 267.
8 Schwebel (1887), p. 117.
9 Bächtold-Stäubli (1927–1942), vol. VI, p. 1672.
10 Ibid., vol. V, p. 1673.
11 Kemble (1876), vol. II, p. 429.
12 Bächtold-Stäubli (1927–1942), vol. V, p. 1673.
13 *Notes & Queries*, 1st ser., vol. V, p. 274.
14 Ibid., 6th ser., vol. I, p. 424.
15 Gomme (1883), pp. 34–37.
16 Evans (1966), p. 198.
17 Cited in Porter (1969), p. 181.
18 Sepp (1890), pp. 165–166; Bächtold-Stäubli (1927–1942), vol. VI, p. 1672.

19 Evans (1966), p. 200.
20 G.R. Owen (1981), pp. 43–45.
21 Johannessen (1974), p. 130.
22 Anwyl (1906), p. 34.
23 Megaw and Megaw (1989), p. 33.
24 Tacitus, *Germania* 3.
25 Davidson (1964), pp. 79, 86–89.
26 Reuter (1934), vol. II, ch. v, p. 1.
27 H.M. Chadwick (1900), pp. 268–300.
28 *Grágás*, K 84. See Johannessen (1974), p. 59, for commentary.
29 Morris and Magnússon (1891), pp. xxviii–xlii.
30 *Landnámabók* 110.
31 The following quotations are taken from the translation by Hermann Pálsson and Paul Edwards, London, Hogarth Press, 1978.
32 Picardt (1660).
33 *Landnámabók* 289.
34 Tacitus, *Germania* 3.
35 Tacitus, *Annales* XIV.30.
36 Quoted in Wallace-Hadrill (1967), p. 57.
37 Brent (1975), p. 38.
38 *Flateyjarbók*, 1.63.
39 *Atlamál*, 91, 96.
40 Hallowell (1926), p. 2.
41 For example, see Nioradze (1925), p. 40, and Hallowell (1926), p. 2.
42 Danielli (1945).
43 Davidson (1964), p. 99.
44 Cramp (1957).
45 Beck (1965).
46 Text in Thorpe (1840), vol. II, pp. 32–33.
47 Text in Thorpe (1840), vol. II, p. 190.
48 Text and translation in Thorpe (1840), vol. II, p. 249.
49 Text and translation in Thorpe (1840), vol. I, p. 379.
50 Borchardt (1971), p. 282.
51 Herrmann (1929), p. 66.
52 *Thuringian Chronicle*, quoted by Baring-Gould (1967), p. 211.
53 Thonger (1966), pp. 15–18.
54 Information from Abbots Bromley Horn Dancers, 1987.
55 Grimm (1880–1888), vol. III, p. 2.
56 Brewster, Sir David, *Edinburgh Encyclopedia*, vol. XVI, Edinburgh, n.d., p. 5.
57 Hadingham (1976), p. 183.
58 Ibid.
59 C.G. Jung (1963), pp. 344–345.
60 Reuter (1934), p. 80.
61 Rochholz (1870), pp. 16, 18, 100.
62 Stober (1892), vol. II, p. 283.
63 Lohmeyer (1920), p. 21.
64 Heyl (1897), Nr. 52, p. 236; Graber (1912), Nr. 58, p. 50.
65 Montelius, Oscar, 'The Sun-god's axe and Thor's hammer', *Folk-Lore*, vol. XXI, 1910, pp. 60–78.
66 Hamkens, Freerk Haye, 'Heidnische Bilder im Dome zu Schleswig', *Germanien*, June, 1938, pp. 177–181.
67 Rancken, A.W., 'Kalkmåningarna i Sibbo gamla kyrka', *Finskt Museum*, vol. 42, 1935, p. 29.

68 Cavallius (1863), vol. 1, p. 230.
69 Laing (1931), pp. 247–248, citing Leroy-Brühl, *La Religion dans l'Empire des Tsars*, p. 113.
70 Borchardt (1971), p. 117.
71 *Landnámabók* 3.12.
72 Kålund (1907); Flowers (1989), p. 34.
73 Moltke (1984), p. 493.
74 Grimm (1880–1888), vol. II, p. 653; Bächtold-Stäubli (1927–1942), vol. III, p. 1653.
75 Bächtold-Stäubli (1927–1942), vol. III, p. 1654.

9   THE BALTIC LANDS

1 Ptolemy, *Geography* III.5.
2 Noonan, Thomas S., in Ziedonis *et al.* (1974), pp. 13–21.
3 Johannes Magnus IV.4.
4 Ibid. IV.5.
5 Ibid. V.2.
6 Ibid. VI.22.
7 *Gesta Hammaburgensis* II.30.
8 Saks (1981), p.41.
9 *Heimskringla* I.6.
10 Henry of Livonia 7.1; 14.1–5; Saxo Grammaticus XIV.40.3.
11 Bartlett (1993), pp. 303–304.
12 Quoted in Fisher (1936), pp. 203–205.
13 J.C. Robertson (1874–1875), vol. IV, p. 90.
14 Tacitus, *Germania* 39.
15 Saxo Grammaticus, 484–485.
16 Schuchhardt (1926), *passim.*
17 Christiansen (1980), p. 31.
18 Albrecht (1928), pp. 45–56, fig. 6.
19 Accounts of the Wends are included in: Saxo Grammaticus; Vyncke (1968), vol. I, pp. 321ff.; Davidson (1981), p. 123; and Pettazzoni (1954), pp. 151–163.
20 Christiansen (1980), p. 32.
21 Neal Ascherson in the *Independent on Sunday*, 19 September, 1993.
22 Cf. Saks (1981).
23 E.g. Adam of Bremen, *Gesta Hammaburgensis* IV.23: 'the land which is called Semland, touching Russia and Polanis, but inhabited by the Sembi or Pruzzi'; Chronicle of Nestor translated by A.L.V. Schlözer, 1802, p. 55, cited in Saks (1981), pp. 25–26: 'Prus – this nation for a long time known under the name Aesty, struck dead holy Adalbert'.
24 Ptolemy, *Geography* III. 5.21.
25 Saks (1981), ch. 1, *passim.*
26 Carston (1954), p. 5.
27 Prutz, H. *Preußische Geschichte*, vol. I, Berlin, 1900, p. 40.
28 Bartlett (1993), p. 296.
29 Ibid., p. 312; Christiansen (1980), p. 136.
30 Quoted in Christiansen (1980), p. 137.
31 Zaprudnik, J., in Ziedonis *et al.* (1974).
32 Jurgela (1948), p. 41.
33 See Wright, Caroline, 'Pagans in Lithuania', *The Wiccan*, no. 101; 'A Special Correspondent', 'Old Lithuanian Faith revived', *The Wiccan*, no. 109; also authors' personal communications from Lithuania.

34 Jurgela (1948), pp. 40–41.
35 E.g. Christiansen (1980); Bartlett (1993).
36 Budreckis, A.M. (ed.), *Eastern Lithuania: A collection of historical and ethnographic studies*, Lithuanian Association of the Vilnius Region, 1980, 1985, p. v.
37 Janis (1987).
38 Rutkis (1967), p. 501.
39 Velius (1989).
40 McCrickard (1990).
41 Rutkis (1967), p. 501.
42 Janis (1987).
43 Baltic Paganism is described in: Enthoven (1937), pp. 182–186; Jurgela (1948); Gimbutas (1963); Dunduliene (1989); and Searle (1992), pp. 15–17.
44 Wixman (1993), p. 427.
45 Schefferus (1704).
46 Manker (1968), p. 39.
47 Rabane, Peter, 'The Jüriöö Mäss Rebellion of 1343', in Ziedonis *et al.* (1974), pp. 35–48; Christiansen (1980), pp. 204–205.
48 Saks (1981), p. 12.
49 *Saga of Olaf Tryggvason* 78, 79.
50 *Gesta Hammaburgensis* IV.16.
51 Pliny IV.90.
52 Diodorus Siculus II.47.
53 Orosius, *Life of Alfred the Great*, ed. R. Pauli, London, 1893, pp. 253–257.
54 Henry of Livonia 24.8.
55 Moora and Viires (1964), p. 239.
56 McCrickard (1990), ch. 13.
57 Manker (1968), p. 36.
58 Raudonikas (1930), p. 78.

10 RUSSIA AND THE BALKANS

1 Descriptions of the Scythians can be found in Herodotus and in Pliny.
2 Details from Fisher (1936).
3 Fisher (1936), p. 383.
4 The Lithuanian word *balta* means 'white', hence Baltic Russia's translation into 'White' Russia: Russian *belo*.
5 *De Russorum, Moscovitorum et Tartarorum Religione, Sacrificiis, Nuptiarum, Funerum ritu* (1582).
6 Fisher (1936); *Cambridge Medieval History*, vol. IV (1966–1967).
7 What follows is taken from McCrickard (1990), ch. 9.
8 Accounts of Russian Paganism are scattered among various works on shamanism, totemism, etc. Some details can be found in J.C. Robertson (1874–1875), vol. V, ch. 7.
9 Oddo (1960).
10 Gunda (1968), pp.41–51.
11 Herodotus IV.33.
12 Leicht (1925), p. 249.
13 Beza (1920), *passim*.
14 Trombley (1993), ch. 1, *passim*.
15 Ibid., pp. 98–99, 147–168.
16 *Cambridge Medieval History*, vol. IV (1966–1967), p. 44.
17 *Bibliotheca*, codex 239.

18 Rodd (1892), p. 58, translation unattributed.
19 Ibid., p. 141, but see comments in Trombley (1993), p. 98, n. 4.
20 Rodd (1892), pp. 148–149.
21 Ibid., p. 139.
22 Ibid., pp. 138–140.
23 Ibid., p. 116.
24 Chuvin (1990), pp. 1–2.

11 PAGANISM REAFFIRMED

1 Bartlett (1993), p. 236.
2 Vesey-Fitzgerald (1973), p. 7.
3 Ibid., pp. 30–31.
4 Ibid., p. 207.
5 Liégeois (1986), *passim.*
6 Pizan (1489).
7 Borsi (1989), p. 96.
8 Valturio, Roberto, *De Re Militari*, vol. XII, Paris, 1532, p. 13.
9 Ricci (1925), pp. 166–199.
10 Authors' personal information, and cf. Hutton (1991), n. 37, p. 370.
11 Scarre (1987), p. 19.
12 E.g. Levack (1987), p. 21, with 60,000 deaths over the two centuries, and Hutton (1991), n. 37, p. 370, arguing for a mere 40,000.
13 Quoted in Scarre (1987), p. 20.
14 Levack (1987), p. 12; Scarre (1987), pp. 27–28, 53.
15 Arntz (1935), p. 268.
16 Flowers (1989), *passim.*
17 See Cohn (1975), chs 9 and 10, for the transformation of magic into witchcraft.
18 Cohn (1975), pp. 232–233.
19 Runeberg (1947), p. 239.
20 Cohn (1975), pp. 161–162.
21 Scarre (1987), p. 22, table 1, p. 25.
22 Anthony, John, 'A guide to tokens and allied "coins"', *Coin Year Book*, Brentwood, Numismatic Publishing Company, 1992, pp. 70–72.
23 Piggott (1968), pp. 178–179.
24 Cited in Scott, W.S., *The Athenians*, London, Golden Cockerel Press, 1943, pp. 43–44.
25 Scott, W.S., ed., *Shelley at Oxford*, London, 1944, p. 61.
26 Merivale (1969), p. 64.
27 Walter (1981), p. 9.
28 Carpenter (1906), pp. 46–47.
29 P. Green (1959), p. 252.
30 Ibid., pp. 139–147.
31 Eric Gill to William Rothenstein, 5 December, 1910, Clark Library, University of California, Los Angeles.
32 Clark (1947).
33 Hayhurst, Yvonne, 'A recent find of a horse skull in a house at Ballaugh, Isle of Man', *Folk-Lore*, vol. 100, no. 1, 1989, p. 105.
34 Bracelin (1960), pp. 153–154.
35 Spence (n.d., *c.*1941), p. 43.
36 *Hitler's Secret Conversations, 1941–1944*, eds N. Cameron and R.H. Steven, London, 1953, p. 51, cited by Yeowell (1993), p. 10.

37 Yeowell (1993).
38 *Odinic Religion Bulletin*, no. 40, November, 1984, p. 8.
39 Information from John Yeowell and Ralph Harrison of the Odinic Rite, Dr Ronald Hutton of the University of Bristol.
40 *The Moot Horn*, no. 1, September, 1992, p. 2.

BIBLIOGRAPHY

(We have not given details of ancient texts, which are available in many editions, or of some of the articles in journals which are mentioned only once per chapter, especially in chapters 5–10. Details of these appear in the notes to the relevant chapter.)

Agrell, Sigurd (1934) *Lapptrumor och Runmagi*, Lund: C.W.K. Glerup.
Albrecht, C. (1928) 'Slawische Bildwerke', *Mainzer Zeitschrift*, vol. XXIII, pp. 46–53.
Anderson, J. (1868) *Scotland in Pagan Times*, Edinburgh: David Douglas.
Anwyl, Edward (1906) *Celtic Religion*, London: Archibald Constable.
Arntz, H. (1935) *Handbuch der Runenkunde*, Halle: Niemeyer.
Ayres, James (1977) *British Folk Art*, London: Barrie & Jenkins.
Bächtold-Stäubli, Hanns (ed.) (1927–1942) *Handworterbuch des deutschen Aberglaubens*, 9 vols, Berlin: Walter De Gruyter.
Backhouse, Edward and Tylor, Charles (1892) *Early Church History to the Death of Constantine*, London: Simpkin, Marshall, Hamilton, Kent & Co.
Baker, Margaret (1974) *Folklore and Customs in Rural England*, Newton Abbot: David & Charles.
Bannard, H.E. (1945) 'Some English sites of ancient heathen worship', *Hibbert Journal*, vol. XLIV, pp. 76–79.
Baring, A. and Cashford, J. (1993) *The Myth of the Goddess*, London: Book Club Associates.
Baring-Gould, S. (1967), *Some Curious Myths of the Middle Ages*, New York: University Books.
Baring-Gould, S. and Fisher, John (1907–1914) *The Lives of the British Saints*, 4 vols, London: Charles J. Clark.
Bartlett, R. (ed.) (1989) *Medieval Frontier Societies*, Oxford: Clarendon Press.
—— (1993) *The Expansion of Europe: Conquest, colonisation and cultural change 950–1350*, London: Book Club Associates.
Beck, H. (1965) *Das Ebersignum im Germanischen. Quellen und Forschungen zur Sprach- und Kulturgeschichte der Germ. Völker*, Berlin: De Gruyter.
Bernheimer, Richard (1952) *Wild Men in the Middle Ages*, Cambridge, Mass.: Harvard University Press.
Bettelheim, Bruno (1976) *The Uses of Enchantment. The Meaning and Importance of Fairy Tales*, London: Thames & Hudson.
Beza, M. (1920) *Paganism in Roumanian Folklore*, London and Toronto: J.M. Dent.
Binchy, D.A. (1959) 'The fair of Táiltiu and the feast of Tara', *Eriu*, vol. 18, 1958, pp. 113–138.
Bloch, Raymond (1958) *The Etruscans*, London: Thames & Hudson.

—— (1960) *The Origins of Rome*, London: Thames & Hudson.

Boardman, J., Griffin, J. and Murray, O. (1986, 1991) *The Oxford History of the Classical World*, Oxford: Oxford University Press.

Bonser, W. (1932) 'Survivals of Paganism in Anglo-Saxon England', *Transactions of the Birmingham Archaeological Society*, vol. LVI, pp. 37–71.

Borchardt, Frank (1971) *German Antiquity in Renaissance Myth*, Baltimore: Johns Hopkins University Press.

Bord, Janet and Bord, Colin (1985) *Sacred Waters*, London: Granada.

Borsi, Franco (1989) *Leon Battista Alberti, The Complete Works*, New York: Electa/Rizzoli.

Bötticher, Carl (1856) *Der Baumkultus der Hellenen*, Berlin: n.p.

Bracelin, Jack (1960) *Gerald Gardner, Witch*, London: Octagon.

Branston, Brian (1955) *Gods of the North*, London: Thames & Hudson.

—— (1957) *The Lost Gods of England*, London: Thames & Hudson.

Brent, P. (1975) *The Viking Saga*, London: Book Club Associates.

Bromwich, R. (1979) *Trioedd Ynys Prydein*, Cardiff: Cardiff University Press.

Brøndsted, J. (1964) *The Vikings*, Harmondsworth: Penguin.

Brown, A. (ed.) (1963) *Early English and Old Norse Studies*, London: Methuen.

Bucknell, Peter A. (1979) *Entertainment and Ritual, 600 to 1600*, London: Stainer & Bell.

Burkert, W. (1979) *Structure and History in Greek Mythology and Ritual*, Berkeley: University of California Press.

—— (1985) *Greek Religion, Archaic and Classical*, Oxford: Blackwell.

Byrne, Patrick F. (1967) *Witchcraft in Ireland*, Cork: The Mercier Press.

Cacquot, A. and Leibovici, M. (1968) *La Divination*, Paris.

Cambridge Ancient History, 3rd edn, vol. I, pt 1 (1970), vol. I, pt 2 (1971), eds I.E.S. Edwards, C.J. Gadd and N.G.L. Hammond; vol. II, pt 1 (1973), vol. II, pt 2 (1975), ed. I.E.S. Edwards, C.J. Gadd, N.G.L. Hammond and E. Sollberger, Cambridge: Cambridge University Press.

—— 2nd edn (1951–), vol. III (1970), vol. IV (1969), vol. V (1979), vol. VI (1969), ed. J.B. Bury, S.A. Cook and F.E. Adcock; vol. VII (1969), vol. VIII (1970), vol. IX (1966), vol. X (1971), vol. XI (1969), ed. S.A. Cook, F.E. Adcock and M.P. Charlesworth; vol. XII (1965), ed. S.A. Cook, F.E. Adcock, M.P. Charlesworth and N.H. Baynes, Cambridge: Cambridge University Press.

Cambridge Medieval History (1964–1967), vol. I. (1967), vol. II (1964), ed. H.M.G. Watkin and J.P. Whitney; vol. III (1964), ed. H.M.G. Watkin, J.P. Whitney, J.R. Tanner and C.W. Previté-Orton; vol. IV, pt 1 (1966), vol. IV, pt 2 (1967), ed. J.M. Hussey; vols V–VIII (1964), ed. J.R. Tanner, C.W. Previté-Orton and Z.N. Brooke, Cambridge: Cambridge University Press.

Campbell, J.F. (1860, 1890) *Popular Tales of the Western Highlands*, 4 vols, Edinburgh (1860), Paisley (1890).

Carpenter, Edward (1906) *Civilisation: Its Cause and Cure*, London: Swan Sonnenschein.

Carston, F.L. (1954) *The Origin of Prussia*, Oxford: Oxford University Press.

Cavallius (1863) *Hyltén: Wärend och Widerne*, Stockholm.

Chadwick, H. Munro (1899) *The Cult of Othin*, London: Cambridge University Press.

—— (1900) 'Teutonic priesthood', *Folk-Lore*, vol. XI, pp. 268–300.

Chadwick, N.K. (ed.) (1954) *Studies in Early British History*, Cambridge: Cambridge University Press.

Chaney, W. (1960) 'Paganism to Christianity in Anglo-Saxon England', *Harvard Theological Review*, vol. LIII, pp. 197–217.

—— (1970) *The Cult of Kingship in Anglo-Saxon England*, Manchester: Manchester University Press.

Christiansen, E. (1980) *The Northern Crusades*, London: Macmillan.

Chuvin, Pierre (1990) *Chronique des Derniers Païens*, Paris: Belles Lettres/Fayard.

Clark, Barrett O. (1947) *Eugene O'Neill: The Man and his Plays*, New York.

Clemen, Carl (1916) *Die Reste der primitiven Religion im ältesten Christentum*, Giessen.

Cockayne, T.O. (1864–1866) *Leechdoms, Wortcunning and Starcraft in Early England*, 3 vols, London: Rolls Series.

Cohn, N. (1975) *Europe's Inner Demons*, London: Heinemann.

Constantine, J. (1948) *History of the Lithuanian Nation*, New York: Lithuanian Cultural Institute Historical Research Section.

Cramp, R. (1957) 'Beowulf and archaeology', *Medieval Archaeology*, vol. I, pp. 60ff.

Crawford, O.G.S. (1957) *The Eye Goddess*, London: Phoenix House.

Cumont, F. (1910) *The Mysteries of Mithras*, London.

—— (1929) *Les religions orientales dans le paganisme romain*, Paris.

Cunliffe, B. (1992) *The Celtic World*, London: Constable.

Curtin, Jeremiah (1894) *Hero-Tales of Ireland*, London: Macmillan.

Danielli, M. (1945) 'Initiation ceremonial from Norse Literature', *Folk-Lore*, vol. 56, pp. 229–245.

Davidson, H.R.E. (1964) *Gods and Myths of Northern Europe*, Harmondsworth: Penguin.

—— (1969) *Scandinavian Mythology*, London: Paul Hamlyn.

—— (1981) 'The Germanic World', in M. Loewe and C. Blacker (eds), *Divination and Oracles*, London: George Allen & Unwin.

—— (1987) *Myths and Symbols in Pagan Europe*, Manchester: Manchester University Press.

Davies, Glenys (ed.) (1989) 'Polytheistic systems', *Cosmos Yearbook No. 5*, Edinburgh: The Traditional Cosmology Society.

Day, J. Wentworth (1963) 'Witches and wizards of the Fens', *Country Life*, 28 March.

Dennis, A., Foote, P. and Perkins, R. (trans.) (1980) *Grágás: Laws of Early Iceland*, Winnipeg: University of Manitoba Press.

De Vries, Jan (1961) *Keltische Religion*, Stuttgart: Kohlhammer.

Dickins, B. (1915) *Runic and Heroic Poems of the Old Teutonic Peoples*, Cambridge: Cambridge University Press.

Diesner, H.-J. (1978) *The Great Migration*, trans. C.S.V. Salt, London: George Prior.

Dillon, Myles and Chadwick, Nora K. (1973) *The Celtic Realms*, London: Cardinal.

Diószegi, V. (1968) *Popular Beliefs in Siberia*, Bloomington: Indiana University Press.

Dixon, J.A. (1886) *Gairloch*, Edinburgh.

Dodds, E.R. (1951) *The Greeks and the Irrational*, Berkeley: University of California Press.

Drake-Carnell, F.J. (1938) *Old English Customs and Ceremonies*, London: Batsford.

Duchesne, I. (1904) *Christian Worship, its Origin and Evolution*, trans. M.L. McLure, London, SPCK.

Dumezil, G. (ed) (1973) *The Gods of the Ancient Northmen*, trans. E. Haugen, Berkeley: University of California Press.

Dunduliene, P. (1989) *Pagonybe Lietuvoje: moteriskios dievybes*, Vilnius: Mintis.

Durdin-Robertson, Lawrence (1982) *Juno Covella*, Enniscorthy: Cesara Publications.

Durmeyer, Johann (1883) *Reste altgermanischen Heidentums in Unsern Tagen*, Nuremberg.

Elliott, D. and Elliott, J. (1982) *Gods of the Byways*, Oxford: Museum of Modern Art.

Ellis, Hilda R. (1943) *The Road to Hel*, Cambridge: Cambridge University Press.
Ellis, Peter Berresford (1990) *The Celtic Empire*, London: Constable.
Enthoven, R.E. (1937) 'The Latvians and their folk-songs', in *Folk-Lore*, vol. XLVIII, pp. 183–186.
Evans, George Ewart (1966) *The Pattern Under the Plough*, London: Faber & Faber.
Evans-Wentz, W.Y. (1911) *The Fairy Faith in Celtic Countries*, Oxford: Oxford University Press.
Ewen, C. L'Estrange (1938) *Some Witchcraft Criticisms*, London: privately published.
Fillipetti, Hervé and Trotereau, Janine (1978) *Symboles et pratiques rituelles dans la maison paysanne traditionelle*, Paris: Editions Berger Lerrault.
Firmicus Maternus (1952) *De Errore Profanorum Religionum*, Munich: Hüber.
Fisher, H.A.L. (1936) *A History of Europe*, London: Arnold.
Flowers, Stephen E. (1981) 'Revival of Germanic religion in contemporary Anglo-American culture', *Mankind Quarterly*, vol. 21, no. 3, pp. 279–294.
—— (1989) *The Galdrabók, an Icelandic Grimoire*, York Beach: Samuel Weiser.
Fol, A. and Marazov, I. (1978) *A la recherche des Thraces*, Paris.
Fowler, W. Warde (1911) *The Religious Experience of the Roman People*, London: Macmillan.
Frend, W.H.C. (1984) *The Rise of Christianity*, London: Dartin, Longman & Todd.
Gardner, Gerald (1941) *A Goddess Arrives*, London: Arthur Stockwell.
—— (1948) *High Magic's Aid*, London: Michael Houghton.
—— (1954) *Witchcraft Today*, London: Rider.
—— (1959) *The Meaning of Witchcraft*, London: Aquarian Press.
Garmonsway, G.N. (ed. and trans.) (1972) *The Anglo-Saxon Chronicle*, London: J.M. Dent.
Gelling, Peter and Davidson, Hilda Ellis (1969) *The Chariot of the Sun*, London: J.M. Dent.
Getty, Adele (1990) *Goddess, Mother of Living Nature*, London: Thames & Hudson.
Gildas (1938), *The Story of the Loss of Britain*, ed. and trans. A.W. Wade-Evans, London: SPCK.
Gimbutas, Marija (1963), *The Balts*, New York and London: Thames & Hudson.
—— (1982) *The Goddesses and Gods of Old Europe*, London: Thames & Hudson.
Glover, T.R. (1909) *The Conflict of Religions in the Early Roman Empire*, London: Methuen.
Godfrey, C.J. (1962) *The Church in Anglo-Saxon England*, Cambridge: Cambridge University Press.
Golther, Wolfgang (1895) *Handbuch der Germanisches Mythologie*, Leipzig: Köhler & Amelang.
Gomme, G.L. (1883) *Folklore Relics in Early Village Life*, London: n.p.
Goodison, L. (1990) *Moving Heaven and Earth*, London: The Women's Press.
Gorman, M. (1986) 'Nordic and Celtic religion in southern Scandinavia during the late Bronze Age and early Iron Age', in T. Ahlbäck (ed.), *Old Norse and Finnish Religions and Celtic Place-Names*, Stockholm: Almqvist & Wiksell International.
Goulstone, J. (1985) *The Summer Solstice Games*, Bexleyheath, Kent: privately published.
Graber, Georg (1912) *Sagen aus Kärnten*, Leipzig.
Graves, R. (1952) *The White Goddess*, London: Faber & Faber.
Green, M. (1986) *The Gods of the Celts*, Gloucester: Alan Sutton.
—— (1991) *The Sun-Gods of Ancient Europe*, London: Batsford.
Green, P. (1959) *Kenneth Grahame: A Biography*, London: John Murray.
Grimm, J.L. (1880–1888) *Teutonic Mythology*, 4 vols, ed. and trans. J.E. Stallybrass, London: Bell.

Grinsell, L. (1972) 'Witchcraft at barrows and other prehistoric sites', *Antiquity*, vol. 46, p. 58.

—— (1976) *Folklore of Prehistoric Sites in Britain*, Newton Abbot: David & Charles.

Grönbech, Vilhelm (1931) *The Culture of the Teutons*, London: Oxford University Press.

Guillaume, A. (1938) *Prophecy and Divination*, London.

Gunda, B. (1968) 'Survivals of totemism in the Hungarian táltos tradition', in V. Diószegi, (ed.), *Popular Beliefs in Siberia*, Bloomington: Indiana University Press.

Guyonvarc'h, Christian-J. (1980) *Textes Mythologiques Irlandais*, Rennes: Ogam-Celticum.

Hadingham, Evan (1976) *Circles and Standing Stones*, New York: Anchor/Doubleday.

Halifax, Joan (1968) *Shamanic Voices*, New York: Dutton.

Hall, Nor (1980) *The Moon and the Goddess*, London: The Women's Press.

Halliday, W.R. (1925) *The Pagan Background to Early Christianity*, London: Hodder & Stoughton.

Hallowell, A. Irving (1926) 'Bear ceremonialism in the northern hemisphere', *American Anthropologist*, N.S., p. 28.

Harding, M. Esther (1955, 1971) *Womens' Mysteries, Ancient and Modern*, London: Rider.

Harrison, Jane Ellen (1903) *Prolegomena to the Study of Greek Religion*, Cambridge: Cambridge University Press.

—— (1906) *Primitive Athens as Described by Thucydides*, Cambridge: Cambridge University Press.

—— (1924) *Mythology, our Debt to the Greeks and Romans*, London.

Haseleoff, Günther (1979) *Kunststile des Frühen Mittelalters*, Stuttgart: Württembergisches Landesmuseum.

Henderson, George (1910) *The Norse Influence on Celtic Scotland*, Glasgow: James Maclehose & Sons.

Henig, M. (1984) *Religion in Roman Britain*, London: Batsford.

Herold, Basilius Johannes (1554) *Heydenweldt und irer Götter*, Basle.

Herrmann, P. (1929) *Das altgermanische Priesterwesen*, Jena: Diederichs.

Hersey, G. (1988) *The Lost Meaning of Classical Architecture*, Cambridge, Mass.: MIT Press.

Heyl, Johann Adolf, (1897) 'Volkssagen, Bräuche und Meinungen aus Tirol', Brixen, Nr. 52.

Hibbert, S. (1831) 'Memoir on the Things of Orkney and Shetland', *Archaeologia Scotica*, vol. 3, pp. 103–211.

Hopf, Ludwig (1888) *Thierorakel und Orakelthiere in alter und neuer Zeit*, Stuttgart.

Hutton, R. (1991) *The Pagan Religions of the Ancient British Isles*, Oxford: Blackwell.

Huxley, F. (1974) *The Way of the Sacred*, London: Aldus.

Jahn, Ulrich (1886) *Hexenwesen und Zauberei in Pommern*, Breslau.

James, E.O. (1955) *The Nature and Function of Priesthood*, London: Thames & Hudson.

Janis, T. (1987) *The Ancient Latvian Religion*, Chicago: Dievturiba Lituanis.

Jeanmaire, H. (1951) *Le Culte de Dionysus*, Paris.

Johannessen (1974) *A History of the Old Icelandic Commonwealth*, Winnipeg: University of Manitoba Press.

Johnson, Walter (1912) *Byways in British Archaeology*, Cambridge: Cambridge University Press.

Jones, Prudence (1982a) *Eight and Nine: Sacred Numbers of Sun and Moon in the Pagan North*, Bar Hill: Fenris-Wolf.

236

—— (1982b) *Sundial and Compass Rose: Eight-fold Time Division in Northern Europe*, Bar Hill: Fenris-Wolf.

—— (1989) 'Celestial and terrestrial orientation', in Annabella Kitson (ed.), *History and Astrology*, London: Unwin Hyman.

—— (1990) 'The Grail quest as initiation: Jessie Weston and the vegetation theory', in John Matthews (ed.), *The Household of the Grail*, Wellingborough: Aquarian Press.

—— (1991) *Northern Myths of the Constellations*, Cambridge: Fenris-Wolf.

Jones, Prudence and Matthews, Caitlín (eds) (1990) *Voices from the Circle. The Heritage of Western Paganism*, Wellingborough: Aquarian Press.

Jung, C.G. (1963) *Memories, Dreams, Reflections*, Glasgow: Collins.

Jung, Erich (1939) *Germanische Götter und Helden in Christlicher Zeit*, Munich and Berlin: J.F. Lehmanns Verlag.

Jurgela, C. (1948) *A History of the Lithuanian Nation*, New York: Lithuanian National Institute Cultural Research Section.

Kålund, Kristian (ed.) (1907) *Den islandske Lægebog*, Copenhagen: Luno.

Kaul, Flemming, Marazov, Ivan, Best, Jan and De Vries, Nanny (1991) *Thracian Tales on the Gundestrup Cauldron*, publications of the Holland Travelling University, vol. 1, Amsterdam: Najade Press.

Keller, W.J. (1975) *The Etruscans*, London: Cape.

Kemble, J.M. (1876) *The Saxons in England*, London.

Kendrick, T.D. (1927, 1966), *The Druids*, London: Frank Cass.

Kermode, P.M.C. and Herdmans, W.A. (1914) *Manks Antiquities*, Liverpool: University of Liverpool Press.

Keysler, J.G. (1720), *Antiquitates Selectae Septentrionales et Celticae*, Hanover.

Kothari, K. (1982) unnamed chapter in Elliott, D. and Elliot J., *Gods of the Byways*, Oxford: Museum of Modern Art.

Kraft, John (1985) *The Goddess in the Labyrinth*, Åbo: Åbo Academy Press.

Laing, G.J. (1931) *Survivals of Roman Religion*, London: Harrap.

Lane Fox, R.L. (1986) *Pagans and Christians*, London: Oxford University Press.

Lasicius (Bishop Ján Lasicki) (1580, 1615) *De Diis Sarmagitarum*, Basle.

—— (1582) *Religio Borussorum*, Basle.

—— (1582) *De Russorum, Moscovitorum et Tartarorum Religione, Sacrificiis, Nuptiarum, Funerum ritu*, Basle.

Legge, E. (1915) *Forerunners and Rivals of Christianity*, 2 vols, Cambridge: Cambridge University Press.

Leicht, P.S. (1925) *Tracce de paganesmo fra gli Slavi dell'Isonzo*.

Leland, Charles G. (1899, 1974) *Aradia, The Gospel of the Witches*, London: C.W. Daniel.

Le Roux, Françoise and Guyonvarc'h, Christian-J. (1978) *Les druides*, Rennes: Ogam-Celticum.

Lethaby, W.R. (1969, 1892) *Architecture, Mysticism and Myth*, London: n.p.

Levack, B.P. (1987) *The Witch Hunt in Early Modern Europe*, London: Longman.

Lewis, Don (1975) *Religious Superstition through the Ages*, Oxford: Mowbray.

Lewis, I.M. (1971) *Ecstatic Religion*, Harmondsworth: Penguin.

Lewis, M.J.T. (1966) *Temples in Roman Britain*, Cambridge: Cambridge University Press.

Liebeschütz, J.H.W.G. (1979) *Continuity and Change in Roman Religion*, Oxford: Clarendon Press.

Liégeois, Jean-Pierre (1986) *Gypsies: An Illustrated History*, London: Al-Saqi Books.

Lindenschmit, L. (1874–1877) *Die Altherthümer unserer heidnischen Vorzeit*, Mainz.

Loewe, M. & Blacker, C. (eds) (1981) *Divination and Oracles*, London: Allen & Unwin.

Lohmeyer, Karl (1920) *Die Sagen des Saarbrücker und Birkenfelder Landes*, Leipzig.

Lommel, A. (1967) *Shamanism*, New York: McGraw-Hill.

Lönnrot, Elias, (1963), *The Kalevala*, trans. Francis Peabody Magoun, Cambridge, Mass.: Harvard University Press.

Lundkvist, Sune (1967) 'Uppsala hedna-tempel och första Katedral', *Norrdisk Tidskrift*, pp. 236–242.

McCrickard, J. (1986) (as Sínead Sula Grián) *The Sun Goddesses of Europe*, Glastonbury: Gothic Image.

—— (1990) *Eclipse of the Sun: An Investigation into Sun and Moon myths*, Glastonbury: Gothic Image.

MacFarlane, Alan (1970) *Witchcraft in Tudor and Stuart England*, London: Routledge & Kegan Paul.

McLean, Adam (1983) *The Triple Goddess*, Edinburgh: Hermetic Research.

MacMullen, Ramsay (1981) *Paganism in the Roman Empire*, Princeton: Yale University Press.

MacNeill, Maire (1962) *The Festival of Lughnasa*, Oxford: Oxford University Press.

Magnússon, E. (1901) *The Conversion of Iceland to Christianity, A.D. 1000*, Saga Book of the Viking Club, 2.

Manker, E. (1968) '*Seite*, cult and drum magic of the Lapps', in V. Diószegi (ed.), *Popular Beliefs in Siberia*, Bloomington: Indiana University Press.

Mannhardt, Wilhelm (1860) *Die Götter der deutschen und nordischen Völker*, Berlin.

Maringer, J. (1977) 'Priests and priestesses in prehistoric Europe', *History of Religions*, vol. 17, no. 2, pp. 101–120.

Matthews, Caitlín (1989) *The Elements of the Goddess*, Shaftesbury: Element Books.

Mauny, Raymond (1978) 'The exhibition on "The World of Souterrains" at Vezelay (Burgundy, France) (1977)', *Subterranea Britannica Bulletin*, no. 7.

Mayer, Elard Hugo (1891) *Germanische Mythologie*, Berlin: Mayer & Müller.

Mayr-Harting, H. (1972) *The Coming of Christianity to Anglo-Saxon England*, London: B.T. Batsford.

Megaw, Ruth and Megaw, Vincent (1989) *Celtic Art, From its Beginnings to the Book of Kells*, London: Thames & Hudson.

Merivale, Patricia (1969) *Pan the Goat-God: His Myth in Modern Times*, Cambridge, Mass.: Harvard University Press.

Merrifield, Ralph (1987) *The Archaeology of Ritual and Magic*, London: Guild.

Meyrick, Samuel Rush and Smith, Charles Hamilton (1815) *Costume of the Original Inhabitants of the British Islands*, London.

Michels, A.K. (1967) *The Calendar of the Roman Republic*, Princeton: Yale University Press.

Mitchell, Sir A. (1862) 'The various superstitions in the N.W. Highlands and Islands of Scotland', *Proceedings of the Antiquarian Society of Scotland*, vol. IV, Edinburgh.

Mogk, E. (1927) *Germanische Religionsgeschichte und Mythologie*, Berlin: Schikowski.

Moltke, Erik (1984) *Runes and Their Origin: Denmark and Elsewhere*, National Museum of Denmark: Copenhagen.

Mookerjee, A. (1988) *Kali, the Feminine Force*, London: Thames & Hudson.

Moora H. and Viires, A. (1964) *Abriss der Estnischen Volkskunde*, Tallinn: Estnischer Staatsverlag.

Morris, William and Magnússon, Eiríkr (1891) *The Saga Library Vol. I*, London: Bernard Quaritch.

Morrison, Arthur (1900) *Cunning Murrell*, London: Methuen.

Müller, W. (1961) Die Heilige Stadt, Roma Quadrata, himmliches Jerusalem und die Mythe vom Weltnabel, Stuttgart.

Murray, M.A. (1921) *The Witch Cult in Western Europe*, Oxford: Clarendon Press.
—— (1954) *The Divine King in England*, London: Faber & Faber.
—— (1963) *The Genesis of Religion*, London: Routledge & Kegan Paul.
Myres, J.N.L. (1986) *The English Settlements*, Oxford: Clarendon Press.
Nance, R.M. (1935) 'The Plen an Gwary', *Journal of the Royal Institute of Cornwall*, vol. 24, pp. 190–211.
Nelli, R. (1963) *L'Erotique des Troubadours*, Toulouse: Privat.
Nennius (1938), *History of the Britons*, ed. and trans. A.W. Wade-Evans, London: SPCK.
Neumann, Erich (1963) *The Great Mother*, Princeton: Princeton University Press.
Nioradze, Georg (1925) *Der Schamanismus bei den sibirischen Völkern*, Stuttgart: Strecker & Schröder.
Norman, E.R. and St Joseph, J.K.S. (1969) *The Early Development of Irish Society*, Cambridge: Cambridge University Press.
Oddo, Gilbert L. (1960) *Slovakia and Its Peoples*, New York: Robert Speller & Sons.
Ogilvie, R.H. (1976) *Early Rome and the Etruscans*, London: Oxford University Press.
Olsen, M. (1928) *Farms and Fanes of Ancient Norway*, Oslo: Bokcentralen.
O'Rahilly, T.F. (1946) *Early Irish History and Mythology*, Dublin: Institute for Advanced Studies.
Owen, G.R. (1981) *Rites and Religions of the Anglo-Saxons*, Newton Abbot: David & Charles.
Owen, Trefor M. (1987) *Welsh Folk Customs*, Llandysul: Gomer Press.
Paget, Robert F. (1967) *In the Footsteps of Orpheus: The Discovery of the Ancient Greek Underworld*, London: Robert Hale.
Paglia, C. (1990) *Sexual Personae, Art and Decadence from Nefertiti to Emily Dickinson*, New Haven: Yale University Press.
Palmer, R.E.A. (1974) *Roman Religion and the Roman Empire*, Philadelphia: University of Pennsylvania Press.
Pálsson, H. and Edwards, P. (trans.) (1978) *Orkneyinga Saga: The History of the Earls of Orkney*, London: Hogarth Press.
—— (trans.) (1980) *Landnámabók: The Book of Settlements*, Winnipeg: University of Manitoba Press.
Parke, H.W. (1939) *A History of the Delphic Oracle*, Oxford: Blackwell.
—— (1967) *The Oracles of Zeus: Dodona, Olympia, Ammon*, Oxford: Blackwell.
Patai, R. (1967) *The Hebrew Goddess*, New York: Ktav.
Pennant, Thomas (1774) *A Tour in Scotland and Voyage to the Hebrides*, London.
Pennick, N.C. (1981) *The Subterranean Kingdom: A Survey of Man-Made Structures Beneath the Earth*, Wellingborough: Turnstone.
—— (1990) *Mazes and Labyrinths*, London: Robert Hale.
—— (1992a) *Secret Games of the Gods*, New York Beach: Samuel Weiser.
—— (1992b) *The Pagan Book of Days. A Guide to the Festivals, Traditions and Sacred Days of the Year*, Rochester, Vermont: Destiny Books.
—— (in preparation) *Celtic Sacred Landscapes*.
Petrie, W. Flinders (1912) *The Revolutions of Civilisation*, London: Harper & Row.
Pettazzoni, R. (1954) 'West Slav Paganism', in *Essays on the History of Religion*, trans. H.J. Rose, Leiden: E.J. Brill.
Philippson, E.A. (1929) *Germanisches Heidentum bei den Angelsachsen*, Leipzig: Tauchnitz.
Phillips, Guy Ragland (1987) *The Unpolluted God*, Pocklington: Northern Lights.
Picardt, Johan (1660) *Korte Beschrijvinge van eenige verborgene antiquiteten*, Amsterdam.

Piggott, Stuart (1965) *Ancient Europe*, Edinburgh: Edinburgh University Press.

—— (1968) *The Druids*, London: Thames & Hudson.

Pizan, Christine de, trans. William Caxton (1489) *The Book of Fayttes of Armes and Chyvalrye*, ed. A.T.P. Byles, London, 1932.

Pomey, Antoine (1694) *The Pantheon, Representing the Fabulous Histories of the Heathen Gods and Most Illustrious Heroes*, London.

Porter, Enid (1969) *Cambridgeshire Customs and Folklore*, London: Routledge & Kegan Paul.

Powell, T.G.E. (1980) *The Celts*, London: Thames & Hudson.

Praetorius, M. (1780, 1871) *Delictae Prussicae oder Preussische Schaubühne*, Berlin: Duncker.

Raoult, Michel (1980) *Genealogical Tree of Occidental Bards, Gorsedds, Eisteddfods and Groves, 1100 AD to 1979 AD*, London: The Golden Section Order.

Raudonikas, W.J. (1930) *Die Nordmannen der Wikingerzeit und das Ladogagebiet*, Stockholm.

Rees, Alwyn and Rees, Brinley (1961) *Celtic Heritage*, London: Thames & Hudson.

Reeves, Dr (1861) 'Saint Maelrubha: his history and churches', *Proceedings of the Society of Antiquaries of Scotland*, vol. III, pt 2.

Reuter, Otto Sigfrid (1934) *Germanische Himmelskunde*, Leipzig: J.F. Lehmann.

—— (1987) *Skylore of the North*, trans. Michael Behrend, Bar Hill: Runestaff.

Rhys, John (1888) *The Hibbert Lectures on the Growth of Religion as Illustrated by Celtic Heathendom*, London: Williams & Norgate.

—— (1901) *Celtic Folklore*, Oxford: Clarendon Press.

Ricci, C. (1925) *Il tempietto Malatestiano*, Milan.

Riehl, Hans (1976) *Die Völkerwanderung*, Pfaffenhofen: Ilm.

Robertson, J.C. (1874–1875) *A History of the Christian Church*, 8 vols, London: John Murray.

Robertson, Olivia (1975) *The Call of Isis*, Enniscorthy: Cesara Publications.

Rochholz, E.L. (1862) *Naturmythen. Neue Schweizersagen gesammelt und erläutert*, Leipzig.

—— (1867) *Deutscher Glaube und Brauch im Spiegel der heidnischen Vorzeit*, 2 vols, Berlin.

—— (1870) *Drei Gaugöttinen, Walburg, Verena und Gertrud als deutsche Kirchenheilige*, Leipzig.

Rodd, R. (1892) *The Customs and Lore of Modern Greece*, London: David Stott.

Rose, H.J. (1948) *Ancient Roman Religion*, London: Hutchinson.

—— (ed.) (1954) *Essays on the History of Religion*, Leiden: Brill.

Rosenberg, Alfons (1988) *Die Frau als Seherin und Prophetin*, Munich: Kösel Verlag.

Ross, A. (1967, 1974) *Pagan Celtic Britain*, London: Cardinal.

—— (1970, 1986a) *The Pagan Celts*, London: Batsford.

—— (1986b) *Druids, Gods and Heroes of Celtic Mythology*, London: Routledge & Kegan Paul.

Runeberg, A. (1947) *Witches, Demons and Fertility Magic*, Helsingfors: Societas Scientiarum Fennica.

Rutkis, J. (ed.) (1967) *Latvia, Country and People*, Stockholm: Latvian National Foundation.

Rutkowski, B. (1986) *The Cult Places of the Aegean*, New Haven: Yale University Press.

Saks, E.V. (1981) *The Estonian Vikings*, Cardiff: Boreas.

Salway, P. (1981) *Roman Britain*, Oxford: Clarendon Press.

Santillana, G. de and Dechend, H. von (1969, 1977) *Hamlet's Mill*, Boston: Godine.

Scarre, G. (1987) *Witchcraft and Magic in Sixteenth- and Seventeenth-century Europe*, London: Macmillan.

Schefferus, J. (1704) *Lapponia, id est, Regionis Lapponum,* 1673, trans. T. Newborough, London.

Scholl, H.-C. (1929) *Die Drei Ewigen,* Jena: Diederich.

Schröder, Franz Rolf (1924) *Germanentum und Hellenismus,* Heidelberg: Carl Winter.

Schuchhardt, C. (1926) *Arkona, Rethra, Vineta,* Berlin.

Schütte, Godmund (1923) *Dänisches Heidentum,* 2 vols, Heidelberg.

Schutz, H. (1983) *The Prehistory of Germanic Europe,* London: Yale University Press.

Schwarzfischer, Karl (1975) 'Study of Erdställe in the Danubian area of Germany', *Subterranea Britannica Bulletin,* no. 2.

Schwebel, Oskar (1887) *Tod und Ewiges Leben in deutschen Volksglauben,* Minden.

Scott, George Riley (n.d.) *Phallic Worship,* Westport, Conn.: Associated Bookseller.

Scullard, H.H. (1967) *The Etruscan Cities and Rome,* London: Thames & Hudson.

Scully, Vincent (1962) *The Earth, The Temple and the Gods,* Yale: Yale University Press.

Searle, M. (1992) 'Romuva, the revival of Lithuanian heathenism', *Odinism Today,* vol. 5, London: Odinic Rite.

Sébillot, Paul (1904–1907) *Folk-lore de France,* 4 vols, Paris.

—— (1908) *Le Paganisme contemporain,* Paris.

Sepp (1890) *Die Religion der alten Deutschen und ihr Fortbestand in Volkssagen, Aufzügen und Festgebraüchen,* Munich.

Shippey, T.A. (1976) *Poems of Wisdom and Learning in Old English,* Cambridge: Cambridge University Press.

Simpson, J. (1967) 'Some Scandinavian sacrifices', *Folk-Lore,* vol. LXXVIII, pp. 190–202.

Skene, W.F. (1876) *Celtic Scotland,* Edinburgh.

Smith, J.H. (1976) *The Death of Classical Paganism,* London: Chapman.

Solmsen, F. (1979) *Isis among the Greeks and Romans,* Cambridge, Mass.: Harvard University Press.

Spence, Lewis (n.d., *c.*1941) *The Occult Causes of the Present War,* London: Rider.

—— (1971) *The History and Origins of Druidism,* London: Aquarian Press.

Stanley, E.G. (1975) *The Search for Anglo-Saxon Paganism,* Cambridge: D.S. Brewer.

Stenton, Sir F. (1971) *Anglo-Saxon England,* 3rd edn, Oxford: Clarendon Press.

Stober, August (1892), *Die Sagen des Elsasses,* 2 vols, Strasbourg.

Stokes, W. (1862) *Three Irish Glossaries,* London.

Storms, G. (1948) *Anglo-Saxon Magic,* The Hague: Nijhoff.

Strömbäck, Dag (1935) *Sejd,* Stockholm: Geber.

—— (1975) *The Conversion of Iceland,* trans. Peter Foote, London: Viking Society for Northern Research.

Strutynski, U. (1975) 'Germanic divinities in weekday names', *Journal of Indo-European Studies,* vol. 3, pp. 363–384.

Sturluson, Snorri (1964) *Heimskringla: History of the Kings of Norway,* trans. L.M. Hollander, Austin: University of Texas Press.

Syme, Ronald (1939, 1971) *The Roman Revolution,* Oxford: Oxford University Press.

Szabó, Miklós (1971) *The Celtic Heritage in Hungary,* trans. Paul Aston, Budapest: Corvina Press.

Temple, Robert K.G. (1984) *Conversations with Eternity: Ancient Man's Attempts to Know the Future,* London: Rider.

Thompson, E.A. (1966) *The Visigoths in the Time of Ulfila,* Oxford: Clarendon Press.

Thonger, Richard (1966) *A Calendar of German Customs*, London: Oswald Wolff.

Thorpe, B. (1840) *Ancient Laws and Institutes of England*, 2 vols, London.

Tille, A. (1899) *Yule and Christmas, their Place in the Germanic Year*, London: David Nutt.

Trede, T. (1901) *Das Heidentum in der römischen Kirche*, 4 vols, Gotha.

Trombley, F.R. (1993) *Hellenic Religion and Christianization, c. 370–529*, Leiden: E.J. Brill.

Turville-Petre, E.O.G. (1964) *Myth and Religion of the North*, London: Weidenfeld & Nicolson.

Velius, N. (1981, 1989), *The World Outlook of the Ancient Balts*, Vilnius: Mintis.

Vernaliken, Theodor (1858) *Völksüberlieferungen aus der Schweiz*, Vienna.

Vesey-Fitzgerald, Brian (1973) *Gypsies of Britain*, Newton Abbot: David & Charles.

Vyncke, F. (1968) 'La divination chez les Slaves', in A. Caquot and M. Leibovici (eds), *La Divination*, Paris.

Wacher, John (1974) *The Towns of Roman Britain*, London: Batsford.

Walker, J.R. (1883) '"Holy Wells" in Scotland', *Proceedings of the Society of Antiquaries of Scotland*, Edinburgh.

Wallace-Hadrill, J.M. (1952, 1967) *The Barbarian West, 400–1000*, London: Hutchinson.

Walter, Nicolas (1981) 'Edward Carpenter', *Freedom Anarchist Review*, vol. 42, no. 4.

Warburg, A. (1920) *Heidnisch-Antike Weissagung in Wort und Bild zu Luthers Zeiten*, Heidelberg: Carl Winter Verlag.

Warde-Fowler, W. (1911) *The Religious Experience of the Roman People*, London: Macmillan.

Wedeck, Harry E. (1975) *Treasury of Witchcraft*, Secaucus: Citadel Press.

Wesche, Heinrich (1940) *Der althochdeutsche Wortschatz im Gebiete des Zaubers und der Weissagung*, Haale a.d. Saale: Niemeyer.

Wheatley, Paul (1971) *The Pivot of the Four Quarters*, Edinburgh: Edinburgh University Press.

Wilson, D.M. and Klindt-Jensen, O. (1966) *Viking Art*, London: George Allen & Unwin.

Wilson, Steve (1993) *Robin Hood. The Spirit of the Forest*, London: Neptune Press.

Wirth, Hermann (1932–1936) *Die Heilige Urschrift der Menschheit*, Leipzig: Köhler & Amelang.

Wissowa, G. (1912) *Religion und Kultus der Römer*, 2nd edn, Munich: Beck.

Wixman, R. (1993) 'The Middle Volga: ethnic archipelago in a Russian sea', in I. Bremner and R. Taras (eds), *Nations and Politics in the Soviet Successor States*, Cambridge: Cambridge University Press.

Wolfram, H. (1988) *The History of the Goths*, Berkeley: University of California Press.

Wood-Martin, W.G. (1902) *Traces of the Elder Faiths of Ireland*, London.

Yeowell, John (1993) *Odinism and Christianity Under the Third Reich*, London: The Odinic Rite.

Zaborsky, Oskar von (1936) *Urväter-Erbe in deutscher Volkskunst*, Leipzig: Köhler & Amelang.

Ziedonis Jr, A., Winter, William L. and Valgemäe, M. (eds) (1974) *Baltic History*, Columbus, Ohio: Association for the Advancement of Baltic Studies.

Zosimus (1967) *Historia Nova*, trans. J. Buchanan, San Antonio: Trinity University Press.

INDEX